A Chance at Love

THE COMPLETE COLLECTION

USA TODAY BESTSELLING AUTHOR
KAT SAVAGE

A CHANCE AT LOVE

THE COMPLETE COLLECTION

KAT SAVAGE

CONTENTS

TAKING A CHANCE

A Fighting Chance

BOOK ONE

A FIGHTING CHANCE

BOOK ONE

For all the bean flickers,
lady-brain thinkers,
and self-sabotagers.
Your Gentry is out there,
waiting to press his front
to your front and write you
sex notes.

LYLA

I'M PROBABLY NOT CHOKING *to death on a spider.*

That's my first thought when I wake up in the middle of the night in a violent coughing fit, gasping for air. I think back on that debunked article I read, about how unlikely it is that people *actually* swallow eight spiders while sleeping each year. So, a small rush of relief hits me. Because even though I sit here, basically dying from this random assault on my esophagus, at least it probably isn't due to a spider having crawled into my gaping mouth. There's a small amount of comfort in that.

I have no idea why I flew up in bed—choking and hacking and coughing up a lung—rising like the undead. All I know for sure is I'm choking on air. Just air. Air is trying to kill me. I don't even inhale correctly. I sip water as I sit on the edge of my bed, trying to clear my windpipe. As it passes, I reach for my phone to check the time.

Three after three in the morning is the last thing I want to see.

But what's more surprising is the text message from my sister.

Given we only really exchange texts about three times a year, and see each other even less, this is...*unexpected,* to say the least. It isn't that we don't get along or dislike each other. We've made very different life choices and don't have much in common, which has resulted in few conversational topic options.

I open the message and her urgency nearly startles me into a new coughing fit.

HARPER

Call me. It's important.

For Harper, this message may as well be a blaring *SOS* in the middle of the ocean. I check to see what time the text came in. Two twenty-seven A.M. This is highly unusual behavior for her. My sister is, for lack of a more precise term, not the type to be up so late without significant provocation. Okay, maybe that is pretty precise. Knowing that, I can tell whatever it's about must *actually* be important.

I press the call button without thinking about what time it is or much else, but it rings until her voicemail picks up. Then my thoughts really take a turn.

Maybe she's pregnant?

No, she wouldn't be texting so late with good news. Or she'd at least use an exclamation.

Maybe someone died? Nan? Paw?

Wow, no. Don't think about that.

Despite my need to wake up in three hours for work, I'll most likely be unable to fall back asleep, thanks to her cryptic text.

Awesome.

I toss my head back on my pillow and roll onto my left side. I'm not sure why sleeping on a particular side of the bed is still important to me. I don't have a boyfriend or husband or even a casual hookup to share the bed with. I can sprawl myself out all over the middle or other side or wherever I want, but I still choose to tuck myself neatly onto the right side of the bed. In which case, lying on my left side makes it so I'm staring into the empty expanse of the rest of my queen pillowtop. It's like a fun little reminder built right in.

Oh, right. Hey, Lyla? You're alone.

Most nights, I don't hate it. I've been single for quite a few years now. And by *quite a few years*, I mean basically each one of my adulthood. I can attest to a few positive points. For one, I don't have to concede television time, food options, or things like sides of the bed. I watch, eat, and do whatever I want. It has its merits. Plus, I don't have to check in with anyone or worry about things like jealousy or how I split my time. My life is drama free. Worry free. Though, I am fairly certain my nan is worried I'll become an old spinster lady with a bunch of cats. Lucky for both of us, I don't really like cats.

Are there spinster dog ladies?

I could get on board with that. Hell, I would probably be on my way to such a glorious life if my apartment was pet-friendly.

I punch my pillow several times, blaming it as the reason for my discomfort and inability to fall back asleep. Time passes in a strange fashion when you're lying in bed, thinking too hard about nothing in particular.

When I check my phone again, it's already four A.M. and I don't know when *that* happened. I shut my eyes tight, hoping the added pressure of holding them closed will help tire me out.

Suddenly, and without context, my high school boyfriend pops into my head.

Don't you just love when that happens?

I really hate my brain.

Why? Why do brains do this?

I don't understand *why* brains decide to use the most inopportune moments to bring up the most painful or random or awkward moments in your past and cycle them up front and center. Like this is the exact moment you might need to resolve your previously unresolved feelings about some ancient happening you've tried so hard to forget.

I slam my head into my pillow over and over again. I haven't thought about Dean Callahan in years. Maybe not even since the day he broke up with me, which incidentally, was prom day—three weeks before graduation and four weeks before I moved away and never looked back. Not really anyway. I've gone back for a few holidays and important events over the years, but that's all. And I never drag it out longer than necessary. I get in and out—usually the same day if I can help it.

So, why exactly Dean is in my thoughts tonight is beyond me. Our relationship would require a chart to understand, and then a whole separate chart for my twenty/twenty hindsight on the matter. Blissful in the moment but torture to reflect on. That about sums it up.

While part of me is genuinely worried about my sister and Nan and Paw, another part of me is secretly wishing and hoping this is not the sort of catastrophe that requires my homecoming. Just thinking about it makes me feel selfish.

Eventually I fall back asleep—with thoughts of Dean and the words from our breakup serving as my nightmarish lullaby.

LYLA

"I'M GETTING A DIVORCE, LYLA," Harper says, sobbing through the muffled telephone line. I can hear my sister sniffling and wiping her nose as she tries to compose herself enough to speak whole sentences to me.

"What happened?" I ask, trying to keep my voice calm and measured, knowing now is the time to lend an ear and try not to ask too many questions. To just be a sounding board.

"I don't know, you know? Just grew apart, I guess. He says he fell in love with someone else. Oh, Lyla, it's awful," and the sobs set in again.

That ass.

My heart cracks in my chest. I see fire and brimstone. I am *raging* inside but again, my voice remains tempered. "Oh, love, I'm so sorry. I'm going to come down," I say. I won't lie, I don't want to. I really don't. But I can't leave her to break alone.

My little sister chose a happily ever after—a quiet life, a husband, and a vow. I, on the other hand, had flown off, career in mind, dating only when convenient or necessary. I've been living mostly in solitude, if I'm being honest. Dating any *one* person never lasted for me because, well, that's how I like it. Dating, settling down, finding love…all that junk has never been my focus. The point is, she'd chosen the opposite, and now it's crumbling around her. As her big sister, I have to go and hold her together.

"No, you don't have to do that—really. Don't go through any trouble for me," Harper says, and sniffs again.

"It's no trouble. I can practically work from anywhere. Plus, I haven't been down in a while and it'll be good for you—for the both of us," I insist.

"Okay," she says.

"Good," I return. I don't bore her with the travel details, I just tell her I'll make them.

However, what I don't make is a promise of how long I'll stay.

The flight I book will get in late the next evening and then I'll make the drive from the airport to the farm, putting me there probably around ten P.M.

I'm not looking forward to packing and hauling myself down there, but it has to be done.

For the most part, I left Harper behind with Nan and Paw to look after the farm. I left her behind to be the one to deal with everything. Our parents died when we were in middle school—me in eighth grade, her in sixth. When I left for college, she still had two more years to go. By that time, Nan and Paw were too old to care for the place the way it needed; so, Harper stayed.

She went to college locally, married her high school sweetheart—and stayed. She was your quintessential small-town girl. Everyone in town knew her name. Hell, for that matter, everyone in town knew everyone's name. All our names.

My grandparents are Louise and Calvin Whitney. Not that it means much to most of the world, but in the backwoods of Kentucky, where there are more horse farms and national parks than paved roads, Whitney is a very well-known name. Our family's farm is at the edge of Scott County, and it's one of the oldest working farms still in the area.

In the fall, they have pumpkin patches and hayrides open to the public. The orchards have always been a popular attraction. City folk always want to come pick their own apples. Corn mazes, sunflowers, fresh laid eggs, you name it. People come from all over to visit and spend the day. Our farm is even on its own road. Whitney Farms is nestled neatly at the end of Whitney Way.

How quaint.

I distinctly remember rolling my eyes any time I had to explain it to anyone as a teenager.

Now, I scroll through my phone until I find a decent ticket for the flight there—a one-way ticket. I don't know how long I'll stay and purposely made no mention of it to Harper so I'm not locked in to any timeline. I'll fly into the Louisville Airport and then make my way two hours southeast.

Oh joy.

I start removing clothes from their hangers inside the closet. I live in a beautiful one-bedroom Boston apartment, on the third floor. I have purposely and meticulously constructed my life. Rebuilt it to be more than it was before.

I worked hard in high school, got accepted into Boston College, obtained an English degree, and almost immediately began writing for various magazines and online blogs. I wish I could say it's that easy for everyone who wants to be a writer. The truth is, I got lucky—*so* lucky. And I knew the right people. I networked like a mother trucker leading up to graduation. I kissed ass like it had never been kissed before.

I throw more items of clothing in my bag and realize I have no idea what or how much I should be packing.

A little of everything?

How long do I really want to stay?

As long as my sister needs me to, I decide in the same moment. Within reason, of course. Whatever that is.

I pack an assortment of items, deciding it's good enough for now. If I wind up without something, I'll just go shopping for it.

After I finish packing, I email some of my needy clients who like to stay in constant contact. I let them know I'll be traveling over the next day but all deadlines will be met, no services will be interrupted, and I'll be accessible just as soon as I settle in.

Then, I text my best friend Cora about the ordeal.

> Harper is getting a divorce. I have to go back home for a while.

CORA

> OMG

> I know, I'll fill you in later. Can I pack you in my suitcase?

CORA

> If it gets me off this date...

> OMG. Pretend this is an emergency and bail!

CORA

> What? Your goldfish died? I'll be right there!

> Flushing Sir Winston at dusk.

CORA

> LOL, travel safe. Let me know when you've made it.

Poor Cora.

The woman is gorgeous. I mean *gorgeous*. But for whatever reason, she has absolute shit luck in her dating life. I'll never understand it. She's also my only friend in the city so, aside from my clients, she's the only person I feel the need to inform of my leaving. I try not to dwell on how sad I find that.

The rest of the day passes rather uneventfully. I text Harper, checking in with her and updating her on my travel arrangements. She lets me know my old room has been freshened up for my arrival. In southern terms, *freshened up* means more like all the bedding has been washed—even though no one's slept there—and everything's been dusted and swept. She's likely even added fresh flowers to the vase on my dresser.

Good ol' southern hospitality.

I can confirm there's nothing quite like it. In the first three days after moving to Boston, I must have been shoulder-checked walking down the sidewalk more than half a dozen times and no one even looked up, let alone muttered a half-hearted apology in my direction. It took me a little while to get used to. Despite their big city indifference, I tried to keep my engrained manners. My nan would have smacked me in the back of my head, or worse, if she thought I was being anything less than the southern lady she raised me to be.

I sit all my bags next to the door. One large suitcase I will definitely have to check. My carry-on laptop bag, which is stuffed with charger cords, my iPad, and all electronics necessary for daily function. My purse with all my essentials. Wallet, contacts, backup glasses, and cash. I tick everything off the checklist in my mind, feeling confident I haven't forgotten anything. I even remember to schedule a car to pick me up in the morning and take me to the airport, rather than trying to get one last minute. I'm feeling pretty good about my overall preparedness.

I return to my bedroom and sit on the edge of my bed, flopping myself back and letting out a long sigh. Then a thought occurs to me.

I sit back up and eye the second drawer of my bedside table. I debate back and forth before opening it.

I am a woman, okay? There's nothing to be ashamed of.

It's the drawer I keep my vibrator in.

How long will I be gone?

What if I need...relief?

Should I...bring it?

Would it be inappropriate?

I mean, I don't have to announce it to anyone. But hello, I am a single woman. Sure, I manage a date here and there for sexual relief, but continued gratification comes at *my* hand. I chortle.

Comes at my hand.

At some point, it becomes an absolute necessity to take care of yourself. I think it's doctor recommended by now. You might even die if you don't. I start to think about all the ways I can pack this in my luggage and have a security check fiasco due to its presence. And those guys who load and unload the bags...I bet they look in them. I bet they take photos and host secret bets about the funniest things they found that day. Maybe I should leave it behind after all.

I reluctantly shut the drawer and decide I can get through a bit of time without self-medicating. Even as I make the decision, I groan. For the sake of my lady parts, I certainly hope Harper isn't too broken up over her split. Maybe she's actually quite resilient. Maybe she'll bounce back in no time. Maybe she just needs a friendly face and some self-medicating as well. I shake the thoughts from my head.

Stop being an ass, Lyla.

Like it or not, Lyla Elizabeth Whitney, by this time tomorrow, your feet will be planted right back on the soil you dug your roots up from all those years ago.

LYLA

I WISH I could say it was a quick drive to the airport, or a smooth flight. I wish I could say, despite the drive being two hours, it went by fast. I wish I could say any one of those things, but I can't. If I had to sum up my travel day in one phrase, it would be *pure hell*. The car was late picking me up and had to haul ass to the airport. The driver didn't help me with my bags, so I had to drag my large suitcase out of the trunk all by myself—I'm short and curvy, mind you. Then, I had to run to the gate—like *actually* run. I didn't get to check in as early as I wanted so I had a middle seat—a freaking *middle* seat—between a not-very-nice woman wearing so much perfume it made my eyes water, and a man who alternated between elbowing me in the ribs and trying to use my shoulder as a pillow. So much for a nap on the way down.

After landing, I discovered the only rental cars still available were either big pick-up trucks or small sports cars. Despite reserving one online, all I got for my inconvenience was an apology and no discount on the Chevy Silverado they rented me. But, to my delight, it was a pretty nice truck. You can take the girl out of the country, but you cannot take the love for big trucks out of the girl.

The drive to the farm was painful and slow and felt like it took so much longer than it was supposed to. By the time I pulled onto

Whitney Way, I could have slept inside the truck until morning and been perfectly fine.

As I pull up to the house and shut the truck off, I inhale a deep breath and take in the sight of my childhood home. While it's true Nan and Paw only looked after me and Harper since middle school, we lived here our entire lives. Nan and Paw are my mother's parents. Mom and Dad moved here before we were born to help work the farm. This place is the entire Whitney way of life. With the exception of me, of course.

If I ever have to describe this house to someone who doesn't know it, I tell them to close their eyes and picture a big white house from the front of a Southern Living magazine. Whatever they'd conjure in their minds would likely be pretty close.

The Whitney home is three stories. Columns in the front, a big wrap-around porch, two porch swings. Tidy landscaping. Black shutters, and lace curtains. The place hasn't really changed at all since I was a child. Each time I visit, I'm amazed at its consistency. Even now, in the dark, I can make out the familiar lines.

As I get my bags from the back, I hear the familiar creak of the back door swing open and slam shut on the spring. Footsteps pad lightly across the wooden planks of the porch and stop near what I assume is the edge of the steps.

"You're actually here!" Harper quietly exclaims, with a tad too much disbelief in her voice. There's a small smile plastered across her face.

Harper is a stark contrast to me. Where my skin is pale and my hair dark, she carries a light golden tan and long, blonde hair. Where my eyes are a strange foggy hazel, hers are a cool and clear blue. I've been blessed with enough boob and butt for the both of us while she's of the petite variety, and much more proportionately sculpted. Which is to say, she was born for small-town life and I was not.

She was prom queen. She competed in beauty pageants. She was crowned Pumpkin Princess at the Harvest Festival and Parade around the same time. She and her jock boyfriend were voted "Cutest Couple" in her senior class.

Now, they're getting a divorce, her small-town life coming full circle.

My poor baby sister.

"Try not to sound too shocked," I say, laughing off her surprise.

She waves her hand at me and descends the porch steps, reaching for the bags in my right hand and gesturing for me to follow her like I don't know my way around. "Nan and Paw are already asleep but they're excited to see you in the morning," she says.

That figures. It's pretty late for them. In fact, it's pretty late for *me*. I own the fact that I like sleep and have no problem being in bed early. Absolutely no shame.

I nod to her in understanding, and then we head upstairs—straight to my old room. She opens the door and I take in the sight all at once. I shift my eyes from one side to the other, looking over all my old stuff with a bit more care. Harper definitely washed the bedding. I can smell the fabric softener in the air. I also note the fresh vase of wild-flowers on the dresser and smile.

I sit on the edge of my bed gently, as if I need to try it out first before fully committing. Harper finishes setting my bags down and sits beside me. The thought occurs to me that we haven't actually seen each other in almost two years, if my math is correct. Despite this, we haven't even hugged hello and it makes me sort of sad.

I seek to correct it and reach for her. At first, her body doesn't respond—undoubtedly surprised by my actions. Then I feel her relax and hug me back. Her shoulders start to shake next, and I know she's crying. I reach up to stroke her hair then, knowing being held is probably what she needs right now.

"I just didn't see it coming, Lyla," she cries. She pulls away from my embrace and wipes at the tears streaming down her face.

"I know, honey," I say, rubbing soothing circles on her back.

"There will be time for all this blubbering later. I'll let you get settled and get some sleep," she says.

I nod and give her a small smile. Harper has never been one to freely cry in front of anyone. She keeps her emotions bottled up. So, I know this whole ordeal is difficult for her in more than one way.

"Okay," I say. "Let's talk tomorrow then."

"Yes," she says. She stands from her spot next to me and walks across the room, to the door. Before she leaves, she turns back to me and says, "Thank you."

Knowing exactly what she means, I simply nod and watch her leave.

I glance around the room once again, remembering moments of my youth brought forth by the books lining the bookshelf and the trophies on the dresser. While my sister was busy wearing dresses and waving gingerly at the judges, I was running. Across tracks and fields. Well enough to become team captain and win some medals and trophies too. Once again, I'm reminded of our paths—such a stark contrast. Not that there was anything wrong with her path or mine, they were just very different.

I fling myself back on my bed, utterly exhausted from the day of travel, and grateful it's over. I want nothing more than to peel out of my clothes and crawl underneath the blankets right away, but I think better of it and decide I should at least wash my face and brush my teeth. Being tired doesn't mean I can forget basic hygiene, after all.

I search through my suitcase for a set of pajamas and settle on a tank top and shorts. Nan and Paw are in bed and it doesn't matter if Harper happens to see me. There are fewer greater joys in life than removing your bra at the end of a long day. Any woman who disagrees should be evaluated. I shrug out of my stiff travel wear and into the comfort of my pajamas, the thin material so light on my skin, I exhale a sigh of relief.

I grab my toiletry bag and slide into the hallway as quietly as I can, walking to the bathroom nearest my room where I turn the knob without a thought. The sight I uncover, however, is enough to make me want to get back in my rental truck, drive back to the airport, and fly all the way back home right this second.

A man. An attractive man—scratch that—a *beautiful* man is standing in the bathroom. Sheer shock paralyzes me. I take in his form. He's standing at the sink in black boxer briefs and no shirt, casually flossing, and I have never had a more thorough appreciation for dental hygiene in my life.

I finally realize I'm staring. "Oh my god, I'm so sorry," I say, turning my back to him. Though, if I just read his expression correctly, he doesn't seem at all disturbed by my invasion of his privacy—or my staring at him for at least one full minute before making an apology.

He lets out a small laugh from behind me. "What for?" he asks, as if I haven't just barged in on him in his skivvies.

"Well, I would think that's fairly obvious, but for starters, barging in on you, not knocking," I start, when his voice cuts me off.

"Don't worry about it," he says plainly, not adding anything else.

"Okay," I say, drawing the word out, unsure of what to say next. "Wait, who are you?"

He turns on the faucet to the sink and fills a cup. "Who are you?" he counters.

I'm shocked for a second time in under two minutes. "Excuse me?"

"No offense, ma'am, but I've never met you, so you could definitely be a serial killer or something," he says.

I think he's teasing me, but I can't be sure. I whirl back around, not caring about his state of undress this time. "First of all, don't call me *ma'am*. Second, what am I going to kill you with? My toothbrush?" I exclaim, holding up my pink travel toothbrush case like a dagger to exaggerate my point.

He shrugs his shoulders at me then leans his hip against the sink, depositing his floss into the trash and folding his arms over his bare chest.

Oh my. His bare chest.

I take a moment to appreciate his form again, as best I can without drawing attention to it. He's about six-foot-three, if I have to guess. He has the lean form of a swimmer, his skin tanned deep. The only way a man gets that kind of deep tan is by working outside. His brown hair is tousled and a little unkempt. It looks as though he'd just dried it with a towel, still a little damp even. He has a young beard. More than stubble but less than bushy. Just a smattering of hair covering his strong jawline and what I surmise would be dimples if he were to smile. His aforementioned bare chest also has some hair. Not too much. Just enough to make your lady parts aware that he's definitely all man.

I stare into his green eyes for a moment and realize they're sweeping up and down my body in the same way I've just appraised his. I watch his eyes travel the length of my legs, dissect my stomach, linger on my breasts and then neck, and finally, make eye contact.

"I'm sure you have other weapons on you," he smirks.

"What?" I ask, confused by his comment. Confused because the sight of him has actually caused me to forget what the hell we were just talking about.

"Your toothbrush shank. I'm just saying, it's probably not the only weapon you're carrying." He uncrosses his arms and turns to the mirror, opening the medicine cabinet and removing a small pill bottle.

I glance down at myself. There's nowhere to hide a weapon. "Have you seen what I'm wearing? I don't exactly have a lot of hiding spots."

"Oh, I definitely see what you're wearing." Another smirk. He winks at me in the mirror and I scowl back.

I furrow my eyebrows and try to shove them together on my forehead. A futile effort. I don't like this man. I like how he looks, but I don't like *him*. I feel my neck and chest warm under his eyes. "Stop looking at me!" I snap.

"You looked at me first," he counters.

I choke and stutter. "You surprised me. I didn't expect anyone to be in here, that's all."

"Listen, calm down. You're getting all breathless and shrill," he says, putting his hands up, making a calming motion toward me.

I don't like this either. "Who are you?" I ask again, putting my hands on my hips this time, trying to make it clear I mean business.

"If I tell you who I am, are you going to tell me who you are? Because I'm not a mind reader, but you seem offended that I don't already know," he says.

I watch his biceps and forearms flex and suddenly notice I have too much saliva in my mouth. I swallow.

Oh my god, am I drooling? Is my mouth actually watering?

This is so stupid. "Sure," I say, rolling my eyes.

He presses his lips together, considering my single word answer, and narrows his eyes at me. He stands and straightens himself, then takes four measured steps in my direction. Before I know it, he's maybe twelve inches from me.

Too close, too close, too close.

I stiffen.

"I'm Gentry. Gentry Bodine," he says, extending his hand out and waiting—a silent cue that it's now my turn.

I straighten my spine. "I'm Lyla. Lyla Elizabeth Whitney," I say, taking his hand in mine and attempting to shake it, but he stops my attempt.

He turns my hand over in his, backside up, and to my sheer astonishment, bends down and slowly plants a damp kiss on my skin. He actually *kisses* the back of my hand like we're straight out of a black and white movie. This man—this beautiful man standing here in nothing but his boxer briefs, no less—just displayed some ancient form of southern hospitality. It doesn't match up. It doesn't make sense.

He looks up at me, a sparkle in his eyes. And the bastard smirks yet again. "Pleased to make your acquaintance, although I doubt we can call it that," he says, laughing at his own joke.

Shock. This is what shock feels like, right?

I'm in utter disbelief and I'm tired. Maybe I'm dreaming. That has to be it. "Um, you too," I say, noting the awkwardness in my own voice.

He gently returns my hand to me and I feel the place on my hand where his lips touched, warm and tingling and wet. "Now, miss, as fun as this has been, I've got to be up early in the morning, so I'm going to get some sleep. I bid you goodnight," he says. He dips his head to me and moves past me in the doorway of the bathroom, almost pressing his bare chest against my body to do so.

I feel the heat of his body through the thin material of my tank top and my breath hitches. Just as quickly as I feel the warmth, it's gone again. I watch him walk down the hallway and into the bedroom across from mine, which was the guest bedroom last time I was here.

What the hell was that? What actually just happened?

I finish my routine in the bathroom as fast as I can and walk back to my bedroom, pausing and staring at his door for a moment, listening for any noise coming from behind it, but I hear nothing.

I shake my head and quickly slip inside my room. After replacing my toiletries, I pull the blankets back on the bed and crawl in. My body immediately unfolds, as if I've been folded up since the last time I was here. I relax my shoulders and nestle my head back into my pillow. If I know one thing, I will sleep hard. My eyelids are already heavy. I don't know what time it is, but if I have to guess, it's past midnight.

The only lingering thought I have is Gentry.

Who the hell is he?

And why is he here?

No one has mentioned a Gentry. Not my sister or Nan or Paw.

And he's staying in the house?

I drift to sleep, thinking about the nearly naked stranger in the bathroom; thinking mostly of his near nakedness.

GENTRY

IN TRUTH, I knew exactly who she was when I asked her. But she seemed so embarrassed and off kilter and well, frankly, it was sexy —*really* sexy. So, I wanted to ruffle her up a bit more. Just for fun. Harper told me yesterday that Lyla was coming, and while I didn't expect to meet her for the first time standing in the bathroom in my boxer briefs while flossing, well...sometimes shit happens and you roll with it.

I feel like I have the distinct advantage of knowing much more about her than she knows about me. Nan and Paw talk about her all the time. Brag, really. Not that I mind. I like their stories about Lyla. Harper's told me about her too. I was careful to avoid asking a lot of questions, though. I didn't want to seem too nosy.

Settling into my bed, I pull my book from the nightstand and replay the bathroom scene in my mind. I can hear her in there now, and visions of her in those tiny pajama shorts keep flashing through my head.

Stop it, Gentry. You perv.

Shaking my head in an effort to rid myself of these thoughts, I refocus my attention on the book and stare down at the words on the paper.

What book is this again? Fuck.

The words blur almost immediately and I'm unable to concentrate. I pinch the bridge of my nose and rub the hair along my jawline.

I can do this; I can focus. I can absolutely *not* think about Lyla—and apparently my lust for her. I cannot think about how I want to walk over to her room, knock on her door, and attempt to kiss her face off when she opens it.

No, Gentry. No. You can't do that.

She may not appreciate me attempting to suck her face off. My lust for Lyla Whitney is very real and very deeply rooted in the fact that her body is something that belongs in a museum. A dirty, sexy museum for the blind so you can feel your way around. Because if there was ever a body built for touching, it's hers. Just looking at it makes me think terribly delicious things. Most of which I'm pretty sure are legal in most states but I can't be sure until I do the research.

When Nan had taken out one of her photo albums and flipped through Lyla's section, I felt like trash. Actual trash. No, trash juice. Here Nan was—the sweetest, kindest old lady— showing me pictures of her lovely granddaughter, and I was staring down at eighteen-year-old Lyla in a sleek prom dress feeling like a dirty old man. Nan had flipped through senior pictures, of Lyla running during her cross-country meets, her college graduation, and then a vacation where she was in a bikini something like ninety percent of the time, and I felt like I was going to die. I finally had to make an excuse to stop looking at the photos. I was a dirty bird, the dirtiest of birds, in need of a cold ass shower.

So, naturally, when Harper announced Lyla's impending arrival, my palms started sweating, my throat dried up, and all my clothes itched. I was excited—*really* excited. My mouth had basically been dry all the way up until I saw her in person. And let me tell you, the photos didn't do her justice.

Her big, hazel eyes impaled me. And her lips. Good god, her lips are the perfect shade of pink I've ever seen. I want to bite them—no, I *need* to bite them. I had half a mind to try right there in the bathroom after about forty-three seconds, but I resisted my urges for this thing called being a fucking gentleman and not a creep.

I set my book back down on the table because it's clear I'm not getting anywhere with that tonight. Then I hear the bathroom door open and shut, followed by Lyla's feet moving quietly across the floor before her door opens and closes. I resist the desire to leap from my bed and bound after her like an idiot.

What am I, some kind of lust-sick puppy?

Get ahold of yourself, man.

I'm glad I managed to keep my composure in the bathroom but there are only maybe two hundred and twenty-seven more possible interactions over the next few days with countless conversations and opportunities to be an idiot.

Awesome.

Lying down in my bed, I reach back and stack my pillows before turning my lamp off. Then it's just me and the dark. I really hate these times. In time, I learned to push myself past tired before getting in bed so sleep would come quickly. But on nights like these, with too much on my mind, I stare up at my ceiling.

My thoughts drift from Lyla to Cassie and back to Lyla. What an odd mix of emotions.

I don't have leftover romantic feelings for Cassie, but a loss is still a loss and the accompanying emotions still linger. Many nights, I find myself examining what Cassie and I had, what went wrong, and how it ended the way it did.

Now, it's like a tennis match in my mind. Lust on one side and loss on the other. I let the ball volley back and forth a few times before planting it firmly on lust's side, deciding it's far less severe for bedtime thoughts.

I finally fall asleep, thoughts of Lyla arresting any others.

As I doze off, I wonder if it's possible, if I have even the smallest chance to be with her. Sure, I know she isn't here to stay. I know she has to go home eventually. But while she is here, while we can, why not? People can have fun, enjoy each other. And then people can shake hands at the end and go their separate ways and there is nothing wrong with that.

A man has to try, anyway.

LYLA

I SMELL BACON. Eggs. Baked goods. But most importantly, I smell coffee—the nectar of the gods. I roll and stretch, forgetting for a moment too long where I am before I stretch right off my bed.

That's right.

I lose my bearings, roll to my right, and fall off the bed. Because this is not my queen pillowtop in my Boston apartment. It is the full-size bed in my former bedroom in the backwoods of Kentucky. And I land with a graceless *thud* on the cold hardwood floor, not even an area rug between us. If I wasn't awake before, I am now. I still want coffee, but I don't need it at this point.

I lie there on the floor for a few seconds and then hear the door to my room fly open somewhere behind my head. I look up, the door essentially upside down to me now, and see Harper and Gentry in the doorway.

Great. Just Great.

"What happened?" Harper asks, her eyes searching over my body, trying to make sense of why exactly I'm on the floor.

I cover my face with my hands. "I fell," I say flatly.

"Off the bed?" she asks, her amusement beginning to crack through her concerned surface.

"Yep." I sigh.

I hear her laughing and look up again. Gentry is attempting a concerned expression. His lips are pressed too hard into a line. He's trying—and failing—to keep himself from laughing and I don't know him well enough for this. I remind myself I don't actually know him at all, which makes it worse.

I point my finger at him. "You. Stop laughing," I demand.

He holds his hands up in mock innocence.

I remember I don't like him and it's easier this time because he's fully dressed.

"Oh, I almost forgot. Lyla, this is Gentry. Gentry, this is Lyla," my sister says. She gestures to Gentry and then to me in turn and I growl.

"Oh, we've met," he says, leaning his shoulder back onto the door frame and winking at me.

I pinch the bridge of my nose.

"Great!" Harper exclaims, ignorant to the embarrassment I'm now feeling twice over.

The strangeness of the situation, the wink he just gave me.

What is she, blind?

"I'll be down in a few minutes," I tell her. "I just want to get dressed."

Harper nods and turns to walk down the hall, but Gentry lingers for a moment—staring down at me. He doesn't say anything, so I look around and then back at him, giving him the universal signal for *"what the hell do you want?"* and he laughs.

"I just want to apologize for last night," he says, and I'm shocked again because I don't understand what he's apologizing for. He must read the confusion because he adds, "I should have locked the door."

"I barged in on you. There's no need for you to be sorry," I say, shaking my head, because there isn't.

He stands there for a moment longer. I look upside down at him again.

What the hell does he want?

"You're different than I pictured," he says.

Of all that's transpired, this is by far the most confusing thing he's said to me. "What do you mean?"

"I mean, based on what your sister and grandparents have told me," he says. "I just pictured you differently."

"I'm sure there are photographs of me around here," I say, still not entirely sure what he means.

"Sure, there are some, but they're all old. And besides, I mean like…you as a whole person. Not just the way you look," he says.

I think about this.

What have my sister and Nan and Paw said to him?

How did they describe me?

Am I different to him in a good or disappointing way?

I have questions but I don't ask them. I don't want to care what he thinks.

Because I don't like him, I remind myself.

So, instead, I shamelessly fish. "Well, I'm sorry to disappoint you," I say, attempting to sound indifferent to his comments.

He draws a long breath and stands from his leaning position just as he'd done the night before. "Oh, you definitely don't."

I snap my head up again to look at him—still upside down—and watch him turn and walk down the hallway. My head is spinning now. Maybe I have a concussion from falling off the bed. Although if I have to guess, that fall wasn't nearly far enough to cause one.

I sit up and grab the edge of the bed, pulling myself up the rest of the way before I finally stand. I stretch and yawn and stretch some more. My phone is somewhere in the sea of blankets and I begin feeling for it. Eight thirty-six A.M. isn't exactly the *sleeping in* I'd hoped for, but it'll have to do.

After putting on an appropriate amount of clothing to be in the presence of strangers who apparently live here now, I descend to the kitchen and make a beeline for the coffee pot. Only after a cup is in my hand do I make it over to the kitchen table where Nan and Paw are seated.

Nan stands first, looking me over with a small smile. "Hi, baby," she says, putting her small arms around me and squeezing me in a tight hug.

I hug her back with a smile, realizing I've missed her so much more than I thought. "Hi, Nan."

She smells like lavender and I inhale deep breaths against her silky gray hair. She has it pulled back in her signature long braid. I hear Paw clear his throat rather loudly behind me and that's my hint.

I turn to him and he stands from his chair, arms out. I lean into his embrace, my head against his chest. Paw is a big man—a sturdy man. Over six feet tall, wide and well-built. Not gym muscles, but the kind you earn from working the land, from mending fences, and raising cattle. His hugs have always been a comfort to me, a safe haven. He releases me and I take a seat between them. I notice Gentry at the other end, a book in his hand.

A book? Weird.

It's tilted just enough that I can't see the front and it makes me even more curious about it.

"Harper is just outside on the porch," Nan says, pointing toward the back door.

I glance in the direction and nod my head.

"She's been so sad, baby," Nan says with a sigh, worry all over her face. Her eyes look heavy with ache.

I put my hand on her shoulder and give her a smile. "She's always been strong, and we can help her. She'll get through this." I give her shoulder a gentle squeeze. "I'll go check on her." I walk to the back door and push it open, looking left and right until I find my sister sitting on the back-porch swing.

She's looking off into the distance, her vision seemingly unfocused. I approach gingerly, so as not to disturb any deep train of thought, and take a seat next to her, matching the slow stride of the swing and falling into sway with her. It remains quiet for a few more moments until I hear her clear her throat.

"Do you think we only get one love?" she asks me.

In truth, I have no idea how to answer. I'm not sure I've ever been in love. Or maybe I have been.

I fell in love once, but he didn't love me back. So, I had to convince myself I didn't love him.

Because is it really love if only one person feels it?

I inhale a deep breath. "I don't think so. I think we get another chance at it," I say, hopeful I'm saying the right things, the things she needs to hear.

"What if I don't?" she asks, tears brimming her eyes.

I keep my voice calm, tranquil. "I think if second chances didn't exist, there would be a lot of lonely people. A lot of people unloved. I know of plenty who've been in love more than once. You will, too. Of course, you will love again—if you want."

She considers my words and her eyes refocus as she turns to me. "I'm glad you're here," she tells me, smiling. It's small and brittle, as if at any moment it will crumble into pieces and fall from her face.

Her lips tremble slightly, and I reach for her. I feel her begin to cry into my shoulder and I stroke her hair. I'm sure there will be more of this and I prepare myself for the coming days. I'm sure she needs it.

It's part of healing. You have to cry it out. All the pain and hurt bottled up inside has to flow from you. Correction, it has to *fall* from you. Like a great rainstorm. Bellowing thunder and lightning so bright your whole world changes color for a few moments. A downpour that floods, destroys, and cleanses. It's the only way to let go of what's inside you.

"Me too," I say, smiling back at her.

She stands from the swing and I catch her by the arm.

"Wait a minute," I say. "One question. Who the heck is Gentry?"

She laughs. "Oh, Gentry manages the farm for Nan and Paw. Once it started to be too much for us, they hired Gentry. He's so great. Everyone here likes him, and he does a great job."

I don't like him, I remind myself.

"Okay, but what's he doing sleeping in the guest room of the house?" I ask, still confused.

She looks around for a moment and then back at me. "Look, everybody's got a past, a story. I can't tell his for him, but I will tell you this: he's single," she says, winking at me and smirking.

I gasp. "Oh my god, no. That's not why I'm asking—not at *all*," I say, rushing to correct any misunderstanding.

"I don't care why you asked, sis. The answer is still the same," she says then opens the door to go back inside to the kitchen.

I follow behind her and notice my grandparents are gone. Gentry, too. "Where is everyone?" I ask.

"Nan is probably over in the store. Paw's probably in the barn. They may not manage the place anymore, but they still like to work. It's good for them. And as the owners, they still have the final say, of course. Gentry consults with them all the time on any changes, improvements, or issues. He's probably having a staff meeting with some of the workers. Then he'll make his rounds and ensure everything is running smoothly before heading to the office." Harper says this like it's routine, and it probably is. One she knows well.

"And what will you do?" I ask.

I watch her expression change a little. "I have to go to the cabin on the back side of the property. That's where Charles and I were living. We made the cabin our home instead of staying here in the main house to give ourselves some privacy and a sense of ownness, if that makes sense," she says—and it does.

"What do you have to do?" I ask her.

Harper lets out a breath. "I have to take the belongings that once made up a whole life and sort them out. I have to sort the one life into two separate lives."

"Do you want me to help?"

"Not today. How about you get dressed and reacquaint yourself with the farm? Tomorrow you can help me if you want. I can't do all I need to do in one day, anyway," she says.

I shake my head, understanding that sometimes mourning is accompanied with a desire for solitude. Or maybe she wants to break a few things that belonged to Charles. I never really liked him, so I wouldn't care either way. The only reason I accepted their relationship was because Harper seemed to be happy. Now, Charles had hurt her. Charles went and fell in love with someone else, which means Charles is a cheater.

And, *by the way*, he always insisted on being called Charles. Not Charlie, not Chuck, not any other shortened version or nickname that would make him sound like less of a snob. It had to be Charles.

If there's one thing I know for certain, it's that Harper definitely deserves the love of a man who is not a cheater and who is not named Charles.

"Wait, what should I do with my rental?" I ask. I mean, let's face it, I make a decent living, but I'm not rich. To have it a day or two is fine but who knows how long I'll be here.

Harper considers this for a moment before a smile spreads over her lips. "I'll ask Gentry if he can follow you back into town and bring you back later. He's the only one with free time."

I roll my eyes because I don't believe a word that's just come out of her mouth. But apparently, I have no choice in the matter.

I go back up to my room and find some leggings and a sports bra. I've jogged nearly every morning since high school and even though this morning has gotten off to a rocky start, I'm not about to let it stop me. A jog through the farm is the perfect solution to both realign my day and do as Harper suggested and reacquaint myself with the place.

I slip my clothes on, opting for one of my thin tank tops to complete the outfit. I pin my long brown hair back into a ponytail and search for my running shoes before stepping back out onto the porch. I put my headphones on and brace a hand against the porch railing while I scroll for the right running music. The irony isn't lost on me when I search for my country music mix. Being back on the farm just seeps right in. I hit play, hop down the stairs, and take off toward the store.

The farm runs a store on the front end of the property. It stocks homemade jams and jellies made right here on the property, fresh apples from the orchards, vegetables from the fields, and even farm fresh eggs from the chickens, plus an assortment of other goodies. People come from town to shop local, and tourists come from the city for the weekend to experience the *farm life*. In truth, they know nothing and experience nothing. Farm life isn't picking apples into a cute little basket or going on a hay-ride. Farm life is blood, sweat, and tears. Early mornings and late nights. A farmer is part veterinarian, part biologist, and part businessman.

I round the row of trees and the front of the store comes into view. It's just as quaint and charming as I remember from childhood. On my rather infrequent visits here, I never manage to make it to the store.

Buckets of mums sit on the porch and the tin roof extends over a patio with rocking chairs and small tables. People frequently eat here after purchasing fresh fruit and deli sandwiches from inside. My favorite has always been our freshly squeezed lemonade. People can buy it by the cup or take home a whole gallon, which they often do.

Making a mental note to come back tomorrow and actually go in, I pass the store and take the trail down to the orchards. In high school, I used to run between the rows of trees, which made for a beautiful and calming scene. I start down the first row when I hear a voice calling to me, just as a song is ending.

"Lyla? Is that you?"

I turn to look over my shoulder and see a face I think I recognize, but I can't be sure. I stop and turn, eyeing the man.

He's about my age. His rusty brown eyes look expectant. His dirty blond hair sweeps over his forehead messily and I notice a small scar over his left eye.

All at once, it hits me. "Dean?"

He was my high school boyfriend. My first love. My *only* love—the aforementioned love who didn't love me back. We dated for a time before he suddenly broke it off. On the day of prom. He'd told me he never loved me. And so, given our love had only ever been my love for him, unreturned, I decided I didn't want to count it as *love* at all.

"Yeah, girl! It's me! How the heck are ya?" He motions me over with his hand in an excited manner.

What the hell is he doing here?

Then it hits me. I recall a conversation with Harper a while back, when she'd tried to bring Dean up. I had told her I didn't want to talk about him. I was pretty rude about it, actually. Now, I wonder if she was trying to give me a heads up that he'd be working here.

"Dean, what on earth are you doing here on the farm?" I ask, making my way over to him.

"Oh, girl, I've been working here...I guess about a year or so now," he says.

The way he calls me *girl* hits me in the face like a brick of nostalgia, makes me remember things. Things I don't want to remember.

"Wow, I didn't know. What do you do here?" I ask.

He stands up a little straighter and rubs the front of his shirt. "Well, I'll have you know, I'm basically in charge of all the cattle now. I'm just over here getting some apples for them that won't sell anyway," he says.

I nod, looking down at his buckets of imperfect apples. It's sad people won't eat the ugly ones. As a kid, I always ate that kind. "Well, good for you!" I say, giving him a once-over.

He sounds proud and he should be. The livestock is no easy task. Sure, the farm doesn't have hundreds of head, but we do have around twenty bovine and half a dozen horses. I never cared for the horses but oddly enough have always loved the cows.

"Thank you, thank you. So, what are you doing back here?" he asks me, looking me up and down, assessing me a little too hard.

I shift. "Well, Harper—"

"Ah, yeah," he says, cutting me off and shaking his head. "It's a real shame what happened."

Wow. Not even thirty-six hours.

News certainly travels fast around here.

"Everyone hated Charles," he says. "We couldn't believe what he did to her—and with Allie, no less."

"Allie?!" I shriek. This is news to me. This I hadn't heard.

Allie's been Harper's best friend since grade school. They went everywhere together, did everything together, and for the longest time, she even worked here on the farm for our family.

He nods at me softly, sadness and disappointment over the whole situation on his face. "It's a real shame. Obviously, she quit working here after it all came out. Broke your grandparents' hearts to see it all," he says.

I can't believe my sister didn't tell me this part of the story. It would have been one thing for it to be a random woman, but the pain Harper must be feeling, the double betrayal from her husband and best friend, I can't even fathom it.

"Unbelievable," I say, shaking my head.

Dean's hand grips my bicep. "Maybe we can catch up while you're here? Get reacquainted?" he asks, but I don't like his tone or the way he's holding my arm a little too tightly.

Suddenly, I feel seventeen again. I study Dean's face once more, really giving it my attention this time. Time hasn't been kind to him. He has a little more chin now and his hairline is farther back than you'd expect for someone in their late twenties. His midsection isn't in the once sleek shape it used to be, but he isn't carrying the majestic appealing hot dad bod either. He's just sort of...frumpy.

"Uh, maybe, I'm not sure. I'll probably be really busy with Harper," I say, trying to sound as noncommittal as possible. I step back and out of his grip.

His eyes narrow and for a moment, I think he might step forward to keep his hold, but he releases me. A smile spreads across his face and he nods—but I don't like this particular brand of smile, and I grow uneasy under his gaze.

"Sure, I understand," he says. "But you know where to find me if you have some time. I gotta get back to work, okay?"

I'm already turning toward the neat rows of apple trees and putting my headphones back in. Truthfully, I need to process the information I just heard. I pick my pace back up to a run, passing tree after tree as I feel the sun overhead.

It's late summer and a small breeze is in the air, rustling the leaves on both sides of me. In a few weeks, everything will start dying. It won't be much longer now before the farm starts to prepare for fall. The pumpkin patches will pop up, and they'll start brewing cider. The sweet aroma of pumpkin rolls will fill the store. The trees lining the property and the ones scattered throughout will turn—being lit on fire by the changing seasons—and it will officially be my favorite time of year.

I make it to the end of the trees and turn toward the barns. I want to check on Paw and Maribelle, my cow. Not just any cow, *my* cow. I helped Paw deliver her when I was in high school and made him promise to never send her to the butcher. She was born premature and I had to bottle-feed her. She was mine from the moment she arrived. Of course, unlike a cat or dog, I couldn't exactly take her with me to college or have her in an apartment—let alone in Boston—so she had to stay here. But I do ask about her all the time—always have—and on each of my short trips here, I make sure to visit the barn as often as I can.

I reach for the barn door and lurch forward, trying to catch my breath. I press pause on the music and remove the headphones only to hear someone calling out.

"Who's there?" Paw asks from inside.

As I lean around the barn door, I catch sight of his face.

He sees me and returns a smile, his shoulders relaxing.

"What's wrong?" I ask, surprised by his unease.

"Just jumpy in my old age, hun, nothing to worry about," he says.

His statement puzzles me a bit, but I decide not to dwell on it. I step inside the barn and see he's examining a hoof of one of the cows.

"Oh, hey again," a voice calls from behind me.

I note that it's Dean and without turning, I greet him and watch him step to my grandfather's side. He's watching Paw with extreme interest, undoubtedly trying to learn everything he can. My grandfather is a genius with animals.

"I just want to visit Maribelle, if that's all right?" I say, looking around in the pins near me. I know which one is hers, assuming they haven't moved her since the last time I was here—which was also nearly two years ago.

Damn, that long?

I look back at Paw expectantly and he smiles.

"Of course, honey. You know where she is," he says.

I walk over to her pin and open the door, stepping inside with care. I reach my hand out to rub her head and she pushes into me. I don't care what anyone says, cows are smart. I whisper greetings to her. Maribelle is light brown all over except for a small white patch on her forehead. Her big dark brown eyes melt me as I rub her head and pet her. Then, I notice something moving behind her. A small figure. I move her to the side and a small calf appears just out of reach.

What?!

"Paw!" I yell.

"Yeah?" he yells back.

"Is Maribelle a momma?!" I ask, barely able to contain my excitement or surprise.

He laughs and says, "She sure is, honey. She sure is."

I stare at the calf in shock. She's a spitting image of her momma—same coloring, same eyes.

"What's her name?" I ask, trying hard to bury my hurt. I can't believe no one bothered to tell me.

"Don't have a name," he yells. After a brief pause, he adds, "How about you give her one?"

I feel a rush of excitement in my chest. I bend down and gently rub the calf between the eyes and back around its ears. She is so sweet. Too sweet. I study her for a moment and she licks my hand and nuzzles me a bit. "How about Lucy?" I yell over the pin gate at my grandfather.

"That's a fine name, honey," he says. "That's a fine name, indeed." Paw has a habit of saying everything twice, as if to really convince you of what he's saying.

I turn my attention back to Lucy and give her and momma Maribelle big smiles before stepping backward out of the pin. I lock it and step farther back, unable to take my eyes off them over the gate. One more step is my doom as my back meets something. What, I don't know, but it moves—wobbles, really. I hear someone cuss under their breath and then I begin to tumble. Certain I'm going to fall for a second time in the same day, I feel hands on my body. Warm hands. Big, sturdy hands. On my hips. I cover them with mine instinctively and turn to see who's caught me, both to thank them and apologize at the same time.

"Oh my gosh, I'm sorry. Thank you," I blurt out.

My eyes meet those of Gentry Bodine. His face is close—too close. Mere inches from mine.

He quickly removes his hands from my waist and clears his throat. "Don't worry about it," he says, and continues walking away from me.

"Hey, wait," I call to him, unsure why or what I'm going to say.

"Yes, ma'am, did you need something else?" he asks.

The comment feels so formal, I'm not sure how to respond. I walk a couple of steps forward to catch up with him and motion in the general direction he's walking. "May I walk with you just for a few minutes?" I ask.

He looks surprised by my request. "Okay, but I'm just headed to the house to get lunch," he says, motioning over his shoulder with his thumb like a hitchhiker.

"That's fine. I just want to clarify a few things," I say.

He turns back, and we proceed to walk out of the barn side-by-side. "Clarify a few things?" he asks.

"Again, please don't call me ma'am. I know you're just trying to be polite, but it makes me feel ancient. Can you just call me Lyla?" I ask.

He swallows, and I realize the weight of this request on anyone who grew up in the south. It's a big deal. Especially given how long we've known each other, which isn't really long enough for this sort of thing.

"I think I can manage," he says, nodding his head. The tension in his shoulders ease.

"Good. I'm just sorry in general about yesterday. In truth, it was a very long day, and I just didn't handle it well on top of being sleep deprived and tired." He considers my words and I add, "Please just accept the apology instead of countering with why I don't need to apologize."

His smile widens at this. "Okay. I accept your apology, but I want the record to show it was under duress and coercion."

I laugh and nod. "Noted."

"Anything else?" he asks.

"How long have you been living with my grandparents?" I ask him.

"A few months now," he says.

When he doesn't add anything else, I'm not sure whether to ask a follow up question or leave it alone.

Then he says, "Let's just say I was living with someone and then I needed to...not live with them anymore."

"Oh, I see," I say.

He shrugs his shoulders, and we continue on in an awkward silence for several more minutes.

"Look, what do you say we start over?" I ask. "Maybe we can just forget the bathroom incident and have a clean slate? Friends?"

A rugged, deep laugh is in his throat, but it doesn't escape his lips.

We near the porch and he turns to face me. It's so abrupt and I'm still moving forward; so, by the time I stop my forward motion, we're close. And by close, I mean there are parts of our fronts touching and I want to concentrate on his smoldering gaze, his hooded emerald eyes, but all I can think in my brain is: *HIS FRONTS ARE TOUCHING YOUR FRONTS, LYLA*.

He places his hand on my side and leans down a bit. I can feel his hot breath on my skin as he says, "Forgive me, Lyla, but no man on earth, no god in heaven, could make me forget the bathroom incident." He smirks, and his gaze travels over my chest and stomach then up my throat, stopping to linger on my mouth for a moment.

He bites his bottom lip—and I can't find any words in my brain.

Where are my words?

Where are the emergency heart paddle things for these chest pains?

The way he says my name—like it's a secret. His growling tone. I can't handle it.

"Um, I, um…" I manage.

He laughs again, a teasing expression on his face. All at once, he releases me. The heat from his gaze is gone, his hand is gone, his front gone. My skin feels cool with his sudden departure, and a shiver replaces the warmth.

"Do you want some lunch?" he asks, his expression now benign, his tone flat.

What the hell?

I nod. It's all I can manage.

LYLA

GENTRY DOESN'T TALK.

He doesn't talk the entire time we eat lunch. He doesn't talk while he clears our plates. He doesn't talk beyond cursory manners. And then, he departs, going back to work, which leaves me sitting in the kitchen, confused and...sort of hot. Like hot and bothered. Not actually hot, since the air conditioner is pretty good in the house.

I mean, during our first encounter, he was in his briefs, all bare chested in front of me. And in the next, he pressed his fronts all over my fronts. And I haven't been laid in...a while, okay. Like, too long. That's the problem. I'm not thinking with my brain-brain, I'm thinking with my lady-brain, which is in my pants.

Focus, Lyla.

I decide Gentry is unavoidably attractive—despite the fact that I don't like him. Like you could be blind, running your fingers over braille, but still know that man is a meat popsicle.

Did I just use the term meat popsicle?

I loathe myself.

A shower. Yes, a shower.

I need to shower after my run and maybe I can make it a cold one. I don't like Gentry and he is hot. But he is also...odd. Very odd. He's

friendly, then he cold shoulders me, then he's friendly again, then…
he's much more than friendly, then cold again.

What the heck?

I pull clothes from my bag, going through the motions without
paying attention, lost in thought. Which is probably why, by the end
of it, I have two shirts, no pants, a bra, and only one sock but no
panties. I need to focus and try this again if I want a full outfit. I
collect all the appropriate items for a shower and make my way down
the hall, just as I did last night. At least this time I know there are no
surprises to be had because no one is in the house.

I feel sort of bad that everyone else is out working on the farm, but
they've all told me to settle in and there isn't much arguing with the
bunch of them once they decide something. Maybe after my shower,
I'll go back out and offer to help in the store, just a little.

I turn the knobs in the shower and feel the water with the back of
my hand. Then, I close my eyes and wait for the perfect temperature,
which I make slightly cooler than usual. I step into the tub and underneath the water, letting it run down my body, and I feel all my muscles
relax at once.

This shower has a small window in it, looking out over the back-
yard and beyond. Since it's on the second floor and only big enough to
show someone's shoulders and head, my grandparents never bothered
putting any blurry coating on it; so, I can see everything. I watch the
cattle in the distant fields and see some workers in the orchards,
picking apples.

I lather up shampoo and start working it through my mess of hair
when I spot Gentry talking to someone I don't recognize. He's close
enough that I can make out most details of his physique. Nothing is
lost to the blurring effect of distance. I study his stance, the way he
leans, one hand in his pocket, the other pointing somewhere. His
shoulders are all business, but still relaxed.

God, he's delicious and it's so inconvenient.

How long has it been?

Wait, shut up.

I don't need to think about that right now. I start rinsing my hair
and counting anyway.

Two years.

It's been two years since I've dated anyone. Since anyone has touched me. Except myself. My eyes shoot open.

No, not here. I can't do that here.

I slide my hands down my neck and pull at the tension in my shoulders.

Although…

Perhaps if I do, it will help me leave behind these thoughts of Gentry.

I listen intently, as if hearing someone downstairs will be of any consequence. I peek out the window and see no one approaching the house. I slide my hands down, over my breasts, pausing to caress them for a few moments. I feel my nipples harden under my touch. My hand explores the skin of my stomach and farther until I part myself. I inhale, a sharp intake, and shut my eyes to concentrate on the sensation I'm creating for myself.

The beauty of masturbation is that you know your body better than anyone else. I stroke up and down, in and out slowly, feeling a climax begin to build. I lean my forehead against the window, pressing my other hand against the glass to steady myself. I can feel myself getting close, so I keep my pace steady, focusing on nothing other than what I'm feeling, then I release against my fingers. When I come, I open my eyes instinctively, releasing the breath I've been holding and panting just to regulate again.

I look over the landscape of the farm and then I see him. Gentry is staring up at me. I duck and nearly fall to into the bath tub.

OH MY GOD.

Did he just see my O face?!

NO. No. Surely, just…no.

He must have looked up after…

I gather the courage to stand back up and look in his direction, peering over the window sill.

Yep, he's still looking at me. Staring is a more appropriate word. Staring hard.

What is that look he's giving me?

Shock? Amusement?

He isn't smiling but he doesn't seem upset or offended. I have a choice to make. Slink down and out of the shower and avoid Gentry as much as humanly possible for as long as I'm here. Or be the woman I know I can be, and own the fact that I do what every red-blooded man does for himself and there's nothing wrong with it, and stop acting like I have something to be ashamed of. I decide I have to be the latter. I stand up, making eye contact with him, and then I grab the conditioner. I pour some into my hand rather dramatically and then begin to lather it into my hair. His jaw drops. I stand there—unwilling to break eye contact first—and watch him pick his jaw back up. Then he smirks and shakes his head, before he turns away and walks toward the barns.

I won. I fucking won. Damn right I won.

Society is strange about masturbation. I personally think it's extremely healthy to touch yourself on at least a semi-regular basis. Although as of late, I haven't really done much of that either, so this shower release was actually much needed.

Diddling yourself relieves stress; this is a fact. I can feel a difference in my body already. I often encourage my friend Cora to do it, which she finds strange but in an endearing way, thankfully. Last Christmas, I bought her and a few of our close friends vibrators and we had a good laugh about it.

But I bet those toys aren't sitting somewhere in the back of their closets unboxed or unused, that's all I'm saying.

In fact, I have it on good authority that none of them are. I know for sure Cora uses hers. As best friends, we share everything. Guys call it *oversharing*, but I think it's completely normal to know what kind and color your best friend's vibrator is.

I finish my shower and head back to my room in my towel instead of dressing in the bathroom. It's too humid in there and I'm not a fan of clothes sticking to my wet body.

When I sit on the edge of my bed I hear a knock at my door. "Who is it?" I call, but no one answers. Instead, there's just another short knock. I call again, this time a bit louder. No answer—again.

Walking across the room, I tuck the towel around me and then turn the knob to my bedroom door, opening it just slightly, not wanting to reveal too much of my toweled body in case it's someone other than my sister or Nan. But no one's there. I look up and down the hallway.

Weird.

As I'm about to close the door, I notice a note stuck to the outside of it. I pull it off and step back into my room, turning the piece of paper over in my hand. It's folded in half, no marks on the outside. I open it and slowly read the words scrawled inside.

Do you endeavor to awaken this hunger within me?
The one I snuffed out so long ago?
You, and your form, momentous in its movement,
seek to coax it from slumber.
It will surely burn me from the inside out.
Be careful, woman.

Now my jaw is somewhere on the floor. I don't even know where. It could have rolled away for all I know. I look over my shoulder like I'm going to see someone there but I'm still alone. I read it again. And again. I blink. I have no words. This isn't like me. I'm not the type of woman shocked into silence by a few words.

But these words?

These words are something else. Something more. Ridiculous in their beauty. Threatening in the way they warn me.

I fold the paper back and set it on top of my dresser. I'm not really sure what to do with my hands now.

Part of me, the really naughty part, wants to do something. Because apparently my shower rub wasn't enough.

Write back?

No, that's stupid.

And god knows, I'm not nearly as poetic.

I shake the thoughts from my head. That's just not a good idea. No way.

What is he hoping for? A fling while I'm supposed to be here helping my heartbroken sister?

That hardly seems appropriate.

I consider all of this. I don't have time for any of it. I turn to the waste basket near my dresser, but I don't have the heart to throw out the note. It's too good, too beautiful. I place it back on the dresser. There's no harm in keeping it.

I finish dressing, choosing a white cotton summer dress. The kind you don't need a bra for, which ranks in the top three reasons for wearing them. I throw my wet hair up in a messy bun on top of my head and slide sandals on before making my way out the door and toward the store.

Part of me desperately wants to avoid Gentry, while the other part hopes to see him. I can't decide which I want more, and it's irritating. Despite my inner war, I make it to the store without seeing him, and slip inside. I take stock of the place. Not much has changed. Bushels of vegetables line the inside aisles and buckets of apples are on display to the right. The left of the store has shelves of honey, jams, and different preserves. I catch sight of the lemonade stand in the back, next to the pitchers of sweet tea and coolers filled with meats and cheeses. Next to them are the deli cases and baked goods.

Nan is speaking to a customer—helping the woman choose apples —when she sees me. She offers me a wave and a smile.

I smile back, stepping farther into the store. I start toward the lemonade, determined to have a glass. As I'm pouring, Nan joins me.

"Hi, baby, what are you doing here?" she asks.

"Well, I've come for some lemonade. And maybe to help you out around here. I can't very well just sit in the house or walk around aimlessly," I offer.

Nan nods at me. "Well, I won't insist you settle in again. I'll put you to work. There's always work, baby," she says, patting me on the forearm.

I pull the glass of lemonade to my lips and sip. I sip until I gulp and then I gulp again. This really is the best damn lemonade I've ever had. I don't even know how people drink the store-bought stuff. I finish with the paper cup and throw it in the trash. Nan will insist I don't pay for it, but later I'll slip money into the register.

I start with restocking, replacing the different types of apples in the baskets, attempting to stack them up so they decoratively occupy the space. I move onto restocking the shelves and even speak to a few customers, giving them my recommendations. A few people from town recognize me and we make small talk, catching up. It makes me think of my actual job and how I'll likely have to get on my laptop later to send a few emails and touch base with some clients, which both bothers and saddens me. I like writing, don't get me wrong. But writing for clients is a tad annoying at times. Annoying only because it means I'm not writing for myself. I'll save that conversation with myself for a later time, though.

As the day winds down, I help Nan clean up and close the store. When we're finished, we walk back toward the house at a leisurely pace, talking about nothing in particular as we catch up on a number of topics and laugh.

After arriving back to the house, we cook dinner together. But my hopes to sit down and eat it are thwarted when Harper comes back from the cabin a few minutes after it's finished, and all hell breaks loose.

Well, not really. But it's hell in my head.

"Don't you and Gentry need to take your rental back before the place closes?" Harper asks me.

"Oh, right," I say.

"I'll text him," she says.

Great. Wonderful.

I'll be stuck in a car with him after what he saw earlier. I can't wait.

"He'll meet you out front in a few minutes. Maybe you guys can stop and eat since you'll miss dinner here?" Harper says, giving me a shit eating grin.

This is exactly what little sisters do: torment you.

After grabbing my purse and keys from upstairs, I slip outside and wait for him. I sit on the edge of the porch and decide it's imperative to text Cora about this.

You're not going to believe the type of shit that's happening here.

CORA

OMG. Tell me everything.

First. There's a hot guy on the farm. Gentry. And he's making me hot. And he saw me flicking my bean in the shower. And I have to take my rental back. And guess who's giving me a ride back?

CORA

OMG.

OMFG.

I want to start driving down the road and throw myself out the door while in motion.

CORA

Remain calm. And just, you know, YOLO.

I hate it when you say YOLO.

CORA

There's no alternative.

There are a million alternatives to that outdated acronym.

CORA

YOLO.

I hate you.

CORA

You don't.

The rustling of gravel catches my attention and I look up to see Gentry sauntering toward me. I didn't even know people actually sauntered but sure enough, the man is actually doing it. The sun at his back casts a long shadow over him and I can see the sweat rolling down his forearms.

He stops a few feet short of me. "Ready to go?"

I stand from my place on the steps and walk forward. "So, you can just follow me and then I'll hop in with you?"

He nods, and we both get into our trucks to head toward town.

After handing over the rental, I'm in Gentry's truck and we're on our way back but it's not exactly a short ride. The closest rental return was forty-five minutes from the farm.

"So, did you have a nice shower earlier?" Gentry asks out of nowhere, and I reach for the door handle, completely prepared to tuck and roll.

"It was fine, thank you," I say, sure I'm turning bright red everywhere.

"I'm sure you felt nice and relaxed after," he says, and I know what he's poking at.

"Look, we're just...we're not going to discuss that, all right? Okay? I'm an adult. That's my shower time. I can do whatever I want to in there," I snap.

I look over at him and he's just smirking with his stupid perfect face and his right dimple is pronounced and I want to put my pinky in it.

Stupid dimple.

"Anyway, on a scale from zero resistance to I'll owe you a favor, how hard would it be for me to convince you to stop for food?" I ask, wanting desperately to change the topic. It's not that I'm playing into my sister's matchmaking idea of getting *dinner* together. It's more like I'm on the verge of starving and my stomach is about to start eating itself if I don't put something in it soon.

"I wish I could pull that favor, but I'm starving, actually," he says.

"Thank you for agreeing to help me take the rental back, by the way," I say, realizing he too gave up a home-cooked meal to help me.

"It's not a problem," he says with a shrug. "What do you feel like eating?"

"I know there's probably a slim chance there's a sushi place around here, but like, is there a sushi place around here?" I ask.

Gentry starts laughing. "As a matter of fact, there is one."

I jump up and down in my seat with excitement and realize in the same moment I'm not wearing a bra, which calms me down.

"Like sushi, do you?" he asks.

"Maybe a little," I say.

He rolls his eyes, teasingly. "I see that."

A few minutes later, we pull into the parking lot of a small restaurant called Osaka. From the outside, it's what you'd expect of an Asian restaurant in this area. The lettering is sharp and bold. Minimal decoration. Small shrubs.

"Wait there," he says. He gets out and walks around the truck then opens my door for me. He holds out his hand to me, looking into my eyes expectantly.

I place my hand in his, letting him help me out of the truck with all his southern chivalry. "Thank you."

Inside, we make our way to a table and place our orders. Over dinner, we discuss the farm, how I grew up on it, how he grew up. Conversation comes easy—scary easy. At some point, I realize this feels like a date and I almost freak out. But it's nothing a shot or two of sake can't fix.

By the time we make it back to the farm, I feel comfortable and warm. We walk up the stairs and I head toward the bathroom.

"Thank you again for your help, and for dinner," I say. Despite my insistence on paying for myself, Gentry wouldn't have it—not that I'm surprised.

"Anytime," he says, and something about the ease in which it rolls off his lips leads me to believe he really means it.

With the bathroom door shut behind me, I walk to the mirror and assess my face. My cheeks are pink from the sun and the saké. With no makeup on, it's only exaggerated. Departing the bathroom a few minutes later, after I've rinsed my face and brushed my teeth, I notice a small note stuck to my door again.

I pull it off and step into my room, opening it quickly, unable to control the excitement bubbling over.

. . .

*I cannot decide if you aim to be
an angel or devil in that dress.
Oh how the wind picks it up,
teases and torments.
Will you come to me?
Still the ache underneath this moon?*

Fuck.

LYLA

I READ the note two more times and fold it back. Then I open it and read it again. His words leave me breathless. My heart is pounding hard in my chest and I don't know what I'm supposed to do right now. Or what I want to do.

What does this mean?

Okay, Lyla. You know what it means.

Does he want me to come to his room? Like...tonight?

Surely, we can't have sex tonight.

I mean, we could...but that sounds like it could get so complicated...

Okay, I need to stop having a conversation with myself and make up my mind.

I pull my hair down from my messy bun while my thoughts wander further down the rabbit hole. I stand in front of the mirror and comb my fingers through my long locks, attempting to calm the waves a little and assessing myself. Even sun-kissed, I've always had pale skin. My hazel eyes and dark hair are a stark contrast. I pull the straps of my dress down and let it fall to the floor, leaving only my panties behind. I reach for sleep shorts and a large oversized sweatshirt, which hangs off my shoulders. I put socks on my feet and grab the notes, intending to get to the bottom of this little game.

I don't know if I'm mad, flattered, insulted, or a little of each, but I'm hoping I figure that out by the time I knock on his door—or at least by the time he answers. I move around the banister to the other side of the hall and stand in front of his door, my fist hesitating before I summon the courage to actually knock. Three brisk taps and I wait.

I hear shuffling inside but get no response. I hear more shuffling and then I see shadows of feet under the door and I brace myself.

He pulls his door open wide, leaning against the door frame with his forearm, immediately making eye contact and smiling.

But I'm not smiling. I can't divert any efforts away from trying not to assault his body with my eyes because Gentry is shirtless again. His gray sweatpants sit low on his hips and the elastic from his Calvin Klein underwear is showing and that's all I notice. There's no focus left for things like smiles.

"Are you always shirtless?" I gruff, sounding more annoyed than I intend to. But he *is* always shirtless. And I mean, honestly, no one needs to be naked this much.

"Only when I'm in the privacy of the bathroom or my own room," he states, and he has a point. It's not like he's been walking around in common areas like this. We're not in the kitchen. He's in his space.

But *still*. He could have put one on to answer the door.

I roll my eyes at him and his smile only seems to grow.

"What are these?" I hold the notes up, changing the subject to the reason I knocked on his door in the first place.

His eyes search mine for a moment and his smile fades a little. "You don't like them?" There's hesitation in his voice, but mischief in his eyes.

I don't want to answer the question. "That's not the point. What do they mean?"

His shoulders gently rise and fall. "You're a beautiful woman, Lyla. And a beautiful woman deserves beautiful words," he says. His voice is low and deep, his words drawn out, resembling both a command and a whisper. Like no other truth exists. Like no other possibility remains.

I swallow the lump in my throat and attempt words. "Thank you," I say, "but this speaks of desire, doesn't it?"

"Is there something wrong with that?" he asks.

I consider his question. Of course, there's nothing wrong with desire. It isn't even something one can help; it just happens to a person.

"But you don't know anything about me," I counter, avoiding directly answering that question, too.

"Your family talks, Lyla. They talk about you. What kind of person you are, what you've done. And I've listened. And now, seeing you... you're just...bewitching." he says.

Did he just use the word bewitching?

Really?

Bewitching?

My lady parts are on fire. "I just don't think it's a good idea. That's not what I'm here for— obviously." I say it before I really even think about it.

I watch his gaze fall to study my legs before his eyes find mine again. "I know you're here for your sister. And I know you're going back to Boston when you're done. But that doesn't really stop me from thinking about your legs wrapped around my neck."

I choke. On nothing at all.

Did he really just say that?

I shake the vision of his head between my legs and my hand gripping his hair then press on. "Regardless, it's just not a good idea." I swallow hard on my words and feel a tinge of regret as I speak them.

He nods his head. "I understand."

I nod, glad we're now on the same page. "Good."

"Can I still write you notes?" he asks.

My face twists a bit, and he laughs. "Why?" I ask, not understanding why he'd want to write me notes without getting anything in return.

"Just because I can't have you doesn't mean you don't deserve stirrings or the knowledge that you stir something in another," he says.

His words come so easy that I begin to wonder if maybe this is just a game he plays with all women. I push away the negative thoughts and focus. "I guess that would be okay," I say.

"Okay, then. Good." The solemn look fades from his face, replaced with a smile once again.

"Good," I say, unsure of what else to say. "So, we can be *friends?*"

Gentry's lips let a small laugh escape, one of quiet amusement. "If that's what you want," he says. "Would you like to come in?"

"Um..."

"I promise to behave," he says, laughing at his own joke.

I peer inside his room and...if I'm being honest with myself, I'm curious to know more about him. This is the perfect opportunity for a little investigative work. "All right, but just for a little while," I say, taking a small step forward into his space.

I'm not sure exactly how long he's been here, but the space is completely transformed. At least from what I remember about it. He's painted the walls deep green and the curtains are black. The room is quite large. I recall Nan having a lot of clutter in here before, but he seems to have rectified that. On the wall closest to the door, his bed and two nightstands are neatly spaced. The linens on his bed are light, an interesting contrast to the dark walls and wood of the furniture. The nightstands aren't cluttered. Simple lamps on both. There's a book opened and downturned on what I assume is his side of the bed.

Perhaps I interrupted his reading.

On the opposite wall is a fireplace. He's left the brick alone, careful not to taint the charm of the old house. But he's installed bookshelves on either side and they overflow with books. From what I can tell, all different kinds, and I walk closer to peer at some of the titles. Some I recognize and others I don't. In front of the fireplace are two enormous bean bag chairs—the kind that are fluffy and definitely meant for adults.

I look at the chairs and then at him, raising an eyebrow.

"What can I say? I'm a kid at heart," he says. "Plus, they're a lot more comfortable than those tall chairs you always see in front of fireplaces."

I laugh. I have to agree that they *do* look very comfortable. "May I?"

He motions for me to help myself, so I carefully attempt to crawl into the center of one of the chairs. These things easily seem big enough for two people each. I cozy down into it and relax, placing my head back and staring up at the ceiling.

"See?" he says, as if to say *I told you so*.

But I have to give credit where it's due. "Definitely, yes." I exhale a breath. This thing is amazing. I almost don't even miss my bed in Boston.

He walks over to the fireplace and turns the knob for the gas.

Some years back, my grandparents had converted all the fireplaces to gas, deciding to save themselves the trouble of starting fires the old-fashioned way. With age comes the desire— and merit—for conveniences you never even thought you'd want. Of course, I had always encouraged them to get or do whatever would make life easier for them. Some battles I won, some I lost. Like when I suggested selling the farm. I'll never make that mistake again. This place isn't going anywhere.

Gentry comes to sit down in the other chair, but I stick my hand up and say, "Wait. Put a shirt on first, for the love of cheese and crackers," my voice stern and pleading.

He looks down at his bare chest and rubs his hands over it.

"And don't do that!" I add.

He laughs louder than I've heard him laugh before. It's deep in his belly, raspy and melodic.

I press my palms against my eyes and shake my head.

He retreats back to his dresser—hands up in a display of mock innocence—where he retrieves a white T-shirt. I watch his back muscles flex as he pulls the shirt over his head, feeling a pang of disappointment when everything is covered up. He turns to me then, and gestures at himself as he crosses the floor and takes a seat in the other bean bag chair.

"Is this better?" he asks.

I nod, not speaking of the war going on inside me or the entire half of me that wants to shout, *Hell no! Take it back off!* Someone needs to gag the horn-dog inside me and throw her in a closet somewhere.

"I like your room," I say, wishing to talk about anything other than the amount of clothes he's now wearing. At this point, I'm willing to ask him what color paint is on his walls, the name of it, and where specifically he bought it.

"Thank you. Don't get me wrong, the room was fine the way it was before, but Nan and I don't exactly have the same taste in decor," he says, grinning.

"You call her Nan, too?" I ask.

He shakes his head and says, "She insisted on it pretty much immediately. I attempted to call her Mrs. Whitney but she didn't like it. Then I tried for ma'am but she wasn't having that either—go figure. I even offered to call her by her first name, but she refused."

This shouldn't surprise me. I haven't heard anyone call Nan by her first name other than Paw, pretty much ever. And the only people to call her by her last were strangers. "Ma'am" is something pretty much all the Whitney women despise, and it's by inherited trait.

I nod my agreement. "Figures. Are you close with them? My grand-parents?"

He nods again. "I think so. I hope so. They've been very kind and have helped me a lot through some hard times."

I wonder what kind of hard times he means, or if he's referring to his previous living arrangement.

Sensing my unasked question, he pushes forward in his story. "In short, I was engaged. It wasn't long ago actually. Not in the grand picture, anyway. When I spoke to them about it, especially Nan, it was like she shared in my sadness and insisted I moved in here. One, because I needed to find a new place, but also because she assumed I needed to do some healing."

"And have you?" I ask.

"The funny thing is, I live in a strange paradox. Almost as soon as my ex broke off our engagement, I felt relief. Because I'm quite sure we didn't really love each other. Not the way we should have—or needed to. So, maybe I was never wounded? Another part of me wonders if we ever truly heal from those types of wounds. Perhaps we always carry them. I wonder sometimes if I'm meant to exist both eternally wounded but also never actually wounded. Perhaps having never been wounded is my wound. It's a hard revelation in love," he says, his eyes staring off into the flames of the fire. The light dances on his face, the glow flickering in his eyes in such a way that I don't know if I'm more captivated by his face or his words.

"I see," I say. And I do. But not wanting to offer so much of myself I ask, "So, when you're done healing, you'll move out?"

"Maybe, maybe not. Maybe I'll fall in love with a good woman and she'll want to be here with me. Maybe Nan and Paw will accept her as they've accepted me," he says.

I don't like this answer—or the jealous feelings it's stirring within me. The thought of some woman here, in my childhood home, with my grandparents. It almost feels like she'd be in my place. Not in *my place* as Gentry's woman because I'm not, but…in other ways. I can't even make sense of my own emotions on the topic at this point.

"And you'll have your little babies running around the farm?" I ask, teasing.

His eyes smile before his mouth does. "I'd like that," he says, looking me in the eyes.

I look away from him and toward the fire, tucking my hair behind my ear. I've never personally given thought to whether I want kids, but Gentry seems like the fatherly type. I can picture it. A toddler at his ankle, another thrust upon his shoulder. The thought warms me, and I nuzzle deeper into the bean bag chair.

Silence falls over us for a few minutes as we both stare into the flames, mesmerized by their ability to be both a beautiful thing and a dangerous thing.

I think that's how I see Gentry, too.

And mysterious.

He is, by all accounts, a stranger. It's not like I know a lot about him. I've been here for twenty-four hours, yet this whole scene is playing out in my head and it's sort of insane.

"Do you want a drink?" he asks quietly, gently startling me from my train of thought.

"Yes, please," I say.

He wiggles up from his seat and walks to a small bar cart next to his window. I hear the clinking of fragile glasses as he pours something for us. He steps back across the floor and holds a glass in front of me.

I take it from him, eyeing the liquid. "What is it?"

"Just try it," he encourages.

I smell it. It doesn't smell like whiskey, which is a good thing because that, I don't like. I put the glass to my mouth and take a small sip. It's good, smooth. I lick my bottom lip. "I like this," I say. I take another sip, this time larger, licking my lips again when I pull the glass away.

"You're going to have to stop doing that," he says.

I look up at him, confused. "Drinking?" I ask, shifting my eyes from left to right.

"Licking your lips," he says. "I have sweatpants on, for Christ's sake."

I nearly spit my drink back into my glass, covering my mouth with the back of my hand to prevent doing so. I feel the heat caused by his words and the liquor in my chest, sure I'm beginning to turn red. "I'm sorry," I say, choking down my drink and clearing my throat. I look over to him then and his face doesn't betray his thoughts. His eyes are heavy, the desire palpable. My hand reaches for my throat instinctively, though I'm not sure why.

"Don't be sorry. Just let me know if you need any help next time," he teases, his voice smooth and wanting.

I press my eyes closed and shake my head. "Stop that." I try to keep my tone light and dismissive. My hand extends beyond the bean bag chair to set my glass on the floor, but it causes me to nearly topple over. I find myself attempting to shift my weight back and catch myself with my hands at the same time, but the effort is futile.

It's also unnecessary, because Gentry has somehow wrapped an arm around me and carefully helped me back into a sitting position. I can feel his warm hand on my side—just underneath my breast—and it causes me to shudder. I start to wonder what his hands will feel like on me, all over me, without the barrier of clothing between us.

NO.

STOP.

STOP THAT.

I'm yelling at myself internally now because clearly the alcohol is making me think things. Dirty things. It isn't me. I'm certainly not thinking about those things. It's the warm alcohol coursing through my veins, causing temporary insanity. I'm a lightweight in truth and between whatever he gave me to drink and the saké earlier, I'm feeling very good right now.

"You okay?" he asks.

"Yeah, thank you. Sorry," I say.

"Sorry for what?" he asks, and it occurs to me that I don't know.

"I have no idea, actually. It's just what people say," I sass, shrugging my shoulders.

"Don't apologize unless you have something to apologize for. Apologies lose their value when given so freely," he says.

I stare at him, my head starting to swim a little.

How strong was that drink?

Maybe I didn't eat enough at dinner.

"What are you, some kind of farm philosopher and poet?" I ask.

He laughs and says, "Nothing so official, no."

I lay my head to the side and stare at him. I feel a yawn and try to talk through it. "Maybe I should go back to my room now," I say, my eyes becoming heavier by the second.

"If you want," he says.

But I can barely hear him or see him. My eyes are shutting, and I'm powerless against how warm and comfortable and relaxed I am.

He whispers, "Let me get you a blanket."

But I protest. The last thing I say—or the last thing I remember saying—is, "No, just stay with me. Stay right here with me."

Then, I drift off and have the most fulfilling sleep I've had in years.

LYLA

I WAKE SLOWLY, one eye at a time.

This doesn't feel like my bed.

I don't feel alone.

I shift slightly and the arm around my midsection tightens. Warm breath is on the back of my neck and I'm sunken into a giant bean bag chair.

It's all coming back now.

I blink the sleep from my eyes and look around. The fire is still going, low and steady. The sun is beginning to peek through the curtains, just a sliver through the middle and from the edges. The room is hazy.

It must be early.

"Gentry?" I whisper, and I feel him stir behind me. We're spooning, his large body cradling my smaller one. I rub my forehead. "Gentry, wake up." I shift, trying to get him to wake.

"What is it? What's wrong?" he asks, sleep in his voice.

I can't see his face, but I'd venture to guess he hasn't even opened his eyes.

I press my fingers into my eye sockets, trying to remember. And I do. I remember. I remember asking him to stay. I asked him to lie with me.

NO.

I did. I asked him.

"Oh my god," I huff. Then he breathes into my hair and I feel a sensation run down my spine. "No, this is not good, this is so bad, I'm so sorry."

"I told you not to make apologies for nothing," he says. He stretches back and releases his grip from my middle.

I turn to face him. "No, you don't understand. This is obviously completely contradictory to what I said last night, and now I just look like an idiot," I groan.

"Lyla, no. Listen, nothing happened, okay?" His voice carries a sincerity I can't describe.

"Well, this can't happen again. Absolutely not," I say, my tone a bit harsher than I intend.

His expression changes at my words. He looks offended—no, he looks wounded.

"Okay, no problem," he says, rolling away from me and out of the giant fluffy bean bag chair. Before I know it, he's across the room and pulling clothes from his drawers, shoes from the floor, and his cell phone from the table. "I'm going to get a shower. I'm sure you can see yourself out," he says, walking out without saying anything more.

And just like that, he's cold again. I am such an idiot. A major ass. I smash my face into the bean bag.

I creep back to my room and shut the door behind me. Then I walk straight to my bed and collapse on it. I hear the shower start down the hall and I hate myself. This is proof I just don't know how to...deal with people. Especially men. Everything is awkward and wrong and never works. When I do seem to get past that part, I'm met with rejection. So, at this point, I'm comfortable in my solitude.

I search for my phone and scroll through emails, social media, and check messages rather numbly while contemplating the recent events in my life. The more I think about it, the more Gentry really *doesn't* have any reason to be upset with me. Of course I'm right. None of this is right; none of it will work. There's no reason for us to be getting cuddly. I want to kick myself for asking him to stay in my little booze haze.

I close my eyes and lie in silence. After a few moments, I hear the bathroom door open and shut. I hear him step across the floor back to his room. He doesn't seem to be in there very long before I hear his door open again. His feet stop in front of my door and my eyes shoot open. I wait to see if he'll knock but it doesn't come. He's only there for a moment and then gone again before I hear him on the stairs and getting farther away, then I don't hear him at all.

I only briefly wonder why he stopped in front of my door and then it clicks. I hop up from my bed and open my door. The paper is taped like the others and I take it, shutting my door again. I don't make it back to my bed before I unfold it.

Holding you, warm against my skin.
Soft, how you melt me.
Dangerous woman,
you don't know how I crave,
how I wish to devour.
Your mouth, it calls to me.

I can't move. I can't deny the fact that I like these notes. No one has ever said these kinds of things to me. But that doesn't mean that pursuing it is a good idea.

I instinctively clutch the small scrap of paper to my chest. I hold it against me for a long time, replaying the words in my head, imagining his voice saying them as I do. I place it on the dresser with the other two, thankful I had remembered to grab them when I left his room earlier.

I shake thoughts of him and his words from my mind a final time before getting ready for the day. I dress to help Harper in the cabin as promised and go downstairs. To my disappointment, Gentry is already gone. Or perhaps, it should be relief. I don't even know at this point. I'm confusing myself. Yes, the attraction is there, the lust. But I'm only here for a short time and the complications are too much. I'm trying really hard to resist but again…my stupid lady-brain. Nan and Paw are in the kitchen and I give them both kisses on their foreheads before finding Harper outside on the porch again. She isn't crying this time, though.

She hands me coffee in a travel mug without a word, but gives me a small mischievous grin.

"What?" I ask.

"Nothing, Lyla. Nothing at all." She raises her shoulders and eyebrows at me in unison.

I grimace. "Obviously something."

She nods in the direction of the cabin as if to signal our departure and we begin walking. "Let's just say, despite how big this house is, it's not as if you can really hide," she says.

I sigh and roll my eyes. "No, no. Don't even *think* what you're thinking."

"What am I thinking?" she asks, raising an eyebrow at me.

"You're thinking I hooked up with a complete stranger after one day, and I definitely didn't," I say, wagging my finger at her.

"No?" she asks, both shock and disappointment lining her voice.

"Of course not," I say, somewhat offended she'd think so. Don't get me wrong, I have no problem if a lady wants to go hooking up with strangers. That's her prerogative. And sure, I've had some flings in Boston. "I'm not here for that, I'm here for you, Harper."

"Look, I appreciate that you're here. I do. And I'm sure we'll have plenty of time for me. But Gentry Bodine is hot—white hot. You know it, I know it, and the blind nuns at the monastery know it."

"That's not the point," I say.

"Then what is?" she asks.

I take a sip of my coffee and consider her question. "The point is, there are several points. I'm here for you, not him—despite his hotness. I don't even know anything about him."

"People have seasons, Lyla. I am in winter. It's cold and desolate here. It's not a time for me to feel. But you're not. You shouldn't deprive yourself of a spring rain just because I'm not ready for one," she says.

"I don't think I've ever had a spring rain," I admit.

"Well, don't you think it's time?" she asks.

I don't know the answer to that question. I think I've avoided it my entire life quite purposefully, actually. She's just in a season of winter and I'm pretty sure I've been in a perpetual state. "It sounds like it could be painful," I say.

"Sometimes it is," she says.

We continue quietly for a few more minutes, and I let her words sink in before changing the subject. "So, how far did you get yesterday?" I ask.

"Not very," she says, her voice growing small, and I hear something in it.

Shame?

Distance?

I'm not sure but I seek to comfort her and pat her back. "That's okay. After today, we'll be all caught up and you can put this part of the ordeal behind you."

There's a new kind of concern or shame written all over her face, and I don't really understand why she'd be feeling so intensely about the belongings in her house. We walk a few more minutes in silence until we arrive at the cabin.

As we approach the door, she turns to me. "I made a mess yesterday," she confesses, her eyes glossy.

I look at her, confused, trying to sort out her meaning without needing to ask. "Well, we can just clean it up while we're here, I'm sure it's not a big deal," I say, waving my hand through the air like it might also wave away her concern.

She exhales a long, deep breath and turns back to the door. She slides the key in and turns the knob, opening the door, and it doesn't take long for me to understand what she meant by her statement.

The place is wrecked. Harper was a hurricane, apparently. A tornado. She had been intentionally destructive. Furniture is flipped over, linens are shredded, pillows are stuffing-less. All the photos of her and Charles now have large holes in his face. Some of the frames are smashed. She'd taken what appears to be his clothing and thrown them into the fireplace, only she hadn't burned them. Some dishes are smashed. I look at my little sister after taking in the scene before me and she looks back at me, her posture clearly expectant of a lecture.

But I just smile at her. A laugh begins to rise in my throat, small at first, but it grows. It escapes my lips and bellows into the air. She stares at me, starting to laugh herself. Her laugh grows louder and soon the two of us are standing amongst the rubble—which used to be her perfect and quaint life—laughing like mad women, clutching our stomachs.

Soon Harper's laughs turn into tears and I take her in my arms. She cries onto my shoulder, her whole body shuddering with each sob. I understand. I understand her need to destroy it, to break this life down. It had been a lie and she needed to take its perfection and make it look as broken as she felt inside.

I untuck her from my arms and hold her by the shoulders at arm's length. I wipe her tears from her cheeks. "Be done now," I say, my voice both soft and stern.

She nods at me, straightening herself. She sniffles and wipes at her face.

"Where are the matches?" I ask.

She looks at me quizzically but ultimately retrieves them from a kitchen drawer. When she tries to hand them to me, I push them back into her hand and point at the fireplace.

"No, Lyla. I wasn't *seriously* going to burn them. I was just angry. I need to box them up," she says.

"No, you will not. Why should you have to do that for him? He abandoned you. And the way I see it, he abandoned everything in this house he didn't take, which means he doesn't want it," I say, folding my arms across my chest and jutting my hip out to one side.

She looks back at the clothes for a few moments, biting her bottom lip, then looks at me again.

I nod again, approvingly.

She walks over to the fireplace and kneels in front of it. She tucks the loose pieces of clothing farther back into the fireplace and inhales.

She strikes a match and watches it calm and flicker. Then she throws it onto Charles' corduroy jacket. No one needs a corduroy jacket anyway. This is a public service. I hear her exhale and reach down to rub soothing circles on her back.

We clean the rest of the cabin less dramatically. We couldn't very well burn everything. We throw away the broken dishes, the ripped photos, and other memories by the bucketful. We go room to room, clearing out *everything*. We have some donation piles as well as keep piles, though the latter are considerably smaller. So much of her life had Charles wrapped up in it. That's what happens after being together with someone for so long. It's hard to discern where you end and the other person begins. There's a memory attached to nearly everything, even things you wouldn't think of. History has a way of lingering like the scent of a corpse on your life, on every part of it. If you're lucky, it doesn't saturate to the core. It you're lucky, some things can be untangled like a fine gold chain and given back to you.

We take a brief break for lunch but don't have to go back to the house for it. She still has food in the cabin, so we sit down on the stools at her counter for sandwiches and sweet tea. I bite into my chicken salad sandwich and audibly moan. I love her chicken salad.

"So, how's Boston?" she asks, words muffled between chews.

"It's good, different from here," I say.

"Different how?" she asks.

"It's not as pretty," I admit, looking past her and out the window over the kitchen sink. I smile as I watch the birds in her feeder try to run each other off.

"Nowhere is pretty like here," she says.

She's probably right. This region heading south and into the Smoky Mountains is unmatched in scenic beauty. I take another bite of my sandwich and just enjoy this moment with Harper. We haven't had many throughout our adult years. We were so different when we were younger but now, it doesn't feel the same. Perhaps a little time and distance has changed us. I've missed her, and I'm glad for this difference now.

Maybe I could come back more, stay longer for holidays, and maybe she could come visit me as well. I think about showing Harper around Boston and that makes me happy. She hasn't come yet, I think mostly because of Charles. He never wanted to go along and she never wanted to come without him. But, I think she'd like it there. I think about going back soon and then realize I don't like the thought. We still haven't talked about how long I'm going to stay, but I'm starting to remember how much the familiarity here calms me, how being here brings me peace. I find myself almost missing this place. My heart lurches.

"We should have brought the truck for all the donation bags," I say, turning my attention back to our tasks.

She nods. "You want to walk back and get it while I keep going?"

"Sure, I can do that." I grab our paper plates and throw them in the trash, then head out the front door.

I take the opportunity on my lone walk back to check my phone and send some emails before I make it to the truck. When I step onto the porch, I reach just beyond the kitchen door to grab the keys and see Gentry. He's reading his book and looks like he's just finished eating.

"Hey," he says, barely looking up from his page.

"Oh, hello," I say, reaching for the keys. I wait a moment but when he doesn't say anything, I feel the need to say more, as is often my default. "Listen, I'm sorry about this morning, and before you make your speech about when to apologize and when not to apologize, just know I'm sorry because the way I acted was dumb, and I shouldn't have, because it was my fault, so I'm sorry." I exhale after that.

Gentry looks up at me from his book with concern in his eyes. "Can you even breathe when you talk that fast?"

At first, I don't know how to react but as the smirk stretches across his lips, I relax. Then I throw the keys to the truck at him.

He ducks and they hit the wall behind him. "Wow, I didn't peg you for the violent type."

"Are you doing anything right now?" I ask.

"No."

"Can you help me?"

"With?" He looks me up and down, a curious expression on his face.

"Harper's at the cabin and we have a bunch of donations bagged up. I was coming to get the truck to load them in, but it'd be nice to have an extra set of hands." I wiggle my eyebrows at him so he can take the hint.

"That's definitely not the kind of help I was hoping you needed, but I can rally for it," he says, rolling his eyes in mock disappointment.

Or at least, I think it's fake. Maybe it isn't. In fact, the longer I think about it, the longer I'm sure it probably isn't.

"But I'm driving," he adds, reaching behind him on the floor for the keys before bouncing out of his chair and heading toward me.

"What? Wait, I want to drive," I say.

"I'll tell you what, if you can get the keys from me, you can drive," he says. He hangs the keys from his index finger in the air and spins them around—teasing me, daring me.

I narrow my gaze at him, considering his proposition for a moment but thinking better of it. "Pass," I say, folding my arms over my chest and turning to head toward the truck.

"Wow, I didn't peg you for a quitter either," he says. He's dancing on my nerves, trying to get a rise, and he's doing a good job.

"I will murder you in your sleep," I say, turning sharply toward him.

His footsteps stop their approach to the truck and he looks around —left and right, back at the house, then back to me again. "How?"

"With a pillow?"

"Does that mean you'd be on top of me?" he teases.

I roll my eyes at him and shake my head. Despite myself, I smile. Then we get into the truck and make the short drive to the cabin. I leave his question unanswered as we enter the cabin. Harper sees Gentry and gives me a look of approval, but I roll my eyes at her, too. We all start carrying bags out to the truck and throwing them in.

"Let's wrap up for the day. It's not like this place is going anywhere. We don't have to do it all today," Harper says after we have the place half-empty. "Plus, I don't want to waste the whole Saturday on it."

I agree with her on this point. She deserves some relaxation. I throw the bags I have into the back and watch Gentry do the same. His muscles flex and his T-shirt rides up. Harper finishes locking up the cabin and I look at the truck. It isn't exactly a big truck. It's an old small pick-up with a bench seat inside, and we're going to be cozy in there.

Gentry climbs into the driver's seat and I wait for Harper by the passenger door. She starts walking toward me and points for me to get in. I point for her to get in. We both silently mouth "GET IN" at each other and take turns pointing again. Ultimately, I lose when she crosses her arms over her chest and starts tapping her foot.

I roll my eyes at my little sister and crawl into the cab.

Gentry's arm is across the back of the seat, and he's sitting slightly turned in the bench seat, as if welcoming me into the embrace of his open arm. Smug smile and all.

"Stop it," I say.

"I'm not doing anything," he says, putting his hands up in protest.

My sister gets in next and this forces me to sit so close to Gentry our legs touch. They don't just touch, they're practically glued against each other from hip to knee. I can feel the heat from his long leg pressed against mine for the entire ride. I'm just glad the damn thing isn't a stick shift and he doesn't have to reach between my legs for the gears at this point.

When we park, I press against Harper to get out of the truck but, of course, she's taking her time. She opens the door and hops out, but not before giving Gentry a very long and sincere thanks for his help.

I turn to exit but feel his grip on my arm just above the elbow, and he turns me back to him. He pulls me in very closely and tucks my hair back, then leans in to whisper against the skin of my jaw. "Don't be afraid of me," he says, his voice low and wanting. Then, as quickly as he grabbed me and pulled me back, he lets me go and exits the truck.

The moment is gone, lost in the breeze.

I sit in the truck alone, catching my breath and wondering if I *am* actually afraid of him.

GENTRY

I TOLD her not to be afraid of me, but she should be. She should be afraid of me because my intentions are not pure. Not even close. I don't know why but something about Lyla drives me nuts. Her body, the banter, all of it. It's like I can't help myself. Like I have no restraint. And that's bullshit but part of me doesn't want to restrain anything. I want to press forward. Into whatever is happening. Into the abyss. Into her.

Whoa. Calm down, man.

I keep busy over the weekend, working around the farm and in town, figuring some distance from Lyla might help. Of course, that's bullshit too. No amount of distance is going to help this situation. I'm acutely aware of her at all times, no matter where I am. As if we both have giant magnets in our pockets and I can feel the pull. Or maybe my magnet is stuffed down the front of my pants. Who knows at this point? What I do know, is it's terribly inconvenient for her room to be so close to mine. I listen for her all the time. I watch her all the time. I'm starting to feel like a stalker. I have no shame. At least none I can seem to locate.

On Sunday morning, I'm in the barn when Harper walks in,

making a line straight for me. I'm nearly wincing as she reaches me, not knowing what this is about.

Is she about to get all weird and protective about her sister?

Is she going to tell me to back off or face facts?

Because believe me, I'm trying. As best as I can, anyway. I might not be doing a very good job, admittedly.

Harper stops a few short steps from me and puts her hands on her hips. "Just what do you think you're doing?"

I look down, confused. I have a saddle in one hand and polish in the other. "Polishing this saddle."

She rolls her eyes at me. "Don't be a smartass and don't be a dummy." She moves her hands from her hips and folds them across her chest.

She really means business when she does this, so I set the polish down and face her. "Harper, I have no idea what you're talking about," I say, at least I don't think I do. But I find sometimes when women start talking, I know more than I think I know.

Her eyes narrow at me.

Wow, I'm failing hard.

"What exactly do you think you're doing with my sister?" she asks.

Ah, okay, there it is.

I choke on, well, nothing at all. "I'm not sure," I admit.

"Listen, I'm not here to berate you."

"Oh? You could've fooled me," I say.

She gives me another pointed look. "I'm here to give you some advice, butt-face."

"Did you just call me *butt*-face?"

"Do you want the advice or not?" She stomps her foot down but it barely makes a sound.

I roll my eyes at her this time. "Fine." I cross my arms and lean back against the post, willing to listen. This *is* Lyla's sister, after all. Maybe she does have something valuable to give me here.

"If you want Lyla, you're gonna have to make some moves. And we're all grownups here, so let's not play games. I mean, if you want her for a night or two nights or a week or forever. Whatever the length of time, you're gonna have to make the moves. I don't think she'd do it. I think she wants to, but she won't. It's a strange situation and she's not one to take chances. I can't explain it, but it's like she's been in a shell her whole life. A protective one. Well, since our parents died, at least. She's kept everyone at a distance in fear of feeling too much and then losing them."

Harper's words sink in deep. They make a lot of sense and I can't ignore them.

"Do you think she likes me?" I ask, sounding like a middle school kid or something.

Such an idiot.

"Oh yeah," Harper says without hesitation.

I press my lips together, not completely sure if I believe her.

"Look, I've been her sister a long time, okay? My whole life in fact. I can tell when she's into someone," she says.

"You're sure?" I ask, not wanting to sound totally desperate, but really wanting to make sure before I go and make a complete fool of myself.

"Look, I know the split from Cassie was weird. I know it didn't hurt in a conventional way. Not the way people expected. And I know you're looking for something. I can't promise you that's Lyla. But I think *something* is there. If I'm wrong about this, I will birth the next calf all by myself," she says, her expression serious.

I nod slowly, letting everything she said marinate. "Okay, okay, I got it."

"Are you sure?" she says.

I nod my head in an exaggerated manner. "I got it, okay?"

She gives me a big smile and turns, walking out of the barn, seemingly satisfied with herself.

Great. Now what?

I go back to work polishing the leather of the saddle in my hands, brushing over it with my thoughts still on Lyla. I like her, sure, but then what? She's going to leave. Why put that kind of pressure on her? Or myself? Wait, assuming she would even feel pressured. I mean, she might look at me like I have two heads. She might look at me like I'm scum. Then again, she might just accept having fun and willingly walk away at the end without any regard for me. None of these things sound like great options.

I walk to the edge of the barn door and peer out over the fields, tracing the tree line with my eyes. I spot Lyla coming down the trail just then, her black leggings hugging her features, tank top blowing in the breeze. Her hair is in a high ponytail and she's running just the way I've seen her do every day she's been here. Her headphones are tucked in securely and I wonder what she's listening to. I watch her as she comes to a stop and begins stretching, reaching down to the earth, leaving her ass in the air. I like it, despite trying really hard not to.

I rub the back of my neck, making every attempt to look away, but my eyes come right back to her bent figure. A tiny part of me feels a little like a scumbag for eye fucking her from a distance like this but, apparently, I don't feel bad enough to actually look away.

Nice. Real nice.

She finally moves into a new position, with her arms stretched far over her head, shifting from side to side. Her tank top rises up to expose a delicate sliver of her midriff and the soft curve of her hip bones peek out from the top of her leggings.

Also, can we talk about leggings for a moment? Because I'm fairly certain the devil herself sewed those bad boys together to assert female dominance over all the horn-dogs in the world. And by all the horn-dogs, I mean all the men. All of them. That's right, we're all horn-dogs, and I can't help but trace the lines of her legs over and over again with my eyes. My mouth is watering.

Awesome.

I attempt to shake the thoughts from my mind and pull my eyes away again. If anything, this only further solidifies my need to do, well, something.

Harper is right. I have to make a move.

And having her blessing has to be a good thing, right?

So, it's settled. I will make a move.

But how?

LYLA

THE REST of Saturday and most of Sunday pass without incident. And when I say "incident", I mean without awkward or intense moments with Gentry. Perhaps it's due to the fact that I was busy writing a couple of articles promised by Monday morning, or because he spent a lot of the time away from the farm, checking on some local suppliers. Whatever the reason, our paths haven't crossed much.

That is, until Sunday evening after dinner. I start up the stairs and feel someone behind me. When I glance over my shoulder, he's right there. And if I'm correct, he's checking out my backside as he ascends the stairs. I turn back around and ignore him, continuing up the stairs. He's so close I can feel the friction in the air around me, the intensity palpable.

I walk to my door and look over to see him walking to his. He looks back at me, a smile wide across his face, though I can't read the reason behind it. I turn back to my door and immediately understand why. Another note is taped to my door. I look back again but he's already disappeared behind his own, so I pull it down and enter my bedroom.

*Do you want to sleep
in my bean bag chair again?*

I roll my eyes but can't contain my smile. Now he's just being an idiot.

Clearly, I don't need to sleep in his bean bag chair.

But part of me does kind of want to.

The chair is comfortable; I can't deny it. I actually slept better in that chair than I do in the bed in my own room.

Or was it because I'd slept with him?

I don't want to take that train of thought to crazy town tonight.

I change into my pajamas, choosing something more modest this time. I decide on a pair of sweatpants and a tank top with thicker straps, so as to cover more than the previous one. I slip out of my room—this time carrying my own blanket—and cross the hall to his, where I knock quietly.

I hear him get up from his bed and come to the door before he opens it. "Hi there," he says, a smile emerging again.

"When you say sleep in your chair do you mean with you or alone?" I ask, getting straight to the point.

"Whichever you'd like more," he says, opening his door wider and gesturing to the chairs in front of his fireplace.

I look past him to the very large, very fluffy, and wonderfully comfortable chairs in the room. "Alone," I say, entering his room and making my way to the chair I'd claimed the other night.

"Are you sure about that? What if you get cold?" he asks, raising an eyebrow at me.

I raise my blanket at him without a word and plop myself down in the center of the chair, fluffing it up like it's a nest. I snuggle under my blanket, solidifying the notion it's all I need around me, and look up at him.

He holds his hands up at me, conceding to the point I'm making. Then, he crosses the room and sits in the other chair.

"What are you doing?" I ask.

"Sitting next to you," he says.

"I assumed you'd sleep in your bed," I say, nodding to his now empty bed.

"That's not how sleepovers work," he says, grinning at me. He nestles down into his chair, covering himself with a blanket of his own and positioning himself so we're staring at each other. I try to close my eyes and settle myself, but I feel his eyes on me.

"Are you going to stare at me as I try to fall asleep?" I ask, opening my eyes and looking at him for an answer.

"Maybe," he says, his smile doing strange things to my stomach and lower region.

"I have a better idea," I say.

"Oh yeah?" he asks eagerly, his eyebrows practically jumping off his face.

"Not that," I say, rolling my eyes. "How about we play a game?"

He looks at me quizzically, studying my expression. "What kind of game?"

"How about...truth or dare?" I ask. Somewhere inside me, a bold and brave version of myself has escaped the closet, removed her gag, and is now playing with fire.

Gentry's face lights up with excitement. "This is the type of game I can get behind."

"Okay," I say. "Who goes first?"

"Ladies, of course," he says, tipping his head to me.

I nod in return. "Okay, Gentry. Truth or dare?"

His eyes narrow for a few moments as he considered his options. "Truth."

"How many times have you been in love?" I ask, not hesitating too long.

He turns his head, looking up, his eyes growing distant as if he's recalling and calculating. After a moment he says, "Two."

I think about this and the two women he loved at one point and find myself wondering what kind of women they were. I nod, satisfied with his simple answer.

"Your turn. Truth or dare?" he asks.

"Truth," I reply. I don't think I'm ready for a dare just yet.

He studies my face again, a smile taking over his lips, forming those dimples I detect beneath his short beard. "Where's your favorite place to be kissed?"

I'm certain my eyes bulge. "You mean…geographically? Like, what city?" I ask, already knowing the answer but buying myself time.

He laughs. "You know that's not what I mean."

I squirm under his playful gaze and sigh. As a woman, I'm completely comfortable talking about sex with my friends. And it's not so much that talking about sex with partners bothers me. But I don't want to talk about anything sexual with Gentry. Because he rattles me. My resistance is wearing thin, but I still think it's a terrible idea. I'm slipping.

I turn my hands over, showing him my exposed and outstretched palms.

He studies my hands for a moment, waiting for more. When nothing else comes, he says, "Your…hands?"

"Specifically, my palms," I say.

He looks at me intensely for a moment, his eyes sharp.

I can tell he's thinking about my response and I interrupt his thoughts with, "Truth or dare?"

He swallows, his Adam's apple traveling the length of his throat and back. "Truth," he says, surprising me.

"Do you want to kiss me?" I ask, surprising myself.

"Yes."

"Why?" I ask.

He takes another long pause to consider the question or his response or maybe both. "I don't think I can adequately explain that," he says.

"Try," I say.

He stares off into the flickering flames. "I almost want to call it a thirst, but when you're thirsty, any water will do, and I don't want to kiss just anyone." A pause and then, "Maybe it's a hunger, but it's more like a craving. Like nothing else will do. No other lips. No other kiss. I just want to taste yours." He grows quiet after that, not saying anything else.

I can only hear his steady breathing as the fire warms my face. But

I'm warm all over. Everywhere. Head to toe. My body is buzzing. I'm not sure anyone has ever spoken to me like this in my entire life

"Damn," I say.

Gentry laughs. "Yeah. Damn."

I sit there in our shared silence for a moment. "Your turn."

"Truth or dare?" he asks.

"Dare," I say boldly, attempting to stifle any hesitation in my voice.

His eyes shoot to me and I can tell he's considering it, but he shakes his head. "I dare you to open your heart."

My face quickly sobers, but he continues.

"I know you can't fulfill that dare right here and now. I just mean... when you're ready to," he says.

I swallow hard. I'm not really sure my heart ever opened back up after my parents died. I stopped letting people in. It was the only way I could survive at the time. A coping mechanism. I've just never made any attempt to wean it off. I nod slowly.

"Truth or dare?" I ask him.

"Dare," he says.

I take a deep, steadying breath. "I dare you to kiss me." My voice is low and quiet, my words slow and measured.

His expression changes from light and smiling to somber and serious. His lips soften to a line. I pull my bottom lip between my teeth. His hesitation is making me start to regret the dare.

Until he pulls himself forward slowly in his chair, and I do the same. We both sit at the edge of our bean bags, legs woven together, knees nearly knocking. As we inch closer, I can feel the intensity and heat in the space increasing. I can feel him even though he isn't touching me.

He tucks loose strands of my hair behind my ears and then trails his fingers from my earlobe to my chin along my jawline. Then his index and middle finger trail from my chin down the front of my throat and he places his hand over my heart.

I can feel it thumping hard and I release my lips from my teeth. His face inches closer to mine until he's only a whisper away. I close my eyes and surrender my face, lifting my chin slightly, parting my lips. I wait. And wait. Until finally, I feel it.

I feel his top lip hover and then meet mine as his tongue and bottom lip follow. I feel his need, his hunger, the *craving* as he called it. He presses his lips deeper against mine and inhales against my mouth. I inhale sharply myself, granting permission to his tongue, meeting it with my own each time it explores my mouth. I feel his hand slide from the front of my neck around to the back, his fingers in my hair. His kiss grows urgent; it feels necessary.

My hand finds his collarbone and wraps around his neck, my fingers finding a home in his hair now, my thumb caressing the edge of his jaw.

I don't know how long the kiss lasts before he pulls away, but when he does, he presses his forehead against mine, planting light pecks on my lips, cheeks, and eyelids as he holds me by my hair.

All I can do is focus on catching my breath. Our chests are heaving in unison, our breaths ragged and uneven.

"Fuck," he murmurs.

LYLA

HIS EXPLETIVE IS MUTUAL. I wholly agree.

Fuck.

I rub my fingers over my assaulted mouth, feeling my swollen lips. That kiss was unlike anything I've ever experienced.

He leans back, half on his chair, half on the floor, holding his own mouth like if he doesn't, something terrible might happen. Like if he doesn't, the kiss will somehow peel itself from his mouth and escape. His eyes are closed and I don't know what to do or say. I know what I *want* to do and what I *want* to say, but I'm not sure either would be the right move.

"Maybe we should stop playing," he says.

"Maybe," I say.

Another long silence follows. Neither of us says anything. Neither of us moves.

Until he says, "Truth or dare?" He finally looks at me, his face dark, expression full of temptation.

I have to decide now. I have to choose what's going to happen next. I inhale deeply, steadying myself as I finally pull my fingers from my lips. "Dare," I say.

His gaze travels over me, from my eyes to my lips, then down my neck and over my breasts and lower. "I dare you to let me kiss you again."

I watch his jaw tighten, his mouth part. I watch his hands grip the chair he's halfway sitting in. I watch his entire body silently beg me to say *yes*, so I do.

His movements are slow. He crawls over to me, on top of me, leaning my body far back into the bean bag chair and hovering over me. He leans down and kisses my mouth again, this time more gently. Then he kisses my jaw all the way back to my ear, where he licks my earlobe. His lips are soft against my neck and down my collarbone. He looks up at me for a moment before placing a kiss right between my breasts. I feel him start to untuck my shirt from around me.

"What are you doing?" I ask, breathlessly.

"I said I was going to kiss you, Lyla. I didn't say where," he says just before pressing his mouth to my stomach and trailing kisses to my hip bone. His fingers linger around the edge of my pants. He hooks them in and my breathing goes haywire. Then his movements pause. "I can stop. Tell me to stop if you want me to," he says.

I shake my head. I don't want him to stop. I don't know what I'm thinking. I should want him to stop but I don't. I look down at him; the expression he's wearing is intoxicating.

He tugs at my pants and I raise up just a little so he can pull them completely off. He inhales jagged breaths as his hands cup my hips. He trails a finger over the lowest edge of my stomach, below my belly button. He bites his bottom lip as he looks down at me.

I'm completely naked from the waist down and in a moment where I should feel vulnerable, I feel nothing but alive. My hands cup around his wrists and we make eye contact.

"I need you to say it, Lyla. Ask me to kiss you," he says. His head dips lower, and he moves his hands from my grasp. They graze my outer thighs, come around my knees and begin to press my inner thighs apart. His face hovers low, his hot breath warming my sensitive skin.

My body shudders in response. But he waits there.

He's waiting for me.

"Kiss me," I say.

He shakes his head at me, a sexy smirk teasing me across his face. His fingers begin to trace up the inside of my thighs and I draw in a breath. "No, Lyla. Ask me. Say my name." He presses his lips together in an O shape and blows his hot breath against me.

My back arches in response. "Gentry, kiss me. Please." I'm barely able to get the words out. My mind is racing, my heart thumping in my chest. My entire body is a vessel of desire and it wants one thing— Gentry's mouth.

I hear a growl in his chest as his face disappears. He kisses the center of me gently and I bend toward him. He places one of his large, warm hands on my stomach, stilling me. He kisses me again, and I struggle to keep my breathing controlled. The third time he kisses me, I feel his tongue against me and I whimper. I actually whimper. After that, I'm gone. Lost to him. To his touch and what he's doing to my body.

His mouth moves against me. He tastes me over and over again and my hand finds his hair, tugging at it, pulling him into me. Somehow, he isn't close enough. I need him—more of him. As if understanding my urgency, his mouth becomes more aggressive. His hands cup my bottom. I place my hands over my mouth to quiet my moans, feeling a climax mounting within me.

"Wait," I manage to say. "Wait, please."

My words stop him. He looks up at me, still caressing my skin with his hands.

"I need you, please. I need you inside me," I say.

He looks at me, hesitant, like he doesn't know whether to give me what I'm asking for. "Let me get a condom," he says. He steps away from me and over to his bedside drawer, pulling out a small package and bringing it back over with him. He stands above me and begins to unbutton his pants.

"Wait," I say, sitting up and reaching for his hands. I place my hand in his so he can help me up. When I find my feet, I kiss his mouth.

He wraps his arms around me and they trail up my tank top. He pulls away from our kiss and silently prompts for me to raise my arms.

I acquiesce, and he lifts my shirt over my head, letting it fall to the floor behind me. His eyes are glowing, lit with lust. He looks down at me and I look away, not wanting to see him seeing me.

His hands land on each side of my face, as if he knows what I'm thinking. He looks me in the eyes. "Everything about you is beautiful," he says, and then he presses his lips to mine again.

I breathe into his mouth, his tongue pressing against mine. My hands find the button on his pants and undo it. Then I unzip them slowly, feeling him grow beneath my hands. The zipper's noise and our breathing are the only sounds filling the room. I play with the edge of his boxer briefs, tugging at them. His hands grow feverish, caressing all over my body. I tug at the bottom of his shirt and he lifts his arms. With him being much taller than I am, I'm only able to get the shirt halfway up before he has to help me, and we giggle.

As if sensing the intimacy of the moment, I watch his face twist from the laugh to something serious and almost painful. I take in the sight of his bare chest as I did before. His chest I've seen, but now I need to know—I *want* to know—what the rest of him looks like.

I step toward him and slide my hands into the sides of his briefs, gently pulling them down until they fall freely from him to a puddle of fabric on the floor. Then I step back and look at all of him. He's an impressive specimen. I don't know how else to say it. Somewhere, there's a sculptor, chipping away at marble, hoping to capture the lines of Gentry's body, the ones he makes so effortlessly.

Gentry stands there, letting me look at him for a moment, and then he holds his hand out to me. "Come here," he commands.

And I do.

He walks me to the side of his bed and begins kissing me again, the backs of my legs pressing against his mattress. As he kisses me, I hear him rip open the condom wrapper and I stop him.

"Wait," I say. I sit down on the edge of his bed and take the condom from him, setting it next to me. I look up at him, his eyes studying me. Then I take his length into my hand and feel his body stiffen. I inch closer to him and when he senses my intention, he speaks.

"You don't have to do that," he says.

"Tell me to stop," I say, my eyes fixed on his as I blow on his sensitive skin, but he says nothing. So I take him into my mouth and hear him curse under his breath. I reach up, placing my hand on his stomach, grabbing at his skin as I work up and down the length of him. When I feel him growing rigid, I pull away and quickly place the condom over him, rolling it down and into place. I look up at him again.

His eyes are glossy, his lips parted. He's panting, hungry with desire. I lie back on the bed and wait.

He lowers himself over me, hovering above me. I can feel the tip of him grazing over where he kissed before and I arch toward him. The soft teasing touches make me want him even more, if that's possible.

"Are you sure?" he asks. He leans down and kisses my mouth hard then pulls away, waiting for my answer.

I reach up and pull his face back to mine, kissing his mouth and jaw, nibbling his earlobe. Then I press my lips to his ear and say, "I want you."

Acting on my words like they're a command, he parts and enters me in one fluid motion.

I inhale and moan against the soft hair of his cheek and then I bite his jaw. I hear him groan and he pushes into me again. I wrap my arms around him, pressing my fingertips into the flesh of his well-formed back. His muscles flex beneath my palms. My breath quickens each time he moves against me. He fills me, rocking against me over and over again. His pace and breath quicken in unison. Then he bends down and puts my nipple in his mouth, and I can't contain my moans anymore. I move my hand over my mouth to stifle them. His tongue licks and swirls and nibbles me. He kisses between my breasts before taking my other nipple into his mouth. I press my eyes closed, my body arching in response.

"Lyla," he moans against my skin.

I look down at him, meeting his gaze. His expression is fervent, needing, one of desire and something else I can't name.

"Tell me you want me again," he says, but I hesitate. "Tell me. Please," he begs. He moves in and out of me, his body rocking against mine, eager and hard.

"I want you," I whisper. "I want you."

His body moves faster then, and I feel my climax building. My breaths become shallow. He's looking down at me, watching me, silently telling me to let go, to unravel. I keep my eyes locked with his and feel myself do just that. My body arches uncontrollably, the center of me exploding in the most delicious way, confetti raining down inside me.

His pace quickens again, his muscles growing stiff. His eyes shut tight for a moment and then open again.

I want to watch him the way he watched me. I want to see him lose control inside of me.

And he does. His lips press into a tight line as he attempts to stifle his moans, his body shuddering before he collapses on me. He kisses my lips again as our bodies shake, our chests heaving. He doesn't move from above me. He just holds himself there, still inside me, for a few more moments.

When he pulls away, I gasp, feeling suddenly empty. He lies beside me and props himself on his elbow. He brushes my hair back from my face and kisses my cheek, the hair of his beard tickling my acutely sensitive skin. My mouth softens, my lips turning upward into a slight smile. His leg is still hooked over one of mine and I like it. I close my eyes and bask in the feelings of the moment. Pure. Perfect. Exhilarating. My body starts to relax, my breathing starting to slow. Gentry's hand sweeps down my arm and he curls his fingers into mine. He pulls my hand up, taking it gently by the wrist, and presses a kiss to the palm of my hand.

I curl my hand into his and pull him around me, turning my body so that my back presses against his front. I wrap his arm over me and tuck it close to me. I feel his breath on the skin of my neck as I begin to drift to sleep, but I feel him start to pull away.

"Where are you going?" I ask, my eyes still closed, already half-asleep.

"I'll be right back," he whispers. "Let me help you to the pillow." His arms pull me upward and gently place my head on a soft, warm pillow. This, his arms leave me.

"Please come back," I say.

"I will. I promise," he whispers.

I can barely hear his words as I drift deeper, as sleep finally over-takes me.

LYLA

I WAKE ABRUPTLY and look around the room. It's still dark out and there's no source of light anywhere. I try to adjust and feel Gentry's arms tighten around me, suddenly remembering what transpired.

Ah, yes. I slept with Gentry.

I slept with Gentry after knowing him for a whopping three days.

Oh my god.

I shift again, this time apparently too much.

"Lyla? Are you okay?" Gentry's voice is gruff, sleepy.

"I'm okay. Go back to sleep," I say, cuddling into his embrace.

His hands travel over me, caressing my skin. They begin to move over my sides. His head nestles into my chest, and he brushes light kisses over my skin.

We're perfectly wrapped up in each other.

Then I feel his hands slide down over my naked bottom and squeeze. This doesn't help any attempt I'm making to fall back asleep. In fact, it's quite the opposite. His caresses cause my body to arch into his. He grips me tighter, his hands moving from my bottom to hip and then sliding up to cup my breasts. I stifle a moan but it's too late.

He heard it. He knows. And he uses it against me.

The tips of his fingers trail gently over my nipple and I feel goose-bumps rising all over me.

He parts my legs with his knee, drawing them upward so they have to open wider. I feel myself getting excited. It's not as though there's a difference in sleeping with him once or twice after three days. It's all the same now.

Except now I want to set the pace.

I prop myself up on my elbow and straddle him. I can feel him growing against me. The skin to skin contact makes my body ache deliciously. I reach over to his drawer and fumble for a condom, glad he's the type of man who's prepared.

I rip the wrapper open and reach down, taking him in my hands. He stiffens and inhales sharply. After securing the condom in place, I lift myself slightly and tease him, rubbing myself against him, again and again. His body shudders with each of my downward strokes. When his breathing increases, I finally envelop him, listening to him cuss beneath his breath.

His hands reach for me, caressing my chest, steadying me by my stomach, then finding their way to my bottom again. He grips me tightly as we find our rhythm. I rock back and forth, trying to keep my moans quiet. When I come, he slows my body down, pulling me to his chest, holding me there against him, my body still slowly rocking against his. He pushes himself deep inside me a few more times, until I feel his body seize against mine. Knowing he's spent, I finally hear him exhale.

And then I fall asleep. Just like that. On top of him, still knotted together, Gentry still inside me.

Given how we fell asleep, to say I'm shocked when I wake up several hours later alone in his bed is an understatement. I roll over, patting everywhere, searching blindly for Gentry. But he's gone. My head shoots up from the pillow at the realization and I look around.

He isn't anywhere in his room. I look from side to side, a few times, as if doing so will somehow make him appear. But the room is still empty. I sit up in bed, partially confused and partially dumb-founded.

That's the same thing, isn't it?

Why?!

What have I done?

I shake my head and draw my knees to my chest, burying my face into my arms and legs.

Clothes.

I should get my clothes.

I need to find them.

Yes.

One step at a time, Lyla.

I search the bed and find nothing, remembering I was undressed elsewhere. I search the floor but there's nothing there either. A pile on the bean bag chair catches my eye. There they are. My clothes, neatly folded, all together. And of course, a note folded neatly on top.

I stare at the pile for a moment, unsure whether I want to read the note or not. I decide, either way, I definitely want to be dressed right now.

I set the note aside and get my clothes on in a hurry, glad for the uncomplicated items I had chosen the night before. Gentry even folded the unused blanket I'd brought over from my room and sat it next to my clothes.

God.

I don't even know what to think at this point. I grab my blanket and the note and slip as quietly as I can out of his door and across the hall back to my room. I sit on the edge of my bed, still not ready to read the note, so I place it down. Maybe I'll never read it. Maybe I should fly back to Boston within the next few hours and wait a very long time to return because I don't want to face anyone after this.

But of course, I'm going to read the note.

And I'm not actually going to fly back to Boston in the next few hours. Though I can daydream.

I pat around on the bed beside me until I feel the paper between my fingers. I hold it there for a second, rubbing my fingers absent-mindedly over it. There's nothing special about the paper and yet, here I am, nervous as hell about what it says.

Is it filled with rejection?

A gentle let-down?

Does he want more?

Or god forbid, is it full of emotion?

The kind he says I deserve. For whatever reason, none of these possibilities settle well with me. I pull the note up and unfold it.

You smell like honeysuckle
and I want to pluck the center of you,
lay your delicate strands flat against my tongue,
worship your sweet nectar.

P.S. Will you go on a date with me?

Well that's not good. Nope. In fact, that's the opposite of good. That's bad. Very bad. Things are tingling, thoughts are swirling.

Nectar!

Date?!

How does he think that's a good idea?

If it goes well, it's bad. If it goes wrong, it's bad. So, no. We definitely shouldn't go on a date. Definitely not. I'll have to speak to him about this.

I grab my stuff for a shower and head to the bathroom, mentally reviewing the list of reasons we can't go on a date so when I see him later, I'll be armed and ready. I drop my clothes to the floor and step into the shower, letting the hot water take my breath as I relax into it.

Ah yes, this is much needed.

Then I hear the door open and shut.

"Someone is in here!" I yell over the sound of the water, but no one answers. I open the curtain and peer out, meeting Gentry's gaze.

"This is where we met, you know," he says, a smile playing on his face.

Despite myself, I laugh. "Yes, it was so romantic," I say sarcastically, recalling our encounter.

"Did you get my note?" he asks.

Nectar.

Date!

I'm not prepared for this conversation. For one thing, I'm naked. And in the shower. And this gives me a disadvantage against my opponent when I need to be serious.

"I did," I say. When he doesn't say anything, I go on. "I don't know how you think a date is a good idea."

"Why would it be a bad idea?" he asks.

"Well, what if we have a terrible time?"

"What if we have a great time?" he counters.

"Exactly," I say, opening the curtain and meeting his gaze to make my point.

He nods slowly. "But hear me out. What if we're just two people, having fun, without expectation or intention?" he asks.

I consider his words.

But can two people go on romantic dates just for fun and then part ways, without it getting complicated?

I do miss dating. Going on dates. Dressing up, holding hands, laughing. I haven't been on a date in a few years.

But...nectar?!

"Nothing will get messy?" I ask, raising an eyebrow at him.

"Cross my heart," he says, using his index finger to draw an invisible X over his chest.

"Or complicated?" I ask.

"Stick a needle in my eye," he says, pointing to his eyeball somewhat dramatically.

I roll my eyes at him. "Fine."

"Try not to sound so excited," he says.

I grimace, but that's fair. "Okay, you're right. Yes, Gentry, I accept."

His face lights up into a big smile and I duck my head back inside the shower because I need to shield myself from his exuberance. It makes him too attractive. I smile in the shower where he can't see it.

"Okay, I need to get going. I'll pick you up tonight at seven," he says.

"Wait, you want to go on a date *tonight*?" I ask. I thought it would be later in the week.

"Why delay what you can do today?"

"Did you really just rhyme?" I ask, rinsing my hair.

"I didn't even mean to. Pretty impressive, huh?" he says, pride in his voice.

I laugh. "Okay, get out. You have to go. I'll see you later."

Then comes the sound of the door opening and closing again and I'm left to finish my shower alone. Considering the pending date, I need to shave now, wash more thoroughly, and possibly condition my hair a second time because I'm suddenly nervous.

I look down out the window and catch sight of Gentry walking away from the house. He turns back over his shoulder and looks up at me, as if somehow knowing I was looking down at that moment. He smiles and winks at me. I wave at him and then turn back to my shower. I can't concentrate on anything if I'm looking at him for any length of time.

When I get back to my room, I dress in jeans and a T-shirt to finish helping Harper. Then I examine all my other clothes, trying to figure out what I should wear for my date. I hold up my black maxi dress. It's an off-the-shoulder dress and dips down to expose a bit of cleavage. More importantly, it's versatile. I can dress it up or down, and because I don't know where or what the date is, it's the perfect choice. But best of all— and I can't stress this enough—it has pockets. Every woman's best friend is a nice versatile dress with pockets. Yes, this will absolutely work. I'll pair it with some sandals, subtle jewelry, and be done. He didn't give me any indication about what the date will consist of, so this will have to do.

I hang the dress back up and refocus my attention on the here and now. I finish getting ready and head downstairs. I'm not sure how I'll keep myself focused, but I have to give it a solid effort. Or so I tell myself.

Harper is waiting for me in the kitchen with a travel mug of coffee. She hands it to me as I approach.

"Oh, bless you, child," I say, taking it into my hands with a feverish need.

"What are you smiling about?" she asks.

I look at her, confused. "What do you mean?"

"Girl, you came in here with a smile big enough to see from the other side of the farm."

"I did?" I ask. I hadn't felt it or noticed.

"Oh yeah." She nods slowly at me.

"You're crazy," I say, rolling my eyes at her as I attempt to suppress another smile.

Her eyebrows raise on her forehead. "Something happened, didn't it?" she accuses, pointing her finger at me.

My mouth drops open and I try to wave her off.

"It did!" she says.

"Okay, fine, fine! Shush, please. Yes, okay?" I say on an exhale.

"Tell me," she demands. "Tell me now."

"I'm not telling you! We aren't in middle school," I say.

She puts her hands on her hips and stands straight, raising her chin at me, demanding more of an explanation without words.

I press my lips together and sigh. "Me and Gentry, okay?"

"You and Gentry *what*?" she questions. "You had sex?"

I nod my head up and down.

The excitement on her face and exuding from her is palpable.

"You know what, it shouldn't have happened, okay? It shouldn't have," I say, reasoning out loud, mostly to myself.

"Why not?" she asks.

"For one, it's been like three days since I met him," I remind her.

"So?" she says, like that's all the explaining she needs to do.

"*So?* So, I shouldn't be sleeping with strangers and people I barely know after three days," I say.

"First of all, you're a grown woman. Sleep with who you want, when you want," she says, like it's the simplest concept.

But, she has a point. Men do it, so why not women, too?

"Okay, maybe you're right."

"Oh, I'm right. You know I'm right," she teases. And then, "So, what are you going to do? Just ignore each other now?"

"Not exactly. We're going on a date tonight," I say.

Harper looks at me excitedly again and claps her hands together. "Yes! Yes! Yes!"

I move my hands through the air in the universal *calm down* movement so she can collect herself and focus. "Let's not make a big deal out of it, okay?" I tell her. "It's just for fun. Nothing serious is going to come of it—obviously."

She gives me a sideways glance then. "I'm just going to keep my mouth shut." With that, she quiets and sips her coffee.

I honestly don't know what to think at this point. Despite my attempts at resistance, which clearly didn't work, I like what I know about him so far. I can't deny our attraction. Maybe I *could* let myself have fun while I'm here. There's no real harm in that.

I could get to know Gentry. Well, the rest of him, anyway.

LYLA

THE DAY PASSES QUICKLY and before I know it, I find myself back in my room, frantically changing my clothes, applying makeup, and fixing my hair. I'm just finishing up, looking myself up and down in the mirror for the seventh time, when I hear a knock at my door. I glance down at my phone and notice Gentry is right on time.

I open the door wide and my eyes immediately meet his. Or at least, I try to focus on his, but they're sweeping over me unapologetically. He makes no attempt to stifle his eager looks. They graze over my bare shoulders, my breasts, my neck, and finally, they come to meet my gaze.

"Hi," he says.

"Hello."

"You look amazing," he compliments, although given his nonverbal reactions, it's hard to assume he thinks anything else.

For the first time, I take in his appearance and he definitely doesn't disappoint. He's wearing dark denim jeans, a dark brown belt and matching boots, with a thin gray sweater over a button-up, rolled up on his forearms.

"You look equally amazing," I say, managing to keep a steady composure and the drool in my mouth.

Damn. Just damn.

He's sex on a stick. He's smoldering delicious temptation. He's a wet dream. Yes, a wet dream.

Calm down, Lyla. Jesus.

"Shall we?" he asks, holding his hand out.

I nod, placing my hand into his just before he laces his fingers into mine, pulling me toward the stairs. "Where are we going?" I ask.

"I can't tell you that," he says, and I can hear his smirk as he speaks.

I'm at his mercy. Not that I find myself taking issue with that, at least in this moment. I smile, concentrating on the feeling of my hand in his. It's nice. His big hand envelops mine and holds me tightly and I find comfort in it.

When we turn the corner, we find ourselves face to face with, well, everyone. Nan and Paw are sitting at the kitchen table, sipping tea. Harper's leaning against the counter, stirring what I presume to be tea. All eyes are on us as we walk in.

Great. Just great.

I hadn't thought this through. It's one thing for Harper to know, but *my grandparents?*

Will they have expectations?

Will they make assumptions?

Oh god.

I feel my cheeks and chest grow warm and know I'm likely pink all over. Gentry nods to Paw, who nods back. We step through the kitchen and as we're walking out the door, I hear Nan call after us.

"Have fun, you two." Her words are punctuated by the screen door smacking against the door frame.

We approach his truck and he walks me to the passenger side, where he opens the door for me. He gestures for me to get in and after I slide up into the seat, he shuts the door. Chivalry truly is a lost art but it's alive and thriving here in the south—and no part of me minds it.

We take off down the gravel road and turn left onto the next. I start to think about where we might be going, but it makes me too nervous so I try to simply embrace the surprise of it.

"Do you want some music on?" he asks.

"Yes, please," I say.

He pulls his phone from his pocket and hooks it to the cord between us. After he hands me the phone, he turns his attention back to the road. "Help yourself."

I scroll through his songs and playlists until I find a country music one that suits me. It seems to be full of slower, more romantic songs. The idea of sultry notes filling the cab does something to me. I watch the side of his mouth hitch up and know he likely approves of my choice.

"How far away is where we're going?" I ask.

As I watch his face, it becomes contemplative. He dips his head from side to side. "Probably only ten minutes or so," he says.

I nod, settling back into my seat and pulling at my flowy sleeves. The space falls silent for a few minutes and I can't tell if it's awkward or not. It seems comfortable enough, but I can't get a read on his expression—or if *he's* comfortable, for that matter. Not wanting to assume or force anything, I decide to be natural. "So, how was your day?" I ask, figuring the question is benign enough.

"Not too bad. Went by too slowly, though," he says.

"How come?"

"Thinking about you too much, if I had to guess," he says, glancing at me then back to the road, a smile plastered to his face.

Okay, that's good. Smooth. Real smooth.

I tuck my hair behind my ear and attempt to suppress a smile. Clearly, he isn't an amateur at this. "I see."

"What about you? How was your day?" he asks, stealing another glance my way.

"Not bad. It didn't really go by too slowly for me, luckily," I say.

"You weren't thinking of me?" he asks.

"No. I mean, I was. A little. But—"

"Calm down," he says with a laugh. "You're not on trial."

Trying to pull myself together is an impossible task around Gentry, but I press on anyway. "I just mean...yes, I was thinking of you, but for whatever reason, it didn't slow down my day."

Gentry nods at this and, as if to further calm my nerves, reaches over and rests his hand on my thigh. For the record, this does not calm anything, least of all my nerves. My body reacts to his touch like it's brand new. As if it had forgotten that we slept with him—*twice*. Heat radiates outward from where his hand is and travels up into my lower stomach then down into my knee caps; and I fight the urge to shake it off because part of me wants to feel it.

"We're here," he announces, interrupting my thoughts of pushing his hand from me and throwing myself from the moving truck just to get far enough away from him to catch my breath.

I look up, trying to figure out exactly what *here* is. We're in a line of cars, and there's a small booth sitting at the edge of the road ahead. I look around, not really seeing any signs, and then turn to him.

If his grin is any indication, he doesn't plan to elaborate. Not even now. He pulls his wallet from his back pocket and removes some cash, then places the wallet in his driver side door.

When it's our turn at the window, he and the man there exchange almost no information.

The man looks inside the cab, tells Gentry the price, Gentry hands him the money, and the man gives him two tickets and tells us to enjoy the show.

What show?

Gentry drives forward until we round a thick row of trees and I immediately understand. In the distance, a large screen is playing previews. Rows of cars and trucks are lined up neatly in front of it. There's just one small building to the side.

"A drive-in movie!" I squeal.

His smile grows with my excitement as he lines his truck up and backs into a spot.

He motions to the truck bed and I look back, noticing—for the first time—an air mattress. He pulls two pillows and a blanket from behind his seat and motions for me to follow him. I slide across the seat of the truck and out of the driver's side. Gentry's arms wrap around me to help me down and for a few brief, delicious moments, our bodies press together before my feet hit the ground. He places the pillows on top of the mattress and spreads the blanket out over it as well before grabbing my hand again and threading his fingers with mine.

"Let's go get some snacks before the movie starts," he says, motioning to the small building.

"What movie is playing?" I ask.

"It's actually a double feature. They're scary movies. Is that okay? I guess I should've asked first," he says, like he's beginning to doubt his plan.

"No, that's perfect! I love scary movies," I rush out, wanting to ease his worries.

He squeezes my hand and then brings it to his mouth, pressing his lips to my knuckles and giving them a gentle but firm kiss.

My eyes and stomach flutter in unison.

This man.

This man does crazy things to my body.

We make our way to the small building and Gentry holds the door open for me. The smell of popcorn arrests my senses and it's heavenly.

"You want popcorn, right?" he asks as if reading my mind, and I nod vigorously. He steps to the counter and orders a large popcorn and two Cokes.

After surveying the rack of candy next to me, I select a box of Snow Caps and place them on the counter. Gentry looks at the box, and then at me.

"Please?" I say, giving him my best puppy eyes and pouting my lip.

He wraps his arm around me, pulling me closer, and leans down to me. Then he presses his cheek to mine and whispers in my ear, "Baby, you can have anything you want."

My center tightens and I swallow hard. His hot, sweet breath against the sensitive skin of my neck causes quakes deep within me.

He straightens and pays but keeps me wrapped in his arm. When he's done, he hands me the candy and popcorn, only letting me go when he needs both hands to carry our drinks.

We walk back to the truck and I stand there, wondering exactly how this will work with both our hands full.

He sits the drinks on the top of the cab and then lowers the tailgate, taking the snacks from me to place there. He helps me onto the back of the truck, careful to keep my modesty intact given the dress I'm wearing. I remove my shoes and crawl onto the mattress.

Then, he wedges the drinks between the mattress and truck bed, and hops up on the truck himself, where he removes his shoes and settles in—snacks in hand.

Overall, I'm pretty impressed with his efficiency with the ordeal.

We prop the pillows against the back of the truck cab and put the snacks in our laps. I look at Gentry, who's frowning down at our bodies.

I look down, not understanding what's wrong. "What?" I ask.

"I don't like this," he says.

Confused, I look down at us again, searching for what could be wrong.

Gentry picks up the snacks and shimmies his body closer to mine, closing the gap that had just been between us. Now, our hips are pressed against each other's. He holds his arm up, welcoming me into his embrace and tucking me into him. He tangles one leg over mine and sets the snacks back down.

I evaluate us now—his left arm tucked behind me, his hand resting on my hip—and it feels more *right*.

"That's better," he says.

From my new spot, I can't look up and see his full face unless he were to look down. So, when I do try to look at him, all I can see is his beautiful mouth curled up into a wry smile.

"I like this, too," I say, leaning into him and nuzzling my head against his chest.

He tilts the popcorn container toward me and I grab a handful.

I'm tossing a couple of pieces in my mouth at a time when I catch him staring at me. "What?"

"That's so *not* how you eat popcorn," he says, rolling his eyes at me. He reaches in to take a large handful, of which he brings to his mouth and proceeds to shovel in. Kernels fall down the front of his chest as I laugh at him.

"I'm not eating my popcorn like that," I say. "No way."

"You basically have to," he says, tilting the popcorn to me again.

I eye him, then I look down at the popcorn. Returning his eye roll, I grab some popcorn and bring it to my mouth, proceeding to shovel it in as he had.

His smile grows large and he nods approvingly. "There you go. See? It's the only way."

"Forgive me. I didn't realize I'd been a failure at eating popcorn all these years," I tease.

"Not a failure, just too reserved. Gotta loosen up," he says, wiggling his body in such a way that it wiggles mine.

Perhaps he's right. Perhaps I have been too reserved in some ways. I prefer to think of it as careful, courteous.

"Are we going to be able to talk during the movie, or is this like the theater? Am I gonna get dirty looks if I whisper to you?" I ask.

"Have you—wait. Have you never been to the drive-in?" he asks, shock scrambling his features.

"Um, no?" I say.

"Seriously?"

"Yes, seriously."

"But this one is right down the street from the farm. Didn't you ever come here when you lived here? Maybe on a date?" he asks.

"My high school boyfriend never took me here. In fact, we hardly ever went on proper dates," I say, shrugging as I recall the memories.

"What do you mean by *proper dates*? What did you do, then?" he asks.

"Well, we used to just hang out at his house a lot," I say.

Gentry studies my face, like he's considering his next words carefully. "What did you do while you were there?"

"His parents were gone a lot so honestly, we had a lot of sex. That's what he liked doing." Saying these facts out loud to another person doesn't seem to hurt as much as I thought it would. I've never really talked about my relationship with Dean outside of how it ended.

"But he didn't want to take you anywhere? Show you off?" he asks.

I shake my head, pressing my lips together and shrugging again. "It's okay," I tell him.

"No. No it's not. You're too much for that," Gentry says.

"Too much?"

"Yes, too much—too good, too amazing. You deserve better. You deserve a man who's proud to have you on his arm. A man who wants to show you off, to make sure the whole world knows you belong to him," he says.

Then he brushes a light kiss on my forehead and I inhale his words.

He's sweet. Too sweet.

"Thank you," I say. "But really, we were kids, you know? I'm sure Dean is different now."

"Wait. Your high school boyfriend was *Dean*? The same Dean who now works on the farm? That Dean?"

I'm nodding before he even finishes his questions. "Yes, that Dean."

Bewilderment fills his face. His jaw tightens several times before finally softening again. "I would never do that," he says.

Before I can respond, he grabs a handful of popcorn and holds it up to my mouth. I open it and he begins to shovel the popcorn in. As pieces fall to my lap in the process, we laugh together.

Then, I reach for the candy and we settle back in to the present instead of reminiscing about my muddy past.

This is going to be a good evening.

I can feel it.

GENTRY

LYLA'S WARMTH radiates outward and sweeps from the side where she's tucked under my arm, to all over my body. She makes my chest tight. Hearing how Dean treated her makes me want to drive back to the farm, wait up all night for him to arrive at work in the morning, and then punch him right in his stupid throat. Guys like him deserve throat punches. My arm instinctively tightens around her.

She's so good.

How could anyone treat her like that?

"To answer your original question, yes, you can talk. No one is close enough to hear you whispering. You just have to make sure you lean in really close to me," I say, refocusing our conversation.

She smirks at me, of course. "Lean into you, huh? You mean like this?" She turns her face to mine, nuzzling the tip of her nose against my beard. She parts her lips, grazing my earlobe, and a tingle ignites the back of my neck, making me close my eyes. "You want me to whisper to you like this?" she asks, her warm breath on my skin.

I nod. "Yes, like that," I say, exhaling the breath I didn't realize I'd been holding. I clench my hand into a fist, resisting the urge to grab her. Because I really want to take her by her thigh and pull her to me. On top of me. And—

Stop. Stop, stop, stop.

Calm yourself down, man.

She takes the popcorn from me and sets it next to the drinks. "Can we lie down?" she asks, her dark eyes moving over my face. They're black now as night sweeps over dusk.

Oh my god.

What's she trying to do to me?

I nod, not trusting my voice to remain calm.

Why am I even nervous?

We slept together. I've been inside her. I have to push aside the delicious recollection of that or I will not remain a nice guy on this date.

Maybe I'm nervous because I want to do it again. I mean, I definitely want to do it again.

But what if she doesn't want to?

My throat tightens as we adjust the pillows and retreat our bodies low into the mattress. "Do you want some blanket?" I ask.

"Maybe just over my feet," she says.

I raise up to pull the blanket over her feet and my fingertips connect with the soft skin just above her ankle. I *really* like her skin— looking at it, touching it, kissing it. I want to bite her and then I want to lick her wounds.

Whoa, okay. Just calm down.

I shake my head. As if her bare shoulders or our legs accidentally grazing aren't enough, I watch her hands slowly shimmy the hem of her dress up higher. My eyes assault her calves, her knees, and just a tiny bit of her thighs before she stops. I blink rapidly, collecting myself.

I settle back into my spot next to her and she turns into me, drawing a leg up just slightly enough to put it over mine. She presses a hand against my chest, and I look to the sky above me, praying for inner strength. Luckily, the movie starts, and I get the slightest reprieve to refocus.

"Have you ever seen this one?" I ask her.

"Yes. It's so good, though. I definitely don't mind watching it again," she says.

"Okay, good."

"Gentry?" she says, her voice barely above a whisper.

"Yeah?"

"Tell me what happened. With your ex," she says.

I inhale slowly. It's a fair question, considering she basically just told me her high school boyfriend used her for sex. I owe her one of my own ugly truths. "We were together for a couple of years. I thought we were good. I really did. But as it turns out, Cassie wasn't. That's her name. She was unhappy, and she cheated on me. Then, she left," I say.

Lyla inhales and exhales a heavy sigh. "You didn't deserve that," she says.

"Thank you."

"How long ago?" she asks.

"She left about six months ago," I reply.

The wounds Cassie left have pretty much healed. Maybe that's because, after two years, I only proposed because it felt like the next logical step in our relationship. I wasn't driven by the want or need to do it. I wasn't compelled. Maybe that had been the problem.

"I'm sorry," Lyla says, pulling me from my thoughts.

In turn, I pull her closer to me. "It's okay," I tell her. She was already pressed to me, but it still didn't feel close enough. "Everything happens the way it's supposed to."

Her head nods slightly, and then we watch part of the movie in silence. Rather, Lyla watches the movie. I seem to be watching her, only taking brief glances in the movie screen's general direction between doing such. When I'm not actively looking at her, I'm memo-rizing the way her body feels against mine in a way I hadn't before, when we were together.

This is different. This is intimacy without sex.

Lyla leans back away from me and raises her face to mine, moving her lips to my ear. "Gentry?" she whispers.

"Yeah?" I breathe out.

"Can we make-out?" she asks, a sultry playfulness in her voice.

My eyes grow wide. I wouldn't have expected such a request but I'm more than happy to oblige. "Yes, ma'am," I say. "Yes, we can."

"Gentry?" she whispers again.

"Yes?"

"Don't call me ma'am," she reminds me, then pulls her lips from my ear and presses them against my mouth.

If this kiss is my punishment, I'll be calling her ma'am pretty much all the time. I kiss her back, tightening my arm around her middle and caressing the skin between her shoulder blades. Her bare skin beneath my hand feels divine. She's so soft, so warm.

Her hand travels from my chest to my abdomen to my hip. She pulls at me, digging her fingers into me. My mouth moves over hers. I part her lips with my tongue and lap it against hers. Feeling her breath quicken makes my hunger for her grow more eager. I pull my mouth from hers and kiss her jaw then lower, and onto her neck. I nuzzle my beard against her smooth skin, delighting in the breaths hitching in her throat.

She claws at my shirt and lets out the faintest moan. Her noises drive me wild. I know I have to stop soon or I won't be able to stop at all and we'll likely find ourselves doing something very illegal in front of an audience.

I pull away from her, peppering her cheeks and eyelids and nose with soft kisses. I kiss her lips again, softly and completely. I pull back, my eyes still closed, and lick my lips. She tastes *so good*. When I finally open my eyes, I look down at her in the faint glow of the screen.

Her eyes are still closed, her lips a little swollen—because despite my gentle intentions, her mouth causes incredibly scandalous thoughts in me, spurring firm and intense assaults instead. Her mouth curls into a small but very genuine looking smile, and I decide then that she doesn't seem to mind.

We both clear our throats, as if sensing the need to move past the moment for fear of it spiraling out of control, and we turn our attention back to the movie. Although, if I'm being honest, I don't have a fucking clue what's going on in the film.

Get ahold of yourself.

Breathe, man.

I blink several times, attempting to still myself and leave my devious thoughts alone in the corner of my mind.

"Gentry?" she whispers again—and she has to stop saying my name like that.

She says it so softly, not quite a whisper, like the whole of it is a request or a wish to be granted. Like a prayer sent up to the stars. Or at least that's how it sounds to me. And she has to stop.

"Yes?" I say, knowing without a doubt she could pretty much ask me to do anything at this point and I would definitely do it.

Buy you a car? What color?

Give you a baby? Hold my popcorn.

Move not just heaven, but earth, too? Where do you want them?

"Do we have to stay for the second movie?" she asks.

No the fuck we don't, I think.

No. The. Fuck. We. Don't.

I clear my throat. "Not if you don't want to. Are you tired?" I ask, praying she isn't.

"No. I just thought we could go back and maybe take a walk or sit and talk," she says.

Talk?

Talk.

Okay, she wants to talk.

I swallow again, nodding. "Sure, yeah. We can do that," I say.

The credits of this movie start to roll and it's safe for us to leave. I climb out of the back and help her down from the truck by her waist. We climb into the cab and head back down the road.

We spend the ride in a comfortable silence. At one point, she reaches over for my hand, lacing her fingers with mine. And that's how we remain for the rest of the ride. Holding hands, music playing quietly over the speakers, and my mind trying to shove all the filthy thoughts about her body into one corner so we can talk.

Talk. Jesus.

Now, don't get me wrong, I thoroughly enjoy talking to Lyla. That's just...not what I want to do at this particular moment.

We park back at the farm and the house is quiet. I know everyone has already gone to sleep, so I try to be as quiet as I can when pulling in and parking.

"How about we get something to drink and sit on the porch swing?" she offers.

"Okay, sure. What do you want to drink?" I ask.

"Something that'll warm me up," she says, giving me a look I can't quite place.

"So like, coffee?" I ask.

She giggles, shaking her head. "Like wine," she clarifies.

Ohhhhhh. Okay.

Yes, let's just lower those inhibitions while I'm trying to be a good boy why don't we?

Great idea.

"Sure," I choke out, swallowing the extra saliva that's collected itself in my mouth because looking at her made me, well, it made my mouth water.

I step inside the door to the kitchen as she saunters over to the swing. I find two glasses—a wine glass for her, a short one for me. I pour her wine, then two fingers of bourbon for me. When I step back out onto the porch, I see she's collected herself into a ball on one side of the swing. Her legs are under her, and her dress is tucked in around her. Her arms are wrapped around her middle and she's rubbing her shoulders.

"Are you cold?" I ask, setting the glasses down on the table next to the swing.

"Just a tiny bit, no big deal," she says.

I reach for the edge of my sweater and pull it up over my head, straightening my button-up back down. "Here," I say, stepping to her. I push the sweater down over her head and help her work her arms into it. Of course, it swallows her. Gone are her bare shoulders and her cleavage. Gone is the entire top of the dress that pleasantly hugs her waist before falling away. This may prove helpful in keeping me focused on the talking. But mainly, she's warm, and that's all that matters.

"Thank you," she says, snuggling into my sweater.

And really, any guy will tell you, watching a woman exist in any of your clothes is sexy. It doesn't matter what it is. They could borrow a T-shirt to sleep in, your hoodie on a cold day, pull your boxers up over their hips, or just steal your hat to wear and the result is the same. Possession. Healthy possession, albeit. We're like dogs, and this is essentially our version of peeing on you—staking claim. Plus, you just always look adorable. We can't help it. We're a slave to our base desires. And our base desires wanted to claim you, in the most respectful way possible.

I sit next to her on the swing but keep my legs down to gently rock us back and forth. I hand Lyla her glass of wine and watch her sip it before I take a long draw of my own drink. She cups her glass with both hands in front of her.

"How's Harper doing?" I ask. I haven't spoken to Harper much about her separation and divorce. It didn't feel like an organic topic for us.

"I think she's okay. I know she's hurting but I know she's working through it," she says.

I nod. "Well, that's good. That's all we can hope for at this point, really."

"I agree."

"I think he's supposed to come by soon to collect his stuff," I say.

The features of her face harden at this. "I hope I'm not around for that," she states.

"Why not?"

"Because I can be very mean. And knowing Chuck, he'll want to play nice, but I honestly don't have it in me," she says, her words sharp.

"You call him Chuck?" I ask, trying to keep myself from laughing.

"Yeah, he hates it. I used to do it for fun every once in a while, but now, I do it based on my inability to give a shit," she says.

She starts laughing with me and then we both stop as our eyes meet.

"Your sister deserved better," I say.

She nods her head in agreement.

A new silence falls over us and we sit there, looking at each other—just looking at each other. I like her face in the moonlight. It bounces off her cheekbones, casting shadows of her eyelashes down onto them. She sips her wine again and I watch her lick her lips.

She needs to stop doing that, too. I take another drink of my bourbon.

"Seems there are a lot of people here that deserved better than what they got," she says.

I raise my glass to that. We've all been screwed over, that's for sure. I clear my throat. "Have you had any other serious relationships? You know, since Dean the dick wad?" I ask, not even a little sorry about the nickname.

She lets out a small laugh. "Not really. I've done what you can call 'dating' I guess. First dates, second dates. I've had some strings of okay dates. But nothing stuck."

I find myself wondering about these men, how they only had one or two dates with her. How they could have let her slip away or found her not worth fighting for. From where I sit, I just can't picture that many men being *that* clueless. It's disgraceful.

"Was Cassie the only woman you were ever serious with?"

"Pretty much. Before her—just like you—I dated here and there, but there was nothing I held onto," I say.

She seems to consider my words. "What are we doing, Gentry?" she asks, her question giving me pause.

Because I honestly don't know. I mean, I want to say we're just having fun, but that feels cheap and, somehow, a shitty thing to say. Though, I don't think I have it in me to say more, because that would make me an idiot. She's leaving, so it can't be more. Which leaves what? Something in the middle? No. The middle of anything is always messy. Always. There's no good way to present the middle.

I suck in a breath and decide to go for complete and total honesty. "I have no idea." With that, I exhale.

LYLA

TALKING TO GENTRY IS EASY, comfortable. Familiar, even. The conversations flow effortlessly, and the lulls between don't make me a mess of anxious knots. I don't spend it awkwardly, wondering what I should say next, which is a relief. After we talk on the porch for a while longer, Gentry walks me to my bedroom door.

We stand there a moment, not really knowing how to navigate this.

Doing things in reverse—sleeping together and *then* going on a date—has confused this particular part of the evening. I tell him I had a good time and he tells me he hopes we can do it again, to which I agree. He slowly wraps his arms around my middle and brings me closer to him. I breathe him in, his scent.

In truth, I'd spent the entire time we were on the swing bringing the sleeve of his sweater to my face and inhaling.

Now, he takes my mouth gently, kisses my lips, parts them with his tongue. The kiss lingers, just long enough to teeter on the edge of something more intense, something that could have us both unravel our carnal desires. We're standing on the precipice of the *want* our bodies radiate.

All we need to do is take a step.

But he pulls back—smoothing my hair, nipping at my bottom lip. His embrace gently recedes, until he's no longer holding me. He leans in close and whispers goodnight against my ear.

And then he's gone, off to his room, while I remain outside mine.

I go inside and sit on the edge of my bed, replaying the moments in detail over and over, my face nuzzled into the sleeve of his sweater. Again, I inhale his scent, glad he didn't ask for it back. I stand and remove the sweater so I can take off my dress and everything else. Then, without shame, I slip the sweater back over me.

I want to be near him. I want to be wrapped up in him. The restraint he'd shown though gives me pause.

Perhaps tonight isn't the night to go exploring him again.

Perhaps we need to pull it back a bit.

Just as I doze off, Harper runs into my room, shaking me by my shoulders. "Lyla! Lyla, wake up!" she says, her voice firm. She isn't yelling, not really, but almost.

Jostled awake, I rub my face and sit up. "What's wrong?" I ask, concern overpowering sleep with every passing second.

"It's Paw," she says.

Those two simple words are enough to wake me the rest of the way up.

Now fully awake, I uncover my legs and go on auto-pilot. I pull on leggings but don't bother to change my shirt or put on a bra. I'm pulling on my socks and shoes while she fills me in.

"I think he's having a heart attack. We called for an ambulance. Nan is with him," she says.

I'm now running down the stairs, hearing his voice echoing in the distance between us. I navigate the halls to my grandparents' room and enter.

Paw is sitting up and I don't know if that's good or bad. He's clutching at his chest and left arm, and I *know* that's bad. His breathing is ragged and shallow.

I run to kneel in front of him. His eyes are wild with pain and he looks scared. I've never seen Paw scared. Nan's gripping his hands, whispering calming words to him. I hear noise behind me and turn to see Harper and Gentry entering the room. Gentry circles around to

Paw's side and clutches his shoulder. We all look at one another, unsure what to do, until someone suggests that he lie down. Though everything is happening so suddenly I don't even register who says it.

I hear the ambulance as we lower him to the bed and Gentry runs from the room, presumably to guide them to us so there's no further delay. He returns with the paramedics only a few minutes later, although it feels like an eternity. Watching my Paw's face twist in agony makes time stand still. The EMTs enter and take over. We all step back and they begin asking Nan questions, their voices becoming watery to me. My vision blurs.

This can't be happening.

Gentry holds me, wrapping his arms around my sides and tucking me into him. I stand there—motionless—and let him. Harper comes to my side and reaches for my hand, taking it into hers and squeezing it tightly. We watch them hook things up to him, transfer him to the stretcher, then hook more things up to him. They call out numbers and codes to one another.

I don't have a clue what any of it means.

They exit the room with him strapped to the gurney and we all follow them out. Nan climbs into the back of the ambulance. Or rather, Gentry hoists her up into it. Then the three of us immediately turn toward Gentry's truck.

We climb in as quickly as we can. I sit in the middle, my mind too far gone with worry to note Gentry's proximity this time. Because it doesn't matter.

Nothing matters right now but Paw.

We drive behind the ambulance as fast as we can, trying to keep up. But as the road opens up, the ambulance slinks farther and farther away until we can't even hear the sirens anymore. We simply chase behind it, knowing our destinations are the same.

We turn into the hospital parking lot and scramble out of the truck, heading into the building together. I hadn't bothered to look at myself, to even pull my hair up in a ponytail, and not a single bone in me cares.

We find our way to the reception desk in the emergency room and explain why we're here. They send us to the third floor—the cardiology wing—and we take the elevator up. Another task that seems to float by in slow motion.

We find Nan as soon as the elevator opens on the floor.

She's sitting in the waiting area, where she explains to us that they have him back there but won't let her go in.

"Have they talked to you?" Harper asks.

"Not yet," Nan says.

"How long did they say it would be?" I ask.

"They said it could be a while," Nan tells us.

"I'll go find some coffee," Gentry says, stepping down the hallway toward the nurses' station. It's probably a good idea, knowing we'll likely be here for some time.

We take a seat in the far corner of the waiting area, Nan and Harper by one wall, Gentry and I by the other, once he returns with each of our coffees. As we sit in our corner, I notice for the first time that I'm still wearing his sweater. Part of me finds it comforting but mostly I just hope Harper and Nan don't notice. I try to ignore the faint scent of him wafting up from the soft fabric as I take Nan's hand into mine.

We sit in silence for a few minutes and sip our coffees. I barely notice anything about it beyond it being hot and that Gentry had added a generous amount of sugar for me. I look down at the small paper cup in my hand, twisting it around and around absentmindedly. Gentry reaches over and takes the cup from me, placing it on the table next to us. He takes my now-free hand in his. I see Nan's holding Harper's hand and now we're all holding hands in a semi-circle.

I've never been a religious person. When I was younger, I explored various options and beliefs, but none of it seemed to fit me the way it did other people. I looked at others and they wore their beliefs so effortlessly, so naturally. It used to bother me, but I settled into it after a little while. Accepted it. But here and now, I wish I believed in something—*anything*. I send up a prayer to all the gods, just in case.

After a few more minutes, a doctor finally approaches and we all stand in unison. I'm pretty sure we're all holding our breath, too.

"Mrs. Whitney?" he asks, directing his question to Nan.

She shakes her head slowly, fear gripping her facial features.

"Your husband suffered a mild heart attack," the doctor informs her. "We have him stabilized but he's currently headed into emergency bypass surgery. The surgery should restore blood flow to his heart."

"How long will the surgery take?" Harper asks.

"It depends on the severity of the damage, but it'll be at least a few hours," the doctor says.

"What should we do?" I ask.

"Right now, there's nothing that can be done. You should just focus on trying to get some rest. We'll update you when we have more information and will let you see him as soon as we can," he says.

"Thank you," Nan says quietly.

The doctor gives us a curt nod and turns away, heading back toward the doors marked **RESTRICTED**. Then we watch him disappear behind them.

We all sit back down slowly, adjusting in our seats as if we'd ever actually be able to get comfortable or rest.

"I'll go make some calls, so the farm will be okay while we're here," Gentry says.

Nan nods her head as she stares forward. She doesn't move otherwise and my heart hurts for her. Nan and Paw have been together since they were both in their early twenties. I can't even pretend to understand a love like that. I know she's worried and I don't blame her. I pull my legs up into the chair and attempt to settle in.

Gentry returns a little while later and lets us know everything will be fine while we're here. He's taken care of everything. I'm so grateful for his presence and authority in this moment. He reaches over and clasps my shoulder, gently massaging me, and I give in to the sensation. I'm so tense, but I let myself melt under his touch, not even caring who might see or what they might think. There's too much stress in my body for that. Even in this situation, I want him to take me into his arms. Not in a sexual way, but for comfort. I want him to stroke my hair, to tell me everything will be okay. To tell me not to worry.

I must fall asleep at some point, though I don't know how or when.

I feel a shift and my eyes flutter open slowly. Harper is across from me, her head propped on her hand, her eyes closed. I realize then that my head is on Gentry's shoulder and his arm is around me. I tilt my head up slightly.

"You should go back to sleep," he whispers.

I look back at Harper and then over to Nan. She's resting similarly, curled into a ball in her chair. She looks pitiful. I want to reach for her.

"She's okay," he says, reading my thoughts.

"How long has it been?" I ask.

"A little over an hour, almost two I think," he says.

"We should hear something soon," I say, hopeful.

"Hope so," he says.

I feel his arm tighten around me and I exhale slowly. I feel so safe like this.

"Get some sleep," he says.

I nod my head and lay my head back down on his shoulder, nuzzling against him. He brushes a light kiss to the hair on top of my head and rests his cheek against me. It takes me several minutes to fall back asleep after that, but I finally manage it. I concentrate on Gentry's heartbeat and breathing, a symphony of peaceful percussion, filling my ears.

LYLA

I WAKE UP LATER. How much later, I can't say. As I open my eyes, I don't know if it's been a few minutes or a few hours. The sterile hospital walls and fluorescent lights overhead give me no hints. Looking around, I notice a few people have joined the waiting area but it's still quite empty. Then I see that Nan and Harper are gone. I start searching around to see if perhaps they've just moved or walked to the nurses' station, but I don't see them anywhere.

Gentry's arm moves underneath me. "Harper convinced Nan to go get something to eat in the cafeteria," he informs me.

I nod my head, relieved to know Nan is eating. I know if we don't force the issue, she won't. "What time is it? How long have we been here? Do we know anything else?"

"It's nearly seven," Gentry says. "The doctor came out again, just to let us know the surgery was progressing well, but he hasn't been back since. Everyone was asleep except for me at that point."

"I'm sorry. I should have stayed awake," I say, sitting up more in my seat.

Gentry's arm reluctantly loosens in response, like letting me go is the exact opposite of what he wants to do. "No, it's okay—really. You

needed rest. And I rested, too. I just happened to be awake in that
moment," he says.

I give him a pointed look.

He brushes his thumb over my jaw and tilts his head slightly, his
eyes trained on my face, as if he's studying it, memorizing it.

I reach up and place my hand over his, closing my eyes and
nuzzling my face into his palm. His touch soothes me and, regardless
of what might happen later on with us, I'm glad he's here right now.
"Thank you for coming," I say.

"Of course," he says. "Do you need anything?"

"I'm actually a little hungry myself," I say, despite not wanting
to be.

He smiles at me and leans up in his chair. "Do you want to go join
Harper and Nan?"

I nod my head and we stand slowly, stretching our bodies out once
we're up. Being cramped in these chairs has really done a number on
my back. Of course, it's the sort of thing you don't realize until you
stand and attempt to move.

As we walk down the hallway toward the elevators, Gentry takes
my hand in his. He laces our fingers together and I let him do it. We
haven't talked about displays of affection in front of others or whether
or not we should indulge in them, so I go along with it.

We find the cafeteria a few minutes later. It's a couple of floors
down and even though I'm hungry, almost nothing looks appealing.
Sure, because it's hospital cafeteria food. But also because suddenly, I
feel a little sick at the thought of eating anything. I settle on a plate of
hash browns and some apple juice.

Gentry meets me at the register and looks down at my plate, his
eyes assessing and judging, all at once. "That's all you want?" he
inquires.

I nod. "I don't think I can eat much."

He concedes, most likely understanding that despite my body's
hunger, I have a mental block to battle as well.

After he pays for our food, we round the corner and search for
Harper and Nan. The cafeteria is a little busier than the waiting area
upstairs, but that makes sense given the time of morning it likely is.

We spot them in the corner next to the windows, where Harper sees us and waves us over. Once we're there, we take our seats—me next to Nan and Gentry across from me, next to Harper.

"Did you guys see the doctor before you came down?" Harper asks.

Nan looks at me, hopeful, and my heart aches for her all over again right then and there over my plate of overpriced hash browns.

"No, nothing yet," I say.

We sit in silence eating for a little while. I mostly pick, moving the potatoes around on my plate, occasionally taking a bite. I try, but it's no use. I can't force myself to eat, as much as I want to. Nan stares out the window, sipping her coffee in silence, while I exchange worried glances with Gentry then Harper and then Gentry again. I don't like feeling helpless. I don't like waiting like this with no way to do anything to help.

"I should go back up. I don't want the doctor to come out while no one is up there and then we miss him," Nan says suddenly. She starts to rise from her chair and Harper follows suit.

"I'll go with you," Harper says, pushing her chair in and collecting her tray from the table. She looks at me and Gentry, and we exchange nods.

I'm glad they're going back up. I hadn't thought about it, but Nan is right. We should make sure someone is up there and available for the doctor at all times. Nan reaches down and kisses me on the cheek, then she disappears with Harper as they cross the cafeteria, leaving the two of us alone at our spot.

I look at Gentry and we smile at each other. It feels like neither one of us knows what to say right now. Most silences that have passed between us have been comfortable, but not this one. Maybe it's due to being at the hospital, or this specific situation in general, but something is messing us up right now.

"You're stressed," he says, and I nod my head in agreement. "And you need a distraction." He stands up and holds his hand out to me.

Confusion takes hold of me for only a second, but curiosity settles in and wins over. I place my hand in his and he tugs me up from my seat, pulling me toward the exit of the cafeteria.

Instead of heading back to the cardiology floor, he takes me one floor down and we exit into the parking garage. He's still tugging me along as he pulls me down a row of cars until we reach his truck. He opens the passenger door and ushers me in.

"We can't leave," I say, but he shakes his head.

"We won't," he assures me.

I climb in and watch him walk around and take his place behind the wheel. Silence falls over the cab, and I wonder for a moment if we're permanently broken.

He shifts in his seat then and lifts the middle console between us up, leaving no barriers between us now. He leans toward me and I feel my heart start to race a little. He reaches his arms out for me. "Come here."

Before I can protest or think better of it, my body instinctively slides over to his.

He wraps his arms around the center of my back and begins rubbing small soothing circles on my skin. Tension begins to leave me, and I exhale a long, deep breath. He brings his face close to mine, hovering just inches away, and I want to kiss him but I resist the urge. Whatever this is, I want him to lead. He sweeps light kisses across my cheek and all the way back to my ear so we're cheek to cheek. I can hear him breathing, can feel it on my skin. It sends a wave of goose-bumps over me.

"I remember you that day," he says. "I remember looking up at the bathroom window and seeing your face twisted in pleasure. I tried so hard to look away, but I couldn't."

As he speaks to me, his hands move over my body. They dip low to the edge of my leggings, and he tugs gently on the front hem, just below my belly button.

"I remember wishing I could have you right then, wanting to be the one who made your face do that," he says. "I wanted to be the instrument of your pleasure."

My chest tightens, my legs go limp. His hand dips into my panties and I shudder.

"I remember wishing I could watch your face do that up close," he whispers.

His fingers travel lower, over my sensitive skin, trailing my folds. My body reacts instinctively, arching toward him, desperate for his touch.

"Will you let me watch you? Will you let me be that instrument?" he asks.

I nod my head, breath ragged in my chest.

"Lean back," he instructs.

I do as he says, lying down on his truck seat. I rest my head against the door, so he can see my face.

He pulls my pants and panties down in one motion, exposing me. He puts each of my legs on either side of him so he's sitting between them—the most sacred part of me on full display for him. He looks down at me, appreciation and hunger gripping his features. He begins again with his fingers, moving over me softly before dipping them inside me.

I inhale a sharp breath at the sudden fullness.

He moves them back and forth slowly, bringing his thumb up to rub gentle circles over my clit.

I moan. I pant. I feel my body arching, my hips lurching toward his touch.

Each time I close my eyes, he tells me to open them. He wants to see me—to watch me.

His mouth hangs open slightly, lips apart. Before I can react, his head moves lower and he takes me all at once, sucking and licking me as if he's starved for my taste. His hands grip my thighs as he rocks me back and forth, my body crashing against his mouth over and over again until I'm close.

Abruptly, he pulls away. His breathing is heavy when he begins petting me with his hands again, his fingers finishing what his mouth had started. His pace quickens, and my body begins to stiffen.

"Come for me," he says. "Please."

His words are all it takes to send me spiraling down a rabbit hole of pure ecstasy. I pulse and twist, coil and uncoil, relentlessly, until my body finally relaxes. For a moment, I'm pretty sure I even saw heaven.

Gentry brings my legs together, letting me enjoy the aftershocks while he gently caresses my outer thigh. He props his head on the seat and stares down at me.

"You're so bad," I say, a small laugh on my lips.

"You make me want to be bad," he says. "And good. And better."

I swallow hard at the entirety of his words and their meanings—at how beautiful and significant they are. "You are good," I manage.

Gentry pulls my panties from my discarded leggings and begins slipping them back onto me. Then my pants.

The smile on his face is strange. There's genuine happiness there, but it's also tinged with sadness. Especially around his eyes. I don't like it. I want to reach out and smooth the darkness from his features. He's *so good*. He's more than good. So much more.

He leans over and caresses my cheek with his palm. I lean into his touch, placing my hand over his.

We sit there after that, just talking. About everything. All kinds of things. The conversation goes on for a little while, transitioning from topic to topic with ease. I know he's just doing it to distract me, and I appreciate it.

After enough time has passed, we both know it's time to go back. I don't want to leave Harper and Nan to deal with this alone for too long.

We exit the truck and walk back to the building. There, we head for the elevator, taking it up to the familiar waiting area that's become our haven.

When we enter, Nan's not there, but Harper is. She's sitting alone in the corner and I can't read the look on her face.

When we approach, she stands.

"Paw's okay," she says. "Nan's gone back to see him." With that, her stoic face finally gives way to a small smile.

Gentry and I both let out a sigh of relief at her good news.

She continues with, "He gets to go home in a couple of days but will have to rest for a few weeks. And by 'rest'…well, the doctor made it clear Paw's not to work or even leave the house. He can go from bed to recliner and back to bed, but that's about it."

I nod along, absorbing the information and agreeing.

The man just had a heart attack, *and* surgery; of course he needs to rest.

However, convincing Paw of that will be next to impossible.

The next few weeks will be rough on everyone.

It looks like I'll be staying here a little longer.

GENTRY

THE NEXT WEEK ROLLS BY, full of watching. Watching and waiting.

I watch Lyla help settle Paw in when we first get him back home, taking care to be gentle. I watch her wrap blankets around him in his recliner, adjust his pillows, bring him food. I watch her make him decaffeinated tea and fuss with him for an hour each time, insisting he can't have caffeine while he argues that he's a grown ass man who can have what he wants.

I watch her have impeccable patience.

I watch her inevitably win him over each time.

On this particular evening, I watch her help Harper with the dishes.

I'm sitting at the kitchen table, drinking my night cap, relieved tomorrow is Saturday. This week, without Paw, had been strenuous. Not because I couldn't handle the farm myself—I could—but because his sudden ailment and needed recovery had everyone talking. I had to field the onslaught of questions. About the events, how he's doing now, when he'll back to normal, and so on. I could nearly script it at this point. Almost the exact same questions in the exact same order by everyone who came by to ask.

Part of me finds it endearing that there are so many worried, but the rest of me just wants them to shut the fuck up about it already and move on. Such is my method with almost everything. Shove it away—so far away that you forget about it—and move forward. I make no claims of it being the best or healthiest way of dealing with stuff, but it does work.

"Charles is coming by tomorrow."

Harper's voice cuts through my thoughts with the mention of her ex. I don't like that guy and I definitely want to know if the asshole is making an appearance here. I sit up a little straighter, paying a bit more attention. I watch Lyla stop what she's doing.

She places down the plate she's drying and turns toward Harper. "Can't we just put his shit in the driveway with a little note that says 'fuck you' and call it a day?" Lyla asks her sister, her tone more serious than joking.

I smile, fighting back the urge to laugh. I love how sassy she can get.

"No, we can't," Harper responds. "That wouldn't be right. Even if it's what I want to do."

"Well, he wasn't supposed to do what he did but that didn't stop him," Lyla counters, her tone harsher than I've ever heard it.

I haven't seen this side of her until now. She's protective, defensive.

Harper looks down then, almost as though Lyla's words have wounded her, which they might've. "Lyla," she says simply. But the implications in only saying her sister's name, in the specific tone it carried, has said everything and then some.

"Look, I know you don't want to see him," Lyla says. "I know you don't. You're just trying to be nice. Tell you what, I'll give him his stuff and you stay out of sight, okay?"

But Harper is already shaking her head. "I can't ask you to do that."

"You're not asking me. I'm offering," Lyla says, shrugging her shoulders.

I admire this sort of care for her sister. I really do.

"Are you sure?" Harper asks her.

"Positive," Lyla answers without hesitation.

The thought of Lyla having to face that jackass alone makes me uneasy. I don't like the idea, but I also don't think he'd hurt her or anything. He doesn't look like the type to, but you can never truly tell with people. Intentions are a strange thing. You mean one thing, do another. Say one thing and mean another. You can never assume to know a person, their intentions, or what they're capable of when their intentions melt away from them and leave them desperate to make a move. Knowing that, I decide to make myself conveniently available for this exchange tomorrow and be at the right place and time. Just in case.

"What time do you want him to come?" Harper asks.

"Tell that asshole—I mean, tell *Chuck*—to be here around ten A.M.," Lyla says. "I don't want to spend my whole Saturday wasting time with freaking *Charles*."

I smile again, bigger this time. We definitely have one thing in common: we both think Charles is an absolute asshole.

I'd seen him around here, before the split. He was always so uptight. To say he'd ever helped with the farm would be a gross over-statement. He'd mainly just walked around, pointed at things that needed to be done, and then delegated them to other people. I'd bet the man had never seen his hands dirty in his whole life.

And the way he treated Harper? Like she was invisible most of the time?

I heard him talk over her more than once, as though what she was saying wasn't important or worth hearing at all. Sometimes he'd look at her after she'd say something, and he'd just give a long sigh and start talking. Not even in response to her comments, but in general. Sometimes, he'd change the topic completely.

I watch Lyla hug her sister, and then Harper leaves the room.

Lyla goes back to finishing her task, drying the last of the items. Then, she sits the towel down on the counter. She reaches back and rubs her neck, twisting her head side to side.

I stand and walk to her, instinctively reaching out to take over and rub where she's rubbing.

She jumps, slightly startled, then relaxes again and lets her hands fall to her sides.

I begin rubbing circles on the back of her neck and outward to her shoulders. I apply some pressure, wanting to help ease her pain. "You're a really great big sister, you know," I say, my voice low but not quite a whisper.

"Thank you. I'm trying. But honestly, up until this visit, I probably wasn't a very good one," she says.

I frown. "What do you mean?"

"I just mean I wasn't around a lot. I wasn't exactly a source of help or comfort," she says, dropping her shoulders a bit as I press my thumbs between her shoulder blades and smooth her muscles. She's tense, but her rigid edges loosen under my fingertips.

"I'm sure that's not how she sees it. You've been living your own life. But she needed you, and you came," I say.

Lyla's quiet for a moment, like she's considering my words.

"Are you done with the dishes?" I ask her.

When she nods, I stop massaging her in this awkward standing position and reach down for her hand.

Since Paw's come home from the hospital, Lyla hasn't spent a single night with me. She hasn't even come to my room to unwind. But she needs it. She needs to relax.

I lead her upstairs, careful not to make too much noise as Paw has all but permanently affixed himself to the recliner. As a result, Nan's been sleeping in the living room, too. I don't want to wake them.

I take her to the edge of my bed and slowly undress her. I point to her shoes and she kicks them off. I unbutton her pants and let them fall to the floor, urging her to step out of them. I pull her shirt over her head then turn her around so her back is to me. Once I unclasp her bra, I bend down and trail soft kisses on the back of her neck. Her breath catches, and I watch a ripple of goosebumps spread over her arms. I let her bra fall, then I point to the bed.

She looks back at me over her shoulder and raises a brow.

"Trust me," I urge.

Her face softens as she crawls onto the bed. There, she lies down on her stomach, tucking her arms under her head.

I unbuckle my belt, then my pants. They fall to the floor with a *clink* as the buckle hits the hardwood and she look backs at me again.

"What is happening right now?" she asks, giggling.

I keep my eyes locked with hers as I pull my T-shirt up over my head and toss it on the floor. Then I open the drawer next to my bed.

"Wait," she says, and I'm sure she's thinking I'm reaching for a condom, but her face relaxes a bit when she sees the bottle of lotion in my hand.

"You need to relax, Lyla. I just want to help," I say, giving her a grin. I open the bottle and put some lotion in my hand. Then I toss the bottle onto the mattress. I straddle her hips without applying any of my weight to her frame. Before I apply the lotion, I rub it between my hands, making every effort to warm it.

But it's no use.

As soon as it touches her skin, she gasps and cusses about its temperature.

She relaxes almost immediately after that, though, when I begin to massage it into her skin. I work delicate circles up and down her back, attempting to focus on the areas in which she reacts underneath my touch. I press my fingers into her harder after a bit, wanting to make sure I do her body justice. I've never really given anyone a massage before, so I try to think about what I would enjoy.

Lyla seems to like it, and every now and then, a moan slips out from between her lips.

I try to ignore all the urges I have. To flip her over. To take her nipples into my mouth one at a time. To reach down and—

No, shut up.

Focus.

"Thank you," she says on a moan. "This feels amazing."

I redirect my attention to her thighs, kneading them softly. "Of course," I say, choking on nothing.

I lift her leg up and palm her calf. I focus on my hands, on what they're doing. On the benign places they're touching. I rub the center of her foot, applying more lotion as I go. I switch to the other leg and then I work my way back up.

My hands freeze above her panties.

I could massage her ass.

No.

Yes.

No.

I skip over it in a hurry. I rub circles down her arms, then I squeeze her fingers between mine and press into her palms.

Touching Lyla is nearly too much. *Every* part of her turns me on. Even her wenis. You know, her wenis. That flabby elbow skin.

I roll my eyes, thankful she can't see my expression.

I loathe myself.

"What about my front?" she asks, her tone dark and suggestive.

Oh god.

I swallow nothing and manage, "Sure." It's the only word I can get out. I don't even try for a full sentence. I lean away from her, letting her twist her body until she's lying on her back.

She looks up at me, almost expectantly. Or at least I think that's the look.

My eyes trail over her. I can't help it. Her soft, pink nipples are perfect. The curve of her breasts, the lines of her ribs. Her hip bones. Her hair is tossed all over, some of it spilling over the front of her shoulders, so I reach for it, tucking the loose strands back and involuntarily inhaling her scent.

Honeysuckles.

She smells like honeysuckles.

Even after everything that's transpired between us, I can tell she wants to cover herself. So, I take her arms and tuck them up above her, trailing my fingers back down her arm and into the dip at the front of her neck.

"You're so beautiful," I whisper.

Lyla tries to shift her eyes away from my gaze.

"Hey, look at me," I demand softly.

She stares back at me then, waiting.

"You are so beautiful, inside and out. And it's taking every ounce of self-restraint I have not to do bad things to you right now," I tell her.

She takes in my words and I watch her swallow, clearly unsure as to what she should do.

"Kiss me," she finally says, more command than question, but I hesitate. "Please."

And that's all it takes. The word "please" from her lips and I'm a goner.

I lower myself down to her, still careful not to put any of my weight on her. My mouth is just an inch or so from hers, and I can feel her body anticipating it. The air becomes thick, her mouth drawing me in.

I'm a lost sailor and she's my lighthouse.

I press my lips to hers. It's innocent at first. Then her lips part, inviting me in. My tongue licks at hers. I suck her bottom lip into my mouth and bite down a little. My entire body is on fire now, desire spilling out from all my edges. I sink down onto her, her tits pressing against my bare chest, and I wrap my arms around her then roll us onto our sides.

We make out like this, my grip tight around her.

I don't want to press forward, don't want to let her go. So, we stay just like this for a long time. We alternate between kissing and talking, then kissing some more, talking some more.

Lyla's eyelids eventually grow heavy, but she doesn't want to go.

We fall asleep in only our underwear, folded into each other, bare chests pressed together.

It's the best sleep I've had all week.

LYLA

I WAKE up in Gentry's arms, which is quickly becoming my favorite way to wake up. A thought which makes me smile but also worries me. I look at his face, just inches from mine, wondering how we managed to sleep like this all night. When I close my eyes again, I focus on how I feel right now. When I close my eyes again, I feel his warmth radiating from his body. The exact placement of his hands on my skin. The way his legs are tangled perfectly with mine.

It sounds awful in my head, but what happened with Paw is going to stretch out my time here...and I can get behind that silver lining.

My eyes shoot open again, remembering Chuck the lame duck will be by this morning and I don't know what time it is. I shift just slightly, and Gentry shifts in response. I know once I start to move, he'll wake up. Though I hate to do it, I know I have to. I stretch my arms out, and Gentry nuzzles his face into my neck.

"Not yet," he whispers.

It's so hard to resist a request like that, so hard to focus on anything when all I want to do is curl back up into him and stay here all day.

"Charles, the royal asshole, will be here soon. I think soon, anyway. And I have to get ready," I say.

"Is that his official title?" Gentry asks through smiling lips.

"I have a lot of nicknames for him, actually," I say, laughing at my own joke.

"Why don't you stay here and tell me all of them?" he asks, making any attempt to keep me here; but two can play this game.

"How about we take a shower together?" I whisper close to his ear.

Gentry's eyes shoot open and he untangles from me at record speed, sitting up in bed and stretching. "I'm up. Let's get this show on the road. Come on, slowpoke." He says this all as he stands from his bed, and I roll my eyes at him.

After retrieving what I need from my room, I meet him in the bathroom.

Gentry has already stripped down, his last remaining items of clothing in a pile on the floor, his body on full display as he adjusts the water. And what a glorious birthday suit it is.

I peel my panties down, flicking them away with my foot. Now, I'm undressed to match.

He looks at me, eyes hooded, then up to the ceiling as if praying to someone.

"What are you doing?" I ask, laughing.

"Thanking all the gods," he says.

"For what?"

"For you," he says, moving to me, pressing his thumbs into the soft spots above my hips.

A smile plays across my lips. He's smooth. Smooth as a baby pig. (*What do you want from me? We're on a farm.*)

We step into the shower and let the hot water run over us as we hold each other. The water pools between us before falling to the tub and Gentry reaches down again, kissing my jaw.

"Hey, Lyla?" he says.

"Yes?"

"You remember that thing you did in the shower?"

I jerk my face to look at him, feeling my cheeks get warm just at the mention. I nod. "I believe I remember."

"Can you do that for me?" he asks.

I look at him, confused for a moment before it really sinks in—what he's asking me. "Oh my god, no. I can't do that."

He pouts his bottom lip out. "Why not?"

"Because, we have to get ready. And I can't look at you while you're watching me do that," I say, blushing so hard I know I resemble a strawberry.

"What if I help?" he asks.

My eyebrow raises at his suggestion because I definitely like the sound of that. "Help me how?" I ask, genuinely interested.

Gentry moves closer to me, his eyes fixed on my mouth. He reaches down and kisses me hard then pulls back again. "Do you want me to tell you or show you?" he asks, then proceeds to kiss me again.

"Show me. Definitely show me," I say eagerly, my eyes still closed, my mouth still drunk from his kisses.

He reaches down, trailing his fingers over my nipples. He rolls them between his fingertips, and they harden under his touch. His hand travels down, parts my legs. He lingers right at the top of my center, hovers there, letting the ache in me build.

"Do you feel that?" he asks.

I nod, biting my bottom lip.

"Give me your hand," he instructs.

I hesitate for a moment, then hold my hand out to his.

He cups it into his, guiding my fingers down my body, until we part me—together.

He growls in my ear and presses me against the shower wall and window. He pushes his knee between my legs, parting me further. He dips my fingers in and out of me, shadowing them with his own hand while rubbing circles over my clit. My toes begin to curl. If I know anything, it's my own body. And maybe it's the heightened sexiness of him helping, or just him in general, but it isn't going to take long for me to come like this.

"Does it feel good?" he asks, his face so close to mine I could reach up and bite his jaw.

"Yes," I moan, inhaling ragged breaths.

"Tell me how good it feels," he demands.

But I don't know what to say. I'm lost to the sensations I feel all throughout my body. Lost to the delicious feeling growing inside me.

"Does it feel better than when I'm inside you?" he asks, grinding his hips into mine, pressing himself against me.

I shake my head because that's an easy answer to give. I feel his length against my hip, long and hard. I ache for *him*, knowing he's so close.

"Pity," he says, rubbing his shaft up and down.

I take him into my free hand and he curses under his breath. My hand slides up and down and he groans, biting his lip.

"I want you," I say.

"And I want you," he says, squeezing his eyes closed at my touch.

"No, I want you *now*. I want you inside me," I beg.

His eyes open, hesitation on his face. "I don't have any condoms in here."

"I don't care. I'm safe. Are you?" I ask.

He nods his head. "What about—"

"I'm on birth control," I say. "Please."

At this, he moves in front of me and dips down slightly. He lingers at my entrance for only a moment before pushing himself inside me.

I moan, covering my mouth with my hand as best as I can manage. My fingers grip his shoulders, and I bite into his collarbone.

He rocks into me over and over again, his hand streaking the glass of the window behind us.

I hadn't remembered it was there until now, hadn't cared about it. Though if someone were to see us, I still wouldn't care. I want this. I need this. He slides into me, over and over again, alternating between fast and hard and slow and soft. I feel every inch of him. He reaches down between us, caressing my clit, and my legs wobble. His strong arms keep me upright. Admittedly, he's doing most of the work. But I don't mind.

"Lyla?" he whispers.

"Yes?" I manage to say.

"Tell me you want me again."

"I want you."

"Say it again," he pleads.

"I want you." I repeat the words over and over again, kissing his mouth, his neck, whispering the words between each one.

We come, not exactly together, but it's a ripple effect—starting with me.

By the time we get out of the shower, the water's run cold. There's no doubt in my mind that the other occupants of the house will put two and two together, but I still don't care.

We dress and laugh; we brush our hair and teeth. I like this— getting ready together. It feels natural, seems normal.

I check my phone for the time just as we're finishing up and it's exactly ten minutes until Chuck the fuck is supposed to arrive. So, we hurry ourselves downstairs. Before we reach the bottom step, Gentry pulls me close for one more kiss, and then we're off again.

Harper is in the kitchen making coffee, and she looks like a mess.

"Are you okay?" I ask.

"This is my fourth cup," she states.

I walk straight to her, taking the cup from her and setting it down. "Yeah, maybe no more coffee for you." I grab her by the shoulders, guide her to a chair at the kitchen table, and sit her in it.

"I don't know why I'm so nervous," she admits.

"It makes sense," I reassure her. "Sure, you were together a long time, but it's different now. He no longer feels warm or safe. He's wounded you. Now, his presence sets you on edge."

"Thank you for doing this. I'm not sure I could see him without crying or throwing up or both," she says.

I take her into my arms, giving her a tight hug.

As if on cue, we all turn as we hear tires barreling up the gravel driveway.

I step back from her, rolling my eyes and nodding toward the living room, silently urging her to go sit with Nan and Paw.

She gets up and walks out of the kitchen.

Gentry cups her shoulder as she passes him, silently reassuring her he's here for her, too.

I walk out on the porch and Gentry stays inside, lingering just on the other side of the screen door. I don't want him out here. I hope

Charles will see me as the least threatening and just take his shit and go.

He parks his car a few feet away and steps out. He's wearing a suit, buttoning the jacket once he's standing.

Who wears a full suit on a Saturday? And for this?

I roll my eyes, unable to keep my disdain completely capped.

His perfectly combed hair looks so stupid, as though it's actually been combed with a comb. I thought that was a practice reserved only for five-year-olds and old men.

"Hello, Charles," I say, impressing myself by using his preferred name and not Chuck.

As if this isn't terrible enough, Allie steps out of the car—my sister's best friend since grade school. The person I consider to be even worse than Charles in this scenario.

A woman doesn't simply sleep with her best friend's husband, no. That doesn't just happen. It's had me wondering just how long she lusted after Chuck before she actually acted on it.

She straightens her shirt and skirt. Despite having worked here in the past and having a good understanding of farm life, the idiot decided wearing high heels was a good idea and now she looks like a wobbly baby deer taking its first steps.

I roll my eyes at her now and know that if she even tries to speak, I won't be able to contain myself.

"Lyla. Where's Harper?" Charles asks. He scans the porch and the door, seemingly confused that she isn't here.

She must not have told him this part.

Well, allow me.

"She won't be joining us. I'll be brokering this little deal today," I say casually, feigning obvious boredom.

"Um, why?" he challenges, bringing his hands to his hips.

"Because I said so." I keep my voice calm and casual.

He gives me a pointed look, like it might intimidate me into going and getting Harper, but I don't cave.

"Will you just go get her?" he asks, his tone growing more aggressive.

"No," I say. "You can either do this with me or not at all."

Charles looks around, like he's deciding.

"You should really go get her, sweetie. We don't have time for these games," *she* says.

Allie's voice hits me like a bucket of ice. I see red immediately. I clench my hands into fists at my sides and square up.

"You should really shut your mouth, *sweetie*. Unless you want to get hurt," I say.

"Excuse me?" she says, exaggerated shock filling her stupid face.

"You heard me," I tell her.

"Are you going to let her talk to me like that?" she says to Charles, looking at him like he should do something to defend her honor.

"Um," is all he manages.

"Yes, you are," a voice cuts in. "Aren't you, Charles?"

I hear the swinging of the door behind me, but I don't move or flinch.

Gentry appears beside me then, his arms folded tightly over his chest. "Tell her you're going to let Lyla talk to her like that because you have no spine."

Charles gulps. "How about we all just calm down?" He extends his hands to further convey his point.

"How about you cut the bullshit, get your stuff, and get gone?" I ask, pointing to the boxes Harper kindly—and against my advice—packed for him, labeled for him, *and* neatly stacked on the corner of the porch for him.

He looks at the boxes, even more confused. "That's it?"

"As far as I know," I say.

"Well, is the ring in there?" Charles asks.

I stare at him, utter disbelief gripping me. I see red again, but this time, I doubt I can play nice. "What the hell do you mean? You want the ring back? You've been married for years. It's her ring!"

"But we won't be married anymore, and I want it back," he says.

"You're crazy if you think you're getting that ring back," I say.

"Look, it's really none of your business," he replies.

"Oh, but it is, Chuck. It is my business. And it'll be a cold day in hell before you get that ring back, even if I have to melt it down and turn it into a tiny dildo myself," I say.

"Dildo?" he repeats.

"Yeah, so you can go fuck yourself," I say.

Gentry laughs, but Chuck doesn't.

"I want that ring back," Charles says in a hard tone. "I'm going to sell it. I have a right to it."

I walk off the porch and straight up to him, squaring my shoulders again. My fists are back to being balled at my sides.

He looks like he wants to flinch. He takes half a step back, but it makes no difference.

"Now you listen to me, Charles. Listen really hard because I'm only going to say this once. You're not getting that damn ring back. So, you can take your shit that's on the porch and pack it into your car, or later, we can have a bonfire. It's your choice. But I swear to all the gods, if my sister's name or the mention of that ring comes out of your mouth one more time, I will knock you all the way back to when you had some fucking manners. Do we understand each other?" I ask him. I keep my eyes sharp and trained on him.

He gives a small nod.

"Charles, you can't be serious?" This comment comes from the winner of the *Worst Best Friend in the World* award.

I turn my attention to her now. "And *you*. You so much as even breathe the wrong way one more time, and I will level you so hard Charles will be picking gravel out of your ass all the way into next week."

She gives me a challenging look, pressing her hand to her hip and studying me but finally thinking better of saying anything more. She crosses her arms over her chest and huffs, leaning back onto their car.

Over the next few minutes, Gentry and I watch Charles put box after box into his car, neither of us offering a helping hand. He's a big boy; he can figure it out.

After he finishes with the boxes, he comes around the car and stands in front of us.

"You don't understand, you know. What it was like," he says.

Gentry and I exchange glances, not sure where Charles is headed with this.

"I was miserable with your sister," he clarifies. "She made me miserable."

I press my eyes closed, trying very hard not to swan dive off this porch onto him and break all the bones in his body.

"She's insane," Charles adds. "And at the same time, completely boring."

With this comment, I know I can't do it any longer. I press away from the column I've been leaning against, but Gentry calms me with a hand on my shoulder.

He gives me a look, one I don't quite understand. Then he slowly steps off the porch toward Charles. "You know what, Chuck, I think we've had just about enough of your mouth to last a lifetime. So why don't you take this last token of our appreciation and head on down the road?"

Charles looks at Gentry, confused. "Take what?"

At that, Gentry rears back and punches Charles right in the gut. Chuck doubles over in response, and Gentry takes this opportunity to knee him in the face. It all happens so quickly. I stand there in shock, unsure what to do. Gentry lets Charles fall to the ground. His mistress —who shall not be named—runs around the car to him, helping him up and into the car. But she says nothing. I'm sure she's assumed she'd have it just as bad. She helps Charles to the passenger seat and then drives away.

"Sorry, I just really hate that guy," Gentry says, turning back toward me and coming up the stairs of the porch.

I still haven't said anything. But maybe that's all right, because Gentry wraps his arms around me and I return the gesture.

As the shock finally wears off, a smile begins to stretch across my face and I squeeze him tighter. "That was kind of hot," I tell him.

"Oh yeah?"

"I'm not usually one to condone violence but the sweet crunching sound of Chuck's face against your knee really has me thinking naughty things," I admit.

"Do you want another shower?" he asks, and at that, we both laugh.

LYLA

ANOTHER WEEK PASSES, and Paw's slowly been getting back to himself. He now goes to bed with Nan in their bedroom, so no one's camping in the living room anymore. He's walked to the kitchen and back, to grab his own water—after the doctor approved it, of course. It's made Nan visibly less stressed, which has been a relief to everyone else.

After Chuck's visit last week, Harper sold the ring herself after hearing his intentions. She went shopping for new clothes with the money, and for whatever reason, the exchange with him seems to have given her some much-needed closure. The reality of Charles leaving doesn't look like it sits quite so heavy on her shoulders anymore. Though she still has her moments.

And since that day, not a night has gone by that I haven't been in Gentry's room. I haven't slept in my own bed at all. I even moved my luggage into his room, because in his words, *it just made sense.*

I wasn't sure it was a good idea at first, but I didn't think about it too long. I didn't *want* to think about it. Instead, I shoved my impending need to leave far off into the corners of my mind and ignored them.

Today, I'm in the barn with Maribelle and Lucy. I brush them and feed them, then sit with them and talk to them. Talking to cows is nice. They don't interrupt you or talk back. They simply sit there, wanting the treats from your hand, quietly listening to you without passing judgment. They're the best sounding boards.

I hear someone walk into the barn and stand to see if it's Gentry but to my surprise, it's Dean. "Oh, hi," I say.

"Well, hello there," Dean says. He does his best to saunter over to me and then he leans against the gate of the pin. "What are you doing out here?"

"Just talking to Maribelle," I say. "She's a great listener." I gesture to her then turn back to Dean, but he's busy staring straight down my shirt. I snap my fingers in front of his face.

"Oh, sorry," he says, laughing. "Old habits."

I decide to let it go, not wanting to get into it with him about *old times*. "Right."

"Speaking of," he says.

Here we go.

"Remember when I used to fuck you right in the back of my car?" he asks.

I don't say anything in return, and he continues with, "Good times, good times. I just figured since you're here...maybe we can go again, for old times' sake."

I cringe at the very thought. "Listen, no offense, but I'm not interested." With that, I wave him off.

He grabs my hand and holds me in place. "What? You mean Gentry's the only cowboy around here you'll fuck?"

My mouth falls open, stunned by the venom in his words. "Let go of me, Dean."

"I've had you before, what's one more time?" he says.

"Dean, let go of my hand," I demand, trying to remain calm.

He pushes the pin open and backs me all the way against the wall of the barn. "Come on, Lyla. You know you want it. You know you remember how it was," he says, licking his lips.

I try to pull away, but the harder I struggle against his grip, the tighter it becomes. "Please, let me go."

"You know what else is nice about this barn? No one can hear you." He laughs after that, a disgusting laugh. One that makes my skin crawl.

In the middle of his sinister, bad-guy laugh, his body is jerked away from me.

Gentry has him by the shoulder, and he whirls Dean around, grabbing him by the neck. "The lady said to let her go. She even said please," Gentry warns, his eyes stone cold and fixed on Dean.

"That's a lady?" He laughs. "Pfft. Nah. She was in your pants pretty fast, and if I remember, she used to beg me for—"

Gentry punches him then.

And when I say Gentry *punches him*, I mean Dean will be lucky if he ever sees out of his left eye again. Or feels the left side of his face. Or is able to chew. Because Gentry doesn't just punch him once. He doesn't show a fraction of the restraint he did last week with Charles. He punches Dean until he's screaming out for Gentry to stop. Like a wuss. And I don't feel bad saying that considering what he just said about me.

Gentry doesn't just let Dean go; he throws him to the ground like a piece of paper he's simply crumpled into a ball and tossed.

Dean's back connects with the concrete floor of the barn and he rolls, wincing and grabbing at his face at the same time.

"I guess I don't need to tell you you're fired," Gentry says, pushing at Dean with the toe of his boot.

Dean rolls to his knees and then to his feet. He looks at me with disgust and rage then turns and leaves the barn.

I run to Gentry, his arms already outstretched to embrace me.

"Are you okay?" he asks.

I nod my head against his chest, but I can already feel the tears welling up.

He holds me tight and starts to run his fingers through my hair.

My hands are trembling from the rush of adrenaline and fear. I try to hold the tears back. I try with all my might to keep them in, but it's no use. My shoulders begin to bob, and he knows.

"Hey, hey, it's okay. You're safe. Fuck that guy."

"Thank you," I manage between sobs.

Gentry kisses my forehead and nudges my face, urging me to look up at him. My eyes meet his as he smiles down at me and says, "Seems I'm punching a lot of people for you girls these days."

I let out a small laugh despite my tears. "I'm sorry."

"No, don't be. You have nothing to be sorry about. The people who got punched brought it on themselves," he says, and he's right about that, I guess; no one told them to be assholes. "Besides, I haven't punched anyone in a really long time. It's nice to know I still got it." He lifts his one arm into the air and flexes his bicep.

At this, I roll my eyes. Although he does have nice arms. "I like it better when your body is making love, not war," I tell him.

He looks down at me, raising an eyebrow. "Oh ma'am, I couldn't agree more," he says, before leaning down to kiss me. He presses his lips gently against mine and the hair on his face gently scratches me.

We stand in the embrace for a long time—teasing and kissing, talking and laughing.

And I don't know when, I can't point out to you the exact moment, but at some time in this barn, I begin to fall.

GENTRY

I'M FALLING in love with her. Or maybe I'm already in love with her.

The fact that I'm unsure of the difference confirms it for me.

Fuck.

Most people would be happy to realize they're in love. Most would rejoice. But all it gives me is apprehension and a knot in my chest. Like a shitty knot. Not a welling up, but a brick.

Do I tell her?

Or do I keep my mouth shut and let her leave?

That's the right thing to do, isn't it?

I have so many questions and no one to give me any answers.

I'm sitting on the porch swing sorting through all these questions when Harper walks out, wiping her hands with a towel and looking around. When she sees me, she puts her hands on her hips.

"What are you doing?" she asks, her eyes searching me for the reason why I look so disheveled.

I look down at myself. My clothes are more rumpled than usual and I'm pretty sure I have two different socks on. I've pushed my hands through my hair so many times, I can feel it pointing in all different directions. I haven't trimmed my beard or even taken the time to tame it in days. "Just sitting here," I say, unsure what else to offer up.

She rolls her eyes at me. "No, what are you *doing*?" she asks, as if asking the same question again will somehow clarify it for me. She gives me a pointed look.

"I'm not sure what you mean," I admit.

"I mean, why aren't you telling my sister how you feel?" she asks, huffing out her frustration.

What the hell, is she all-knowing?

I rub my hands over my face. "I don't think she wants that."

She looks up toward the sky and shakes her head. "Listen, I don't know how many times I have to play matchmaker or whatever the hell this overtime is where I have to come back and keep you on track, but my sister is feeling something, too."

I sit up straighter, eyeing her. "She told you that?"

"Of course not, but I know," she says, and I slump back down. "No, you listen to me, I know what I'm talking about. I know she feels something."

"She could be feeling a lot of things," I say, stating the obvious.

"And she could be feeling what you feel," Harper says.

I think about that for a moment.

Is it possible?

Could a woman like Lyla feel something for me?

"She has a life somewhere else," I argue.

Harper waves her hand in the air, dismissing the fact. "An inconvenience."

I huff. "Right, just a tiny thing."

"You listen to me. When it comes to love, almost everything that stands in its way is a minor inconvenience to be dealt with. As for the two people in love? If they really want it, they'll move mountains to make it work," she says.

"Heaven and earth," I mutter under my breath.

"What?"

"Nothing, just something I said to her before," I say.

"So, do you know what you're doing now?" she asks.

I nod my head. "Yeah, I got a pretty good idea," I say, standing from the porch swing.

"Good," she says, disappearing back into the kitchen door as though we've just settled the most mundane topic.

I step off the porch to go find Lyla. I'm pretty sure she's still on her run, so she could be anywhere, but I know her route well enough to hunt her down.

I round the barns, but she hasn't made it this far yet.

I walk through the wildflowers near the store, but she isn't there either.

When I round the trees, I spot her legs behind a particular row in the orchard, only she isn't running. She's just standing there, sort of pacing.

I quiet my footsteps, hoping to surprise her. But when I get within earshot, I realize she's on the phone, and I catch too much of her conversation.

"I don't know, I guess about one more week or so?" Lyla says into the phone. "I should be home after that. Yeah, I've kind of been seeing that guy I told you about. What? No, nothing serious. Just having some fun and stress relief while I'm here. Yeah, totally, we can get drinks when I get back into town. Yeah, I'll book my flight soon and let you know when it is. You want to get me from the airport? Awesome! Okay. Well, I'll text you later. Love you too, Cora."

I back away slowly, very sure I don't want her to see me there now.

One week or so?

What's 'or so'…?

That's it.

She's leaving.

She hasn't even told me.

Nothing serious, she'd explained on the phone.

Why would she bother telling me she's leaving if we're nothing serious?

It makes sense.

I walk back toward the farm house in the opposite direction she's going.

Nothing serious?

How can she feel that way?

Maybe I've been misreading the situation. Maybe this time hasn't meant as much to her as it has to me. The thought makes me sad.

I've tried so hard to be a comfort to her, a relief, a shoulder. I tried to make myself a safe place she could unravel in, be herself in, come undone in if she needed to. I really thought I had.

I'm back on the edge of the porch, pushing my hands through my hair again.

As if by some divine torture, Lyla rounds the path and strides toward me. Her hair is floating in the air behind her, her legs powering her body forward. The lines of her body belong to a seasoned runner. Soon, she'll be running home. Running away from me.

I don't know how to get through the *next week or so*, how to pretend for her, but I'll try.

She slows to a walk just before she gets to me. Her breathing is hard and jagged, her hair a mess. She isn't wearing makeup, and a sheen of sweat covers her skin.

She's so beautiful.

"Hey, you," she says casually, situating herself between my legs.

"Hey," I say, leaning my face back, away from her.

She stretches toward me, silently asking for a kiss, and I can't help myself. I lean in and brush my lips against hers, keeping it brief.

"You okay?" she asks, somehow sensing that I'm not, but I can't tell her what's wrong.

"Just a little tired. It's been a long couple of weeks," I say, which is true. It has been, and I am tired. But neither is the reason for my mood. I want to grab her by the shoulders, I want to tell her to open her eyes. Instead, I just sit there quietly, staring at her, pleading with her using only my eyes.

"I understand. You want to take a nap with me?" she asks.

I think about wrapping my arms around her and falling asleep peacefully, the way I have each night she's slept with me. I think about how, maybe, if I only have such a short amount of time left, I should take every opportunity I can to hold her. To memorize everything about her so that, after she's gone, I'll still be able to feel her for a little while.

"Sure," I say, not entirely sure it's a good idea but willing to roll the dice.

She takes my face into her hands, cupping my cheeks and staring at me. "Gentry, I..."

I wait, but too many seconds pass. "What?" I ask her, my voice low and urgent.

"It's nothing," she says, shaking her head, and it's painfully clear that whatever she was going to tell me, she thought better of it.

Nothing serious.

"Come on." She takes me by the hand and pulls me all the way up to my bedroom.

My feet feel like they're moving especially slow as I watch her walk in front of me. The twist of her hips as she moves drives me wild. But I won't have sex with her.

Not this time.

Maybe not ever again.

The last time we made love, it was cloaked in happiness.

Never mind. That was a lie.

Still, it'd been a joyous occasion, enjoying each other the way we had. But if we were to do it again, the memory of it would only be tinged with sadness, with longing. With the knowledge that she didn't feel the same way. I'm not sure I want that.

I close the door behind us and sit on the edge of my bed, where I pull my boots off. From the corner of my eye, I see her pulling her tank top over her head and unsnapping her bra. She lets it fall to the floor. She kicks off her running shoes, then peels out of her pants, leaving only her panties on.

She turns to me, tilting her head to the side, silently questioning why I'm not undressing. And then, "What's really wrong?" She walks over and kneels in front of me.

I really don't need her kneeling; that's not helpful. I brush my thumb over the edge of her bottom lip and force a smile. "Nothing," I say. "I promise."

I start to unbutton my shirt and she takes over, pushing it from my shoulders. Then she tugs my T-shirt over my head. I stand, and she stays kneeling, while I push my pants down my legs. She reaches for me, but I take her hands in mine, pulling her up and embracing her.

We curl up on my bed and I wrap around her as tightly as I can. I get as close to her as our bodies will allow.

From her position, she keeps pressing her backside into me, inviting me to make this a sexy nap.

But I resist.

I press my lips to her shoulder, inhale her honeysuckle scent, and actually fall asleep.

LYLA

I STAND in Harper's cabin, spraying the kitchen window with glass cleaner and wiping it down. I offered to clean it for her during the day since she and everyone else have jobs to do to run the farm. Plus, cleaning has always been my go-to for when I'm stressed. Anytime I have a surge of panic or anxiety, I know the very next weekend I'll be cleaning all the way down to the baseboards.

I move to the next window in the dining room and begin spraying. Gentry has all but ignored me for the last two days. He hasn't been his usual self. I can't put a finger on it. And we haven't had sex, either. Or any hot moments that felt like they might lead to sex.

What's happening?

I don't like this uneasy feeling in me, caused by the growing distance between us.

Doesn't he understand how much I want to savor these last few days before I have to leave?

Doesn't he understand how much it's hurting me?

Just then, I hear the front door of the cabin open and Harper walks in—a much needed distraction from my own thoughts.

"Oh, hi," I say. "Have you come to check on the progress I'm making?" I ask, as I gesture around the space. Overall, I'm pretty impressed with myself. I've already finished the kitchen and dining room, and swept and mopped all the hardwood floors on the first floor. I was currently going back around to get the windows before moving upstairs.

"Actually, I came to ask you what the hell you're doing." She stops at the entrance of the kitchen and crosses her arms over her chest.

I look at her, utter confusion taking over.

"Do I need to spell it out for you?" she asks.

"Um, I think I'm going to need you to because I have no idea what you're talking about." I sit down the glass cleaner and turn to give her my full attention.

"I swear, people around here act like we're all blind or something. Then, they act weirded out if or when we prove we're not," she says, and it only further confuses me. "Let me be more specific. What the hell are you doing about Gentry?"

Oh. That.

"What do you mean?" I question.

Harper rolls her eyes at me. "You obviously have feelings for him." A pause and then, "Don't you?"

I can't seem to say anything, so I simply nod my head.

"Right. Now, I'll ask you again," she says. "What the *hell* are you doing?"

I let out a sigh and move to sit down at her kitchen table, where I rest my head in my hands.

She frowns at me but comes to sit next to me.

"I don't know, Harper. I mean, I have to leave soon. I don't know what to do," I confess.

"Who says you have to leave? You're a grown up. You can decide where you want to be," she says.

"What about my life in Boston? I have an apartment, friends, clients. I can't just abandon all that to come back here for a guy."

"But is he just any guy? Or is he the guy?" she asks. "Because no matter the answer to that question, your choice should be simple. If he's just a guy, you go. But if he's *the guy*, don't you owe it to yourself to keep him in your life?" Her eyes search mine, and I can feel the tears beginning to fill my eyes. She places her hand over mine.

"Oh, Harper, what do I do? How do I know if he's the guy?" I ask.

Harper sits back, her eyes growing foggy as she looks past me to some faraway point. "Do you remember when we were kids and we'd play all day outside in the snow? We'd come in numb from head to toe, our clothes soaked, our skin so cold it was pink?"

I nod and she goes on, saying, "Do you remember Nan always having warm blankets waiting for us? She'd have us strip down next to nothing and wrap a blanket straight from the dryer around our bodies?"

I nod again, unsure where she's going with this story.

"Do you remember the warmth spreading all over?" she persists. "Like...you could feel it—your body almost coming back to life, from numb to alive again?"

I understand what she means then.

"That's what it feels like when you meet the guy. Like your whole life you've been in the cold and your body is numb. Then he comes in like a warm blanket and suddenly, you're alive. Suddenly, you're home," she says.

I stare off into the space in front of me, absorbing what she's saying.

We both sit there in silence for a while, enjoying the comfort of it.

"Is that how it was when you met Charles?" I finally ask.

Harper gives a small smile and nods. "Yes, but lucky for me, I think we get more than one warm blanket in our lives. Or at least, I hope."

"I think we do," I say.

But what do I know?

I've never even had one warm blanket unless you count Dean, which I *definitely* don't now.

She smiles again, this time wider.

"Thank you," I say, and her hand pats mine in response. Sometimes I'm pretty sure she's a better big sister than I am.

She leaves me then, silently exiting the cabin to head back toward the main house. I watch her through the window for a few minutes, her long blonde locks flowing in the breeze.

I put the glass cleaner away and walk upstairs. Harper's packed up everything, all of which has been put in the outside storage shed except for her clothes, which she took. She still isn't sure if she wants to live here. So, for the time being, she isn't. That means the cabin is completely empty. Almost all the furniture is gone besides a few stray pieces that still need to be handled, but nothing major.

I reach for my phone in my back pocket and scroll for Gentry.

> Can you come help me at Harper's for a bit?

GENTRY
> Sure. Be there in a few.

This has been his standard lately. Short on words and a lot of using the word *sure*, which is partially why it's been so difficult to accuse him of anything. He's being polite, even helpful still. We still sleep in bed together, we just…don't have sex. And I don't want to be one of those women who beg for it or seem crazy when we just… don't.

I look out the bedroom window and see Gentry pulling up in his truck. He gets out and smooths his hair, messing with it for a moment. Then he starts walking toward the porch and looks up. I wave for him and he walks inside. In the process, I hear the door open and close downstairs. I hear his boots on the stairs and down the hall. Then I hear him stop in the doorway behind me. I'm still looking out the window and I know he's probably confused.

As I turn to him, I start unbuttoning my shirt at the top.

"What's going on?" he asks.

"I need your help," I say.

He looks around the empty room. "With what?"

"With this," I say, as I open my shirt, revealing my bra and torso.

He pinches his eyes shut. "Lyla, I was working," he says, and his voice is serious.

"You can spare some time for me, can't you?" I ask, letting my shirt drop to the floor.

He clears his throat. "Don't."

"Don't what?" I ask, slipping my thumbs into the top of my pants and pushing them down.

"Undress. Stop undressing," he says.

"You don't like it?" I ask, reaching back to unclasp my bra before I let it join the rest of my clothing on the floor.

"You know that's not it," he says.

"Then what is it?" I ask, hooking my thumbs into my panties and pushing them down. They fall into the pile and I step back toward the window, leaning against it.

He presses his eyes shut again. "Don't do that," he says. "Don't make that face."

I part my lips and nibble on the end of my finger. "Look at me," I tell him.

He clenches his hands into fists but opens his eyes. I hear his exhale from all the way across the room.

I slide my feet across the floor, parting my legs a bit. The sun streaks into the window, casting my shadow onto the floor.

"What do you want from me?" he asks, his question loaded.

"I want you to come here," I say.

He steps into the room, hesitation all over his face, still keeping his distance.

"You don't want to help?" I ask, trailing my finger down my chin and to my breasts. I draw delicate circles around my nipples.

His fists clench and loosen, on repeat.

I trail my fingers lower, around my belly button, pausing there to see if he'll react, but he remains still. His jaw tightens.

"You're really gonna make me do this alone?" I ask, and then I part myself with my fingers and inhale sharply.

His eyes are on fire—as is my whole body.

Having him watch me like this is making me feel almost drunk.

His eyes darken, and he bites his bottom lip as he watches my hand.

"Please," I say, begging for his touch.

His lips part but he says nothing. He raises his shirt over his head and throws it to the floor. He unbuckles his belt, slides it out in one fluid motion, throws it down. He kicks off his boots and reaches for the button on his pants, his hand lingering there for just a moment.

The next thing I know, he's walking toward me, wearing nothing but a sinister look. If I didn't know better, I'd say I'm about to pay for this little game I've played. I don't know if he wants to worship me or punish me, but maybe it's a little of both.

He leans in close to me, his breath ragged. He takes me by the jaw and lifts my mouth toward him. He kisses me gently at first, then harder, his mouth covering mine until I open my lips for him. His tongue presses into mine, relentlessly, with fervor.

My arms come up and wrap around his neck. He presses me to the glass window behind me, his hands touching me everywhere. He cups my breast and I suck in a breath, our lips only parting because of it.

He bends down then and takes my nipple into his mouth, licking and sucking it. His hand presses against my neck just a little, his thumb rubbing over my jaw. He presses his knee between my thighs, spreading my legs wider. Then he rubs himself against the outside of me. I feel him slick with me on him as he agonizingly rubs himself against my entrance, teasing me.

My body arches toward him, pleading for him.

"You want me?" he asks, and I nod. But he says, "Tell me."

"I want you. Please," I beg.

That's all it takes.

I feel him enter me, stretching me open. I inhale against his mouth again.

His eyes are pinched shut so tight, it's like he's concentrating on something specific or trying hard to restrain himself. He moves back and forth inside me, his hands gripping me, his fingers pressing into my skin. His body is hard against me—all rigidity, no softness. He pushes, harder and harder. He bends and kisses my neck as my hands run through his hair and tug at it. He bites the soft spot at the base of my neck then licks. My hands dig into his back next. One of my legs hooks around him, and he cups my backside with his large hand.

This is a frenzy, an act of desperation.

Our bodies collide again and again, like we can't get there fast enough, like we're both starved.

"Lyla?" he whispers.

"Gentry," I exhale.

"I love you," he says. Then he presses his mouth to mine, not waiting for any sort of reply.

I'm too far gone to the pleasure of the moment to stop or fight against it.

Before I know it, we're climbing—both of us. We come, right there against the window of my little sister's old bedroom.

He holds me close for a few minutes, then gently lets me down, pulling out and away from me.

I lean back, catching my breath.

He turns from me and places his hands on his hips, shaking his head like he's disappointed in himself.

I'm not sure if I should say something, ask something. He just told me he loves me, and I don't know what to do. So, I walk to him and press my face against his back, wrapping my hands around him and holding him over his chest. I find his heartbeat beneath my palm and keep my hand there.

He doesn't move to stop me—or to reassure me. He just stands there, letting me exist with him.

Somehow, I just know.

I know this is what's been plaguing him for the past couple of days, and I understand why. Because I'm leaving. And he doesn't want to complicate it or make it worse for either of us. For some reason, this sacrifice he's been trying so hard to make only makes him more wonderful to me. His failure of mission at the end doesn't do anything to diminish his efforts.

This is all we have.

This.

We simply exist with each other, neither of us pushing or pulling, neither of us asking for more. We don't expect things from each other. We don't ask for anything we know the other can't give. And that's why he isn't standing here now, asking if I love him too or asking me to stay. A greedier man might have, but this is Gentry.

And he isn't going to ask for anything.

LYLA

"WILL you go on a date with me?" I ask him as we're driving back to the house from Harper's cabin.

We're holding hands, my hip against his. His face still isn't right, though. It's as if he's in a perpetual state of pain. And perhaps he is.

"Where do you want to go?" he asks.

"I think I'll plan this one," I say. "But you'll need your dancing boots."

He gives me a quizzical look, apprehension playing on his face. "Okay."

I bounce with excitement and he gives me a genuine Gentry smile.

"Great, meet you on the porch in, say, two hours?" I ask.

He nods and drops his hand to my thigh, squeezing it. "I'll go, but I just want you to know, I'm an excellent dancer," he says.

I laugh at that. "Well, that's a relief. I was afraid you were a two-step, elbows to your sides man."

"No way," he says, his familiar bantering voice beginning to return.

"Okay. I shall see you soon." I kiss his cheek and skip off inside the house.

I have the perfect outfit for this occasion. I step into Gentry's room and head for my bags. I pull out the dress I packed for a *just in case* situation, relieved to know that in doing so, I'd covered my own ass. In reality, it's a simple garment. A white sundress with delicate lace straps and a lace hem at the bottom. It dips down in the front to expose cleavage and the aforementioned hem is asymmetrical, cutting up in the front. It's the perfect dress to pair with boots. I pull out white lace panties, and then my gold jewelry to accent it. I hide the outfit in my room across the hall so he doesn't see it and then head to the bathroom to shower.

Now, every time I'm in the bathroom, I think of our shower together. Shower time has since had so many more implications than simply getting clean. I make my actual shower quick, knowing Gentry will need to start getting ready soon as well. I wipe the fog from the mirror over the sink and take note of the golden tan I've been blessed with since being here. It'll only serve to make the dress look better.

After brushing my teeth, I head down the hall to my room when Gentry comes walking up the stairs.

"What are you doing in there?" he asks, as I turn the knob to my room.

"I hid my outfit in here," I say.

He nods slowly, raising a curious eyebrow in my direction.

I shut the door and towel off before slipping on my panties and then the dress. I look at myself in the long mirror on the back of my closet door, brushing my hands over the soft cotton fabric and studying my figure. The dress cut is a few inches above my knees and the straps sit perfectly on my shoulders. Content with my appearance, I towel my hair off and grab the blow dryer. I run my fingers through my hair as I twist the damp locks between my fingers. As my hair dries, it rests into twisty tendrils. I use a fair amount of product to set the look and then get to work on my makeup, deciding a rosy bronze palette will pair nicely with my newly tanned skin.

After my makeup is done, including a light layer of pink lipstick, I put on a gold necklace that rests between my breasts, two gold stackable bracelets, and my favorite rings—one on my thumb, and one on my middle finger of the other hand. After I slide the boots on, I go back to the long mirror and assess the finished product.

Oh yes, this will work.

Not too shabby, if I do say so myself.
I text Gentry.

> Are you ready?

GENTRY
> I thought you said two hours?

> I'm impatient.

GENTRY
> It just so happens, I'm already on the porch.

Damn.

Men are always faster, of course, but I thought my time management had been good. I wanted to beat him down there.

> Be right down.

I grab my purse and stuff my phone in it as I tuck it under my arm. I still myself and leave my room, getting down the stairs and through the kitchen as quickly as I can. I step out onto the porch and see Gentry standing there.

He's leaning against the post with a bouquet of wildflowers in his hand. His lips part slightly when he sees me. "Wow," he says, his voice barely above a whisper.

I step toward him as his eyes scan over me from head to toe and back up. Stopping just a few steps short of him, I take in his appearance. He's wearing dark brown boots and a matching belt with dark denim jeans and a gray T-shirt. Not one of those regular looking T-shirts, but a nice one, coming down to a slight V-neck in the front. It's tight on him, exposing the lines of his pecs and biceps beneath it.

"You look amazing," I say.

"You're beautiful," he says.

I step closer and lean into him, inhaling his scent.

"The most beautiful girl I've ever seen naked," he adds.

I laugh out loud and push against his chest. "Shut up," I say, just before I lean up and kiss him.

"These are for you," he says, handing me the wildflowers.

I peer down at the small violets, daisies, and honeysuckle. "Honeysuckle?" I ask, blushing and pointing to it.

He nods, smirking at our secret.

"Thank you." I step back inside to put them in a vase of water, leaving them on the counter before joining him back on the porch.

"So, where are we going?" he asks, pulling his keys from his pocket.

"Well," I start, "I need you to let me drive."

"My truck?" he asks, his eyebrows shooting up on his forehead.

"I am licensed," I tease.

"But...it's my truck. It's like my baby," he says, patting the hood of his truck.

I roll my eyes at him and move my body closer to his, getting *very* close. "Do you want me to beg?"

A shudder overtakes his body and the keys jingle in his hand. "Maybe," he says, leaning down to kiss my neck.

"Please," I whisper against his ear.

He straightens up and holds the keys out to me. "It's not fair when you do that."

I laugh and jingle the keys in a dramatic manner.

He opens the driver side door for me, chivalrous even in his surrender.

"Thank you, sir," I say as I hop into the seat behind the wheel and buckle my seatbelt.

He leans in and kisses me before closing the door. Then he rounds the truck and gets in, fastening his seatbelt and pressing his hands together as if in prayer.

"Oh, don't be so dramatic." I roll my eyes and rev the engine, wagging my eyebrows at him.

His eyes widen, faux fear gripping his features.

We roll onto the road and head toward town, Gentry's hand on my thigh, my eyes on the road.

"So, now do I get to know where we're going?" he asks.

"Not specifically," I say. "But I will tell you this. When I lived here,

I wasn't old enough to drive into the city to drink and dance, but I always heard it was what people did when they were older."

Gentry nods toward me, appearing to understand. "Fair enough," he says, settling into his seat. He peers out the window and I wonder if he's watching the passing trees the way I try to, the way your eyes can focus and blur and focus again on the next one.

"Are you hungry?" I ask him.

"We can just get food at the bar," he says.

"Oh yeah, I'm getting mozzarella sticks for sure," I say, my mouth salivating at the very thought.

"And onion rings," Gentry adds.

"Yes. Mmmm."

"I didn't peg you for a junk food eater," he says, laughing.

"Are you kidding me?" I ask. "Junk food is my reward for all the running I do."

"I noticed your trophies. You've been running for a long time," he says, and the way he phrases it makes the statement feel so much heavier.

You've been running for a long time.

Yeah, that's probably true…

"I really enjoyed it, and after school, I just kept doing it," I say.

His hand squeezes my thigh and silence falls over us again.

"Did you play any sports?" I ask him.

"I was a swimmer, believe it or not," he says.

But judging by his long, lean form, and the way his stomach forms a perfect V, it isn't hard to believe at all.

"I figured you were captain of the football team—quarterback or something," I tease.

He scoffs. "No thank you to brain injuries." He has a point there, but I assume that, even without that title, he was popular in high school.

"I bet you still had all the girls chasing you," I say, glancing at him.

"Not really. Or, if they were chasing me, I was unaware," he says with a shrug of his shoulders.

Now, *this* surprises me. He's so confident, so charming. "Interesting," I say.

"What is?"

"You were just completely unaware of your beauty, and I wouldn't have guessed that," I say.

His gaze is on me, his eyes sweeping over me, assessing me. "Were you aware of yours?"

I definitely was not—not even a little. Perhaps that's why Dean had his run of me. Why I let him do whatever he wanted when it came to me. Maybe I hadn't known I had options. "I guess you have a point," I say, not wanting to offer the full spectrum of my thoughts on the topic.

He squeezes my thigh again, only a little higher than before.

We fall into easy conversation for the next several minutes before we finally arrive at our destination. I pull into a parking spot and turn the truck off. Neon signs are everywhere. They're open, they're serving Bud Light, they've got a mechanical bull, *and* a live band. All this in various colored neon writing.

I turn to Gentry with the biggest grin I can manage. All my teeth are showing.

"Why are you smiling like a psycho?" he asks, trying hard not to let his cool exterior crack into a smile.

"Because I'm excited, duh!" I say vigorously and louder than necessary.

"And now we're yelling. Okay." He rolls his eyes in mock disdain and opens his truck door to get out. "Wait, are you going to get white girl wasted? That's what they call it right? When you're all sloppy and take your shoes off, and there's like a boob hanging out of your dress?"

"Okay, I might definitely take my shoes off at some point, but there's no way my boob will come out," I say, shaking from side to side to show him they're securely in place.

He laughs so hard, raising an eyebrow at me like he needs more proof. He doesn't need to worry, though; my boob doesn't need to see a place like this.

At the door, we present our IDs and then push our way inside. It's pretty full. Not shoulder to shoulder, but definitely busy. We head to the bar first, deciding a drink is the first item on the to-do list.

"What do you want?" he asks. He has to lean into me, brushing his lips against my ear and pulling me close so I can hear him over the music.

In return, I have to speak into his ear so he can hear me. "I want something sweet. And a tequila shot," I say.

He pulls back just enough to give me a look of surprise.

I motion for him to lean back in. "I want to feel the burn tonight, Gentry."

He nods and leans in so the bartender can hear him but he's out of my earshot now.

I finally look around and take in the details of the place. There's quite a lot happening in here. Given it's the only decently sized bar not overrun by bikers for some miles, I guess that shouldn't be surprising. In the far left corner, there's a rise with pool tables. To my right, the mechanical bull is tossing a girl to the inflatable floor. The DJ booth is opposite the bar where we're currently standing, and people are dancing, well, everywhere. The dance floor is overflowing into the tables and corners of the place.

"Here," Gentry says. He places a cloudy drink in one hand and the tequila shot in the other.

"Can you hold my drink? I want a lime wedge and salt for the shot," I ask.

He shakes his head, then licks his finger and sprinkles salt over it. Next, he produces a lime wedge and places it between his teeth, sticking it outward toward me. He lifts an eyebrow at me—a silent dare.

I nod for him to lift his finger to me and he offers it. Taking his finger into my mouth, I slowly begin to suck and work my way down it. Once all the salt is gone, and his eyes are fixed on my every move, I down the shot without hesitation and then reach for him. I bring his face to mine, slowly leaning in to bite the lime, careful not to touch his lips with mine. I feel his arms wrap around me, the heat of his palms through my thin dress. He presses the lime into my mouth and watches me suck on it before dropping it into my now empty shot glass.

He leans in close to me again. "How long do I have to stay here and pretend I don't want to take you back home and watch this dress fall to my floor?"

"A little while," I say, setting my shot glass on the bar.

He smiles down at me and takes a long sip of his beer.

"No shot for you?" I ask.

"Maybe later," he says. "Do you want to ride the bull?" He winks at me.

"I'll ride the bull when you take your shot," I say, raising a brow in challenge.

"Well, I'll definitely take a shot now," he says. "But not before we dance."

I sip my sweet drink, still unsure what it is as we stand there looking at each other. If anyone is watching us, I'm not sure what they'd think. First, we do a scandalous body shot, and now we're gazing at each other like long-time lovers. I've got to get ahold of myself.

"Do you want to get a table to finish our drinks before we dance?" I ask him.

Gentry nods and holds out his hand to me. He leads me through the swells of people grouped together until we find a small table along the wall and take a seat. We're both scanning the crowd, taking in the people and the scene when he asks, "Do you go out a lot back in Boston?"

His question catches me off guard. "Not really. Believe it or not, I lead a pretty quiet existence," I say.

"Oh, come on, you mean you and your city friends aren't out on the town getting chatted up by eligible men like every weekend?" he asks.

"Well, I'm not. But my friend Cora is always dating. Or trying to. She doesn't have a lot of luck for some reason. I just spoke to her the other day actually," I say.

"Why doesn't she have luck?" he asks.

"I'm not sure. She's beautiful, talented, and smart. And on, like, every dating app there is," I say, laughing a bit. "Believe me, she's trying."

"I guess those city guys just don't know a good thing when they see it," he states.

"I guess not," I say. "I'm sure she'll find the right one. It just may take a lot of bad Tinder dates to get there."

Gentry laughs in the bar and I can hear his sincerity before it's swallowed up in the noise. He takes another drink of his beer and I notice it's nearly empty.

I look down at my own drink and realize I'm a little behind. I start sipping faster, gulping through my straw. Not only to catch up, but because I really want to dance. I watch a couple on the floor in front of us. She's swaying her hips, her guy keeping up with her impressively well. I wonder if Gentry is as skilled.

"Are you ready to dance?" he asks.

I cut my gaze to him, realizing he's putting down his empty beer bottle. My drink is nearly gone now so I sip the last bit and set my own glass down, hopping up from my chair. "Born ready," I say, and he holds his hand out to me.

A country song I don't recognize is playing overhead. It's fast-paced but sexy. Gentry leads me onto the floor and spins me around before grabbing me by the hips to guide me.

I can start to feel the burn.

Down my throat, in my chest, the back of my neck, and lower.

And lower.

GENTRY

I PULL Lyla to me under the strobing lights above. The flashing soft pinks and greens illuminate her skin and eyes in such a way that I have to remind myself to breathe. I spin her, then wrap an arm around her waist, lining her hips up with mine.

I know Lyla likely isn't expecting me to be able to dance. For whatever reason, there's an overwhelming presumption that men can't dance. There's also an overwhelming amount of men that can't actually dance, which doesn't do the rest of us any favors. But I'm not one of those men. I grind against her and sway in perfect rhythm to the music. Make no mistake, this isn't the same type of grinding you'd see in your average club in the city. No one is humping anyone's ass. This is more like the staff-only clubhouse watermelon scene in *Dirty Dancing* where everyone drools over Patrick Swayze. The only difference is we're swaying to a sexy country song.

My eyes are locked on hers and I watch her eyes turn from hesitation to surprise before settling into a comfortable pleasure. In this whole world, there's no better feeling than having the body of the woman you want pressed against you, her eyes drunk on you. Knowing you did that, you made her feel that. I press against her lightly to push her away from me and spin her around, bringing her back to me effortlessly. The song changes and the tempo calms. A slow song called What Could've Been by Gone West comes on, and the irony isn't lost on me.

I pull Lyla in closer and tuck her into me, wrapping my arms tight around her and pressing my cheek to hers.

"You've got moves," she whispers.

"My mother insisted," I say. I lead her around the floor, my hands gripping her skin. Her hands are warm on the back of my neck and in my hair. This is the feeling they should write epic poems about.

"Really? Did you take lessons?" she asks.

"Yes, for a while when I was younger."

"Little Gentry, wooing all the preteen girls. I bet they were putty," she says.

"I can assure you they were just an extension of high school. I'm pretty sure most of them thought I was very strange for being in lessons."

"Their loss. My gain," she says.

Yes, Lyla. Your gain.

Do you know how much more you stand to gain?

I grip her tighter and she returns the gesture, fueling my hope. I lose myself to my thoughts for just a few moments while the song binds us, while the song tells us what will happen if someone doesn't say something.

But can I do that? Do I have the right?

Sometimes I can see it. I can see the words tumbling from my open and pleading mouth. I can see a smile spread across her lips right before she hugs my neck and tells me she will stay with me.

Then I snap back here, back to her half-packed bags, to her inevitable leaving. And the words catch. I can't force them out.

The song starts to change again, the pace picking back up, and I decide to change gears.

"Another drink?" I ask.

She nods, and I grab her hand to lead her back to the bar.

This time, I order two shots of tequila and her sweet drink. I hand her one of the shots and take the other. I give her a lime next and take one for myself.

She's staring at me, amusement playing across her face. "Cheers?" she says, raising her shot to me.

I clink mine to hers and then we both lick salt from the back of our hands before downing the gold liquid. We're biting limes and looking at each other when I raise my eyebrow and nod in the direction of the bull.

Lyla looks back over her shoulder and then to me again. "Oh my god, you're serious?"

"I'd never joke around when it comes to watching you ride something," I say, making every attempt to suppress my smirk. When I fail, she smacks me in the arm.

"I'm wearing a dress," she protests.

"Are you wearing panties?" I ask.

Her eyes bug just a little. "Of course."

"Then you're good," I say. "Come on." I drag her by the hand toward the short line. And by short, I mean there's one person in front of her.

The bull attendant hands her a clipboard with a waiver attached and then looks her up and down. I don't like it.

"You're going to ride in that?" he asks.

Lyla looks down at herself and then at me.

My glare is fixed on the barely-of-drinking-age guy getting excited over her figure. "We're both riding," I tell him, pulling the clipboard from his hand.

"What?" Lyla looks up at me in confusion and I scribble my name on a form.

"I'll sit behind you since you're worried about your dress," I say, attempting to clear any possessive tone from my voice.

"Oh boy," she says with humor, then jumps up and down in place.

I pull my boots off, placing them on the floor next to the booth, and she follows suit.

We watch the girl currently riding the bull, jerking back and forth. I place my hand on the small of Lyla's back. I want to touch her all the time; I can't help myself.

We watch as the girl gets flung to the inflatable mat at the far side of the ring. Then, she exits.

"Okay, you guys ready?" the same clipboard guy asks.

We nod, and I push Lyla toward the entrance. "Don't worry," I whisper to her. "I got you."

Her shoulders relax just a little at my reassurance and we bounce our way over to the bull.

"This is crazy," she says as I hoist her up onto the bull by her waist.

When she has her leg over and is sitting in place, I help tuck her dress edges beneath her and then I hoist myself onto the bull behind her. "Yeah, I know," I say, smiling and sliding closer to her, pressing my front against her back.

She shifts and leans into me.

I can smell her hair, feel her warmth. I shake my head. I have to focus so we don't get tossed from this contraption in two seconds flat. I lean forward into her and wrap one arm around her. I wrap the other hand underneath the rope in front of her, but she's already gripping it tight with both hands. "No, put one of your hands in the air," I remind her.

"Oh, right," she says. She unclenches one of her hands from the rope and lifts it into the air, signaling that we're ready to ride.

A buzzer sounds from behind us and we feel the bull start to sway. It makes a figure eight then pops up and begins shaking back and forth. We tilt and sway with it as best we can, riding forward and tipping back. The bull whirls to the right and we counter. We think it's going left but it doesn't and dumps us onto the mat below.

I keep my grip on Lyla and tuck her against me, so she rolls onto me instead of away.

She's laughing so hard she can barely breathe. Her chest heaves against mine as she tries to wipe the small happy tears from her eyes.

Watching her laugh causes me to laugh. It's infectious. Soon, we're trying to stand, dizzy in a fit of laughter and tears.

I push her toward the exit, trying to help her keep her balance as I make every attempt to gather mine at the same time. We wobble out onto the regular floor and pull our boots back on.

"Water?" I ask.

When she nods, we head over to the bar again, still laughing. She's trailing behind me as she reaches out for my hand. I grip it tight and its urgency in my palm calms my breathing.

"Well, that was an experience," she says, taking another sip of her water.

We're back to being seated at our previous table and I nod in agreement. "I couldn't very well claim to have shown you the real deal down here if I didn't get you on the bull," I say.

She tilts her head at me. "You know, you're right. I'll be sure to write a raving Yelp review," she teases.

Then her eyes lock with mine, sobering me.

"Do you want to get out of here?" I ask, daring to dream.

She nods her head slowly at me and we both get off our chairs at nearly the same time. We're making our way across the bar and out the door before either of us have a second thought. We're halfway to the truck when a slow song starts to play. Music fills the entire parking lot. I'm watching Lyla walk just ahead of me and wonder if this is both the first and last time we'll ever dance.

"One more dance?" I ask her.

She turns to me, a small smile on her lips. "Okay."

We're close to the truck now, so I take her in my arms like before, cheek to cheek, my arm wrapped tight around her middle.

I hear Brett Young singing Mercy into the night sky and I grip her tighter.

Lyla's hands are clinging to my back and I'd give anything to freeze this moment. To play it back over and over again. To never let go.

But I know I have to let go of her at the end of the song. I know I have to get into that truck and drive her home. I know I have to make love to her like it's the last time I might.

And later on, in a couple of days, I'll have to really let her go.

I pull my face back from hers to look at her. I run my thumb over her jaw and stare into her eyes, perhaps longer than I should. Then, I lean in and kiss her like it's the last time I have the chance to. Just in case it is.

Because nothing is guaranteed.

LYLA

THE RIDE back home is quiet. Gentry is behind the wheel, my hand in his and my eyes on the passing trees. My mind, though, is back in that parking lot. Replaying those moments.

I can still feel his thumb drawing circles on my skin, and a trail of goosebumps crawls up my arm. Back in that gravel lot, he held me so tight. His arms gripped my hips and I felt totally enveloped. I'd wrapped my arms up around him, gripping his back.

I can't explain what I'd felt. The rocks beneath our feet, scraping and scuffing. The neon lights dancing in the background. The rest of the world falling away to just a blur. I'd felt his heart beating against my own chest, the slow rise and fall of his lungs, pressed against my body. We swayed in the darkness—completely alone and completely together. There are moments in life, moments so significant and perfect you will never forget them. And that will always be one of mine.

We pull onto the long drive of the farm and the truck rocks from side to side as it dips with the earth. I can see the tire swing ahead and the house beyond, drawing closer. But I don't want this night to end. Time is pushing me forward and I can't seem to pause it or slow it down even a fraction. I can't seem to dig my nails in and stay a little longer.

The truck stops rolling and I watch him shift it into park then turn the key. Gentry is just sitting there, and I wonder if he's going to say something. He looks like he wants to. He even turns like he might. But then he simply offers a smile that doesn't quite reach his eyes before he moves to get out.

I sit for a moment longer, and I want to call to him but think better of it. I hop out of the truck and make my way to the porch, passing him.

He slows behind me. "Stay," he says.

I feel a lump form in my throat, my heart starting to pound. I turn to face him. "What?"

"You heard me," he says. A pause and then, "Please."

"Gentry...don't do this."

"Before you say no, before you throw this away, tell me you don't feel something for me. Tell me you're going to walk away in a few days and never look back and never think of me. Tell me you don't want me," he says.

But I can't. My throat is dry and tight. I have no words for him and I can feel my bottom lip begin to tremble. "Don't make this harder than it already is," I manage to whisper.

He hangs his head, looking at the ground, kicking at some imaginary thing there. "We could be something. And you know it. And you're scared of it," he says.

"I'm not scared," I counter. "I left this place, and it wasn't so I could get sucked back here by some man who thinks he loves me after a good fuck."

Gentry flinches at my words and I immediately know I've hurt him. It's quiet, only for a moment, but it feels like so much longer.

"Some man," he says. "I'm just *some man*." He swallows, and I can see him thinking about it, trying the words on.

"Gentry, I—"

He holds his hand up to me. "Don't. It's okay. I just needed to know, and now I do."

We stand there and I'm not sure what to do.

"I don't want things to end like this between us. I didn't want it to be like this," I say.

He lets out a small laugh and shakes his head. His hand rubs the back of his neck and I watch him roll his shoulders. "Well, it's a little late for that, Lyla. Because they already have." He steps backward, to his truck, and then turns and opens the door.

He climbs in and sits there for a moment before turning the key in the ignition and driving away. He doesn't drive away from the property, but rather deeper into it, and I wonder where he's going to lick his wounds.

It's better this way, I remind myself.

It's better to end things now than let them get messier later on. It just gets more dangerous.

The inevitable crash swells, and if left unchecked, it will get too big to survive.

In heartbreak, it's about balance.

How much of the flood can you take on before you drown?

Too little, and you're left wanting.

Too much, and you're left dying.

I walk up the stairs of the porch and look out, hoping to see him, or his tail lights—*something*. But there's nothing out there. I don't know where he could've gone, where to look for him. I think about texting him but it's clear he needs time, space. Perhaps it's better like this. Perhaps in the heat of anger, it will be easier to let go. A sweet goodbye may have been too painful.

I wrap my arms around myself, rubbing my shoulders, suddenly cold.

Pain will do that to you—make you feel cold on a warm night.

I walk inside and up the stairs, grateful everyone is sleeping. I get to the top of the stairs and look between Gentry's door and mine.

Right.

My stuff is in his room.

Should I still sleep in there?

No, that's fucked.

Can't.

I open his door gently, like he might be in there somehow. I look around in the dark and the room's stillness is off-putting. So much has happened in here. I flip the light on and go to my suitcase, folding things inside, picking the clothes up from the floor that are near it. I walk to the nightstand and remove my charger, my personal stuff.

I try to remove all traces of me. Soon, it will be like I was never here at all.

Except that's not how memories work. They remain in your skin. You can't strip them away. Not with soap and water, distance, or even time. They scar up your insides, take root, refuse to leave.

I finish and look around the room. There's nothing left of me here in this space. My luggage is by the door and I should just leave. I should go back to my old room and try on the aloneness waiting for me there—*my old friend.*

My hand is on the doorknob, but I can't turn it. Not yet. I look at the fireplace, the bean bag chairs. My eyes study the folds in his unmade bed. The unfinished book on his nightstand. His closet door is half-open—and I can't fight the urge. I walk to it quickly, opening it the rest of the way. I step inside and run my hands over the fabrics of his shirts. I can smell him in here, like a fresh cut fir tree for Christmas. I raise the sleeve of his one shirt up to me and inhale, understanding right then that the actions in romance and stalking are the same. Before I realize what I'm doing, I rip the shirt from its hanger and tuck it under my arm.

Then, I leave his room for the last time.

I walk into my room and it dawns on me that I haven't been in here for a couple of weeks aside from earlier today, to get ready. My suitcase gently crashes to the floor, flopping over onto its overfilled belly and teetering. I sit on my bed, clutching Gentry's shirt in my hands and willing myself not to cry.

Please don't. Please don't cry.

I smell his shirt again, soaking in the clean scent of him.

Don't. Not yet. Don't do it.

After kicking off my boots, I lie back on my bed. When I tuck a pillow beneath my head, I feel the rustling of paper.

I flip over onto my stomach and reach for the papers—two folded notes. On the outside of one, in Gentry's writing, it says, *"If you decide to stay"*; on the outside of the other note, it says, *"If you must go"*. My lip is quivering again.

No. Not yet. Don't cry.

I set aside the note for staying. I'm not meant to see that one. It's not the choice I've made. I unfold the note marked for leaving and inhale a deep breath.

We all make choices in life.
Some are easy, some not so much.
I wanted to pretend this was an easy one,
that you could see it the way I did.
The worst thing about falling in love
with a temporary situation
is the inevitable shatter.
If you must go, know that you
take a piece of me with you.
I just wish you'd have given us
a fighting chance.

Any hope I had of not crying goes out the door as soon as I read the first sentence.

By the last one, I'm sobbing.

I fall asleep balled up in the center of my bed—Gentry's note clutched in one hand, his shirt in the other. Mascara streaks down my face and there's no warmth in this bed; I wake up and search for it again and again but it's not here. I pushed it away with poisonous words.

In one of my fits, I reach across my bed, still searching, and I wonder if I'll be able to live with this choice I've made. I swallow the answer down into my gullet, here in the dark, wearing my aloneness again.

And it fits just like I thought it would.

Too well.

LYLA

THE NEXT MORNING, my eyes are closed but I'm awake. I can feel the dried drool at the corners of my mouth, the gritty feeling behind my eyelids. Everything has crusted over. Light is dancing in the room and I want to open my eyes but I'm afraid. Afraid of what's out there. What I'll see. What I'll have to face. I roll over and finally unclench the shirt, searching for my phone.

It's nine twenty-three in the morning, earlier than I want it to be but later than I expected. In two days' time, I will be on a plane back home to Boston. Just two more days, and maybe, I can put this behind me and remind myself of all the reasons I've been alone most of my life. I can go back to casual dating to satiate the occasional need, the occasional want. I can focus on my life, travel to the places I want. Except in all the freedom of my adult life, I still haven't traveled anywhere. Maybe I'll finally start.

I roll to my side and see the folded note marked for staying. Holding my breath, I push myself up and reach for it. I brush my fingers over the words written on the outside of the note. The thought of opening it frightens me, so I walk to my suitcase and place it in the front pocket. Maybe one day I'll be brave enough to read it, but today is not that day.

As I stretch my arms up over my head, I decide to spend the entire day with Nan. To get my fill of her before I leave. Maybe I'll ask her to go shopping with me. I'll invite Harper, too. Make it a girls' day.

Yes.

That's exactly what I need.

I want to go shopping for some local things to take back with me anyway, and this is the perfect scenario. I rush to get dressed and wonder if Gentry ever came back.

While I walk downstairs, I can hear people in the kitchen. I take a deep breath, preparing to see him sitting in his usual spot, reading the way he always is. I turn the corner wearing a small smile, but it falls immediately. Nan and Harper are the only ones at the table. Part of me realizes that, as much as I was dreading it, I was looking forward to seeing him. The sorted emotions are confusing for me.

"Good morning," Nan says.

"Good morning," I say, kissing her on top of her head.

"Did you sleep okay?" Harper asks, a look of concern briefly crossing her face.

"It was fine," I lie. "I was actually wondering if the two of you could step away from the farm for a little while today and go shopping with me? Maybe grab some lunch? I'd really like to get in a girls' day before I fly back."

"Oh, I would love that," Nan says.

"Me too!" Harper says.

A wave of relief washes over me, realizing I don't have to spend the day here—or alone, replaying everything that happened last night. "Great, I can be ready in twenty minutes if you guys can?"

We agree to meet at the car after everyone collects their purses and freshens up, then I walk back upstairs to grab my stuff. While I'm up there, I throw my hair in a messy bun. Once I check the mirror, I understand why Harper shot me a concerned look. My face is still puffy and red, my eyes a bit dark and tired looking. I'd managed to wipe away most of the mascara from the night before. But it'll have to do; nothing a good day of distraction can't fix.

I walk out to the car and realize Gentry's truck isn't here. I look around, as far out as I can see toward the barns and road, but it's nowhere in sight. I hear Harper and Nan coming down the stairs behind me, so I turn my attention to them. In the back of my mind, I wonder if I should ask Harper if she's seen him, but I think better of it.

We pile into the car and head down the gravel drive. Harper is driving with Nan in the passenger seat since I elected to take the back. It feels more concealed somehow, less in the spotlight. I can hide away back here a little until we get to our destination. Nan is chattering on about the ladies in her church group as Harper and I listen as best we can.

Harper keeps giving me looks in the mirror and I keep looking away and down at my phone, making every attempt to avoid eye contact.

I'm scrolling aimlessly through social media accounts as we pull into a parking spot in the center of town. There's a strip of small boutique stores on this street that are perfect. We all fall out onto the sidewalk and decide to hit each shop before stopping for lunch at the corner diner on the other end of the street.

"I really want to get some new pants," Nan says.

Harper and I both look at each other, knowing we're in for a few hours of listening to Nan be very indecisive about several pairs of pants just to put them all back and not buy any. It's classic Nan. I laugh, knowing I wouldn't have it any other way.

We walk into the first boutique, immediately greeted with the scent of lavender. The aroma fills the small space without overwhelming it. The place is all clean white walls and rustic accents. The shop features clothing, accessories, jewelry, and an assortment of home goods. I stop at a rack of shirts while Harper browses purses, and Nan makes her way to the pants. Country music plays softly overhead and I find myself relaxing. This whole experience is much needed.

Nan approaches with her first pair of pants. "What do you think of these?"

"I like them," I say. "You should try them on."

She nods and tucks them under her arm as she makes her way toward the dressing rooms. Once she's inside, Harper makes her way over to me.

Oh boy. Here we go.

"So, what's going on?" she deadpans.

"What do you mean?"

She tilts her head at me and presses her lips together, giving me a look that dares me to act ignorant.

I sigh. "We had a fight. Do you know where he is?"

"He texted me asking if he could stay at the cabin for a few days, but that was it," she says.

"He's on the back of the property at your cabin?" I ask, making sure I heard her correctly.

"Yeah, he wouldn't say why."

"He asked me to stay," I say, biting my bottom lip.

Harper's eyes grow wide. "And of course, you can't." Her response throws me off guard.

"Right, that's what I said," I say.

"And he didn't like that," she says.

"No."

"And he's hurt," she predicts.

"Yes." I nod my head, staring at the shirt in front of me. All I can see is a block of dark color.

"Because you can't stay," she says.

"Right, that's what I said," I repeat.

"Except…"

"What?" I ask.

"Except, you could if you wanted."

"Harper." I say her name like a warning.

"Listen, I'm not saying you should stay. I'm not pushing one way or another. I'm not telling you what to do. I'm just reminding you that you have a choice, and there's nothing so big in Boston waiting for you that says you can't stay here if you really wanted to," she says.

I consider her words, flipping through the rack of shirts and stopping on a black tank top with lace at the bottom. I pull it from the rack and tuck it under my arm without hesitating. The next shirt is an emerald green V-neck T-shirt and I tuck that under my arm as well. "I can't stay," I say.

Harper nods, flipping through the rack until she stops on a shirt, running her hand over the material. She pulls it off and tilts her head to the side. "What do you think of this one?" she asks.

Just like that, we're off the topic.

She holds up a light pink peasant blouse that falls off the shoulders and I tell her she should get it. She keeps it with her, and we continue on like this for a little while. The silence between us stretches, aside from the cursory questions about clothing.

In the end, I buy three shirts, a necklace, and a pair of ballet flats before we move on to the next boutique. At this rate, I'll need an additional suitcase just to fly back. Harper and I convince Nan to buy a pair of pants and Harper buys the shirt I approved, along with a purse and matching wallet. After we put the bags in the car, we head to the next shop.

"You know, I think you should definitely get a few new outfits," I say to Harper.

"Why do you say that?" she asks.

"Well, now that you're not with Chuck, you're going to want to date. Maybe not too soon, but at some point. It'll be nice to have clothes that don't have memories attached to them, you know? I mean, at least not Chuck memories. I know you got a few things from selling the ring, but you need post-Chuck clothes," I say.

She laughs and nods. "I think I agree. Although, I don't see myself dating anytime soon."

"Well, I think the sooner you move on, the better," Nan declares.

We both shoot a look of surprise at her. She isn't usually so forward.

"Oh, don't look at me like that," Nan says. "No offense, honey, but he was an asshole."

I burst out laughing.

"Nan!" Harper says, trying to stifle her own laugh.

"I only put up with him because you loved him," Nan says.

Harper blinks her eyes over and over again in complete shock. "Well, everyone do me a favor, okay? Next time you hate the guy I'm with, tell me. Maybe I shouldn't be with him and I just can't see it," Harper says.

"Oh, baby," Nan says. "Some things you just gotta learn on your own. Some aches you just gotta live out, so you know how to avoid the ache the next time. We couldn't save you from that." She pats Harper on the arm.

I smile, though Nan's words of wisdom hit me hard. And I know they've hit Harper, with her eyes glossing over.

We step into the next shop, this one low lit and romantic. The music is instrumental, and everything is just a bit more sensual. Nan blushes toward the rack of lingerie. The clothing selection is more intimate, sexy.

"I don't think they have pants here for me," Nan says, laughing.

"Get some panties," I suggest.

Nan jerks her head and glares at me. "You hush about my underthings."

"Prude," Harper says, and we all start laughing.

I make my way to a rack of nightgowns, rubbing the silk from one between my thumb and index finger. It's black and has a slit in the side that travels pretty high. I want it. I think of Gentry looking at me in it. I want to feel him touch it. To touch me wearing it. I press my eyes closed and realize if I buy it, it'll sit in my drawer in Boston—unworn, untouched.

"You should get it," Harper says.

"Why?" I ask.

"For you," she says.

"I don't have anyone to wear it for."

"Who says you need someone to wear it for? Wear it because you like it."

I take the hanger off the rack and hold it up to my body, rubbing my hand down the front of it. As I continue around the store, I keep it in hand. I don't know if I'll buy it yet. I do this a lot, just carry something around that I want, unsure if I'm actually going to go through with buying it or not.

There are jewelry racks on the far wall and I make my way over to them. A pair of silver dangly earrings catch the light and shimmer. I pull them off and hold them up to my ear in the mirror on the counter. It's a mistake. My face reminds me of what happened. It's still worn. No amount of shopping can reverse the effects of sobbing myself to sleep.

For a little while, I let my mind indulge the idea of staying. As we go from shop to shop buying countless things for ourselves and others, I daydream. It's only right. I figure if I'm going to make the choice, I have to live it out. I have to really explore the decision I didn't make so I know I'm making the right one.

Of course, I would have to go back to Boston. I would have to pack up my stuff, give my rental apartment notice. I would have to close out some clients, though most would be fine with me working remotely. It wouldn't be too hard. Two weeks tops and I could be driving back with a moving truck.

Where would I live when I got here, though?

On the farm? Somewhere else?

Move straight into Gentry's room with him?

That seems a little too much. I stick a pin in that variable for a moment. My logical brain sorts through issues one at a time.

I'd be down here, living somewhere, working remotely. Gentry and I would be together.

And what?

What if it doesn't work?

Then we're in close quarters and it's awkward.

What if we can't even be in the same room?

Would he quit working on the farm?

That hardly seems fair.

Would I move away again?

That seems like a lot of work—a lot of *risk*.

"Want to get lunch now?" Harper's question snatches me from my thoughts.

I realize we've made it through all the shops on the street. We're standing in front of the diner on the corner.

"Yeah, sure," I say.

As we go in, I know.

I know it's not a good idea to stay. I know if it ends, it's too much, too complicated. The ripple effects are too great.

It's better that the two of us shatter now than potentially shattering the great big world we'd build around us later.

GENTRY

THIS MORNING, I was relieved to find out Lyla had left the farm for the day with Nan and Harper. It meant that avoiding her would be a little easier—at least for today. One more day and she'd be going home. Just one more day, and I won't have to hide. I can fall apart and start to heal.

I couldn't think of anything else to do last night but go to Harper's cabin. I decided to stay there until Lyla leaves. It's for the best at this point. I can't be in such close proximity to her and not want to say something, do something. Beg. I'm not above begging for the sake of her—of us. But I already tried. She wants me to let go, and distance is all I can offer now.

Perhaps I'm not built for flings. For summer romances and hookups. That culture seems so disingenuous. I can't stomach it, not for myself. I don't judge other people—good for them. Do what you want, you're an adult. I can't, though.

Or maybe it's just with Lyla. Maybe she makes it impossible.

I stare out at the fields of sunflowers on the back lot of the farm as the sun sets and it almost looks like it's on fire. Like my life. Like my heart. Everything hurts. She'll be gone soon. One more restless night. One more night where she is close by and my body wants to go to her, but my mind stops me from indulging. After that, she'll be farther away and it'll be easier to stifle the impulses.

I walk back into the barn and hear the sounds of a vehicle pulling up the gravel drive. My heart begins to thud—not pound…*thud*. Like it's going to fall out of my chest cavity and into my stomach. I get close to the door but try to stay concealed. The car pulls up to the porch and I watch Lyla exit the back seat. Her hair is a mess on top of her head and she doesn't look like she put on fresh makeup today, even from here. I like her best like this. She collects bags from the back with Harper. She's smiling, but it's dulled. Not big and bright like I've come to know it over the weeks. Not genuine. Not the real Lyla.

Even now, I want to go to her. I want to apologize for putting her in an impossible situation. To soak up every moment I can with her before she goes. I want to touch her, feel her skin. Make love to her again and again up until the moment she has to leave. Kiss her lips until they're swollen, inhale her honeysuckle scent.

But I can't. I won't.

I recede back into the barn after she walks into the house. Making my way back to the cabin, I seriously consider stopping and picking honeysuckles to shove into my pillowcase. I kick at the ground over and over again, cursing myself for getting us into this mess. Because that's exactly what it is—a big fat fucking mess. My heart is messed up, more than it was before her. But I don't blame her. It isn't her fault. She didn't do anything wrong. She was just a woman who came down looking for nothing and found a sappy guy and didn't know it.

It's my fault. Everything about this is my fault. I'm the one who pushed her to have fun. I'm the one who wouldn't leave it alone.

I pursued. End of story.

I'm a dumb shit. What's worse is, I'm a dumb shit who hurt her. And she deserves better.

Inside the cabin, I kick my boots off and look around. It's a nice place. For a moment, I wonder if Harper will eventually move back in or if it holds too many memories. If she's not going to, maybe I can. I need more than a room. I need a whole place again. I think it's time. I consider speaking to her about the cabin after Lyla leaves. Harper could even have my room since it's bigger than the one she's in now.

I walk over to the kitchen, where I pour two fingers of bourbon into a glass. Downing it in two gulps, I sit the glass back down and sit on the couch. The cabin is quiet. I've been used to the noise of the main farm house. I think if I do move here, I'll need a dog or something.

Yes, a dog.

That's what people do, right? Get pets to help with their loneliness?

Yes, that's a plan. I open my phone and start scrolling pet ads. The bourbon warms my chest faster than I realize and suddenly, I want more.

Scrolling through more ads, I pour another glass. A few gulps in and I see a German Shepherd puppy on the screen. He's a little blurry —maybe as a result of the bourbon. He's close by, full-blooded and farm-raised. I click the contact button, type in a message of interest, and hit send before I can change my mind. Once I gulp down the last of my bourbon, I put the glass back down and walk over to the couch. I keep scrolling for more puppies and then I hear what I think is a knock at the door, but I can't be sure. So, I wait.

Another knock comes, and I call for the visitor to come in as I'm looking over my shoulder at the door.

Lyla walks in and I'm dumbstruck.

Fuck.

I'm too buzzed for this. I don't move. She's staring at me and I'm staring back and I don't know what to do. She's a little blurry, too, but I know it's her.

"Can we talk?" she asks.

"I don't think that's a good idea," I admit.

"Well, will you listen?"

"If you want me to," I say.

She takes a long, deep breath as she walks toward me. While she makes her way around the couch, she tucks the loose strands of her hair behind her ear and exhales. "Listen, I didn't want things—"

I hold my hand up. "Look, if you're here to make some kind of apology or say you didn't want things to go down this way, just don't.

You don't owe me any apologies and I don't think either of us wanted it this way."

"But I do owe you an apology," she says.

"It's my fault, Lyla. I'm not an idiot. Well, I am, but not about knowing whose fault this is."

She's looking at my face—studying it—so I clarify and tell her, "I knew what was happening and I tried to fight against it, despite everything telling me not to."

"I'm still sorry," she whispers.

"Jesus, for *what*? I put you in an impossible situation, you deliver the only answer you were ever going to give, and you're sorry?" My words are starting to slur.

"Have you been drinking?" she asks.

"I may have had some drinks," I say, shrugging. "I'm a grown man."

"Maybe you should get some sleep," she suggests.

"You were never going to stay," I say, pausing before I go on. "You were never going to stay, and I asked anyway—like an idiot. I did the one thing you didn't need me to do and for that, I'm the one who's sorry—the only one who *should* be sorry."

There's a long silence stretching between us, and I feel myself wanting to reach for her. The warmth in my chest slowly grows to courage in my hands and I ball them into fists at my sides a little too hard as a reminder not to do it. If I touch her now, nothing will put out the fire in me.

"Do you want me to help you to bed?" she asks.

"No," I say. Of course, I want her to, but I can't let her. She should go, and I tell her as much with my suddenly icy exterior.

"Gentry, please…"

"Please, don't," I beg her, pressing my eyes shut. Her hand covers mine, and I want to cry or rip out my heart and throw it against the wall. I can't be sure which at this point.

She removes her hand just as quickly as she placed it and I feel her shrink beside me. "You should get some sleep," she says.

I let my head fall back on the couch and I stare up at the ceiling. "It's a little difficult," I say. "Hence the alcohol."

"Yeah," she says. She stands, and I hear her walking into the kitchen behind me, followed by the clink of a glass.

I look over my shoulder and watch her pour herself a shot of bourbon. She tilts her head back and downs it. I watch her neck work, the delicate muscles flexing and relaxing. Biting her comes to mind. She likes that.

I sigh too loudly and catch her attention. "You should go," I say, despite my own desires. No part of me actually wants her to go. I find myself wanting to beg again.

"Okay," she says. But she steps toward me, hesitating.

"What?" I ask.

"Just one last thing," she says, standing right in front of me now.

I try to stand but she pushes me back down. Her hand caresses my jaw as she pulls her legs up to straddle me and sits on my lap. My hands find her skin instinctively.

"Just one last kiss," she says, then she tucks her hair behind her ear and leans close.

Her lips are so close, it wouldn't take much. I'd just have to lean in a bit.

But she closes her eyes and presses her lips to mine.

I kiss her back, pressing my mouth into hers, devouring this last bit of her she's offering me. My tongue parts her lips and I bite and suck and lap her up. My hand pushes into her hair and I pull her against me.

If I can't leave my mark on her heart, I'll leave it here. She'll remember the taste of me, the way I kiss her.

LYLA

I WAKE up on my last morning here and I've never felt so conflicted about anything in my life. When I moved away from this place, there was no hesitation. I never even looked back or gave a thought to who I'd miss or who might miss me. This time feels different.

After spending this time with Harper, I feel closer to her. Seeing Nan and Paw, the fragility of their lives, puts a few things in perspective. I at least need to visit more. And Gentry.

How can you miss someone you were never meant to hold onto?

I spend part of my morning packing the rest of my bags, stuffing all the things I bought yesterday into every open crack I can. The overflow is stuffed into a gym bag I borrow from Harper and promise to mail back to her. While I might have gone a bit overboard on the shopping, I don't feel guilty about it. I needed the distraction.

I'm sitting on the edge of the bed, looking around the room, taking in all the details. A farewell breakfast waits for me downstairs, but I'm stalling.

Last night, Nan came into my room and lay down on the bed next to me. She tucked my hair behind my ear and pressed her palm to my cheek. She asked me why my heart had been so sad all day. That's when I lost it. I began to cry right into her hands and told her every-thing. About Gentry, what he asked, how I'd kissed him one last time the night before. How I sat there holding him on his couch until he fell asleep then left and hadn't seen or spoken to him since. All she did was hold me—no judgment, no lectures.

When I stopped crying, she asked me about my life in Boston, if it made me as happy as he'd made me these past few weeks. But I couldn't answer her. I couldn't bring myself to lie to her or tell myself the truth. So, I started crying again, and she wrapped her arms around me.

She let me fall asleep like that. When I woke up in the middle of the night, she was gone. At first, it alarmed me, but as reality sank in, it made sense. She needed to get back to Paw. Despite his near perfect recovery, she's still been keeping a sharp eye on him. I'd walked to the window then and looked out over the farm cloaked in the night sky. The moon illuminated the swaying trees in the orchard and the tin roofs on the barns. I stared out over the field toward the cabin. You couldn't see it from here, it being just over a hill and tucked behind trees. I'd wondered if Gentry was awake before finally turning back to bed. It took me a long time to fall back asleep.

This morning, waking up felt dream-like. I wondered if it was a dream within a dream for a moment. If perhaps I was still asleep, and it wasn't the day I was supposed to leave. But then my phone went off. When I reached for it, I felt a sudden sense of urgency, like maybe my phone would tell me something I desperately wanted to hear. Or rather, I would hear from the person I was desperate to hear from. But it was only Cora telling me to travel safely.

Now, I look down at my untied running shoes and lean over to remedy them. I know in my heart, I will not hear from Gentry today or see him. I know he will not say goodbye. We've already done that in our own way. I broke this, us. Whatever it was, I broke it. Him. Myself. All of the above. I'm not even sure anymore.

The clock tells me there are only a couple of short hours left before my flight. There's a strange relief in going, in knowing I am walking away. Running is familiar to me. I've been doing it my entire life. It's predictable, familiar. The physical act of running makes your lungs burn, makes everything heave and swell. You're standing there trying to catch your breath, but you feel freer, better, more in tune with yourself. This feels no different. I'll get back to Boston, back to my freedom, and be more aware of every part of myself.

I walk downstairs with all my bags and stack them out on the porch. When I walk back into the kitchen, I head for the coffee, knowing caffeine will be an important component in order to survive today. Part of me can't wait to be back in my bed in Boston, curled under my blankets. I'll order in food and avoid leaving my apartment at all costs for no less than seven to ten days.

"You all ready, honey?" Paw asks.

I nod. "Yeah. Everything's good to go."

"We're sure gonna miss ya around here," he says.

"I'll come visit more, I promise," I tell him.

He smiles at me and my heart wants to burst. I sit down next to him and Harper comes in then. She sits across from me.

Nan is last to join us and has a small box in her hand. "This is for you, baby," she says. She places the small box into my hand and sits down.

"What is this for?" I ask, confused.

"Just something I think you need," she says, shrugging her shoulders as she starts to butter the toast on the plate in front of her.

I look down at the box in my hand and finger the red ribbon tied in a bow around it. I slide it off and set it down, then pull the top off. Inside, there's a necklace. A small pendant with the word *"Live"* dangles from the silvery chain.

"I found it in one of the shops yesterday. I thought you needed a reminder," Nan says.

I swallow hard. "It's beautiful. Thank you so much." I slip it over my head and pull my hair through, adjusting it over my shirt. I rub it between my fingers and feel the grooves of the letters.

We eat breakfast mostly in silence after that, sharing the occasional comment about something arbitrary and all the while, I thumb the charm, giving a lot of thought to the word.

"I'm going to drive you to the airport," Harper says. "Is there anywhere you need to stop beforehand?"

"No, I think I have everything," I reply.

She gives me a tight smile, and it feels sad.

I reach for her hand and squeeze, doing my best to be a comforting big sister.

After we finish breakfast, I walk out to put my bags in the trunk while the dishes are being cleared. Lifting my suitcase into the car, I realize Gentry's other note is still tucked into the front pocket. It's not that I want to torture myself *per se,* but I stuff the note into the pocket of my leggings and finish loading my bags.

As I sit on the porch swing, I take one last look around the farm. I'll miss running the property, its unique challenges I'd never find on my runs in the city. I'll miss the fresh air, counting the stars overhead because I can actually see them, and the way the sun sets over the fields and bathes everything in pink and orange.

And him.

I don't even let myself think his name.

Nan, Paw, and Harper pile out onto the porch for the goodbyes. Nan hugs me tight and I squeeze her back, not wanting to let go.

"Promise you'll come for Christmas," she says.

"I promise," I say. And I actually mean it. A long visit.

Paw bear hugs me and despite his recovery, I'm gentle with him at first. "Hug me like you mean it, you ain't gonna break me," he says, laughing.

So, I squeeze. "Take care of my cows," I say.

"Of course, honey, of course. You take care of yourself, okay?" he says.

"I will," I say.

Harper and I walk down to the car and I wave before ducking into the front seat, trying not to cry in front of them. As my little sister gets in behind the wheel, I realize I'm actually holding my breath and I release it.

She turns the ignition over and buckles her seatbelt. "You ready?" she asks.

Her question gives me pause for just a moment. Because no, I'm not ready.

"Yes," I say, buckling my own seatbelt.

As she turns the car around and starts down the driveway, I pull the note from my pocket and inhale sharply.

"What's that?" she asks.

"A note from Gentry I haven't read," I say plainly. I press my fingertips to the ink on the paper once again and know it's now or never. I read it now or I might as well throw the damn thing out the window as we're driving down the road. I open it slowly, and I can see Harper glancing between me and the gravel drive in front of her. My eyes well up.

> The truth is, I never thought you'd stay.
> I never wanted to ask.
> If you're reading this,
> I'm equal parts surprised and elated.
> Because whether it makes sense or not,
> I love you.
> I think I loved you the moment I met you.
> And I'm not afraid to tell you that.
> I guess what I'm trying to say is,
> Thanks for giving us a fighting chance.

"Stop the car," I say. Wiping tears from my eyes, I look up to see we're about to pull onto the road.

Harper hits the brakes and we both jerk forward. "What's wrong?" she asks.

I'm already unbuckling my seatbelt. "Everything and nothing," I say as I reach for the car door. "I have to go."

"Lyla wait—"

But I don't hear her.

I tuck the note back into my pocket and I run. I run as fast as I can, as hard as I can. I run up the driveway, and the house is in sight. I can't stop—won't stop. The air in my lungs burns, but my legs have done this before and I know they can do it again. When I pass the porch, Nan calls out to me, but I don't answer. I just wave. It's just a little farther now.

I can't see the cabin yet, but my body propels forward, sure of my destination. I know he's there. It's like I can feel him, just beyond the trees. I want to call out, get to him faster somehow. I round the edge of the tree line and I see his truck sitting in front of the cabin porch.

Gentry.

I run again, up the stairs and in the front door without knocking, without hesitating. "Gentry?!" I call out into the empty room, gasping for air. I lean over, putting my hands on my knees. My legs wobble but I can't care right now.

I hear the boards on the stairs creak and then he's there—standing at the bottom of them. His eyes are red and glossy, and it hurts me.

"Lyla?" He looks me up and down, taking in my appearance and ragged breaths. "Are you okay?"

"No," I say. "I'm not okay."

"What's wrong?" he asks, his face twisting with concern.

I inhale a few more deep breaths and stand upright, finally able to compose myself somewhat. "I want to hear you say it," I say, and his eyes search mine. "If it's true, I want to hear you say it."

"Say what?"

"Tell me you love me," I say.

His fists balls at his sides and I can see his jaw clench from across the room. "Lyla, I don't know…"

"No, nothing else. Just, if it's true, tell me. And if it's not—"

"I love you," he says, interrupting me.

I walk toward him, cutting the space between us in half and stopping again. "Ask me again," I say.

His eyes narrow, like he doesn't understand, like he doesn't trust what I'm saying.

So I smile. "Ask me again, Gentry."

He moves one foot forward, then the other, slowly, until all the space between us is gone. He's close enough that I can feel the heat from his body. I can see the laugh lines around his red-rimmed eyes. The green flecks in his irises and the bloodshot whites. I press my palm to his cheek and he leans into it, pressing his hand against the back of it. He moves it down slowly, over his chest, and holds it there.

"Lyla, I love you. Please stay with me," he says, his bottom lip quivering.

Tears are gathering in his eyes and I want to kiss his pain away, erase the hurt I've put there, but I can't yet.

I lean in close to him and press my forehead against his, gathering all my strength. "I'll stay with you, Gentry. Because I love you, too," I whisper.

I feel his body relax, every rigid muscle growing soft as he wraps his arms around me so tight I think he might never let go. I hug his neck, and his lips find mine. He kisses me over and over again and I realize I can taste salt. My hands fly to his face and I wipe gently at his cheeks as I kiss him back, reassuring him with each one that I mean what I've said.

"Is this real?" he whispers against my mouth.

"This is life, my love," I say.

He kisses my mouth again and then lifts me up over his shoulder.

"Where are you taking me?" I ask, but I already know.

"We have to make up for lost time," he says.

I don't object but I also know we have all the time in the world now. Because despite the details, this is where I'm going to be from now on. "I still have to go back to Boston, you know. I have to pack my apartment and give notice."

"Okay, I'll go with you. I've always wanted to see Boston," he says, and I smile. "But not right now. Right now, I'm going to show you how much I've missed you these past few days."

And he does.

Later, we lie in bed and I watch him sleep. His chest rises and falls slowly, and it hits me all at once.

I can memorize these moments all I want, but more are coming. This is my reality now—my life. Gentry is mine and I am his.

My eyes grow heavy and I drift to sleep with a smile on my face, knowing I will wake up in Gentry's arms. Nothing has ever felt so right.

And I realize...*this* is living.

EPILOGUE

GENTRY

I'VE BEEN CARRYING this ring around in my pocket for weeks now, but I think tonight is finally right. Why, I can't say. Nothing special is happening. Lyla and I just plan to spend a quiet evening at home, but it feels like the time.

It's been eight months since she officially moved here from Boston. We've been living together the entire time. I know it sounds crazy, but not for us. It fits us.

I sat down with Paw maybe three months in and asked for his blessing. He asked me what took so long, if that gives any indication as to how things are around here with us.

Even now, as I watch her push the cart down the cereal aisle in front of me, I want to get down on one knee right here next to the leprechaun on this box and ask her. But I won't. I've been waiting patiently. I will wait a little longer.

"Do you want anything in this aisle?" she asks as she stuffs three different boxes into the cart.

I've come to learn that one of Lyla's favorite snacks before bed is a bowl of cereal, but she almost never eats it in the morning. In fact, I've never seen her eat it in the morning. I appreciate these things about her.

"No, I'm okay," I say. I rub the pouch with the ring inside between my fingers. I can't keep it in a box because it's too bulky and she touches me too much—not that I'd ever complain about that.

We move to the next aisle for dog food. Because even after I sobered up, I still wanted the German Shepherd puppy I drunkenly inquired about. Our fur baby—Mack—is basically our pride and joy, and I've watched Lyla show no less than ten strangers his picture at random. She's the best dog mom. Of course, we've talked about real babies. We both want them eventually. My heart flutters a little at the idea but I tuck it away. There'll be plenty of time for that later.

I pull a bag of dog food from the shelf and hoist it into the cart.

Lyla is comparing two bags of dog treats then shrugs before throwing both in the cart. "I think he'll like both," she says.

Mack may also be a tad spoiled but that's all right by me.

"What do you want for dinner?" I ask.

I watch her chew the pad of her thumb the way she does when she's thinking really hard. I don't know why I've asked her this.

"I don't know, what do you want?" she asks—and I knew she would do this.

"How about we just grab sushi on our way home?" I ask.

Her eyes light up because I know, no matter what, sushi is always the right answer. The woman has a serious addiction. She nods enthusiastically, and I know I've set the tone for the evening.

"Can we get dumplings, too?" she asks.

"What kind of question is that?" I say. "Of course we can."

She claps her hands like she's just won a prize.

"And wine," I add.

"Wow, I feel so special," she says.

I lean in close to her and whisper, "Baby, you are special." With that, I kiss her cheek.

"I love it when you do that," she breathes.

"Do what?" I whisper again, my voice gruff.

"Whisper things to me," she says. "I get all hot."

And just like that, I'm hot. "We should get out of here," I whisper. She nods.

I load everything into the back of the truck and we head back to the farm.

Lucky for us, Harper had been two things: super excited her sister was moving back, and totally willing to move out of the cabin for our sake. So, we live in the cabin, and Harper basically has the entire second floor of the main farm house to herself.

Of course, Lyla and I renovated a lot of the cabin. We transformed one of the bedrooms into an office for her, updated a lot of fixtures, and repainted nearly every room. It really is *ours* now.

I unload the truck while she takes the food in and, as always, Mack runs out to greet us. It pains me to know he's already turning one soon. We've talked about getting an addition so he can have a playmate, but we don't want to disrupt our dynamic just yet.

I wrangle the bags and Mack inside, but Lyla isn't in the kitchen with the food. I look into the living room and she's not there, either.

"Lyla?" I yell out as I pull our items from the bags.

"I'm upstairs. Can you come here for a second?" she yells down.

I finish stacking the groceries on the counter and walk upstairs toward our bedroom. I push the door open and my jaw drops.

"I thought maybe we could start with dessert," she says, her clothes on the floor.

Lyla's tan skin fills my eyes. Her perfect body is on display as she lies on the bed, her posture inviting me in. I step into the room and close the door behind me because Mack shouldn't see this. I swallow hard and realize even after more than eight months of this, she still makes me just as excited, just as hungry.

"Fuck," I say as I pull my shirt over my head. My eyes take in every inch of her body like I've never seen her before. I press my palm to her thigh.

She sits up and unbuckles my belt, taking everything from my waist down off in one motion, freeing me. I'm already hard for her and she licks her lips. She reaches for me, but I grab her hands.

"Wait," I say. "Not like that." I lay her back gently onto the bed and part her legs with my knee, holding the weight of my body over her. I lean down and kiss her softly on the lips.

"Not like what?" she asks.

"I want to take my time with you," I say, before kissing her again.

And I do. I make love to her slowly, tenderly. Her moans give me life. I kiss every inch of her. Her jaw, neck, between her breasts. Her stomach, hip bones, and all the way down. I push into her slowly, fill her up over and over again until she comes for me. And then I come for her.

"I love you," she says.

The light in the room is nearly gone but I know she's smiling. And I know it's time.

"That's good," I say. "It makes this next thing easier." I reach down over the edge of the bed for my pants and fumble with the pocket until the ring is loose.

"What are you doing?" she asks, and I know she has no idea.

I prop myself up over her, my chin even with her chest, and she's trying to look down at me through the darkness.

"Lyla Whitney," I say, "I love you. In some ways, I think I've loved you since the moment I met you. I want to spend the rest of my life waking up next to you, slow dancing in parking lots with you, eating sushi with you, and making love to you. Will you marry me? Please?"

Her ragged breathing turn to laughing. "Yes," she says as her voice cracks. She's laughing and crying at the same time now. "Yes, I'll marry you," she says again, and I realize I've been holding my breath since I stopped speaking.

I exhale and my forehead dips to her chest. Her hands are reaching for me, trying to pull me up, but I'm frozen.

"Give me your hand," I say, and we feel our way toward each other until our hands meet in the darkness. I slide the ring onto her finger and she gasps.

"Oh my god, turn on the light—any light," she yelps.

I reach for the side lamp and click it on, then look back at her.

Tears are streaking her cheeks and she's staring at her hand.

"Do you like it?" I ask.

"It's perfect," she says.

I bring my face to hers and kiss her tears away, then her lips. "You realize you're going to be stuck with me forever pretty soon," I tease.

She sighs and nuzzles my neck, sending a wave of goosebumps down my spine. "You promise?" she asks.

"Oh, baby, with all my heart," I whisper.

She shivers. "Say it again," she says. "Please."

I lean in close to her, pressing my cheek to hers as I put my lips right against her ear. "With all my heart," I whisper.

Her body arches toward me, her hands reach for me—and I know.

This is how love is supposed to feel.

And I will fight every day to keep it.

ACKNOWLEDGMENTS

I would be nothing without Jen and Christina. My bitches. Thanks for hanging in there with me all these years. Thanks for pushing me. Thanks for letting me push you.

Thank you to Christina, again, for making my book perfect. And thank you to Amanda for proofreading my book and making it more perfect. You guys are my dream team.

I do everything I do for my goblins: Mattie, Kali, and Kaden. When you read this book ten years from now when you're old enough, just know you kept me going on the days I felt like quitting.

Chris. My lover. Thanks for picking up the slack so I could cry at my laptop and write down the words and do the things.

The wonderful peeps who beta read and provided feedback to me: Maryjo and Autumn. You're the tits.

Thank you so much to Cynthia, Dee, Talon, Maria, Briana, K Leigh, Daniele, Shelly, the #TEAMQUEEN ARC Crew, and so many other fellow authors and bloggers who championed this book and Gentry. Your support is everything.

Thank you to every single reader out there who gave this book a chance. You guys are awesome. You're the reason I do this, the reason I keep going and fighting. I love you so very much.

One More Chance

BOOK TWO

ONE MORE CHANCE

BOOK TWO

For anyone who's ever accepted subpar love,
for the divorcing and divorced.
For those desperate for a love that puts a fire in their
belly
and a quake in their panties.
Your Jensen is out there, ready to shake up your life.
He will probably scare the shit out of you.
But YOLO.

HARPER

I CAN BARELY SEE the line I need to sign through the blurred mess my tears have created, but I scrawl my name in blue ink across it as fast as I can and it's done. I'm officially divorced. It would have been sooner, but my now *ex*-husband Charles is an asshole and decided to draw it out for a while. *Why? I'm not sure. To torment me, is my best guess.* We've been over and done with for more than a year and a half now. And still, crossing the "t" in my reclaimed maiden name of Whitney on my divorce paperwork, hurts in a way I can't exactly explain. I don't miss him, but I hate this sense of failure.

The next envelope in the pile of mail I've avoided cuts in a way it shouldn't. I run my fingers over the embossed stamp on the back before slipping my finger inside and tugging it open.

Mr. & Mrs. Whitney
request the pleasure of your company
at the celebration of marriage between
Lyla Elizabeth Whitney
&
Gentry Tucker Bodine
on Saturday, June 20th

at six o'clock in the evening

Whitney Farms
The Big White Tent
100 Whitney Way

Dinner and Dancing to follow

I don't know why my sister insisted on giving me an invitation. We live on the same property. I helped her stuff the damn envelopes myself. Don't get me wrong, I'm happy to see my sister's day coming. But the *"plus one"* she slapped next to my name on the front of my envelope feels more like a slap to the face. Despite telling her several times there's no way I'm bringing a date, she still suggested keeping an open mind in case *an opportunity presented itself*.

I gave that advice a big eye roll.

After Lyla moved back to the farm, she and Gentry took the old cabin I once shared with Charles at the back of the property, and I moved into the main house with Nan and Paw. I suppose moving back in with my grandparents post-divorce really completed the small-town narrative. Married my high school sweetheart, never left town, got cheated on, got divorced, and still haven't left town. *Pathetic.*

In my nearly two years of single life since Charles left, I've done a lot of reflection, and I've generally arrived at the same conclusion. My life is small. And there's a big difference between a simple life and a small life.

I check my calendar because I'm terrible at remembering what day it is. We're two weeks out from Lyla's big day but that doesn't mean anything around here is chill. People are arriving tomorrow actually—including her friend Cora, who's coming in from Boston for all the wedding shenanigans. We have the bridal shower, the bachelorette and bachelor parties, a brunch, rehearsal dinner, and the list goes on. The Whitney family, along with almost everyone in the South, takes weddings pretty seriously. This is an event. One to be talked about. It's been in the local newspaper. Everyone in our small town is talking about it. Roughly two hundred people will be in attendance.

After Cora arrives, we'll still have so many details to finalize. Thinking about all this only dredges up my own wedding memories. When I married Charles, there was a similar chain of events. Charles was so annoyed by all of it, he made me cry three times in the week leading up to our wedding day. The morning of, he told me he wished I came without the package of my family. But here I sit, with tears in my eyes as I sign the divorce papers.

I walk out onto the porch and watch the setting sun cast long shadows over the fields. Taking a seat on the porch swing, I'm just in time to be greeted by Lyla and Gentry pulling up. They're back from town. Mack, their German Shepherd, jumps out and rushes toward me as soon as their door is open. I lean down to be greeted with his gentle licks and nudges.

"Hey, Mack baby. Who's a good boy?" I say in my best baby voice.

"Hey, Harper," Lyla says.

"Hey, where are ya'll coming back from?" I ask, and my sister holds up a bag of dog treats and an iced coffee. "Isn't it a little late for coffee?" I add, laughing at her buzzed cheerfulness.

"Never," she says. "Listen, I'm glad I caught you. I was thinking. Starting tomorrow when Cora gets here and up until the wedding, I vote Cora and I stay here in the big house with you and Gentry, and Cora's brother can stay in the cabin. What do you think?"

"Oh, sure," I say. "Sounds fun."

"Not to me," Gentry interjects, his bottom lip jutting out. He's clearly not happy about this arrangement.

"Not happy about your boy's only slumber party?" I tease.

"You sister thinks it'll be fun not to have any sexy time until our wedding night," he pouts.

"That's so much more than I needed to know," I say, holding my hands up in front of me. My face involuntarily scrunches up and I gag.

"Oh, come on! It'll make it more special. But I also know myself, and thus another reason Cora and I should stay here while her brother stays in the cabin with Gentry," she says, giving me a knowing look.

And I know my sister too. She's not one to keep her hands off Gentry. They're electric. This entire ordeal will certainly be a challenge for them. So at the very least, they need distance.

"I didn't know Cora was bringing anyone," I say, wanting to change the topic to anything other than their sex life.

"She convinced her brother to come with her because she has an awful track record in the romance department and didn't want the pressure of finding a date. She tempted him with an open bar. He's single, you know," Lyla says, wiggling her eyebrows at me.

I roll my eyes at her. "Okay, that's my exit cue. I'm going to bed." With that, I turn toward the kitchen door and wave over my shoulder at Lyla, who's still jabbering on about Cora's little brother. But I'm not listening to any of it. As far as I'm concerned, he's a leper. A leper with some other sort of disease affecting his genitals too. As a matter of fact, he's a leper with diseased genitals and hairy moles all over his back.

Since Charles left, I've taken up stock in the middle of the bed. Which is exactly where I tuck myself in now. I glance around my room. This used to be the room Gentry was staying in for a while. I decided to keep the dark green paint job and black curtains he left behind. Well, I kindly requested he leave the curtains. I liked the calming effect of the dark palette. It didn't feel too manly. Just comfortable.

I flip from my left side to my right, trying my best to get comfortable. My long blonde hair cascades over my shoulders and I take it between my fingers. Every now and then I consider cutting it but can never work up the courage. My entire life, I've never had more than a trim. When I started dating Charles, he would frequently remind me that short hair *was not my look* and I should keep it long *for both our sakes*. A very small part of me occasionally got the urge to cut it just out of spite, but then I'd think better of it.

At some point I fall asleep, with white wedding gowns twirling in my head. I can't see the woman's face or hair. Just wisps of white flowing outward and falling all over everything.

HARPER

I SPEND ALL MORNING CLEANING, preparing for Cora's arrival. I make up the guest rooms and put fresh towels in the closet. Lyla is in town dealing with wedding stuff, so Cora dutifully told her not to worry about picking her up at the airport. She should be arriving anytime, and I'll be greeting her and showing her around until my sister makes it back.

I finish up in the bathroom and make my way down to the kitchen, pouring myself a glass of lemonade before stepping out onto the porch. Deciding this is the best place to wait for everyone, I take a seat on the porch swing and scroll through my phone when someone catches my attention from the corner of my eye. I look up to see a man walking up the driveway. He's still a way's off, and then he stops, looking around. He's alone, and doesn't seem to be from around here.

Maybe he's a new employee? No, he doesn't look the part. Maybe he's visiting the farm and got lost? He does look like he's from the city. I watch him for a few more minutes. He checks his watch and then adjusts the strap on his shoulder. I look up and down the driveway for a car but see nothing.

"Can I help you?" I finally call out.

Startled, he looks up in my direction. I have to shield my eyes from the sun to get a better look. He's standing too far away to see much. The man starts walking in my direction and I grow a little nervous. It's times like these I wish someone was around.

"I think I'm in the right place," he calls back to me.

I stand from the swing and step to the edge of the porch to get a better look at him. I'd be lying if I didn't say the first thing I noticed was his tight pants. His jeans sit low on his hips and hug from his thighs all the way down to his calves. Oh yeah, he definitely isn't from around here. Those are city pants, for sure. So is that haircut. The man's hair is shorter on the sides and longer on top, slicked back in place a little with one of those hard parts. Classic but apparently coming back into trend. He only has a little stubble, which is a blessing. Otherwise, I wouldn't be able to see his devastating jawline. As he gets closer to the porch, I can't help but take in his sheer beauty. And I'm not sure I've ever called a man beautiful before. As least not a real one.

"Who are you looking for?" I ask, folding my arms over my middle to protect myself from, well, I don't know. He just looks like the kind of man you need to protect yourself from.

He fishes for something in his pocket and pulls out his phone. "I was told to ask for Harper?" he says, presumably scrolling through looking for the information. But why the hell is he looking for me?

"What do you want with her?" I ask, not sure I want to give myself away just yet.

"She won a prize," he says.

"I did?" I asked, more confused than excited.

"Well, no. But at least I know you're who I'm looking for," he says.

Damn, he got me. If I had to guess, he's maybe my age or a year or two younger. "I'm Harper," I say.

He steps onto the porch, bringing himself face to face with me, but not really because he's probably seven or more inches taller than me. He looks down at me, and it's the first time I can really see his bright gray eyes. "I'm Jensen," he says. "Cora's brother."

Oh. *Ohhhhhh*, yes, okay. Not a leper. Definitely not a leper. But no, not okay. Because I can't have this kind of hot guy just hanging around here for the next two weeks either. Excuse me, not even hot.

Beautiful. Like actually beautiful. I'm already an emotional train wreck.

"Oh, nice to meet you," I say, putting my hand between us for a shake.

He studies me for a second, a smirk on his face. I watch his shoulder shrug, and his bag falls effortlessly to the porch. He reaches for my hand, his arm flexing all the way up, his tight T-shirt doing nothing to conceal his form.

On the other hand, having something to look at for a few days might not be so bad. His large hand envelops mine, and its warmth spreads through me.

"Nice to meet you, too," he says, a wide smile spreading across his lips.

"So, where did you come from?" I ask.

"Um, well, I'm originally from Boston like Cora but—"

I laugh. "No, I mean just now? You were walking."

Jensen starts to nod his head, understanding my question. "I had my Uber driver drop me off at the end of the driveway, but to be fair that's because I didn't know the driveway was like, a whole additional road. So I had to basically hike the damn thing."

I laugh again, looking down at Jensen's once pristine white tennis shoes, now covered in a layer of fine dirt. A dusting, really. "You can probably save your tennis shoes," I say, pressing my lips together to keep from laughing at his misfortune.

He looks down at his feet, his eyes growing wide. "I just bought these sneakers, too."

"You call them sneakers?"

"You call them tennis shoes?"

"Interesting," I say. We stare at each other for a moment, unsure what to say, and I watch him reach for his bag again. "Oh, I can take you back to the cabin if you want, so you can put those up. Or you can leave them here on the porch until your sister arrives? I thought you'd be arriving together?"

"No, I had to travel in from a business conference in Raleigh," he says.

"What do you do?" I ask.

"I'm in pharmaceutical sales," he says, and I didn't see that coming. I'm a little impressed. Also a little intimidated.

"Can I get you something to drink?" I ask him.

"I thought you'd never ask," he says.

Slightly embarrassed at my lack of hospitality due to my general distracted thoughts of him, I retrieve a glass of lemonade for him and we sit on the porch swing to wait for his sister, or literally anyone else. Lyla, Gentry, the Pope. Anyone will do. I need a buffer.

I watch him sip the lemonade at first, and then it turns to gulps. I watch his throat muscles work down the liquid and for a moment I'm transfixed by his Adam's apple. I shake my head. *Holy crap. I've got to get ahold of myself.*

"Looks like we've got some time to kill, Harper," he says, and I like the way my name sounds when he says it. I can't explain why. The inflection, the tone, I don't know what it is. Like it could be a song. "So, tell me about yourself."

Oh no.

JENSEN

I WATCH Harper shift in her seat. Well, in the swing we're sharing. I can't be sure but I think asking her to tell me about herself has made her uncomfortable, and I don't know why.

"I'm afraid there isn't much to tell," she says, her head down, a curtain of golden blonde hair covering her face.

And may I just add, it's a gorgeous fucking face. I'm not a blind man. Anyone who didn't notice her beauty definitely had to be. Harper has piercing blue eyes, and I do mean piercing. Even from a bit of a distance, it felt like she was looking into my soul. Her long blonde hair is straight but not lifeless. It cascades off her shoulders like a golden waterfall and I've stopped myself from touching it three times already. But her lips. Her pale pink lips look so full and soft. She has those naturally full lips, and I think bad things when I look at it so I'm trying really hard not to look at it.

"I'm sure there has to be," I say, and she shrugs her shoulders, giving me a look I don't quite understand. "You want me to go first?"

She nods her head.

"Okay, but for every one thing I tell you, you have to tell me something. Deal?" I ask. I don't really understand why I'm trying so hard to know what's behind her pretty face, but she seems a little guarded and that just further spurs my curiosity.

She reluctantly agrees.

"Now let's see, what can I tell you first?" I say, looking up and away as if in deep thought. I even rub my thumb and index finger along my chin to really give her a show.

"Technically, you already told me your job. So, I should at least tell you I work here on the farm," she says.

I nod my head, taking this information in and trying to understand what exactly one does on a farm. "So, do you milk cows and stuff?"

Harper lets out a small laugh, and I'm confused. Don't farms have cows?

"Not quite," she says. "This isn't a dairy farm. We do have cows but they're not for that. We have a store we run. Plus an orchard. And in the fall, we have pumpkin patches and hayrides. That sort of thing."

"I never knew farming was so intense," I admit.

"It can be," she says.

"What else do you like to do?" My question gives her pause and she starts to wring her hands together in her lap. This woman really has anxiety about talking about herself. "For example, aside from my boring sales job, one of the reasons I took it is because I like to travel. And it allows me to do that. I've been to forty-three states and six countries."

"I've never been anywhere," she says. "Do you want more lemonade?" Harper stands and reaches for my glass.

She disappears inside, and I sit there comprehending her statement. It's interrupted by the kicking up of gravel not far off and I look down the driveway to see a car followed by a truck making their way to the house. Harper is saved by the intrusion for now. I stand and walk to the edge of the porch, seeing my sister driving the car and Lyla following behind. The door swings open and shut behind me, and I see Harper join me from the corner of my eye.

She stands away from me by a few paces, quite careful and aware of her proximity. I can feel it radiating from her. She seems very measured, not that it's a bad quality to have. But I wish she'd loosen up a bit. She seems knotted up pretty tightly. Maybe all the stuff with her sister's wedding has been stressful. Weddings can be stressful, right?

I don't know why I'm so concerned about her demeanor or the stressors of her life. Maybe my job in sales and ability to read people is spilling over right now; I can't be sure. I did just finish traveling, and I'm always in need of a nap after that. I walk down the porch steps to greet my sister.

"Hello, bub!" Cora says as she steps out of the car.

Since childhood, Cora has called me bub. There have been some phases in my life. Like when I was sixteen and she would say it in front of all her hot friends. I begged her not to call me that anymore, but she refused to stop.

So here we are. I'm a twenty-seven-year-old bub. I smack my head even now because there are people around. Attractive people. I give her the look as I lean in for a hug. "Hey, sis. How was the trip?"

"Not terrible. I was seated next to this super cute guy who, as it turns out, lives here. Well, not here. But close to here. I told him I was coming for a wedding, and one thing led to another and now he's gonna be my date!" She exclaims this to everyone very loudly and proudly.

I look back at Lyla who's out of her truck and listening intently as well. "You invited a stranger to the wedding?" I ask, since everyone else has been shocked into silence.

"He's not a stranger. We talked the entire flight. It was practically a date in itself," she says, shrugging her shoulders.

I can see the torn expression on Lyla's face, but she finally says, "Well, great!"

"Wait, what about me?" I ask, raising my hand into the air. "I'm supposed to be your plus one, remember?"

"Bub, listen, it's nothing personal. But a real date with the chance of some dancing trumps a family date any time," my sister says.

"Yes, that's in the invisible rule book for crazy single people who haven't been laid in a while," Lyla says.

Everyone except Cora laughs.

"You can be Harper's plus one!" Lyla says, with aggressive enthusiasm—a *lot* of aggressive enthusiasm.

I'm somewhat startled hearing this change of plans. For starters, I would've assumed Harper already had a date. *Why wouldn't she have a date?* "Oh, okay."

"Yeah, of course. I mean, it doesn't mean anything really. It's just a numbers game for seating and catering anyway, right? So yeah, of course," Harper's saying.

I'm watching her sister attempt to discreetly elbow her in the ribs to get her to stop rambling and I successfully suppress a laugh. "Great, it's settled. I'll be your date," I say.

I watch Harper's eyes grow wide and if I didn't know any better, I'd say she's stopped breathing, but I pretend not to notice.

As we're all standing there starting to pull bags from Cora's car, a man joins us, walking from the direction of some barns.

"Jensen, this is Gentry," Lyla says.

The man walks next to her and wraps an arm around her, kissing her on the forehead.

"Good to meet you, man," I say, shaking his hand.

"It's nice to see you again, Gentry," Cora says.

Cora's been down to visit Lyla a few times since she moved here, and has gone on and on about how perfect these two are as a couple. And, how perfect Gentry is. Then she starts in with her *why-can't-I-just-find-a-man-like-Gentry* talk and even though I'm the little brother, I do my best to comfort her.

Lyla turns to Gentry. "Babe, a little change of plans. Cora met a date on her flight. So Jensen is gonna be Harper's plus one instead."

Gentry's head shoots up in my direction again and he looks me up and down in an assessing manner. I don't exactly know what he's looking for but I just sort of stand there and tuck my hands in my pockets while he's doing it.

"All right, I guess," he says. "Come on, I'll show you where we'll be staying." He motions to me, and I climb the porch stairs and grab my bag then follow after him.

I stop and turn briefly. "Oh. Hey, Harper?" I call out.

She turns toward me, her long blonde hair flowing in the breeze. I watch her gently tuck it back over her shoulder. "Yeah?"

"It was really great meeting you. I hope we can get back to our game later?" I say, and I catch Lyla look at Harper.

"Oh, uh, sure," Harper says. Then she wrings her hands in front of her again.

"Great," I say, smiling at her. When I turn back, Gentry is looking at me now. More like staring at me. The man has sort of an intimidating glare going on. I catch up to him and we begin our walk back further onto the property. "So, what's the story with Harper?"

Gentry looks over to me again, a little less severity in his eyes. "Listen, around here, we don't go telling each other's stories. It's not our place. But I'll tell you this, and you can take it as a warning. Tread lightly. Lyla and I aren't married yet, but Harper's been a little sister to me for a while now." Gentry's quiet again as I contemplate his words.

"Okay then, I'll just have to ask her about it. I'll find out for myself. I can appreciate that."

"Yeah, you can try," Gentry says, almost snickering.

Challenge accepted.

HARPER

TODAY IS BRIDAL PARTY HELL. Granted—and luckily—it's only me, Cora, and the bride herself. It could be much worse. But it's still hell. Cora couldn't come down to shop for bridesmaids' dresses before due to her work schedule. Now we're in a boutique in town, trying on lace and satin and everything else the day after she arrived.

Lyla's dress is ready, so it's just Cora and I who need to find dresses. But we're built differently, so finding a dress that works for both our figures, while also being comfortable, is proving to be difficult.

Lyla wants a classic look. Something sleeveless or with thin straps. For my frame, that's not a problem. I'm not working with a lot up top. It's a decent handful. A small handful, though; nothing will spill out of any dress. Cora, on the other hand, is built similarly to my sister. All boobs. Lots of boobs. Boobs everywhere. So some strapless numbers won't work.

"What about this one?" Cora says, holding up a lilac floor length goddess number. It flows nicely, and I think the straps would be okay for both of us.

"I don't really want lilac. Do they have it in another color?" Lyla asks from two racks over.

Cora replaces the dress and starts flipping through color options. "Green?"

"I shouldn't even have to tell you no," Lyla says.

"Gray?" Cora says.

"Wait, gray could work," Lyla says.

We converge to where Cora is and rifle through the dresses. They have a few sizes in the gray and we find some that could possibly fit us.

"Dressing rooms?" I ask, and then we make our way toward the mirrors in the back.

"Okay, I think these are gonna work!" Lyla says. She's standing there staring at me and Cora while we twirl and turn in front of the mirrors.

In truth, I actually like this dress. It feels light and comfortable, and it looks good on both of us. The color is approved. "What do you think?" I ask Cora.

"Girl, if the bride loves it and we even like it a little, I say we go for it." Cora laughs.

We finish changing and pick out shoes and accessories to match the dresses then head to the register.

"Hey, ladies," I hear from behind us.

We all turn to see Gentry and Jensen stepping into the shop, but I know Gentry's voice, and Jensen is definitely the one who greeted us.

"Hey there," Lyla says. "What are ya'll doin' in town?"

"I had to come pick up my tux and Jensen needed a suit," Gentry says, gliding past everyone to wrap his arms around my sister. They're disgusting. Like in that overly affectionate way that annoys all single people.

My sister wraps her arms around Gentry's neck and asks him if he missed her last night.

"No! No, you're not doing this here!" I exclaim in protest to the scene.

"I second that," says Cora.

"Third," says Jensen.

"We're just about to pay. Does everyone want to get lunch?" my sister asks as she wrenches herself away from Gentry—finally—and we all nod.

"Ladies, if you'll allow me." Jensen steps up to me and Cora, reaching for his wallet.

"What are you doing?" I ask.

"Paying for my sister and my date's wedding attire as a small token of my gratitude for letting me tag along. And also for the open bar that I will be killing." Jensen laughs.

"Oh, no. I can't let you do that," I say.

"But I insist," he says.

"But I insist harder," I say firmly. Even though he's already giving his credit card to the lady behind the counter, who's smiling at him. Because he's smiling at her. Not in a flirtatious way, but a naturally charming way. I can see why he's a salesman.

"I'll pay you back," I say.

"Don't even try," Cora interjects. "This is just Jensen being Jensen." She pats her baby brother on the shoulder and collects her shopping bags.

I collect mine and am utterly confused as to what just happened. Why exactly did he pay? What does *"Jensen being Jensen"* mean?

"Well, thank you," I say. "But I still don't really like it."

"Well, you're welcome," he says. "And I guess I'll just have to live with that knowledge."

We all walk out onto the sidewalk and decide to get lunch at the diner across the street. After throwing our bags in the car, we walk over. Gentry and Lyla hold hands and bite each other's necks like two idiots in love. Cora texts her stranger mystery date from the airplane and smiles like an idiot. And then Jensen and I bring up the rear, walking next to each other in an awkward silence like a different kind of idiots.

"I like the dresses you guys picked," Jensen says.

"Oh, thanks. It was quite the ordeal for a while, but we finally managed." More silence. His proximity alone causes me anxiety. I want to wring my hands but catch myself and force away the familiar habit.

I try to think back to the last time I was around any man who caused this sort of reaction in me. When Charles and I first met, he gave me butterflies. I remember that. It was so long ago, though. No one before or since has been in my life in that way. No one has caused my body any reaction. Stupid Jensen was at least proving I wasn't dead inside, so I could thank him for that.

We enter the diner and take one of the larger, round booths in the corner. Everyone slides in until we're all seated. Jensen is to my left on the outside of the booth and Cora is to my right, in the center of the booth. I'm wedged between the Reed siblings and becoming alarmingly aware of how beautiful they are as a set. Cora's brilliant red hair and freckled pale skin feel radiant next to my dull blonde hair and farmer's tanned skin. Jensen's hair isn't red, though the shade of brown is on the warmer side. Both of them have the silver-gray eyes. Mine are just blue, the most common color ever. So boring.

"I can say the alphabet backwards, you know," Jensen whispers to me.

His statement startles me from my thoughts, and I realize for the last several minutes I've just been staring at the same spot on my menu. "What?"

"The alphabet. I can say it backwards," he says proudly, still in a whispered tone.

"Um, okay."

"It's part of our game, Harper. Remember?"

Oh. Right. The get-to-know-each-other game that makes me want to die. "Oh, I see."

"Now, it's your turn," he urges.

I try hard to think of anything about myself that sounds interesting and nothing comes to mind. "Um, well. I was a cheerleader in high school." Even as the words leave my mouth, I know I sound like an idiot.

"Do you still know the cheers?" he asks.

"Unfortunately. They're like the songs stuck in your head you desperately wish brain damage would fix." I laugh.

"Do you still have the uniform?" he asks, his smile doing something weird now.

What the fuck is his face doing? Is he flirting? I swear to the gods, I don't even know what that looks like. So maybe he is. I wouldn't know, but his smile looks kind of sinister now, mischievous.

"Um, I think so actually. Somewhere in the back of my closet," I say.

"I was in marching band," he says, and this surprises me. Because he doesn't look like a marching band kid. Maybe a soccer guy. Not football, because he's leaner than that. He could've easily been in track like Lyla.

"What did you play?"

Just then, the waitress interrupts us for our orders and we each take our turns. I notice we order the same drink—sweet tea. I also notice he orders all his condiments on the side. She takes our menus and leaves.

"Saxophone," he says.

For a split second, I think he just said 'sex-ophone' and I have to play it over in my head. "What?" I ask, and Jensen looks at me. "Oh, right." I start laughing because I feel like I've forgotten how to have basic conversations with people.

"What's so funny?" he asks, halfway laughing himself.

"I thought you said sex-ophone."

"I'm not sure I know how to play that one." He laughs.

Our drinks arrive and we both opt not to use straws, drinking instead from the side of the glass. When he notices I'm doing it too, he gives me a sideways look.

"I like eating the ice intermittently." I shrug.

"I do it for the sea turtles," he says proudly.

We both sip our tea again and set our glasses down.

I have to admit, this isn't terrible. Being around people. Happy people. New people. It's not as bad as I thought it would be.

The food arrives to our table and we all dig in, shoveling fries down, laughing and talking. Lyla steals Gentry's pickle and he bites her neck. Cora is giggling and going on about this great date she's going to have. I'm watching the whole thing play on and on and it's nice.

I look at Jensen, who's taking a bite of his double bacon cheese-burger; and by bite, I mean like a quarter of the thing that fits in his mouth at once. Ketchup and mayo are all over the corners of his lips and I laugh.

He closed-mouth grins at me and I resist the urge to nudge him. It came over me so naturally, like I'd be nudging a friend.

I have to stop myself from going there. But I could enjoy the company, the new friends. I could welcome in these distractions.

Right now, I need them.

HARPER

"HOW DO you set up one of those online dating profile things?" I ask.

Lyla looks at me, saucers for eyes, like I've grown an additional head. "Are you serious right now?"

"Yeah, why not? I mean, I figure it's time to try something, right?" I shrug my shoulders.

"Yes! But also just let me mentally adjust to this. I was surprised. Caught off guard, if you will." She takes my phone from me and stares down at the app I'm attempting to download.

"I think Cora has used this one. Let me get her." She runs from the room and back in, with Cora in tow, leaping onto my bed.

"Okay, girl. What's going on?" Cora asks.

I look at both of them. They're staring at me all starry eyed. "Nothing. I just think it's time to at least try to put myself out there a little, you know? But I don't know how to work these damn apps."

"Hold on," Cora says, grabbing my phone. She clicks, swipes, and clacks for several minutes and then hands me my phone back.

"Is that it?" I look down at my phone, and there seems to be a whole profile there. Even pictures of me.

"Yep. I've been on enough of these things. I can throw a profile together pretty fast," she says.

I scroll through my newly formed profile and the pictures she chose. *Not bad, not bad at all.* She mentions I'm divorced, that I want to take things slow, and so on. The photos she chose are pretty good too. Nothing too revealing, but they capture me pretty well. "Now what?"

"You just scroll through photos of available men in the area and read down here about them. If you're interested, hit the thumbs up. If not, thumbs down. If you both give each other a thumbs up, you'll match and be able to start a chat," Cora tells me.

"Give it a try!" Lyla says, her voice carrying more excitement about this than my whole body can manage.

I start scrolling through some photos. The first guy is bald. I don't consider myself superficial, but at twenty-eight, a man with some hair would be nice. Thumbs down. The next guy is shirtless in the mirror with a tattoo of what appears to be his fraternity symbol on his chest. Thumbs down.

"What was wrong with him?" Cora asks.

I look up at her, wondering what sort of man is about to show up at this wedding based on that one comment. "Just not my type."

The next man is fully dressed, which is promising. He also has hair. That's two checkmarks on a list of an undetermined number of checkmarks. I read his short bio and everything is great until he says he just wants a girl to "kick it with" and something about that has me turned off. Thumbs down.

"Okay, wait. What was wrong with him?" Lyla asks, staring over my shoulder. The two of them are both huddled in, watching my every move. "You know, some of these guys might not be perfect, but they might be good practice."

"Practice?"

"Yeah, you know, no future but maybe some fun," she says, wagging her eyebrows at me.

On reflex, I scrunch up my face. "Even if I wanted that kind of fun, I'm not having fun with a guy who says 'kick it' or has a fraternity tattoo." I stick my tongue out, disgusted both at the thought and their assumption that I'd want to.

They both shrug their shoulders at me and exit, leaving me to flip through this pool of eligible suitors. But from what I can tell so far, it's more like a cesspool and I think I should've brought my boots to wade through this shit.

I lie back on my pillow and keep going, hoping at the very least this little exercise will help me identify what I'm looking for in a guy. When you've only been with one man in your entire life, it's hard to know. Because you haven't thought about any man beyond him. Do I want a tall guy? A fit guy? Funny guy? Thick? Does he need to work out? All good questions. Right now, all I know is he needs to have hair.

I give my first thumbs up to a guy who, by all accounts, seems to be normal. He didn't use any hideous language, has hair, and there are no shirtless pics. Right after, a screen pops up saying we matched. If I recall my brief tutorial, this also means he gave me a thumbs up. I briefly consider messaging him, then decide to wait and see if he messages me first.

My phone dings with a text from a number I don't recognize, so I exit the app and go into my texts.

> **UNKNOWN NUMBER**
>
> Hey! My favorite nostalgic food is pizza. But not just any pizza. Crappy thin cheese pizza dipped in ketchup. Reminds me of simpler times.

I read the text twice, trying to make sense of who and why.

> Who is this?

> **UNKNOWN NUMBER**
>
> Jensen, of course. We have to play our game somehow. Thought this would be easier for when we're not around each other.

> How did you get my number?

And I genuinely want to know, because I sure as hell didn't give it to him.

JENSEN

Gentry gave it to me. I asked him if I could
have it in case of emergencies. You know,
wedding emergencies. Plus, I'm your plus one.
I mean, we have to coordinate.

JENSEN

Maybe?

I hesitate, knowing just how badly this game can go sideways. Pushing my anxiety aside and figuring human interaction could be good for me when I eventually go on a date, I indulge.

My favorite nostalgic food is grilled cheese
with pickles.

JENSEN

That actually sounds delicious and I want to try
one immediately.

Oh. Well, I guess I could make you one?

JENSEN

You would do that for me? :)

Sure. For lunch tomorrow?

JENSEN

Deal!

He seems really excited about the sandwich. A little too excited. I feel extremely awkward about all of this.

JENSEN

Am I bugging you? Is it your bedtime?

No, I barely sleep these days.

JENSEN

Same. I'm a night hawk.

Several minutes go by and I wonder if he's lost interest, actually thinks I'm crazy, or has fallen asleep and isn't really the night hawk he's claimed to be. While I wait, I save him in my phone as "Night Hawk" and laugh.

JENSEN

I don't like sleeping alone.

I'm divorced.

I typed and sent it before I even thought about stopping myself. I'm not sure why I did. I mean, if I can't tell Jensen, harmless Jensen, how am I going to be able to tell a date? I have to press onward.

JENSEN

That sucks. I'm sorry. What happened?

He left me for another woman.

JENSEN

Jesus. What an idiot.

I smile at his attempt to make me feel better about the ordeal. I mean, Jensen doesn't know me or the marriage, so I know he's just being nice, but still.

It's been over a year and a half, so I guess it's time to move on.

JENSEN

Oh yeah? Move on how?

Date other people, I guess.

JENSEN

Well, technically, you are. I'm your plus one DATE, remember?

How could I forget? You've only reminded me like four times.

The texting grows quiet again and I flip back to the dating app. I give three more thumbs downs and two thumbs ups. And then a flashing message appears in my inbox. *Holy shit, someone messaged me.*

Before I can click on it, I'm distracted by a knock on my bedroom door.

I push the blankets down and stand, phone in hand, still partially looking at the screen as I open the door. I glance up and back down and then immediately up again, making eye contact with Jensen.

"I really want that grilled cheese with pickles," he says, holding up a paper bag full of what I can only assume are the ingredients.

I glance down at my phone and it's ten-thirty. *He wants a grilled cheese this late?* "As a bedtime snack?" I ask, raising an eyebrow and folding my arms over my chest.

"To be fair, neither of us are sleeping," he says.

I grab the bag of items from him and look inside. Everything for the sandwiches seems to be there. I motion for him to follow me to the kitchen and tuck my phone into the pocket of my sweatpants.

When we're downstairs, I pull a pan from the cupboard and start warming it. He sits and watches me carefully butter the slices of bread then sit them aside. I hear my phone ding again and realize the app has its own set of sounds.

"Do you need to get that?" he asks, his arms crossed over his chest now, a smirk on his lips.

"No, it can wait."

"I hear those dating app guys can get impatient." He chuckles.

I shoot a look in his direction. "How did you know?"

"First, everyone knows that alert tone. Second, I've been on that app."

"Any luck?" I ask, finding myself curious as to what kind of girls he'd be looking for on there.

"It's served its purpose from time to time," he says.

Ew. That sounds mildly...*ew.* "Oh. So you're a player?"

"No?" he says, his words falling out more like a question than an answer and I wonder if he knows if he is or not.

I place the pickles on the melting cheese and then the other slice of bread on top. Then I flip the two sandwiches over, revealing the other side to be golden brown. I smile at myself and my good job. I give the other side of the sandwiches a few minutes, then lift them from the pan and place them on the plate.

I turn and extend the plate to Jensen. "Your snack," I say, smiling at him.

"Oh, you're having one," he says. He sits down at the table and rubs his hands together. I sit across from him and wait for him to take a bite. He reaches for his sandwich but then gestures for me to reach for mine.

I roll my eyes and pick up the sandwich.

"Okay, at the same time. Ready?" he says excitedly.

I nod, readying my sandwich in front of my mouth. We both bite into our sandwiches at the same time and I watch his eyes grow big then sort of roll back, and he makes a moaning sound in the back of his throat.

I'd be lying if I said that noise wasn't extremely sexual and extremely distracting. "Does it always sound like you're having sex with your food?"

"Only when my food is making love to me," he says, and then he winks at me.

For a moment, I think that's stupid. *Who even winks anymore?* Then I realize he can actually pull off winking. *Then,* I get distracted wondering how long it's been since someone winked at me, and I can't remember ever being winked at by anyone other than Charles—during my freshman year of high school. At the time, Charles definitely couldn't pull off winking.

"Thirsty?" I offer.

"Parched," he says.

I get up to grab us some glasses of lemonade, if only to avoid having to make eye contact with him for a few moments. Then I sit back down and I watch him guzzle half the glass. I look to his plate and realize his entire sandwich is gone. *Jesus, does he have a tapeworm?*

"Do they feed you where you're from?" I ask him, laughing.

"Of course. I just really like your signature sandwich," he says, laughing in return.

His gaze settles on my plate. I look down and see I've only eaten a quarter of my sandwich. As I glance back up at him, it's obvious he's salivating.

"Do you want the rest of mine?" I ask, watching his features immediately perk up. I hand my plate to him and watch him dig in. It's satisfying to watch someone like something you made this much.

"Thank you for the sandwiches," he mumbles, still partially chewing.

"You're welcome. I'm glad you like them."

We sit in silence for a few minutes while he finishes eating between sips of lemonade. He stands and takes his plate to the sink, which I find low-key impressive. As if that wasn't enough, he then rinses the plate and sets it in the drainer. Jensen turns, leaning back against the counter, and places his hands on it on each side of him. "Let's see those guys," he says.

"What?"

"The guys messaging you." He laughs. "Let's see who's interested."

"Oh my god, no." I laugh.

"Come on," he prods. "I'll be nice."

I roll my eyes and take out my phone.

He walks over to me as I open the app and click on the inbox. "Steve?" he asks, his nose crinkling.

"What's wrong with Steve?"

"Nothing, just not a very cool name," he says, shrugging his shoulders.

"Well, not everyone can be a *Jensen*," I tease.

"Damn right, they can't." He smirks.

I open Steve's message and Jensen leans in close to read with me. A little too close. I can smell him, and I like the way he smells. Spicy and clean. *Shut up, Harper.*

STEVE

Hey :)

JENSEN

"HEY, WITH A SMILEY FACE?" I laugh.

"What's wrong with that?" Harper asks.

"You can't be serious," I say.

She shrugs her shoulders and messages the guy back. *Actually* messages the guy back, if you can believe it.

"I have to get some practice in, anyway. Even if he isn't a winner," she says.

Practice? What kind of practice is she talking about? I study her face for a few minutes as she navigates back to the screen where you scroll through people. "Practice?" I decide to ask.

"It's your turn, I think," she says, clearly trying to detract from my question.

"In high school, I had a crush on the most popular girl in school. I mean, she was the prom queen and everything. Her boyfriend didn't like it too much, not that I was a threat. He broke into the band room and wrecked my saxophone. My guitar too," I say.

"You weren't popular in high school?" she asks, her tone giving the impression she's a little shocked.

"Not exactly. Unless band kids who don't play any sports and go to college still as virgins are what you'd call *popular*," I say, laughing.

Harper's face is sheer shock at this point. "I never would've guessed."

"I guess you could say a lot changed my freshman year of college." I think back to when I met the few decent popular guys I did, and how they helped me bloom. I put some weight on, which filled out my tall frame. Then I learned how to dress, talk to people, and be more confident in myself.

"I was prom queen," she says, cutting into my thoughts.

I look Harper up and down, taking in her petite frame, golden hair, and overall demeanor. "I can see that."

She looks down at her feet, as if my words have bothered her. "You wanna go sit out on the porch?"

I nod, following her out to the swing we'd sat on the previous day. "Wow, look at that sky. You'd never see a sky like that in Boston or another big city."

"I wouldn't know," Harper says.

"What do you mean?"

"I mean I've been looking at the same sky my whole life. I don't know any other skies."

I think about that for a few minutes, leaning back against the porch swing and listening to it sway.

"When I said I needed to practice earlier?" she says.

Here it comes. "Yeah?" I ask, turning to give her my full attention.

"I meant I was with Charles since high school and I've never dated anyone else."

I blink at her several times, processing what she just said. "Wait, wait, wait. Let me see if I have this straight. *You?* Have only been with one man? Your entire life?" I ask, punctuating my statement to give it the necessary emphasis to portray my bewilderment.

"That's correct," she says.

"A man named Charles?"

"Yes," she says.

"So, let me see if I have this. You divorced a man named Charles and you're gonna practice dating with a guy named Steve? Because you've only been with one guy ever. And you basically have to learn how to like...do what we're doing now?" I ask, looking at her quizzically.

"Well, I mean I guess," she says.

"Why don't you just practice with me?"

"I'm sorry, what?"

"Look, I'm your wedding date anyway. Let's get to know each other. Be friends. Have conversations. Spend time together. That's what dating is."

"And the sex?" she asks.

I nearly choke on nothing at all. "Sex?"

"People who are dating have sex. Surely you don't expect me to—"

"God, no," I say.

Harper pulls her head back, my knee jerk reaction sounding a little offensive.

I have to recover. "No, wait. That sounds wrong. Look, don't get me wrong. You're a beautiful woman, truly. But maybe given the circumstances, we practice the non-sexual dating components. Then when I leave, you'll be ready to date with sexual components maybe?" I offer, holding my hand out for her to shake.

"You're crazy, you know that?" she says.

"Probably."

Harper reaches out, and I take her hand so we can shake on it. "Yeah, sure. Why not? What could possibly go wrong?" She laughs.

"Great. In the meantime, keep the app. Maybe it'll help you with your flirting skills or something." I laugh and stand.

"I know how to flirt," she says.

"Okay, then. Hit on me," I challenge.

"What?" she says.

"Come on. Stand up and hit on me," I say, ushering her to me. I stand square in front of her and watch as she stares down at our feet, wringing out her hands so hard I fear she may start rubbing off her skin.

"Um, okay. Maybe I don't know how to flirt. But I don't flirt anyway, right? The guy does. I just stand there and take it," she says.

Oh dear. This is far worse than I imagined. I didn't know it was possible to be this clueless as to how to interact with the opposite sex.

"Um, no. There was this whole feminist movement. You guys are allowed to hit on us now too," I joke.

"Well, laughing at me isn't gonna help," she says, sitting back down.

"I'm not, okay? Stand back up."

Harper stands and I usher her forward, guiding her by the small of her back until she's standing much closer to me. She's just a whisper away from pressing her entire front side against mine.

"Proximity is everything," I say. "Now, tell me you had a nice time."

"What?"

"Pretend it's the end of a date—our grilled cheese pickle date. Pretend you're interested in seeing me again, and right before you walk into your place, you're gonna tell me you had a really nice time in such a way that I'm definitely gonna want to whip out my phone and hit you up for a second date."

Harper swallows, clearly unsure how she should proceed.

"Do you want me to show you? And then you can think about it and practice later?" I ask.

"Okay," she says.

I bend down slightly, bringing my face close to hers so our cheeks are almost touching. I blow my breath against her neck and ear as I exhale slowly. My fingers reach for hers and I lace them together, playing with them. "I had a really great time tonight, Harper," I say, letting her name fall from my mouth slowly, every letter getting time on my lips. I pull away slowly, letting more of my breath tickle her cheek.

I watch as goosebumps trail up her arm and I unlace my fingers from hers. Slowly backing away, I give her my signature Jensen smile. Not the one I give my customers or clients. Not the one I give family or friends. I give her the one I give specifically when I'm trying to seal the deal with a woman. That's what I'm trying to show her after all, right?

Her leg wobbles just a fraction and she swallows. "Um, me too."

I back away from her and toward the steps of the porch. "I'll see you tomorrow."

"All right."

"Goodnight, Harper."

"Goodnight," she says. She's still staring at me, her eyes fixed on some spot on my face.

I head down the stairs and back toward the cabin, the night sky so bright with stars, I can't take my eyes off it.

If I have to guess, Harper has finally gone inside. She's such an interesting person. I've met a lot of people while traveling and in my line of work, but no one quite like her. That's what I love about traveling in general. No two people are the same, although you get your types. But Harper, she's so delicate. And I have an appreciation for that.

I get back to my room in the cabin and undress, peeling out of my jeans and shirt. I'm not too proud to admit that even men assess themselves and their flaws in the mirror. I haven't been to the gym in almost a month and I can see the toll already. My work schedule has been pretty hectic, but it's about to slow down. Maybe I'll ask Gentry if there's a gym around here tomorrow.

I flex in the mirror and poke at my stomach. Still flat but softer than it was when the carbs were less frequent and the gym was more often. I shrug, knowing in the grand scheme I'm probably the only one able to see what I see anyway. That's not arrogance talking, just a willingness to remind myself we all see ourselves in a different light than everyone else.

I lie back on the bed and my phone dings.

> HARPER
> Okay. I get it now.

> I will teach you how to use the force.
> Worry not.

> HARPER
> Are you speaking Jedi?

> Obviously.

HARPER

Okay. How about I'm Eminem and you're Dr. Dre instead?

What the hell? I stare at my phone in awe. I mean, that's probably the coolest analogy ever, but I never would've expected it from her.

Doesn't everyone down here just listen to country?

HARPER

Um, no.

I'm impressed yet again.

I set my phone down. Maybe Harper isn't that much of a lost cause after all. She probably just needs a few reminders. Her self-esteem seems like it could use a serious boost. I can't imagine what her husband leaving her for another woman did to her confidence. But she *should* be confident.

Again, she just needs reminding. And I can definitely help her with that.

HARPER

LET'S just say the past two days have been interesting. From the moment Jensen did his flirty fake goodnight whatever on the porch, he's been...interesting. We've continued to play the getting-to-know-each-other game, divulging random facts to each other throughout the day either by text or when we're together in person. Some are trivial, some more serious. Our favorite snacks, how our first kisses went down, our celebrity crushes, and whatever else the mood calls for.

As if that's not enough, he fucking flirts with me. And he expects me to flirt back. Which I've discovered I'm horrible at, except when I'm impressing him with how many Eminem lyrics I've memorized and can recite. Of course, I can't rap them fast like he can, but I know them by heart all the same.

"What's in two days again?" Jensen asks me as we walk a trail through the property.

"The bridal luncheon."

"Where women have tea and sandwiches on the lawn?" he asks.

"This isn't a country club," I say, laughing. "More like, women eating platters of meat and doing shots of bourbon in a plowed corn field."

"Wow, okay. Party time," he says.

"Pretty much." I laugh, recalling my own bridal luncheon. One decent memory I have because Charles wasn't involved.

"Wait, does this mean you're going to get drunk?" he asks.

I nod. "Probably."

"Are you gonna drunk text me? Or want to make out?" He pokes his elbow into my ribs.

"What? Oh my god, no." As I say it, I feel my cheeks getting hot.

"You know, maybe liquor will be just what you need to be a little more flirtatious."

I roll my eyes. "You're ridiculous." When I look over at him, I notice he's stopped.

Jensen's staring out over the back field, at all the sunflowers in full bloom. "Wow," he says. "This is incredible."

I look out over the field, the heads of the tall sunflowers bobbing as the breeze passes through them. "They are pretty."

"I read somewhere that they face the sun, but when they can't find the sun they face each other."

"As beautiful as that is, it's not true," I say.

"No?"

"Unfortunately not. By the time they're full grown, they're pretty well stationary but will follow the sun a little."

"They're pretty like you. And I don't know why, but they feel kind of shy. Like you," he says.

"You think I'm pretty like a sunflower?"

"Yes. Somehow so grand but understated. A little overlooked, or underappreciated. Maybe that's what I mean," he says.

I know I'm blushing at this point. I feel the heat over my cheeks, spreading down my chest. "And shy, too?"

"Yeah. Like, you don't realize you're a sunflower," he says. "Look at that field. So breathtakingly beautiful, just existing, but content just following the sun."

I swallow hard. *He said breathtakingly beautiful. Whoa.* That's a bit more than pretty. I don't know that anyone's ever called me something like that. Of course, he's got the "content" part wrong. Very wrong, I think. I feel it more and more each day.

Jensen looks at me, pulling his eyes from the flowers as he smirks.

"Content," I whisper.

"What?" he asks.

"You said *content*."

"You're not?" he asks.

"I don't think so."

"Why not?" he asks as we turn, continuing our walk toward the main house.

"I'm not sure why exactly. I guess if I knew why, I could fix it. I've just felt less and less content with my life every day since Charles left. Not because he left, necessarily. I don't think his return would make me feel *more* content. Just in general, like I'm missing something."

"Maybe you should try new things, see new places. Meet new people until something clicks," he suggests, like it'd be so easy to just leave and go somewhere else.

Where would I even start? "Where would I go?" I ask aloud.

"Wherever you want." He shrugs. "That's the beauty of being an adult with nothing tying you down. You can fly free."

I think about his words as we approach the porch. Lyla and Gentry fly out of the side door in a hurry.

"There you are!" she says, rushing toward me. Her tone is shrill and nervous; it's the one she uses when she's panicking.

"What's wrong?" I ask.

"We have a wedding problem. The guy who was supposed to sing our song for our first dance just canceled. I've been on the phone all morning trying to find a replacement, but no one's available this late. It's awful," she says.

"Can't the DJ just play the song?" I ask.

"I guess, but that's not special. It's just not how I imagined it at all. I wanted our song to be live," she huffs.

"Excuse me," Jensen says, "I don't want to intrude, but I can sing. And play guitar. I'm pretty decent at it, if I can say so without sounding like I'm bragging too much."

"Are you...are you saying you would do it? I mean, could you? Would you even have time to learn the song?" Lyla asks, her voice getting high again but this time with excitement.

"I just need to be taken to a guitar shop. I didn't bring mine with me. And I need to know the song. I'm sure I can manage," he says.

What is he, some kind of musical savant?

"Oh my god," Lyla yelps, rushing toward Jensen and bear hugging him, pinning his arms to the sides of his body in the process. "Let me pay you for your trouble."

"No way," he says. "Totally unnecessary."

"At least let us pay for the guitar," Gentry offers, giving Jensen that man-to-man look of an unspoken something I can't quite explain.

"Okay, sure," Jensen agrees. "But I'd be happy to do it as a wedding gift."

Jensen and Gentry make plans to go into town to the local music shop to grab a guitar the next day, while I stand off to the side running through a mental checklist.

So, let's see. He's been to a million places around the world, has a super impressive well- paying job, is devastatingly beautiful, and now I learn he can sing and play guitar. Yeah, that seals the deal. He's way too good for me. Way. Too. Good. A man like Jensen probably has women lined up around the block for dates, or even just the chance to smell his hair.

There's no way he'd be into a simpleton like me. This whole fake flirting, getting to know each other, and buddy buddy plus one talk feels more and more like pity as I tick off all the things he has going for himself.

Pulling out my phone, I walk up the stairs while the rest of them are still talking. In the kitchen, I'm greeted by Cora.

"Oh hey," she says.

"Is your brother always…um, I don't know…like that?" I ask, not even sure what I'm asking.

Cora doesn't appear to be caught off guard considering I skipped right over the greeting and straight to the questions. "Yep." She takes another bite of her fudge bar.

"Well that's…"

"The words you're looking for are *infuriating* and *intimidating*," she says.

"Yeah, maybe."

"Listen, he comes off like that, sure. But he's not doing it on purpose. He's not arrogant. He's actually a really genuine person," she says.

I narrow my eyes at her, unsure if she's being truthful.

"Trust me. I saw him before he was this way, too. When he was just skinny little Jensen no one paid any attention to," she adds.

"And he was the same?"

"At his core, yeah. The package is a little different. And the flare, sure. But he's never stopped being who he's always been." Cora finishes the last bite of her fudge bar and walks out of the kitchen, taking a call from her mystery date.

We've all come to learn that his name is Alan, and he's a minor league baseball player of some sort, but we don't know of the team.

I think about what she said, the things Jensen has said, and while he's a great friend so far, I realize that's all he'll ever be. And, it's a little difficult to practice dating with someone who isn't actually interested in you. You can only take the practice so far.

I should set up real dates. I think I have to.

Jensen steps inside the kitchen, interrupting my thoughts and looking around like he expected someone else to be in here.

"Cora's upstairs I think," I tell him.

"What's your idea of a perfect date?" he asks.

"Me?"

"Of course you," he says.

"I don't know. I've never thought about it," I confess.

"Well, think about it." He laughs.

I sit back in my chair at the kitchen table, my eyes darting around the space to avoid landing on him. "I always wanted to take one of those cooking classes for couples, where you prepare the meal together then sit and eat it at a nice little table. Charles thought it sounded stupid. He never wanted to go camping, either. I always loved camping when I was a kid. Sorry, this is turning into a things-Charles-hated list," I say, laughing.

"Maybe they're sort of the same list," he says, and I never thought the truth could sting so much. Such a simple truth. But perhaps he's right. "What else?"

"Campfires. Swimming in the lake. He never bought me a teddy bear. I thought everyone did that. He said they were stupid and we were adults."

Jensen stands there quietly, like he's calculating a plan, like he's sorting out the details of something. "Okay. Tomorrow, after I get back from the music shop, meet me on the porch. I'll figure everything else out."

I nod, not entirely sure what I've signed up for, but on board nonetheless. I shrug. How bad could it be?

I scroll through my phone until I get to where I was going before I was sidetracked.

STEVE

Hey :)

Hi there.

I don't put the smile at the end of my response because it's stupid. However, I'm willing to overlook it on his end because desperate times and all. Beggars and choosers and whatnot. Maybe it won't be so bad. It's not like the smile will be at the end of every single text he sends. Maybe he's just trying to seem non-threatening in the beginning.

I hear the unmistakable and apparently very specific app notification tone ding.

And here we go.

HARPER

JENSEN TEXTED me when they were on their way back from the music shop. So I'm on the porch, sitting in the swing and tapping my foot. I'm tapping my foot to keep from wringing my hands, although I'm not sure one nervous habit is better than another.

A million thoughts have popped into my head today. Where are we going? What are we doing? What do I need to wear to be prepared? Do I need to bring anything? All excellent questions. All unanswered by Jensen.

Gentry's truck comes into view down the driveway and I fight the urge to stand. If I stand, I'll definitely start wringing my hands. The ding of the dating app sounds and I turn the ringer off, opting for vibration only. I don't need everyone around me to know exactly when people are messaging me.

Gentry and Jensen exit the truck, a new guitar case in Jensen's hands.

"Did you find what you were looking for?" I ask.

"Sure did," he says, smiling.

"He listened to the song in the truck, too. Doesn't seem to be worried about learning it by next week," Gentry says.

"That's good," I offer.

"Ready to go?" Jensen asks me.

"I don't know. Am I dressed okay?" I ask.

Jensen looks down, realizing I'm in a sundress and flipflops. "Okay, your sister did you the favor of packing your overnight bag, but that won't work. Go dress like you're going hiking."

"Overnight bag?" I ask. "We've got the luncheon tomorrow. I can't go somewhere overnight."

"Don't worry, I've cleared it with Lyla. We'll be back in plenty of time, and she's already approved it," he says.

I curse my sister, wherever she might be at the moment. She's probably lying low on purpose because she knew how I'd react to this. I huff out a sigh, and Gentry looks from Jensen to me and back to Jensen, pressing his lips together and smirking. I don't like that. Not at all.

I run upstairs and search my room for appropriate hiking attire. Considering I haven't been hiking in ages and there's no fucking mountains around here, my leggings, sports bra, a flannel shirt over it, and my tennis shoes will have to do. I look ridiculous, but when I get back out to the porch, Jensen is in the driver's seat of Gentry's truck.

"Wow, you make flannel look adorable," he says.

I want to face palm. I can't tell if he's joking or being serious.

As if reading my mind, he says, "I'm serious."

"Oh, thank you." I jump into the passenger seat of the truck and realize for the first time that either Jensen's borrowed some of Gentry's clothes or recently bought some of his own. Instead of his signature tight jeans, he's in relaxed fit cargo pants. He's in a plain white T-shirt with a flannel shirt thrown over it as well.

Are we actually fucking matching right now? Are we for real going hiking?

"So, where are we going?" I ask, eager to kill the suspense. I'm terrible at surprises.

"Camping, of course," he says.

"What? Really?" My brain is having a hard time processing what he's saying.

"Yeah, really. I worked everything out. All the gear is in the back. I borrowed it from Gentry and Lyla. They were eager to help," he says.

I bet they fucking were. Especially Lyla. Her words ring in my head. *He's single, you know.* Yeah, single and perfect and not interested in me.

Let's fake date, he says.

Swell. I attract people who pity me and want to fake date me to teach me how to real date. *Awesome.*

"Camping where?" I ask, to shut my own thoughts up.

"Now that's a surprise." Jensen pulls the truck out onto the road in the opposite direction of town, which piques my interest even more. There isn't much out this way other than other people's properties.

That is, until you hit the next town.

"Your sister has a really pretty song picked out to dance to," he says. "I've never heard it before."

"*Lady May* by Tyler Childers is one of my favorites too," I say, smiling. I agree, she picked a good one.

"What was your song at your wedding?" he asks.

I think back to that day, the way I had to pat at my cheeks with tissues in the bathroom right before our first dance because of how emotional the whole thing had been—both good and bad. In some ways, I was so happy. In others, I was completely scared I'd made the wrong decision.

"I don't remember the name of it. Charles insisted on picking it. The whole thing is a blur." I'm not saying anything that isn't true. Charles picked this dreadfully boring song he called *a classic.* I swear, sometimes it was like he was an eighty-year-old man trapped in a young person's body.

"That sucks," Jensen says.

I shrug, not really bothered either way about the memory anymore. "What about you? No marriages or divorces under your belt, but have you been close? Thought about it with someone?"

Jensen's jaw tightens for a second as he stares off. "There was one girl. It was a long time ago."

"What happened?"

Jensen's shoulders rise and fall slowly as he exhales. "Just wasn't meant to be."

Getting the impression he doesn't want to say much else, I quickly change the subject. "Are we almost there?"

Jensen laughs at my paper-thin attempt as he turns the wheel of the truck onto a road I'm not familiar with. "As a matter of fact, we are."

I look down the road and see a body of water not far off in the distance. A lake. We're camping at a mother-effing lake.

"We're also gonna build a campfire," he says. "That's like, three things in one or something, right?"

I think back to our conversation about dates turned things-Charles-hated and indeed, this will be like combining three of those things. Well, if we go swimming. *OH MY GOD. Are we going swimming? Is he going to be shirtless and stuff?*

More importantly, how many fucking tents did he pack and why haven't I asked myself that question until now?

Jensen parks the truck on a patch of gravel off the road and hops out, pulling bags and a cooler from the back before I can even make it out of the truck.

I watch him stack everything neatly and note there only appears to be one tent. One two-person tent. That's...snug. I'm going to file my panic away for later in favor of remaining calm while he needs my help setting up the campsite.

We walk toward the lake, bags in hand, and set it all down on a flat stretch.

"Let's set up the tent first," he says.

I walk over to him and the tiny tent he's holding in his hands, and then I place my hands on my hips. "We're both gonna sleep in there?"

"Yes?" The word falls from his mouth like a question.

"It's awfully small..."

"You don't want to spoon?" He smirks, lifting his eyebrow.

"What?"

"If it makes you feel better, there are two separate sleeping bags. I promise to behave," he offers, pointing to the bags on the ground.

I nod slowly, surrendering to the situation.

After we set up the tent, collect wood for the fire, and set up the cooler and two chairs, he hands me the bag Lyla packed for me. "She said she packed everything you'd need. I was thinking we could have dinner, then swim?"

"Sounds good," I say. "What's for dinner?"

Jensen pulls out long metal spears and a pack of hot dogs. He lays out buns, condiments, potato salad, and chips.

"When did you even have time to pack all this or shop or whatever you needed to do?" I ask.

"I told you, I had help." He winks at me.

Okay, yep. We're going to have to talk about the winking. He shouldn't be doing that.

He strikes a match against the package and throws it in, the flames starting to flicker higher and higher until we've got ourselves a decent sized fire. Then he hands me a beer and my spear, a hot dog already jammed on the end.

As we sit and roast hot dogs, I take a few sips of the beer. The sun is lower in the sky and I realize this is actually really nice. Hell, maybe if I had been able to convince Charles we should do this, we wouldn't have split up. Although there's no way to know that. His reasons for leaving seemed inconsistent at best.

"What are you thinking about?" Jensen asks, and I don't exactly want to admit I was thinking about my ex-husband.

I pull the hot dog from the flames and cup a bun around it, setting my spear aside. "I was thinking this is actually really nice. Thanks for bringing me."

"Hey, it was your idea. I just executed it. Just goes to show you, you have really good ideas," he says.

Maybe he's right. Maybe I'm not boring or passionless. Maybe I do know how to have fun, *be* fun. We settle into a comfortable conversation as we eat, alternating between our getting-to-know-each-other game, wedding stuff, and the occasional Charles informational.

As we're cleaning up, Jensen looks at me, rubbing his hands together and grinning wide. "Ready to go swimming?" he asks.

Shit.

JENSEN

I DON'T ENVY BEING a woman. Well, I mean, sometimes I think it'd be cool to have boobs but mostly, I don't envy the struggle. Harper disappeared into the tent to change into her bathing suit while I simply slipped out of my pants and shirts, leaving just my swim trunks. That was it. I've been waiting for about six minutes now while my grand transformation took all of thirty seconds. Maybe she has strappy things she's struggling with, I don't know. The point is, I respect the effort. Because I like boobies. Because I'm a typical man in that regard.

"Okay, I'm ready."

Her voice travels from behind me and I turn, giving up my view of the lake for...something so much better. Harper is wearing a small, red bikini. *Ugh, why did it have to be red?* The bottom ties on either side. There's a tie at her neck and back. Four little knots. That's it. Women are goddesses.

I clear my throat rather loudly, averting my eyes from all the perfect skin to the ground. Because again, I'm not here to cause trouble but I'm not fucking blind either.

"Okay, let's go," I say, rushing toward the water.

Everything will be better when she's wet. *No. Shit.* I mean, covered in water. Under the water where I can't see her.

We walk down toward the edge of the lake, which has a nice little bank that lets you walk right in. I let the water hit my ankles and it's surprisingly warm. I expected it to be at least a little cool. I wade in deeper, the water hitting my knees as I look over to find Harper.

She's already in deep enough to let the water hit her upper thighs. She walks further in, skimming her hands along the top of the rippling water. I watch her shoulders dip, like she's just unloaded a burden.

"It's nice, huh?" She turns toward me, her eyes trailing up my body and finding mine. Her long blonde hair bounces and sways, the ends of it just starting to get wet. Her face is calm, serene. "I really love the water," she says.

"Have you ever seen the ocean?" I ask.

"No. I was supposed to go on my honeymoon, but there was a change of plans. That's sad, right? I'm a grown woman and I've never seen the ocean," she says.

"No. I'm sure plenty of people haven't seen it. But if you love the water, you should."

Harper nods her head, silently agreeing with me as she steps deeper into the water, letting it hit her chest.

Most of her is submerged now, and I'd be lying if I said I wasn't a little relieved. Her petite frame still has plenty of womanly curve, I can confirm that much. Parts of her look surprisingly soft and round and squeezable. *Okay, no. Abort that thought train.*

I dive into the water head-first, and come up several feet past her. Little droplets fall from my now wet hair. Harper is smiling at me like I've extended some sort of challenge, and then she dives into the water, disappearing for several seconds.

I look all around, until she finally surfaces near me.

"Are we racing? Because I didn't shave my body," I say. "That's gonna slow me down."

"See that buoy over there?" she says, pointing out into the water.

I peer out and see a little yellow dot bounding on the water.

Harper waggles her eyebrows at me and then yells, "Go!"

To be fair, I'm not mad she gave herself a head start. One of my strokes equals two of hers and I catch up with ease. But I'm also not in the mood to dust her, so I swim right next to her, watching her paddle and breathe, paddle and breathe.

When we get closer to the buoy, I stop in the water several feet short of it, letting her pass and touch it.

"It's not fun if you let me win." She laughs.

"Yes, it is." I lie back and float on my back, looking up at the sky. It's getting much darker now. If it weren't for our fire on the shore, I'm not even sure we'd be able to see our way back.

"Wanna head back?" she asks.

I nod, rolling over and starting to swim toward the light, this time at a more leisurely pace. "I'm sorry I couldn't figure out a way to add in cooking lessons. That will be the next thing we do."

Harper splashes water at me, laughing. "You're crazy. Why do you want to take me on these dates anyway?"

"We're practicing, remember?" I remind her. And myself.

"Right," she whispers.

The rest of the swim is silent, only the lapping water and sounds of our breathing filling the night sky.

As Harper starts to get closer to the shore, the water level getting lower, her wet skin emerges from the surface. The moonlight licks at it, illuminating it.

I stop in the water, watching as she gathers her golden hair to the side and wrings droplets from it. Watching her get out of the lake is equivalent to every movie scene where the beautiful woman is getting out of the body of water, slick wet skin, hands running through her hair. We've all seen them.

And me? I'm the dorky, nerdy, weird guy always standing some-where off to the side with big cartoon heart eyes.

"Aren't you getting out?" she asks, looking back at me.

I realize I'm still standing in waist deep water, staring at her. "Yeah, sorry. I thought I felt something move," I say, whatever that means.

"Like a fish or a snake?"

"There are snakes in lakes?" I ask.

"As much as I want to laugh at the rhyme, yes," she says.

If I didn't want to get out before, I definitely do now. I evacuate the snake filled body of water and grab the towels I laid on the chair next to the fire, handing her one and wrapping one around my shoulders. "I'm sure if we sit here, we'll dry out in no time," I tell her.

Harper sits in the other chair, patting at the water on her arms and then wrapping the towel around her hair to dry it more. "I'm sorry it took me so long to change before," she says.

"Oh, it didn't. No problem."

She smacks her forehead with her palm and shakes. "No, no. I was just checking through the bag Lyla packed me and saw she didn't pack...appropriate pajamas." She squeezes her eyes shut and presses her lips into a line.

I laugh as I watch her turn a little pink. "What do you mean appropriate?"

Harper looks up at the sky, whispering under her breath. I can't hear what she's saying but if I had to guess she's probably cussing out her sister. I know the look well.

"She packed like, a lingerie nightgown thing," she says.

Oh. OH.

Oh...

"I see," I say, smirking.

"I think I can just sleep in my outfit that was packed for the morning," she says.

"I have extra clothes," I offer. "Probably more comfortable than jeans."

"What do you have?"

"A T-shirt and some basketball shorts. You can probably roll them up." I stand and rifle through my bag next to the tent, pulling out a plain white tee and black shorts. I pull out a nearly identical outfit for myself and then return to Harper, handing her a set.

"Thanks," she says.

While Harper ducks into the tent, I look around, realizing we'll have to take turns changing in there. When she emerges a few minutes later, I can't help but think she's completely adorable.

Harper tucks her hair behind her ear and hangs her wet suit over the back of her chair to let it dry out.

"You look cute." The words pop out before I can stop myself.

She looks down at herself, the baggy shorts falling all the way down to her knees even after she's rolled them a couple of times. The T-shirt swallows her, the collar of it so wide it exposes her clavicle.

"Oh, thank you," she says, pointing to the tent. "Your turn."

I duck into the tent and quickly change, careful not to get our sleeping bags wet. When I step out, Harper's facing the lake, her arms wrapped around her middle, staring out into the darkness.

"Hey, twin," I say, approaching her.

She looks back at me, noticing my matching outfit and giggling. "Hey, yourself."

"What are you thinking?"

"It's just so peaceful here," she says, inhaling deeply. Then she exhales, dropping her shoulders.

I nod, looking out to where her line of sight falls. The sky and the water disappear into each other, into the blackness. I rub the scruff on my chin and yawn.

"Are you ready for sleeping bags?" she asks.

I chuckle, stretching my arms over my head. "I could be convinced, as long as our pillow talk is interesting."

Harper's throat works up and down as she presses her lips together. I'm sure she's giving my remark some thought. "Okay," she finally says. "But I get two passes for things I don't want to answer. Same goes for you."

"I can live with that."

We make our way to the tent and I let her crawl in first. Harper gets in her bag and zips it up to her chest, nestling against her pillow. She's as close to the wall of the tent as she can get, clearly nervous about sharing the space.

I crawl in my own bag after her, slipping in and flipping it up to my waist, but I don't zip it. I lie back on my pillow, tucking one arm underneath my head and making zero effort to hug my side of the tent. Turning to my side to face her, I can't help but notice she's trying to hold perfectly still. "So, Harper, got any questions for me? Or should I go first?"

"How many sexual partners have you had?" she asks, not even hesitating.

I shake my head. *Wow.* She had that one locked and loaded. "Uh, I don't know exactly. Why?"

"I'm just trying to establish a baseline so I know what to expect when I go on actual dates," she says. "What's an average person's number?"

"Uh, well, first, I don't think you need to ask the people you date that question. And second, is it important criteria to you?"

Harper seems to give it some thought, her top teeth sinking into her bottom lip. "I guess it's not important. But I've only been with one person and I know that's probably not typical so I was just curious what their...level of experience might be, I guess."

Ohhhhhh, okay, okay. I see where she's going with this. "So you're afraid you might not be...as good?"

"Maybe? Oh my god, why am I telling you this?" Harper puts her hand over her face, attempting to hide her reddening cheeks.

I reach for her wrist, gently pulling it down. "There's nothing to be ashamed of. I'm glad you can talk to me about this stuff," I offer, trying to reassure her.

"Did you know I've only ever kissed him, too?" she says.

Whoa. Okay, that's intense. I can't even imagine what that's like. I mean, I know I was a late bloomer, but after I did, I went pretty wild for a second. "That's okay too."

Harper looks over at me, her eyes rolling back a little. "Somehow I don't think going on a date and being like, 'Hey, did you know you're only the second guy I've ever kissed?' is gonna go over well."

I inhale, thinking about how I would feel on a date if a woman told me that. I don't think it would matter to me. I mean, it doesn't now. Then again, we're just friends so the information is of no consequence. "Well, would it help if you could say you've kissed two guys and they would be lucky number three?"

Harper narrows her eyes at me, then they grow wide. "You mean you?" Her voice takes on a tone of disbelief.

"Um, well I am a man. With lips."

"No way. That's too weird," she says.

Ouch. Okay. Try not to be wounded, Jensen. "What exactly is weird about my lips?"

"Nothing. I just mean it would be weird with you—kissing you. I don't think we should do that. Do you?"

I shrug, trying to keep my cool. In theory, it's not a big deal. Just two people kissing. "It's just a kiss, Harper. It doesn't have to mean anything. Just a notch on your belt and then you can walk with the confidence of having kissed multiple guys."

She turns on her side toward me, studying my face as if she's finally starting to consider my offer. Her eyes are still narrowed. "And you think it'd be that simple?"

"Yeah, why not?" I say, shrugging again.

"Okay," she says. "Let's do it."

HARPER

JENSEN IS STARING at me and my heart is pounding so hard, I'm pretty sure he can hear it in this tiny tent. His eyes float from my mine down to my mouth and then stop there, watching me chew on my bottom lip.

"Close your eyes," he says.

Oh god, oh god, oh god.. Despite the panic in my throat, I do as he instructs, gently pressing my eyelids shut. I can feel him shift closer, his hot breath on my skin. He sweeps his thumbs across my lips and it's electric. Warmth runs over me. And I mean it runs...*everywhere*. He might be doing it simply to get me to stop chewing my lip, but the way the rough pad of his thumb feels across my soft lips is intoxicating.

His hand moves across my jaw, resting at the base and tangling into my hair as he cups my face. *Oh god, oh god, oh god. This is it.* I part my lips a fraction, unsure what sort of kiss to prepare for. His breath feels closer now, and if I had to guess, his lips aren't far from mine. I curl my toes, attempting to suppress all my nervous energy.

"Open your eyes," he whispers.

When I do, Jensen's face is only an inch from mine. I swallow, unable to move or breathe or think.

"I'm going to kiss you now, Harper." And then he does. He pulls me closer, snaking his hand further into my hair. His lips press against mine, softly at first and then harder.

To my surprise, I don't hesitate to kiss him back. I lean in, pressing back against him. I part my lips and his tongue is in my mouth, lapping against mine. Everything is so fuzzy. I reach for him, pulling at the collar of his shirt.

His other arm comes around my back, pulling me flush against his body. And what a hard, delicious body it is. I press my hands against his chest and stomach, feeling the definition of his muscles through the thin fabric. My fingers make my way up over his shoulder and into his hair.

He leans his body into me until he's practically lying over me, his elbows resting on either side of me, supporting most of his weight as I try to pull him down closer to me. His knee presses against the outside of my sleeping bag and forces my thighs open. My lungs fill with air so rapidly, I feel like I might pass out. Jensen's tongue moves inside my mouth with such hunger, so fervent. I bite his bottom lip, sucking it into my mouth. He inhales sharply and pulls away.

"What?" I manage, breathless.

"Nothing, nothing, I just didn't expect that," he says.

"Is it bad?"

"God no," he says, clearing his throat. As if finally realizing he's halfway on top of me, he smooths his hair back and pulls away. *But, but…nooooooo.*

"You stopped."

"Uh, yeah. Probably don't want to get too carried away, you know?" He settles back into his sleeping bag space.

But, but…kissing. "Right," I whisper. "Yes." My fingers run over my swollen mouth. Between the intensity of the kiss, his teeth, and the scruff of his face, my lips feel wounded. Not that I'm complaining. It's the best kind of ache.

Charles never kissed like that. Ever. Not even in the beginning. I don't ever remember that kind of heat between us.

I chance a look at Jensen from the corner of my eye and he's now the one chewing on his bottom lip. *Give it to me; I'll chew it. Okay, no. Shut up.*

"Not that I have a lot to compare that to, but you're a good kisser," I admit.

"Thanks," he says. "And, while I won't give you an exact number, I do happen to have some comparisons. And you're a good kisser, too. So, you shouldn't be worried."

"I am?"

"Definitely," he confirms.

I look up at the tent, a little relieved to know this might not be something I need to worry about. But less relieved about how I can't stop thinking I wouldn't mind making out with Jensen some more. I know people have friends with benefits, but can that benefit just be kissing? Make out buddies? Is that a thing? Maybe I'll Google it tomorrow. And if he's that good at kissing, how good is he at other stuff? What else can he do with his mouth? *Oh my god. I didn't just think that.*

I press my eyes shut, attempting to push those kinds of thoughts of Jensen way, way down. In truth, he's been very nice to me. A good friend. Albeit, this is a very unconventional friendship. But I don't want to mess it up. I'll just have to settle for this one perfect kiss on this one perfect date I've always wanted. This is turning into some sort of sappy twilight zone. I swear to god.

"Hey, Harper," Jensen whispers, cutting into my thoughts.

"Yeah?"

"Remember how I said I hate sleeping alone when we first started playing the game?" he asks.

"I remember."

"Thanks for being here, for making it possible not to sleep alone tonight," he says. "And sorry if I spoon you in my sleep."

I laugh. Over the past few days, I've found it's Jensen's pattern to say something incredibly genuine and follow it up with something sort of silly. Perhaps it's some kind of defense mechanism.

"No problem, on both counts." Who knows, getting spooned might be nice. I tend to get cold at night. I could always use the extra body heat.

"Goodnight, Harper," he says, exhaling my name like a long sigh.

"Goodnight, Jensen," I whisper.

Sometime after that, I hear the faintest snore coming from him. Not so loud it's annoying or disruptive but just enough to know he's asleep. I look over at his face, attempting to see any of it in the darkness. I can only make out the faintest silhouette.

But it's a really beautiful silhouette. I fall asleep, studying the slope of his nose, the slant of his forehead, and the way his chin dips to his throat.

HARPER

MAYBE I'M DREAMING. Light flickers behind my eyelids and I don't know if it's real. The faint sound of a guitar strumming fills my ears. A muffled voice hums a melody, sings a few lines of a familiar song under their breath. They sound far away. Not too far, but not next to me either.

I blink my eyes open. The light blue fabric of the tent wall is so close to my face, I snap back, startled. Then I turn, realizing Jensen isn't in the tent. I hear more strumming, a voice growing louder as they sing. *Is that Jensen?*

Straining my ears as I sit up, I remember he must still have his guitar with him from yesterday. I can't be sure, but his voice sounds like it's traveling from somewhere around the campfire.

What time is it? How long has he been awake? So many questions as I pat for my shoes at the end of the sleeping bag, still listening to his loverly voice. It's deep and warm with just a hint of rasp. So surprising. I know he said he sang but I didn't expect it to be so well.

I peek my head out from the tent and see his back is to me. He's leaned over the guitar in his lap, looking at something on his phone and placing his hands on the strings of the guitar. His voice starts again, and I realize it's Lyla and Gentry's wedding song. Presumably, he's looking down at it on his phone and attempting to learn it.

I gently step the rest of the way out of the tent, trying my best not to disrupt him. I'm halfway to him before I realize I'm practically sneaking up on him and now I'm not sure how to announce myself without startling him or being obvious. "Good morning," I say, a little too abruptly.

Jensen jerks toward me. "Jesus, are you part ninja?" He laughs.

"Sorry, I was just listening to you play and didn't want to interrupt. You have a beautiful voice." *And face. And mouth. I like your mouth. Oh, wow. Okay, Harper.*

"Thanks. Just trying to learn this song," he says. "Want some breakfast before we head back in a bit?"

"Sure."

Jensen reaches into one of the coolers and pulls out sausage links and pancake mix. He weaves the links onto the spears from last night and hands them to me, then grabs a skillet and sets it in the edge of the fire. "You roast the breakfast weenies," he says. "I'll make the breakfast buns."

"Breakfast hot dogs?" I ask.

"Basically. And instead of ketchup, I have syrup. Pretty brilliant, huh?"

I have to admit, it is. I give him my most approving nod and focus my attention on the sausages.

"So, about last night," he says. *Oh god. Oh no.* "I know I woke up a few times spooning you. I don't know if you noticed. I'm sorry about that. You're just very warm, and small. So you fit very well."

I giggle until my giggle turns into a full-blown laugh so loud he's staring at me. "God, I thought you were about to say something about the kissing. Now I find out you spooned me all night. This is getting so weird," I say, still laughing.

Jensen rubs the back of his neck. "I guess it is a little weird, huh?"

"You think?"

"We can be less weird friends if you want?" he says, offering up his best attempt to steer this shipwreck waiting to happen away from the iceberg.

I tilt my head back and forth, wondering if that would even be fun, if that would even feel like friendship at this point. I guess becoming used to this hasn't exactly helped. Can I be friends with Jensen the way I'm friends with Gentry? I inwardly snarl my lip. That doesn't seem right. But maybe what's best isn't always what's right. Is that a thing?

"Maybe it's best?" I question back.

"Maybe. I guess we can't let this get too muddy," he says.

"Time for me to spread my wings. Prepare to fly."

"Isn't that a Mariah Carey song?" he asks, starting to laugh at me.

"Her song is about butterflies. I'm clearly talking about dating." I giggle again, trying to press my lips together into a serious straight line.

"Whatever you say." He laughs.

We finish cooking and eating breakfast, then we pack everything up, which admittedly is the worst part of camping. It's all fun and games when you're unpacking to set up camp. Packing up camp to leave, however, just really sucks. With a little effort, and maybe some whining on my part, we get it done and hop into the truck.

I grab my phone to check my messages. I didn't even realize I left it in here until this morning. I must have been having a pretty good time to not even think about checking it. Lyla sent me three texts, all of which suggest I should wear the lingerie and then follow up with how my silence must be a good thing. There's one text from Gentry telling me to ignore Lyla and do what I want. And then I see three messages from Steve.

We've been messaging on and off since I messaged him back. It's been going pretty well.

I open those first, choosing to ignore my sister for the time being.

STEVE

Hey, would you maybe want to do something tomorrow night?

No pressure if you're busy.

Oh god, am I being ghosted?

I laugh at both his persistence and mini panic attack. It definitely feels like something I would do.

> Hey! Sorry, I was just a little tied up with something. I have a wedding related event today, but I think I can be free later. Play it by ear?

"Wow, you prepare to fly fast," Jensen says, laughing and rubbing his neck.

I look up to see him glancing over at me, and he nods toward my phone. I put it down in my lap. "It's the same guy," I tell him.

"Wait. Steve?" he asks in disbelief.

"Yeah, we've been messaging on and off."

"Uh, okay," he says.

"What?"

"Nothing. I'm just surprised, that's all," he says, gripping his hands tighter on the wheel.

"He wants to know if I'm free tonight but I don't know if the event will be over in time. So I said maybe."

"Tonight? Wow, that's fast." He adjusts his position in the driver's seat.

"It is?"

"Well, I mean, we just kissed last night. Don't you need a cooling off period?"

"Right, but that wasn't real," I remind him. "It was just practice."

"Right," he says. His jaw flexes as he stares forward.

And now I'm not sure what to say or do. Is he mad? No, that can't be right. Maybe he just genuinely thinks I deserve better than a Steve? Maybe he really feels like I'm moving too fast? Am I? Hell, I don't know how all this works.

The last time I did this, I had a curfew and zero need for a bra. I don't know what it's like now. Too fast, too slow. I know I'm tired of sulking and crying about Charles. I know I'm over my marriage. I know I'm ready to move on. I think. And maybe it won't be love, but eventually, maybe I'll find it again. But until then, I want to have fun. I want adventures. I want to make out and go camping and dancing and take cooking classes and travel. I want to go see the ocean and swim with turtles.

And I don't want to do it alone.

I want a partner in crime. I'm ready for that.

I'm ready for something not even Charles gave me.

JENSEN

FIRST OF ALL, I'm not jealous. That's not what this is, okay? I dropped Harper back off at the main house and headed back to the cabin and found Gentry, who immediately needed my help with the wedding tent setup while the women did their bridal luncheon thing.

And I am not jealous. I keep reminding myself of this as we push support poles into place and hammer stakes but really, I don't even need reminding because Jensen Reed? Not a jealous guy. Besides…*Steve? Really?*

"You okay, man?" Gentry asks, cutting into my fourth reminder.

"Yeah," I say. "Just thinking."

"You wanna talk about it?" he asks.

Gentry's a good guy. But he's on Harper's side. I'm not sure he can be trusted with my side of things. Though I don't have anyone else to talk to here. I could text one of the few close friends I have but we're all so scattered and on different schedules, it's nearly impossible to sync up.

I consider it for several more seconds and decide to risk it. "It's just…Harper, okay? She might be going on a date tonight, apparently."

"And that bothers you?" he asks.

"No. Yes. No. Maybe."

"Well, that's clear." He laughs.

"I mean, no. It shouldn't. We're friends. But it does. Steve. His name is Steve. That's not better than *Charles*. You know what I mean?"

"So you don't approve of his name?"

"No, I don't."

"But it would be okay if he had a different name?"

"No. Yes. Maybe."

"Again, so clear," he says, hammering another stake into the ground and tying a rope around it.

"I'm just saying, we spent last night together. Maybe give yourself a breather before the next date," I say.

"Was last night a date?"

"Well, yeah. Maybe not a real one. But we kissed."

"So it wasn't a date, but you kissed?" Gentry asks, stopping and squinting. I can tell he's trying desperately to understand what the hell I'm saying and I'm not even sure I do.

"Right. But it's like it meant nothing to her."

"Was it supposed to?"

Crap. Double crap. I finish hammering the stake into place and stand. I guess it wasn't—isn't. I press my eyes shut. I can't very well go and press the issue and get her to feel something or have it mean something to her when I leave soon. Because then what? That's not fair. Besides, what would it mean? A fling? No way. She's better than that. I could never do that to her.

Okay but wait. Thinking all of this means...I would want something to happen. Or I *do* want something to happen and I'm just not acting on it for the sake of being decent. Is that what's happening right now? I press the palms of my hands to my eye sockets. My train of thought is making my brain hurt.

I push it all away and focus on the mindless work of this damn wedding tent. Why is this thing so fucking big, anyway? We finish placing the last support poles and raise the canopy. White sheer fabric drapes over the entire massive expanse. I step inside. Okay, yeah. This was worth it. Southerners really know how to do this.

Gentry steps in next to me and looks around, inhaling a big breath with his hands in his front pockets. "Why don't you just tell her you like her?"

"What?"

"You do, don't you?"

"I don't know," I admit.

"Then I guess you can lie to yourself long enough for Steve to win her over," he says, before walking back out of the tent.

Ugh. Steve. The faceless bane of my existence. Probably works in finance or accounting. *Ugh.* Or worse, what if he's like Gentry? Some fucking Southern gentleman cowboy rancher man? *Double Ugh.* Must find out what I'm dealing with.

Crap. Excuse me, Jensen? It would appear you fucking like Harper. At the very least, I'm attracted to her. Or whatever. *Awesome.* I should find her. I should definitely go find her before this lunch thing kicks off.

I run back toward the main house where they've set up tables and chairs for the event. Harper told me something like thirty women were coming. Aunts, cousins, old high school friends, people from their grandparents' church. It all sounds so exhausting to me just thinking about it. I round the corner of the barn and see a crowd gathered in the yard right next to the house. Their laughter is filling the air and it appears the party is already in full swing. I'm too late. I try to step a little closer to see if I can catch a glimpse of Harper.

Shielding my eyes with my hand, I roll up on the front of my feet, attempting to peer over heads and through the crowd like somehow these two actions give me X-ray vision. I catch sight of her long, blonde hair flowing behind her. She's standing with her back toward me, leaning against a table, and appears to be in conversation with someone. I pull my phone from my pocket and shoot her a text, then wait to see if she pulls it from her pocket, but nothing. Maybe she doesn't have it on her.

I'm not going to be the one guy that causes a scene and goes walking into lady territory. No way. That's too much. I'll just have to wait. I can do that. Granted, it might be impatiently.

I tuck my phone back in and head back toward the cabin. A guitar and a beer await me.

I have a song to learn.

HARPER

THESE OLD LADIES from Nan and Paw's church are insane. Like certifiably. And they drink more than most men I know. They don't want to sip on wine, either. Oh, no. They want the hard stuff.

Annette, the organ player, comes up to get her third red cup of peach moonshine and cocks me a sideways smile. "You're so young and pretty. Why aren't you out getting into trouble?" she slurs.

"Who would serve you your moonshine, then?" I laugh.

Annette hiccups. "Good point." She turns back, laughing, and then carries on with the others.

At least they all brought presents. Lyla and I don't know half these people. They're here by extension. A courtesy. It's the way of the South. I don't understand it; I just live it.

I watch Lyla as she parts the crowd, nodding and smiling and trading small talk with each woman here. She looks dreadfully uncomfortable as she attempts to make her way over to me. She presses through the last few people and exhales.

"Why don't I remember it being like this with your wedding?" she asks.

"Because you spent the entire time half-drunk, asking me if I wanted to run away, and the other half making out with Charles's best man Toby," I remind her, laughing.

"Oh god, I forgot about Toby," she says. "He wasn't even good at kissing."

I clear my throat. The mention of kissing sends me into a panic, as if the mere mention of it means she knows. "Speaking of kissing..."

"Kissing? What about it?" she asks.

"Nothing. Well, something." I shift my weight from one foot to the other and back again and before I realize it, I'm wringing my hands.

"What?"

"I kissed Jensen. Actually, he kissed me. We kissed." I breathe out as fast as I can.

"Oh my god, when?" she says, her voice rising.

"Shh," I say. "Last night."

"And then what?"

"Nothing. We went to sleep."

"Wait, what?" she asks, clearly confused.

"I told him I only ever kissed Charles so we kissed and then we went to sleep." I can tell she's as confused about it as I am.

"Well, did you like it?"

I drift off for a second, recalling his lips pressed against mine, the way his tongue flicked and lapped against mine. If I think hard enough, I can still feel the pressure of his hands against my back and warmth spreads all the way down to my—

"Well?" she asks.

"Yes," I admit, the skin across my chest warm.

"And him?"

"I think he did." I shrug. "I didn't exactly ask him."

Lyla crosses her arms across her chest, eyeing me. "You like him, don't you?"

"What? No. Don't be absurd. We're just friends. He's being nice, helping me figure out how to even talk to guys, flirt. You forget, Lyla, that I don't know shit about shit."

"And now you're kissing." She narrows her eyes.

"Imagine going on a real date. Imagine trying to date after divorce and only ever having kissed or slept with one man," I say, the last part of my statement turning into a whisper. I don't exactly want to announce this to the crowd around us.

Lyla nods, considering my words. "That's fair."

I nod too, raising my eyebrows in that universal told-you way. Perhaps she understands a little better, but she'll never fully understand where I'm coming from. With that in mind, I don't think she exactly has the right to judge my actions or the way I'm trying to handle this.

"So, are you gonna try to go on real dates?" she asks.

"This guy Steve asked me on one for tonight, but I told him it depends on when this wraps up. He's from the dating app," I say.

"Oh my god, Harper. If you have to leave this early, then do it."

"No way. He can wait. What do people say? Chicks before dicks," I say, laughing.

"That's fair." She laughs. "I'm just saying, if you want."

"Maybe I will just drink and then drunk text him later," I tease.

Lyla raises her glass up, clinking it against mine. "I'll drink to that," she says, and we slam back our moonshine together.

Maybe I can't go meet up with Steve. Maybe I don't even want to just yet. But I can certainly step this whole texting thing up, get a little flirty. I can be risky or sexy or whatever.

As long as Steve-o doesn't flash his dick at me via textual romancing, I'm good. My phone is a no-dick-pic zone. I take another shot of moonshine and think better of a third before having more food. This is a marathon, not a fucking sprint.

Looking through the crowd, I realize there are a lot of people between me and the table full of food. I'll just wait a minute. I sit and pull out my phone, noticing I have a message from Jensen.

JENSEN

Save me some of that moonshine!

Shaking my head, I giggle and look at how much is left. Plenty as long as I can keep Annette away.

I will save you some!

JENSEN

Good! Are you going on your date later?

Probably not. Just gonna brush up on my text flirting.

A text bubble pops up and then disappears and then pops up and disappears again. I go to text Steve, letting him know I can't make it but I'll text him later.

JENSEN

Maybe I can come by for another grilled cheese and pickles later?

I say sure and then tuck my phone in my pocket and stand, ready to brave the people to get my hands on some rolls and mac and cheese.

After a few steps, I realize I'm a little tipsy for sure. I'm definitely swaying.

Like a sunflower.

I smile at the thought.

HARPER

THE CEILING of my room is spinning a little, so I throw one foot over the edge of the bed and plant it on the floor to try to get it to stop. Maybe I had one too many moonshines. All the ladies left about an hour ago and I've been trying to sober up enough to use my phone ever since.

I hold it above my face and it's like I have two phones. I try closing one eye and it helps enough to navigate to Steve's messages.

> STEVE
> How did it go?
>
> Hope you had fun!

See. He's nice. He's a sweet guy. I attempt a reply, clicking and erasing and clicking more.

> It wass good time. Send me picc.

Close enough.

A text comes in from Jensen as I wait for Steve's reply. Maybe it will be a shirtless photo. He looks like he could have an okay chest. I navigate to Jensen's messages.

> **JENSEN**
> You okay?

> I'm drunnk

> **JENSEN**
> You need help?

I stick my tongue out, somehow believing that will help my texting capabilities.

> Imm ok juss trying too flirt. Send me pic

My hands slip, and the next thing I know, my phone flips sideways and falls right out of my hands, hitting me in the face. "Fuck."

Relieved no one was around to see that, I re-adjust my phone, trying to hold it in an angle so it's not directly above me. Noticing Steve replied, I navigate back to his messages and open the image. Steve has what we'll call curly hair. Not totally curly, though. It's sort of wavy and dark. I can't say I like how it's styled but it's not bald. I shrug. He did send a shirtless picture like I was hoping, but it's a little lackluster. He's pale. Really pale. I can't exactly make out a lot of muscle definition but maybe it's just the angle and lighting. I still have hope. I think his smile is supposed to be sexy but it's not. *Ugh.* This is going to have to do.

A notification from Jensen comes in and I click on it, flipping back to his messages. *Oh my.* He's shirtless too. He's also not pale, nor does he lack muscle definition. He's just so deliciously perfect, from Adam's apple to navel. It's not like I didn't see it while we were camping. How could I forget the swimming, the water dripping down his rippled muscles? His hair is a tousled mess, partially wet, like maybe he just got out of the shower. His smirk is so genuine and natural.

Let's be logical here, Harper. You're probably going to sleep with maybe a couple of guys before you find someone. So why would you sleep with Steve when you can sleep with Jensen? Jensen is much...

better looking. Steve isn't the one. I know that for sure. Practice is practice. I shrug again. *Yes, okay, new plan.*

> Come ovverr

Throwing my phone down beside me, I close my eyes and wait. This is a good idea. *Okay, don't think about it. Just focus on something else. If you think about it too long, you'll chicken out.*

Should I take my clothes off? No, I'll wait. He can take them off.

Maybe I should put more comfortable ones on. Or sexier ones on. I sit up, wondering if I even have anything sexy.

Making my way over to my dresser, I pull open the top drawers and rifle through my panties and bras. Nothing here screams, "Let's have sex!" *Oh wait!* The lingerie nightgown in my bag from camping. *Yes.*

Whirling around to the chair where the bag is, I lose my footing and stumble, catching myself on the footboard of my bed. I reach for the bag, pulling it onto the floor in front of me. I slowly ease myself down onto the floor and search the bag for the garment Lyla tucked in. A mess of black strings and lace spills out. *Okay, this is fine. I can do this.* I lie back on the floor, unbuttoning my pants and shimmying out of them. Sitting up, I try to pull my shirt over my head and my arms get caught in the sleeves. My arms are like jello as I try to pull and tug and shimmy it up my shoulders but sure enough, it's up over my face when I hear my door open.

"Harper?"

Jensen's voice hits my ears through the fabric of my T-shirt, and my hot breath starts to suffocate me in here.

"Help. I'm stuck," I plead. I hear my door shut and if I'm not mistaken, he's attempting to suppress a laugh as he steps closer to me. His hands run down the length of my arms, rolling my shirt down.

"No, I need it off," I say.

His hands stop, reversing their movements and lifting my shirt over my head.

I finally get a look at him and he's staring off, away from me. "What are you doing?" I ask him.

"I'm trying not to look," he says.

"Why?"

"Because you're shirtless."

"It's the same as a bathing suit." I laugh.

"Oh, right."

Looking down, I realize I didn't make it into the lingerie, which is still balled at my feet.

His eyes sweep down, seeing the same pool of lace, and he reaches for it. "Were you...trying to put this on?" he asks, one eyebrow raising.

"Yeah," I say, hiccupping. *Oh great. The hiccups.*

"Why?"

"To be sexy."

"You don't need this to be sexy," he says, shaking his head and smiling.

I look down again. My sports bra is slightly twisted to the side. I've had it for so long, there's a hole right at the elastic. The panties I'm wearing are pink with white polka dots. Not exactly sex panties. Nothing even matches. "Right, I've got so much sexy going on." Sarcasm drips from every slurred word as I sweep my hands down over my body.

Turning to lift myself up, I hear him mumble something that sounds like, "If you only knew," under his breath.

But when I ask him what he said he tells me, "Nothing." Then he helps me sit on the bed and looks around.

"Do you still want to put this on?" he asks, holding up the lace contraption.

"Too late now," I say, throwing my body back on the bed, legs still hanging over the side.

"Okay, I'll find something else," he offers.

"Forget it. You've already seen me, doesn't matter now," I slur. I look up out of one open eye and Jensen's standing there, his hands in his pockets, eyes skimming the room. "Sit down, silly."

He sits on the bed but not close enough that I can easily reach out and touch him. I have to stretch and lean just to put my fingertips on him.

"Maybe I should get your sister," he says.

"I don't want my sister. I want you." I roll my body toward him and even through glossy eyes, I watch him swallow as his eyes sweep over my body. "Just lie with me."

I reach my hand out for him, but every move he takes is measured. He slowly leans back, propping an elbow up underneath him. We're face to face now and if I scoot a little closer, I can kiss him again.

"Does this mean we aren't having grilled cheese with pickles as promised?" he asks.

"Oh man, that sounds so good right now. I can make it to the kitchen, I think." I attempt to lift myself up, but Jensen pats me back down into place.

Laughing, he says, "Even if you could make it down there, I think you'd burn them. We can have them tomorrow."

Silence settles over us after the laughter subsides and I can feel the heat now. "I know what we can do instead of eat sandwiches," I say.

"What?" he asks.

I silently reach for the collar of his shirt, pulling him closer to me. His lips part as he scoots closer and I fix my eyes on them. I reach up and press mine against his, feeling him exhale against me. His hand, previously in the air and unsure what to do, wraps around me and pulls me closer. I part my lips, and immediately feel his tongue against mine. He sucks on my bottom lip and leans in, pressing his chest to mine so my back falls flat against the bed. His knee parts my legs and I claw at his back as the intensity of his kiss deepens.

Lowering my hands, I feel for the edge of his shirt and tug on it. *Off. This has to come off.* Suddenly desperate to feel the warmth of his skin against my own, I peel it over his head and watch him cast it aside. My hands continue exploring his chest and stomach, his flexed muscles growing rigid under my touch.

Jensen's mouth drops to my neck and I moan in his ear. This causes a reaction in him because his hands fist into the skin on my thigh and into my hair. My hands explore lower still, my thumbs pressing into his hip bones. I feel the edge of his briefs graze my fingertips and a jolt of excitement travels my spine. My fingers slip in against his warm skin and I reach lower. I'm almost to my naughty destination when he grabs my hand.

"Harper, wait. What are you doing?" he asks, breathlessly.

"Let's have sex," I whisper back, leaning up to bite his bottom lip.

He moans and as I release, he presses his lips together, exhaling a long sigh. "I don't think that's a good idea. You've been drinking."

"No, it's fine. I want to." I can practically hear the begging in my own voice.

"You can't even dress yourself, babe," he says, voice low and husky.

Oh. Babe. He called me babe. "I don't need to get dressed. I need to get undressed."

"You can't do that either," he says, laughing.

"Don't laugh. I'm sexy," I huff.

"Yes. You're very sexy. But sloppy drunken sex isn't what you should be having with the second man you've ever have sex with," he says gently.

"I don't need this kind of logic in my life right now." I make another attempt to reach for him, making contact with his hard length outside his pants. *Ope.*

Jensen's head rolls back as he feels me stroke him, and then he starts to shake his head. "No, no, Harper. It's not right."

"Come on. I need it."

Jensen bites his bottom lip and I pout, poking mine out. I can see the wheels turning. All this adrenaline has sobered me up a little.

He leans in close, tossing my hair behind my back before pressing his lips to my ear. "How about a compromise?" he says.

"What?"

"Lie back and lie still," he says, and I do as he commands. The last time this happened, I wasn't disappointed.

I watch Jensen lift his hand, pressing his fingers to the edge of my jaw and caressing them down over my throat. He sinks them down lower to my collarbone and then lightens his touch, trailing his finger-tips over the tops of my breasts. His whole hand melts over me, cupping me and massaging. My back arches instinctively. His face comes closer to my chest and he takes my nipple into his mouth through the thin fabric of my bra, nibbling and sucking at it. Moans escape me without restraint at this point.

He leans up to meet my eyes and his hand continues its decent, down my ribs, around my navel. His thumb presses against my hip as his other fingers slide into the top of my panties, lingering there. He presses kisses against my chin and throat, never taking his eyes from me as his fingers dip lower.

I can't breathe, a feeling of warmth and tingling spreading over my body so intensely. It's the best kind of suffocation. I grip the sheets as I feel his fingers part me, my eyes growing wide and wild. His are hooded, staring at me with a feverish anticipation. He licks his lips, nodding, some sort of silent encouragement to enjoy what's happening.

He strokes against the outside of me over and over again, my body writhing and building. Then, without warning, he sinks them into my center, filling me up. My body shudders and I moan so loudly, I cover my mouth with my own hand. His hand rocks back and forth against me and he leans down, pressing kisses along my cheek. I give him my lips, letting him take me by the mouth.

He pulls back long enough to whisper, "Come for me." Then continues to kiss me as the motion of his hand becomes quicker and more intense.

My body responds, arching as a delicious knot builds inside me. Then, fireworks. Wonderful, dirty, sexy fireworks from the tips of my curling toes to my clenched hands to my lips pressed to Jensen. Everywhere is warm and fluttering.

He lies back, pulling his hand away and cradling me in the crook of his arm. I try to right my erratic breathing as I wallow in the aftershock.

"Are you okay?" he asks.

"More than." I shut my eyes and relax into him, letting my body melt.

"Maybe I should go. Let you rest," he says.

"No, please don't," I say. "Let's just sleep here."

Jensen pulls me up onto the bed, turning us so our heads are on the pillows. He wraps his arms around me, folding me into his big body. "You make a great little spoon."

"Only because you make a great big spoon." I lace my fingers into his, holding his arm and sometime after that, I drift to sleep, still a little drunk. On alcohol or Jensen, I'm not sure.

Perhaps, a little of both.

JENSEN

FALLING asleep last night was difficult for the same reasons it was amazing. I held Harper, pulled her closer to me, and desperately wanted to sink into sleep. But my body, my body was very aware of her presence. It was overflowing with desire and about seventeen percent of me regretted not having sex with her when she offered it up. The rest of me—the better part of me—knew it would have been a shit move.

Now I lie here as the morning sun barely makes a dent through these black curtains, watching her sleep. I don't know if she knows this but she snores, just the tiniest bit. It's so soft it might go unnoticed if you weren't listening for it in the silence.

Ugh. What is happening right now? Why am I watching her sleep like a creep?

I brush a loose strand of silky hair away from her face and loop it over her ear. Harper is definitely going to have a hangover when she wakes up. No doubt about it. That much moonshine would always return with a vengeance. I'll make it easier on her, at the very least. I peel my body from hers, slowly retreating to the edge of the bed to look for my shirt. Surely this house has some breakfast, aspirin, and caffeine in it.

Stepping quietly out of her room, I turn to see Cora staring at me and press my eyes shut.

"Hey there, bub," she says, a wide grin across her lips.

"Sis," I return.

"What are you doing here so early?"

"I slept here."

She gasps. "I knew it!" Cora starts dancing around, and I wave at her to calm down.

"Shh, stop that. She's asleep and for sure gonna wake up hungover. Where's the medicine and food and stuff?"

Cora leads me down the hall to the bathroom, retrieving the aspirin from the medicine cabinet. Then we head downstairs to the kitchen where Nan and Paw are sitting. Learning upon my arrival that that's what literally everyone calls them was a pretty interesting experience. Calling them that myself does nothing to damper the nervous emotions I have about being here and having spent the night in Harper's room.

"Good morning," Cora greets them, and I nod silently, hoping to avoid eye contact.

"Mornin'," Paw says.

Cora crosses to the coffee pot and pours three cups.

"Do you happen to have a tray?" I ask, knowing this will definitely arouse suspicion.

"Harper's gonna need a bit more than coffee this mornin'," Nan says, laughing. *Oh god.* She retrieves a tray, loading it with the coffees, a shot glass full of an unknown liquid, and a plate of giant greasy hash browns with two forks. "Here, dear. This'll help," she says.

She pats my arm and I look at Cora and then Paw, who raises his coffee mug to me as if he's saluting me. I'm not sure I've ever been more mortified in my life.

I turn and slink back up the stairs, unsure if I've been given some sort of blessing or if this is mere entertainment for them. I crack open Harper's door, careful not to make too much noise when I notice she's awake, rubbing her head.

"Oh god," she says.

"Hey there, fish."

"Fish?" she asks.

"Yeah. Because you drank so much."

"Oh my god," she says, pressing her eyes shut.

"I got some stuff for you. A feel-better kit, if you will." I sit on the edge of the bed and she sits up, leaning onto her elbow. Handing her three aspirin, I reach for the coffee.

"No, that," she says, pointing at the shot glass.

"What even is this? Nan gave it to me."

"Hangover remedy. I have no idea what it is but it works. I think it's mostly alcohol and maybe something else. I don't know. I don't ask, I just take it," she says, shooting the liquid back and swallowing the aspirin.

I exchange the shot glass for the mug of coffee as she sits up all the way and I scoot back, putting the tray between us. "Fork, my lady." I extend my hand toward her, and she takes it, immediately digging in.

Honestly, I'm surprised she's this calm at all considering I fondled her all the way to O-town last night. *Oh shit, what if she doesn't remember?*

I shove my fork into the hash browns and take a bite.

"Thank you," she says.

"No problem. Just wanted to nurse the hangover."

"No, I mean for last night. Well, this too. But, I meant for last night," she clarifies.

"It feels weird to say you're welcome for an orgasm," I admit, starting to laugh.

Harper starts choking on her bite of hash brown and slaps me in the arm. *What the hell is happening?* This is officially the strangest fucking friendship ever. *Can this even be classified as a friendship anymore?*

I take a sip of coffee and clear my throat. "Harper?"

"Yeah?"

"What are we doing exactly?"

She exhales, her shoulders sinking a little. After a moment, she says, "I'm not sure. Maybe we should stop the rest of the stuff and just be normal friends. Keep it simple." She sighs, shrugging.

Okay, ouch.

Can't say it didn't suck to hear that. I'm not one of those men with a fragile ego, but come on. I send you spiraling down Orgasm Drive and you put it in reverse and wave goodbye? I thought we were going to be full steam ahead on this thing, not going backwards.

"Right. Got it," I say. "No problem."

Harper shovels more hash browns into her mouth. "Probably for the best, you know?"

"Heard you loud and clear." I nod, not needing any further explanation for what's happening. She's not interested. I get it. She needs a Steve in her life. Maybe a Donald. I'm clearly not what she's looking for.

"Are you okay?" she asks.

"Yeah, I'm good. I'm gonna go, let you get rested up and on with your day. I need to get going too." I stand, rubbing my hands down the front of my pants before I head for the door.

"I'll text you later?" she asks, uncertainty in her voice.

"Yeah, sure." I step out, shut the door behind me, and head downstairs. Stepping out onto the porch, I notice Cora on the swing.

"Hey, bub, how's it going?"

"Terrible. This is terrible."

"Come sit," she says.

I do, and throw my head back in the swing, pressing my eyes shut and pinching the bridge of my nose.

"Tell your big sister what's going on," she says.

"I've just royally fucked up. That's all. I overestimated my ability to be detached. And underestimated Harper's ability to unknowingly charm me and then wound me."

"That's a little dramatic, don't you think?" she asks, giggling.

"No."

"Why don't you just tell her you like her?"

I rub my forehead, realizing how complicated the truth makes things. "Then what? Leave in a week?"

"Oh, little brother. What a pickle."

"Anyway. How's your man stuff going? What's his name again?"

"His name is Alan," she says. "And he's been really nice. We've been texting. He called me. He's sent a few pictures."

"No red flags so far?" I ask, skeptical considering her history.

She shakes her head. "Not that I can detect."

"Good, I'm glad." I sigh, and she leans her head against me. I flop my head over on top of hers. We certainly make a pair.

I head back to the cabin after that, deciding to focus my efforts on learning the song I need to instead of wallowing. I can do that. I can channel my energy into something more productive. No problem. It's basically what I've been doing my entire life.

I scruff my feet against the dirt and rocks, stuffing my hands into my pockets. Maybe I should leave well enough alone. Let her go on her dates with her normal guys—*safe* guys. Let her do whatever she thinks she needs. She knows best.

I leave in a week, anyway. Onto the next city, the next adventure. Alone. Always alone. Is it too much to want a partner for my adventures?

No. The answer is no.

HARPER

I TRY TEXTING Jensen twice but get no response. The mood felt weird when he left a little while ago. After I shook off the rest of the hangover and got a shower, I wanted to check in on him, but he hasn't answered me. *Is he mad at me?*

I think back through the fogginess of last night and wonder if I pushed it too far. Maybe my pathetic attempts at seduction turned practically begging were more unwelcome than I anticipated. I mean, when I said we should cool it this morning, he certainly didn't object. I'll give him some space and try to talk to him about it later.

Meanwhile, Steve sent me eight messages last night. Eight unanswered messages sit in my inbox from him and it feels a little excessive but I ignore his enthusiasm and open them.

> STEVE
>
> Hey you!
>
> You okay?
>
> I'm just sitting around thinking about that date we missed.
>
> Did you like the pic I sent?

Can I have one back?

Did you get drunk and pass out? Lol

ext me later?

Well goodnight

Poor Steve. I just up and disappeared on him. He didn't deserve that. I'll text him back in a little while. I don't have the energy to juggle Jensen's mood and Steve's excitement at the same time. If Jensen has a mood. That's yet to be determined.

Perhaps putting them both out of my mind and focusing on the fact that Lyla's bachelorette party is tomorrow night is what I should be doing. Cora and I are supposed to go shopping for stuff, so we agreed to meet downstairs in ten minutes. While part of me is looking forward to it, the other part is thinking about how I'll be trapped with Jensen's sister all day.

Making my way downstairs, I check my phone again but nothing. I shoot Steve a quick apology and shove it back into my pocket. I need the distraction of shopping at this point. I walk out onto the porch and Cora's already there.

"Ready to go, fish?" she asks.

"Okay, so fish is like a thing?" I laugh.

"Huh?"

"Jensen called me that this morning," I say.

"Oh, yeah. It's a thing where we're from. Or maybe just our family. I don't really know," she says.

I nod in understanding, telling her I'm ready to go.

"Great, let's go buy some penis shaped stuff!" she yells loudly.

I slap my forehead. *Yeah. This should be super fun.*

We travel into the city, knowing full well our small town will not have the necessary items for a bachelorette of the expected magnitude these women are looking for. We park and walk into a place called "Spank It"; lovely, I know. But let's face it, all the really good bachelorette stuff is in the sex shops. We make our way to the aisle with all the penis shaped stuff as Cora requested and we're not disappointed. Dick lollipops, straws, dick beaded necklaces, and anything else you could ever want in the shape of a shlong is here. There's even a cake pan. Yes, a penis cake pan, complete with a ball sac.

"We have to get this!" she yells, picking up the cake pan. *Okay, we are baking now.* "And these!" She picks up the lollipops.

Before I know it, ten of every dick shaped thing is in our basket, plus sashes that say, "BRIDE TO BE" and "BRIDESMAID" and then one for me that says "MAID OF HONOR"; apparently, we have to label ourselves to go dancing and drinking. My stomach rolls at the very thought of drinking again, but I'm not going to be able to avoid it. It's a necessary component of the party shenanigans. And besides, if I'm going to suck on a dick shaped lollipop in front of people, I'm going to need to have drinks in me.

We check out and head back to the car, satisfied with our haul.

"What are you gonna wear tomorrow?" she asks.

"I haven't thought about it. Something normal I guess?"

"Normal? Honey, this is a sexy bachelorette party. We must sex you up. You know what, I'm in charge of your look now," she says.

Oh boy. But I don't bother putting up a fight. Ultimately I will lose, so why waste the energy? "Oh, okay."

"Let's go shopping for an outfit," she says, rubbing her hands together and pointing to the sign of a leather shop.

By the time we finish and are actually in the car on the way back to the farm, I want to die. The outfit she picked for me is so tight I might not be able to breathe. Leather pants? People actually wear these?

"So, what's going on with you and my brother?" she asks abruptly.

"Oh. What do you mean? We're just friends," I say.

"Right. You're about as bad at being *just friends* as I am at trying to get a second date," she says, laughing.

"I guess it's been a little muddy."

"Honey, if it were any muddier, we'd all need boots," she says.

"He's just helping me. I've only been with one guy. He offered to help me get comfortable with a guy other than my ex. That's all," I say, shrugging.

"So you don't like him?" she asks, flipping her long red hair back.

Cora's profile is intimidating. Not because she's trying to intentionally intimidate me, but because she's just so striking. The light freckles on her face are so naturally gorgeous and she embraces them, choosing not to cake on foundation and cover them. She seems so confident in her skin, so sure of herself. It's hard to believe she has trouble dating. I'll have to take everyone's word for it.

"I think he's nice. And really good looking. But I'm not sure I can really like him. I mean, he leaves soon."

"What does that have to do with anything?" she asks, as if his leaving is inconsequential.

"Well, he'll be gone and then what?"

"Go with him?" she tries.

"I'm sorry, what?"

"Oh, stop acting like you couldn't or like it's such a radical idea," she scoffs. "The fact is, you're both adults. You can do what you want. And Lyla told me you've never traveled. Hell, that's all he does. Travel with him. Do something you like to do along the way."

"I don't even know what I like to do," I admit.

"Lyla said you used to take pictures. Why don't you do that anymore?"

"I'm not sure. I just sort of stopped."

"Well, get out your damn camera and start again. Think about it. Listen, my brother, I love him, and he's happy enough. He likes his life enough. But I know he's lonely," she says.

"He is?"

"We all crave connection, Harper. We all want that person, the one person we can share something with. I know he wants it the same as any of us," she says.

"I don't think he likes me like that. He's been nice, but the help he's given me has been clinical, I think. Or at least that's how I read it. He's never said anything."

"Listen, I take no pleasure in saying this, but these walls are thin, and I don't think my brother ran the bases without being attracted to you." She laughs.

"Ran the bases?" I ask.

Cora raises her eyebrows at me, giving me a knowing look.

"Oh my god, no. We didn't have sex."

"Well, whatever he did to you, you seemed to enjoy it," she hints.

I slap my forehead, running my hand down my face and trying hard to suppress the oncoming heat filling my cheeks and chest. "He was very clear from the start that he was only helping me so I wouldn't seem like an idiot when I dated for real."

"Just think about it," she says, letting the car grow quiet for the rest of the ride back.

Therefore, I'm forced to think about it.

The truth is, I'm not good enough for Jensen. I'm plain, living in small-town nowhere, and divorced. Jensen is lively and beautiful and successful. He's a total catch. Any woman would be lucky to have him. So asking me if I like him is a silly question. Who wouldn't like someone like Jensen? But liking someone and being able to do something about it are two different things. That's decided.

I pull my phone from my pocket, sixty-two percent sure I'm making the right decision.

STEVE

No worries about last night!

Are you free tonight?

STEVE

Yeah, you wanna get dinner?

Sure, let me know where to meet you.

I slip my phone back into my pocket, careful not to reveal what I've done to Cora. Besides, I still didn't have any returned texts from Jensen, so how interested could he really be?

We pull onto the farm and collect the penis stuff, careful to hide it all from Lyla. I stash it in my room along with the outfit Cora selected for me. Then, I start getting ready for my date with Steve.

Yes, focus. Steve is nice, seems excited to meet you, has a decent job, is mildly attractive. Steve will do fine for a post-divorce first-date experience. Except maybe I'm supposed to count Jensen as that? I don't even know anymore.

I finish getting ready and check myself out in the mirror. Not wanting to go too over the top, I chose a simple maxi style dress, which hugs the top of my torso nicely and then flares from just the right curves. I apply light makeup and finish the look with a few jewelry pieces, then curl the ends of my hair into soft waves. This will do nicely, I decide.

Grabbing my clutch, I make my way downstairs and head for my car.

I still have time to turn this day around, to make it suck a little less.

HARPER

THIS IS ACTUALLY GOING BETTER than I expected. Steve held the door open for me, recommended a wine to pair with the menu, and even recommended his favorite dishes to me. Steve is shaping up to be pretty good, indeed. This may have actually been an excellent idea.

I read over my menu as Steve explains his job in more detail. Something about banking and loans and he drones on about it but I don't mind. He seems passionate about it.

"That's fascinating," I say, pretending to have heard the last few bits.

"It's okay," he says. "Pays the bills."

I appreciate his modesty. Points in the positive column for Steve. "I don't do anything quite as fancy on the farm, but I always have fresh air and every day is a little different," I offer, hoping it doesn't sound as lame as it feels.

"I would love to come out there. I've been meaning to but haven't had the chance," he says.

"You definitely should."

"Would you give me a personal tour?" he asks, his gaze meeting mine.

Okay, Steve, not too bad. Smooth, pretty smooth. "I'm sure that can be arranged." I laugh.

"What day is best?" he asks.

"Oh, um...this week is busy with my sister's wedding, so—"

"Oh, right. You mentioned that. How's that going?" he asks.

I get into the details of the wedding plans and upcoming bachelorette party, appreciating what appears to be his genuine interest in the topic. More points for Steve. Maybe this whole ordeal doesn't have to be so terrible.

"Wow. Sounds like you have your hands full. You need any help, just let me know. I'd love to help if I can," he offers.

Oh, Steve. Where in the white knight have you been? "Really?"

"Yeah, I'm your guy," he says, smiling. "Do you have a date?"

"Technically yes but it's not a real one," I answer honestly.

"Not a real one?" He laughs.

"Just a numbers game."

"Ahh," he says. "What a shame."

Honestly, I don't know what I was working myself into a frenzy over. This is pretty easy so far. Of course, it's just talking. Who knows how anything else will go.

After the waitress takes our orders, we settle into easy conversation, both of us exchanging information and questions. There's no lull, even when our food comes or as we begin to eat. Each bite of food is punctuated with an exchange and everything feels...nice.

"Would you like another drink before we go?" he asks.

I look down at my empty glass, weighing the question.

"I'll be honest, Harper," he says. "I know once we leave, the date is over. And I don't want it to end just yet."

Ugh. Break me down, Steve. Break me right down. "Okay, yeah. Let's have one more," I say. Why not? I can be the woman who has one more.

Our drinks come and we sip them slowly, laughing and talking. My stomach flutters as I think ahead to the possibility of a goodnight kiss or embrace of some kind. I look down at my drink and realize there's only one sip left. After I down it, Steve calls for the check and pays, insisting we don't split it.

He walks me to my car, guiding me by the small of my back. He's not as tall as I would like, only just slightly taller than I am. I'm not tall to begin with, so that's pretty short for a man. But whatever, it works. He's nice. Everything else has been very delightful. *Okay, Harper, are you describing chocolate or a date?*

We stop just shy of my car and I stand there, clutching my purse in front of me, unsure what else to do.

"Well, I had a great time," he says.

"Me, too. Thank you so much for dinner."

"Of course," he says. "So um, would you want to do this again sometime?"

"Yeah, I think so." I smile. "That would be nice."

"Great. Text me when you get home so I know you made it, okay?"

I nod as Steve's hand comes up to my face and he brushes a length of hair behind my ear. He sweeps his finger down my jaw and tugs my chin toward him. *Oh my god. Okay, don't panic. He's going to kiss you, Harper.*

Steve leans toward me, his lips beginning to pucker, and he slowly presses them against mine. And it's...okay. He presses harder, attempting to work his tongue into my mouth but only gets about halfway in, suddenly pulling back and breaking the kiss. "Wow," he says. "You're a really good kisser."

I don't know how he would know that. We barely got started.

Excuse me, Steve, but my half-kissed lips are still waiting for the rest of whatever that was.

"Oh, thank you," I say, because it's all I can manage. I can't lie and say he is too. Because it was just...*okay.* His lips were sort of rough, like maybe he needed chapstick. They weren't warm, either. I felt no electricity or flutters anywhere in my body. That can't be good.

Fuck, fuck, fuck. Wait, calm down, Harper. Sometimes first kisses aren't all fireworks and awesome. Sometimes people are nervous, trying too hard to concentrate. I've seen enough romcoms to know that much. Yes, we were just nervous. Things will warm up. Things will flutter later.

We say our goodbyes and he opens my door for me, then shuts it and waves me off.

Besides, there are other important key factors in a person you're dating. Stable, good job, nice, and so on. Lots of things to list off before "electrifying kiss" comes up.

Maybe I'll talk to Lyla about it, just in case. Then it hits me. Who I really want to talk to about it is Jensen. I don't necessarily mean about the kiss. I just realize I want to talk to *him*, seek him out, because I've grown used to having him to talk to this week.

I don't want to tell him I kissed Steve. I won't lie to him, of course, but for whatever reason, I feel weird about it.

After less than one day of silence, I miss talking to him.

The car ride home is quiet, and I spend most of it sighing and shrugging and sighing some more. I hate the thought of not speaking to Jensen like we have been. I hate the thought of not spending time together. And I especially hate that he's leaving so soon. What then? Are we going to be friends via text message who never see each other again?

None of these thoughts are sitting well with me as I pull back onto the farm and park.

Getting out of the car, I rifle through my clutch to pull my phone out so I can text Steve.

"Hey," Jensen says, his voice carrying down to me from the porch swing.

I snap my head up, startled by his presence. "Shit, you scared me. I didn't expect anyone to be out here."

"Sorry," he says, hands in his pockets. "You look nice."

"Thank you," I say. "I just got back from the raincheck date with Steve."

I watch Jensen's face scrunch up a fraction, clearly not liking what I've said. He presses his lips together into a line and nods. "Right," he says. "I just came to talk, but never mind."

"What? No, let's talk." I step up onto the porch toward him.

"Did you have a good time with Steve?" he asks.

"What?"

"It's a simple question, Harper," he says.

"Uh, yeah, it was pretty good. Why?"

"Did you make plans to go out again?" he asks, his legs twitching back and forth.

"Yes."

Jensen swallows, like what he's about to say next is painful or awkward for him. He looks away from my face. "Did you kiss him?"

"Jensen, what's this about?"

"I'm just trying to talk," he says, still not looking at me.

"Yeah, we kissed, but—"

Jensen steps past me off the porch, shaking his head. "Well, that's that then. Good for you, Harper. I'm glad it worked out for you." With that, he starts walking back in the direction of the cabin.

"Jensen, wait!" I yell, but he doesn't. He keeps walking, hands in his pockets, back to me.

Ugh. Damn it. What the hell was that about?

Men are driving me absolutely batshit crazy today. Okay, that's not fair. *Jensen* is driving me batshit crazy today.

I take out my phone and text Steve that I made it home safe, getting an immediate return text full of sweet sentiment. These men are clearly total opposites.

This little moment just confirms that I probably made the right decision.

Obviously, the good stable choice is Steve.

And the kissing? We can work on the kissing.

JENSEN

I'VE BEEN LYING in bed for what feels like hours this morning. Then again, when you barely sleep all night, maybe time just blends together and it all feels like morning because that happens to be what time it is now. But there are no black curtains in this room in the cabin. Light filters through the windows, almost unhindered. It's so bright in here, I couldn't fall back to sleep if I wanted. I've been staring at the ceiling and trying my best not to reach for my phone. I really, really want to be stronger than that right now.

I want to text Harper, but I don't know what to say yet. She clearly had a good time with Steve and I don't want to mess that up for her. What can I offer? A life traveling or waiting for me to have a day off in between trips to see her? That's not a life.

Perhaps it's part of the reason I'm still single. It's not that I want to be, necessarily. But between my job and what I'm looking for in a partner, nothing has lined up. I think about Harper. The color of her eyes. The way her hair sweeps down her back. The way her teeth sink into her bottom lips, her cheeks turning pink when my voice gets low. She feels different to me. Not inexperienced or simple the way she believes. But authentic, natural. She's not trying to impress anyone or convey any false ideas about who she is. She's just genuinely and uniquely herself. And she doesn't understand how fucking sexy that is.

I press my eyes shut, wishing more than anything that I could rewind and play this all out a little differently. I have to get up. This is pointless.

After all, I promised to help Gentry with some wedding stuff today. I don't know exactly *what*, but I agreed nevertheless.

Pulling on my shoes, I reach for my phone and see a missed message from my sister.

> CORA
> What have you done?

I scratch my chin, not fully understanding what the hell she's talking about.

> Huh?

> CORA
> Lyla and Harper are sitting here talking about potentially rearranging the wedding so Harper can bring some guy named Steve?!

> Look, if that's what she wants to do, I'm not gonna stop her.

> CORA
> You're an idiot.

I shove my phone in my pocket and meet Gentry in the kitchen, where he's sipping coffee and flipping through something on his phone.

After a quick greeting, he says, "Sleep okay?"

"Not really."

"Oh boy." He chuckles.

"You and Lyla seem happy. Like, really happy?" I say, not quite sure if I'm asking a question or making a statement.

"Yeah, we are. Granted, we have our days. And the starting line was rough. But we figured it out."

"What happened?" I ask, leaning forward.

Gentry tells me about their first weeks together, how resistant Lyla was, how in the end fighting for her didn't matter if she couldn't see it for herself. In the end, she had to want it. Which feels more than vaguely familiar. I take in his story, what it means. And it means I have to let Harper do whatever Harper is going to do.

"So, you ready?" he asks.

"Yep," I say. "What's on the agenda?"

"We're going to pick up my brother from the airport, stop to approve the rehearsal dinner arrangements, pick up the marriage license, and then there's a bachelor party to get to." He rubs his hands together.

"Oh, now you're talking." I wasn't looking forward to running errands but knowing it'll end with drinks and a good time certainly sweetens the deal.

"You think the girls are the only ones who get to have some fun? No way. There may even be a stripper who can rub your worries away and leave body glitter behind," he jokes.

"Sounds perfect," I say, laughing and heading for the door.

I have to admit, Gentry is a pretty likeable guy. A balance of responsible adult and what's shaping up to be a bit of a partier. Or at least, he knows how to throw one.

We head out toward the airport to pick up his brother Graham, who lives in Oregon. Gentry explains that Graham is his older brother who's married, but his wife isn't coming to the wedding. Apparently, tragedy struck, and they suffered a miscarriage. She's okay and recovering well but can't travel. At the same time, she didn't want her husband to miss his only brother's wedding, so sacrifices were made. Although, it sounds like everyone would've understood if Graham didn't come, his wife insisted.

Gentry throws his brother's suitcase in the back and they hop in. "Jensen, this is my brother, Graham. Graham, this is Jensen. He's Lyla's friend's brother. If you can follow that." He laughs.

"Hey, man. Good to meet you," Graham says, extending his hand to me.

I shake it, nodding and returning the sentiment. I note the similarities and differences between them. Maybe I can't help but do this considering I have a sibling of my own.

Gentry and Graham have the same dark hair, the same color eyes, and are built nearly the same. Where Gentry keeps a short beard, Graham is currently clean shaven. They have the same dimples, but you can see Graham's more due to this. Under the right circumstances, they could pass for twins. Minus Graham being an inch or so taller, and the thin jagged scar he has slicing right through his eyebrow near the corner of his eye.

We make our way back through town, fulfilling the other errands we need to run, Graham filling most of the silence. He's a pretty funny guy and I find myself laughing as he reminisces with Gentry about their teenage years.

"Okay," Gentry says. "Who's ready for a good fucking time? Just the boys?"

"Hell yes, brother," Graham says.

"Let's get me drunk," I say.

Gentry pulls onto a road that's essentially an entire street full of bars and clubs, explaining that a few more guys will be meeting us here.

As we wait for their arrival in the parking lot, I pull out my phone. My head flips back and forth as I debate. I know Harper's going to be out having a good time tonight and I don't want to dampen that. I need to squash this. I pull up her messages.

> I hope you have a good time tonight.

HARPER
> Thanks. You too.

I'm a little surprised at how quickly she responded, even if it is a short response. I try again.

> I mean it. I'm sorry about my behavior.

HARPER
> I appreciate that. I hope you have a good time too.

Ugh. I don't like that. I'm ready for alcohol. Lots of alcohol. We're celebrating, right? Let's fucking celebrate. I put my phone away and shake out my arms from shoulder to fingertip, mentally preparing myself for a long and much needed evening of meaningless shenanigans. Maybe I'll even hit on a waitress or bartender, I don't know. The sky is the fucking limit.

All I know is I will definitely *not* drunk text Harper later.

I will do just about anything to avoid that.

HARPER

I HAVE a strawberry flavored dick in my mouth. Not a real one, of course. Although it would certainly make blow jobs more entertaining.

No, I have a strawberry flavored dick shaped lollipop in my mouth. Because that's what we do at bachelorette parties. We wear tight leather pants and crop tops, sashes displaying our titles, too much makeup, and shove phallic shaped candy in our mouths, all while sipping brightly colored overpriced drinks.

Remind me again why I'm doing this? Oh right, my sister is getting married, I'm divorced, and I don't give a fuck about life right now. Maybe it's the aforementioned colorful drinks, but I'm dancing, singing off-key, and some guy named Teddy from a college fraternity is grinding on my ass. And, I really don't care. Which is so unlike me. *Bless the booze.*

"Let's get some air," Lyla shouts over the music, her plastic tiara swaying on her head. Fuck yes, she's wearing a tiara.

I nod and we make our way toward the patio, squeezing between people. Teddy calls out to me, but he'll have to find someone else to dry hump for now.

We push open the doors and a blast of cool night air hits me in the face. I inhale deeply, feeling the essence of sweaty bodies fall away from me.

"Having fun?" Lyla asks, giggling and sipping her drink.

"Yeah, actually. Mine wasn't like this. It should've been, though."

"Hell yes it should've," she says. "That stuck up asshole Charles sucked the fun out of you. He was literally a fun sucker."

"Speaking of suckers," I say. "This lollipop is actually delicious."

Lyla sticks her blue raspberry one in her mouth, her lips and mouth all stained blue. She looks like she gave a smurf a blow job but I don't have the heart to tell her that. The blue dick in her hand sways like she does because we're all sauced at this point. Last time I saw Cora in the crowd, she was rubbing up on two different frat guys. Apparently college boys have no issues with your age, marital status, or level of intoxication. If you have a pulse, you're fair game.

I check my phone for the time, realizing the clubs will be closing soon. I'm proud I'm not so drunk I see two phones but I have a heavy enough buzz that everything is very fun. I'm carefree, which isn't my natural state.

"We have to go soon," I huff, disappointed that the night is nearly over.

"Gonna hook up with that teddy bear frat boy?" Lyla asks.

I crinkle my nose. *Gross.* "No, thank you. I have my hands full enough." I laugh at my own mess of a life.

"With Steve?"

"And Jensen," I add.

"Jensen?" she repeats. "I thought that was over? Or well, never really started?" She leans in closely as she adjusts her weight from one foot to the other.

I sigh loudly. Right, I thought the same thing. You can always depend on alcohol to make you feel your truths. "I fucking like him," I say on the tail end of an exhale.

"So go for it." She waves her hand. "He's fucking hot. And you should definitely sample the goods."

"Oh my god."

"What? Just do it. You know you want to," she says.

She's not wrong. I really do want to. It's an itch I desperately want to scratch. A sexy itch. What am I even talking about right now?

Planting myself on a bench, I navigate through my messages and stare at the names. Jensen and Steve are both right there—one right above the other. Theoretically, I can make whichever move I want. Fuck it.

> Hey

Several minutes pass before I get an answer, which makes sense considering he's probably not waiting around with his phone in his face.

JENSEN
Hey!

> What are you doing?

JENSEN
We just left a bar in an Uber and we're headed back to the cabin.

Okay, let's think about this, Harper. If you pull the trigger, there's no going back. You can't undo it.

> Okay, I'll meet you there.

He says okay and I gather the ladies just as last call is being announced, rounding them into an Uber of our own. I have to act quickly or I'll start overthinking all of this. The driver makes rounds, dropping some of the party members off until it's just me, Cora, and my sister remaining.

My stomach starts to flutter as we pull onto the farm's long drive-way. He pulls next to the main house and we all jump out, and I take care of tipping him. Cora and Lyla start up the porch stairs but I'm still on the ground, looking toward the cabin, biting my bottom lip.

"Are you coming?" Lyla asks.

"Nope," I say, marching off in the direction of Jensen.

I watch them over my shoulder as they give each other a surprised look before going inside.

I'm full steam ahead. One foot in front of the other. I'm making my way back there and I mean business. Sexy business. I'm dressed for it this time, too.

I knock on the cabin door, hoping Jensen answers. But that's not my luck.

"Hey, what's up? Everything okay?" Gentry asks.

"No time to talk," I say. I walk past him into the cabin but don't see Jensen and assume he's already in his room. Making my way upstairs, I give myself one last pep talk in my mind. *You can do this. You want this. Make it happen.*

I knock on the guest bedroom door and wait several seconds before he swings it wide open. I don't even let him get a word out before my mouth is on his.

I press my mouth against his, his arms coming around me and pulling me against him. I reach back and shut the door behind us, then press him further into the room until his legs hit the bed. I push him down, immediately reaching for the edges of my shirt as he stares up at me. The cropped black shirt falls to the floor behind me, my red lace bra putting everything I have on display.

"Fuck," he whispers under his breath.

I lower myself onto him as his hands come up to reach for me, gripping my flesh and pulling me down further. I sink down onto him, my lips meeting his again. Reaching down, I grip the bottom of his shirt and tug it up and off his body. My hands explore him the way I've wanted to ever since the night in the tent. His hands grip my ass, grinding me down against him. I pull back from the kiss and bite his earlobe, feeling his grip on me tighten.

"Fuck me," I whisper.

Jensen's movements pause, like he's not sure he heard me correctly. "Are you sure?"

"Yes."

He flips me over, his large body now above mine, my back on the mattress. He leans down, kissing me, his lips trailing from my mouth, down my neck, and between my breasts. He takes my nipple between his teeth through the fabric, gently nibbling and sucking as he reaches around and unclasps the bra. His kisses continue down, over my stomach, around my belly button until he reaches the edge of my pants.

In one motion, they're off, along with my panties and shoes. Everything is in a pile on the floor and I'm completely naked beneath him. He stands and removes his pants but leaves his boxers in place, then tugs me in one swift motion to the edge of the bed and kneels as he licks his lips.

He doesn't take his eyes from mine as he leans in and blows hot air on the center of me. My back arches my body toward him and he licks me, his tongue wet and flat against my tender flesh. I can't even say what comes from me is a moan. It's more like a whimper. He sucks me into his mouth and continues sucking, my body twisting in response.

I grip the sheets, my eyes closing tight as my stomach knots. "Wait," I say. "Not like this. I want you inside me."

Jensen lifts his mouth from me, smiling. "Don't worry, babe. I plan to give you more than one." Then he presses his mouth to me once again, his movements more rapid this time. He applies pressure, building me up quickly, pressing his fingers to my thighs to keep my legs open.

"Oh my god," I yell as I lose my mind to the most delicious orgasm I've ever had. Jensen kisses and licks gently up my body as he makes his way up to my lips. I kiss him and press my forehead to his chest as I catch my breath.

"I hope you're not tired," he says.

I shake my head, and Jensen stands and walks across the room, pulling something from his suitcase before coming back to the bed. He places what I see now is a condom on the edge of the bed and then pulls down his boxers. My eyes are fixed on his hard length as he touches himself. I shamelessly watch him stroke from tip to base as he looks down at me.

"Come here," he says.

Something inside me, low inside my stomach, does flips, and I crawl to the edge of the bed. He lets go of himself as I take him into my hand and I watch his head roll back, his chest expanding as he inhales sharply.

I press my tongue to the tip of him and his hand reaches for my shoulder, steadying himself, gripping me. I open my mouth further and take him in, his body shuddering in response. I work up and down the length of him, wanting to make him feel as good as he made me feel.

His hand cups my jawline and he stops me, pressing me back away from him. When I look up at him, his hooded eyes are fixed on me, his bottom lip trapped between his teeth.

"Lie back," he whispers as he reaches for the condom and rips it open.

I do as he says and watch as he sheathes himself.

Jensen lies down then, pressing his chest to mine, and for the first time, I can feel his dick rubbing against my entrance. He presses his lips to mine, his mouth hungry for me. My hands press into his lower back as I wrap my legs around his thighs, my whole body begging him to be inside me.

"Jensen," I whisper, and as I say his name, he pushes into me, filling me with every inch of him. I inhale against his mouth.

"Fuck," he murmurs, rocking back and forth into me. His eyes shut, and one hand holds his weight while the other cups my breast. He presses his forehead to mine. His movements, slow and intense, cause me to feel every sensation. I hook my legs over his, like I can't get him close enough, all of me needing more of him.

"Open your eyes," I beg.

Jensen looks at me, our eyes fixed on each other as he presses into me over and over again. He kisses me again, his tongue lapping against mine, then he moves away to look at me again.

"Harper," he says. "Oh my god."

His movements grow faster and I hold onto him. I feel the delicious build in me all over again and then I unravel just before he does. His body shudders and jerks before collapsing onto me. I hold him tight against me, drawing circles on his back. Inhaling the scent of his skin, warm and salt licked, I close my eyes and attempt to right my ragged breathing.

Before I know it, my eyelids grow heavy, and I succumb to sleep, with Jensen still inside me.

HARPER

I HAD sex with Jensen last night. Correction. I had a lot of sex with Jensen last night. After dozing off the first time, I woke him up two more times throughout the night to go again.

Now, as I lie here in his bed, very awake and very aware of all the reasons that was a terrible idea, panic settles in.

What now?

Do I shake his hand and say thanks? Smack him on the ass and tell him good game? What do people do after they hook up? *Awesome predicament, Harper. Totally awesome.*

Jensen stirs beside me, his arm tightening its grip over my middle. *Shit. Don't wake up. Not yet. I'm not ready. I don't have a plan.*

"Good morning," he whispers.

"Oh hey, good morning," I reply, feigning a sleepiness in my voice, attempting to disguise the fact that I've been awake for probably the last forty-five minutes.

"Hell of a night, huh?" he says.

"Uh, yeah," I say, unsure if he's referring to us or the parties.

As he starts to laugh, I'm even more unsure. "Certainly didn't think I'd be waking up next to you," he says.

"Oh, sorry. Should I have left?"

Jensen laughs again, and I clearly have no idea what's going on.

"No, silly. I just mean it's nice," he says, nuzzling his face into my neck.

Weird. Really weird, actually. I sit up and break his grip around me, searching for my pants. "Oh, yeah. It was nice."

Jensen recoils, his brow wrinkling. "Wait, what's going on?"

"What do you mean?"

"I mean where are you going?" he asks.

"I'm leaving. Gotta get home and shower and change."

"Oh. Okay." He exhales, dropping his hand to the mattress in an exasperated manner.

"What? I have to meet Lyla later and then Steve after that. I assume people leave after they hook up. Not that I know for sure because I've never done it but that's what everyone does in movies."

"Wow, okay, Harper. I got it," he says, his jaw tightening.

Fuck. I did this wrong. "Are you okay?"

"Yeah, I'm good," he says.

I dress in silence, neither of us saying anything else. Jensen doesn't move from the bed. I attempt to tell him I'll see him later, that I'll text him, but he's short, only giving me one-word answers.

I slink out of the room, unsure what I've done to warrant such a response. We hooked up; I left. That's the deal, right? We have to keep everything outside of the bedroom as normal as possible, anyway. The way it's always been. That's the system as far as I can tell. Maybe I should ask my sister later when I meet with her. Right now, I've got to get a shower and find some coffee pronto.

As I walk back to the house, I try hard to examine my own emotions. What is this I'm feeling? I'm relieved not to be feeling shame. Far too much of that goes around for enjoying sex. It feels more like worry, but I can't understand why. Why am I worried? And about what? The worry seems to be knotted up along with dread and a whole mess of other stuff on the spectrum, but none of that seems to be connected directly to actually having sex.

The sex was amazing. Sex with Jensen was incredible. Far superior to anything I'd experienced with Charles. I can't begin to explain or describe the differences adequately. The way Jensen navigated my body was nothing short of wizardry.

As I ascend the porch, thoughts of Jensen's hands last night still clouding my mind, Lyla steps out from the kitchen.

"Hey there, sis," she says, a wide smile across her face.

"Oh my god."

"What?" she asks, holding her hands out in innocence.

"I know it's coming. Just do it," I say.

"I can't just enjoy your little walk of shame?" She laughs.

"Who says I'm ashamed?"

"Atta girl," she says, patting me on the back.

"I feel a mess of other things, but shame isn't one of them," I admit.

"Oh no."

I tell her we need to talk when we meet for lunch later, and then I make my way to the shower where I peel out of the stupid leather pants from the night before. With any luck, this will be the last time. They're so uncomfortable. I make a mental note to shove them to the back of my closet and never look back.

I let the hot water run over my body for what seems like forever before I even make a move for soap or shampoo. Steam fills the room while I let everything run off me and down the drain. I finally lather shampoo in, scrubbing from my scalp all the way down. My hair nearly touches my ass and I pull it around, examining it in my hand. And then, it hits me.

I finish my shower as quickly as I can, conditioning next and then washing my body. I dry off and dress then brush my teeth. I throw my hair up into a bun on top of my head, not bothering to dry it. I collect my purse and phone from my room and put on shoes. Running downstairs, I'm yelling for my sister before I hit the bottom floor.

"What is it? What's wrong? Lyla yells, coming into the hallway from the kitchen, concern in her voice. Her hand is clutched to her chest as if I've been screaming that someone attacked me.

"Nothing's wrong. I need to you take me somewhere. I don't want to go alone."

"Okay, where are we going?" she asks.

"I need you to take me to the salon."

Lyla's eyes grow wide, not fully comprehending what I'm asking. She looks up at my hair. "Okay. Let's go."

JENSEN

I CAN'T SAY this morning didn't sting. It definitely did. But if Harper only wanted a hookup, I have to respect it. It's a little surprising though, coming from her. I guess I just assumed more would come of it. Even if assumption is rude. She's entitled to what she wants, regardless of her past or how I feel.

Lucky for me, she left the farm a little while ago and I have an amazing view of the property from this little bench under a tree near the orchard. My fingers strum the strings of the guitar, trying to recall the melody of the song for the wedding. I've almost got it down. I should have it today if I can focus, and I figure now is as good a time as any to crack down.

I also took the liberty of scheduling my flight out of here for the day after the wedding. I called my boss and asked for somewhere warm, somewhere near an ocean if at all possible, so he's sending me to an account close to my current home in North Carolina. Hopefully after client meetings, I can sneak away to the beach for a few days. That will recharge me.

My thoughts float back to Harper, how she's never seen the ocean, how I wish I could show it to her. Now I really am crazy. I shake my head violently and turn back to strumming the guitar when I hear a car coming down the gravel driveway.

I peak over my shoulder even though I know it's probably Lyla and Harper coming back. They've been gone for a while now and I don't think anyone else is gone or expected. Sure enough, I'm right. Between the tint of the windows and the reflecting sun, I can't see inside the car, so I stare as they pull up and exit. It takes all of two seconds to realize Harper's hair is gone. Well, not all of it, but from where I am, about half. Her golden locks fall just below her shoulder now, no longer cascading down her back and swaying as she walks. I swallow, choking on my sudden intake of breath catching in my throat. *Good god.*

Before I realize what I'm doing, I stand and walk toward them. Harper's back is to me as she twists her now shorter locks around her fingers. Lyla's eyes catch mine as I approach and she presses her lips together in a sly smile, retreating toward the house.

Harper turns to face me, her eyes meeting mine with a hesitant smile. "Hey."

"Hi there." My eyes sweep over her face and hair, taking in her appearance, her face somehow glowing.

"I got a haircut," she says, as if it isn't obvious.

"I see that. I like it."

"You do?"

"Yeah, it looks great. Why did you decide to cut it?"

Harper bites her lip, reaching up and taking her short hair in her hand. She can't seem to leave it alone. "Because I never have before, aside from trims. Because Charles never wanted me to."

"Well, I'm glad you did then."

Harper smiles, fully, her rosy cheeks bright and warm under my words. "Are you sure it looks okay?"

"Harper, I don't think it matters what anyone thinks but you. You have to love it. That's the point, right?"

She tilts her head at me, considering my words for several long moments. "You're right."

"But for the record," I say, pausing for effect. I lean in close to her, giving her my low voice, the one that pinks her cheeks. "I think it's fucking hot."

Harper presses her lips together and pushes me back, shaking her head. "Don't do that. I can't think when you do that."

"Then my work here is done."

"What are you doing with your guitar?" she asks, changing the subject.

"Practicing for the wedding. Almost there," I say proudly.

This is awkward. Or at least, it doesn't feel like it did before. *Did we fuck it up? Did sex make it weird between us?*

I watch Harper dig the toe of her shoe into the gravel and I *know* we fucked it up.

"I don't like tomatoes," I blurt.

Harper laughs, nodding her head. And even though I don't think it actually happened, I would swear her shoulders eased a bit. "I don't like wearing socks," she says.

In this quiet moment, our game continues on as it has before. I quite enjoy it. It may be my favorite thing about this entire trip, surpassing both the promised open bar and the sex. Not that the sex wasn't amazing. But this feels special.

She taps her foot again, her hand rising to touch her short blunt bob. "Well, I better go get ready."

"For what?"

"I'm supposed to meet Steve in a little while," she says plainly, like we didn't just have sex, like there's no reason in the world I'd be jealous.

Like I don't want to kick Steve in the shin or crash a shopping cart into the side of his car or—*relax, Jensen.* "Oh."

"Yeah, we made plans the other day," she says, her voice trailing off.

I want to tell her to cancel them, to tell him she's not going to see him anymore, to ask her to choose me, but that's me getting carried away in a moment. And moments don't make for wise decisions.

"Yeah, I get it." I scruff the bottom of my shoe along the gravel, mimicking her earlier movements. Then I shove my free hand into my pocket. "Have fun." I twist my hips and spin in the direction of the bench I occupied before, deciding the view it offered was better than hiding myself away in the bedroom that still smelled like her, sitting on the sheets still holding her shape.

Harper doesn't move from behind me right away but eventually I hear her steps kicking up rocks. To my surprise, they're not away from me but toward me.

"Jensen, wait," she calls.

I turn back to catch her tucking her hair behind her ear and then wrapping her arms around her middle. Whatever she wants to say is caught somewhere in transit.

"What is it?" I ask.

"I don't want to go," she says.

"So reschedule."

"No. I don't want to go. Ever," she clarifies.

I swallow hard, knowing what I'm about to say may have severe consequences but unsure I can stop myself at this point. "What do you want?"

"You. Even if it's just for a little while." She exhales.

I lay the guitar down at my side and walk toward her, both hands in my pockets, a smirk playing across my lips. "Well then, I guess you should cancel the date. And then come here," I say, my voice dropping low at the end of my statement.

Harper runs toward me and then jumps up, filling my arms.

I lean down and press a kiss to her neck then bite her collarbone. "Besides, I'm sure you can find twenty more Steves after I leave," I say, biting again.

Harper moans into my neck.

Somehow the mix of my own words, my leaving, and her delicious sound, leaves just a tinge of sadness in my gut.

HARPER

HERE'S WHAT I KNOW: The next three days are a dream. We don't spend every waking minute together. It's not some romance novel come to life. But it's a dream. We text when we aren't together, still playing our game, still getting to know the random nuances of each other. The evenings transform us, from our casual selves to something more romantic. A base desire sets in around dusk and I can't turn it off. It's as if he can't either. We both seem to watch the clock, count down the minutes until we can tangle up together, unravel in each other.

It's strange. I know it was never like this with Charles. Granted, we were so young when we started dating. Virgins have no carnal desires, and everything was so vanilla. With extra vanilla on top. And vanilla sprinkles. We never had sex outside the missionary position, we never displayed affection in public beyond holding hands or a kiss on the cheek, and we definitely never did any of the things I've done with Jensen over the last three days or am about to do again right now.

Jensen leads me out into the field of sunflowers. There are large paths running through the patches, and sometimes we allow guests to take walks through them, depending on the weather. However, it's never at night like this.

He leads me by the hand, the other holding blankets tucked beneath his arm. The only sounds filling the air are our giggles and the crickets.

"Where are we going?" I whisper.

"You'll see. I found it the other day," Jensen says. "We're almost there."

A few more steps and he veers to the left, stepping through some sunflowers and into a clearing. It's not on the path, but a patch of soft earth that was somehow missed during planting.

Jensen spreads out the two blankets he has, one on top of the other, and I look at him quizzically.

"Extra padding," he teases.

I shake my head as I watch him lie down and place an arm under his head, then he pats the blanket next to him as he looks up at me. I crawl next to him, using his shoulder as a pillow as I follow the direction of his gaze up toward the sky.

For all the stars, it almost doesn't feel like night. They're shining so bright, they're nearly lighting up the sky. I exhale deeply, letting all the air from my chest out until it feels like nothing is left.

"Almost kinda makes you feel like there's nothing else in the world except us, huh?" Jensen's whispered question against my hair sends a sharp spike of goosebumps down my spine and I curl my toes in.

"Almost." I think about the last three days, how everyone's pretty much left us alone, and the fact that we have to give it all up in a few hours. Because tomorrow it's all about Lyla and Gentry. Which is fine, and completely the way it should be. I've never been happier for two people. After tomorrow, I'll officially have a brother, and they'll be living their happily ever after. But it reminds me that everything is on a clock. They leave for their honeymoon the next morning, and Jensen will leave to go back to his own life around the same time.

And I'll be here.

Two more nights. That's all I have. Then I'm back to no direction, no clue what I want, and no idea how to figure it out. Okay, that isn't entirely true.

I want Jensen. Right now.

In the future? I don't know.

I can only speak for now.

Running my fingers over his chest, I wrap my leg over his and dip my knee between his thighs. A soft groan escapes his throat.

"What are you thinking about?" he asks.

"Time."

"Like the song?" he asks. "By Hootie and the Blowfish?"

"The what?" I laugh.

Jensen belts out two lines of the song and I can't control my giggling. He really puts on the theatrics. Even from a horizontal position, he's giving it a good show.

"Stop, stop," I whisper. "You're going to make the dogs start barking."

"You don't want me to serenade you?" he says, feigning offense.

"Not that song, please," I say, finally catching my breath.

"What song, then?" he asks.

Looking back up at the stars, I let my head fall back on his arm, giving thought to his question. "I don't think I'd want to pick a specific one. I think I'd want you to pick one that reminds you of me. If that makes sense."

I feel his head move slightly above me. "Yeah, it does, actually," he says, and I can't be sure because I don't look, but I think I can hear a smile on his lips.

I lean back into Jensen, wrapping my arm around his chest and looping my leg back over his, my knee drawing up between his legs once again.

"Mmmm," he says. "I like this."

"Me too." My words fall out more like a sigh than anything else.

"Can we make out now?" Jensen asks, his question cutting through the calm silence in such a way it nearly throws me into a fit of laughter again.

I giggle. "Yeah."

Jensen pulls me on top of him with the arm resting underneath me, curling me into his chest. His mouth presses against mine in a balance of hunger and playfulness. I think this is what I adore most. His ability to be both unbelievably sexy and insanely adorable at the same time. He's somehow all man while maintaining his devilish boy qualities and I am weak in the knees for all of it.

I wrap one hand around the back of his neck and dig my fingers into his short locks, pulling his mouth closer to mine. His hand begins to reach up my shirt and I pull back.

"Oh my god, are you feeling me up outside? Are we about to have sex outside?"

"I don't know what you're talking about," he says, as his hand continues its way up my shirt. I place my hands on my hips, my legs straddling him. Jensen cups my breast and tugs downward.

"Are we really doing this?" I laugh.

"Come on," he whines. "Adam and Eve did it outside."

"Adam and Eve were sinners."

"We're definitely sinners," he says, laughing and raising his eyebrows at me.

He licks his lips slowly, in a way I definitely can't resist, as he rolls my nipple between his fingers and I whimper.

"Fine, but if I have bug bites in my bathing suit areas, I'm going to make you kiss them better tomorrow," I say, leaning back down toward him so he can continue his fondling.

"Is that a threat or a promise?" he asks as he pulls my shirt over my head.

Thankfully, I hadn't bothered with a bra for our late-night walk. Considering I don't technically have enough to really need one and I was wearing an oversize sweatshirt, it didn't matter. His shirt is the next to go, and I rub my fingers all over his chest and stomach, getting my fill before unbuttoning his pants and ripping them down, along with his underwear. I stand and remove mine next while he sheaths himself with a condom.

I settle back down on top of him, hovering just above him. One little dip and he'll be inside me, but if my time with him has taught me anything, it's that I like to tease. I kiss his mouth, lapping my tongue against his and then pulling away. I lower my body closer, rubbing myself against his shaft and his grip on my thighs tightens. "Do you want me?"

"Yes," he says on a sigh.

The center of me slides over the tip of his dick and his fingers dig into my hips. "Tell me."

He groans. "I want to be inside you, Harper."

In one fluid motion, I slide up and over the tip of him, taking him into me, letting him fill me. The sudden fullness takes my breath. I inhale sharply, as does he. Each time he enters me, it never fails to take my breath away.

I rock back and forth, one hand on his chest for balance, the other cupping my own breast. He likes watching me touch myself like this and I like touching myself like this. In this short week, I've learned a lot about myself.

"There you go, babe," he whispers, his voice low, eyes hooded. He licks his lips, then bites into the bottom one.

I'm in rhythm now, slowly rolling my body, feeling every inch of him inside me. Jensen reaches for my hand on his chest and moves it toward my clit, encouraging me to touch, to play.

He grabs onto my hips and helps hold me steady as I rub circles around myself. The sensation of both him inside me and my fingers outside is maddening. My pace quickens, sending sparks through my body in every direction. One of his hands slides up my side and replaces mine on my breast, cupping and massaging, as he pushes and pulls me to and away from him.

"Look up," he whispers.

I always do as he commands, and this time, my eyes are filled with hundreds of thousands of tiny lights, all flickering above us. The night sky is a canvas of deep blue and stars, so vast I feel my eyes welling. Before I know it, my cheeks are wet. I bear down on him, headed for the finish as tears silently run down the sides of my face. God, this is so strange. I can't summon the courage to look back down at him, so I keep staring up at the infinite expanse above us. His body knows how to please mine, how to soothe it, how to bend it to his will. His voice commands me, and I find myself mesmerized by it, almost a slave to it in these intimate moments. More than all of that, I realize now, his soul feeds mine, gives me something I didn't know existed until now.

I collapse onto him in the throes of an orgasm and he follows right behind me, our breaths short and heavy.

"Who knew you were such freak," he murmurs.

"What do you mean?"

"You just had sex outside, sinner," he says, laughing.

"Someone has corrupted me."

"Sounds like an awesome guy," he says, and I grab for him, his body arching in response. "Oh my god, no, truce," he pleads.

We settle back down and no sooner than our giggling subsides, he can't help himself.

"What do you want to try next? Nipple clamps? A butt plug? Getting tied up?" He laughs.

"Um, nothing is going back there, I can assure you." I start giggling.

"So, you're saying there's still hope for the nipple clamps?" he asks.

I elbow him in the ribs, laughing uncontrollably.

Maybe I don't have forever. Maybe I don't even have another week with him. But I will enjoy this. I will live *this* moment. I will make the most of it.

HARPER

DESPITE THE LATE-NIGHT FIELD ROMP, I woke up this morning feeling extremely refreshed. No, I didn't wake up in the field this morning. After our shenanigans, he walked me back to the house and he went back to the cabin. We spent the night apart, which actually felt sort of strange. But I had to wake up at five this morning, so it's a good thing I'm refreshed.

By six, all the ladies are on their second cup of coffee and we're all seated at the kitchen table as Nan sits plates of delicious breakfast food in front of us. Cora and I dig in, but Lyla isn't touching hers.

"Lyla, eat. You have to," I say.

"I can't. I'll throw up for sure," she says.

"If you don't eat, you'll throw up," Cora says.

Lyla huffs and picks up her fork.

"Drink this. It'll help settle your nerves," Nan says, sitting a shot of clear liquid in front of Lyla.

"I can't start drinking this early," Lyla protests.

"I'm not saying to keep drinking, baby. Just the one. It'll knock the edge off," Nan says.

Lyla takes the shot in her hand and shoots it back without even asking what it is or smelling it. Her entire body shivers as she sets the tiny glass back down. Then she stabs her fork into a piece of French toast and stuffs it into her mouth. *Wow.* Seems to have done the trick.

By my count, there are no less than fifty-three or so things to remember or do today before this thing kicks off, so I can't blame her for being nervous. That's a lot of opportunity for something to be forgotten, go wrong, or ruin her day. Maybe I should have Nan prepare a flask of that stuff, just in case.

"Okay, how about we all shower after this then we head to town for hair and makeup at the salon?" Lyla asks, and because this is no time to protest or even ask questions, Cora and I nod quietly, continuing to eat.

My phones dings and I look down to see an incoming message from Jensen. A smile stretches wide across my lips and Lyla clears her throat to get my attention.

"Who's that?" she teases.

"Shut up."

"Is my brother seriously awake this early texting you?" Cora inquires.

"Apparently." I untuck my hair from behind my ear to cover my blushing cheeks and then open my messages as they shake their heads at me.

> JENSEN
>
> I can't believe you guys have to be up this early.
>
> Also good morning.
>
> Also I really wish we were spooning right now so I could touch your butt.

Despite trying to keep a straight face, a giggle escapes me as I read the last one.

"Smitten," Lyla says.

"Shush," I snap.

> Why are you up? I also wish we were spooning.

JENSEN

Just to text you before you go all no contact
for several hours.

I should still be able to text a little.

JENSEN

I can't wait to feel you up in your dress.

You're so bad.

JENSEN

What does that make you?

I guess I'm bad too.

Placing my phone in my pocket, I finish my breakfast and bound upstairs for my shower. It takes all of us over an hour to rotate in and get ready. Afterward, we pile into the car fresh faced and legs shaved.

We made special arrangements at the salon for some sort of special bridal spa package, which includes a massage to get us nice and relaxed first before they tweeze us, wash us, tug at our hair, and smear makeup all over our faces with forty different brushes. At first I wanted to object, but the complimentary mimosas sealed the deal for me.

When we walk out of the place three hours later, we're practically magazine ready from the collarbones up, but still donning our zippered jackets and leggings. Did I mention there's a small tent attached to the big tent where we'll be getting ready? It's equipped with everything we'll need, including mobile air conditioning, lighting, and mirrors, and Nan is transferring our dresses, shoes, accessories and anything else she can think of there while we make our way back. Until right before the ceremony, we're essentially chained to this room. And until she walks down the aisle, Lyla is completely chained to this room. Yes, there's bathroom access.

As we walk into our tent, I find my old camera sitting on one of the mirrored tables. I had asked Nan if she knew where it was, and she said she'd dig it out for me.

"Are you going to take pictures?" Lyla asks, her voice filled with excitement.

"I was thinking about it."

"Please do it. You haven't in so long," she says.

I run my hands over the top edge of the lens and shrug my shoulders. "Why not? I'm sure I can get some decent shots."

I start unpackaging the new battery and shove it into the back of the camera, then hold it up, adjusting the lens focus. I look through it, all around the tent until it lands on Lyla standing in front of her dress, staring up at it. The look on her face is pure elation and I can't help but adjust the focus and snap the photo.

Cora and I dress quickly, then help Lyla into hers and adjust her long veil. It falls down over the backless gown so beautifully, it brings tears to my eyes. Speaking of tears, we all take turns freshening each other's makeup for that very reason, making sure our hair is perfect as well. By the time we're completely ready, there's only thirty minutes before the ceremony begins.

I desperately wanted a moment with Jensen before the ceremony began, but it doesn't look like that's going to happen. Luckily, he'll be seated in the front next to Nan and Paw and we'll be able to see each other the entire time. Unfortunately, he'll be so close I'll have a hard time concentrating. I'm willing to make the sacrifice, though.

Nan enters the tent to check on us. Her beautiful gray hair is pulled in a simple elegant braid to the side. Her make up is light and refined. She's wearing a pale pink dress that sways when she walks. "You girls ready?" she asks, but her smile falls away when her eyes find Lyla. Tears begin to well up and her hand clutches her chest. "Oh, baby."

"How do I look, Nan?" Lyla asks, smoothing her dress with the palms of her hands.

"Like an absolute angel. I'm so glad I'm here for this," Nan says. "Let's go. It's time."

We collect our bouquets. Pale pink flowers mixed with white honeysuckle are wrapped in gray lace. Lyla won't tell me the joke behind the honeysuckle but her and Gentry give each other a look every time someone brings it up.

We shuffle out of the tent and around to the entrance of the larger one, readying ourselves to step in as the song begins to play. Cora's in front, then me, and Lyla is hidden behind us with Nan and Paw on each side of her. She insisted they both do it.

"Ready?" I whisper to her.

"Absolutely," she says.

The song *Wild Horses* by The Sundays begins to play softly, and it's time.

JENSEN

ALL DAY, I've wait for this moment. Granted, I'm not the one getting married. Not even close. But I'm standing here in this navy suit, right at the edge of the first aisle, looking down it just like everyone else, and I'm waiting. But I'm not waiting for Lyla. No. That guy off to my left with tears brimming his eyes is waiting for that honor. Not that Lyla isn't hot, because she totally is. At the moment though, I only have eyes for one Whitney sister. I'm the guy waiting for the other woman walking down the aisle.

My sister clears me, and then I see her. The long gray dress falls from her hips, the perfect amount of curve and sophistication. I want to run my fingers over the thin straps that hug her clavicles. Her shoulder length locks are twisted into soft waves and pinned back loosely into a bun with flowers. Her makeup is wedding makeup, that flawless look you only find after the professionals have been through. She's a vision, so breathtaking. I swallow hard as I grip the back of the chair.

Her eyes catch mine as she nears, and she smiles a secret little smile just for me. My eyes follow her as she steps around in front of me to the left. I turn back to watch Lyla, only because this day is about her and she deserves the next five minutes of my attention. For what it's worth, from what I know of them, she and Gentry seem perfect for each other and I'm glad they're getting their day. It so rarely happens like this for people anymore.

The ceremony is typical. The pastor walks them through their vows and exchange of rings. When they kiss, I wiggle my eyebrows at Harper who's been looking at me more than them.

Everyone proceeds out after the couple, for cocktails on the lawn while the tent is transformed for the reception. It's hard to believe what these catering companies can do in such little time, but when we step back in, the space is completely remodeled, complete with a dance floor, small stage, and dinner tables lining the area. A DJ is set up on stage alongside a microphone and my guitar. It's almost show-time for me, but first I have to get a moment with Harper. In fact, I'm dying for it. The bridal party was swept away for photos during cock-tail hour, and if I don't speak to her soon, I may actually shrivel up on the floor. *Exaggerate much, Jensen?*

"Hey, you," Harper says from behind me. I'd recognize her voice anywhere, in any crowd.

I turn and take in the sight of her up close, finally. "Oh my god, at last," I breathe, wrapping my arms up and around her. I inhale the scent of her hair and she giggles.

"Are you okay?" She laughs.

"That was too long."

Harper wraps her arms around my back, resting her head against my chest. "I totally agree." Her shoulders rise and fall as she inhales deeply, sinking into our embrace.

"Can we make out yet?" I ask her.

She laughs again, and I swear to god, it's one of my favorite sounds. "Not yet. But we can regular kiss?"

"I'll take it." I lean down and press my lips gently to hers, tempted to take more, knowing if I push the issue, she'll give in to me. I slip my tongue in for just a moment and then pull back. "Is that regular enough?"

Harper sinks her teeth into her bottom lip, her eyes drifting shut. "Unfortunately." She sighs. Her small hands are gripped onto the lapels of my suit jacket and I know she wants more.

"You'll have to unhand me now, woman. I have to go sing," I tell her.

"Oh, dear," she says.

"What?"

She leans in close, pressing her lips to my ear. "I think it's gonna make me wet," she whispers.

I swallow hard, because suddenly there's a lot of fucking saliva in my mouth. "Better get to it, then," I say, pressing a quick kiss to her cheek.

I watch her saunter—*yes*, saunter—to her table and melt into her chair, eyes on me the entire time. If I didn't know any better, I'd say she mentally undressed me twice over. Not that I'm complaining.

I wait at the edge of the small stage as announcements are made. The DJ welcomes Gentry and Lyla in to an eruption of applause. I clap for them, their joined hands in the air, but still my eyes trail over to Harper, who's looking at her sister and new brother with joy on her face.

This plan of mine, while I've been assured by Gentry is great, is pretty bold. And while I've been confident in my ability to charm for a while now, there's always a chance it can backfire. But that's life, right? Risk for reward. Besides, Harper deserves it.

I ready myself as the DJ introduces me, shaking out my arms all the way to the tips of my fingers, pushing out the last bit of nervousness I have.

Here goes nothing.

HARPER

JENSEN STEPS across the stage to the microphone and throws the strap of his guitar over his shoulder, adjusting and strumming it. God, he looks good up there. The suit, the guitar. His hair is slicked back on top, all city boy like. I want to run my fingers through it and mess it up and maybe nibble his bottom lip while I'm doing it. *Lord, get a hold of yourself, Harper.*

His hand grips the microphone, adjusting it, and I watch a wry smile spread wide across his lips, exposing his gorgeous dimples and bright white teeth. There's a sparkle in his eyes as he looks at me, then winks. He introduces himself to the crowd and clears his throat. I swallow, nervous for what's about to happen. I barely heard him before when we were camping, not enough to know how talented he actually is. But as I sit here about to listen to him sing, my hands are clutching the napkin in my lap and I can barely contain myself.

Gentry leads my sister into the center of the otherwise empty dance floor and grips her in his arms. I watch only this much before my eyes travel back to Jensen, and he begins to strum the opening notes of *Lady May* by Tyler Childers, the song their first dance will be to. It's a beautiful country song, so soft and gut wrenching. One of my favorites.

Then it happens. Jensen starts to sing.

His voice bellows out over the quiet tent and everyone is watching the newlyweds on the dance floor. Everyone except me. I'm stuck in a trance, watching Jensen's mouth move. His deep raspy voice sings the words of this song and I'm in awe. If I didn't know him, I think I'd still be impressed. But having had that mouth on me, having kissed those same lips, it's like I'm carrying around a secret, like I know just how far the talent of that mouth extends. And Jensen might be singing their wedding song, but he's looking at me. From the start of the song to the last note, he hardly takes his eyes off mine.

When he's finished, everyone claps. Gentry and Lyla even turn and applaud his talent. I stand and clap for him too, because he deserves it. Just when I think he should be putting his guitar down to come off stage, he clears his throat again and steps back up to the microphone.

"Thank you, thank you very much. Now, I got special permission from the groom to do this, so you'll have to excuse the interruption. I know it's their day, but I have a surprise for a special girl. Her name is Harper," he says.

Oh god. Oh no, oh god. What. The. Fuck. Panic!

Everyone's eyes shift toward me because everyone here knows me and suddenly I'm set ablaze with embarrassment. My skin is hot. I know I probably look like a lobster. I crouch low in my chair, but Cora elbows me.

"Stand up," she says.

I cover my face with my hands but it's no use because everyone's starts to clap and cheer. So I stand slowly, wrapping my hands around my waist and pressing my lips together to suppress the I-can't-believe-this-is-happening grin I have.

Jensen points down at me. "This one is for you."

Every last ounce of resistance I have melts away as he starts to strum the guitar and sing the words to *Ocean Eyes* by Billie Eilish. I laugh as tears brim my eyes because it's the sweetest thing anyone has ever done for me. I don't know how he found out this is one of my favorite songs.

In all my life, no one has even come close to doing anything like this. I swallow again, not fully understanding the entire range of emotions I'm feeling in this moment. I try to push away everything and just enjoy it, getting lost in Jensen's voice as he serenades me.

He finishes to another eruption of applause and sets the guitar down. Then, he rushes off the stage and straight toward me, wrapping his arms around my waist once he reaches me. I meet his embrace, wrapping my arms up around him and burying my face into his chest. He snarls into my neck and I giggle.

"You're ridiculous," I whisper.

"Good ridiculous?" he asks.

"The best kind of ridiculous." I kiss his lips, gripping tightly onto his lapels to bring him down to me.

He inhales against me. "Careful, woman." His warning sends tingles all over.

"Or what?" I tease.

"Or we won't make it through the whole reception, and that would be rude," he whispers.

A shiver travels my spine and I straighten up. "Wanna dance?" I ask, hearing the DJ start up in the background.

Jensen nods and our hands fall in unison, mine into his as he leads me out onto the floor. He turns, pulling my arms up around his neck, and sways back and forth to this slow song I couldn't name for all the money in the world because all my attention is on him. His hooded eyes are dark and fixed on mine. They're everything sex and heat with a hint of playful mischief behind them.

"I have a proposition," he says.

"A dirty one?" I ask.

"Well, it can involve dirty stuff," he says, tilting his head back and forth, lips pouted.

"Go on," I say, pressing my lips together in curiosity.

"Well, I have to leave tomorrow. I fly back home to North Carolina. And I want you to come with me for a few days," he says, his words stopping abruptly.

"What?"

"You could take a little vacation. See the ocean. I want to show you the ocean, Harper," he says.

His words dig into my lungs, into my heart. Suddenly everything in my chest is so heavy. *He wants to show me the ocean.* "Really?"

"Yeah. You can bring your camera, sight see. I'll have to work a little during the day, but we can have the evenings together. And the weekends. Maybe you could stay a week? Or even two?"

"Wow, I don't know." I swallow against my words. I look down at our feet moving in perfect rhythm. I think about the farm, if everything will be okay while I'm gone. I think about the fact that I've never been anywhere worth speaking of in my whole life. I think about what something like this could mean.

"I just, I really want to do this for you," he says. "You deserve it."

"I would have to make sure everything is covered here."

"Oh, I already did," he says.

"What?"

"Yeah. Everyone says to have a good time and not to worry," he says.

"Um, well...shit." I sigh. "Okay, let's do it."

Jensen exhales, his eyes fluttering shut, then opening again. "Good, because I already bought your ticket."

"Oh my god, see. This is what I'm talking about! Ridiculous," I say, laughing and pushing at his chest.

He grips me tighter. "It's gonna be great, Harper. I'm gonna show you so much." He presses his cheek against my temple, inhaling deeply and returning to silence as the song finishes.

Like it or not, I'm going on an adventure with Jensen. Who I am kidding? It sounds amazing. But also a bit scary.

Actually, it scares the shit out of me. I've never flown on a plane. I've never been out of the state, other than driving into a bordering state for day trips. I've never seen the ocean. And I was about to plunge head-first into all of it with none other than Jensen.

Part of me is riding the high, enjoying the ride while it lasts, hanging onto every delicious moment and making a mental scrapbook of this time to flip through later. Another part of me is absolutely terrified for when the ride ends, when it's time to get off.

Will the memories be enough? Or am I setting myself up for a terrible tailspin?

Sure, I was alone before Jensen and I was fine. But I was acutely unaware of how lonely I was.

Could I return to it as easily?

HARPER

TWENTY-FOUR HOURS after he asked me on the dance floor to go home with him to North Carolina, we arrive in Raleigh. I peer out the window of the airplane, watching the bright city lights blur as we land. I've never seen such a sight. And for all my fear of flying for the first time, Jensen made it a breeze. Maybe it's because he flew us first class and kept me liquored up. Or because he talked to me the entire time, forcing my mind elsewhere. But I barely noticed when we took off or landed.

In the back of the Uber, he points out buildings in the city, places I can visit during the day if I want. Apparently there are some nice parks and museums here. I'm just in shock at the size of the city, and apparently Raleigh isn't even that big when compared to larger ones. It makes me wonder about Boston, where my sister ran away to all those years ago. If it's anything like here or bigger, I'm certainly starting to understand the appeal.

"We're here," he says, stopping in front of the door on the right side of the hall.

When the Uber had dropped us off in front of this building, my jaw dropped. It's gorgeous. Jensen's "small downtown loft" is bigger than he lets on. Big bright windows overlook the city, bright white countertops line the kitchen, and a brick fireplace is nestled in the open living room. Stairs lead up to what I assume is the bedroom. Though, for whatever reason, thinking about it makes me super nervous.

We've slept together several times for Christ's sake. Why does the thought of his bedroom make me nervous now? Maybe because it's *his* bedroom. Maybe because being in it will feel so much more intimate. Maybe because I want to open his underwear drawer and medicine cabinet and fridge and just expose all the things right now.

Jensen sets our bags down and walks into the living room, grabbing a small remote and clicking a couple of buttons. The fireplace roars to life and then he lowers it. *Wow, fancy.*

"Are you hungry? Thirsty?" he asks.

"Both, actually."

"I probably don't have much to eat, but I can order whatever you want. I have some drinks and water," he says, rounding back toward the fridge.

"Water is fine," I say, leaning against the counter.

His long arms stretch up into the cabinet next to the fridge to retrieve a glass, the muscles in his sides flexing as I let out an audible sigh. "What?" he asks.

"Nothing. You just look really good getting water."

"Well, if that's how you feel, I will fetch you water anytime you like," he teases.

"Can I really have anything to eat? Because I can't do that at the farm, obviously."

Jensen finishes filling my glass of water and brings it to me, then opens the drawer next to me, revealing an entire collection of takeout menus. "I'm not home a lot. And the thought of trying to get groceries and watch them go bad before I can use them doesn't sit well with me."

I rifle through the menus, and there seems to be a little of everything. "And all of these will deliver here? Now?"

He checks his watch and nods. "Yeah, pretty much."

Amazing. Most everything back home closes by nine and nothing is close enough to deliver to the farm. "Okay. I'll have this, please." I raise up a menu for a fancy sounding steakhouse.

Jensen cracks a smile, flipping the menu open. "That's my girl."

The sentiment he uses does something to me. *His girl. His. Girl.* Excuse me while I retrieve my lady parts that have fallen out all over the floor.

"Let me guess," he says. "Steak and shrimp? Loaded potato? Tell me you want your steak a medium rare, please?" His eyes are pleading.

"Yes to all those things."

He clutches the menu to his chest and presses his eyes shut. "You just get better and better."

"Are you still drunk from the airplane booze?" I joke.

"Maybe," he says. "Maybe not." He makes a face and I can't help but laugh harder.

"Again, ridiculous."

"How about you go upstairs, put on comfy clothes and freshen up or whatever you need to do, while I order? I know after I travel, I can't wait to get out of my travel clothes," he says.

"That sounds like a great idea," I say. "Do I have time to shower?"

Jensen nods, explaining to me where the towels and things are upstairs as he takes out his phone to order.

I grab my bag and head up the steps, taking them slowly. I don't know why, it's not like there's a freaking monster up here. What am I expecting?

I reach the top and peer around, surprised for whatever reason at how neat it is. He probably cleaned before he left. Or maybe he's just always this neat? The bed is made. There's nothing piled up anywhere. No laundry on the floor. I thought guys were messy?

After I flip the light on, the cool gray bedding catches my eye first. His large bed sits on the far wall and looks comfortable. I walk over to his dresser, noticing everything on top is so organized. *Fuck, he's more organized than me.* A couple of watches are laid out next to a small cup with change in it. I rub my hand over the knob of the top drawer, betting myself it's his underwear drawer, tempted to pull it open and peak in. Why? I don't know.

A closet door is next to the bathroom, and across from it on the opposite side of the room is another room that looks like an office.

Maybe he can work from home and we can have naughty office sex. *Wow, Harper. Where did that come from?*

I step into the bathroom, my cheeks hot from my own thoughts, and it's just as clean and tidy as the rest of his place. White tile and a floor to ceiling glass shower with multiple shower heads intimidate me. I set my bag down, praying you turn it on just like any other shower, and begin to undress. As I step out of my clothes, I realize it's so tidy I don't even know where to put them. On the floor seems so out of place. So I ball them up and place them on the toilet, thinking to myself I need to get a separate dirty linen bag or something.

"What are you doing?" Jensen's voice travels from behind me and I spin around, realizing I hadn't even bothered to close the door.

"Um, nothing? Just getting in the shower. I didn't know where to put my dirty clothes," I say.

But he's not listening. He's staring. Because I'm naked. Jensen sucks his bottom lip into his mouth as his eyes travel my legs, up my middle, over my breasts, and finally come to rest on my face.

"I have a hamper," he says, his voice low, nearly a growl as he steps toward me. He stands in front of me, pulling his shirt over his head.

"What are you doing?"

"I'm dirty too," he says. "Let's shower together."

Oh. Fuck.

I hear the unbuckling of his pants but I don't take my eyes off his as he unbuttons and slides them down. Now there are clothes on the floor.

He steps back toward the shower and reaches in, eyes still on me. The water shrieks on and then comes to a steady stream, the water so hot the glass steams instantly. Jensen pulls the bathroom door shut and then nods toward the shower, inviting me in.

And I know, I know they say money can't buy happiness but damn, five shower heads in a giant floor to ceiling shower big enough for two people sure is a lot of happiness.

I tried to get Charles to shower with me once. He agreed after a long while but got frustrated that we had to keep switching in and out of the water and refused to do it again after the one time. But this, this is nothing like that. This is bliss.

I stand under the falling water, letting my coiled muscles relax, rolling my neck and shoulders, eyes closed.

The warmth of Jensen's hands hit my senses next, gripping my sides tenderly and sliding up my ribcage to cup beneath my breasts. The water makes everything slick, our skin gliding against each other's with ease. I return his touch, the palms of my hands stretching over his chest and down his tightened stomach. He inhales a breath as tiny beads of water trickle down his forehead and the ridge of his brow before falling. His wet eyelashes make his eyes look darker, more intense, and I hold my breath as he trails a single finger down the center of my stomach, looping around my navel.

Jensen's other hand reaches to the shower wall, retrieving a bottle of shampoo. "Turn around," he says, his voice low and breathy.

I turn my back to him as he tips the bottle, and I hear the click of the top behind me. Then I feel his fingers in my hair, massaging my scalp, running through the short lengths and back up again. He repeats this over and over again, working the suds until he moves me back, tipping my head into the shower stream and rinsing it, then moves his body against mine, pressing his front to my back. His fingers comb through my hair one last time before he tugs it to the side, exposing my neck to his mouth. Jensen leans in slow, his hot breath tickling my wet skin.

He presses his mouth to my neck, but I realize it isn't his lips. His teeth glide along my throat, not biting, just pressing against me, sending a wave of goosebumps over me, even in this heat.

"You make me want to do bad things, Harper," he whispers. "You make me want to be a good man but a bad boy."

Before I can respond, he spins me, bringing his mouth to mine and pressing his kiss deep. His tongue laps and takes, no hesitation. One of his long arms wraps me up, coils my body into his while the other cradles my head. I am entirely at his mercy and I wouldn't have it any other way.

My fingers comb through his hair and grip his back, his muscles tightening under my touch. Before I know what's happening, he breaks his kiss and falls to his knees. Jensen runs the palms of his hands up the backs of my thighs and looks up at me, licking his bottom lip.

I brace myself, placing one hand on the shower wall and the other on his shoulder. Slowly, he leans in toward the center of me, mere inches away, and stops. His teasing is achingly hot, sending chills up my spine. He parts my legs slightly with his hands, just a little, just enough. My back arches toward him and he grins, blowing hot air onto my sensitive skin. A moan escapes my lips, echoing against the shower walls.

"Harper?" he says, his voice nearly inaudible.

"Yes?"

"Tell me a secret," he says. His fingers trail further up and he swipes two over me slowly, my knees buckling slightly under the delicious sensation.

I moan again. *A secret? Now?* "I can't...think," I admit.

"Just one little secret," he says, swiping his fingers over me again. "Please?"

Oh god. Oh god. Oh god. A secret. Okay, focus, Harper.

His fingers trail up me again, slow and deliberate, flicking at the end.

I double over, whimpering. "Fuck."

"Surely, you can think of one?" he teases.

"I...I...I'm scared," I blurt, my eyes pinching together.

"Yeah," he says, pausing for a beat. "Me too."

My eyes shoot open as Jensen's face plunges between my thighs, his tongue replacing his fingers. Both my hands come to his shoulders, gripping him tightly as his tongue works circles around my clit. I struggle to catch my breath as his mouth moves against me, hungry and precise.

"Oh god," I cry. My thighs begin to clench as I feel an orgasm begin to build inside me.

He backs away, looking up at me, licking his lips.

Jesus. But really, Jesus has nothing to do with this.

Jensen stands and leads me out of the shower, water pooling all over the tile floor, but he doesn't seem to notice or care. He presses me against the sink before lifting me onto the counter, resting my ass on the edge and parting my legs so he fits between them. He rubs his hard shaft against my already wet entrance and I moan, my knees pressing against his hips.

"Be right back," he whispers, as he steps back and opens the bathroom door. He disappears into his room for mere seconds, returning with a condom in his hand.

Yes, good call. At least one of us is thinking straight. Technically, I'm on birth control, but still. We haven't discussed enough to go without.

He sheaths himself and is back between my legs again in record time, pressing his lips to mine. I don't know if he's hungry for me, or if like me, he's remembered there's food on the way, but he's in a frenzy now. His tongue laps against mine at the same time I feel him press into me and I dig my fingers into his back. I arch toward him, my moan echoing out into the loft.

Jensen stills me, waiting until the initial rush of being intertwined calms, and then he begins to rock back and forth, gripping me tightly against him. He moves in and out of me slowly, then picks up the pace. He thrusts into me harder and deeper each time, sending a wave of delicious sensations crashing over my body from my toes all the way up to my throat. The heat has crept into my cheeks as well. I return his frenzied movements, rubbing my hands over his back, pressing kisses to his collarbone. I open further for him, giving myself over to him completely, offering myself up like a sacrifice splayed out right here on his bathroom sink counter.

We rock together harder and faster, the pace quickening still, a groan in the back of his throat nearly constant, gutting me.

"Fuck, Harper," he says.

I feel myself unraveling around him and I know he can feel it too. He stills, his orgasm rocking his body hard. He leans toward me, pressing his forehead to mine, pecking soft kisses to my lips and cheeks.

Just as he exhales, we hear the buzzer at the front door downstairs.

The food is here.

Thank fuck, because now I'm starving.

JENSEN

IT DIDN'T TAKE LONG for us to clear the food we ordered. After a day of travel and only a few airport snacks in our bellies, Harper and I finished our steaks, potatoes, and shrimp like champions. For as petite as that woman is, she can put away some food. Not that I'm at all complaining whatsoever. Quite the opposite, actually. If anything, I'd brag about it.

I watch her as she clears our empty takeout containers from the counter, wearing nothing but one of my white V-neck T-shirts. I know she's not wearing any panties because I watched her dress in a hurry to come downstairs. I'd tossed the shirt at her when she was completely naked and she quickly threw it over her head, pulling her hair up in a cute little ponytail. But that's it. So no. There are no panties under there. The T-shirt comes down past her ass cheeks a little, but I know if she were to, say, reach up into a high cabinet, things would begin to peak out. *God, I'm such a perv.*

Look, I know I *just* had her in the bathroom, but did you hear me? She's wearing my white T-shirt and nothing else. Her slightly hardened nipples press against the thin fabric and I shift my weight from left to right, taking another sip of my whiskey. The warm liquid hits the back of my throat and I'm hoping, more than anything, it will calm me the hell down.

"Are you finished with this?" she asks, picking up the last container in front of me.

I nod, letting her take it, knowing it's in her Southern nature to clean up after dinner, even though she doesn't have to. I tried assuring her, reminding her that she's the guest. It didn't work. I figure why not let her be comfortable and do what makes her comfortable?

I go back to silently studying her. Harper's graceful movements mesmerize me. I don't know if she actually knows she's graceful, but she is. Perhaps it's just a natural state for her.

"Did you ever take dance lessons or anything?" I ask.

"No, why?"

"Just curious." So, it is a natural state. I move toward her, taking her gently by the wrist, forcing her to drop the forks she has onto the counter.

Harper instinctively wraps her arms up around my neck and I know this means the T-shirt she's wearing has ridden up.

I resist the urge to drop my hands low enough to take advantage and instead focus on her face. "Let's go sit in front of the fireplace," I suggest.

She nods, leaving the rest of the kitchen mess for morning.

I lead her by the hand to the couch, the fire still roaring low and steady from earlier.

I sit and Harper coils herself up in my lap, drawing her feet in. Her head rests just below mine, nestled partly on my shoulder and partly on my throat. I inhale against her hair, something floral and fresh filling my senses.

"Jensen?"

"Yeah?"

"Will you sing to me?" she asks.

"What do you want me to sing?"

"Surprise me," she says.

I lift her, then place her back into the corner and throw a small blanket over her legs so she isn't chilly. Sure, the fire's warm, but just in case. Retrieving my guitar, I sit on the couch near her feet, strumming and tuning it. "Have you ever heard of a band called Radio Company?"

Harper shakes her head. "No."

"This is a song by them called *Off My Mind*." I begin to sing the words as Harper's eyes study my face and mouth. I don't know why this song popped into my head. Or maybe I do and just didn't realize it. As I sing the words, they feel too familiar, too true in some ways, anyway. I sing for her, to her, quietly, my voice echoing into the expanse of the empty loft. *Always so empty.*

As I finish and strum the last chords, Harper begins to clap and whistle as if I've just performed a miniature concert. "I think I could listen to you sing every day."

"Well, I can sing for you every day," I offer, realizing too late the weight of my words, what they mean.

We let the silence fall over us for a beat, and I store away the guitar while I find myself thinking a lot of things I shouldn't. I think back to our sexy shower time, but not the parts I expect to be reminiscing about.

I settle back behind her, her body nestling into mine again. She spreads the blanket back over us and I'm thankful I don't have to go into the office right away in the morning. All I want to do is lie here with her, hold her, have a little more of this.

"So, what are you going to do tomorrow when I go into work?" I ask, hopeful she's excited and not regretting coming.

"I think I'm just going to take my camera out and explore. We're close to downtown, right? I could walk?" she asks.

"Technically we are downtown," I say. "And if you go a couple of blocks that way, you'll be in the heart of the city. Museums, good places to eat, a nice park."

"Perfect," she says.

Yeah, she is, my thoughts echo and I do my best to quickly shake them away. "You ready for bed?" It's been a long day, and as much as I don't want the evening to end, her eyes are starting to look tired and I can feel the same in mine.

She nods against my chest, releasing a long breath as I take her by the chin and turn her face to mine.

I press my lips to hers gently, and everything aches. *Why does every-thing ache?*

She's pulling back now, away, standing up and letting the blanket fall to a mound at her feet. She stretches her arms over her head. "Okay, bedtime. But I have an issue." Harper turns, giving her back to me as she steps toward the stairs, placing one foot on the first step.

"What's that?" I ask.

"We haven't had dessert yet." She turns away again and steps up to the next step. Her hands glide down over her body to the edges of her shirt, and she lifts it over her head in one swoop then tosses it down to the floor.

She peeks at me over her shoulder, pausing for only a moment, giving me a knowing look, then turns back, a silent invitation to follow.

My god, this woman. I stand, crossing the floor slowly toward her, my eyes never leaving her backside. She makes it to the top as I still ascend—all long legs, ass, and beautiful spine. She's not trying to cover up or shield herself. Her arms hang to her sides in a relaxed, comfortable manner. She disappears from my line of sight and I move faster to get to her, pulling my shirt off as I get to the top.

Harper's lying on my bed wearing nothing but a knowing grin, legs crossed at the ankles, propped up on her elbows. My eyes travel up and down her body as I leave my shorts in a pile on the floor and step toward the bed.

"I want you," she says, running her own hand over her tit, her voice low and breathy.

And just like that, I'm not tired anymore.

HARPER

WHEN JENSEN KISSED me goodbye an hour ago, he tried hard not to wake me. He trailed his hand over my hip, up my side, and caressed my cheek before placing his lips to my forehead. Of course, I was awake the entire time, listening to him quietly navigate his morning routine. So when he leaned in to kiss me, I opened my eyes, pulled his face back down to me, and kissed him gently on the lips. This only served to make him want to stay, however. While I wish he could, I knew I had to let him go.

I lay in his bed for a long while, just staring up at the ceiling and smiling like an idiot. Then my phone dinged, pulling me out of my thoughts and back into reality.

> **JENSEN**
> Why do I even have to have a job?

> For money?

> **JENSEN**
> I will sell all my worldly possessions to crawl back into bed with you right now.

> Sounds good to me.

JENSEN

sighing

What time will you be back?

I ask because I realize I didn't have a chance to this morning. This morning had been centrally focused on kissing.

JENSEN

In time to pick you up for dinner at 6:30pm?

Sounds good. What should I wear?

JENSEN

I want to take you somewhere nice. I left a credit card on the counter downstairs in case you need anything at all. A ride, an outfit, anything. You can even shop for food or drinks that you like, since I don't have any and don't want you to starve.

I can pay for stuff.

JENSEN

Please let me take care of it.

Not wanting to argue, I agree with him, making a note to place his card in my wallet before I go out. I brought several items of clothing, but nothing really fancy. I guess I'll add shopping to my agenda today.

Pushing the covers back, I cross to his full-length mirror and stare at myself for a moment. The genuine smile planted across my lips for the past few weeks is something I haven't seen in quite a while. I relish in this moment before getting dressed and throwing my hair up into a ponytail, deciding to shower later, closer to date time.

I check my camera, shove extra film in my bag, and head downstairs. His card is on the countertop with a note neatly folded in half, my name on the front.

Harper,

If I were to write you a song, it would go like this…
You're beautiful, got a great smile,
you're beautiful, got a nice ass,
but none of that compares to
the way I feel when I'm inside you.
Okay, I'm shit at writing songs. I will try to get better.
But all of it is true.
xo
Jensen
P.S. Have fun today.

I giggle at his note, pressing it to my chest and rolling my eyes. That man is so ridiculous. I know I say it and think it a lot, but it's true. I slip it into my bag along with his card, and the spare key he gave me so I and come and go as I want, and then leave the loft.

———————

I can confirm I love everything about this city. And the shopping? So much better than home. I stepped into the first store a bundle of nerves and left with two outfits and two pairs of shoes because I couldn't decide which to purchase in the moment. Plus, I thought the second outfit might come in handy if we went somewhere later in the week as well. Oddly enough, I didn't feel strange using his credit card. I thought I would feel guilty or have remorse, but I didn't. Each time I used it, I handed it over in a proud sort of way, like doing so meant I belonged to Jensen. Except, that was a weird thought to have.

I get back to the loft in plenty of time to get ready before Jensen arrives home, so I rush upstairs, hanging both outfits in his closet. Then I run to the bathroom to make quick work of the much needed shower in favor of saving any time I have for hair and makeup.

Pulling a towel around me, I walk into the bedroom and pull the two dresses from the garment bag, trying to decide which to wear. Maybe I can let him pick? *No, Harper. Be ready and sexy when he gets here.*

The first dress is black, cut just above the knee and tight all the way up. It hugs my body in all the right places, with a V cut in the front for some cleavage. The second dress is a deep shade of red and long, grazing the floor just a tad. It flows from the hips and hugs my center and chest but is sleeveless, exposing my collarbones and neck in the most eloquent and delicious way. *Decisions, decisions.*

I return to the dresses after drying off, applying a decent amount of going-on-a-date makeup, and curl my hair into soft waves that bounce off my shoulders when I walk briskly. I finally play the catch-a-tiger-by-his-toe game just to fucking decide because I'm running out of time. When it's settled, I slip the short black number on just as I hear the front door open and close.

"Honey, I'm home," Jensen calls out.

I giggle at his apparent joke and take one final look in the mirror as I yell back, "Be right down!" I smooth my hands over the soft fabric of the dress and slip my feet into the black heels I got to match. *Here goes nothing.*

Bracing myself at the top of the stairs, I peer down, seeing he's looking down at his phone. I begin descending, my eyes still on him, and I manage to make it to the bottom without him looking up.

Jensen finally looks up toward me, the sound of my heels on the hardwood seemingly capturing his attention. He straightens himself from his leaning position over the counter and releases the grip on his phone. His eyes travel up the length of my body, his mouth agape. He doesn't say anything right away, just watches me walk to him. His eyes are dark and hooded, mischief playing in his irises. His lips tug up just a touch, giving his mouth the most sinister grin.

"I'm not worthy of you," he whispers.

My breath hitches in my lungs at his words and I blink. "What?"

He paws his hands over his rumpled suit he's been wearing all day and I connect the dots. "I need to change really fast. I'll be back in two minutes." Jensen reaches out to touch me but stops himself. "Nope, I can't. Not yet. If I start touching you now, we'll never make it to dinner."

A rush of goosebumps pricks my spine and the thought of skipping dinner and spending the entire time in bed with Jensen is more appealing than I care to admit. But I'm dressed up. And a part of me wants to go out with him, see the city with him, and experience it as he does.

He presses a chaste kiss to my temple and bounds upstairs, taking them two at a time.

I walk to the windows, realizing I haven't even looked out of them at a close distance since arriving. Floor to ceiling, they look out over quite a bit of city landscape. The streetlamps are all beginning to flicker on. An impressive amount of traffic is still on the road. By this time back home, everyone would be home.

I hear Jensen's steps behind me as he comes down, keeping his promise that he wouldn't take long. I turn and suck in a breath. He's wearing a sharp black suit and crisp white shirt but no tie. Instead, the top two buttons are left undone for a more relaxed look.

As I step toward him, I smell his spicy cologne and catch a glimpse of dampened hair. "Did you shower?"

"Told you I can be quick," he says, winking.

"You look amazing."

Jensen stills his movements as he finishes buttoning his cuffs and holds his hand out to me. No sooner than I place mine into his, he pulls me in toward him, pressing me tight against his chest and inhaling a deep breath.

"Do you remember when we went camping?" he asks.

My stomach flips, delicious knots coiling low in my belly as I recall our first kiss. "Of course."

"Every time I breathe you in, that's what I remember. Lying next to you in that tent, your sweet scent in the air. Your hair damp from the lake." He breathes in, dipping his head to my neck and pressing kisses along the front of my throat and down the top of my chest.

"Do you want to know what happens when I breathe you in?" I ask, trying to steady my breathing.

He looks up at me expectantly, letting his bottom lip trail up from my skin slowly. "What?"

I bring him cheek to cheek, so my lips are close to his ear, as if this room is filled with people and I have to keep what I'm about to say a secret. "I think about that blanket in that field of sunflowers with all those stars above us," I whisper. "I think about lying there, looking up at them with you."

His lips part as a wide smile spreads over his lips, baring his teeth. "That's a good one."

"We have a lot of good ones," I point out.

"Let's go make another good one," he says, as his hand squeezes mine.

I nod, eager to go wherever he takes me.

Eager for a lot of things.

HARPER

JENSEN LEADS me down a quiet walkway, only a few streetlamps filtering through the trees. The night is warm, with gentle breezes fluttering my short skirt. All I hear is the quiet shuffle of our shoes, his hand resting on the small of my back.

"Where are we going?"

"A quiet little place, you'll see," he says, a gentle smile across his lips.

We walk a few more paces, rounding a corner and I see a red door, no signs. Jensen pushes the door open, and I take a step inside, greeted immediately by a woman at a hostess stand.

"Two for Reed," Jensen says, replacing his hand on my back, rubbing small circles over my spine.

"Right this way, Mr. Reed," she says, checking something on the sheet in front of her and then stepping in front of us.

The hostess seats us in a quiet booth toward the back of the restaurant. After sitting, I take a look around. The lighting is low, a small candle between us on the table. Plush seating envelops me. It certainly doesn't feel cheap. I don't know that I've ever been to such an upscale place. The walls are smooth, neatly decorated with modern art. Instrumental music plays overhead and it takes me a moment to realize it's not through speakers. There's a small stage where musicians are playing. My hands involuntarily clench in my lap, intimidation flooding me.

"Do you like it?" he asks, interrupting my observations.

"It's beautiful."

"Should I order us a bottle of wine?" he asks, and I nod, still taking in the grandeur of the room. He gives our order to a waiter and I finally look down at my menu.

Holy shit. Okay, this place is expensive. Clearing my throat, I sip my water and eye Jensen, who looks more than relaxed. His eyes rove over the menu with calm interest.

"So what's good here?" I ask, hoping to take my mind off these prices.

"You have to try the orange duck," he says. "If you're in the mood for poultry."

I scan my menu until I find the dish he's talking about, noticing it's one of the more expensive items. "Maybe I'll just have some chicken."

"Babe, you can get chicken anywhere. Where's your sense of adventure?"

"This place is expensive."

Jensen's head tugs back, surprise appearing on his face. "I want to treat you. Don't worry about the cost, just get what you want. It's not a problem." He attempts to give me a reassuring smile, reaching across the table for my hand and lacing his fingers between mine.

Inhaling a deep breath, I try to shake the feeling I have. Jensen has money. A lot of money. I feel like I knew this but didn't really realize what it meant. Or the extent of how different his everyday life would be compared to mine.

Then it hits me.

I trust him. I trust him completely. So if he says this isn't a big deal, if he says not to worry, then I shouldn't. I won't. "You're right. I'll have the orange duck," I say, squeezing his hand in return and flashing him a smile.

"That's my girl," he says, turning his attention back to his menu.

There it is again. *That's my girl. His girl.* I swallow hard, sipping my water again. I want to ask him about it, to get clarification. But I won't do it tonight, not while things are so nice. *Where is that wine? I need a drink.*

As if on cue, the waiter rounds the corner with our bottle and two glasses. He opens it tableside and pours a small taste into Jensen's glass, offering it to him. Jensen sips and nods his head. *Wow, I've only seen people do that in movies.* After the waiter finishes pouring our glasses, he leaves the bottle and takes our food orders before disappearing.

"Thank you," I say, staring across the table at him.

"For what?" he asks.

"For this, for inviting me here. For everything."

"You don't have to thank me. I wanted you to come," he says.

"Why?"

"I told you, I wanted to show you another city, take you to see the ocean," he says, furrowing his eyebrow slightly like he doesn't know what other answer it could be.

I nod in agreement, afraid to ask what I really want, afraid to push for more. The questions swarming my mind seem to be building up. "What day are we going to the ocean?" I ask, deciding to steer the conversation somewhere less tense, at least for me.

"I'm thinking this weekend. I'm hoping to get out of the office early on Friday and head down so you have a couple of days there," he says, his grin wide with excitement.

"Sounds great," I say. "I might even pick up a new bikini or something this week."

Jensen narrows his eyes. "Oh my god, I get to see you in a bikini again."

I giggle. "You've seen me completely naked," I whisper.

"I know, I know, but seeing you in a bikini is essentially the same concept as lingerie. It's teasing and delightful."

I laugh harder this time, shaking my head. "You're silly."

"Now I'm having thoughts of you in that red bikini at the lake," he says. "You look so good in red."

Our food arrives, disrupting the bikini talk, and we settle into more conversation while I still steer clear of heavier topics. And he's right, this orange duck is fucking fantastic. We sip wine and laugh. Jensen orders dessert, which comes with chocolate covered strawberries, and he feeds me one across the table. This simple act of feeding me, of holding the strawberry to my lips while I take a bite, feels sensual. He watches my mouth the entire time, biting his bottom lip.

"Okay, it should be illegal for you to eat," he says.

"You want me to starve?" I laugh.

"Okay, it should be illegal for you to look like that when you eat," he says. "Maybe that's a better way of putting it."

We both laugh as the check is delivered to the table and he immediately swipes it, pulling a card from his wallet and laying it at the edge of the table. The nosey part of me, not that I condone her behavior, wants to know how much an evening like this costs. But I resist the urge to look.

The mood changes when we arrive back to his loft. Suddenly, it's as if we're both aware of the proximity of a bed. Or perhaps that we're in a space we can have sex in.

Jensen removes the items from his pockets, setting them on the counter, as I step out of my heels.

I turn to see him leaning against the counter, staring at me. "What?"

"Come here," he says, reaching his hand out to me.

I oblige, walking back to him, my bare feet hardly making any noise against the floor. His face turns dark as he licks his lips, biting the bottom one again. I wrap my arms up around his neck as his slide around my waist.

"I want to take you to bed," he whispers, as he leans down and presses soft kisses to my neck, just underneath my ear.

"How about right here against the counter?" I tease.

Jensen groans, his grip tightening, fingers digging into my flesh. But it doesn't hurt. "I want you in the bed," he says. "I want to watch your face as I make you come." He walks me back, ushering me toward the stairs.

"You can't do that against the counter?" I laugh.

"Not the way I'm craving it at the moment," he says.

I ascend the steps, his hands trailing down over my ass as he walks behind me. I can't place a finger on it, I can't say exactly how, but tonight feels different. We've had sex plenty of times, but this feels more intimate, more serious.

As Jensen kisses me near the foot of his bed, his hands lace into mine. His mouth is slow but not teasing. He kisses me completely, passionately.

Then it dawns on me.

We're not just having sex tonight.

We're making love.

JENSEN

THIS WEEK HAS PASSED TOO QUICKLY. It's already Friday, and while I'm excited for the weekend, for time with Harper, I realize before I know it she'll be going home. The thought makes me sad. Actually, not just sad. Sick to my stomach, like there's a large rock in the pit of it, weighing me down.

"Okay, I'm ready," she says, bounding into the bathroom, interrupting my thoughts.

My eyes wander over her body. Her short hair is back in a messy ponytail, her face carries no makeup, maybe only a little lip balm. I sweep my gaze down over her legs, which look great in her cutoff jean shorts, then back up again over her tank top stretched over the black string bikini tied up beneath it.

"Oh my," I say, exhaling.

She pushes sunglasses up on her head and clips a fanny pack around her waist. "What?"

"You just look," I pause, "really good. Even if you are wearing a fanny pack."

"Don't make fun of my fanny pack. It's badass," she says, attempting to suppress a laugh.

I hold my hands up in mock innocence. "Let's get out of town."

We hop in and hit the road early, attempting to avoid traffic. Harper plugs her phone in and hits a button. "I made a road trip playlist," she says.

"I hope it's good," I tease.

"It's the best," she says. "Don't worry."

We're thirty minutes down the highway before I realize the music is all songs we've referenced since knowing each other. I smile both outwardly and inwardly. Harper leans over toward the center console and reaches for my hand, tangling her fingers with mine. This is contentment. This is that comfortable silence people always seem to talk about. Neither of us feel the need to fill the space with words, both of us relaxed and just enjoying being around the other.

"So, where are we staying when we get there?" she asks after a little while.

"I found a little rental right on the water. An Airbnb."

"Right on the water?"

"Yep," I clarify. "The patio opens right up to the beach."

"Oh my gosh, that sounds amazing," she says.

There's a reason why I hadn't let her see the place, although I could easily show her photos. There's a reason I didn't just book a hotel room, too. I want Harper to have the very best experience, one where we wouldn't have to waste time driving to the beach or seeing it from a distance first. I squeeze her hand instinctively. Harper deserves perfection.

My phone rings but I quickly dismiss the call, seeing that it's work. I told them I wasn't coming in today, that I wouldn't be available this weekend. They can wait.

We pull into the driveway of our small rental after another two hours of driving and rest stops. The small bungalow sits in a nice area, and I all but abandon the car to get Harper to the beach as quickly as I can.

"Leave everything in the car, I'll come back for it," I say, hopping out and waving her to follow me. I lead her to the gate on the side of the house, the one I know leads straight to the back, straight to the water. "Close your eyes," I urge.

She gently closes them, allowing me to lead her through.

I position her a little way's away from the water, her eyes still shut tight. Walking behind her, I wrap my arms around her waist and lean down, pressing my lips near her ear. "Okay, now open them," I whisper.

I can't see her face, but I hear the ragged sharp intake of breath filling her. She smooths her hands down over mine on her hips, leaning back into me. "This is amazing," she says.

For a moment, I think she might be crying or near crying. There's so much emotion in her voice, so much raw feeling.

"So you like it?" I ask.

"I love it," she says.

A rush of air leaves my lungs, relief washing over me. I press my eyes closed and listen to the water lap onto shore. My favorite part of being near the ocean has always been the sounds it makes.

"You go dip your toes in. I'll get our stuff from the car." I press a quick kiss to her lips before turning back.

Inside, I place our bags in the bedroom and peer out the sliding glass door toward her.

Harper is walking along the water's edge, her feet squishing into the wet sand, her eyes fixed on the horizon. She pulls the camera hanging around her neck up and snaps a photo of the water.

Pushing the door open, I suppress my greed, my desire to call for her, in favor of watching her for a little while longer. The winds coming in from the ocean blow her blonde ponytail back and forth as she constantly fights to keep loose strands tucked behind her ears. In this moment, I am in awe of her.

She must catch me looking at her from the corner of her eye, her head suddenly whipping in my direction as she gifts me with a smile, wide and genuine. "Hey, you," she calls as she kicks her foot through a puddled bit of ocean water.

"Hi there," I say, clearing my throat.

Harper begins to walk slowly toward me, and I have a sudden urge to pause this moment, memorize the way she looks in the darkening sky behind her, the setting sun casting a glow across her beautiful face, the way her bright blue eyes practically twinkle.

"Come here," I say, reaching for her with one arm and pulling my phone from my pocket with the other.

"What are you doing?" she asks.

"I want to document this moment," I say. "Smile." I turn us so the ocean is behind us. I lean down, pressing her to me so we're cheek to cheek, and snap a photo of us.

"Did it turn out good?" she asks.

I bring up the photo and examine it. From the smile on her lips to her body pressed close to mine and comfortably tucked beneath my arm, the picture is prefect. It's everything I wanted to capture.

"It's perfect," I say, leaning my phone down to show her.

"Will you send it to me?" she asks.

"Of course. But first, let's have some dinner and a bath."

She sighs. "That sounds amazing."

We walk back through the sliding doors, my arm still wrapped around her and I can't help but notice how close we are to the bed. I mean, obviously, we're in the bedroom but what kind of person would I be if I didn't take advantage of it?

"Wait," I say. I press her up against the bed and push her back gently, leaning over to take her mouth with mine.

"I thought we were making dinner?" She giggles.

"We are," I say as I tug at her shorts. "But first I want a little appetizer." I part her naked legs and drop to my knees, a need to taste her overcoming me.

Her laughter turns to moans in the back of her throat when my mouth finds her and later when I joke with her, I'll ask her if she remembers that time I ate before dinner.

HARPER

DO you know how difficult it is to stand and chop vegetables right after you've been cunnilingus-ed? Is that even a word? After you've been eaten out? *Ew, gross, don't like that phrase.* After you've been given an orgasm with a mouth? *Okay, yeah that will have to work.* My legs are jello as I try to concentrate on chopping the mushrooms and onions. Meanwhile, Jensen marinades two steaks as he hums. *FUCKING HUMS.* He's pleased as punch with himself and the "eating before eating" jokes he keeps making has caused the blush on my cheeks to remain there since we've entered the kitchen.

"You know, we eat steak a lot," I observe, in an effort to change the topic.

"I should probably make sure it doesn't exceed the number of times I've eaten—"

"Oh my god, no. Stop it," I say, laughing, despite myself.

"What?" he asks, feigning innocence.

"You know what."

I bring the bowl of onions and mushrooms to the stove so he can sauté them in butter and then start on the baked potatoes. Moving around the kitchen with him like this feels so comfortable and familiar. To any outsider, it might look like we've made dinner together hundreds of times. I sigh at the thought.

In reality, we've made dinner four times together. This past week, I went grocery shopping and stocked his nearly empty kitchen with some simple meals for us to make in the evenings. He tried insisting I not cook or that he could just have dinner delivered but I rejected both. I enjoy cooking. Plus, there's something intimate and almost sensual in the way two people can cook together.

As he throws the steaks into a hot pan, I prepare two place settings at the small table on the deck. The sun has set and the sky is deep purple and inky blue. I light the torches on the corner posts and they illuminate the space just enough to set a romantic mood. *Romantic mood. Weird.* Those words feel strange to me in some ways, and I hesitate for a second, realizing this is all sort of an illusion. But one I'm not ready to leave.

We sit down to our meal a few minutes later and Jensen pours us some wine.

"Tomorrow, I'd like to take you to the pier. There's a Ferris Wheel and shops and booths," he says.

"Oh fun." The words come out feeling a little flat, but not intentionally. I'm still thinking about the curtain that will be pulled back soon. The plane ride home I'll have to take. The farewell.

Sensing my mind is elsewhere, Jensen attempts to suggest we go elsewhere.

"No, really. The pier sounds really fun." I shake away my negative thoughts and refocus on enjoying the moment. Yet again. I think I've done that probably a dozen times over the past week. Leave it to me to self-sabotage a good time.

After dinner, he draws a bath in the large whirlpool tub. The steam rolls off the hot water and sends a ripple through my stomach. He adds bath salt and bubble bath.

"I even have a rubber ducky," he says, pulling a small yellow children's bath toy from the bag.

I can't help but laugh. He really does think of everything. He's made me laugh more in the time I've known him than I did in my entire relationship with my ex which I find both sad and illuminating.

Because laughter is going on my permanent list of requirements in a relationship after this. *After this.*

We undress and step in, the water rising a couple of inches as we settle.

He cuts the water off and suddenly his eyes aren't so playful. His gaze feels serious, almost a hint of somber. "Are you having a good time here with me?" he asks.

"Of course I am. I've really enjoyed the last week." I don't have to lie or even exaggerate.

"Good." He smiles, his hands rubbing over my thighs. We're facing each other, our legs crossed over the other's, my feet resting on either side of him.

I consider saying thank you to him again but it doesn't feel right.

"I got an email on my phone from work earlier when I didn't answer the call," he says. "They need me to go to California on Tuesday."

Oh. Oh my. That's sooner than I thought I'd have to go home. "Oh I see," is all I can manage to say.

"Apparently one of our clients there is having some issues, so I have to go smooth things over," he says, but I barely hear him. His voice is growing fuzzy as I come to the realization that means I'll have to go home on or before Tuesday.

I nod along as he continues to explain the situation. "Well, I guess we should grab my ticket to go home soon, then," I suggest.

Jensen grows quiet, not answering me directly. His hands smooth over my skin under the water and he tightens his grip on me, as if that's some sort of answer.

"We're just going to have to make the most of these last few days," I say, leaning up and moving to him, straddling his lap and pressing his wet body against mine. His hands find my ass and rest there. Jensen stares into my eyes with so much intensity, I'm convinced for a moment he can see right into me. Afraid of what he'll find there, I break eye contact and press my mouth to his, savoring his lips.

I have to remember this, I think to myself. *I have to remember all of this.*

My hands grip his back, my fingertips digging into his flesh. I have to savor every moment, collect them like rain drops in a mason jar.

Suddenly overcome with emotion I don't understand, I feel tears begin to well up in the corners of my eyes. I can't let him see me cry over this so I push back what I'm feeling and focus on the full-on make-out session we're having.

I reach down between us to touch him as he presses hard against me. His hands squeeze my biceps and he inhales a sharp breath as my hand cups him.

"Jensen?" I whisper close to his ear.

"Yes?"

"If I asked you to do something, would you do it for me?"

"What?" he asks, his teeth biting into his bottom lip as soon as he mouths the single word.

"I want you to make love to me," I say, kissing his jawline.

He pulls back, capturing my eyes with his. "Baby," he says, his voice barely audible. "I thought that's what we've been doing?"

Overcome with emotion, I capture his mouth with mine again. *I thought that's what we've been doing.* His words echo in me as he wraps his arms around me and stands.

"Let's go to the bed," he says, stepping out of the tub with me still around him. If I had any time to think about it, I would commend him on his athletic abilities and sheer strength for pulling that off.

He walks me back to the bed we visited briefly earlier and lays me down. Before he can pull away from me to retrieve a condom, I pull him close and tell him I'm on birth control.

He looks down at me, his features dark and wild. "Are you sure?" he asks, and I nod, clawing at him to be closer.

"I want to feel you," I say, nearly begging.

He presses kisses along my jaw, down my neck and over the top of my breasts.

"Please, Jensen," I breathe, unable to control my need for him in this moment. It's as if I'm floating, hoping to be anchored to something, hoping he'll reach out and pluck me from this state.

He tugs my hand up over my head, then the other, lightly pinning them there as he rubs himself against the outside of my center. My breath catches in my throat, unable to regulate it any longer. Short, jagged gasps escape me and when I think I can't take it for a second longer, he pushes into me slowly, all the way, unburdened by any barrier. My hands grip his where they're pinned. He moves in and out of me painfully slowly. Every time he gives me all of him, it takes my breath away. I don't bother checking my moans or noise level. They escape my lips freely, unabashed.

He releases my hands only after I've begged to be free, begged to touch him. My hands move over his back, around to his chest, up to the back of his neck. I wrap my legs up around his thighs, pressing him into me.

His pace quickens, and I hold onto him as he moves over me. His muscles tighten and ripple, his grip on my ass getting tighter, more possessive.

"Come for me," he urges.

I press my eyes shut and feel it building inside me. I unravel around him, which only spurs him on as he pushes deeper, like he wants to disappear into me.

He groans in the back of his throat and his body begins to shudder. I feel him between my legs. I feel him like a wave lapping over my entire body. Jensen collapses against me, his chest pressing against mine. I kiss him everywhere. His lips, his cheeks, his eyelids, as he steadies his breathing. I cradle him, almost unwilling to let him go. I don't want him to go. Not yet.

"Let's just stay like this for a little while," I whisper, and he hugs me tighter, obliging my request.

Somewhere in the middle of steadying our breathing, we fall asleep just like that. Anchored to each other, intertwined. Joined together.

HARPER

"HARPER," he says, his voice floating into my still half-asleep mind. "Harper, wake up."

I peer through one barely open eye and it's still dark out. "Why are you waking me up before the sun?" I groan.

"Have you ever seen a sunrise over the ocean?" he whispers, and both of my eyes pop halfway open.

"No," I say. "I've never seen any sunrise if I can help it. Because I like sleeping."

"Come on," he says. "It'll be worth it."

The weight of him disappears from the bed and I roll over, still naked from when we went to bed. At some point in the middle of the night, we woke up long enough to untangle ourselves and get under the blankets. I sit up, rubbing my eye sockets with the balls of my palms. I don't even want to check what time it actually is.

Jensen walks back into the room with a mug of coffee. "Here, thought you might need this."

"Oh, bless it." I sigh, my body melting into relief. At least he had the good sense to brew coffee. On my third sip, I realize it's perfectly creamed and sugared. He knows how I take my coffee. *Strange.* Of course, I know he likes his black with a little sugar. Exactly one and a half spoonfuls to be precise. So maybe it isn't so strange.

"Get dressed," he says, opening the sliding glass doors. Cool air rolling off the water fills the room and sends a shiver down my spine. I tug at the covers, but he tugs from the bottom and I surrender. I roll on sweatpants and throw a tank top over my head. Even dressed, I'm still chilly.

"Here," Jensen says, stepping toward me with one of his large sweatshirts.

He places my coffee down and slides the garment over me. It's warm and smells like him. I find myself inhaling against the collar several times.

"Okay," he says. "Now you're ready."

With one hand wrapped around my warm coffee cup and the other held tightly in his, we step out onto the back deck and sit at the edge of the stairs. Jensen digs his bare feet into the sand, but I keep my socked feet up. There's nothing worse than a sock full of sand. He wraps his long arm around me, tucking me into him, against his chest. I inhale a deep breath of fresh ocean air and release it with a sigh.

"Just a little while now," he says, rubbing his hand over my thigh.

"Then can we go back to sleep?"

Jensen laughs. "You're welcome to nap while I take a run. I like running on the beach. I can wake you later for a shower."

"Sounds amazing," I say, fighting back a yawn.

"We should get to the pier early, before the crowds make it impossible," he says.

"Okay, that's good too," I say, lazily nodding.

"I promise it will all be worth it." He laughs again.

We sit talking for a few more short minutes when I realize the sky is beginning to lighten just a little. The horizon is glowing now, subtle streams of golden orange light highlighted with pink begin to show over the water's edge.

"This is it," he whispers.

Mesmerized, I don't take my eyes off the horizon. Slivers of the sun's bright globe melt over the water, making it sparkle. Each wave holds beams of light before disappearing and being replaced with the next wave. When the sun is halfway up, it sits there, almost suspended in time, before completely rising. It's as if the sun has risen straight out of the water.

Jensen closes my jaw with two fingers under my chin and until now, I hadn't realized I was sitting here with my mouth hanging open.

"It's so beautiful," I say, the sleepiness suddenly gone.

"I told you," he teases, a warm smile stretched wide across his face.

We sit there for a little while longer in the silence, taking in every bit of the sunrise.

"Okay, time for that run," he says, standing and stretching his legs. I only now notice that he's already dressed for it.

"I feel so awake now, I don't know if I'll be able to go back to sleep."

"You can always run with me?" he suggests.

"Oh, no, thank you. If it's not toward food or for my life, I'll pass."

Jensen laughs and smacks me on the butt as I turn to the door. "Suit yourself."

I turn and watch him jog down the sandy beach. I admire his sheer willpower. I have none of my own to speak of when it comes to exercise related things. I am blessed with a naturally slim figure and I thank my lucky stars regularly for it.

Sliding the door shut behind me, I wrap the blanket further around me and plop back onto the bed. I definitely wasn't lying when I said I might not be able to go back to sleep. I feel very awake. Too awake. Pulling my phone from its charging cord, I notice a text from Lyla that came in not too long ago. *What is she doing up at this hour?*

LYLA
So...how's it going? ;)

Why are you awake so early?

LYLA
It might be our honeymoon, but I still try to get in a run each morning.

Gross. You and Jensen have that in common. Anyway, it's going great. I only wish it didn't have to end so soon.

LYLA

End?

Well I have to come home. Things will be over then.

LYLA

That's dumb. They don't have to end. Also, it's not like you really HAVE TO come home.

What are you even saying?

LYLA

I'm saying stay if you want. For as long as you want. Forever, if you want.

Don't be ridiculous.

LYLA

I'm not. You're a grown woman. You can decide what you want to do. You're not tied down.

I consider her words for a few minutes. She's insane, obviously, but it doesn't stop me from thinking about it. For a brief moment.

My ticket home is already booked.

LYLA

So?

So don't make this any harder or more complicated.

LYLA

I'm just trying to help.

The fact is, I have to come back home. I can't just uproot my life and I can't just assume he would even want me here.

I set my phone down because I can't deal with this right now. I don't want to dwell on the completely pointless *what ifs* of this situation. It is what it is. We had fun. We're still having fun. And in a few days, I'll fly back home and he'll go off wherever and probably have fun with someone new. The thought actually makes me lurch forward, like I'll vomit if I think on it too hard. Going back to sleep definitely isn't in the cards now. And I don't want to shower until Jensen gets back, because why shower alone when I can shower with him? Tossing my feet back over the bed, I decide the only thing I can do is cook breakfast.

And drink more coffee. I'm definitely going to need more coffee.

JENSEN

I WISH I could say with certainty I knew what the hell I was doing. This morning I thought I'd go for a run, clear my head, really give this some thought. But when I came back, Harper had cooked breakfast and damn if it wasn't delicious. Then we had what I can only assume was the longest, sexiest shower in history. This didn't help with my muddled mind at all.

Now, we're driving down the highway and her bare feet are tucked up beneath her in the passenger seat, her hand resting in mine. Every now and again I give it a little squeeze and she squeezes back. Every time she does, the corners of her mouth turn up a little. She's staring out her window and yawning, still tired from the early morning. Apparently she didn't fall back asleep like she wanted.

"You can nap in the car, if you want," I suggest. "The drive is about an hour."

"I don't want you to have to drive in silence while I sleep," she says.

"I don't mind. I want you to rest if you need to."

"Really? Well, maybe I will. If I happen to fall asleep, I won't fight it," she says, and I give her hand another squeeze and smile.

Shit, maybe I can use a quiet drive to help with this whole clearing-my-mind thing I need to do. *Fuck*. Of course I got myself into this messy thing. I know two things to be true: Harper leaves in a few days, and it will go too quickly.

Also, I am starting to feel something for her. Is it love? God, I don't know. I want to say no. I want to say it's too soon for that. I want to say it's more than like but less than love. Is that a thing? Now I'm fucking confusing myself.

Harper's hand goes limp in mine and I glance over to see she's indeed fallen asleep. Good. She needs rest. I want her to enjoy the pier. A quick nap will do her good.

I'll just...stew in my thoughts. Great.

"Wake up, sleepyhead," I whisper, gently shaking Harper by the arm.

Her body stretches out like a cat in the sun, and her eyes blink open. "Shit, I fell asleep. I was so certain I wouldn't."

"You went pretty fast," I say, laughing. "Are you ready for the pier?"

"Yes, definitely," she says, and I gesture over to it, its tall Ferris Wheel stretching upward into the sky. Harper dips her head to look up. "Okay, I definitely want to ride that," she says.

"Let's go," I say, opening the car door and stepping out. I stretch out my back and walk around to meet Harper. After pressing a kiss to her lips, I grab her by the hand and tug her toward our first stop.

"What do we need tickets for?" she asks, as I hand money to the teen in the ticket booth.

"Lots of things, including the rides."

"Are you going to win me a teddy bear?" she asks, giving me her best pouty lip.

"I will win you whatever your heart desires." I plant another kiss against her mouth as I shove the tickets in my pocket. "But I suggest we win stuff last so we don't have to carry it all around."

"Good call," she says.

We walk together, holding hands, and every now and then she leans into me. To anyone who sees us, this is natural and normal, like we've been together forever. That thought makes me smile. *Finally I have a thought that's making me smile. Jesus.*

"Can we ride the Ferris Wheel first?" she asks.

I nod. "Of course. Today, it's whatever you want."

We stand in line for the wheel, which thankfully isn't too long. I made it a point to get us here earlier than the rush at lunch. That's usually when everyone filters in.

As we step into our bubble, the attendant tells us not to try opening the door while in the air and not to rock it.

"Oh that's scary," she says.

"Why?" I ask her.

"Because he wouldn't be telling us if someone didn't actually do it before. It's like the warning label that says don't drink the shampoo. It's only on there because someone drank the fucking shampoo." She laughs.

I can't help myself and start to laugh hard too. "You're insane."

"Whatever. Just don't rock us, you jackass." She giggles again.

I hold her close to me, pulling her to me and kissing the top of her head. "Scout's honor."

"Were you ever really a Scout?" she asks.

"No, but that's not the point. I would never dishonor them."

Harper punches me in the chest and I catch her wrist, pulling her even closer. I press my forehead to hers and her eyes close. I nip her bottom lip and then lick. This is all it takes before her mouth is pressed hard against mine, parting my lips with her tongue. I open for her, letting her tongue lap against mine. It's as if she's trying to devour me and it's so fucking hot I have to pull back lest we have a boner situation on this family friendly ride.

"Fuck," I breathe.

She lays her head on my chest and sighs. "The feeling is mutual."

The feeling is mutual. But is it? Is it really? I think about what it would mean if it actually was, if she really knew what I was thinking and feeling. Would she still say it's mutual?

"What are you thinking?" she asks, like she can just fucking sense that I'm having a moment here.

"Nothing really," I lie. "I'm just thinking about the places we can eat for lunch." *God, that's pathetic.* I could've at least been semi-truthful.

"Well, I don't know about you, but I'm in the mood for seafood. Specifically shrimp. Some sort of battered shrimp. Is that possible?" she asks.

And even though I'm a fucking liar who wants to tell her the truth, I don't. "Yeah, of course. This is the coast." I press my eyes shut, willing myself to get a grip. *There's still a lot of day left, Jensen. You can't go ruining it this fucking early.*

Harper leans up, looking out the bubble toward the ocean, her eyes lighting up as we reach the top. "Wow," she says. "This is amazing."

She looks back at me, her lips pulled back into a wide smile. This is her best face. I love all of her faces. Serious. Sexy. Even the sad ones. But my favorite is when she's happy. Not just a little happy, but so happy she smiles with her teeth.

I watch her as we go around. I watch her watching the world around us, taking everything in. I can't help but admire her, be in awe of her. She deserves so much more than what she's been given in the past. I hope in some small way, I've helped make up for what she's been through. At the very least, I hope she sees not all men are like her ex-husband. That guy was a total asshat.

When the ride ends, we step off and I push my thoughts to the side so I can stay in the moment with her.

"What next?" she asks.

Exactly, I think to myself. *What next?*

HARPER

AS WE TAKE a short walk from the Ferris Wheel to the next ride—the Scrambler—I try to ignore that Jensen seems unusually quiet. His face portrays a happiness, though I can't help but feel like it's masking something else. Not that I can really say anything, it happens to me from time to time too. All I can do is try to pull him out of his fog.

We step into this Scrambler thing, which I've ridden at county fairs in the past and know there's no chance in there to really talk. You spend the majority of the time hanging on for dear life, squishing the person sitting on the outside and laughing uncontrollably. Jensen wraps one arm around me and holds the bar in front of us with the other.

I hold onto the bar tightly with both hands, my face buried into his chest. "Are you ready to be squished?"

"Please. Have you seen you? No way you're gonna squish me," he teases.

"We'll just see about that."

The ride starts up and as it builds momentum, I feel myself thudding into the side of his body with each spin. As the ride goes on, I move my hands from the bar to around him and notice his tightened stomach muscles. Tears stream from the outer corners of my eyes I'm laughing so hard. We rock back and forth in our spots, the inertia of the ride pressing us together and then apart, over and over again.

As the ride slows to a stop, Jensen's even wiping tears of his own.

"So did you get a little squished?" I ask him.

"Not even," he says, giving me the side eye.

"Whatever, I felt those muscles tighten." I trail my fingers up his stomach as we exit the ride.

He lets out a long, "Pshhhh," and tugs me toward an old school looking diner called 'Jim's'—that's it. That's all it says. I want to question it further, but I trust Jensen to make good decisions.

As we approach the door, he says, "I know it doesn't look like much, but it's the best. Trust me."

We seat ourselves in a corner booth, per the instructions yelled out to us when we enter, as is customary with a lot of diner settings.

The waitress—a young woman, maybe college age—sets two waters down in front of us along with straws and pulls her pad from her apron. "What can I get ya'll?" she asks, her deep accent punctuating each word.

"We'll need just a few minutes." Jensen smiles up at her.

Her eyes meet his for just a moment, and it's long enough to fluster the girl. She twirls a strand of her hair and pushes it behind her ear, a shade of pink brushing her cheeks now, before she steps away.

Yeah, girl. I know the feeling. "Seems you have an admirer," I joke.

"Huh?" he says, sounding genuinely confused.

"You caused her to blush just by making eye contact with her. You didn't notice?" I laugh.

"Not really," he says, shrugging his shoulders and turning his attention back to his menu.

"Is that how all hot guys respond to obvious attention? Just a shoulder shrug? Of course you must be so used to it." I giggle.

"I didn't notice because I'm here with you. And I don't care about anyone else," he says, bringing his gaze up to lock with mine.

I'd be lying if I said I didn't feel a chill trail my spine. If this is what she felt when she met his eyes, I can understand the blushing.

I reach across the table and lace my fingers into his, suddenly feeling like he's too far away with this table between us. Not that I want to be one of those couples that sits on the same side of the table. That's ridiculous.

Then again, so is my use of the word "couple" to describe us. We're not a couple. We're friends at best. Friends with benefits? Part-time lovers? *Shit, I hate this.*

Shoving thoughts of labels aside, I ask him what he's ordering and tell him to make it two. I excuse myself to the restroom and immediately pull my phone out once I'm locked in my stall.

> This is too much for me.

LYLA

> What do you mean?

> I mean this might have been a mistake. What happens when I leave?

LYLA

> I don't think it's a matter of WHEN. It's more like IF you want to.

> Stop saying that. I'm in trouble here. I just excused myself to the bathroom to panic.

When she asks what has me panicking, I hesitate, giving her question a bit of thought.

> My feelings. I can't deal with what happened with Charles again.

LYLA

> I thought you got back out into the dating world?

> Yeah, but I expected to date around, have bad first dates, make out with a couple of men before I felt anything real.

LYLA

> So, you're feeling something real?

I shove my phone away, leaving her question unanswered for the moment. I'm not ready to answer it and I don't want to lie. The truth is, I have no fucking clue what is happening with me, with us, right now.

Returning to the table, I notice our food is already here but Jensen hasn't started eating. "Wow, how long was I in there?" I joke.

"Not long, it just got here. They're quick," he says.

The basket of golden beer battered shrimp on top of a bed of French fries looks nothing short of amazing. "I'm going to be so fat after this." I laugh.

"Good, I'll rub your belly while we cuddle." He winks.

"What are we doing after lunch?" I ask right before I pop the first crunchy shrimp into my mouth.

Jensen looks at his watch. "Well, we have some options. We can start the games and try to win something, then get back on the road to the rental after that. Or we can stay later but not get back until pretty late, which means dinner will likely be fast food somewhere."

Thinking about the options, I shove three fries into my mouth and look up at the ceiling like I'm deep in contemplation. "I don't think I want fast food," I admit. "Let's win stuff and check out the souvenir shop, then head back. I really want to swim in the ocean."

"Deal," he says, shoving two shrimp into his mouth at once.

On the way back, I don't fall asleep. I do hug the bear Jensen won me —as promised—to my chest. The soft little guy is wearing a bowtie; and though I've never been into stuffed animals, I definitely feel like I'll be keeping this one forever. The souvenirs I got everyone back home sit in a bag on the back seat. Picking them out was yet another small reminder I'll be going home soon. Seems it's written everywhere, though it's the last thing I want to think about. The fearful woman in me can't help but wonder, though.

Will this bear be the only thing I have left of our time together?

Will this fluffy little stuffed animal be the only thing I'll have left of Jensen?

HARPER

WHEN WE ARRIVE BACK to the rental, Jensen suggests we swim first and eat afterward, so we make quick work of our bathing suits. Despite wanting to straddle each other while dressing, we manage to make it out to the beach without incident.

Hand in hand, we step into the waves lapping onto the shore, walking further in as we get used to the temperature. The water is cool and refreshing compared to the heat of the day. The sun overhead beats down on everything and I'm glad I remembered sunblock. I might be used to being outside in the sun, but it's different here somehow. It's not like back home.

We wade deeper until the water is approaching my chest and stop there as Jensen lets go of my hand so he can dip under and wet his hair. I do the same and lie back to float after I come up. The ocean water feels so amazing against my skin.

"I hope this trip has been everything you wanted, Harper."

Jensen's voice cuts through the calming sound of the waves and I find my legs again, moving toward him as quickly as I can. Wrapping my arms around his neck, I lift myself and curl my legs around his hips. He grips my backside as I look deep into his eyes.

"This trip is so much more than I ever thought possible." I lean in and nudge my nose against his, coaxing him to give me his mouth. One of his hands trails up the side of my body and cups my jawline. I don't know that I've ever been more desperate for someone's touch.

He presses his lips to mine, my mouth immediately opening for him. I didn't know it was possible to enjoy kissing this much.

We stay like this for a little while, holding each other and making out. I push away, a giggle escaping my throat, and start to swim. Jensen swims after me, catching up to me in no time, despite giving me a head start.

"Remember when we went swimming while we were camping?" he asks.

"Yeah?"

"God, I thought you were so sexy in that red bikini. This black one is equally sexy, by the way, I'm just saying. All I wanted to do was stare at you, but I tried so hard not to look directly at you." His confession pours out like he's been waiting to tell me ever since.

"I thought you were just as sexy in your swim trunks. I kept catching myself staring at your chest and had to look away."

"I wouldn't have minded if you didn't," he says.

My eyes meet his as I slow my swimming to a halt, his arms scooping under me once again. This time he begins carrying me up toward the shore, out of the water, trailing kisses down my neck, over my collarbone. I hold on as tightly as I can, realizing there's more than one way I don't want to let him go. I suppress everything for this moment, his hands gripping my flesh tightly, his lips moving over me, his chest pressed to mine.

"I want you," I whisper against his ear. "I want you." My breathing is shallow and jagged but my confession will be masked by the moment. I can say it without letting him know all that it means.

"I want you, too," he groans, the words coming out almost pained.

For a moment, I allow myself to believe they could mean more, too.

We made love three times before bed. Once when we came in from swimming and two more times after dinner. Each time, the movements became more passionate, more intimate.

After our shower, we let ourselves air dry, lying in bed naked together without touching. We talked until we started to yawn, laughed, and poured out more random confessions. Jensen hates wearing socks but also hates flip flops, which I find odd. I tell him I've been able to touch my tongue to my nose since I was a kid and he makes me show him multiples times. Of course, he fails when he tries.

He tells me after his parents got a divorce, he wasn't sure he ever wanted to get married but he eventually came to understand and accept not all couples are the same. I told him after Charles, I felt the same way. He tells me he hopes to be a father one day. I tell him I've always wanted to be a mother.

Now we're lying here beneath the blankets, my head on Jensen's chest as he snores lightly, his arms around me. I can hear his heart beating just beneath my ear. I've listened to him sleeping for the last several minutes and have decided if I could, I'd stick a recording device into his chest so I can hear his heart, always. As ridiculous as that sounds, I still find myself wishing for it.

A thought hits me like a sack of bricks as we position ourselves for bed. After this, I only get to sleep in his bed with him two more times. Two more times and then I'll be on my flight back home.

Home is a funny word. We let things like houses define home, when really it's the people who make it. Knowing this, thoughts of leaving feel more and more unsettling. The farm waits for me; the ground it rests upon is the only home I've ever known. I know no other and yet, part of me wants to. Part of me thinks maybe I could, that I'm ready. The rest of me is still the same girl I've always been. Too scared to leave, too worried about everyone else.

I try to think back to a moment, any moment, where I was just a little selfish. Any memory where I put myself first. Several silent moments float by, Jensen's heartbeat and the gentle rhythm of his breathing the only sounds filling the air.

I realize I can't think of a single one. No moment where I truly only focused on what I wanted.

That's sad to me. It's sad to think I've done that to myself. What's worse is some things I know will never change.

This thought process is probably one of them.

JENSEN

WE ARRIVE BACK at my loft after what can only be described as a very quiet, almost somber drive. We probably didn't say more than a handful of things to each other the entire way.

Two more nights, that's all I get. Maybe…maybe long distance can work? Maybe, we can visit each other? People do it, right? Yeah, and how many times does it actually work out? I let out an audible sigh because I'm going insane talking to myself like this. The angel on my shoulder is like, "Anything is possible!" in all his delusional optimism. The devil on my other shoulder is like, "Face facts, bro. Ain't happening," in all his shitty realistic gut punches.

"What do you want to do tonight?" Harper asks as she leans over the kitchen counter toward me.

I'm on the other side, plugging in my phone and removing my wallet. I think it's weird when men carry their wallets around their own house. Women don't carry their purses from room to room. Do I have a need for my wallet to be in every room I'm in? No. I'll save my sciatic nerve the trouble.

"I don't know, really. I was thinking we rent a movie and binge on movie snacks?" I offer. I don't have the energy to go out anywhere, although if she asks, there's no way I'll say no.

"Oh, thank god," she says, laughing out a relieved sigh. "I don't think I can muster the strength to be around a bunch of people."

I smile at the realization that we're on the same page. In fact, we're almost always on the same page. "I'll pop the popcorn. You rummage the cabinet for cookies and candy."

"Deal," she says.

I watch her pull Oreos and gummy bears from the cabinet and empty them into bowls. I heat a pan on the stove because the only good popcorn you can make at home is on the stove. Who even invented bagged popcorn? Was it for astronauts? No, thank you.

Harper grabs sodas and takes all her things over to the coffee table in the living room. "I'm putting on pajamas while you finish up," she says just before she bounds upstairs.

I finish the popcorn and meet her back at the couch. We both take a seat and I start shuffling through movies, the new releases first and then back to older ones, classics really. Like the original *Jumanji* with Robin Williams and *Romeo and Juliet*, but the Leonardo Di Caprio version. It's the only version worth watching.

"What's that movie?" she asks, my remote hovering over *The Princess Bride*.

"Don't tell me you've never seen it?"

"Nope," she says. "But this transgression sounds serious. Should we remedy it?"

"As you wish," I say, quoting the movie. Not that she knows, but we'll fix that.

Harper narrows her eyes at my response, just as I thought she might. She'll understand soon enough.

Selecting it, I settle back into the couch and tuck her close to me. After the second time Wesley says, "As you wish," in the film, Harper turns her head toward me, giving me a knowing smile. I give her a playful wink as she turns back to the movie.

We take turns trying to throw pieces of popcorn into each other's mouths at her persistence. I didn't know people actually did this. I thought it was one of those cheesy things that only happens in movies. But here I am, dipping and diving for each piece she tosses at my face. Admittedly, she looks adorable even as she throws her head around, mouth wide open, trying to catch the pieces I pop up.

About halfway through the movie, she picks up an Oreo and twists it in half, giving me the half-barren of cream. Harper keeps the side with all the cream on it and I raise an eyebrow at her.

"I want some cream," I tell her.

"This is my cream, get your own." She laughs.

I look down at my cream-less cookie and frown, jutting my lip out.

She rolls her eyes at me. "Fine," she says. "We can share." Harper licks some of the middle from her cookie and then extends it out to me. The look on her face suggests she doesn't think I'll lick the cookie after she has. Challenge accepted.

I lift her hand to my face, cookie still between her fingers, and slowly lick the cookie clean. Harper swallows hard. Who knew eating Oreos could be so sexual? There's licking and cream and tonguing cookies. You know what, on second thought, the Oreo is definitely the most sexual cookie.

Harper leaps to me, straddling her legs around me, and my arms embrace her instinctively. Her back is to the movie now as she kisses along my jawline, her hands reaching down my body.

"You're going to miss the movie," I laugh out between stifled groans. I love everything about her hands on me.

Harper brings her eyes to meet mine, her bottom lip between her teeth, a teasing look playing on her features. "But I want you to lick my cookie," she says.

And I swear to God Himself, I die in that moment. Because it's so dirty and so unexpected and so hot, I can't even contain myself. My hands grip her ass and now I'm the one swallowing hard. She begins to giggle, probably assuming what she said was absurd and cheesy, and it was. But it's something else too. I don't know why that silly erotic innuendo caught me like it did, but I realize in the split second I give it thought, that Harper is finally all the way out of her shell. The one she built, or maybe the one Charles built around her, I really don't know. Perhaps, it's both. But all of it is gone.

I cup both hands on her jaw, giving her my widest, most sincere smile. Her lips are still pressed into a playful line and most of me wants to coax them open with my own. But I pause us for a moment, holding her just far enough away, so I can memorize everything.

"What?" she says.

"Nothing. You're just perfect."

Harper huffs a laugh. "You've had too much sugar."

"I'm not sugar high. If anything, I'm drunk on you."

Harper laughs harder, but takes note of my serious demeanor and stops, maintaining eye contact.

"Let's go to bed," I whisper.

She nods as she lifts herself from my lap. She leads me upstairs by hand, the noise of the movie melting away into the background. I'm not remorseful she didn't finish the movie. There's plenty of time for movies; not enough time for us.

Harper drags her shirt up over her head, giving me the expanse of her naked back, and I have an urge to trace the curve of her spine with my index finger.

It's in this moment, this exact moment, that I realize I'm in love with her. I don't know when I actually fell in love with her, and I suspect it was before now. But this is the moment I'll remember as when I knew it, when I got my head out of my ass and realized it.

I love her.

Because she asked me to lick her cookie.

HARPER

I TURN to face Jensen after removing my shirt and I can't read the expression on his face. There's something more to his hooded eyes, something he seems to be fighting away. His hands come to my waist as he approaches, gripping me tightly. I sweep my palms over his chest and around his shoulders, feeling his warm skin against me.

He reaches down and tugs at my shorts, sending them down to the floor, and I'm left completely exposed.

"Lie down on the bed," he whispers. "Face down."

I do as instructed because I trust him, because I know I have nothing to fear in this moment. I rest my head against my crossed arms, belly to the mattress. The cool fabric sends a sensation down my body.

Jensen undresses next, the sound of his clothes hitting the floor being my only clue. His weight dips the mattress a bit as his hand reaches out to tuck my hair behind my ear. "You're so beautiful," he whispers. "I don't think I could ever get tired of saying that."

Feeling like I've had the wind knocked out of me, I inhale, trying to steady myself.

His fingers trace down along my neck from my ear, stopping to draw delicate circles between my shoulder blades before moving down. He lingers every few inches, like he's memorizing the exact way my spine feels beneath the pads of his fingers.

When he reaches my tail bone, he dips them in the dimples right above my ass before cupping it. I part my legs instinctively and he reads my invitation, letting his hand pass over me and dipping two fingers into my wet center. There's something deliciously different about this angle, and I find myself pressing up and arching each time his hand rocks back and forth.

"Turn over," he says, sliding his hand away from me.

He's still sitting on the edge of the bed and when I turn, he pulls me to him, wrapping my legs around him, so we're face to face. My chest is pressed against his as he clings to me, like he can't get me close enough. He lifts me gently, pressing his lips to mine and sets me down again, this time entering me slowly as I melt down over him. I claw at his back as he fills me, my insides immediately twisting into lovely knots of pleasure.

"Fuck," he groans against my mouth, the expletive coming out more growl than actual word.

Moans and panting are the only noises escaping me as I lose myself to this moment. My body bounces up and down slowly, the pace set by him. I shudder over and over again each time he pushes all the way in. He strokes the outside of me with his thumb so slowly, the intensity is almost unbearable.

"I'm gonna come," I manage between shallow breaths.

Jensen doesn't change pace; he doesn't change a thing. He wants it now, just like this, his expression hopeful and coaxing.

The delicious knots unravel inside me as I grow limp around him, basking in the pleasure of the orgasm ripping through my limbs. Three more slow thrusts and Jensen tenses head to toe, his own orgasm overcoming him. He collapses back onto the bed, bringing me with him.

He's still inside me but we make no effort to move. We pant together, trying to catch our breath, wrapped up in each other. Jensen's heartbeat is beneath my ear again, a lullaby I've come to rely on.

"Do you think there's a way to record a heartbeat without medical technology?" I ask.

Jensen chuckles, his hand gently rubbing up and down the length of my back. "I'm not sure. Why?"

"Just need a recording of yours," I say, my eyes blinking lazily as I succumb to relaxation.

"I'll see what I can find out," he says.

It's the last words I hear before drifting to sleep.

I wake up suddenly, sitting straight up in the bed, confusion and concern mounting in me. The room is completely dark and I reach out, realizing the bed is empty. *What time is it? How long have I been asleep? Where's Jensen?* All these questions are like an avalanche in my mind, once I remember where I am. I hate the split-second moment when you wake up so disoriented you don't even remember where you are.

Peering toward the bathroom, I realize he can't be in there. The light is off according to the crack at the bottom of the door. Then I hear it. The soft strumming of a guitar floats through the air. It sounds like it's coming from downstairs.

Gathering the sheet around me, I tiptoe to the edge of the stairs. The glow of the fire paints Jensen in a golden orange glow. He's sitting on the edge of his couch as he works his fingers over the strings on his guitar. I can't be sure, but it sounds like he's humming. As quietly as I can manage, I descend. I'm not more than four or five stairs down before he speaks.

"Sorry if I woke you," he says. He's not at full volume but it's not a whisper either.

"You didn't. I just sort of woke up, I guess."

Jensen pats the couch next to him, inviting me to sit. I curl up into a ball against the arm of the couch, my feet pressed against the side of him. His hands continue strumming and I'm mesmerized by the way they float over the instrument. His humming grows until it becomes words.

He sings in a hushed tone, the words barely echoing across the space. I close my eyes, a lazy smile over my lips. Being serenaded intentionally or by accident is so peaceful. A quiet rhythm causes me to loosen the tension in my body.

"Any requests?" he asks, but I have none.

I shake my head gently. "Surprise me."

His fingers start up again and I don't immediately recognize it so I listen closely, trying to figure out if I've heard it before.

Baby, you don't know how wild you drive me,
The time it seems to fly right past us,
Just when I think I'll be able to get past this,
I see your face and can't resist
this feeling in me,
so unfamiliar,
so foreign to my heart,
just has me singing
baby, you don't know how wild
you drive me

Jensen starts laughing after the last line, his head shaking back and forth. "I told you I can't write songs for shit."

"I think it's beautiful," I tell him.

"Well, thank you. I appreciate the lie," he teases.

"I would never lie about something so serious."

"But you would lie about something not so serious?" he asks, lifting an eyebrow in my direction.

"Probably not. Unless you asked me if you looked fat in your outfit or something. Then I would probably lie." I giggle. It's not even a full giggle. It's lazy and tired.

"Go back to bed, weirdo." He laughs.

"Can I sleep right here while you play? I don't want to go back up to bed alone."

"Of course."

"Okay, just wake me when you're ready to go upstairs." I yawn, twisting my body to lie on my side.

Jensen throws the blanket from the back of the couch over me and tucks me in before returning to his guitar.

Sweet notes float through the air as I drift back to sleep.

This lullaby is almost as good as his heartbeat.

HARPER

WAKING up this morning alone isn't how I imagined I would be starting my day. I listen for Jensen to see if he's in the bathroom or his closet. I stand and peek into his office but he's not there either. I walk back to the bed and there's a note on the side table.

> *Had to get to work*
> *but didn't want to wake you.*
> *You looked so peaceful.*
> *XO*

Since I've been here, I've never woken up alone. Jensen always wakes me up to kiss me goodbye and I always get to tell him to have a good day. This is weird. Certainly out of the ordinary at least. Then again, can I really call out patterns after a week? Maybe I'm reading too much into it. Tonight is our last night together and I don't want to ruin it by being whiny or accusing him of anything. There's no need for it.

Shaking off these feelings, I head back upstairs to shower and start my day. I want to go shopping for a couple of things to make tonight truly special. Because the reality is, I might never see him again. Not like this.

To hold onto hope that our paths will cross again is probably unhealthy at best. At worst, it creates the opportunity for pain. I don't need an unhealthy obsession or a chest full of pain all over again. I barely survived the last one.

With all these thoughts running through my head, I pause. *Did I wash my hair yet?*

I lather shampoo for what I'm pretty sure is a second time and decide to give my shower some focus long enough to get through the routine. I get out, dry off, dress, and rush through my hair and makeup so I can get going.

As I walk downstairs, I grab the film from my camera so I can get it developed while I'm out. I've been taking pictures the entire trip and made sure to snap plenty of our time together. It's one of the surprises I have brewing for Jensen.

Out on the sidewalk, I decide to put this whole mess of thoughts I'm having behind me and only focus on now. Seems I'm doing a lot of that. There's plenty of time to sort my head out later.

For now, I have to keep my focus on here.

I arrive back to the loft after a few hours. That took so much longer than I anticipated, but I'm back before Jensen and that's all that matters. I slip the photos I had developed into frames. There's five of them. I considered more but it felt like too much. Just as I'm placing the last photo, a thought occurs to me. *Is this... problematic?*

Giving a man framed photos seems like it sends a message. The wrong message. *Crap, I didn't think this through. No. You know what, it's fine.* He'll understand my intention. Of course, now I feel like once he moves on and starts dating someone, what the hell is he going to do with them? *Shit. Just shit, fuck, and hell.* I press my fingers to my temples, willing myself not to worry this much. It's just a few pictures. No big deal.

In my moment of panic, I pick up my phone and text Cora. She's his sister, she'll know what to do. She knows him.

> I need your help.

CORA

Is everything okay?

> Yeah. I mean sort of.

CORA

Are you and Jensen all right?

> Yes, of course. We're fine. Well, I mean okay, I framed some of the pics I took to give him.

CORA

Okay? That's good right?

> I don't know. Is it? Will it be weird?

CORA

Um, no? I think you're overthinking this one.

> Right, but what happens when he dates someone new?

CORA

Maybe he doesn't want to date anyone new?

> Technically we aren't dating. I mean when he does.

CORA

Honey, you can call what you're doing whatever you want. But it's dating. You're dating.

> No, we made very specific plans.

CORA

Yeah, those have been derailed.

I don't think he thinks we're dating.

CORA

You guys avoid talking about this shit,
don't you?

There's nothing to talk about so why would we
talk about it?

CORA

I think you should talk about it.

Okay, you know what, you're not helping.

I put my phone down, releasing a heavy sigh.

When I get back home, maybe I won't jump right back on that dating app. When I started things up on the hot and heavy side with Jensen, I deactivated my profile rather than deleting it. But I have a feeling I'll need a break after all this. I'll flip that switch at a later date.

I run upstairs to the bathroom to reapply my makeup a bit sexier—smoky eyes and all. Checking the clock, I realize he should be home very soon. So I slip on surprise number two. It's got quite a lot of straps but the lady at the lingerie store assured me it would be worth it. *That's right. Lingerie.* Don't get me wrong, I'm not one of those women that has like forty-three sets tucked away in a bottom drawer for special occasions. In fact, this is the first set I've ever owned. I tried to wear something for Charles exactly one time on our honeymoon and he said I looked ridiculous. He actually used that word. *Ridiculous.*

How does a woman wearing lingerie pull that adjective from someone? So I threw it away and never revisited the option.

Stepping in front of Jensen's full-length mirror, I don't think I look the way Charles described me all that time ago. My breasts fill out the cups and the lace hugs my body gently, accentuating every curve. I turn to take in my profile and see the lace cut diagonally across my ass cheeks. This is when I realize maybe for the first time, at least to this extent, that Charles is a complete and total donkey ass. Not just a regular ass. Specifically a donkey ass.

I pull on the silky robe I purchased to accompany the lingerie. Everything is black and sleek and I feel like a goddess for maybe the first time ever. Growing up, I might have been the popular girl. I might have been the prom queen and harvest princess and all that. But what people saw outwardly, I didn't. It's not that I considered myself ugly necessarily. More like plain. I felt just plain. A scoop of vanilla ice cream in a sea of the rest of the flavors. But tonight, wearing this, I feel great. I'm not vanilla. I'm mint chocolate chip. I'm rocky road. I'm something else entirely.

As I slip on high heels to complete the ensemble, I hear the front door open and shut.

Jensen's home.

And I can't wait to show him what I've been up to.

JENSEN

TO SAY today was rough would be wholly understated. Distracted all day by thoughts of Harper—tomorrow, seeing her tonight—left me unable to concentrate or have a single moment of inner peace. Leaving this morning without saying goodbye to her like I've been doing all week was such a shit thing to do. It's not that I didn't want to. I was desperate for it, actually. I wanted to call in sick, wrap my body around hers and stay there all day; and I was afraid if I woke her, that's exactly what I would've ended up doing.

To make matters worse, she didn't text me all day. She's probably mad at me and I don't blame her. Or maybe she assumes I just needed space. I don't know. I tried to leave a note, a thinly veiled sort of lie. Which I also hated. So my distracted thoughts today volleyed back and forth and around and over and through like a fucking maze. One minute, I was thinking I should leave work, run home, and profess my love to her like a maniac. The next minute, I was wondering how I could avoid her until she left because telling her I loved her would be disastrous. Then I thought, *but would it?*

Finally home, I drop my keys on the counter with one hand and use my other to loosen the tie around my neck. I keep my eyes shut, decompressing from the day, and trying to figure out how to navigate this evening. *My last evening with her.*

Hearing her footsteps on the stairs, I open my eyes. She rounds down the last step and she's a fucking vision. Not good. All I can see is the silky black robe cut above her knees and high heels. The robe is tied in the front with a bow, like a gift waiting to be unwrapped. Whatever she's wearing under it, it can't be much. The thin material of the robe clings as she walks and I can't detect any bulges or lines underneath.

"Hey, you," she says, her voice low and sultry.

Fuck. I'm dead. I'm a dead man. "Hi," I say, my voice clipped.

"How was your day?" she asks, wrapping her arms around my neck, eyes locked on mine, expectantly.

I wrap my arms around her waist, a gesture fully ingrained and reactive now. "Long. And a little rough."

"Aww, poor baby," she says, pressing her lips to mine.

I lean into the kiss, somewhat desperate to memorize everything I can. How soft her lips are. Her scent. Her taste.

"Hopefully I can make it better," she says between kisses.

My hands move over her back. It seems no amount of bad day, no amount of sadness, makes me want her any less. I grip beneath her shoulder blades, pulling her closer as the kiss deepens. My mouth moves over hers and I realize I have to shake off this mood and do my best tonight. For her. She deserves an amazing last night here.

Suddenly, she steps back, breaking the kiss and releasing her hold on me. I stare at her for several seconds as her hands come up, gently unraveling the bow holding her robe closed. The strands of the tie hang loose as she hooks her fingers around the edges, slowly pulling it open and exposing her body underneath.

Black lace covers over her breasts, letting her nipples show through. The lace stretches down her torso, stopping just above her belly button. A couple of inches of skin are exposed there before the black lace panties cover lower, but still, I can see through them. Her bare legs look almost glossy all the way down to her black high heels.

Harper opens the robe further, pushing it off her shoulders and letting it fall to a silky black pool on the floor. I quite literally stop breathing for a full ten seconds. My breath hitches on inhale and I'm suspended there, taking in the sight of her, committing every line, every curve to memory.

"Do you like it?" she asks, a smirk playing across her lips. Despite her confidence, I can still detect a light pink to her cheeks. This is what I love about her. Slightly embarrassed and yet still so vulnerable and brave.

"I more than like it," I admit, finally exhaling the breath I've been holding. "I love it."

Her eyes widen the slightest amount, then settle a bit as she bites her lip. It's not a shy gesture, but more sensual. "Come here," she says, her demeanor gentle wanting.

I push my hands into my pockets and take two quiet steps toward her, my lips pressed together in a small smile. "What are you trying to do to me, woman?"

Harper feigns innocence and shrugs her shoulders. "Just trying to make tonight special."

A half-hum, half-growl forms in the back of my throat as I pull my hands from my pockets. I finger one of the thin straps, just over her collarbone. Looking into her eyes, her bright blue eyes, nearly rips me in half. I don't want her to go tomorrow.

"What if you could just travel around and take pictures?" I ask suddenly.

"Like a traveling photographer?" she asks, startled in this moment. "Yeah."

Harper shifts from one foot to the other, presumably due to the heels, as she gives it some thought. "I mean, I would love it," she says. "I think it would be awesome, why?"

I shake my head, realizing I have no idea what I'm saying. "Just thinking," I say.

She tilts her head to the side, studying my face for a moment, then straightens again. "Come on," she says. "Let's get you out of those clothes. I ordered dinner so we wouldn't have to spend time cooking."

Harper leads me upstairs by my hand and I get a full view of her backside on our way up. The smooth expanse of her upper back, the delicate lace, and cheeky panties showing off her perfect ass should be enough to distract me. But I don't know how I can touch her now, knowing it'll probably be the last time. Long distance relationships never work. Ever. Everyone knows that. What would I do? Fly down there every couple of months? Have her fly to wherever I am? That would probably only work for six or eight months at best. After a while, it would become tiresome.

I could wait. I really only have about another year of traveling around before I'm promoted to something a little more stable. Once I'm manager for a region, with people under me, I would be home every day and only have to travel occasionally. But wait a year to be with her? I can't exactly ask her to wait for me. A year from now, she could have moved on already.

Leading me to the edge of the bed, she steps to the side, patting the mattress and instructing me to sit. After I'm seated, she immediately straddles me, her knees resting on either side of my hips. She wraps her arms around me, and I return the gesture, the pads of my fingers rubbing against the silky texture of the black lace covering her lower back and sides.

She leans in closely, her cheek barely grazing mine, and presses light kisses along my jaw. I still, the gentle touch causing ripples of sensation down my spine. By the fourth kiss, my breaths have gone shallow and she rubs her teeth against my skin.

I press my eyes shut as a groan escapes me. "Harper, wait," I say, gripping her bicep just above her elbow and pushing her back from me.

"What's wrong?" she asks, startled by my sudden reaction.

"Nothing. Well, something. Listen, just hear me out, okay?"

"Okay, yeah, of course. Tell me what's wrong?" she says.

I inhale the deepest breath my lungs can manage, never taking my eyes from hers, then exhale. "Come with me?" The question falls from my mouth sounding more like a plea than anything else.

"What?" she asks, shaking her head, startled by my question yet again.

"Don't go home. Come with me to California. That's where I have to go next. Come with me. Travel with me."

Harper's face is twisted up in confused emotions and I don't blame her for that.

I hold my breath, her eyes searching my face. I'm not sure if she believes I'm actually saying this but I hold firm all the same, hanging on the silence between us, desperate for her answer.

HARPER

MY EYES BLINK three times in rapid succession as I take in what Jensen's just said, just asked. *Is he serious? Maybe I heard him wrong.*

I would ask him to repeat himself but I already said "what?" once and saying it again won't change it.

He said what he said.

"You're serious?" I manage to say, as he stares straight into my fucking soul.

"Of course I am," he says, like what he's just proposed is as normal as getting breakfast at the diner down the street. "You can take photos, explore, we can explore together."

He must read the hesitation on my face because he continues on.

"You can see so many places. And if you need to go back and visit family, or aren't interested in the city I'm headed to, you can fly back and visit the farm and meet me in the next city. Just think about how amazing that could be for you. And us. We could be together."

His speech shocks me silent as I take in all that he's saying, the conviction in his tone. He's definitely serious.

"Are you crazy?" I blurt. It's in the air between us before I can snatch it back. No turning back now. "That plan, it's crazy. It's too soon for that kind of commitment. We've known each other for like a month, not even." I can hear the panic in my own voice.

"I'm not asking for a commitment. Well, I guess I am, but Christ, I'm not proposing. We just date, but also you can travel with me. You're not locked into anything."

I'm pacing his room now as he sits on the edge of the bed, calmly pleading. "I don't know, I don't know. My divorce is barely final. I can't just hop from it, straight to you, to such a big thing. This was just supposed to be a little fun."

"I get that. But I think you know we passed 'just fun' a little while ago, and we're teetering right on the edge of more." His words come out hard as stone. He's not playing around. All lighthearted fun, all playfulness, is gone from him.

Between his tone and pleading hopefulness in his eyes, I am struck silent all over again. I don't know what to say, so I tell him exactly that.

He exhales long and hard. "People only say they don't know what to say when they want to say no," he says, his words clipped.

"I don't. I just..." I pause, collecting my thoughts. "I just don't think it's a good idea. It'll never work."

"Why not? Why won't it work?" he asks.

"Because," I fumble. "Because we'll get tired of each other, or you'll get tired of me being around all the time. Or you'll want space. And then what? You hand me a plane ticket and send me on my way?" My voice is high, unforgiving. I sound as panicked as I feel, but Jensen doesn't react in anger.

He lets out a gentle sigh and I almost detect disappointment. "Is that really what you think of me?" he asks, sounding wounded. "Harper, I'm not your ex-husband. I'm not that guy. I don't throw people away like that. And I would never, under any circumstances, throw you away like he did."

"Right. I bet all men say that at first." I fold my arms across my chest. I've stopped pacing and now, I'm just staring at him.

"What would you know about men? You've experienced one kind of man. Hell, one man in your whole life," he says, his words biting and hard.

"How dare you," I say. "How fucking dare you."

"Harper, I love you," he says. "Are you listening? I fucking love you. I'm in love with you."

"Stop saying that!" I yell, surprising both of us.

"I can't. It's the truth," he says.

"Well, you know what, Jensen? I didn't ask for that. I said I was ready to date, ready to kiss another man, ready to fuck another man. But I never said I was ready for love, or even wanted it."

"You're just scared," he says. "You're scared of what we could be."

"No, I'm protecting myself."

"Harper." He sighs. "You can try that all you want. You can push people away because you got hurt. But you deserve to be loved, really loved. You deserve one more chance at that. And if that chance doesn't work out, you have another after that. And another. Because life isn't about avoiding love, avoiding connection. It's about finding the right love, the right connection."

"And you think you're that connection?"

"I think I could be," he says, his words barely audible, something hovering just above a whisper.

I can't fight the sigh I'm holding in my chest, shutting my eyes as I let it out. "I just can't do this," I admit. "I can't be this. I'm not ready to be this."

Jensen nods, hanging his head low, shoulders slumping more and more. "Okay," he says. "All right. I get it."

He wipes his hands down his face before finally looking up at me again. Several silent minutes pass before he speaks.

"I'm sorry I ruined our last evening," he says. "I'm gonna sleep down on the couch. I'm sure you need some time alone. You take the bed."

Jensen stands, collecting himself for a moment, hands coming to his pockets again. He walks toward the stairs as I wrap my arms around myself, covering my middle. I'm wearing nothing but lingerie and high heels and it seems so ridiculous now.

Did we just have a heated fight while I was half-naked? Suddenly, I feel the need to cover as much of myself up as I can.

I don't have the strength to watch him. Listening to his footsteps behind me, I hear him getting further and further away. It's only when I know I'm alone do I crumble to the floor. I can't breathe. It's as if this lace corset is constricting me. I rip at it until I'm lying on the floor in only my panties. *I'm an idiot.*

To make matters worse, I'm a crying idiot. I sob gently, careful not to make any noise that might carry downstairs. The last thing I need is for him to come back up here and see me sobbing and naked on the floor. Because that's who I am. Raw to a point. Open to a point. Caring too much about appearances and expectations.

It's as if I'm devolving right here on the floor, seeing myself for the first time in a new light. Is this stubbornness? Cowardice? A mix of both? Probably that last one.

When I finally manage to stand, I crawl into my side of the bed, hopeful Jensen will come up and get into bed later when he's calmed down. But he was calm, wasn't he?

I try to wipe the look of defeat in his eyes from my memory. I replay the scene again and again. When I tuck the blankets beneath my chin, his scent saturates my senses. Woods and spice. I dip my face, pressing it against the cover, inhaling deeply.

There's nothing left for me to do but cry myself to sleep. I thought I'd gotten past this. I thought after all the nights following Charles leaving, I'd never do this again. I would never be here again. This is exactly what I wanted to avoid. But here I am. Saltwater on my pillow. A deep sense of emptiness washing over me. All of my own making.

I don't deserve one more chance at anything, least of all love.

HARPER

WAKING up after crying yourself to sleep is taxing on the body. You spend all day stiff, a discomfort all the way down to your bones that doesn't go away no matter how much you stretch or bend or try to relieve it. Despite knowing there's nothing I can do, I stretch my arms up over my head, arch my back, wiggle my toes.

Last night was my second night home, back on the farm. It was my third night crying myself to sleep. Like all healing, I'm sure it will take time to get past this blip in my life. In a little while, this will be nothing more than a dark memory—the moment Jensen walked in, to the moment he walked out.

Of course, until then, I'm left replaying our last interactions over and over again.

Jensen never came to bed that last night. I woke the next morning to him packing his bag for California. We moved around each other in silence, packing and avoiding. The car ride to the airport was filled with more silence. It was so deafly quiet and tense in the Uber, the driver turned on music just for the sake of noise.

When we arrived at the airport, Jensen silently helped me with my bags, handed me a ticket home, and for a moment, I held my breath as he leaned in and kissed me on the forehead. He ran the pad of his thumb over my jaw as he gave me a halfhearted smile, and then turned toward his gate in the opposite direction of mine.

Since I've been home, he hasn't tried to contact me. He called Cora and had Cora call my sister just to make sure I made it home safely. It would seem even Cora didn't want to contact me directly. Of course, Lyla's not here, so then she called me. I broke down and confessed everything to her, sobbing into the phone all over again just yesterday. Luckily, she's coming home today.

She and Gentry spent their honeymoon backpacking through Ireland, seeing every inch of the countryside they could fit in. They even extended their trip just to see more. Hence, why they're not back yet. But I'm excited to see her, excited to hug her. Shamefully, I need to lean on her yet again to heal my heart. Or at least to distract me from it. Either would do at this point.

After I shower and dress, I find Nan on the porch and offer to help her snap the green beans she's working on. Mindless repetitive work will be my distraction and help pass the time until Lyla arrives.

Taking a bowl into my lap, I start snapping the ends off and throwing them into tub between us.

"Tell me what's on your heart, baby. I waited to ask. Seemed like you needed a little time," she says, her voice gentle and caressing.

"Oh, I've gone and made another mess, Nan. No surprise there."

"What was the first mess you made?" she asks.

"Charles."

"And the second?"

"Jensen." I huff out his name, trying my best to hold back the tears brimming my eyes.

"I need to tell you some hard truths, baby. Are you ready to hear them?" she asks.

I nod, unable to actually speak.

"Now, first, let's talk about this Charles mess. I fail to see how that was your mess. A devoted partner, that's what you were. Even when it got tough."

I press my lips together as she continues.

"The way I see it, Charles is the only one who made a mess. Didn't know what he had, didn't want to know," she says, stilling the swinging porch with her feet. "And that's okay because sometimes people don't deserve to see you, the real you. I think deep down you knew that. You were never your whole self with him. Ever."

"I tried to be," I croak, my voice breaking mid-sentence.

"I know you did," she says, patting my knee with her hand.

All bean snapping operations have stopped. I stare down into my bowl, unable to move my hands or anything else.

"Now, this Jensen mess. Tell me about it."

I recount all that happened between us. By the end, I'm crying again, but I don't try to stop. I just let it all out. After several minutes, I finally pull myself together.

Nan sits there quietly, absorbing all I've told her. "Well, my dear, that *is* your mess. A man—a good man—opened his heart to you. Maybe that wasn't his intention in the beginning, maybe it happened to him the same way it happens to everyone. Suddenly. Without rhyme or reason or sense. And you denied him. But why? That's the part that truly baffles me. Why did you do that?"

I wasn't prepared to answer that. I wasn't expecting to be asked why.

I straighten my back, sniffling and tell her what I've been telling myself. "Because, Nan, it's too soon. It's too complicated. My home is here, and he travels. And I know I already said it, but it's too soon. I shouldn't be jumping from one serious relationship to the next." I breathe all this out as fast as I can, gulping in a breath when I finish.

Nan looks at me, studying me, taking in my rushed excuses with a precarious look in her eyes.

"Well, I'm sorry to say this, but that's bullshit," she says.

"What?"

"You heard me," she says, reaching into her bowl for her next bean. "That's bullshit. He resolved the traveling issue. You can go with him. Too soon, too shmoon. Time is no one's business. Time is a thing not to be wasted. Too soon? What is too soon when we're talking about love?"

"I don't know..."

"And another thing," she says. "Let's not forget you've been separated from Charles, and alone, for a long time. What's this jumping from one to another nonsense?"

Everything she's saying seems to be poking holes in everything I've said.

"And, baby, listen to me now. This will always be your home. Always. You know that. But home is also wherever your heart is. Now, I know some of your heart will always be here, with us. But where's the rest of it?" she asks.

I swallow hard, my lips trembling. I can feel another wave of sobbing trying to break through, but I try to hold back.

Nan turns to me, caressing my cheek with her hand so gently, it's nearly feather-like. "And I think she's gonna tell you the same thing," she says, nodding her head toward the driveway.

I've been so distracted, I didn't hear the car pull up. I look to find my sister hopping out of the passenger seat before the car even comes to a complete stop. She runs up on the porch and I nearly trip as I set the bowl down and leap toward her, wrapping my arms around her for a long embrace.

"Lyla," I manage to say between sobs.

"Oh, baby sister," she whispers into my hair. "I missed you."

"I missed you too," I say.

"Okay," she says. "Let's go get this whole mess sorted out over some ice cream." Lyla looks back at Gentry and he waves, nodding his head as he collects their bags from the trunk of their rental.

"I'll just be home if you need me," he says, passing the bags over to their truck and hopping in, presumably to drive back to their cabin.

Having replayed in detail all that transpired between me and Jensen, I curl into a ball in my bed, my head resting in Lyla's lap. On the phone, when I told her what happened before, I had to skip a lot. I gave her the abridged version. This time, however, she got the fullest picture I could paint.

"Damn," she says.

"Damn? All that and all you have to say is one little expletive?"

"Um…" she says, thinking for a moment, "yeah, pretty much."

A small giggle erupts from my lips, despite everything. "This is serious. I need your help."

"My help with what? You've already made your choice, haven't you?"

"I don't know. Healing?"

Lyla looks down at me, curiosity playing across her features. She arches an eyebrow, pensive. "I think you want me to tell you that you made the right choice. I think you want me to validate what you did, to reassure you."

"No," I snap. "I mean, maybe a little." *Maybe a lot.*

"Well, I can't do that," she says, folding her arms over her chest.

Sitting up, I reach for the tub of ice cream on my side table and dig my spoon in. If I was going to hear this, I was going to be medicated while I did. "Because?" I ask, shoveling a scoop of chocolate chip cookie dough into my mouth.

"Listen, Harper," she starts, "I can tell you that you made the safe choice. I can tell you that you made the easy choice. But the right choice? I'm not so sure. Because deep down, I think you love him. And deep down that scares the shit out of you."

I scoff, making a noise in my throat that isn't even words.

"I've never seen you more yourself than when you were with him. Gentry even said so. You were so vibrant and happy when Jensen was here for the wedding. Seeing you flirt and banter and truly enjoy your-self in a way I never saw with Charles…that's the Harper that deserves to exist."

"Fuck," I whisper, shoving another scoop of ice cream into my mouth. I will not cry a forty-seventh time, or whatever this would be if I actually allowed it. I simply can't. I don't even think I have any tears left.

"Yeah. Fuck," Lyla repeats, digging her spoon into the tub.

After some time passes, with the two of us silently sitting there eating the mostly melted treat, I place it back down. Unable to eat anymore, I lie back on my pillow and stare up at the ceiling.

When there is a lot at stake, the body does one of two things. It either goes into action mode, seemingly moving on instinct to make it to the outcome. Or it shuts down completely, unable to move, para-lyzed by fear and anxiety.

Until right now, my body had done the latter, hollowing itself out, wanting to feel nothing. But, I feel something slowly start to unravel in me. I grab my phone.

Cora, I need your help.

CORA
With what?

I need you to find out exactly where Jensen is, but keep it a secret.

I put my phone back down while I wait for her reply.

There's something I need to tell Jensen, and I can't do it over the phone.

HARPER

THE HALLWAY of this hotel smells like a hospital. It's clean, too clean. A chemical scent fills the air all around me, as if they've attempted to disinfect every inch of it. The door, to room four-ten, stares back at me as I trace each number with my eyes. My hands are at my sides, trembling and coiled into fists. Jensen is just beyond this door and I've been standing here for a full seven minutes, willing myself to knock. After the first few went by, I wondered if he'd open the door before I got the chance to knock. Although, I don't know where he'd be going at this hour.

I caught a red-eye flight from Kentucky to Los Angeles, took an Uber here, and now it's four-something in the morning. Yes, four. Good ol' time zone working for me. I had Cora find out exactly where Jensen was staying and confirm he hadn't left yet and wouldn't check out before I got there. She asked for his room number *"in case of an emergency"* and passed the information along to me.

Now, I'm standing here, too chicken shit to knock. I practiced a speech all the way here. On the airplane, in the Uber, in the elevator to the fourth floor, and for the last seven minutes I've been standing here. Sure, I could've called him. I could've texted or emailed or even sent a telegram, but none of that felt good enough. How would that text read? *Sorry, I think I made a huge mistake. Will you forgive me and live happily ever after with me? Dumb.*

No. It had to be like this. With that thought, I lift my hand and knock before I can convince myself to turn away. I wait for several seconds and hear nothing. *Probably because he's still asleep, dumbass.* I knock again, this time harder and louder, realizing I likely have to wake him from sleep just to get him to come to the door.

A few more seconds go by so slowly, I think I might pass out. Then, I hear something. *Finally.* A shadow underneath the door moves closer and I hear the lock on the other side twisting. I suck in a breath, anticipation winning out over fear. *This is it.*

Jensen appears, rubbing his left eye with his palm as he leans his other hand against the open door. He finally looks at me, blinking several times as he brings me into focus. "Harper?" he says, his voice giving the impression that he isn't quite sure it's me.

"Hi," I squeak. *Smooth.*

"What are you doing here? Is everything okay?" he asks, shifting his eyes up and down my body and side to side, as if someone else is going to appear in the doorframe.

"No, everything is most definitely not okay," I breathe out.

Jensen looks startled, clearly not expecting this answer to fall from my lips. "Come in," he says. "Come in and tell me what's wrong." He moves back into the room, allowing space for me to pass him.

Walking to the edge of the bed, I survey my surroundings. His suitcase is open on a bench, most of his belongings not in it.

I take a deep breath, adjusting myself as I sit. "The thing is," I say. "I'm in love with you."

This admission catches Jensen off guard and stops him in his tracks. He stands at the room's edge, staring at me.

So I go on. "And that's a problem, or I thought it was a problem. I mean it's a problem because I didn't realize it in time. And I hurt you. I didn't mean for that to happen. You were just there in your apartment, saying all these things and I couldn't process it all. Or rather, I don't think I wanted to. Maybe I wasn't ready to. Does any of this make sense?"

Jensen only nods, offering no words of his own.

"Anyway, I got home, I cried a lot. And the short story is, I realized I'm an idiot. Or rather, in so many words, I was told I am."

Again, Jensen only looks at me, rubbing his hand over his bare chest as if he's been wounded and the place is still tender.

"So I had to tell you. I had to tell you I'm in love with you. And I want to be with you. And that scares me but I still want to do it." My foot begins to tap the carpeted floor as anxiety washes over me again. The only sound in the room for several minutes is the *pat pat pat* my toes make as they bounce.

"You love me?" he asks.

I nod before I speak. "Yes."

Jensen walks across the floor, falling to his knees when he's right in front of me. His hands graze the backs of my bare knees and his thumbs press into the tender flesh of my thighs.

"I love you, too," he whispers, relief softening his rigid shoulders.

The whole of him slumps, as if a tremendous weight has been lifted. I lift his face up to make eye contact with him. The smile playing across his lips widens and he removes a hand from my knee to wipe at the tears on my cheeks.

"Why are you still crying?" he asks.

"Because I'm happy," I whisper, the words catching in my throat.

"Say it again," he says.

"I love you."

Jensen exhales, like he's hearing it for the first time all over again. He brings his face level with mine, leaning up on his knees and pulling me down toward him. His forehead presses to mine and his eyes flutter shut.

"I feel like I've been waiting a lifetime to hear you say that," he says. His lips meet mine in a gentle kiss at first and then it deepens. His arms come around my back as he stands, pushing me back on the bed. He lifts me further onto the bed, pressing a knee between my thighs.

My hands cup his face; my kiss consumes his mouth in a desperate frenzy. I hunger for him. I need him. I know this now. There's no more denial. No more fear. My fears have been overpowered, swept away and replaced with hope, with love.

I don't know exactly what the future holds for me, for us. Jensen and I could be together for years to come or we could decide by next week this won't work. Either way, I'll know I didn't run.

I will know I gave us a chance.

And for now, that's enough.

EPILOGUE

JENSEN

I WATCH HARPER METICULOUSLY place pickles onto a grilled cheese in the pan. Her precise placement is out of character as she generally just pops them on without much thought to where they land. She's taking her time crafting our sandwiches.

During this brief travel interlude, we've gone back to the loft in North Carolina, the place we now both call home. Of course, we're not here often. Over the past year, I've been able to show her so many cities across the states, places she's always wanted to see. We've taken two trips outside the country. The first was to London, the second to Paris. Harper takes photos everywhere we go, capturing something special with her lens in each place, something I can't explain, but people love. She began sharing her photos on Instagram, and soon captured the attention of a gallery who wanted to feature her photos in a special exhibit about how ordinary places hold beauty. Since then, her photography has really taken off and when we travel, she's never bored or restless.

Now, I help Harper carry the plates to the table, her quiet demeanor giving me pause. As we sit, I can tell she's in deep thought.

"Are you okay?" I ask. "You're quiet."

"Yeah, I'm fine, just thinking," she says.

"I can see that." I give her a knowing look. Harper wears everything on her face. Every emotion, every change in mood can be detected. She has no poker face.

Harper takes one triangle of her sandwich and cradles it in front of her mouth but doesn't take a bite. Meanwhile, I'm already starting on my second half.

"You're not hungry?" I ask, somewhat worried when she isn't even eating our favorite sandwich. We eat them any time we can manage on the road, and when we're home. We still sneak in nights of staying up late, talking, and eating the sandwich that brought us together.

"It's not that I'm not hungry. I'm just not hungry for this. In fact, I think this pickle is going to make me sick," she says, pressing the back of her hand to her lips, as if she's fighting the urge to vomit.

Taking the sandwich from her hand, I put it back on the plate and shove it far away from her. I slide my plate to the side too, not wanting my sandwich to make her ill. I take her by both hands, studying her face. It's pale and I briefly wonder if she should make an appointment with her doctor.

"I'm pregnant," she says, her eyelids squeezing shut.

It takes me a full twenty seconds to register what she's just said and still, I can't help myself.

"I'm sorry, what?"

"I saw a doctor yesterday to confirm it," she says, removing her hands from mine and opening her eyes to dig into her purse next to her.

Harper slides a black and white sonogram across the counter toward me. I stare down at a small white blurry dot in the center. A tiny arrow points to it, with the word "baby" written beside it.

"You're pregnant," I say on an exhale, more statement than question.

"Yes," she says, emotion in her voice.

I pick up the photo, rubbing my fingers over the little dot. "When? How long?"

"They said about eight weeks," she says, some sort of hesitation in her voice I can't place.

"Eight weeks," I repeat, working my way back through a mental calendar. "We made a baby in Texas," I say, recalling that's where we were then.

Harper nods. "I'll understand if you're upset," she says.

"Upset?"

"Yeah, we didn't exactly plan this, you know. I'll understand if you're mad or panicked or want to consider our options."

"Harper, stop."

She pulls her bottom lip into her mouth, seemingly preventing herself from saying anything further.

I smile, a small but genuine smile, attempting to ease her fears. "I'm not mad. Or panicked. Okay, maybe a little panicked because we're going to be parents, but not panicked in a bad way. More like oh-my-god-am-I-going-to-be-good-at-this panicked," I say. "I'm happy."

"You are?"

"Hell yeah." I squeeze her hand tight, trying to make her really see me.

She slumps her shoulders. "But what about all the traveling? What about our way of life?"

"It will change. I'm due for my promotion next month. I won't be traveling for work anymore. We'll have to find other reasons to travel. Vacations." I shrug my shoulders because it all sounds so simple to me, but Harper's worry isn't gone.

Several moments pass as she thinks about what I've said.

"Harper?"

"Yeah?" she says, coming back to the conversation.

"I love you. And I want to have this baby with you. And I want to marry you."

Her eyes widen, a smile finally beginning to form on her lips.

"But I'm not going to ask you yet because I don't have a ring and I want to ask you properly."

"Have we ever done anything properly?" She laughs.

"That's a fair point," I admit. "But still."

"Can we get married in Las Vegas?" she asks.

"Really?"

"I've had the whole traditional experience. Unless you want it for yourself, I'm okay with not having it again," she admits, shrugging her shoulders.

"So you mean to tell me we're going to elope to Las Vegas after I've knocked you up?" I laugh.

"It feels very *us*, doesn't it?" she says, giggles floating from her mouth freely.

"I don't want to answer yes to that." I rub my hand across the stubble of my chin, absorbing all that this means, all that this will mean moving forward.

I've never actually pictured myself as a dad. I mean I've always wanted to be a father, but never gave thought to what kind I would be, if I'd be good at it. Wanting kids and being ready for it or good at it is another train of thought entirely. But I'm oddly calm now, visions of a baby in my arms, visions of Harper holding a baby. She will be an excellent mother.

And me? I'll learn.

"We can elope to Las Vegas as long as our sisters come, and Gentry. I want some people involved," I tell her.

"Deal," she says.

"So, we're doing this?" I clasp my hands together in front of me as I stare her down, a smirk on my face.

"We're doing this," she says, her hand coming up to cover her mouth.

"Hey, Harper?"

"Yeah?"

"I think this will be our best adventure yet," I say, coming around the table and pulling her up into my arms. I kiss her lips again and again, attempting to drive away any hesitation remaining in her.

Harper and I, we've never been conventional. Nothing about my life since meeting her has been ordinary or predictable. I have a feeling I'm in for a lot more of that. I owe everything to this woman, and I will spend the rest of my life proving to her that I'm the man she was always meant to be with.

Sometimes the road to where you're supposed to be isn't straight, isn't easy. Sometimes you get sidetracked along the way, you think you're at your destination but you're not. Somewhere deep down, you know. The failure of first loves can be difficult, they can create doubt and fear in you.

But, like Harper and I, when the right person comes along, you'll feel it. A shift in the cosmos, an awakening.

I'm grateful every day for Harper's willingness to finally leap. I don't want to know a life without her.

My life is made more whole by her love.

ACKNOWLEDGMENTS

First of all, I hate writing acknowledgements. I feel like I'm saying the same shit over and over again in every single book. Are you even reading these?

I would like to thank whoever created acknowledgements. I really needed a part of the writing process to loathe, so good job.

I want to recognize the pandemic. I'm a "silver linings" person and try to seek out the positive in the negative so thanks COVID-19, for making me over-commit to a shit ton of writing this year. Fuck you, 2020.

I 100% can't do this without my support team, aka Christina Hart and Jen Rogue. Christina also doubles as my editor so everyone can thank her for turning this sack of hot mess into a polished sack of hot mess. Jen Rogue does her formatting magic so I don't have to rip my hair out doing it. Without them, I probably wouldn't even write anymore so someone please make sure they stay alive.

#TEAMQUEEN ARC Crew, you people are the bomb dot com. Thanks for being the most amazing group of cheerleaders I could ever ask for. You guys go hard and I'm so happy to have you.

Bloggers in the house! You all show up and that is fucking amazing. Like wait...you actually want to read and review and post about little ol' me? Fucking cool. Thank you so much. From the bottom of my heart, you guys rock.

I always like to thank my children. I don't know why. Like what did they do? They didn't even bring me snacks while I was writing this. Like...thanks for existing I guess. Just kidding, I fucking love those little assholes.

Mattie, Kali, and Kaden, thanks for pushing me to be an okay mom.

Chris. My dude. My lover. My man. Partner in crime. You're like Fred Savage at the beginning of *The Princess Bride*. You aren't about to read my kissing books. But you show up every day, you support me and my writing, and you respect that this passion of mine is important to me. You love me and I love you and that's all I can ask for in someone.

And lastly, but most importantly, every single person that flips this book open and gives it a chance, thank you. Every single reader out there that keeps me going, keeps me pushing forward, keeps me trying to do this for really real, just fucking thank you. You're awesome.

Thanks for coming to my TED Talk.

Until next time. Peace out. Mic drop. Deuces. Buh-bye.

Taking A Chance

BOOK THREE

TAKING A CHANCE

BOOK THREE

For anyone who's had bad luck in love;
for the hopeless, and for those still looking.
Your Declan is out there,
ready to paint you peony pink
and tie you to a bed.

CORA

I WISH I could say exactly how I got here, how I arrived at this moment. Where did I go wrong? What god or goddess did I piss off? What sin from a former life followed me to this one? And the answer is: I don't fucking know. I don't know why I'm sitting across from Frank, a junior accountant at some-white-man's-name accounting firm. I know he said the name, I just don't remember it. Of course, that's not my fault. You remember that FRIENDS episode where Ross and Charlie are with professor what's his face and he's listing off all his allergies in a monotone monologue? Yeah, I'm pretty sure Frank is that guy's slightly better looking brother. This is the price I pay for Internet dating.

"So, Frank," I say, interrupting his ramblings about accounting and how tedious the job can be. "What do you like to do for fun?"

I don't take my eyes from my menu as I interrupt him, or as he begins to answer. I chew on my top lip as he describes a game called frisbee golf and I want to stab myself with the butter knife next to my plate. In fact, the only thing that stops me is the thought of Frank possibly crying. He looks like a crier.

I peek up over my menu, assessing him. The photo he used on his profile must be old. Possibly filtered. Frank's not...ugly. He's not overweight or balding. His face is okay, plain, unimpressive. Frank is a giant scoop of cheap vanilla ice cream. Not even specks from the real vanilla bean. He's wearing a lavender polo shirt. It feels like something you'd wear while golfing, or maybe frisbee golfing if the rules are the same. Or maybe you'd wear it in a business casual office setting. A lavender polo shirt doesn't say "first date" to me, but who am I to judge? Oh, right. You've been on fifty-seven first dates in the past two years, Cora. Judge all you fucking want!

The waitress takes our menus from us and I take several gulps from my glass of red wine. Frank ordered sparkling water, if that tells you anything.

"So, Cora. That's an interesting name," he says. "Feels very exotic."

"I guess when you compare it to Frank, it is."

"Well, I'm German, and my mother's side has a little French. I studied French in college, you know? I like to woo the ladies with it," he says, raising an eyebrow at me.

I swear if this guy starts trying to speak French, I'm out of here.

"I've been to France. Didn't really like it," I say, keeping my tone flat.

"Oh," he says.

I let the silence fall over us after that, choosing instead to focus my efforts on the basket of bread in the center of the table. I love bread. I don't care if I do have a few extra pounds in the rear, I will not give up bread. All bread. Any bread.

Frank clears his throat uncomfortably loud as I slather butter onto a freshly baked chunk of Italian loaf.

"Did you want some?" I ask, licking butter from my thumb and making a smacking noise in the process.

"No, I'm okay," he says, studying me with his head tilted slightly. "So, why online dating? And have you had any luck?"

"Well, Frank," I say, leaning back into my seat and ripping a bite of bread off with my teeth, "if I'd had any luck, I wouldn't be here with you."

"Oh," he says again—apparently his favorite one-word answer.

"No offense, Frank," I offer, "I've just done a lot of online dating. Like, a lot."

I don't know why I'm being so cold to Frank. It's not his fault. Actually, I take that back. His vanilla-ness is putting me in a sour mood, so it is his fault.

"Well, maybe I'm the right guy for you," Frank quips.

Before I can stop it, a snort escapes me. I actually fucking snort at the guy. I make eye contact with him and he looks hurt. Now I feel bad, though only a bit.

Our food arrives, and I welcome the silence while we eat. Lucky for me, he's not a talk-with-your-mouth-half-full type of dude. I swear, the next first date I go on better take me to pole dancing lessons or to pick fruit in an orchard. Or maybe kayaking. I realize none of those things are similar, but I need some fucking spice in my life.

I think there's a potential candidate for something like that in my dating profile inbox. What's his name? Ian? Aaron? Something like that. I'll check when I get home.

I know if I told anyone I was planning my next date while still on my current date, I might face a little judgment. But honestly, I know what I'm looking for, and I know Frank isn't it. Why waste time? Precious time I could lose with *the one*. And when I put it that way, people don't tend to argue. I figure I've earned the right to be picky, to treat these damn first dates like an interview. Frank is the fifty-eighth man I've gone on a first date with in two years. That gives me the right to be a little angsty, right?

Frank walks me to my car, after paying the bill—which he was very proud of paying for. As he cupped it on the table and slid it in front of him, he said, "Don't worry, I got it." I found it very odd, because I didn't reach for it or offer to pay. He was just very adamant for no reason. Fine, Frank. Go ahead and pay. You should since I feel like I just sat through one of Ross's paleontology conferences.

I push the button on my key to unlock my car and Frank is right on my heels, an eagerness to him I haven't seen all night. Where was this excitement all night, Frank? Where? I turn and extend my hand. "Well, thank you so much for a lovely evening."

"Oh," he says, grabbing my hand and giving it a limp shake.

Surely he didn't think we'd kiss after...*that.*

"Goodnight," I say, opening my car door and throwing my purse in the passenger seat.

I learned some time ago it's shitty to give false hope. So I don't tell him we should do this again. I don't tell him to call me. I don't even insinuate I will call him only to ghost him later. It's the mature thing to do.

I head home, blaring my "Another Dud" playlist I curated specifically for the drive home after a shitty first date. The fact that I was in deep enough to feel the need to do that could be pathetic. Or awesome. It depends on your perspective.

At home, I unenthusiastically walk up three flights of stairs to my apartment. The building is old and there's an elevator, but I don't trust it. I don't trust any elevators for that matter. To say moving into this place was a nightmare is an understatement.

I push my key into my door and hear the door across the hallway behind me begin to open.

Great. Probably my jerk neighbor escorting one of his ladies of the night out. I'm not even sure he catches their names; I only know that he and I have a very different approach to being single and dating. He casts a wide net, and pretty much drags in anything it catches. I use very specific bait in an effort to attract a very specific fish. My problem is, all the other fucking fish get to my bait first.

I hear him whisper something inaudible and look over my shoulder just in time to see him kiss a blonde on the cheek. I can feel her blushing from all the way over here. I roll my eyes and pretend to have trouble with my key so I can eavesdrop longer. I'm nosy, and I'm not ashamed to admit it.

She steps into the elevator at the far end of the hall, past the stairwell, and my neighbor watches after her, smiling. When the elevator doors close, he turns toward me, leaning against his doorframe with his arms crossed over his chest. I turn back to my key, all the while feeling the heat of his gaze on my back.

I've lived in this building for three years. Declan Walsh was already here when I moved in, and I only know his name because it's on the mailbox downstairs. And because of the one interaction I've had with him.

A package addressed to him was delivered to my door. So, being the good neighbor I am, I walked it over to his apartment and knocked on his. He then proceeded to answer it—shirtless. I explained about the package, he took it from me. And then he stared at me, his eyes sweeping up and down my body for way too long. Then the jerk proceeded to ask me to come in. And I don't think it was for a glass of lemonade, given the way he perused me. I called him a jerk, told him I'm not that kind of woman, and that's quite literally the only time I've spoken to him other than occasionally muttering "jerk" under my breath in his presence.

"Hey, neighbor," he says as I open my door.

Oh, right. He still continues to try to talk to me.

I huff and slam my door, as is my customary response to him.

Not that I'm complaining about the comfort of my own apartment, or the pajamas I slip into as soon as the door is locked behind me. It's not even that I hate watching FRIENDS reruns or the bowl of popcorn perched in my lap. I love all of those things. Really, I do.

But the fact is, I'll likely allow myself to fall asleep here on the couch, thankful I don't have to work tomorrow. It comes down to one sad truth: I have grown to hate being alone, sleeping alone. I refuse to compromise and bring just anyone into my bed. I make self-deprecating jokes about my loneliness and dating life frequently. But mostly it's to mask how sad I find it, how I long, how I yearn—yes, yearn—for someone.

For *the one*.

CORA

LET the record reflect his name is Ian. And while we're not exactly ziplining or picking fruit, he is taking me miniature golfing. It doesn't quite get my blood pumping, but it's not nearly as stuffy as dinner and a movie. As a matter of fact, he apparently has an entire day of activities planned. Normally I wouldn't make such a lofty commitment on a first date, but what else was I going to do all day?

I lock up my apartment and meet him in the lobby downstairs. He's not bad, not bad at all. Ian's taller than me by a couple of inches, and standing at five-nine myself, you'd be surprised at how often that doesn't happen. He's also well-dressed but casual, has thick brown hair, and sparkling blue eyes. The longer I look at him, the more promising this feels.

A wide smile spreads across his lips as I approach. "You must be Ian," I say, extending a hand.

"And you must be the beautiful Cora," he says. Okay, laying it on a little thick, but I can stand to have my ego stroked a bit.

"Nice to meet you," I say.

He takes my hand in his and twists it at the wrist, bringing it to his lips and pressing a chaste kiss on top. *Not bad, not bad.*

"Are you ready for a good time?" he asks.

I nod, and he proceeds to open the door and wave me on. *Wow, okay, holding the door open.* Chivalry might not be dead after all.

At the miniature golf counter, he lets me pick my color ball first. I go for black, like my soul, and he raises an eyebrow at me as he picks up the red ball.

"Is darkness your friend?" he teases.

"Sometimes it's my only friend." I shrug and smirk, doing my best to be flirtatious. I'm not going to lie, flirting isn't something I'm super skilled in, but I seem to do well enough to land dates.

He guides me out to the first hole with his hand on the small of my back, and I don't mind. It's actually nice. I take note of the warmth of his hands. They're not clammy or sweaty. Believe it or not, as many dates as I've been on, that's actually something I have to check for.

"Ready to get your ass kicked?" he asks, stepping back from the hole to let me putt first.

I raise an eyebrow at him, placing my ball down on the mark and studying the curves of the course, making some assessments. I line up and hit my ball, watching it bounce off bricks from one side of the hill to the other. The little black ball disappears into the hole and I look back at him, grinning innocently, as I just shot a hole in one.

Ian gives a low whistle, crossing his arms over his chest. "Didn't you say you've never been mini golfing before?" he asks.

"I did." I shrug.

He laughs. "I feel like I've been swindled."

"No, I'm telling the truth," I quip, not offering any more information.

Ian steps up to the putting spot and whacks his ball, bouncing it from the wall all the way over to the other one. His second swing is a little more controlled, and his ball goes in. We mark our card appropriately and move to the next hole. This pattern of me doing one or two strokes better than him continues throughout all eighteen holes and at the end of the course, I win by about fifteen strokes. I sign my name on the top of the card for him and date it, then hand it over to him.

"Here, a souvenir of our first date," I say, laughing. "Or rather, a souvenir of that time you got your ass kicked by a woman."

"Okay, okay, tell me what's up. How did that just happen?" he asks.

"My father was an amateur golfer, good enough to play in a few events in his day," I say, still laughing.

Ian slowly nods his head up and down and rubs the stubble on his jaw, as all the pieces fall into place in his mind. "And little miss Cora was along for those practice rounds, I see."

I nod, confirming his suspicions.

"Would the winner like to claim her prize?" he asks, his tone flirty and bold.

I rub my chin between my thumb and index finger, pretending to think about it. "I suppose a prize is in order."

He steps closer, and for a moment I think he might try to kiss me, but I don't know if I'm ready for that. Ian leans in and then to the side, pressing a kiss against my cheek. *Okay, cheek kiss. That's acceptable.*

He leans back from me, grinning. "Ready for our next activity?"

"Yep!"

He nods beyond me and I turn, looking over my shoulder and taking in the sight of a go-cart track. Now this might get my blood pumping a little. I take off toward the gate, Ian trailing behind me, my eyes likely as big as saucers. Maybe I'm a big kid, but who doesn't love go-carts?

Just when I think there are no fun men in this city anymore, Ian steps up and delivers. We race and Ian wins, then we head inside to play video games, eventually cashing in our tickets for a teddy bear that Ian gifts me. After that, we grab food next door at a burger place —and he doesn't even judge me for ordering extra fries.

I check the time as we finish eating and note it'll be getting dark soon.

"I know the best place for ice cream," he suggests.

"Yeah?" I ask.

"How about a cone before I take you home?" he asks.

"Deal." Hell, this is definitely one of the better dates I've been on.

A little more time with Ian before he drops me off doesn't sound like a bad thing at all.

As we walk back to his car, I text my friend Lyla. All I send are heart eye emojis, and she knows what that means. I'll be texting her later about this date for sure.

Right as I'm about to give up hope on ever finding a decent guy, the clouds part and the sun shines on me. *Finally.*

DECLAN

I SHOVE my paintbrush into the glass of cloudy water, exasperated and stressed. I rub my hand over the stubble of my chin and exhale with so much force, it turns into a groan. The canvas on the easel in front of me is mocking me. The colors aren't right. The composition is flawed at best. I knew this would happen. It always happens when I try to paint without a live subject.

This canvas is dead. I pull it off and set it down against the back wall full of unfinished canvases—also known as the graveyard.

A new, blank one is collected on my way back to my stool; and now I'm just staring at the white. This is almost worse than the fucked up canvas, but at least it feels like it could be something other than a failure. Maybe I can get that postal service worker lady to come back and sit for me. Did she want to do more than sit? Yes. Will dodging her advances in an effort to paint her be worth it? Also yes.

Maybe I need a fresh subject, too. Not someone I've painted before. I wonder if soliciting strangers on the street is against the law.

"Excuse me, ma'am, I know I'm a stranger, but will you come back to my apartment and remove some of your clothing so I can paint you?"

Yeah, that'll go over swell. I laugh out loud in my empty apartment at the thought. Maybe I need to step away from the project completely and stop trying to force it. Get some fresh air or drown in something else. I swivel around on my stool and notice the stack of bowls next to my full sink and three empty pizza boxes next to the fridge. Or maybe I could clean my apartment and stop living like a fucking slob.

From outside my front door, a noise interrupts my thoughts. It's subtle at first, like someone approaching, and I realize they're coming up the stairs. *Cora.* My neighbor Cora is the only one who uses the stairs. I don't know what it is about the elevator, but I've never seen her use it. She also hates my fucking guts, so maybe it's an attempt to avoid being inside it with me by surprise. I don't particularly like her either, though. She calls me a jerk every chance she gets and I hardly think I've warranted such hostility. I mean, okay, sure, there was a little misunderstanding. But that was forever ago, and I've still never had the opportunity to explain that I wasn't inviting her into my apartment for sex. I just wanted to paint her.

The noise outside gets louder. So, I move to my door and try to peer through the peep hole to see what's going on. It looks like she has a man with her, which rarely happens. I know she dates a lot, but most never come back to her apartment with her. I watch the man slide his arm up and around her like an embrace, but if I didn't know any better, I'd say it looks like she's trying to push him back. I press my ear to the door to have a listen.

"Come on, baby," the male voice says.

"No. Stop," Cora says.

"We had a good time. You owe me," the male voice sounds again.

At that, I swing my door open wide, letting my presence be known to both of them. I lean against my doorframe and they both snap their eyes toward me.

"Hey, neighbor," I say, my eyes finding Cora's.

"Buzz off," the male voice says. "We're in the middle of something."

"No, we're not," Cora says, her fist pressing against the man's chest as his arms are still trying to hold on around her waist.

"Yeah, I don't think she likes that," I say, my eyes ticking to his, my jaw clenching.

"Yeah? And how would you know?" he asks, following it up with, "You had a piece?"

I press my eyes shut, thinking back to the last time I punched someone and hoping I wouldn't need to update that record.

Cora's eyes look pleading. Her lips mouth the word *help*—and I know, no matter what happens, this guy's gotta go.

Stepping away from my door and further into the hallway, I take a more aggressive stance, dropping my hands to my sides and balling them into fists.

"Yeah, I'm going to need you to go now," I say calmly.

"I'm sorry, are you the fucking police?" he asks, laughing.

I don't know what gives this man his streak of confidence. He's at least three inches shorter than me from what I can tell and doesn't look all that beefy.

"Take your hands off her and back away before I make it impossible for you to walk down the stairs you just walked up," I say. It's not an empty threat. I will do it, and I hope my body language and facial expression give off that impression.

He stands there for a few moments longer, eyeing me, almost as if he's sizing me up. I can tell in his eyes he wants to ignore me, but after a few moments longer, he finally lets her go.

Cora clutches her purse to her middle, like she's protecting herself, and I hate that. Sure, she hates me, but I don't like to see any woman in this state. He backs away slowly, all the while his eyes are attempting to burrow into me. But I'm unfazed. *Jackass.* I don't know where men get off thinking they have a right to a woman's time or body.

Once he's down the stairs and out of sight, I finally look over at Cora again. Her bottom lip is trembling, and I can tell she's moments away from crying. I chance moving closer to her, slowly, my steps measured until I'm close enough to reach out and touch her.

Without warning, she leaps at me, her arms coming up around my neck as she sobs against my chest. At first, I stand still, unsure what to do. Eventually, I gently return her embrace and pat her back.

"It's okay now. The prick is gone," I whisper.

"Thank you." She sniffles.

"Don't worry about it," I say.

We stand there for several more minutes and I get swept away in my thoughts. I don't know if I ever realized how tall she is. Standing at six-four, I tower over most women by nearly a foot. Her red hair has always captured my attention. It was one of the reasons I'd asked her into my apartment in the first place. I had an itch to paint those vibrant locks. I can't say for certain the itch to do that has completely gone away.

Cora finally steps back from me, patting at her eyes and rubbing her hands over her disheveled clothes. She looks up and her eyes meet mine. The silver glow of her irises would look beautiful in paint, especially with the glossiness the tears are causing. Mascara is running down her freckled cheeks and her nose is pink from crying. She's beautiful in her sadness. *This. This is the humanity I want to paint.*

"So," I say, hesitantly. "Do you want to come in for a second?" I throw my thumb over my shoulder, knowing this'll probably end the way it did last time, and I hold my breath.

"What is it with you men?" she scoffs, turning back to her door. She steps in quickly, and that's exactly the way I thought that would end.

Fuck.

CORA

IT'S NOT like I need a lot from a knight in shining armor. Just rescue me, make sure I'm safe, and don't fucking hit on me two seconds after you save me from peril.

For a split second I thought, *wow, Declan is actually a decent guy. Maybe I was wrong about him.* Then he goes and tries to lock me in his tower—for conquest, no doubt.

"Wait," he says. "It's not what you think."

"Oh, right. It's not what I think. You're just a nice guy who invites women back to his apartment practically every day, even strangers like our postal worker, and it's not what I think."

"It really isn't, and I've tried explaining many times," he says.

"Okay, well, you're either a sex fiend or a fucking drug dealer and either way, I'm not interested."

Declan throws his head back, shaking it back and forth as he looks up at the ceiling. His hand rubs down his face and over the stubble on his chin and neck.

"I don't have to defend myself to you. This is so pointless," he says.

Without another word, he turns back toward his apartment and steps inside, the door slamming behind him.

Standing inside the doorway of my apartment, I step back and slam my own door. My legs give out, and I slide into a puddle on my floor.

I can't believe my date actually attacked me. Never, *ever* did I think that would happen, in all my online dating experience. I mean, I know it happens, but you just never think of it happening to you. Ian seemed so sweet, so genuine. Just goes to show you how supremely fake people can be.

I'm so mad at my bullshit meter right now. It's usually pretty good at detecting scumbags, but it really let me down this time.

The tears start again as I reach for my phone to text Lyla. Here she is, expecting this great news, and I have to flip the switch on the whole thing.

> Well, that was a shit show.

LYLA
> Oh no, what happened?

> He fucking attacked me at my door.

LYLA
> OMG are you serious?! Are you ok?!

> I'm fine, my neighbor came out and ran him off.

LYLA
> The neighbor you hate?

> Yeah.

LYLA
> I thought he was a jerk?

> He is, but apparently he has his limits. Like not watching a woman be assaulted.

LYLA
> Well, either way, thank the gods he was there.

> Right. But then he tried to get me to go to his apartment.

LYLA

What?! For what?

Isn't it obvious?

LYLA

Wait, you're just assuming he was being sleezy? You don't actually know?

I think about her question for a second. I mean, of course he was being a jerk. Why else would he invite me in? What would he want to do? Pour me a cup of hot tea and talk about our feelings?

He's a guy. It's not that hard to guess.

I throw my phone down, uninterested in listening to Lyla want to see the good in people. Who just invites woman after woman into their apartment with good intention? No one, that's who.

Pulling myself up off the floor, I replay the events of the evening as I make it into my bedroom and look for pajamas. Declan is taller than I realized or remembered. Perhaps the fact that I avoid being near him at all costs is to blame. Well, I suppose I avoid him in all cases except distress, like having just been assaulted.

I think about how I flung myself at his body and gripped him like he was some kind of damn life raft and I was stranded at sea. I bet I got tears and snot all over his shirt. *Damn.* I should've offered to wash it. When I finally stepped back from him, he looked as though he'd been running his hands through his hair, over and over again. His nearly black eyes seemed to penetrate my soul. It was all very unsettling. But I won't deny that he smelled heavenly. There's something purely intoxicating about a man's scent. He was all woodsy and spice.

He's attractive, for sure. Maybe I'd blocked that fact out due to my hatred for him. Not that his attractive face or solid muscled body is of any consequence. I still hate him. I simply hate him a little less for rescuing me.

I shake off these unwelcome thoughts, focusing instead on my presentation for work tomorrow. My marketing team and I have been waiting for months to be able to present this information to the board of directors for one of the biggest companies in town; and now, we finally have our chance. Last year, the board saw decreasing profit margins in several product lines and contacted us for a proposal on creating new campaigns for all the failing ones. Our hope is that they like the campaigns enough to not only adopt across those failing, but the entire product line in general. Tomorrow we'll present our ideas and show statistical market research in effort to prove the changes will be lucrative.

Admittedly, I'm nervous. Our ideas are quite progressive, and this company is old school—very set in their ways. My team has to convince them that forward thinking is the only solution. We hope to gain them as a permanent client through this challenge, which feels more and more like an audition every day.

Despite being straight out of college with dual advertising and marketing degrees, I flailed for a little while. I had no idea what to do. Then, one day, I woke up and decided I wanted to start my own company. After about a year of being a one-woman business, I finally had enough clients and steady income to hire a few employees. Now, we're one of the most well-known woman-owned marketing companies in Boston. I also purposely hired all women. Now, we're five strong on the team and continuing to expand.

I still live somewhat modestly, only because I know at any moment there could be a downward trend, a growing pain, or some other hiccup to set us back. If my parents taught me one thing, it was to always be prepared for the future. The company's money is not my money. We do our part to donate to charitable organizations and update our technology. Plus, the entire team goes on vacation together every year as a team building exercise, and we set aside money for that.

When I finally lie down in my bed around midnight, I'm confident about tomorrow's presentation. But thoughts of the way the rest of my evening went, linger heavily. Perhaps I need to lay off the online dating for a little while. Most annoying of all the thoughts swirling in my mind are Declan's dark eyes, peering down at me—hell, through me.

I'm affected, and I don't like it.

CORA

"A TOAST!" Claire yells over the crowd, holding up her glass of champagne.

Claire was the first employee I ever hired, and she's been by my side through the thick and thin of this company's growth. I'm happy to be celebrating this victory with the entire team tonight, but especially Claire.

"To the woman who taught me everything. The leader of this team. Cora!" she says, as the rest of the team joins in at the end to cheer.

"Thank you, ladies. But honestly, it took the whole team to get here," I say, clanking my glass against all of theirs.

As I sip from my flute, I look around at them, thankful for each of their talents and contributions. When I hired Claire, she recommended Anna, who's a wizard with market projections. She's also one of the coolest people I know and sports a pixie cut she often pushes up, making it resemble a faux-hawk. She and her wife Liliana adopted their first child last year.

Monica is the introvert on the team—quiet until you get to know her. I worship her complexion and keep begging her to tell me what her skin regimen is, but she won't give it up. Her dark skin looks so smooth she gets complimented on it literally everywhere we go.

Sara was the last to join the team. She's also the youngest. She's still in her carefree non-committal phase, single and mingling with much better luck than I tend to have. She rounds out the team and provides a youthful energy when we're in a slump.

"Hey," Claire says, interrupting my thoughts. "Doug is out of town, so I was wondering if you could do me a favor."

Her husband, Doug, is one of the best men I know. They're so in love it's almost disgusting, and I'm inclined to believe their love is the reason I'm so picky and won't settle.

"What's up?" I ask.

"I have tickets to an art exhibit opening and I don't want to go alone," she says, eyes wide and pleading.

"Ugh, is this one of those stuffy fancy exhibits with classical music playing all night?" I ask, recalling the last one she took me to. Silver platters of snails and tiny desserts the size of croutons had me starved all night.

"No, no, nothing like that. This one is in the new modern art gallery that just opened up," she explains.

"When is it?"

"Tomorrow night," she says, pouting her lips out.

Probably because she knows I hate going to these kinds of things during the week. They always drag on so late, and while I'm not necessarily one of those people in bed by nine, I don't want to drag myself home at three in the morning either.

"Fine," I say, rolling my eyes. "But you owe me."

"Yes!" she says, making a fist in the air.

I was inclined to tell her to fuck off, but she's been there for me in similar situations and it's my turn to bite it. We do this back and forth, being the other's plus one to events we don't want to attend alone.

I reach for another glass of champagne from the tray in front of us and slam back half of it. I'll regret it in the morning. But tonight, I'm happy and feeling good. The board loved our ideas. They plan to implement them as soon as possible, with a promise to expand their services with us if all goes as planned. This is when I cross my fingers and pray our projections were accurate.

"Let's dance," Anna says, already wiggling back and forth in her seat.

Monica immediately starts shaking her head, but she's already being pulled up from her seat by Sara. And no one has to tell me twice, because dancing might be one of my favorite things in the entire world.

We make our way to the dance floor of this crowded club in a train-like manner, holding our drinks above our heads and bumping into one another. I hate the fact that I have to take my drink to the dance floor with me. But what can I do? Leave it behind? We don't have that luxury. We aren't men.

Instead of trying to balance it the entire time, I slam back the rest of it and discard it on an empty table close to the dance floor's edge. The rest of the girls follow suit and then we're off, pushing our way to the middle and forming our own little circle in the crowd.

Almost everyone around us are coupled up and I can't help but envy how their bodies fit together. I should clarify that dancing with a man is my favorite, while dancing alone is a close second. I start to feel myself sync to the rhythm after closing my eyes and swaying back and forth to the music overhead.

"Cora!" Claire yells through the music.

I stop and open my eyes, catching hers staring past me and pointing.

"Isn't that your neighbor you hate?" she says.

I whirl around, eyes searching the crowds dancing and then beyond.

Declan and another man are sitting at the edge of the bar on the other wall. He's sipping a drink and laughing. I've only seen him in public a few times. We shop at the same grocery store due to the proximity to the apartment, but he's usually dressed in joggers and a white T-shirt. I saw him in the park too, again due to proximity.

I've never seen him in a place like this, though. From here, I note his shoulder-length hair is styled, which I don't think I've ever seen. In spite of myself, I start walking in his direction. I don't really have an intention; I sort of just want to observe him in the wild.

Is this the type of place where he collects his women to bring back? Is this his hunting ground?

Must. Know. More.

After approaching the edge of the floor, I try my best to crane my neck while still blending into the people dancing. Declan laughs and throws his head back. I think this is the first time I've ever seen him laugh, and I'm oddly fixated by his Adam's apple as the muscles in his throat work up and down. Also, his teeth are really white. I wonder if he uses whitening strips. I wonder if there's a way to find out without asking him. In this moment, I briefly consider digging through his trash and realize I've reached my alcohol limit for the evening.

Switching to water, starting now.

Declan's eyes scan over the crowd and then lock onto me.

Fuck. I'm caught. I'm busted. Do I make a run for it? A wry smile stretches across his lips, and he holds up his hand and waves. He's actually waving at me. In my alcohol induced niceness, I wave back. That's right, I get nicer when I drink. Everyone's heard of "mean drunks" but I'm the total opposite. *Am I smiling too? Damn it.*

Declan waves me over as he finishes off the drink in his hand and signals the bartender for another.

I start to walk toward him, hesitation in my steps. I'm not even sure why I'm going over there. I hate his guts and yet, here I am, willingly walking toward him in a social setting. When I reach him, I stand there awkwardly for a moment, my hand resting on my hip.

"Hello, asshole," I say, smirking.

"Hello, love," he replies, his smile unwavering.

Oh shit. I was not prepared for that.

DECLAN

I TRIED ALL DAY. Correction. I tried and failed all day to paint the details of her face. As soon as I walked back into my loft last night, I got to work, trying to put it on the canvas as fast as I could before the memory faded. I managed to get some of it right. The shape of her face, the arch of her nose, the color of her eyes, and even a good outline of her lips.

But today, I tried remembering the placement of her many freckles. The pained look in her irises, and the exact shade of the flush in her high cheeks along with the precise way her mascara was smeared. That sounds horrible to anyone who isn't an artist. Trying to explain how badly I want to splash someone else's pain onto a blank canvas to beautify it is always difficult. But at our core—humans at their core—really only have one thing in common: The way they process and express those emotions. Humans from all different corners of the world, one way or another, all know love, pain, and grief.

So when my agent called me up asking about my current projects, I dished about my frustrations; and he insisted I come out and have a drink with him. Of course, one drink turned into three, and here we are. Generally, I hate places like this. He knows it, but he convinced me under the guise of *looking for a muse*. Given my recent failures, I'm a desperate man, willing to try anything at this point.

Imagine my surprise when none other than the neighbor who hates me made eye contact with me from across the floor and then called me an asshole.

"Looking for your next victim?" she asks now, even after what I consider a pleasant greeting on my part.

I chuckle, shaking my head as I tip back the glass of Jameson in my hand and finish it off.

"Something like that," I say, not wishing to reveal too much about myself to her.

She's got her own perceptions, and I'll let her wallow in them if she desires to be so presumptuous. A noise escapes her throat that sounds half-groan, half-huff.

"Who's this lovely little slice of carrot cake?" my agent—and admittedly my best friend—says. He runs his eyes up and down the length of Cora's body and licks his bottom lip.

Unfortunately, this is very typical of Ryan. I've been his best friend since college, and he was just as terrifyingly idiotic toward women then as he is now. I roll my eyes, scoffing at his attempt to get her attention.

Cora peels her eyes from me, smirking at my reaction to him. She holds her hand out to Ryan to introduce herself.

"I'm Cora, Declan's neighbor, and thereby a witness to his many indiscretions," she says.

"Indiscretions?" Ryan asks, beginning to laugh.

"Yeah, yeah," I say. "This one has some strong opinions about me and how I live my life."

Ryan looks from her face to mine and back again, clearly confused. He knows as well as I do that I haven't slept with anyone in so many months it's almost laughable.

Cora snaps her head back toward me, narrowing her eyes.

Sensing the tension, Ryan attempts to break it. "How 'bout we get some shots?" His suggestion draws Cora's attention back.

"Yeah, sure," she says, surprising both me and Ryan by the looks of it.

He flags down the bartender and orders three shots of Patron, because apparently, he wants us to get wasted. That on top of what we've already had will be enough to do me in for the night.

When the shots come, Ryan raises his high into the air. "A toast! To new friends," he says, eyeing Cora. "And to the old ones that drive me nuts." He clinks his shot glass against mine as he says this last bit.

Before I can shoot mine back, my gaze snags on Cora as she takes hers, quickly and efficiently. Her body shakes as she swallows, and I study the heaving of her chest as a result. I shoot mine back then, licking at my bottom lip, eyes still on Cora's profile as she drowns in cheap conversation with Ryan. *Who the fuck calls a woman carrot cake? Ugh.*

"Let's dance!" Ryan shouts, seemingly invigorated with a new surge of energy.

He's such a jackass.

"No, thanks. I'll pass," I say, holding up my hand.

Cora gives me another look; and if I've observed anything, it's that she really likes giving me dirty looks.

"Well, I'll dance," she says, taking Ryan by the hand. *Of course she would.*

Ryan hops off his stool and tugs her toward him, his intentions written all over his face. I tip my drink toward both of them and they turn, stepping toward the dance floor. It's no surprise he's got his sights set on her. For as long as I've known him, redheads have been his thing. And let's be clear: I'm not an idiot.

Cora, in all her anger and angst, is an attractive woman. Anyone can see it. I can even look past my particular way of seeing beauty in everyone as an artist and know I could be attracted to her, under different circumstances. You know, like if she were fucking nice or didn't have this prejudice against me. As it is, that's not our path. Not this time around.

I turn, watching Ryan and Cora dance, which consists mostly of Ryan attempting to fondle any part of her he can get his hands on. Or rather, any part she allows. I can appreciate that about her. She seems headstrong, certainly doesn't bite her tongue. She's strong-willed. Sometimes, I think the world needs more of that. More people who know what they want and don't accept less. I've observed Cora enough over the years to know that much about her.

I watch her lean into Ryan, not in an attempt to accept his advances, but because she's suddenly unbalanced. I think someone's had too much to drink. I stand, knowing I can't trust him to be a gentleman about things. Not that Ryan would ever make a move if she refused. But he probably wouldn't care if she was too drunk to be aware of what was happening, and I can't allow that to happen.

Despite how she feels about me, I can't stand by and watch any woman be...*persuaded*, into something she's unaware of. Looks like I'll be the one making sure she gets home safe. *What fun.* She probably won't even thank me in the morning. No matter. My mother would kill me otherwise. She didn't raise a bystander son. She raised me to do what's right, no matter what. Doesn't matter if it's not my fight, doesn't matter if I did start it. I have to *make* it my fight if it's the right thing to do.

I reach them in the dancing crowd, leaning into Ryan so he can hear me. "I'm going to get her home safe," I say. "Let's link up later this week." At that, I lean toward Cora, linking my arm around her waist to keep her upright. "Let's go, princess."

"I'm not a princess," she slurs.

I laugh. "Okay, princess."

"Stop calling me that," she says, louder now but just as slurred. Her feet zigzag back and forth while her head bobbles like one of those dolls stuck to someone's dashboard.

This is going to be an adventure.

CORA

THE SUN ASSAULTS MY FACE, causing me to wince and roll to the opposite side of my bed. That's how I wake up. Light filtering through my window, burning my eyes out of their sockets. An audible groan escapes me, and I realize I have little recollection of what happened last night. Good thing I'm the boss and can be late to work. *God, I also have that thing with Claire tonight.* I stretch out my body and it hurts. Everything hurts. I don't even remember undressing. *How the fuck did I get home?*

A noise comes from my kitchen. A cabinet opening and shutting. *Oh my god, did someone break in?* Panic fills my chest and I reach for the bat I keep beneath my bed. So what if I'm only wearing panties and a tank top? I'll clobber someone half-naked. I don't care.

I quietly slip out of my bedroom and tiptoe down the hall, careful not to step on the floorboards that squeak. I peer around the corner and see someone bent over in my kitchen, their back toward me. My heart pounds in my chest so hard I'm pretty sure I'm going to vomit it up.

I jump out from the corner and yell, "Who the hell are you and what are you doing in my apartment?!" I keep the bat raised high as I step toward the kitchen.

The figure straightens and turns toward me. "What the hell are you doing?" Declan asks.

What the hell is he doing here?

"Why are you in my apartment?" I ask him.

He turns back to the counter then to me again, holding a cup of coffee toward me. "I thought you might need this," he says. "And these." His other hand has two pills in it.

I lower my bat a little, stepping into arm's reach of him. "What is it?"

"Aspirin," he says.

I breathe out a sigh, relieved Declan isn't an intruder I need to beat with my bat but also still confused.

Setting my weapon down, I take the coffee and aspirin from him. As I put the pills in my mouth, he hands me a glass of water. *Good call.* I don't want to swallow pills with hot coffee.

After swallowing them, I say, "Thank you, but this doesn't explain what the hell you're doing in my apartment."

"You don't remember?" he asks, leaning back on my counter. A smug smile is plastered on his face.

Oh god. Did we sleep together? Oh god. Oh god. Panic sets in again.

"Um," I hesitate, "no?" I wince again, the single word coming out pained on my lips. God, if he says we slept together, I'll have to move out of this building. Possibly out of Boston completely.

"Well, princess," he starts, and I think I might die right now, "you were pretty drunk at the bar, and I made sure you got home safely. You threw up almost as soon as you got here, and I was afraid you'd do it again in your sleep. So I stayed to make sure you didn't choke to death on your own vomit."

Declan doesn't take his eyes off me as he sips his coffee, looking at me over the rim of the mug. *Oh. Shit. Okay.* On the one hand, relief. We didn't sleep together. On the other hand, it sounds like I made a complete ass of myself and he most likely witnessed me throwing up. That's only mildly less embarrassing, but I'll take it.

"Oh," I say.

Declan continues to grin at me, like he's waiting for me to respond with more. When the silence stretches, he continues. "You're welcome," he says.

"Thank you," I say, a little mad at myself for not saying it before.

Declan drinks more of his coffee, and I've completely run out of things to say. So I sip more of my own as we stand in the kitchen in silence. *God, this is awkward.*

"Oh my god, I'm fucking naked," I blurt out, realizing I'm still in my undies. This tank top barely covers anything and I don't have a fucking bra on. My cheeks warm at the realization as Declan laughs. He. Laughs. *Is he laughing at me?*

"Don't worry, princess," he says. "I've already seen it."

"What's that supposed to mean?" I snap.

"It means you gave me quite a show when you undressed for bed last night. I had to intervene and help, otherwise you'd have kept stumbling around like a baby deer," he says.

And. I'm. Moving.

"Oh my god," I say, slapping my hand over my eyes. This is the worst.

Declan's face is sheer amusement as he continues to look at me. To my surprise, his eyes haven't fondled anything below my chin. Given the way he's looked at me before, I thought he'd be all over it.

Hm. Maybe he doesn't find me attractive?

Holy fuck, Cora, why do you even care?

Right, I don't care.

"Anyway," I say, "I need to get ready for work. Thank you again for making sure I was safe last night. I really appreciate it. Now, I'm sure you have things to do or women to hit on, so," I say in a rush, nodding toward the door.

He places his mug in the sink and runs a little water into it. I find this gesture oddly polite. Finally, he walks to the door.

"You know," he says, wagging his finger as he turns back to me, "I'm glad you appreciate what I did for you, but I can't help but feel like maybe you owe me."

My jaw drops, and I'm utterly concerned for his safety at this point. The next words out of his mouth better not be what I think they're going to be.

"Hear me out," he says. "Are you busy tonight? Actually shit, I'm busy tonight. Are you busy tomorrow night?"

"Um, no," I say, hesitantly.

"Great," he says, rubbing his hands together. "Can you come to my place around six?"

I give him the look. The same look I give him every fucking time he tries to get me to go to his place, and he holds up his hands to me.

"It's not what you think, and I'm going to prove it to you," he says.

I weigh my options. I could tell him to go to hell like normal. On the other hand, he probably could've had his way with me last night and didn't, so maybe I should consider letting him at least *try* to prove his case.

"Fine," I say, agreeing in frustration.

He opens my door, shouting back to me as he walks out, "See you later, princess."

"Ugh, stop calling me that!" I yell as I shut my door.

Princess? That sounds familiar. Then, a flood of memories from the night before come crashing in and the scene plays out in my mind. *Ugh.* He had to all but carry me out of the bar. How humiliating.

I check the clock on the stove and *fuck, fuck, fuck,* I've got to haul ass to work. Today has gotten off on the wrong foot. All I can do is pray it improves.

DECLAN

I'M at the gallery early to oversee the setup, and I have a bit of a pep in my step. It could be jitters. Or it could be due to *finally* convincing Cora to come over so I can paint her. I may never know. Of course, she doesn't actually *know* she's being painted…

I figure that'll be a fun little surprise to beg for when the time comes.

There are two kinds of artists: Those who don't concern themselves and only show up exactly when they're supposed to, and those who want to make sure every painting goes in exactly the right spot based on lighting and flow. I'm the latter. My exhibit— "Women in Motion"—is part of a larger exhibit featuring other artists.

We all have our own rooms in the gallery. I've filled my space with twelve pieces I recently finished, including women I know and strangers alike. Why, I'm not sure, but this particular show has me a little more nervous than usual. Perhaps because these pieces are really important to me. I find the more attached to the art I am, the more anxiety I feel about sharing it.

I make a few adjustments to the originally planned layout, and then the exhibit workers begin to mount them. My top priority is making sure there's a flow to it. Certain works need to be beside one another to make sense, at least in my mind. A few are intentionally opposing—sharp lines next to soft ones. I'm excited to see how the crowd reacts tonight.

After finishing up, I head to a room in the back to change. Tonight, I have to play the part of a *fancy artist* type. It's my least favorite thing about this. I'm just a guy who paints. But half the people I've met while doing this are surprised by me, having expected me to be gay. The other half assumes I use my talent as a way to get women into bed. I can't win. So, I just let everyone think what they want. I live my life exactly the way I choose to. If they're going to judge me no matter what, I might as well be happy.

I throw on a black suit, keeping my white collared button-up open at the top, and try to tame my shoulder-length hair into submission. It's mostly smoothed down, not that it matters. I'll likely run my hands through it ninety times before the night is over. I secure a hair tie around my wrist, just in case, then emerge from the back. Some people have started to trickle in. It's always slow for the first half hour or so.

"There you are, man," Ryan says, pulling me over to a group of people to introduce me.

"Which exhibit is yours?" one of the women asks, and I point in the direction of my pieces.

They *ooo* and *ahh* as they make their way across the floor to the first of my pieces. As they ask me questions, I explain my perspectives. My reasons for the choices in each piece. Anything they want to hear. I'm pretty much a dancing monkey for the rest of the night. Ryan needs me to talk them into buying. That's the game. Not that I mind, but I'd much rather feel like I don't need to perform for a sale.

Then again, the entire reason I have Ryan is so I'm not a literal starving artist. Back in college, when I began painting, it didn't matter if the pieces sold. It didn't matter if they were chosen for exhibits. I had my righteous artistic outlook and that was it. Unfortunately, you can't eat or pay bills with that, so Ryan offered to help. He majored in business anyway, and felt I could be doing a lot better for myself.

After graduation, I got a day job but kept at it. Eventually, with his help, I was able to quit that shit job and make a decent living painting full-time. Sometimes commissioned pieces, other times gallery exhibits that sell out. Honestly, Ryan made the whole thing possible. Without him, I'd likely be eating Ramen every day and living in someone's basement, painting away and earning shit.

The crowd begins to grow, with more people filtering in by the minute. An hour into the event and the place is crawling with collectors.

I grab a flute of champagne from a passing waiter and scan the room, taking in all the spectators. That's my favorite part of this. All those faces, all those emotions. Turning my attention to the window, a flash of red catches my eye and I halt my scanning. Outside the gallery on the sidewalk below, Cora's standing with someone. She's chatting away with them and laughing. It dawns on me that she's in line to come inside, but it's not moving quickly. They tend to make sure the space isn't overfilled, only letting people in as some let out.

"Ryan?" I yell over my shoulder to my friend.

He's just behind me, taking a break from entertaining buyers and hitting on one of the waitresses. *Typical.*

"Yeah, man?" he asks, coming up and placing a hand on my shoulder.

"Go make sure they get in," I say, tipping back my flute and swallowing the last of the liquid in my glass.

"Whoa, is that the carrot cake from the other night?" he asks, licking his lips.

"Just go," I say. I swear to god, if he doesn't stop calling her *carrot cake*, I'm going to punch him.

He slips through the crowd and makes his way to the front door. I step back from the window, watching Cora's red hair cut through the crowd, presumably at the request of Ryan and the doorman.

I find a waiter, swiping three flutes from his tray before I move back toward my paintings. If I know anything, it's that Ryan will lead them straight over. I sip from one of the flutes, balancing the others by the stems tucked between my fingers. Big hands come in handy sometimes.

Sure enough, I hear Ryan's voice behind me, and I turn as it grows louder.

"Here he is, the man of the hour," Ryan says, clasping my shoulder again.

"Hello, love," I say, stretching out my hand to give Cora and her friend the champagne.

Cora's jaw hangs open, and I have no doubt she's shocked as hell that I'm here. She blinks several times in rapid succession as she takes the glasses from me, handing one to her friend who's smiling wide and staring at me.

"Hi, I'm Declan Walsh," I say, reaching out to shake her hand.

"Oh my god, I'm sorry. Declan, this is my friend Claire. Claire, Declan," Cora says, clearly waking up to the situation at hand.

"So nice to officially meet you, Declan. I've seen you outside Cora's apartment. She's told me so much about you," Claire says, shaking my hand. Her smile grows even wider somehow.

"Oh, she has?" I tease, eyeing Cora, who shoots back half her glass at the mere mention.

"What are you doing here?" Cora asks as she lowers her flute.

"I should ask you the same thing," I counter, sipping casually.

"Claire invited me. Just a girl's night out," she says.

"I thought that's what last night was? I didn't peg you for someone who goes out two nights in a row during a work week," I say, offering a wry smile.

"Oh, she's not. I had to drag her out," Claire offers.

I like Claire. It almost feels like she's on my team. I can't tell what game we're playing just yet, but still.

"Anyway," Cora says, "what are you doing here?" Her attention is on me, her eyes assessing my features.

I think she's deeply rooted in annoyance at the moment, so I take a long sip, holding my finger up in the universal *just a minute* to further agitate her before answering. "I'm working," I say simply.

"What are you, like, a waiter?" she asks. Her tone is genuinely curious, which only amuses me more.

"Uh, no, carrot cake," Ryan interjects. He pulls Cora to him, tucking her under his arm, then turns her toward the bulk of my work. His Vanna White arm gestures over the wall. "This is his work."

I watch Cora from the corner of my eye as she scans the pieces, putting two and two together. The realization washes over her face.

"Oh, fuck," slips from her lips, muttered under her breath. She cranes her neck toward me, her eyes wide and wild, asking me without words.

"Guilty," I say, raising my glass toward her.

CORA

THE SWEAT on the outside of the champagne flute has dripped down onto the stem, saturating my fingers, and I'm suddenly nervous I'm going to drop it. Maybe it's because my hand is shaking from the news I just received. *Declan paints.* He's a painter. Declan is a motherfucking artist. And not just for fun. Apparently, he's reached exhibit level artist.

I try my best to wipe the shock from my face, but I doubt it's working. I'm sure he can see it as clearly as the dark purple lipstick on my face.

Did I mention he's like...dressed up? His black suit looks tailored, not off the rack. It hugs his shoulders and tapers down his waist beautifully. I can appreciate a well-cut suit, even if a man slut is wearing it. His wild hair is slightly more tamed than usual, but still frames his stubbled face. I swear, I don't think I've ever seen the man clean shaven.

Declan watches my face, studies my reaction, a small smile almost indiscernible on his mouth. He has a pretty mouth, too. His lips sort of roll up when he smiles, and the crow's feet at the corners of his eyes deepen. I've observed that it doesn't matter how big or small the smile. His whole face seems to wear it either way. I even sort of like his imperfect nose and the way it just *fits*.

Oh my god. Why are you analyzing his face, Cora? Shut up.

"So, what, you're like...a famous artist?" I ask, the question stupid but relevant. Or at least it is to me.

"I don't know about the famous part, but yes, I'm an artist," he says. "I do okay."

"Just okay? I mean, you're in an exhibit. That seems a little more than okay."

"Ryan has helped me evolve, I guess." He shrugs, noncommittally. He's very matter of fact about his accomplishments. I can't tell if it's a façade or if he's really this humble.

I turn my attention back to the paintings. They're all women, displaying different emotions; and they have a certain level of nudity to them, which makes them feel so much more vulnerable in these emotional states. Some are happy, some are sad, some look worried. I study each face; his level of detail immaculate. The paint strokes appear to convey their own amount of emotion as well, making each one come to life. I can't believe I'm going to say this, but I'm actually impressed. I'm impressed by Declan. That's wild in itself.

I turn, taking in more of his work when my eyes snag on one in particular. This woman is older, her face slightly wrinkled, but her bright blue eyes look so tranquil. She looks...familiar. I feel Declan's presence behind me. It's as if he's studying me as I study his work.

I rub my thumb over my jawline, and it hits me. "Is that...Sandra?"

Declan nods, confirming that I am indeed looking at a painting of our postal service worker.

"Wait, so..."

I trail off. My head snaps to Declan, who's very slowly and deliberately nodding. Even though he isn't saying anything, it feels like *I tried to tell you.*

"Oh," I manage to squeak out.

I walk to the wall furthest from us, my eyes still tracing over the forms in each piece as my mind works on processing this new information about Declan. *Why is he standing so close?* I need distance. I need space to regain my composure.

"So, what, you have sex with them and then paint them? Do you seduce the women you paint? What's the game here?" I blurt it all out before I realize what I'm saying.

Declan takes a step back from me, sighing. He doesn't look wounded by my accusation. He sort of looks amused.

What the hell is so funny?

"I just like painting," he says. "I see someone I want to paint, and I ask them to let me. That's all."

"You don't sleep with them?" I raise my eyebrow in his direction.

Declan looks up and away, as if he's thinking hard about the questions I've asked.

"You know," he starts, "I don't think I've ever slept with anyone I've painted."

"Really? I find that hard to believe."

"No, you mistake me. I've never invited someone over to paint them and then slept with them as a result. But I have slept with women I've then later painted."

I shift my eyes back and forth, sorting through his answer, trying to find the difference. It makes sense, but when I think about the women I've seen come over, I can't help but feel like it's suspect.

Let's not forget, Declan is hot. Like, really hot. I'm sure he has women swooning over him all the time. So, a woman sits half-naked for him, gets painted by him, and then doesn't want to sleep with him? I feel like if I was attracted to a man on any level and then he painted me, I'd be beyond turned on. Being painted by someone sounds so intimate, like you're sharing something with each other no one else gets to experience.

My friend clears her throat behind me, interrupting my thoughts, and I realize I've been carrying on with Declan like we're the only two people in the room.

"So, Declan," Claire says, "what are you working on next?"

"I have a couple of things going, and a few more I've planned out. Are you in the art scene?" he asks her.

"Well, I studied art in school, and I love it. I have a few pieces but would love to grow my collection. I enjoy the process behind the art as well," she says.

"If you'd like, you're welcome to come see my studio, see what I'm working on?"

Declan offers this to her like it's no big deal. And maybe it isn't. Maybe I'm the only one here who feels like it's an extremely intimate and personal thing.

"Oh my gosh, that would be wonderful," she says. Claire presses her hand to her chest, both surprised and elated by this. She's obviously appreciative of such an opportunity.

"Great. Why don't you take my number and we'll set it up sometime?" Declan waves his hand as Claire reaches in her bag for her phone, rifling around for several awkward minutes.

After he gives her his number, he encourages us to walk around and see the other exhibits. So, I link my arm into Claire's and practically have to drag her away from Declan.

"Oh. My. God," she says. "Your neighbor is awesome! I thought he sucked and was like, a whore?"

"Oh, I'm pretty sure he's still a whore," I correct.

"Right, but he's an awesome whore. Maybe you can—"

"Don't even," I snap, cutting her off. I know Claire, and she's been very much in favor of me abandoning my search for *Mr. Right*, in favor of *Mr. Right Now*. She thinks I should just have fun and *leave it to fate*, whatever the hell that means.

"I'm just saying," she says. "You seem to perk up in his presence."

"You're mistaking my being on high alert for perkiness," I say.

"High alert for what?" she asks.

"For whatever happens to those women who get sucked into these relationships with slutty men. And I use the term *relationship* very loosely," I say.

We stop in front of another artist's exhibit, studying their work for several silent minutes.

"I don't like these," she whispers to me. "They make me feel uneasy."

I nod my head in agreement, still not saying a word. Then we move on, cutting through the crowd to the other side of the gallery.

"He doesn't seem so bad," she starts again.

"Okay, fine. He's not that bad. Sure. He's my slutty artistic neighbor who also happens to be really good looking and he's not that bad of a human." The words leave me on a breath, pushed out quickly and with force.

Claire side-eyes me. "Whoa, girl. He like...*affects* you."

"Shut up," I say, realizing we've worked together too long. She knows me. She knows the things I say, how I act under different conditions.

"Look, for better or worse, you react to him. Your body reacts to him. When's the last time that happened, huh?"

If by *that*, she means I feel a strong urge to punch him in his pretty face every time I see him, then yes, she's correct. But if she means I get tingly feelings in my lady parts, she's definitely wrong. There's a big difference between rage and sexual desire radiating throughout your body. Isn't there? I don't think those feel the same.

How would you know, Cora? When's the last time anything sexual radiated throughout your body?! Ugh. My inner sex goddess is right. At this point, I'm a born-again virgin.

We walk through the rest of the exhibits, her question hanging in the air, unanswered. I contemplate leaving early, but I know Claire will never let me live it down.

Once we've rounded the place, we find ourselves back in Declan's space. He's deep in discussion with Ryan and some other people, so we don't interrupt. Instead, we try to slide past the group. But Declan reaches out, grabbing me at the bicep. He puts a finger up to the group, leaning in close to me. So close, in fact, that I can smell him again.

"This wraps up in about another hour, if you'd like to talk?" he says.

Talk? Us? Umm.

"I can't exactly abandon Claire," I start.

"Yes, you can," she offers, presumably perking up at the idea of us talking like it's a big deal. "I'll just grab myself a cab and we can chat tomorrow."

He looks to her and smiles, then looks back at me for confirmation.

I nod, reluctance flooding me.

My friends are the worst.

CORA

I HUG Claire right before she steps into a taxi and drives away, leaving me standing on the sidewalk next to Declan. Apparently, he sold all the paintings he had on display tonight. After seeing his work, that shouldn't surprise me, but I'm still surprised in general about this side of him. It feels very important to him, not just an exploited talent. And that's something I can respect.

"So," he says, interrupting my thoughts, "wanna share an Uber home?"

When I think about it, I don't want to punch him, which is different. My skepticism still runs deep, though. Even with that considered, I don't see the harm in taking him up on his offer. I nod as he pulls his phone from his pocket and clicks some buttons.

"There's one seven minutes away," he announces.

I fold my arms over my chest, suddenly chilly. The air in Boston is getting crisper by the day. Soon, we'll be well into fall—my favorite season.

"Are you cold?" Declan asks.

"A little," I admit, realizing while the leggings and boots were fine choices, the thin fabric of my three-quarter sleeve top leaves something to be desired. Which is warmth. I desire warmth.

"Here," he says, sliding his suit jacket off and advancing.

"Oh no, I couldn't. Then you'll be cold."

He laughs. "I'm Irish. I don't get cold."

"You're Irish?" I look him over, his dark hair certainly making me question his statement.

"Mostly. We're not all gingers, like you," he says, his lips pressing together to form a closed-mouth smile as the jacket slides over my shoulders.

I adjust, pulling it further on and uncoiling a little in its warmth. I suppress the urge to inhale its scent deeply or ask him what kind of cologne he wears, even though it might be the number one question I have at the moment.

"Thank you," I say.

Declan nods his head as he fastens one of the buttons on it so it stays in place. His mane hangs into his face, dangerously close to mine. I release a breath I didn't realize I'd been holding as he steps away.

We make eye contact for the briefest moment before his phone dings and a car pulls up to the curb behind him. *Saved by the Uber.* Declan holds the door open for me as I crawl in and slide to the far end, allowing him to step in on the same side rather than run around the car.

"Are you hungry?" he asks me, leaning across the center of the car.

"A little," I admit.

He leans forward, giving the driver a new destination. The street he names intersects with ours, so it's not far from home.

"You ever been to Saints?" he asks, leaning back into his side of the seat.

I shake my head. "I've heard of it, but never been."

"I think you'll like it," he says as he looks out the window.

Oh you do, do you? Jesus, why am I giving him so much attitude in my mind?

A few minutes later, we pull up in front of the place, which is known for delicious fusion creations and a custom drink menu. I've been hoping one of my Internet dates would suggest this place, but no one ever has. I'm not sure why. It has a wonderful tone with low lighting and a rich, warm dining room palette. Not that I can complain about a free meal, but those guys always seem to suggest somewhere really boring and commercial.

Declan steps out onto the sidewalk, giving me his hand to help me as I slide across the seat. I place my hand in his, realizing this is the only contact outside of me sobbing into him that we've ever had. His grip is light but possessive as I make it out of the car. His fingers curl around mine, like he doesn't quite want to let go. He holds onto it until he's opening the door for me to walk inside before him. *So chivalrous.*

The door closes behind us, and he ushers me forward by the small of my back until we're standing in front of the hostess's station.

"Hey, Declan," the petite young woman behind it says. "Your usual spot?" She leans way over the podium between us, and her tits practically pop out at Declan. She bats her eyes up at him, her stance forcing him to look straight down into her shirt to make eye contact. I internally roll my eyes.

"Yeah, that'll be good, Bri. Thanks," he says.

Of course, she doesn't give me a second look. Hell, she didn't even give me a first look. I'm a ghost during that interaction.

I don't like to be one of those women who pass judgment on other women, but could she *be* trying any harder for his attention? Even as she seats us in what is apparently his *usual spot,* she doesn't even glance at me. His usual spot is a small booth tucked back in the corner, further away from the rest of the patrons, and I can see why he's claimed it.

I remove Declan's jacket, attempting to hand it back to him, but he stops me, insisting I keep it for when we leave.

In this light, his bright white button-up is practically glowing against the dark of his suit and complexion.

"Why don't you check out the wine menu, and I'll be right back," he says, standing almost immediately after we've been seated.

I browse the selection, keeping my eye on a red blend that looks pretty good. I'm not even all the way through the entire thing when Declan re-emerges, his reason for leaving apparent. He's tied his long hair back into a knot, somehow still looking a tad disheveled, but I like it. It fits him.

"Didn't want hair hanging down in your food?" I tease.

"Contrary to what you might think, I can be civilized," he says, pushing his menu to the side without even looking.

Choosing to make the best of this weird situation, I ask, "So, what's good here?" Because this is weird, right? *Well, Cora, you've loathed the man for years and now you're sitting down with him and having a meal and your hate is shrinking ever so slowly, so yeah, it's fucking weird.*

"Try the blackened salmon," he says, not giving any more information.

"I don't really like fish," I say.

"Trust me," he says.

Uh, okay. I squirm in my seat, adjusting and readjusting as I read the menu. His eyes are burrowing a hole into me. I can feel them on my face and they're causing a heat to bloom over my cheeks and down my neck.

"What are you looking at?" I finally snap, looking up from my menu to make eye contact.

His finger traces the edge of his water glass as he leans back. "Your freckles."

"What about them?"

"I like them," he says. "That's all."

"You're staring at me like I'm the first person you've ever seen with them," I say.

"But no one's freckles look the same. And I'm not inspired to paint just anyone's freckles," he says.

This must be the beginning of one of those out of body experiences, because I no longer feel the chair beneath me or the menu in my hand. I stare at him for several minutes, neither of us saying anything. Growing up, I hated my freckles. I was the redheaded, freckled girl who was too tall for her age group, all knobby knees and sharp elbows. To hear someone speak so nicely about my skin is soothing decade old wounds.

"Did you just say you're moved to paint my freckles?" I ask, clearing my throat.

"Would that be okay with you?" he asks, lacing his fingers together in front of him.

I swallow hard against the lump in my throat and quiet the twenty questions plaguing my mind. *Why mine? Paint them how? Am I going to be naked like some of the women in the other paintings?*

"Um, I think that would be all right," I say, not quite sure what I'm getting myself into.

"Can we start tonight?" he asks.

Oh my god. What have I done?

DECLAN

I SLIDE my key into the door and twist, pushing it open and then flipping on the living room light. I step to the side to let Cora in. From the moment she agreed, up until now, she's asked me no less than seventeen questions and I can tell more are at the ready.

I watch her step into the space—*my* space. Her footsteps are timid compared to her usual. Anytime I've ever seen her, aside from when she was practically assaulted in front of her apartment door, she's always had an air of confidence. After closing the door behind me, I push my hands into my pockets and continue to watch her. She looks around, her face portraying she's deep in thought as she studies her surroundings.

"I'm going to change," I say, unbuttoning the cuff links at my wrist. "Make yourself comfortable."

I leave her to go change out of my suit. Boy, Ryan would love it if I showed up to the next exhibit with paint on my suit. It's not that I don't have other suits, but let's just say I've ruined as many as I have.

I return after making quick work of changing. The old jeans with paint splattered all over them and a white T-shirt are a stark contrast to the crisp black suit, and I read as much on Cora's face. Her eyes trace down my body to my bare feet.

"Not even socks?" she asks, a teasing quality in her voice.

"Not if I can help it." I shrug. Bare feet are as essential to me as the brushes when I'm painting. I can't explain it. I just feel better when my feet can feel the floor beneath them without a barrier.

"Interesting," she says. "Do I have to be naked?"

Her question catches me off guard and I choke a little bit on nothing at all. "Um, do you want to be naked?"

"I just noticed that most of your subjects seem to be some degree of nude," she says.

"That's up to them, really. I let them decide," I say, clarifying a bit of the process. If I'm being honest, most women do want to be some level of nude. Perhaps when they run it through their minds, it's exhilarating or feels like a once-in-a-lifetime thing, and they take full advantage.

Cora pulls her top lip between her teeth, like she's giving this a lot of thought. "You let them have a say in how you paint them?" she asks.

"I let them get comfortable, then I observe them until I find what I want to paint," I confess. I hook my thumb into my belt loop and notice her posture relaxes a fraction.

"May I use your bathroom?" she asks.

I point down the hall and then turn to position my stool and canvas while she's gone. After I pour paint onto my palette, I hear her footsteps behind me a few moments later. When I turn to show her where to sit, I stop at the sight of her. Gone is Cora's top layer of clothing, leaving behind a black lace bra and panties. But she's still wearing my suit jacket. And, dare I say, the image of Cora wearing nothing but her underthings and my jacket, makes something low inside me do a somersault.

She's wringing her hands together in front of her, biting her bottom lip. "I thought," she pauses, "I thought to myself this might be the only time I ever get painted by a professional. And I want to step outside my comfort zone. Be a little vulnerable. Maybe even sexy."

The tension in my jaw draws tight and I resolve to nod, understanding what she means. For some women, they want the painting to be a reflection of themselves in a manner that's outside their normal character. Something bold. Something sexy. Something wild or carefree. They all have their own preferences. And just like I said, they often take full advantage.

"Sit over here," I urge, pointing to the space in front of me where the light filters in from the street. Given it's dark out, all the streetlamps are on, casting delicate shadows in different directions.

She steps lightly and I notice she's barefoot too, her toes painted black to match everything else she's wearing. Cora stands a bit awkwardly in front of the chair at first and finally sits, pulling her knees up as she looks around and finally, at me.

"What do I do?" she asks.

"Just talk to me, and I'll tell you when to stop moving," I say, giving her a smile. I want her to relax, to feel comfortable so her personality comes through.

"Talk about what?" she asks.

"Anything you want," I say. "I can ask questions if it helps?"

"Okay. Do that." She laughs nervously.

"What do you do for a living?" I ask. Something simple to get the ball rolling.

"I own my own boutique marketing company."

"Wow, that's actually really cool," I say.

"And all my staff are women," she adds.

"Also impressive," I say, nodding. I don't say that as a means to blindly compliment her. It actually is very impressive to me.

"Yeah, I pretty much have everything I wanted in my five-year plan," she admits.

"You made a five-year plan and actually stuck to it?" Everyone I know derailed almost immediately. Life has a way of reading your plan, laughing in your face, and ripping it up more often than not.

"Pretty much. I wanted a certain amount of growth within my startup, which I've achieved. Other things escape me though," she says.

"What other things?" I ask, leaning in to her words as they trail off into nothing.

Cora's eyes falter, drifting down to the ground and then back up.

My suit jacket slips from one shoulder and before she can pull it back up, I hold out my hand.

"Wait. Leave it."

Her eyes connect with mine over her bare shoulder and I lean in closer to my canvas.

"Don't move anything. You can still talk, but try not to move anything else," I say.

"I wanted to be married by now," she continues. "I wanted a house and a husband and it's all terribly cliché but it's what I wanted."

I press my paintbrush to the canvas, swirling colors to form her silhouette, framing her arm and chest on the canvas. "And no one you've been on dates with had that potential?"

It's as if her entire body sighs, even while sitting still. "Something like that," she says. "I think I'm defective or something."

My eyes sweep over her limbs, across her breasts, and up her neck. I do this in the most professional manner I can muster. It isn't like me to ogle who I'm painting, but there's something in Cora's raw vulnerability coupled with the way she looks right now that I can't ignore. The freckled patterns across her shoulder and clavicle are a constellation of questions I want the answers to. *Whoa. You're getting carried away in the paint, dude.* I shake the strange thoughts from my mind and return to my strokes.

"I doubt you're defective," I scoff, with a laugh.

"Oh yeah? I've been on almost sixty first dates in the past two years," she says on a breath.

If I didn't know any better, I'd say I just detected a slight wobble in her chin. "I doubt that's your fault."

"I'm the common denominator," she argues.

"Or about sixty men weren't good enough for you. And that's a pretty low number considering how many truly undeserving people there are in this city alone," I say.

"I can't tell if you're trying to make me feel better or mocking me," she says, her body still, face holding a confused expression.

"I'm trying to make you feel better, but if you can't tell, I'd say I failed." I laugh.

Cora laughs too; it's small and breathy. Then, her face returns to a melancholy state. Is it wrong to admire the beauty in her sadness? Can I tell her she's beautiful when she's sad without it coming off terribly wrong? I consider this for a moment before dismissing the idea of telling her.

Ryan tells me all the time that one of the reasons I eventually strike out with the women I date is because I get weird and tell them stuff like this. Not that I'm trying to score with Cora, but I'm on thin ice with her as it is.

I should leave well enough unspoken.

CORA

TIME IS LOST on me as I sit here, unable to discern if ten minutes or two hours has gone by. Realistically, I know it's somewhere between those two figures. More than ten, less than one hundred and twenty, which doesn't seem all that great in terms of judgment. I've made every attempt to sit as still as possible like Declan's instructed, and I think I've done pretty well at it so far. No complaints from him, anyway.

I've been filling any silence between us by studying his face as he paints. He's focused and serious, and while he's always struck me as a serious guy, this is different. It's a side I didn't even know existed.

"I think I'm done for the night," he says. "Have to let some of this dry for layering."

"So I can move now?" I ask, making absolute sure I won't mess anything up.

"Yep," he says, followed by a small laugh.

I arch my back and stretch my arms up overhead, bending and cracking my neck. Sitting in one position for so long really stiffens the body. I stand and turn, looking behind me to a far wall, and something catches my eye. I tilt my head to the side, taking in the sight and blinking several times.

"Is that me?" I point to the half-finished canvas and stare at him in disbelief.

Declan begins rubbing the back of his neck, like he's nervous. "Uh, yeah."

Blinking back in the direction of the canvas, I trace my eyes over the cascade of mascara running down my painted cheeks. *He painted me crying? When the hell did—*

Wait. "Is this from the other night? When I was practically assaulted?" I question.

Declan nods, not lending an actual audible answer.

"You painted me after I was fucking sobbing? You thought to yourself, *wow, I think I will paint her terrified and a complete mess,* and that sounded like a good idea to you?"

"It's not like that," he says.

"Then what's it like?" I press.

"It's hard to explain," he says, rubbing his neck some more.

"What do you think gives you the right to paint my vulnerable moment like this? And without my permission?" I ask, voice stern.

Declan is quiet behind me for several long moments. "I'm sorry," he finally says, his voice barely above a whisper. "I couldn't help myself."

A snort of derision escapes me, unfiltered and loud, and it cuts through the silence abruptly. "I bet the guy who groped me at my door would say the same thing." I march over to the unfinished painting, tuck it under my arm, and then walk out of his apartment back to mine.

It isn't until I'm in my apartment and no longer fuming that I realize I'm still in my fucking underwear and his suit jacket. I just walked from his apartment to mine in my panties. Hell, I just yelled at him in my panties. *Oh my god. Great job, Cora. Stellar fucking plan.* And in true dumbass fashion, I still have his jacket and my clothes are in his bathroom. *Awesome.*

After I stop pacing and calm myself down a bit, I study the painting more closely, bringing it toward me. I trace over the lines of myself on the canvas—now immortalized in paint—and the black pools, dissecting it all. The mascara streaks are alarmingly accurate. If I wasn't so mad, I'd be impressed. Maybe it's possible to be both.

I need to talk to someone about this; someone rational, logical. I can't talk to Claire. She'll hear he painted me, and the rest of the story won't matter. To her, it'll be the most romantic gesture she's ever heard of. I can't call Lyla. She's been begging me to take Declan up on his offer to come over since the beginning. Of course, that was when we both assumed it was for sex.

I pick up the phone and dial the only person I can think of who might be impartial. Harper—my new sister-in-law—is practical enough to see my side of this. *I think. I hope.*

She answers on the second ring, her voice slightly labored. "Hello?"

"Sorry, did I wake you?" I ask, realizing it's a little late to be calling people.

"No, not really," she says over the line. I hear her adjusting or repositioning, possibly a ruffle of blankets. "I haven't been sleeping much this past week. I have to pee like, every four minutes."

Harper also happens to be pregnant with my niece or nephew. They find out the gender next week and are supposed to come for a visit after that. Before she gets too big to travel.

"I need to talk to you about something, and I need that pragmatic side of yours," I start.

"I'm all ears," she says.

Taking a seat at the edge of my bed, I breathe out a sigh and relay my past with Declan. I feel like she needs the whole picture for this. So, I spill everything all the way up to a few minutes ago when I stormed out.

Harper is silent on the other end for a few moments before replying. "Okay, let me see if I have this correct," she says. "You hated him, then you shared a meal with him and chose to be painted by him half-naked, but you're mad he painted your private emotions?"

"Well, when you put it like that, I sound like a crazy person." I sigh.

"I'm just wondering why your emotions on canvas felt more vulnerable to you than partial nudity," she says.

You know what, on second thought, Harper is making too much sense. I shouldn't have called her. She has the unique ability to be completely objective and serve up a very different side of the issue at hand than the one you see.

"Harper, that's not the point. The partial nudity was with my permission, and I wasn't *totally* nude. The important parts were covered. As for the emotions, he didn't ask permission. He just used what I was going through for his art. It feels like a violation," I spit out on a hurried breath.

A few more quiet moments of contemplation go by and I hear her shift again. "Something inside you allowed you to trust him in your moment of need. Something also had you accept a dinner date. And something definitely made you feel like it was okay or safe to be undressed in front of him. So do you really think it was a violation or do you hate that you hate him less?"

An unidentified noise escapes my throat. A scoff? Another snort? Some combination of both? I'm not sure, but whatever it is causes Harper to sigh in response—loudly.

"Look, that's definitely not it," I say, unsure if I'm lying or not. *Am I?*

Let's examine the facts. Do I hate him less? It's probable. And by that, I mean yes. Do I hate that? Also probable. What else is probable? That I'm lying to Harper. But can I hate that yet also feel violated? This is a lot of questions. I feel my brain compressing against the walls of my skull.

"Okay, then I guess continue to be mad at him and hate him like you did before," she says.

I can practically *feel* her shrug through the phone line. "I should go. You get some sleep. I'll see you guys next week, right?" I say, changing the subject before she reaches through the phone and chokes me.

"That's the plan," she says.

We say goodbye and I end the call, not really feeling much better than before. Shrugging out of Declan's suit jacket, I set it down next to my bed and crawl beneath my blankets, making a mental note to have it dry cleaned for him while I'm at work tomorrow.

Maybe I'm mad at him, and maybe I never want to speak to him again, but that doesn't mean I shouldn't have the decency to wash his jacket after wearing it most of the night.

As I doze off, my emotions are all jumbled. It's unsettling and annoying, which is sure to make for a night of tossing and turning. *Perfect.*

CORA

AFTER LEAVING WORK, picking up Declan's jacket, and then stopping to get my favorite Japanese takeout, I arrive at home, ready to tackle laundry night. Despite having a great day at work, it was still clouded by last night's events. It took me forever to fall asleep last night and as a result, I woke up groggy as hell this morning. Only after two cups of coffee was I able to start functioning like an actual human being.

The day turned around during lunch and ended on a good note in terms of progress on our current catalog of projects. But picking up Declan's suit jacket—which I paid the cleaners to expedite—served as a stark reminder of the cloud overhead. That was when I decided to pick up Japanese. Because nothing does a better job at improving my mood than a big Styrofoam container of shrimp hibachi.

I unpack everything onto my kitchen counter, then separate my takeout containers and pour myself a glass of wine. I don't even bother going to sit down. I crouch over the sink, alternating between sipping from my glass and shoveling rice in my mouth. It's not until about halfway through that I realize how pathetic this seems.

I'm ashamed to admit the number of meals I eat this way. Unless it's a date night or I'm out with friends, this is usually where I am. There's a certain kind of sadness associated with eating so many meals alone in this manner. Is it so much to want someone to sit down with? To light a candle, talk about our respective days, and laugh? Do dishes together or fight over whose turn it is?

For a long time, my brother Jensen and I shared these same goals for our lives. Before he met Harper, he'd been single a long time. Now that he's found his happiness, it casts a harsher spotlight on my own life. Don't get me wrong, I'm happy for my little brother. It's awesome for him. But I can't help but feel pangs of jealousy.

I shovel the last bite of rice and teriyaki shrimp into my mouth as I turn to toss the container into the garbage, which is full. Not surprisingly, having someone to take out the trash is closer to the top of my list of desires than I care to admit.

I down the last of the wine in my glass and then go change my clothes, throwing on a ratty old pair of leggings I refuse to part with and an oversized T-shirt with a wide neck. Since I'm staying in the building, I don't even bother with a bra. I hoist my laundry bag over my shoulder and descend the stairs to the basement. Yes, it would be easier to use the elevator when carrying a large laundry bag. No, I still won't use that elevator.

In the basement laundry room, I toss my clothes into the wash and pop in my headphones. Waiting is the worst part. But no one is here and I see no occupied machines anyone would come back for, so I scroll through my music and put on my laundry playlist. Why exercise when you can just dance? That's my motto.

The music plays in my ears and I start dancing, immediately zoning out right here in the laundry room—no audience, no restrictions. I swing my hips and snake my body, running my hands down my sides before dipping low. All is right in my world when I'm dancing. Granted, it's not like I've had professional training, but I happen to think I'm pretty good. Maybe it's not the foxtrot, but I can do those *Dirty Dancing* moves with the best of them.

When the washing machine stops, I transition my clothes to the dryer, all while moving and shaking what my momma gave me. And between you and me, my momma gave me a lot.

With the exception of the bar the other night, I haven't danced since Lyla's wedding. She and her hubby Gentry threw a hell of a

Southern wedding. *God, what a mess that was.* Well, for me. Not the wedding itself. My date flaked on me halfway through and started flirting with a waitress on the catering staff, leaving me alone at my table most of the night. I managed to sneak a few dances in with other people here and there, but for the most part, I got to sit and watch Lyla and Gentry be in love and Harper and Jensen fall in love. Let's just say it's a good thing my friend made it an open bar.

One of my favorite songs fills my ears, and it's a dirty one, so naturally my dancing gets dirtier. I grasp the edge of the folding table in the laundry room so I can dip all the way down to the floor and back up, swaying my hips and letting my booty shake away.

With no warning, I feel a yank at my headphones, and they fall out of my ears before dangling at my waist. "What the hell?" I yell, whirling around to see what the fuck is happening.

I come face to face with Declan's arms folded neatly across his chest. A wide smile is plastered across his face and I want to claw his eyes out for what I'm sure he just saw.

To make matters worse, the headphones disconnect from my iPhone then, causing the song that was privately playing to now echo throughout the entire room. The basement acoustics are surprisingly good. So, let's stop right there; because do you remember that song *My Neck, My Back?* The one your parents probably refused to let you listen to because of how filthy it is? And by filthy, I mean filthy good. Well, Elle King covered it, and that's what I'm listening to. And she's going on about *my pussy and my crack* as I make eye contact with Declan.

"Sorry," he says. "I just wanted to see what song had you feeling so good." He pauses, listening to another line of the song and how the man needs to put his neck into it. "This makes sense." He nods his head gently up and down, as if there's no more confusion.

"Do you always sneak up on people and yank their headphones out or am I just that unlucky?" I accuse.

"To be fair, I stood in the doorway for several minutes and you didn't even notice me," he says.

"So the next logical thing to do is rip something from my ears?" My voice is slightly elevated, the song continuing to play out loud from the machine in my pocket. Maybe my cheeks are red with embarrassment or maybe they're red in anger, I'm not sure, but I can feel the heat.

"Like I said, I wanted to know what song you were listening to," he says, so matter of fact. His shoulders pull up and slump back down in the slightest of shrugs, like it isn't a big deal.

"Do you just like pissing me off on purpose?" I ask, crossing my arms over my chest.

"I mean, you are kind of cute when you're yelling at me, but no," he says.

Cute? I'm cute. The confession throws me slightly off kilter and I fumble to form my next sentence.

I roll my eyes, not conceding my original point. "Anyway," I say, changing the topic when I realize a more thorough apology isn't coming, "I have your jacket upstairs. I had it cleaned. I'll bring it over after I'm finished here."

"I take it this means you won't sit so I can finish your painting?" he says, unfolding his arms. His jaw tightens, hands gripping and loosening over and over again at his sides.

"I think it's best I don't," I say.

"Why are you so stubborn?" he asks.

"Why are you so stoic and oblivious to social norms?" I reply.

Declan rubs his hand over his stubbled chin, releasing a long, deep sigh. "I wish I knew the answer to that."

He turns to leave without another word. My dirty song is still playing, the last verse about rolling your tongue from the back to the front serenading me. I stare at Declan's back as he leaves. Once he's gone from my sight, I stare at the empty space he previously occupied.

Flabbergasted. The word is flabbergasted. That's what I am.

What the hell is that guy's problem?

DECLAN

SOCIAL NORMS? What's a *social norm* anyway? The majority group decided what's acceptable behavior and what makes you a weirdo? That seems unfair.

More importantly, since she left my place last night, I've felt like a total shit.

I don't know if she knows this or if it's mere coincidence, but Cora does her laundry the same day, every week, at almost the same time. So, I went down to apologize. I truly wanted her to know I didn't mean to violate any sort of boundary, even if I am slightly unaware of them. My inability to perceive one is no excuse, though. Really, I should just learn from past mistakes. It's not like this is the first time there's been a mix-up.

My last girlfriend, Vanessa, didn't appreciate when I painted her while she was sick with the flu. She'd fallen asleep on the couch, representing the epitome of a frail humanity. Needless to say, she didn't appreciate her reddened nose or the beads of sweat glistening on her forehead plastered across a large canvas.

Women, I find, have an issue with unfiltered vulnerability. More often than not, they make attempts to hide certain parts of themselves or only want to present a polished, in-control version. But that's really only a small fraction of what makes a person, and that's not what I want to paint. Women are beautiful in every light. I don't care if they're thin, thick, white, of color, old, young, blonde, freckled, pregnant, crying, or laughing. They're something to be celebrated, worshipped even. Apparently though, they have very strict guidelines as to when and how you're allowed to do this. I don't like that. My goal, to wake them up to the beauty of their mess, remains.

I head back up to my apartment, taking the elevator for the short ride. I don't know why Cora hates this thing. It seems fine to me. After stepping out onto our floor, I'm greeted by Ryan at my door.

"Dude, I've been knocking forever," he says.

"Yeah, I'm not there," I say, in true jackass fashion.

"And I called you," he says.

"My phone is in my apartment," I add.

"Where were you?" he asks, his attention split between my phone screen and his.

"Downstairs," is all I say. I don't need to get into conversation about Cora or anything that happened.

"Okay, well, we're supposed to be leaving in like twenty minutes so hurry up," he says.

"Where are we going?" I ask.

"You don't remember agreeing to that buyer's invitation for dinner? He's supposed to introduce us to several friends of his—avid collectors, a.k.a potential business for us." He's stopped typing now and is staring straight at me as he says all this.

I open my apartment door and we step in. "Let me just get changed." Not that I want any part of this. I don't remember agreeing to any stuffy dinner. But if he's here, it's important. I guess it beats eating dinner alone at my tiny two-person kitchen table that's shoved in the corner, or while standing and staring at the painting I now cannot finish. *Damn it, Cora.*

Leaving Ryan to click away on his phone, I run back to my bedroom and rummage through my closet for my navy blue suit. I don't have time to shower, so my hair goes back in a knot and a liberal amount of deodorant and cologne are applied. I slip my father's class ring on my right middle finger and my mother's wedding band on my pinky—the only finger it fits. To be clear, this is her first band. She wears a new one now that my father got for her on their fortieth wedding anniversary. The one I'm wearing is much more modest, with an inlay of tiny diamonds.

She gave it to me back when I was dating a woman named Teresa, encouraging me to take the next step and give it to her. But Teresa wasn't right for me. Or maybe I wasn't right for her. Either way, she's gone, and I wear it now. My mother hasn't broached the topic of marriage in regard to anyone else I've dated since, and I prefer it that way.

I head back to the living room several minutes later and catch Ryan staring at Cora's painting.

"Dude, is this who I think it is?" he asks, excitement in his voice.

"Probably," I say, huffing out the word in frustration.

"When are you finishing?" he asks.

"I'm not. I mean, I can't." I sigh.

"What? What not?" he asks, cutting his eyes to me.

"She's pissed off at me," I admit.

"Why?" His question comes out sharp, full of surprise.

"For existing. At least, I'm pretty sure that's why." I shrug.

Ryan shakes his head back and forth, his look turning sympathetic. "That's rough."

He pats me on the back as I bend to grab my wallet and keys. Then, we're out the door. I turn to lock it behind me and hear Ryan's voice at my back.

"Oh, carrot cake. I'm so glad we bumped into each other again," he says.

I turn, seeing Cora round the top of the stairs and stop in front of her door.

"Hello again. Ryan, right?" she asks him.

My friend nods enthusiastically, no doubt pleased she remembers him. "That's right."

She turns to her door, juggling the basket on her hip as she attempts to jam her key in the lock.

"Let me help you with that," Ryan says, pulling the basket from her grasp so she can focus.

"Thank you," she says, her tone flat but kind.

"Say, what's this I hear about you not letting my dude over here finish that painting of you?" he asks.

Oh boy. Here we go.

"I just don't think it's a good idea," she says, taking the basket from him and setting it inside her apartment.

"Oh, psh, you're beautiful. That painting deserves to be finished. Come on, what do you say?" Ryan clasps his hands together in front of him, jutting out his bottom lip as he pouts.

Cora shifts from one foot to the other, as if she's actually thinking about it. I thought for sure it'd be an instant hell no.

"Fine," she says, her gaze sliding from Ryan to me. She doesn't look happy, but it's not a death glare so I'll take it. That's progress as far as I'm concerned.

"You're an angel," Ryan says. He takes her hand in his and kisses her knuckles.

Cora snorts, rolling her eyes; and if anything, I can appreciate her response to being buttered up.

"Tomorrow," she says, shooting me another pointed look.

I give a silent nod, afraid any words I might speak will cause her to change her mind.

Ryan does tend to come in handy when I need him, helping without even having to be asked. Of course, some of it is rooted in self-interest. But I like to think it's mostly rooted in the spirit of friendship.

"Okay, lover boy," he says, though I'm not sure why. "Let's wine and dine these artsy farts."

Artsy farts. Great.

On second thought, eating cold pizza alone in my apartment *might* be better than what's about to happen.

Only time will tell.

CORA

WHAT IN THE actual hell is happening in my life? Three years I've lived here. Three years and up until a few days ago, I could count on one hand the number of interactions I've had with Declan Walsh. But now...now we've hung out at an art exhibit, shared a meal, I've sought comfort in him, been almost naked in front of him, and he's seen me dance to a very dirty song. That's a few too many activities for my comfort.

The increased frequency with which we've seen each other has caused me to think about him in the middle of my workday. That's right. I'm sitting at my desk, minding my own business, and keep wondering about his cologne. I didn't see it when I changed in his bathroom, and I obviously haven't asked him about it.

I minimize my project window and pull up my browser to search for *pine and spice men's cologne* and see what results come up. Maybe I can figure it out from the descriptions or product reviews. I'm halfway through the third page of browsing when Claire approaches.

"What are you doing?" she asks.

"Nothing," I blurt, quickly minimizing my screen. "What's up?"

"Do you want to get dinner after work? The hubby is on a golf course today," she says.

"Oh, I can't," I say. "I already have plans."

"A date?" she asks, raising an eyebrow at me.

"Uh, no. I'm going over to Declan's place so he can finish the painting of me he started," I clarify.

Claire's eyes bulge. "Wait," she says. "I've clearly missed a whole chunk of information."

I regale the details of the past couple of days to her—my anger about some of it, my reluctance about the rest, and my general displeasure with Declan.

"Um," she says, her eyes portraying her bewilderment, "this is great."

"What?" I blink at her several times, not fully understanding how she got *great* from what I've just told her.

"Look, Cora. My dear friend, Cora. All I'm saying is, this feels like one of those times when someone needs to remind you there's a fine line between love and hate. And lust and hate for that matter," she says.

"Oh my god, no. The line between me and Declan is so thick, you can barely see from one side of it to the other," I reply.

"Uh huh," she says, crossing her arms over her chest.

I hate it when she gives me that dismissive response. "You don't have to believe me. It's true," I push.

"Okay. Well, when he's done painting you, I want to see it. And I want to see the unfinished one you stole from him, too," she says.

"It's my face!" I snap, my voice raising higher than intended.

"It's his hard work," she counters, turning to leave my desk.

My friends are good for nothing. No one is on my side. Not a single one. They're all mesmerized by the hot guy across the hall with his long wild hair and nice smelling skin, and artistic ability, and large hands, and—I'm going to stop there.

I shake my head and turn back to the task at hand: Identifying his cologne.

I collect Declan's jacket from the hook in my bedroom where it's been since I brought it home. I'm back in the same set of undergarments I was wearing the other night, thanks to doing laundry last night. I throw a comfy dress on over it; one that's easy to slip off. I thought about walking the short distance in only his suit jacket again but decided against it.

I knock on his door promptly at seven, just as the note I left taped to his door this morning indicated. I hear some shuffling around, and finally, the door opens. Unfortunately, Declan is shirtless. *Is that actually unfortunate?* The expanse of his bare chest is just below eye level for me and I take in the sight of him. The lightest layer of hair spreads over his chest, not so thick it borders on too much, but it's enough to shove aside any notions about the matured state of his body. *How old is he, anyway?*

"Hi," I say, stepping past him and trying not to make eye contact with his nipples.

Shutting the door behind me, he clears his throat. "Thanks for coming."

"You can thank your friend with the slick tongue," I say. I set the jacket down and slide the dress up over my head.

"What are you doing?" he asks, which causes me to pause mid-lift, because aren't I supposed to be taking this off?

I finish pulling the dress over my head and toss it aside. "Um, getting ready." I slide his jacket over my shoulders and sit where I was the other night. While I make every attempt to re-create my position exactly as it was, I feel his eyes on me.

"What?" I ask.

Declan's eyes carry confusion, though I'm not sure why. His hands haven't left his pockets, and I watch him swallow.

"Nothing, nothing," he says. "Sorry."

He positions himself in front of his canvas and squirts some paint onto a palette from various tubes. I watch as he carefully selects a brush and swirls it into a dark shade. The man does have very large hands. They're nearly twice the size of mine. And yet, as I watch him, they seem so gentle at the same time. He's definitely capable of a soft touch, which makes sense given he paints in fine detail. *God, Cora, stop staring at his fingers.*

His hair is down tonight, not back in the messy knot like usual. It cascades down over the edge of his shoulders, the ends falling just below his collarbone. Admittedly, I've always wanted to touch it. Even in the midst of my most heated moments with him, part of me has always secretly admired his hair. I wonder if he uses some kind of product in it. I'll have to excuse myself to the bathroom again at some point to check.

"You left your clothes here, and after hearing about cleaning my jacket, I washed them for you. They're over there," he says, pointing to a small table in the corner.

My clothes are neatly folded in a pile on top. I'm slightly impressed by the kindness of the gesture, considering how hateful I've been.

"Thank you," I say softly.

Declan nods in response, biting into his bottom lip as he paints stroke after stroke on the canvas. Part of me wishes I could watch him make them, but I can't very well do that from this side of the canvas.

Silence fills the room for a little while; me, concentrating on being still, him on his work. This time allows me to simply reflect. It's almost meditation. The stillness, the inability to act on any thought that might pop up. I can't answer my phone or get on my laptop. Sitting in one attitude, in this case, is a little refreshing.

"So, did you boys go out looking for more cake last night?" I ask.

"Cake?" he repeats.

"Ryan calls me carrot cake," I say. "I assume he lovingly flavors all his women."

To my surprise, Declan laughs. It's deep and genuine. "No, we didn't. And yes, he does and for the record I hate it."

"You hate cake?"

"God no. I hate that he calls women *cake*," he says. "I love actual cake."

"Me too," I say. "But not carrot cake."

"My mother makes a lemon blueberry cake. It's my favorite," he says.

"Oh my god, that sounds amazing." It's no secret I love cake. All kinds of cake. One of the reasons I'm okay with a few extra pounds in my trunk. I have thick thighs, so what? I hear they save lives. It's worth it for the damn cake.

Silence falls over us again as I realize we were almost having a whole damn conversation without arguing. *So close.*

"Where does your mother live?" I ask. The question seems innocent enough not to spur a heated debate.

"Not far from here, actually," he says. "My parents have lived in the same house since I was born."

"Wow, long time. Exactly how long would that be?" I ask, thinking it's a sly way to discern his age.

"Since I was born? Are you asking me how old I am?"

Damn. Caught. Okay, maybe it wasn't that sly.

"What? No. But since you brought it up, how old are you?" I ask, doing a poor job of covering my tracks.

Declan laughs again, flicking his wrist and turning the direction of the brush against the canvas. "I'm thirty-four. How old are you?"

"Thirty-two," I say.

He raises an eyebrow. "Thirty-two and you own your own company? Impressive."

"Yeah, well, apparently most men find it intimidating. Or at least that's the reason they give me for not wanting another date sometimes." I shrug, exhausted from the mere mention of it. I've heard that excuse more times than I can count. I don't fully understand it. I'm not intimidated by their jobs or success. I'm not intimidated by talents.

Declan, for example, is an extremely accomplished artist, a truly talented guy. But I don't sit here and compare my lot to his or size my achievements up next to his. That's stupid and sets you up for constant dissatisfaction with life in general.

"Intimidated?" he asks. "Sounds like bullshit to me. Or just a whole lot of weak men."

Oh. Yes. Yeah, that. Weak men. "Well, it would seem that's the only kind attracted to me." I offer a self-deprecating laugh, but Declan doesn't join in. His eyes study my face. For the painting or because of what I've said, I'm not sure, but something gives him pause. He makes a barely audible *hm* sound and returns to his work.

"What?" I ask, too curious to let it go.

"Nothing," he says, shrugging. "I just don't understand men."

"Meaning?" I ask.

Declan tilts his head back and forth, as if considering his words carefully. "I'm not sure I should say."

"Well, now you have to," I reply, giving a little laugh.

"Just don't get mad and storm out, okay?" He sighs.

"Fine. I promise," I say.

He swirls his brush on his palette and lifts it to the piece again. "I just think you're really beautiful and strong and I don't understand anyone who wouldn't want that."

Oh. My. I swallow hard, making every attempt to calm my emotions. *Don't cry, don't cry, don't cry.* And fair warning, that's the sort of thing that will definitely make me cry.

Hell, that's the kind of thing that lands me smack in the middle of trouble.

DECLAN

CORA IS SHORT OF WORDS, her eyes glossy and full of some emotion she seems to be trying to hide. She doesn't respond to me immediately. Instead, she inhales deeply a few times.

"Thank you," she says, her throat tight.

Her response makes me think not many people say such things to her. Maybe I've caught her off guard. Maybe she wants desperately to believe me but her past doesn't help with that. Either way, it's clear the sentiment is rare.

I shrug my shoulders, not wanting to make a big deal out of the moment. "It's nothing."

"When did you start painting?" she asks, sounding genuinely curious.

"I think I've been making some kind of art since I was little, but this particular medium and my concentration on it took hold around fifteen. Of course, I was terrible then." I chuckle.

"Did you go on to study it in college?" she asks.

"Not at first. I went into business management then changed my major," I say.

She nods, taking this information in and processing it.

We fall into silence again like we have many times, and I concentrate on the freckle pattern peppering her shoulder. The artistry is in the details, those subtle nuances that can make or break a painting. Of course, not all paintings call for it. But my particular style, my relentless need to paint a certain level of realism, demands it.

Why did I choose this style? No idea. I think I just believed if I was going to paint someone on canvas, it needed to feel like *them* as much as possible. Now, it's sort of become a strange addiction. I've never gone more than forty-eight hours without painting something. Crazy, right? Needless to say, I don't take many vacations. It might also be why I can't keep a girlfriend.

I make a final stroke across the jawline on the canvas and stop, standing back to take in the whole picture. My shoulders slump and it's almost as if when I finish a painting, I uncoil just a bit.

"It's done," I say. "I'm finished."

Cora finally moves, standing and pulling the jacket closed around her. She steps gingerly toward me and the canvas, then around to my side.

I turn, now interested more in her reaction to the painting, than the painting itself. Her eyes grow wide as her mouth drops open. They're growing glossy again as she blinks back her emotions.

"It's beautiful," she whispers.

"My paintings are only as beautiful as the people in them." I genuinely mean that. It's true. I think all people are beautiful in their own ways and I'm drawn to their humanity first. But I can't deny that painting a truly beautiful woman is a treat. That sounds bad in my head. *Don't say that out loud, man.* I guess what I mean is it's always a privilege to paint someone I could be attracted to. You know, if I weren't trying to be professional. Or if that woman wasn't kind of mean. Like Cora.

"Thank you," she says. "Thank you for doing this. And I'm sorry I'm such a bitch."

"Well, love, if you weren't such a bitch, things might not have turned out like this." As soon as I say the words, I regret them. They sound like they're implying something. Maybe they are. Maybe if she hadn't been presumptuous all that time ago, I would've hit on her rather than asked to paint her. Or maybe it would've been both. Who knows, really.

Cora turns to me, holding her chin up and looking me straight in the eyes. She doesn't say anything right away, just holds my gaze. For how long, I can't be sure. Maybe only a few seconds, maybe full minutes.

I study the silver flecks in her irises, the way they catch the light even in this dim room. It takes all my strength not to want to pick up a pencil and catalog them. I settle on standing here, unmoving, wondering if they resemble confetti falling mid-air.

"I should get dressed," she says, breaking the tension.

It was tension, right? I'm not that out of practice, am I?

"Yeah, of course," I say, pointing back toward the bathroom.

She collects her previously discarded dress and her clothes from the table, then disappears into the bathroom. We make eye contact for a brief moment as she slides the door shut, and then she disappears out of sight.

I turn my attention back to the canvas, wondering if by some turn of events I'm attracted to her, or if I'm riding the high of finishing the painting. I don't get to ponder it too long before Cora's out of the bathroom and back in my sights, walking toward the door.

"If it's all right with you, this will be in my next exhibit," I say. I don't generally ask permission. Most of the time when I paint someone, I make it perfectly clear what's going to happen with the piece once I'm done, and get them to sign an agreement. This time though, with the history between us, with the tension balanced ever so precariously, I feel the need to ask.

"I think that would be nice," she says. "Thank you for asking."

I nod, shoving my hands in my pockets, unsure what else to do or say.

She stands still for a few more silent seconds, a small smile on her lips, rocking back on her heels. "Well, I should get going."

"Thank you for letting me paint you," I say, walking toward the door to meet her.

"I never thought I'd say this, but I'm glad I finally came in," she says, lightly giggling.

I smile at her, feeling relief in her statement. Perhaps this is the start of less hatred between us.

"Goodnight," I say softly.

"Goodnight," she says, tucking her hair behind her ear as she steps past me.

I catch a faint scent, something that smells all too familiar. Once I close the door, I make my way to the bathroom to find my suit jacket hanging on a hook on the back of the door. Pulling it down, I inhale at the collar.

I'm not sure how I didn't notice it before. Perhaps I was too distracted by her crying when she hugged me. Either way, I recognize it now.

And nothing about this is good.

CORA

OVER THE PAST SEVERAL DAYS, I've barely seen Declan, let alone spoken to him. It's almost as if upon finishing the painting of me, he disappeared into a hole. Well, that's not entirely true. I waved at him in the hallway at one point, but that's been it. It's like we're back to the way it was before he painted me. The exception being I waved at him rather than scoffed in his general direction.

Is this what he meant when he said he's professional? Life just goes back to before and we don't acknowledge the forward progress? I don't have a lot of time to ponder this. Jensen and Harper arrive for their visit today and I have to haul my ass home to clean before they get here.

Still, like, we can't be friends? Wait, what am I even saying? I want to be friends with Declan Walsh? No, no, no. I shake the idea away as soon as it registers and walk up the stairs to my apartment.

It seems I'm not out of the woods yet; because as soon as I'm close to my floor, I hear distinct voices coming from the hallway. Declan, Jensen, and Harper are all laughing.

I turn the corner to see Declan leaning against his doorway like always. Jensen and Harper are standing at my door, their luggage on the floor. Apparently, someone just said something hilarious, because they're all cackling.

"What's so funny?" I ask.

Jensen turns in my direction and the other two follow, all eyes on me now. "Sis! Surprise! We're early," he says.

"I see that," I say, putting my messenger bag down as my little brother throws his arms around me. Sure, I say *little*, but he's been taller than me for most of our lives. I think we're fortunate to be so close. I've seen the other side and want no part of it. Some of my friends only speak to their siblings on holidays or when someone has died, and I find the idea of it so sad.

"It was this guy's idea," Harper says, pushing Jensen out of the way so she can come hug me.

Harper and my brother have been together since they met at my friend Lyla's wedding. I brought Jensen along, and he found himself occupied with Lyla's little sister, Harper. Who would've thought the two younger siblings of best friends would find love? Actually, I say that like it was shocking, but at the time, everyone except them could see it happening.

I lean down and rub Harper's belly. She's not super big and round yet, but she's got a little bump emerging and I can't wait until the bundle gets here. I'm going to be the best aunt.

"Well, you guys certainly surprised me. And my house is a mess and I have no dinner started as a result." I laugh.

"Let's go out," Jensen suggests, shrugging his shoulders.

"Really? After traveling?" I turn to Harper. "Don't you want to rest?" I don't know a lot about pregnancy, but I know you're tired more often. I imagine the last thing she wants to do is go out.

"Yeah, let's go out. Declan, why don't you join us?" she says, turning back toward him. Of course she would invite him. For a moment, I'm embarrassed about not acknowledging him as I realize he's been standing quietly in his doorway the entire time.

"Oh, I wouldn't want to intrude," he says.

"I see you've both met my neighbor," I say, interjecting myself into the conversation. I turn to him and smile. He returns a pleasant expression, and some other emotion is there too; though I'm not sure what.

"Yes, we did. He was just telling us about your laundry room dance party," Harper says, giggling.

My eyes shoot back to Declan, and this time, his face is teasing, like usual. I narrow my eyes, hoping laser beams will shoot out if I want it bad enough. *This.* This right here is how he goes from being okay to back on my list of people I want to make voodoo dolls of and stick pins in.

"Anyway," I say, trying to redirect and manage the situation. "Declan, will you be joining us?"

"Do you want me to?" he counters, baiting me.

No. Yes. I don't fucking know, okay? "Well, they invited you, so obviously they want you to," I say, skirting around the question.

"That's not what I asked," he says, folding his arms over his chest in that stupid way he does.

I see Harper press her lips together into a line as she tries to keep herself from smiling. Jensen on the other hand looks pleased as punch with the interaction. His big toothy grin is hard to miss, even with most of my attention on Declan.

I roll my eyes hard. "Just meet us downstairs in fifteen minutes," I say, moving to unlock my door.

"So is that a yes?" he asks, his tone carrying amusement.

"Don't push it," I say, stepping in and ushering my brother and Harper in after me.

Declan backs into his apartment, hands up in mock surrender. I shut my door hard, bordering a slam, and exhale loudly.

"He really pushes your buttons, huh, sis?" My brother is leaning back against the kitchen counter now, his elbows propped behind him, and I want to punch him in his smug face. I mean that in the most sisterly way.

"Shut up and follow me," I say, leading them back to the guest room. Luckily, I had enough sense to make sure it was clean. It's the rest of my apartment that needs some attention. Living alone has a tendency to make me a little sloppy, but it's so easy when you don't have to worry about anyone in your space.

"Babe, leave your sister alone. She's not ready," Harper says.

"Thank you," I say. "Wait, not ready for what?"

"To hear about the possibility that you and Declan might like each other," she says, matter of fact.

"Excuse me?" I snap.

"See, I told you. Not ready." She laughs.

"That's insane," I say.

"Maybe. Or maybe not. Only time will tell," she says.

I find myself rolling my eyes again. "I'm going to get changed. I'm sure you might want to as well. I'll be ready to walk down in a few minutes."

Leaving them in the guest room, I retreat to mine to peel out of my work slacks and into something a little more casual and a lot more comfortable. After dressing and freshening my makeup and hair in about six minutes flat, I examine myself in the mirror. Simple ripped jeans, a loose top that hangs off one shoulder, and ankle boots. I scrunch up the long sleeves of my shirt around my elbow and grab my purse.

As we walk down the stairs to meet Declan, I'm at war with myself yet again. Part of me wants to get this over with quickly. The rest of me is oddly excited to dig a little deeper into who Declan is. He's so reserved and guarded in so many ways. I just want to peel back one or two layers. *No big deal.*

"Why aren't we taking the elevator?" Harper asks as she grips the railing.

"Don't ask," Jensen says, a husky laugh in his throat.

"I'm afraid of the elevator here, okay? Actually it's all elevators, but this one in particular is old and rickety and I don't want to plummet to my death," I say, like it's the most reasonable explanation anyone has ever given.

As we reach the bottom, I catch Declan in my peripheral and turn. He's leaning against the wall next to the mailboxes wearing dark denim and a gray V-neck T-shirt. His hands are in his pockets, which I've observed is a common stance for him.

"Let's get this train wreck going," I say, pointing toward the door.

The ghost of a smile plays across his mouth. "Whatever you say, love."

I simply cannot even with this pet name.

DECLAN

JENSEN AND CORA are very different people. Jensen's brown hair and tan complexion next to Cora's red hair and fair, freckled skin would have you thinking they're not related at all. Although, I'll say their eyes are nearly the exact silvery shade. For a man, I suppose he's not a bad looking guy so the one thing they have in common is they're good looking people. After that generalization, you'd never guess.

Plus, Jensen's really laid back. I watch him settle back into his side of the booth where we're seated and casually rub his wife's stomach. This is while he relays the story of how they flew off to Vegas and got married a few months ago upon finding out Harper was pregnant.

"So we're at this chapel, right? And the lady there hands us a form to fill out. No shit, one of the questions was whether or not we wanted an Elvis impersonator." He laughs. "And the crazy part is, having Elvis marry you costs more."

I laugh, lifting my glass to take a sip of my whisky. "Sounds like you had fun."

"I barely made it there in time," Cora says. "This prick thought he was going to get married without me there." Beside me, she leans over the table, tonguing the straw in her bright pink drink, and I find it a little distracting.

"So, you didn't have anyone come?" I ask, genuinely curious about the merits of elopement versus traditional ceremonies.

"Well, I called her grandparents to make sure they'd be okay with it," Jensen says. "But doing that caused a chain reaction. Lyla found out and she called my sister and the next thing I know, they're both showing up to the chapel, along with Gentry, Lyla's husband. So it wasn't quite the traditional elopement."

"What made you decide to do it that way?" I ask, Cora's straw tonguing still in my peripheral.

"I'd already done the big fancy wedding," Harper interjects. "And there was no way anyone was going to convince me to do it again, especially while smuggling a watermelon under my wedding dress."

The whole table laughs, and they both very much seem to treat their accidental pregnancy as a blessing, and why shouldn't it be? If both people want it, it doesn't matter what comes first.

"Oh my god!" Cora exclaims out of nowhere. "You didn't call and tell me the sex of the baby!"

Harper smiles wide and leans back, rubbing the top of her bump. "We thought we'd wait until we got here because we got you something." Harper pulls a small box from her purse and hands it to Cora, whose eyes grow big and bright. I don't think I've ever seen her face filled with so much excitement.

Her hands work to untie the ribbon and then she opens the lid. She pulls a necklace from the box, her hand cupping the charm. Then I notice her chin beginning to wobble.

"It's perfect," she says. Cora leans over to me, showing me the pendant. It's a hand stamped square with a little blue gemstone in one corner. The stamped letters read *I love Jackson*. I smile down at it and then up at her.

"I'm having a son!" The pride in Jensen's voice is tangible. It's no secret most men are desperate to have a mini version of themselves. And Jensen seems like exactly the type to tell anyone who'll listen.

"Congratulations, man," I say, holding my glass up. The rest of them follow suit and we all clink our glasses together. Even Harper, who's sipping on iced tea while the rest of us opted for booze.

When our food comes out, we settle into easy conversation

between bites. As for me, they ask about my work. Harper pokes around about my previous relationships, inquires if I'm in one now, and whether or not I've ever painted a pregnant woman.

For the record, I have. Only once though. Not because I don't want to paint more, but because it's even harder to convince a pregnant woman you're not a creep for asking to paint them.

"Well, you can paint me while we're here, if you want," Harper says.

"Really?" I ask.

"Yeah, why not?" She shrugs her shoulders, taking another sip of her tea.

"Actually, I would love to see that," Jensen says.

"Um, you guys," Cora interrupts. "I don't think that's a good idea. The women he paints are usually half-naked."

"Didn't he paint you?" Jensen asks.

I feel my body tighten. *Is he going to be mad I painted her like that?*

"Yeah, but I'm single and it was no big deal," Cora says.

"What does relationship status have to do with painting?" I ask.

Cora whips her head to look at me, seemingly surprised by my interjection. I've painted married women before. *Doesn't she believe me when I say I'm a professional?*

"Well, nothing. I'm just saying maybe certain people would feel uncomfortable with it," she says.

"What people?" Jensen asks.

"You," Cora says, looking back at her brother as if it's obvious.

"Why would I feel uncomfortable? I have a hot wife. I impregnated my hot wife. I don't think Declan's the type of man who's going to hit on her," he says, challenging his sister.

"Oh," she says. "Well, I mean, it's none of my business anyway."

Her tone turns dismissive and I can't quite tell why she's so put off by the idea of me painting Harper.

"How long will you be staying?" I ask the couple.

"Three days," Harper says. "Will that be long enough?"

"As long as you don't mind some long sessions of sitting in the same spot?" I laugh, despite the fact that it's true.

"As long as you don't want me standing on one leg or holding something heavy above my head, I think I can manage." Harper laughs.

"Good, it's settled," I say.

I turn toward Cora, who's made herself busy with her food and I watch her shove a giant bite of mashed potatoes into her mouth. I know it's not conventionally sexy, but something about a woman who's comfortable enough in herself to eat freely the way she does is sexy. Most women take small, measured bites, careful not to be too *unladylike* or whatever people call it.

As we leave the restaurant, Harper and Jensen are in front while I walk next to Cora behind them. We picked the place just around the corner from where we live for the sake of convenience, so it won't take us long to get home.

I observe the couple in front of me, so at ease with each other. Harper rests her head on Jensen's shoulder as they walk in step. Their hands are intertwined between them and it's moments like this I envy couples. Most of the time, I'm fine alone. I even prefer it. But every now and then, someone to hold hands with would be nice.

I glance over at Cora and trail my eyes down her arm to her hand closest to me. She has long, delicate fingers and I briefly wonder if she's ever played piano.

"Stop with the public displays of affection," Cora yells as her brother and Harper lean in and kiss each other. "We get it, you're in love."

"You don't approve of public affection?" I ask.

"Maybe if I had a boyfriend with which to also grope in public, I wouldn't be so annoyed," she says, half-laughing.

"Here, I'll hold your hand." I scoop her hand into mine, lacing my fingers between hers. Even with her long fingers, her hand is easily only half the size of mine.

Cora tries to pull from my grip. "I don't think that's a good idea."

"Calm down, woman. It's not a big deal." I feel the tension in her hand slowly dissipate. *This is weird, right? Why did I even do this?* Sometimes I do things without considering how they look to the outside world and sometimes the results aren't great. "Why do you suppose people like holding hands?"

Cora looks at me, and from the corner of my eye, I can't read her expression. "I don't know. I assume people enjoy the comfort in it." Her shoulders lift and fall the smallest distance. A tiny shrug to accompany her thoughts.

"Do you feel comforted?" I ask, nodding down to our hands intertwined.

"I'm not sure," she admits.

"Fair enough," I say, and it's true. Given the way things are between us, I'm not sure my presence does much by way of bringing peace to her.

"There are other positive emotions that come from affection. Comfort isn't the only one," she adds.

"Well, do you feel any of them?" I ask.

"Also not sure," she says, starting to laugh.

I shake my head as we enter the building. I realize this is the second time we've shared a meal together. It's also the second time I've allowed myself to wonder if she feels like we're on a date. For that matter, I briefly allow myself to wonder if *I* feel like we're on a date.

CORA

OH MY GOD. *Oh my god. Oh my god.* Walking up these stairs feels like it's taking forever, like time has suddenly slowed down. Because what the hell are we going to do when we get to the top? Surely, he didn't consider this a date? Then why the fuck are we holding hands? Is he going to try to kiss me? *Okay, calm down. Deep breath.*

With my free hand, I pull my keys from my purse and grip them between my fingers, adjusting them so my door key is in position to unlock it.

"Thanks for coming along," I say.

"It was my pleasure," Declan says.

"We're getting pretty good at this, huh?" I laugh.

"Good at what?" he asks.

"You know, not arguing or giving each other dirty looks," I say, giggling.

Declan's face grows wide with a smile, genuine but mischievous. "I suppose that's true but to be fair, you're the one who gave most of the dirty looks."

I elbow him playfully in the ribs as we all reach the landing. The love birds settle into making out next to my door as Declan lets go of my hand so I can unlock my apartment. Jensen and Harper take the opportunity to basically jog inside and continue kissing each other.

"God, they're sickening," I huff.

Declan is standing next to me, watching them giggle and kiss each other. I turn just as he slides his hands into his pockets. "I don't know, they seem pretty in love. It's cute."

I make an audible gagging noise. "Yeah, yeah. They're in love, we get it."

"Bitter, much?" he asks.

I twist, folding my arms over my chest. "Always."

Declan catches my eyes with his, holding my gaze for a moment longer than is comfortable. I shift under his stare, unsure what to do now.

"Well, I better get in there before they start having sex on my couch or something," I say, trying to keep the moment light.

Declan begins to lean down, his face coming straight at mine. For a second, I consider backing up but something inside me urges me not to budge. I part my lips like I'm about to protest, except I have no idea what I actually want to say.

A mere few inches away, Declan begins to lean to the side. Then, ever so delicately, he places a kiss on my cheek. "Goodnight, love." His mouth hovers just over me and the breath of each word tickles my skin.

With that, he's gone. Declan straightens up and backs away so quickly I don't have time to even process what just happened before he's in his apartment and out of sight.

My hand cups my face where his lips pressed. The sensation lingers as I stand there staring at his closed door. I have to physically shake my head back and forth to snap myself out of it and finally go inside my own apartment.

What the hell was that? Surely it was just a nice gesture, just being cordial. *Right? Yes.* I'm still rubbing my cheek when my eyes meet the scene on the couch.

"Please don't have sex there," I say. My brother and his wife are making out like two teenagers. "She's pregnant. You're going to squish the baby if you're not careful." My warning does nothing to curb their behavior so I resolve to retreating to my bedroom to avoid looking at it.

"Don't worry, sis. I have excellent depth perception," Jensen calls out toward me as I walk down the hall. His comment causes me to gag yet again and I hear Harper berating him behind me.

Once in the safety of my room, I undress for bed, my hand still occasionally finding its way up to my cheek. I can confirm Declan has soft lips. Very soft lips. The lingering effects of them on my skin lead me to believe he's probably a very good kisser. And I bet he leaves his hair down during sex so it can pool all over your skin and make you tingle. And I bet he's generous. And—

Holy shit, Cora. That spiraled quickly. Calm yourself down.

I lie back on my bed wearing nothing but my panties, twisting my hair around my fingers, examining the ends as a hundred questions race through my mind.

I trail my fingers down my neck and caress my collarbone before following the line of my sternum between my breasts and finally around my belly button. I suppose I could go for a little release to get rid of all this tension. Closing my eyes, my fingers trail down further and dip into the waistline of my panties.

"Oh my god, yes!" Harper's voice travels through the walls of my apartment and I rip my eyes open and my hand from my underwear. I wait a few moments and then more moans and muffled words ring in my ears. *Oh. My. God.* They're having sex. Those bastards are having sex. In my apartment.

So much for releasing tension. I can't touch myself to my brother and sister-in-law's moans. That's like incest or something, right? I'm turned off. Way off. So off I may never turn on again.

I dress quickly into some pajama shorts and a tank top, then shove headphones into my ears so I can drown them out and try to get some sleep.

Not surprising, an hour later I'm still tossing and turning. I slowly remove one of my earbuds, ready to shove it back in at the slightest onset of sex noises again. But the coast seems clear. *Horny jackasses.* What kind of people can't even wait a couple of days until they're back in their own place?

I swing my legs over the bed, my feet gently padding against the floor. Perhaps a nice middle of the night cocktail is in order. I don't work tomorrow, so no need to worry. Making my way out to the kitchen, I grab the throw from the back of the couch and pour a glass of wine. Fresh air, that's what I need. I gather my blanket up around me, glass in one hand and slip out onto the balcony, leaving the sliding glass door cracked behind me.

The cool night air hits me and I inhale deeply, smelling the city scent and letting my shoulders fall as I sit down in my chair. The streets below are relatively quiet. Only a few passing vehicles and pedestrians fill the air with any noise.

"You can't sleep, either?" Declan's voice comes from my left, startling me. I jump and grab my chest, breathing a sigh of relief at the immediate realization of who it is.

"Jesus Christ, you scared the shit out of me," I say, attempting to calm my nerves with another sip of my wine.

"Sorry about that," he says. "I didn't expect anyone to be out on their balcony this late."

"Well, likewise," I say. "And for the record, no. I can't sleep. Although, this isn't exactly new to me."

"I don't sleep a lot either," Declan admits, his voice low and calm. He sounds resolved in the fact, not frustrated or restless.

"You sit out here when you can't sleep?" I try to recount all the times I've been out here, which actually aren't many. He wasn't out here for any of them, or I'd have likely marched back inside.

"Sometimes," he says. "Although, now that I'm out here, I think I should do it more often."

It's silent for a moment. I can't see Declan through the dark, but I can hear him shuffling around a little, perhaps repositioning himself.

I take another sip. "What makes you unable to sleep?"

A long sigh escapes him. "Probably the anxiety. Lots of racing thoughts, too."

"I don't think I'd have guessed you have anxiety," I admit. "You seem so calm."

"I think anxiety manifests differently for everyone. I'm not the bouncy, unable to sit still type. I don't look overwhelmed outwardly.

But I don't sleep much, I tend to avoid crowds unless someone drags me out. And the exhibits? They take everything out of me," he says.

"I can relate to some of that," I admit. Suddenly, Declan's demeanor doesn't seem so strange. He carries himself in a quiet, reserved way, even when he's attempting to socialize. And he's not exactly chatty, almost as if he only gives what he needs to.

"Most people don't get it. And they think I'm rude. It doesn't help that I awkwardly ask people to come to my apartment. I'm not a smooth talker like Ryan," he says, exhaling a chuckle.

"You're right, that doesn't help." I laugh. "Maybe you should wear a button or a T-shirt? Hi, I'm Declan and I'm socially awkward."

"Probably a good idea." He laughs.

"Well, thanks for telling me. I'm sorry I busted your balls all this time," I say, and I mean it. After getting to know him over the past couple of weeks, it's clear he's not who I thought he was.

"I appreciate that," he says.

We grow quiet again and I listen to the buzzing of the streetlamp next to me.

"Do you have plans this weekend with your brother and his wife?" Declan shifts in the dark again and I try to focus on him, to see if he's turned toward me.

"Yeah, we're going to do a few things," I say. "Nothing too crazy or intense, given Harper's condition."

"Well, if you need an extra person, a buffer so to speak, I'm here," he says.

"Really? Wait, I thought you were going to paint Harper?" I ask, my eyes still searching the darkness for his face, but I can only see part of a silhouette.

"You don't seem like you want me to," he says.

He's right, but I don't want to tell him that. I can't explain why. Hell, I don't even know myself.

"Well, you want to tag along instead?" I ask.

"Yeah, sure. They're nice, but I'm sure watching them make out all weekend will get old." He laughs. "I don't have any new paintings started. It might be refreshing to step away from the studio for a little while."

"Well, okay. Actually, that would be nice," I say. "Do you want to come to brunch with us in the morning?"

Declan's black shadowy figure grows tall as he stands and moves toward the edge of his balcony. His face comes into light, cast from the streetlamps, and the first thing I notice is his toothy smile.

He leans into the railing, rubbing his palm over the five o'clock shadow on his jaw. "What time?"

"We were going to leave at about ten," I say, swallowing the sudden lump formed in my throat. *Am I nervous? Is that what's happening here?*

"Then I guess I'll see you then," he says. "Goodnight. Again."

My lips curl up and I fight to suppress the smile that wants to emerge. I nod as he disappears into his apartment. The glass door slides shut, there's a click, and then he's gone.

This is the second time I've been left, staring at a door, and wondering why the hell I'm filled with both elation and disappointment.

CORA

I'VE BEEN awake for hours. No amount of wine was going to help me sleep last night. Not even switching to chamomile tea helped. The idea was to sleep in, lazily go to brunch, and drink my weight in mimosas. Not be too tired to even want to go. Plus, Declan's coming now, so here I am in my bathroom, attempting to conceal the bags under my eyes and praying no one says the cursed *you look tired* to me.

"Ready to go, sis?" Jensen yells from somewhere near the living area, probably looking pristine as always. I hate to say it, but maybe Harper hasn't hit the glowing phase of pregnancy yet, and I'll look less tired by comparison.

I set my makeup sponge down as I examine myself in the mirror and resolve to the fact that this is the best I can do given the circumstances.

Of course, Harper's a fucking vision when I walk out. Does she even walk or does she have a hoverboard under that dress? I swear to god, she's floating. Her blonde hair falls across her shoulders in soft waves and I want to poke my eyes out. I mean, I really love my sister-in-law. I do. I do, I do, I do. But also, can a girl get a break?

"Are you okay?" Harper asks, interrupting my self-loathing. "You look—"

"Don't say it." I hold my hand up. "Just don't."

"Okay. Well, let's get you a mimosa then, shall we?" Harper points over her shoulder to the door using a hitchhiker thumb, and I nod.

I thought this was going to be a very casual thing, so now I get to stand next to the pageant queen in her flowing maxi while wearing my workout leggings, a loose sweatshirt, and Vans sneakers. So that's fun.

Opening my door, I jump back abruptly, met by Declan. He's standing right in front of my door, his hand up like he was about to knock. In his other hand, he grips a bouquet of pink peonies.

"Jesus, you scared me," I say, clutching the strap of my purse across my chest.

"I'm sorry." He laughs. "I just wanted to give these to you. I didn't want to do it downstairs, so you could leave them here."

I examine his outstretched arm, the fragrance of the flowers lingering in the small space between us. "Oh, thank you."

Declan nods, first at me and then past me, where Jensen and Harper are standing.

I back into the apartment and grab a vase, quickly. From the corner of my eye, Declan takes one step across the threshold into my space. For whatever reason, I find this nerve wracking.

"Nice move, man," Jensen says, his attempt to whisper out of my earshot a big fat failure.

I roll my eyes. Isn't he supposed to be more protective of me? Isn't he supposed to dislike who I date and give them a hard time? *Wait. Oh my god, did I just say date? What the fucking fuck. Freudian slip? No, no.* Just, by appearance, I mean. You'd think Jensen would be asking him his intentions or something.

"Okay, let's go," I say, peeling out of the door and pointing down the hallway. I lock the door after everyone exits and we make our way downstairs. Jensen and Harper lead the pack and with Declan by my side, we're bringing up the rear once again. Strange, considering we're the locals and they're visiting.

We make it to Bluff's, the best place in the whole city to eat breakfast or brunch. The place is busy as hell but we get a table pretty quick. The staff here is nothing if not friendly and efficient. We all immediately order water and coffee, and three of us order mimosas while Harper pouts.

"They're my favorite," she whines. "Let's be rational here. Is having a kid, like even really worth this kind of sacrifice?" She motions to her belly while asking this, drawing a laugh from our whole table.

"Tell you what, babe. As soon as he's here, you can go on a week-long bender while I take care of him. Deal?" Jensen offers, rubbing gentle circles over her back.

Harper smacks his arm with her menu and I turn my attention to Declan, who's sitting next to me. Despite opening the door to him this morning, I didn't notice much about him until now. His fresh black T-shirt hugs his arms and chest all too well. His hair is pulled back in a low knot. He rests his elbows along the table's edge while one hand holds the menu at an angle and the other rubs his face like before. His stubble is still there, clearly having skipped shaving for several mornings.

For the first time, I notice a ring on his pinky—a thin, white gold band with tiny diamonds set into it.

"It belonged to my mother," he says, as if he can read my thoughts. "Her first wedding band, actually. It's the only finger it would fit."

"Why do you wear it?" I ask.

"A couple of years back, they celebrated forty years together and treated themselves to new rings. She held onto it and gave it to me when I was dating someone," he says, shifting in his seat.

"Wow, forty years," I say. "That's amazing."

"Yeah, crazy. Talk about big shoes to fill," he says.

"What do you mean?" I continue the conversation as I browse the menu and take a sip of our delivered drinks.

"I mean when your parents are that great of an example, it's intimidating," he says, sipping at his black coffee.

"Really? I just look across the table and think that," I say, laughing. Declan's eyes cross over to Harper and Jensen as he holds her hand in his and brushes kisses across her knuckles.

"Maybe it's just a pregnancy thing?" Declan offers. The thought had crossed my mind, actually. Maybe they're being this extra due to the life change occurring. *Does pregnancy make couples more affectionate? Interesting.*

"So what happened?" I ask, unashamed of my curiosity.

"With?" he asks.

"The woman you were dating," I clarify.

"Oh," he says. "Nothing really, she was great. But it just didn't feel right."

I nod, taking in this new information as the waitress takes our orders and I use the opportunity to get a conversation going with the love birds before they can start sucking face again. We talk about the baby, their plans for moving from my brother's loft in Raleigh to a house outside the city. I suppose that's what happens when families start growing; you need more space and priorities change.

Jensen asks Declan about his next exhibit and I catch Harper's stare across the table. She nods her head in the direction of the bathrooms and we excuse ourselves, leaving the men behind.

Once we're in the safety of the restroom, she attacks. "Okay, girl. Spill it."

"Spill what?" I ask, examining my face in the mirror. The puffiness beneath my eyes has gone down a bit.

"You know what. Don't play like you don't know what I'm asking about," she says, her eyes meeting mine in the reflection.

After turning the knob of the sink, I push the button on the soap dispenser and begin absentmindedly washing my hands. "There's nothing to dish."

"So, this guy you've claimed to hate is going to meals with us, bringing you flowers, and—I can't emphasize this one enough—he's painting you half-naked. But there's nothing to say about it?" Harper crosses her arms over her chest, giving me the look. You know, the *I smell bullshit* look.

"Honestly, I have no idea, okay? Obviously, for the longest time, nothing. I loathed him. And he mostly annoyed the shit out of me for that fact. Now, I don't fucking know. I think we're becoming friends. Maybe?" I pull a paper towel from the dispenser and dry my hands, one finger at a time, drawing out the process.

"Sweetie, I don't think friends bring friends flowers," she says.

"Let me start over. This isn't the right question to yield a response I can use."

I turn, facing her, and brace myself.

"I know you've loathed him for a while, I get that. But how do you feel now?" She stares at me, straight into my eyes, like she's looking into my soul. She's serious and like a dog with a bone, she's not letting this go.

"I don't know, I—" I stutter, the words not finding me. "I don't loathe him anymore. I don't think. He's...different than I thought."

Harper nods, urging me. "Go on."

"He's nice. Respectable. He's got layers," I say.

"And he's hot," Harper adds.

"Right, there's also that. Which apparently I can see better when I'm not blinded by hate," I huff.

Harper places her hand on my shoulder, patting lightly and sighing. "Well, I guess you should look into that a little further then."

I laugh and shake my head, wondering how Harper always finds herself in the middle of everyone else's drama. "Do you just intentionally insert yourself into people's love lives or is it a happy coincidence?"

Harper checks her face in the mirror, smoothing her hair. "When it comes to people I care about, it's intentional."

I smile, both of us stepping toward the exit. She cares. I get it.

DECLAN

WHEN THE GIRLS arrive back at the table, I breathe a sigh of relief. It's not that Jensen put on a big brother act about his sister or isn't nice. It was actually the opposite, though it didn't make me any less uncomfortable having him ask me when or if I was going to make a move.

To be honest, I had no idea what to say, how to respond to his line of questioning. I dodged most of his attempts to probe me for information on the topic, but I'm no less relieved. Because what the hell do you say to that coming from the brother of a woman who has hated you for years and now maybe doesn't hate you but you're definitely not at a *make a move* level?

Do I want to make a move? Maybe I should decide that first.

Cora lays her napkin across her lap then looks up at me and I realize it looks like I was staring at her lap. I guess I was, but not for the reason she probably thinks. I just like the way she laid her napkin down. She folded it into a triangle so precisely, her long fingers running along the hem of the white fabric. *Yeah, that's not weird at all. Jesus.*

"Sorry," I mutter.

"For what?" she asks, her eyes narrowing, not in an upset way but more confused or curious.

"Staring," I say. "It's a bad habit."

"I don't mind." She shrugs.

Wait. She doesn't mind? Is this a trick? It feels like a trick. "Oh." That's all I got. *God, I'm terrible at this.*

We begin eating, everyone settling into mostly silence, with an occasional comment about the food, weather, and other mundane things. It seems Cora has good people in her life. Jensen and Harper feel good. Sometimes I find you can tell a lot about a person by the people they surround themselves with. On the other hand, I hope no one judges me based on the way Ryan interacts with women, so the theory has its limitations.

"After this, can we go shopping?" Harper asks, before she stuffs a forkful of pancakes into her mouth.

"For what?" Cora asks, as she cuts a piece of her omelet away.

"I'm not sure, maybe some baby outfits," Harper says, shrugging.

"She's starting to nest." Jensen sighs. "We've been buying a lot of baby stuff lately." Jensen rubs Harper's back in a reassuring, comforting way and I find the display warming.

"I'm sure you'll find some great stuff to take back with you. Unfortunately, I have to meet with my agent at a venue for my next exhibit," I say. I would've liked to have gone, to have spent more time with them and Cora especially, who's now looking at me. *Is that a hint of disappointment?* I can't be sure, but I'm going to say yes to make myself feel better.

"Bummer," she says, her one-word reply more a mumble than anything.

The slow realization creeps in, her comment confirming it. She's bummed I'm not going. *This is new. This is interesting.*

I lean in closer to Cora, making every attempt to conceal what I'm about to say next from the others at the table. "If you want, I'd like to make it up to you."

Cora stiffens slightly, obviously surprised by what I've just whispered to her. Or perhaps it's my close proximity.

"What did you have in mind?" she asks, leaning in toward me.

"I'll handle the details. You just tell me when you're free. Maybe after your guests leave?" I suggest.

"We can occupy ourselves this evening," Harper announces loudly.

We both shoot looks in her direction, obviously startled. Clearly, we weren't nearly as quiet as we thought.

"I can't just leave you guys alone," Cora protests. "You're here to visit me."

"Nonsense," Jensen says. "I mean, yes, we came to see you. But we're adults. We don't need a babysitter. And it doesn't mean we need to see you twenty-four seven or that we should get in the way of your plans."

The man has a point. One of which I'm grateful for.

"Um…" Cora stalls. "Okay, then. Tonight?" She looks back toward me and I nod.

"Perfect," I say.

We all turn our attention back to eating, but my thoughts unravel to somewhere else entirely. Sure, Cora hasn't exactly been the nicest to me. I suppose if I were truly the man whore she thought I was, I could see her perspective. Women have to protect themselves. Then again, that's never stopped me from thinking she's beautiful. And dare I say sexy. Because she is. Definitely.

I've done a lot to intentionally warp my perceptions of her due to how she's treated me, but it hasn't been easy. It became most apparent to me the second time I worked on her painting, when she was in my space and slipped her little dress over her head. The fabric looked soft and silky, floating over her. When it bunched up into her hands, exposing all that skin underneath, I nearly choked. I had to rip my eyes away from her. And that? That doesn't happen to me with someone I'm painting. Ever.

So when I say I have no idea what I'm doing or why I just asked her out on what I consider an official date, it's true. But I think part of me has always wanted to, despite the obvious hurdles up to this point.

After we finish eating, we gather out on the sidewalk as they decide where they're going first. "I'll pick you up at seven?"

"Okay, that works for me," Cora says, her smile small and almost nervous. I can feel the nervous energy radiating from her, so I cup her elbow, stilling her.

"Don't worry," I whisper close to her. "It will either be just another bad date to add to the pile or the first good one."

Cora's lips curl together, fighting a bigger smile, but I accomplished what I wanted to do, which was calm her.

Before I release her, I lean in, giving her another kiss on the cheek. This time, it's longer, heavier. Then we part ways; I head toward home, and they go in the other direction.

I have some work to do. Because not only was asking her out a spontaneous act, but I have no idea what the actual date will be. So yeah. Now I need a plan.

I guess I'm making a move after all.

CORA

WHAT THE FUCK have I actually done? What exactly have I agreed to? I mean, I know what I agreed to, but I'm looking around my empty room trying to figure out which of my masochistic personalities I need to cuss out. What has this bitch done?

I pace back and forth at the foot of my bed, making every attempt not to chew my nails. I'm fairly certain if I don't stop pacing soon, I'll break a sweat, which isn't a good look on a date. *A first date. With Declan Walsh. Holy shit.*

Sitting down on the edge of my mattress, I press my feet into the wedges I decided on. Usually, I would never opt for a shoe that makes me even taller than I already am. The men I usually go out with already teeter on the edge of shorter than me when I'm in flats. But Declan towers so far over me, I know I'm safe. Which is sort of nice, considering I love heels. I guess that's one mark in the *pros* column.

I check my phone for the thirteenth time. He should be here any minute. The love birds are watching scary movies on my couch with snacks, though I'm not sure why they opted for a movie at all. They've been talking through the whole damn thing. I hear them even now, laughing and carrying on.

I stand, taking one last look in the mirror. Without knowing anything about this date, I opted for black jeans, black wedges, and a bright blue top that hangs off one shoulder; the sleeves come down to the elbows. I figure it's not too dressy but enough that I won't look like a slob if we go somewhere a little more upscale.

A knock echoes from the front door all the way down the hall. And with it, my heart beats so hard I'm convinced it's trying to answer in some sort of heart attack Morse code. Smoothing my hands over my hips, I grab my clutch and step out.

"I'll get it," Jensen chirps, jumping off the couch in a hurry and bounding toward the door. If I didn't love him so much, I'd kill him.

Jensen swings the door open wide, offering a big welcoming gesture with his arms. Then I see him. *Declan.* My eyes start at his black boots, travel up his near-black ripped denim, over the crisp white V-neck T-shirt, and up to the most shocking part of the image. His once long locks are gone. His hair is trimmed into a short fade on the sides, the top quite a bit longer and pushed back, still looking so touchably soft. I could still run my hands through that. *Whoa.*

"Oh my," I say, involuntarily. "You look great." I step toward him with less hesitation now, closing the distance between us quickly.

Declan runs his hand through the top of his hair, just as I imagined doing only a moment ago. "You look beautiful," he says, a smile spreading over his mouth. He tucks his hands in his pockets, and through the art of observation, I've come to connect this habit of his with nervousness. I can't be totally sure, but I'm starting to hone in on the pattern.

"Thank you," I say. I look to our right and realize my brother is still standing there, a very pleased look on his face as he continues to stare at us. Just standing there, with his goofy grin. I make eye contact with him and he wiggles his eyebrows. *Oh dear god.*

"Should we go?" I ask, wanting to get the hell out of here as quickly as I can.

Declan nods, stepping back into the hall and waving toward my brother and Harper.

"Stop making that stupid face," I say through gritted teeth at Jensen as I pass him.

"Okay, no problem," he says, holding his hands up in surrender. Except his face looks the exact same. *Ugh.* I step out the door and just as he goes to close it behind me, he says all too loudly, "Make sure you use protection." Then the door clicks. My feet halt and I close my eyes. *That did not just happen.*

Declan walks ahead of me, seemingly unfazed by my little brother's suggestion. Maybe he didn't hear it.

Downstairs, he holds the door open for me as I step out onto the busy sidewalk, the cool air hitting my skin and causing a ripple of goosebumps down my spine.

"So, where are we going?" I ask, adjusting my clutch under my arm.

Declan takes me by the hand, lacing his fingers into mine the way he did last night. His large warm hand envelops mine, causing a sensation to radiate through me. Suddenly, I'm unaffected by the cool evening air; and I don't resist or stiffen. I close my fingers through his and fall in step next to him.

"Somewhere I doubt you've ever been," he says. "And somewhere else after that you've probably never been to either."

"How cryptic," I tease. I notice the side of his mouth hitch up from my peripheral and a small dimple forms just above the corner.

"Well, if I told you now, you might back out," he says, giving my hand a squeeze.

"I'm not one to do that," I reply.

"I had a feeling," he says. "It's something I like about you."

So he's thought about things he likes about me. *Interesting.* Okay, but I've done the same so it's not a big deal. *Unless…it is a big deal.* Even through my blinding rage moments concerning him, it's not like I didn't notice a few things.

"I see you cut your hair," I note.

"Don't like it?"

"I do, actually," I say. "Although, I will admit, even in the midst of hating you, I always wanted to touch your long hair."

"You did, huh?" Declan looks over at me, surprise and amusement mixed together on his face.

I nod. "It just looks really soft and touchable." I shrug.

"Well, you're welcome to," he says, tilting his head toward me.

Without hesitation, I use my free hand to glide my fingers through the length at the top. It's exactly like I imagined. No feel of sticky products; just soft, thick inky hair that does its own thing. Fortunately for him, that includes staying in place without assistance and looking amazing.

"Well?" he asks, looking back up at the sidewalk.

"Impressively soft," I say, my hand now flexing at my side. "Also, I like your cologne." I couldn't help myself. He smells so good. In this close proximity, I'm surrounded by his rich, warm scent.

"Oh, thanks," he says. It almost feels like he wants to say more but stops himself.

The streetlamps flick on a few minutes later, and I've always loved how the city streets look all lit up. We pass a couple of bars and restaurants then come to a stop in front of an unmarked red door. I look up and around for signage, or anything to give me an indication of where we are, but there's nothing. A single bulb hangs over the entryway. Declan knocks three times, sharp and deliberate.

I look around as we wait, observing that no one else seems to be huddled together or lining up. I snap my attention back to the sound of the door opening where a man greets us, his sharp all black suit capturing my attention.

"Walsh for two," Declan says to the man, who then proceeds to open the door, welcoming him in with a handshake.

He leads me in, hand still in mine, and it brings a comfort to me as we walk down a dimly lit hallway. A few overhead lights burn low, barely illuminating the intricate black and red wallpaper. I'm sure if I touched it, the black would be velvety. It seems to pop against the red in contrast. But I keep my free hand to myself. It also looks like it costs more than my entire apartment.

Declan leads us near what I assume is the back of the place, weaving us through a small crowd. I note a bar to our left. It's not terribly busy but steady. We curve to the right, where small tables are set up and a stage is in the center, colorful spotlights shining above.

"Here we are," he says. He brings us to a small two-person booth, and motions with his hand for me to sit on one side. He sits on the other and adjusts his jacket.

"What is this place?" I ask.

"Do you like blues?"

"Yes," I whisper, not wanting to be louder than the rest of the noise in the room, which isn't very loud at all.

"Good," he says. "This is a speakeasy. It was renovated a while back, expanded to include more seating and a stage."

"What's the name of it?"

"It doesn't have one. I mean, technically I guess it has one somewhere on paper for tax purposes, but it doesn't have one as far as people know. You either know about this place or you don't. It's not advertised anywhere. Total word of mouth," he whispers.

"Wow." I pick up the small menu in front of us. It only has a few options. I imagine, like most upscale places, the limited menu aids in making sure quality is the most important thing. Too many items to worry about and it becomes something else entirely.

A waiter comes by to take our drink orders and Declan insists on ordering for me. Somehow, it doesn't come off as domineering or alpha, which I appreciate. He's sweet about it. Cute, even.

I agree and then sit back, listening to him speak with the younger guy taking our order. He chooses a vodka-based signature cocktail for me and a steak dish, and I have zero complaints. He also asks for a basket of bread for the table and again, no objections from me.

"Sorry, I just love the bread here. They bake it fresh," he says.

"I love bread too," I say, jokingly pinching my side. "As you can see."

Declan narrows his eyes, clearly not amused by my self-deprecating joke. "Um, you're beautiful." He clasps his hands over mine on top of the table, leaning in much closer. "And, if you like bread, you should eat the fucking bread." His voice is low and playful. Then he winks.

Oh shit. A man after my own heart. *Wait. Heart? No, probably not.* I shake away the thought, feeling it hit all too seriously, which is insane. *It's just bread, Cora. Calm down.*

The waiter delivers said bread and our drinks just as a three-person band takes the small stage and plays the first few notes. The music is sad and passionate. A man with a deep gritty voice sings of heart-break. I feel the emotion deep in my soul as I take a sip of my drink, and then I reach for a slice of the bread in the basket.

Declan turns in his seat toward the band for a few minutes and then back to me, studying my face.

"They're very talented," I remark, still keeping my voice low.

"Yeah," he says. "I don't like to brag, but I know all the best places in the city for this kind of experience."

"Oh you do, huh?" I bite into my bread again. It's warm and soft, and possibly the best restaurant bread I've ever had.

"My clients tend to be upscale people. They want to meet in upscale places. I have the privilege of holding onto a few luxuries from their universe." He takes a sip of his bourbon, the amber colored liquid hitting his lips and leaving a wet trail behind when he sets his glass back down. I don't even drink bourbon, but I find myself tempted to have a taste, to lick the remnants from his mouth. *Good god, woman. Get a grip.*

"I'll have to remember that for when I need to lay it on thick with one of my own clients," I say, attempting to get back on track from my distracted and quite frankly terrifying thoughts.

"I'll definitely help you out if you ever need it," he says, lending a wide smile with his response.

The waiter comes with our food, and everything looks like it's ready to be photographed for a damn culinary magazine. "Wow," I exclaim, when he walks away. "This looks amazing."

"It tastes better than it looks if you can believe it," he says.

I cut through my steak and it's like butter. So soft and perfectly red in the center. Even if this is a terrible date, I will forever be grateful I know about this place now.

Several bites in, Declan breaks the silence. "When you were a kid, what did you want to be when you grew up?'

I stop mid-bite, thrown off for a moment by his random question. But then I think about it, searching back to my childhood years. "For me, it changed a lot, but what I remember most is wanting to live on a farm. I wanted to raise chickens and goats, maybe even a cow."

Declan studies my face, appearing to be surprised by my admission. "That's not what I expected you to say but I like it."

"What did you want to be?" I ask, as I cut another bite from my steak before eating it.

"An astronaut," he replies. "I think like, half of all boys dream about being one at some point so it's not exactly original."

"I see the appeal, though," I say, smiling. "It's no chicken farm, but it has its merits."

Declan laughs; the smooth throaty noise is an octave above everything else in the restaurant and I almost look around to see if anyone is staring, but he seems unconcerned.

"I'm glad you think it has its merits. Otherwise, I might be in trouble," he says.

"What do you mean?" I ask.

"All in good time, love," he says. Again with calling me *love*. I never knew I could be a fan of any pet name. But the way he says it...well, let's just say I can live with it.

We finish eating and Declan pays the check. I note that he in no way makes it seem like he's doing me a favor by paying it, which I can appreciate.

"Ready for our next stop?" he asks, standing from the booth and holding out his hand for me to take.

"Definitely," I say, and there's more enthusiasm in my voice than I expect. I place my hand in his without hesitation, letting him lead me to the exit.

We pass several blocks and I begin to wonder where the hell we're going when we end up in front of the planetarium. Then it clicks. His comments about space, being an astronaut.

"I think this place is closed," I say as we approach the doors.

Declan peaks through the glass doors and waves at someone I can't see. Seconds later, the door opens and we step inside, the only light coming from the exhibits themselves. All the overhead lighting is turned off.

"Hi, Carl," Declan says, shaking the man's hand. Carl, who wears a blue suit and name tag, shakes Declan's hand and nods.

"The place is all yours. Just let me know when you're leaving," he says, then disappears through an **EMPLOYEES ONLY** door off to one side.

"Ready?" Declan asks, smiling as he squeezes my hand.

I nod, slightly nervous, mostly excited, and ready for anything that's about to happen.

DECLAN

THE ONLY SOUND in the entire place is that of her heels and my own leather soles tapping against the polished floors of the dimly lit planetarium. I know; the planetarium? It sounds strange, but I couldn't help myself when I was planning this out.

"Through here," I say, stepping out of the way to let Cora pass through the door leading to the dark dome-shaped room.

"I can't see anything," she whispers.

"Why are you whispering?" I laugh.

"I don't know," she says, laughing. "It seemed like an appropriate time to whisper."

"Just wait here," I say, walking her down the path a bit, then letting her hand go.

I step to the far end of the small stage in the center of the room and feel for the familiar switch. Flipping it up, a thousand tiny lights fill the dome.

Cora's eyes dart up, growing wide as she takes everything in. "Oh my god."

I walk back to her, staring up at the swirling constellations. "Pretty incredible, isn't it?" Most people skip over the planetarium when seeing the sights. Most don't even understand how incredible it is.

Sure, they're not real stars. But the simulated sky does a pretty damn good job of capturing your attention like the real one.

"This is amazing," she says. I look down at her, her face glowing from the lights above. But mostly, I'm overcome by her stretched neck, the way her jaw makes the muscles twitch ever so slightly, tenderly.

Without a second thought or hesitation, I lean down and press a kiss to the center of her throat. I feel her tense for a split second then relax again. I pull back, realizing I took her by surprise. Hell, I surprised myself.

"I'm sorry," I whisper, my voice low and breathy, my mouth close to hers.

"Why are you whispering?" she asks, mocking my earlier comment.

"It seemed like an appropriate time to whisper," I mimic.

Her eyes meet mine and my whole body sighs. Her hand trails up and she rubs her thumb across my jawline, her eyes studying my face. The next thing I know she's pulling me in, leaning up, and our lips touch—gently at first, then harder. I wrap my arms around her waist and pull her to my chest. I don't part her lips or press forward. I simply embrace her, inhale her, enjoy what she's offering me.

I pull back, catching my breath as I open my eyes. Cora's open slowly, her mouth still slightly puckered and wanting. There's a tightness in my throat I attempt to swallow down.

"I'm sorry," I whisper again.

"Are you going to apologize every time you kiss me?" she asks, a small, playful smile spreading across her mouth. *The mouth I just kissed.*

"It's possible," I say, rubbing my thumb over her full bottom lip. "Come sit with me." I nod to two seats near the stage and take her hand in mine.

As we sit, she asks me what I'll paint next.

"I'm not sure yet," I admit. Because I truly have no idea. It's unsettling when I don't know what's next. I usually have a general direction. It might be time to start panhandling for models soon.

"You can paint me again, if you want. Or if you need something to work on while you find something else," she says, her words coming out less confident than usual. Perhaps she thinks I wouldn't want to.

"I'd like that," I say, squeezing her hand in mine.

I watch her smile widen from my peripheral as she looks up, her eyes glossy under the movement of the lights above us. I lean back too, taking in the full simulation of the cosmos.

For a little while, we do nothing more than sit there, quietly, our hands tangled together. Neither of us say anything and a comfort washes over me. Usually, I'm uncomfortable in situations like this. I find the need to fill the silence or excuse myself entirely. But this is nice. I like it.

"Should we head home?" I ask after some time. After checking my watch, I realize we've been here for over an hour.

"Yeah, probably," she says. If I didn't know better, I'd think there was a reluctance in the tone of her voice.

On the walk back to our apartment, she notes the convenience of living in the same building and we share a laugh. Internally, I continue to ponder both the pros and cons of this particular situation. On one hand, it is convenient. On the other, it gives me several more opportunities to fuck it up. And I do have a tendency to fuck things up.

I don't do it on purpose. It just happens. Things unravel and I find myself holding an empty spool.

At her door, she places her hand on the knob, then stops. As she turns back to me, the ghost of an emotion on her face I can't place becomes a smile.

"I had a really good time with you tonight," she says, her hands wringing in front of her. She wants me to kiss her again. This much I can tell.

"I really enjoyed tonight," I say, cupping her elbows to bring her closer to me.

Cora leans in, bringing her nervous hands up to my chest. Her eyes are full of need, of desire. I've never seen her like this.

I run my thumb over the edge of her lips again, tilting her face up. Kissing someone has never felt so significant. Perhaps it's because of the way we've evolved. Or maybe it's the way she smells. But it scares me a little.

I lean down, brushing my lips against hers. Softly, tenderly. I increase the pressure and feel her whole body give over to the moment. Her hands travel up over my chest and around the back of my neck, her fingers tangling in my hair as my hands wrap around her waist. I inhale against her mouth, parting her lips with my tongue. I feel her own jagged inhale, her tongue connecting with mine.

The hunger brewing in my chest takes over and the next thing I know, I'm backing her up against her door, pinning her there with my body. I lace my fingers into hers and press her hands to the door above her. I trail kisses down her jawline and nip my teeth at her collarbone, gliding my tongue over her skin.

Just when things are getting too hot for the hallway, her door gives way, and it takes all my balance and strength to prevent her from toppling back and falling. Holding her against me by her waist, her face buried in my chest, I can't help but laugh. And I laugh hard.

"Well, hey there, sis," Jensen says, his hand still on the doorknob. "Sorry, I thought the thud was someone knocking."

"It definitely wasn't, little brother," she says, attempting to stifle her laughter, her shoulders shaking up and down.

I press my lips into a line to keep my own laugh at bay. "Goodnight then," I manage, releasing her from my grip.

"Goodnight," she says, a smile playing over her whole face. Cora backs away slowly, then she and Jensen both disappear behind her closing door.

I turn, taking the few strides to reach my door, and press my forehead against my door.

Fuck.

CORA

I HAVEN'T BEEN able to concentrate on anything for three days. After seeing my guests off yesterday, I spent the rest of the day having an internal panic attack about the whole situation with Declan.

The day started off swell. Jolly even. Declan came over, realizing we didn't have each other's numbers, and we exchanged them. He said his farewells to Jensen and Harper, saying he hoped to see them again soon.

I dropped them off at the airport, stopped by work to check on some things, and pulled Claire out for lunch to recap the developments for her. Then I had to call Lyla, repeating all the details to her. Of course Harper had jumped me for them as soon as I made it into the apartment after our date, so she was already up to speed. Which rounds out all the people I needed to tell.

It's now been a couple of days of texting with Declan, making plans for a second date and checking my phone with a giant grin on my face like a teenager. I feel so ridiculous.

"You okay?" My employee Sara rounds the corner to my desk, apparently noting the blank look on my face.

"Yeah, I think so," I say, not even sure if I believe myself. "Just having an internal meltdown."

"So, the same as any other day?" She laughs, and admittedly, she's not wrong.

"Except this one is about a boy." I sigh.

"Declan?" Her whole face perks up as she asks.

"How did you—" I start. "Oh, right. Claire." Nothing is a secret around this place. News for one team member is everyone's news. Doesn't matter what it is. It makes its rounds; a perpetual game of telephone. Not that I'm mad about it. Everyone would've found out sooner or later.

"Yeah, Declan," I say, clicking at my computer mouse extra hard. The aggressive clicking only further points to the notion that a very different mouse needs clicking.

"Have you seen him since your date?" she asks, leaning against the wall and settling in for all the details.

"We exchanged numbers the next morning and have been texting. He says he doesn't want to use the fact that I live across the hall as a reason to get lazy," I say.

"What does that mean?" Sara tilts her head at me, crinkling her eyebrows.

"It means that, instead of just coming over to my place or having me come over and settling into a routine like that too early, he's kept his distance. Out of respect for my space." I sigh again. Because I both admire this and hate it.

I mean, it's been one date. That's it. But there's something about the idea of him just being able to come over at any time with such ease that I really want to take advantage of. Of course, in his mind, we need a few more official dates established before we're that couple who just *Netflix and chills* all the time out of convenience.

"I think that's good though," Sara says.

"Yeah, it is," I say. "But do you know how many times I've almost gone over and knocked on his door?"

"It must be weird to know he's *right* there," she agrees.

"Well, he's had some work obligations with his agent that's kept him away in the evenings," I say. "But I'd be lying if I said I didn't listen for him to get home."

It's true. I've been on the couch both nights when he's made his way down the hall. I heard him outside my door in the hallway, his keys rattling. He was alone and I swore I heard him get closer to my door, then he hesitated before walking to his apartment. If I didn't know better, I'd think he's been tempted too. Perhaps that's why he's trying to stick to official dates for the time being.

"I'm sure whatever the reason is, it's smart," she says, leaning over and placing her hand on my shoulder.

"Maybe after our second official date tonight, I'll have more to say about it." I shrug.

When I return back to the project on my screen, I'm still thinking about Declan. This is so unlike me. I'm not a *let a guy consume all my thoughts* kind of woman, but this feels different. Or rather, seems that way, because how can I go from loathing someone to making out with them against my apartment door? *Oh, the making out...*

I'll say this much. Declan is a damn good kisser. And his lips are perfect—soft and full. The stubble on his face scratched gently at my skin. His tongue. His very skilled tongue. Maybe the line between loathe and love is the trail his tongue makes across my skin.

My phone buzzes, pulling my attention from work once again. At this rate, I'm not going to get much done.

> LYLA
>
> So, do you know where he's taking you?

I shake my head, preparing my reply. She knows I don't know. When we spoke about it yesterday, I told her as much.

> The answer is the same as last night.

> LYLA
>
> You're much better at surprises than I am. I'm dying to know and I'm not even going.

> I like his mysterious ways.

> LYLA
>
> Ok, well use protection and give me all the details after!

Jesus. What is it with her and my brother? She always tells me this, though. Every date, it's the same advice. *Use protection.* I could be squeezing in a lunch date during my workday, and she'd still say it.

I put my phone away, flipping it over so the screen faces down. Somehow, everyone thinks this is a magical way to pretend it doesn't exist. Like you can't just flip it back over to procrastinate.

I stare back at my computer screen, realizing I've lost all interest in this project. I wonder if switching to another will help. Then I wonder if Declan is on social media. Of course, I'm sure his art has its own page, but does he have any personal accounts? *God, this is going to be a long day.*

By the time I make it home, it feels like the longest day in the history of days. I'm so tired, I'm tempted for the briefest of moments to reschedule with Declan, but I can't bring myself to do it. Three days ago, we kissed. And I fully intend to do it again.

I slip out of my work attire and into jeans and a T-shirt with a cardigan sweater over it. I slip on my bright pink Vans and freshen my hair and makeup. Declan said to keep the outfit casual, so that's exactly what I've done. I'm not complaining, either. I don't have the energy for high heels or binding clothing this time around.

After I've yawned no less than half a dozen times since I've been home, there's finally a knock at the door.

I open it wide and Declan fills the doorway, his head close to the frame. He's wearing jeans and a T-shirt too. Not the crisp, pressed T-shirts he normally wears. This one is worn, a more relaxed look.

"Hey," he says, a smile growing over his face.

"Hi, come on in," I offer, just in time for another yawn to escape me.

"Long day?" he asks. "Or am I already boring you?"

I laugh. "Oh no, super long day actually." I turn, collecting my purse. "We've got a couple of hard-hitting projects we're working on as a team, and I'm pretty sure if I stop moving, I'll fall asleep standing up."

"Do you want to reschedule?" he asks.

I turn to him, but I don't detect any negative emotion on his face. He doesn't seem upset about the idea.

"I briefly considered it, but I'm not going to lie, I couldn't bring myself to do it. Or rather, I didn't want to do it, no matter how tired I feel." I shrug, offering him a smile so he understands I really want to be here doing this.

"I know I wanted official dates first, but let's stay here. I'll be right back," he says, then disappears to his apartment.

He's back in a few minutes, with a paper sack in hand. "Let's break the rule." Declan extends the bag to me. Inside, there's a bottle of wine, movie snacks, and a TV remote, which I hold up at him with a quizzical look.

"Yeah, that's just meant to symbolize watching a movie. No one has DVDs anymore." He laughs. "Except we'll use your remote, obviously."

I laugh, his attempt both adorable and sincere. "Thank you, really. A movie night sounds great. It means I can wear my pajamas, and I'm a big fan of any activity where that's okay."

"Well, I'll go get mine on then," he says. "And be right back. Pick a movie?"

"All right, what genre?" I ask.

"Anything on the creepy side is okay with me," he says.

I grab my chest, surprised and relieved. "A man after my own heart."

The phrase escapes my lips before I can call it back, and my brain and mouth really need to stop using that. It's just one of those playful phrases people use, but I realize all too late the more serious insinuations.

But Declan's smile doesn't waver. In fact, his expression only deepens as he steps back once again and then disappears to change into his pajamas. *His pajamas. We will be in our pajamas. Christ, I did not think this through.*

I sit the paper sack down and run to look for something to wear that's both cute but not too revealing. And this is the exact moment I realize I don't have anything that fits that criteria. My nighttime wardrobe consists of sweatpants, long fluffy socks, and baggy T-shirts. And you know what? That's just going to have to work. It will be a test, I suppose. *Will he still find me attractive when I'm dressed like a hobo?* Let's find out.

I return to the living room, setting the snacks out on the coffee table and grabbing two wine glasses from the kitchen. Half a minute later, as I'm pouring wine, I hear my door shut behind me. I turn in time to see Declan walk toward the couch, and I note his appearance. He's wearing a T-shirt that has the collar ripped out and bits of paint on it. My eyes travel down, and *damn, damn, double damn*. He's wearing the gray sweatpants. *The. Gray. Sweatpants.* Talk to any woman, and it doesn't matter which gray sweatpants specifically, they are *the* gray sweatpants. Because boy, those sure do something to a man. They hang low on the hips, somehow hugging curves. Then, there are the *impressions*. I swallow hard, trying not to look directly at them, but it's more of an eclipse.

"You ready?" he asks.

No. The answer is no.

CORA

I TRY to recall the last time I had a man in my apartment. At least one I was dating or attracted to, anyway. It's so far back there, I don't even think it counts anymore. *Born again.*

Declan sits down on the couch next to me, not too close but not hugging the opposite end. If either of us were to move our legs an inch toward the other, we'd be touching.

"Did you decide on a movie?" he asks, cupping one of the wine glasses and bringing it to his lips.

"Oh, right," I say. "I was thinking a classic. Jason or Michael?"

"Ooooh, tough choice," he says, rubbing his fingers over the stubble on his chin. "I'm going to have to go with big Mike."

"Big Mike?" I laugh.

"Well, he's not small," he says, laughing and shrugging.

"Fair enough," I say, as I click through the options to find *Halloween.*

The movie starts and I realize two things: One, I need a blanket; and two, for all the snacks here, we don't have popcorn, which is essential to me.

"I'm going to make popcorn real quick. Do you want some?" I ask, standing from the couch and stretching my arms over my head.

"I'll help," he offers. "Oh, and I know this is a strange request, but can I have a blanket? It's not a proper movie night without a blankie over my lap."

Is he reading my mind? Has he been spying on me? "Yeah, there are some bigger ones in the hall closet if you want to grab one. I was just thinking about that, too."

Declan smiles, then heads down my hall as I make my way to the kitchen.

Ten minutes later, we have a fluffy blanket stretched over both our laps and Declan scoots closer, his thigh pressing against mine as he holds the big bowl of buttery popcorn between us to share. I lean into the bowl—and him, pulling my feet underneath me.

Declan launches a piece of popcorn in the air and it comes down, landing in his mouth. He's so much more relaxed like this than I've ever seen him. Anytime I've been witness to him interacting with someone, he's so quiet, stoic even. He feels like one of those people that chooses every word they say carefully.

"This is my favorite part," he says.

I focus, realizing I've only been staring at the screen without actually comprehending what's happening. Michael Myers has a sheet over his head, and I get the sinking feeling *I'm* in over my head. I need both hands to count how many months it's been since I last had sex. I'm so pent up at this point, I could probably get to O-town from a firm handshake.

"Hey," he says. "Are you okay?"

Apparently, I'm so spaced out that Declan feels the need to check on me. *God, that's bad.*

"Yeah," I say, shoving a handful of popcorn into my mouth. "Just a long day, like I said."

"Come here," he says, taking the bowl of popcorn from between us and setting it on the table. He turns his body toward me, throwing one leg behind me on the couch, urging me to turn my back to him.

I scoot backward until I'm cradled between his thighs, and he presses his big warm hands against my back. He starts a circular motion with his thumbs, pressing into my flesh over and over again, concentrating on the knotted muscles between my shoulder blades.

My shoulders drop of their own accord and I exhale, immediately relaxing into his touch. A small moan escapes my lips, unfiltered and deep. I'm powerless to stop it as his hands glide up my spine, his fingers pressing into the tender parts of my neck.

"Feel good?" he asks.

I roll my neck around, savoring each touch. "You have no idea." I sigh.

Declan works his way down my spine, massaging as he glides lower. His thumbs press into the dimples of my lower back, his hands wrapping halfway around my hips. A chill rushes over me, causing me to lean further forward and grip the fabric of the blanket in my lap, moaning again.

He clears his throat behind me, his body squirming against mine. I wonder for a moment if my slightly sexual noises have caused a reaction in him. *Only one way to find out.*

I twist my body around, readjusting the way I'm seated so I'm facing him. His hands are still in the air, the absence of my skin beneath his fingers surprising him. Declan's eyes meet mine, and I see a mixture of emotion in them. *Confusion? Attraction? Perhaps a bit of both?*

I can still feel the kiss from two days ago lingering on my lips and I want to feel it again. I never thought I'd be saying that about him, the presumed man whore across the hall. My next-door neighbor with a reputed sex addiction. Whatever I thought of him in the past, it's all gone now.

I lean in toward him, his body unmoving. His hands lower to his lap and he watches me, my advancement. I press my hands into the couch on either side of him, balancing myself. I'm probably only two inches from him, his hot breath tickling my skin.

"Declan?" I whisper, pausing for an answer.

"Yes?" he replies, his voice low and gritty.

"Kiss me again," I say, the words falling out more like a plea than anything else.

His lips part slightly as he inhales sharply and presses his eyes shut. For a split second, I think I've made a mistake. But then his hands fly up, gripping my sides, his fingertips pressing into my flesh.

His mouth takes mine, not the soft way it did before. He kisses me hard, aggressively coaxing my mouth open, and I let him. No hesitation on my part. His tongue laps against mine as I lose my breath to the moment. *Good god.*

He leans back against the arm of the couch, bringing me with him, until my body is pressed on top of his at an angle. My legs trail after, drawing up until I'm nearly straddling him. His hands caress my sides, down my hips, dig into the backs of my thighs. I kill the moans in my throat before they can escape me, but that won't last long. Not at this pace.

I press my hands against his chest, gripping the front of his T-shirt between my fingers. I pull my mouth from his for a moment, sinking my teeth into his bottom lip. A groan escapes him and I smile in satisfaction.

"What are you smiling about?" he asks, before he takes my mouth again, trailing kisses from my lips down to my jaw. His teeth sink into the edge of my throat, and I am powerless to stop the next moan as it leaves my lips.

"I like the way you kiss me," I say. I lift my hand, combing my fingers into his hair the way I've imagined so many times. Although, doing so while making out had never been the vision. Yet, no part of me is complaining about the upgrade.

It's been so long since I've kissed someone like this, so long since I felt the warmth of lips against my skin. I feel the dormant fire in me starting to roar again. It's a hunger, one I stamped out long ago for the sake of my own sanity. But now, the once familiar feeling low in my belly is alive again.

"I've only kissed one part of your body, love," he whispers close to my ear, between kisses. He presses his lips to the sensitive skin just below my lobe. Declan licks where he just kissed and then blows air over it, sending a wave of goosebumps down my entire body. "Do you want to know what it feels like when I kiss other places?"

And just like that, the fire spreads all over. Every inch of me is awake with want.

For Declan.

DECLAN

GOD, *why did I say that? Am I possessed?* I feel possessed. I tug at the edge of her shirt, inching my fingers underneath it, scratching my nails against her skin. Cora's body reacts, arching and pressing into me.

She's so beautiful, so fucking sexy. I can't focus on anything else except her. What's right or wrong, what we should or shouldn't do, be damned. *I want her.* And from the feel of it, she wants me, too.

"Yes," she whispers back. *Yes.* She *does* want me to kiss her in other places. She said yes. Her answer only seems to spur me on. I tug her shirt further up, the curve of her ribs beneath my fingers as I continue upward.

I cup just below her breasts on both sides, the warmth of her body heating my hands. Cora has all but stopped breathing. I can feel her trying to hold it, the occasional jagged inhale and sharp exhale escaping her. She's nervous. Hell, I'm nervous too.

Her eyes meet mine just before my hands slip up and over her soft, perfect tits. For the briefest split second, we're both holding our breaths. Cora exhales, pushing into the palms of my hands as she does so. Her body arches when she throws her head back. She shudders, dipping down against me.

Her nipples harden under my touch and I feel myself harden

beneath her center. She presses her body down against my dick, causing me to grip her tits a little harder. She doesn't seem to mind. She bites down on her bottom lip right before bringing her mouth to mine again.

I don't know if she knows this, but she's a different creature now. She's all hunger and base instinct and it's goddamn divine. She trails kisses down the side of my neck before biting my shoulder and that's all it takes for me to become completely unhinged.

I push her back from me, laying her down on the other end of the couch, her legs on either side of me. Pressing my hands to her thighs, I look to her face for permission. Cora gives me the slightest nod. My fingers hook into the top of her sweatpants and even in the midst of this heat, I can appreciate her willingness to be comfortable around me, to not try too hard.

Slowly, ever so slowly, I pull them down along with her panties. She lifts for me, allowing me to bring them all the way off. Tossing them aside, my eyes never leave hers. There's a vulnerability in her face now. For a moment, she presses her knees together, and all I can see is the beautiful Y shape her legs make as they meet the rest of her.

Then, like a gift, all at once she opens for me. My thumbs press into the soft flesh of her inner thighs, just above her now parted knees. I slide my hands up, the sensation of my touch causing goose-bumps to rise over her soft skin.

I cradle the soft flesh at the apex of her legs, her hip bones in my palms. Leaning over, my eyes trail down from her face, taking in the rest of her, and back up again. I need to see her, watch her face while she takes pleasure. And god, I want to give her pleasure.

I press my tongue to the sensitive skin at her center, sucking her into my mouth. Gone are the soft tame moans that escaped her earlier, now replaced by something louder, more guttural. It does nothing to tame me, but rather spurs me on. I lick and suck, bite and blow. Her legs flex and shudder, her back arching as she presses herself harder into my mouth.

In all the time I've known her, I've never imagined what she'd taste like. But, damn, if that wasn't a mistake. She's a ripe peach, a dark cherry pit. I hope she stains me.

Her hands reach for me, tugging at my hair, a silent plea for more. I pull her to me, lifting her ass from the couch and spreading her wider. I pull back from her only for a moment, only long enough to tell her what I want her to do. "Come for me." I don't ask it of her, I demand it. I need it from her.

I reach for her, cupping one of her tits in my hand, my mouth still working her over. She starts to shake beneath me but I don't ease up, I don't let her go. I want to feel her against me. She reaches for my hands, lacing her fingers with mine as she cries out and her body seizes.

My movements still, letting the wave of her orgasm wash over her before I ease her back down to the couch. I swipe the back of my hand across my mouth as I catch my breath. I still can't peel my eyes from her. She coils up, pressing her legs together tightly. There's no doubt she's overwhelmed with sensation. Her ragged breathing begins to regulate.

"Fuck," she manages on an exhale. "That was incredible."

A smile grows on my face as I drop back on the arm of the couch. "Good."

"Is it your turn now?" she asks, easing herself up from the couch.

"Huh?" I look up at her. Her hand trails over the tie at the top of my pants.

I sit up, pulling myself out of reach. Cora pulls her hand back, likely startled.

"No, trust me. I want to," I say. "But we have plenty of time. And tonight was about you."

"Wow," she says. "That's different."

"Different?" I ask. "From?"

"Every man I've ever met, or heard about. Ever. In my whole life," she says, laughing.

I return a laugh, nodding. "Right. Well, I'm not very manly, I guess."

"Oh, I beg to differ," she says.

"I know I'm odd," I admit. "People don't really understand me most of the time."

"I don't think you're odd," she offers. "Okay, you know what? To be fair, I used to think you were weird. And slutty. But now I have a different opinion."

"Yeah, it only took like three years," I say.

Cora laughs harder, reaching for her panties and sweatpants. "Do you want to finish the movie then?"

I nod, letting her dress. When she settles back onto the couch, this time she tucks herself close, under my arm.

There isn't much of the movie left, but I'll sit here with her and enjoy what's left, despite the overwhelming urge I have to leave and paint. I can feel the itch to hold a brush in my palm. Something inside me is begging to make it to a canvas, though I don't even know what it is.

This is rare for me these days. Most of the time, I have to make an effort to find a project that interests me. In fact, I can't recall the last time I didn't.

All I know is once the feeling takes hold of me, it will not be silenced. I have to purge it in paint.

When the credits start rolling, Cora sits up and stretches before standing. I stand and move toward the open space near the door.

"I should get going," I offer. "You need to sleep."

"And you don't?" she asks.

"I have the luxury of sleeping in. An artist's life." I laugh. "Long nights, late mornings."

Cora nods. "Well, I'm jealous." She comes to stand right in front of me, her arms wrapped around herself.

I lean in to kiss her on the cheek, but she takes my mouth instead, her hands suddenly around my neck. I reach for her, gripping her sides like before, pressing her body to mine.

I break the kiss before it evolves into something I can't stop and press my forehead to hers. "See you tomorrow?" I ask.

"Yes," she breathes.

I say goodnight, leaving her apartment before I change my mind and lift her off the floor, carry her down her own hallway, and lay her on her bed. I leave before I can do all the things I'm desperate to do to her.

Inside the safety of my own apartment, I grab a blank canvas from the wall and position it on my easel. I mix pinks and flesh tones on my palette, cracking my neck as I move it side to side. Without hesitation, brushstrokes begin to fly across the white surface.

I still don't know exactly what it will be, but I trust my hands. I trust myself here in this space better than anywhere else.

CORA

A WARMTH SPREADS across my cheeks as I recall what took place on my couch last night. Declan kissed me. *Declan. Kissed. Me. In all the places.* This is an extremely inconvenient time to replay those memories, considering I'm standing in front of the microwave in the break room at work.

I replay a flick of his tongue against me and everything south of my belly button quivers. My hand grips the edge of the counter as heat spreads down my chest.

"Are you okay?" Claire asks from behind me.

I whirl around, startled in the assumption I was alone. "Yeah, fine, why?"

Claire stares at me. She's known me a long time, so she's not buying it. Her eyes narrow, arms folding over her chest. "What happened?" she asks. It's not really a question so much as a demand for information.

"Jesus, nothing, what?" I reply, my voice high and shrill.

Claire tilts her head at me, giving me her *I smell bullshit* look.

"Okay, okay," I huff. "Declan came over for a movie last night…"

She squeals, moving closer and leaning in. "Tell me everything."

I give her the PG-thirteen-ish version. She doesn't need every dirty detail. Some of them need to be kept for myself. I wipe away fake sweat from my forehead. It's not there, but shit, it feels like it is.

"Most excellent," she says.

I exhale, long and hard. "It was pretty amazing."

"When do you see him again?" she asks, her eyes wide with excitement.

"Tonight," I say, shooting her a look. "And I'm nervous as all fuck."

"Why?"

"Um, because I have plenty of experience with first dates, but I'm a little rusty with anything beyond that if I'm being honest," I admit.

"Oh, honey. Riding a man is like riding a bike. A woman never forgets," she says, patting the top of my hand.

I laugh. Leave it to Claire to say something like that. "You're an idiot."

"I speak the truth," she scoffs, retreating back to her desk.

I was so preoccupied with telling her what happened that I completely forgot about my food in the microwave. I reach in, retrieving my now lukewarm chicken teriyaki meal I got from the freezer section on a whim. Looking at it now, I have much regret. It definitely looks nothing like the photo. After depositing it into the trash, I walk back to my desk.

Great. Now I'm horny and hungry.

After work, I rush home as quickly as I can, wanting to give myself plenty of time to get ready. I feel like I need to step it up after last night's sweatpants episode. Although, it certainly didn't seem to bother him.

My closet is divided into very distinct sections. The left is where all my work attire hangs. Slacks, button-ups, polos, pencil skirts and the like. The middle and veering right are my after-work items. Leather, tank tops, halter tops, skirts that can't be worn to work, and ripped jeans. All the good stuff. But right, way right...that's a part of the closet I rarely go in. Slinky dresses, things with slits, and backless items I never get to wear.

I don't ever make it to this level of wardrobe for dates. Or I haven't, until now. Not in a long time anyway. My hand glides over the soft fabrics, stopping on a long black dress I've been dying to wear. It's crushed velvet, with a slit in the side that runs high enough to make people look twice. The back is open, and there are some strings at the top that hold the whole thing together. It screams *please take me off*. In short, it's perfect.

I re-shave my legs in the tub. This isn't the sort of thing you wear with even the tiniest hint of stubble. I top off the look with smokey eyes, a purple stained lip, and soft curls in my hair. When I step back from the mirror, I'm actually more than pleased, which is rare for me. This will definitely redeem me.

There's a knock at my door as I grab the clutch from the back of my closet door and stuff my things into it.

Declan has precise timing. I guess living across the hall has other advantages. Not that being on time is at the top of my list.

I swing the door open wide, excited and nervous to see his reaction to what I'm wearing, and I'm not disappointed. He goes from biting his bottom lip to mouth hanging slightly open almost immediately and I'm pleased with the impact.

"Jesus," he says. "You're bewitching." His eyes float over me, inspecting and admiring.

Bewitching, huh? I'll take that. "Thank you." I smile, tucking my hair behind my left ear as I take in Declan's appearance.

He's traded his jeans in for black pants, a stark contrast to the pristine white button-up and skinny black tie. Instead of a jacket, he has on a black vest, and his sleeves are rolled to his elbows. *Fucking yum.* There's something about a man wearing a vest that makes my mouth water.

"You look amazing," I say. "I love a man in a vest."

"I'll make a note to buy more," he says, before he leans in and brushes a kiss against my lips. As he pulls back, he inhales deeply. "Did I ever tell you that you smell like peonies?"

I giggle. "I don't think so."

"Well, you do. And they're my favorite," he whispers, kissing my cheek.

"I'll have to make a note of that," I say, using his own words against him.

"Oh, please do," he says.

Walking through the lobby, hand in hand, I realize we're like, *dating*. Not just that we've gone on a date, but we are continuing to go on more dates. Multiple dates. That's the very definition of dating. *Right?*

I'm still asking myself, *are you really dating Declan Walsh? Are you really dating the man you've loathed for years? Did he really defile you on your own couch?"*

The answer is yes, and it hasn't lost its shock value.

Declan holds the door open for me, and a brisk wind rushes in. I'm glad I grabbed a jacket before we headed down.

"So, where to?" I ask. "You didn't tell me why we were dressing up."

"Well, it's nowhere we can walk to," he says, strolling toward the black sedan near the sidewalk. He opens the door, holding his hand out to me to help me inside. It's not a limousine, but it is one of those fancy town cars, complete with a driver.

Surely, all this isn't for a date?

"Wow," I say, sliding into the back, the plush leather seats already warm. A woman could get used to this. "What's with all the fancy?"

"I hope you're in the mood to socialize," he hints.

I nod, unconcerned about public gatherings. The job I do doesn't afford me the luxury of being nervous around new people.

We head downtown, the smaller buildings turning larger the deeper we go. The sky is already dark, but the city is lit up and alive. The streetlamps illuminate the sidewalks, casting a warm glow on everyone that walks by.

The warmth of Declan's hand overtakes mine, his skillful fingers lacing between my own. Slowly, he pulls my hand away from my lap, into his. I turn from my people-watching out the window as he continues lifting my hand to his mouth. His lips slowly brush across my knuckles and a warmth fills my chest. *Yes, we're definitely dating.*

The car pulls in front of a venue I don't recognize, and there are people out on the street, all gathered around a path.

"What the hell?" I say, peering out his window.

"I have an event tonight. It's all very high society. My work is on display and I have to rub elbows with fancy people." He smiles.

Oh my god. "Shit, I didn't even wear pantyhose," I say. "Don't let me drink too much. You know what, don't let me drink at all." I'm suddenly nervous, sure I'll make a fool of both myself and Declan in front of important people.

"Relax," he whispers, as the driver opens the door on his side. "You'll be great."

He exits, his hand reaching back for mine as I slide over and out, gaining my footing without incident. He wraps his arm around my waist and someone snaps a photo of us.

"I didn't realize artists were such celebrities," I tease.

"We're not. Pretty much anyone at this event is getting their photo taken," he says.

Where the hell are we?

I get my answer immediately upon walking into the massive event space. A sign welcoming guests lets me know we just walked into the grand opening of a new contemporary art museum, and honored guests such as the mayor and pretty much every executive from any company in the city is here tonight. *No big deal.* I might even run into some of my own clients at this thing. *Awesome.*

"I think I dressed too...too something," I whisper.

"I think you look perfect," he says, tightening his grip around my lower back.

We deposit my jacket at the front desk and I slip the ticket into my clutch. Declan continues to guide me through the thickening crowd toward the tables at the far end of the hall. When we make it to one marked **RESERVED**, I see his name and mine on cardholders at two of the spots. *Wow, so he had this thing planned.* My name is printed on the card and everything.

"Declan!" a slightly familiar voice says, cutting through the general noise.

We both turn to see Ryan heading straight for us. It didn't register that he'd be here, but thinking about it now, it seems obvious he would be. On his arm is a tall blonde with zero body fat, a smirk more than a smile playing on her face.

"Ryan," Declan says, extending his hand to his friend.

Their casual handshake is similar to what you'd see any two men do when greeting each other. It always makes me wonder why women don't do it. Sure, sometimes we hug hello, but that's usually rare for someone you see frequently.

"Oh, carrot cake," Ryan says, turning his attention to me. "What a lovely surprise."

"Hello again," I say.

Declan's hand flexes and settles back against my skin. "Her name is Cora," he says.

I look up at him, sensing something in his tone. His jaw is tight as he looks sternly at his friend.

Ryan throws his hands up in the air in a show of innocence. "Of course, of course," he says, half-laughing. "This is my date, Natasha. She's the senator's cousin." He doesn't bother mentioning which senator.

The woman extends her hand to Declan, who shakes it as professionally as he can considering she reached toward him palm down, like she expected him to kiss the top of it. When she looks in my direction, I get little more than a curt nod.

I know women like this. Privileged, self-centered, and pampered are a few words in my vocabulary for them. The others are less kind. Natasha thinks the world owes her something. Be it because of her last name, her money, or her perfect face, she's clearly waiting for everyone to pay up.

"Honey, I'm a little parched," I say, looking up at Declan. I've never called him *honey* before. I've never called him any pet name. But here, in front of Natasha and Ryan, I feel the need to pee on his leg. Mark my territory. Just a little, subtly, so they can grasp the situation.

"Then let's get you something to drink, love," Declan says, but he doesn't take his eyes from Ryan. "If you'll excuse me."

He leads me away from our table and to the bar in the corner, where the bartender hands him two flutes of champagne. He deposits one in my hand before downing half of his. My sip is more reserved, although I have half a mind to follow his lead.

"Sorry about that," he says. "Ryan is a great agent and a good friend, but man, he likes to show his ass. He's mostly harmless, though."

"It's okay." I laugh. "I know the type better than I'd like to admit. He doesn't bother me." I wish I could say the same for Natasha. *Bitch.*

"Let's go meet some less offensive people," he says, tangling his fingers with mine.

We walk the floor and sip, stopping only when he wants to introduce me to someone. I meet the owner, some board members, and one of the curators for the gallery before spotting someone I know.

Dr. Richards, both former client and one of the many bad dates I went on, steps toward us. I can't say too many bad things about him. After he learned of my work on our date, he hired my company for some marketing. To be fair, the date wasn't terrible. We're just extremely different people. Luckily, he didn't hold it against me when he chose to hire me.

"Cora? Is that you?" Dr. Richards' eyes light up, as they sweep up and down my body. Declan's head jerks in my direction, presumably surprised someone here knows me.

"Hello, Ken," I say. After we started working together, he insisted I call him by his first name. I wanted to continue with the formal title, but after the third time he insisted, it felt wrong not to oblige.

"What are you doing here?" he asks, looking first at my hand in Declan's and then fully toward Declan.

"I'm here with—" I start, but Declan interrupts.

"Her boyfriend," he says, extending his hand toward Ken. "Declan."

I try to look at him without expressing any of the surprise I feel. His shoulders are squared, his posture a fraction stiffer than it has been the entire time we've been mingling. *Is he pushing his chest out?* Declan already towers over Ken by a few inches. There's really no need for this peacock display. Then again, after what I just did in front of Natasha, maybe it's fair. Plus, I kind of like it. But, let's revisit this boyfriend thing for a moment. Because...*boyfriend? When did we get there?* He's probably just saying it for Ken's benefit.

"Oh wow, great," Ken says. "Nice to meet you, man. And what brings you all here tonight?"

"I'm one of the artists on display," Declan says.

"Oh, okay, nice," Ken says.

They volley back and forth for a moment, asking each other things, seemingly sizing each other up. They infer that Ken's a urologist, I worked for him, Declan's my neighbor, and so on and so on. Then they discuss where Declan's art is hanging. I simply stand back and watch the exchange happen.

"Declan, there you are," Ryan says, interrupting.

Thank fuck. I thought Declan and Dr. Richards were about to start playing tug of war or some shit. I never thought I'd be happy to see Ryan, but here I am, eating those words.

"If you'll excuse us," Declan says to Ken, nodding and turning us in Ryan's direction.

"Natasha's interested in commissioning a painting," Ryan says. "Of herself."

What. The. Fuck.

DECLAN

THERE ISN'T a single bone in my body that wants to paint that woman. Not even a little. Not even in the name of science. Nothing about her appeals to me; on an artist's level or otherwise.

"I don't know, man," I say, but I already know what his reaction will be.

"Are you kidding me?" Ryan shrieks. "She's related to the senator. Do you know the potential work that can bring our way?"

"I'm working on some other things right now," I say, attempting to avoid outright saying I don't want to fucking do it.

"Listen, she's willing to pay a premium price for a premium service, if you know what I mean," Ryan half-whispers.

Cora's hand tightens around mine, and I'm oddly comforted by it. *Is that jealousy? A protective instinct?* I don't know, but I like it.

"Let's talk about it later," I say, settling the matter for now.

"Sure, sure. I'll call you tomorrow about it," Ryan says.

Looking down at Cora, she seems unruffled by it, which is good for several reasons. I don't want her to be uncomfortable. But this sort of thing happens sometimes, and it's good knowing she can handle it. And by *this sort of thing*, I mean there are a certain number of women in powerful positions who want me to paint them. They want a lot more too, but that's another story. I think they've all seen that Leo and Kate scene in *Titanic* one too many times and they're all dying to be painted like French girls. They all want the scene after that too, the one in the steamy car. But no, thank you. I'll pass.

We head back to the table to sit, since dinner is about to be served. I motion for a waiter to bring us two more flutes then pull Cora's chair out for her. Ryan sits, leaving Natasha to pull out her own chair, which she looks less than enthused about. Luckily, I'm not sitting next to her, and neither is Cora.

"So, what's for dinner?" Cora leans over to me as I settle into my seat.

I watch as she delicately places her napkin over her lap. A simple gesture, but I like the way her hands move as she does it, just as she'd done at brunch with Jensen and Harper. I like her nude-colored nails, the delicate gold band she wears on her right thumb. The details capture me for a moment before I realize she's waiting for a reply.

"Oh, uh, some sort of steak dish, I think. Unless people opted for a vegetarian plate, which I did not," I say.

"Good call," she says. "I hope there's bread."

Her reaction makes me laugh, not like I'm laughing at her but because I find her so fucking cute.

"I'm sure there will be, love," I say, trying to put her stomach at ease.

As if on cue, waiters begin to deposit baskets of freshly baked bread onto the tables and I can't help but peek over at her to see her reaction, which is nothing short of a child being handed a Christmas present.

"Ohhhh, and they have the fancy butter, too," she delights.

The evening goes on in complete bliss. After we finish eating, I take her around the exhibits, showing her mine last. Several of the pieces will be on permanent display while others will be for sale. Then, we dance. I hold her close, my fingers gliding over the skin of her exposed back with a certain amount of desire bubbling in my chest. I'll be good here. Though, I can't say what'll happen in that tinted rental. There's a visor between us and the driver, so all bets are off.

At the end of the evening, we collect her coat but can't escape another run-in with Ryan and his tagalong.

"Don't forget. I'll call you tomorrow," Ryan says as Natasha drags him away, and he gives me the universal call symbol, his thumb at his ear and index finger stretched to his mouth.

I nod, helping Cora into her coat. Ryan can be so exhausting.

"What a night," Cora declares.

"Did you have fun?" I ask, stepping in front of her to open the car door.

She slides in before me. Once we're in the warmth of the car, she takes my hand. "I did," she says. "Thank you."

I say, "So, about—" just as she says, "Are you—"

Then, she stops. "Oh, sorry. You go."

"No, you first."

Cora takes a deep breath. "Are you going to paint her?"

I sigh, knowing she'd probably end up asking this at some point. "I really hope I don't have to."

"Isn't it your decision?" she asks.

"More or less," I say, running my hands through my hair. "But I also agreed with Ryan a long time ago that his role in my life means he gets a certain amount of say so in projects, in terms of good business decisions, anyway." A conversation I'm now regretting.

"Oh," she says simply.

"You don't want me to, do you?" I ask.

"Oh, what? No. I mean, no. But, well, I just…I was just asking," she breathes out. I'm not even sure it was a whole sentence, or at least one that made sense.

I chuckle. "All right, then."

"Don't laugh at me," she jokes, laughing herself. "If I'm being perfectly honest, I don't like her."

"Yeah, I don't either," I admit.

Silence fills the car for a moment, our hands still tangled together. It's not an awkward silence but a comfortable one.

"So," she says, breaking the quiet. "About this whole boyfriend thing..."

She trails off, presumably so I can pick up the topic and run with it. Or maybe so I can explain myself.

Fuck.

"Yeah, I'm sorry about that," I say, rubbing the back of my neck, slightly embarrassed about my behavior. "I don't know why I did that."

"Were you jealous of Dr. Richards?" she asks, a playful smile plastered across her face.

"Were you jealous of Natasha?" I counter, deflecting, knowing full well she was.

"Please," she says. "Jealous? More like annoyed." Her eyes narrow but her smirk doesn't dissipate.

"Well, same for me. I was just annoyed." I shrug, returning a grin.

Cora presses her lips together, knowing full well we're at an impasse. We were both jealous, and now we both refuse to admit it. But neither of us are idiots either. We're just playing the game.

I help her out of the car after we pull up to our building, the night air a bit chillier than when our evening began. It almost makes me wish I'd opted for a jacket, but a few strides later we're tucked inside and already making our way up the stairs. I haven't exactly figured out what's about to happen. I mean, I know what I *want* to happen. But what I want and what happens in reality are rarely in line with each other.

Cora's steps slow in front of me as she rounds the corner, approaching her door. She turns and I notice her hands fidgeting on the clasp of her clutch.

"I had a really great time," she says. "Even if we were both a little annoyed by other people." The look on her face when she says this lets me know all I need to in that regard.

I smile down at her, my hands instinctively reaching for just above her hips. Pulling her to me, we both inhale a deep breath as we embrace, her arms coming up around my neck. It's now or never. Well, maybe not *never*, but it sure feels that way.

"Would you like to come over?" I ask, pulling back from the hug. I find it ironic this is where we are. Over the years, I've slipped this question in a couple of times for an entirely different reason than I'm asking now. Asking this question prior had set years of distance and hate into motion. Now, here I am, asking it for the exact reason she assumed I did before.

"Yes," she whispers.

CORA

THE KEYS in Declan's hand make a dainty jingling sound as he unlocks his door and then pushes it open for me. Upon stepping inside, it feels both familiar and, strangely, like I'm here for the first time. Perhaps the circumstances cause it to feel different. Or the ball of nerves in the pit of my stomach. I can't be sure.

"Would you like something to drink?" he asks, closing and locking the door behind him. The click of the lock echoes into the otherwise quiet room, jarring my senses.

"Sure," I say, my voice suddenly less steady.

He takes long strides across the open space between the living room and his kitchen, pulling at his tie as he opens a cabinet for two glasses. He deposits his tie on the counter as he pops the cork from a bottle, then pours red wine into the delicate stemless glassware. I'm oddly fascinated with his movements, studying the discarded tie longer than necessary. *It's just a bit of black fabric.* Perhaps this is my mind's way of calming itself down.

"Here you go," he says, placing the glass of wine in my hand. *Good. I'll need this. Liquid courage, right?*

"Thank you," I say. I turn to find his easel empty, the various canvases previously against the wall now all covered in white sheets. "Are you redecorating?" I tease.

"Something like that." He laughs. He motions to the couch and we sit, our legs crossed toward each other. In the words of Cher Horowitz, that's an *unequivocal sex invite*.

Declan takes a sip of wine, his eyes never leaving mine. I watch the glass tip back, then his lips part, the dark red liquid wetting them. His outstretched arm over the back of the couch aligns his hand with my shoulder, his index finger drawing circles there on my skin. Between the wet lips and gentle caresses, I'm more than a little distracted.

"I didn't mind it, you know," I say gently, taking another sip of my wine. "When you said you were my boyfriend."

"No?" he says. "I assumed it was a little too soon for those kinds of labels."

"Maybe so," I muse.

"Then again, I've never been one for labels or an imaginary timeline."

"Neither have I," I whisper, my breath shallow.

Declan takes my glass along with his and places them on the table in front of us. Then, he inches closer to me, his legs touching mine. "Cora," he says, his voice low and gritty.

"Yes?" My voice is barely above a whisper, my nerves making me jittery.

He runs his thumb across my lower lip, his fingers pressing against my jawline. "I don't want to ask to kiss you. I'd just like to kiss you. Anytime I want." His words come out with a raw tenderness I didn't expect. But they're also lined in firmness, edging on a hunger that makes my lower stomach flutter.

This man is stone. This man is fire.

"Yes." My answer is simple, breathy, begging in nature.

Declan presses his mouth to mine, harder than our previous kisses. He coaxes my mouth open, his tongue exploring and needful. One of his hands runs along my neck and tangles in the hair at my nape. The other skillfully wraps around my waist, pulling me toward him.

I run my palms along the length of his arms, up over his biceps, gripping his shoulders, moving to his collar. His hand runs down my naked spine, his fingertips digging into the expanse of my exposed back. *One little tie.* That's all he has to unknot. One little tie and this dress will slide all the way down.

I reach for the top button of his shirt, slowly undoing it between my thumb and index finger. The next button comes faster and I slide my hand in, feeling the hot skin of his bare chest against my palm. *God, that's amazing.*

"Wait," he says, pulling back from our kiss, stilling my hand. "I don't want this to happen here."

Before I can ask him what he means, he stands and lifts me to my feet. "Hike up your dress," he says, nipping my lips with his teeth.

Without a second thought, I pull the dress up, cradling it just below my hips. Declan dips down, his large hands cradling the backs of my thighs, then hoists me into the air. My parted legs slide up over his body, his hands settling on my ass. My body straddles his, the muscles in his arms tightening as he effortlessly carries me from the couch. My arms gather around his neck while he kisses and nibbles the tops of my breasts, taking my breath away.

A moan escapes my lips as it dawns on me that he's carrying me into his bedroom. For a split second, I realize I've never been in here, but the urge to look around is stifled by my unfiltered need for *him.* His steps stop when he reaches the edge of the bed, his mouth taking mine once again as he sinks us onto the mattress, me beneath him. With one knee on the bed, he slides me upward until my head hits a pillow.

Declan's kisses move from my mouth to my throat yet again, the stubble of his jaw scratching softly against my skin. "Cora," he whispers between breaths.

"Yes?" I'm all sharp inhale, ragged exhale.

He stops kissing and looks up at me, his eyes searching my face. I stare back, taking note of his thick black eyelashes, the way they shadow his cheekbones.

"Tell me what you want," he says, one arm propped up, his other hand caressing my hip and thigh. I don't know how he expects me to concentrate on anything beyond that.

"I want," I start. "I want," I try again, swallowing as his fingers trail over my belly button. "I want you."

A grin spreads across his lips, one more sinister than any I've seen before.

"Tell me what you want," I ask of him, hopeful his answer is the same.

"I want this," he says, kissing my mouth. "And this," as he kisses the tops of my breasts. "And this," his mouth glides over my bare shoulder. "And this," he whispers, his hand sliding between my legs and cupping me.

I throw my head back against the pillow, his touch causing a wave of sensation over my whole body. What escapes my lips is more of a whimper than a moan.

"Take it," I breathe out. "Please."

Declan's eyes meet mine in the soft glow coming through the window, the only source of light in the room. There's an intensity in them, something I've never seen before. He retreats from me and I find myself grabbing for him, arms outstretched, beckoning his warmth to come back against me.

He walks to his dresser near the opposite wall, pulling out the top drawer and retrieving something, then turns back to me. I can't make out what's in his hands as he sets it on the edge of the bed, but I'm intrigued.

"Untie your dress," he says. "And slide it down."

I reach for the tie at the base of my neck, slowly, biting into my lip as I pull at the thin string. I don't even hesitate. His voice is melodic, demanding, and I want to do everything he asks of me. With both hands, I pull the sides of the thin black material down and over my breasts, exposing them. My nipples harden, but I'm uncertain if it's because of the cool air or the look in his eyes.

I continue to pull the dress downward, lifting my bottom off the bed. He places a knee on the mattress, leaning over me. Declan takes over then, pulling the dress the rest of the way down and off my feet. All that's left are the dainty lace panties and goosebumps over my flushed skin.

"Your turn," I whisper.

He reaches for the third button on his shirt, then stops. "You do it."

I sit up, running my hands down his chest, undoing one button, then the next, until I can push his shirt over his shoulders and off completely. He kisses my lips and then gently pushes me back down onto the bed.

My mouth waters as he begins to unbuckle his belt and unzip his pants. He pulls them down just enough to expose his bare hip bones and I reach for him, desire controlling my every move.

"Wait," I say, lifting up again. "I want to taste you." I don't know what's come over me, my mouth saying things I never imagined I'd have the courage to mutter. The filter is gone, the inhibitions lowered.

His hand falls away as he lets me take control. I pull his other knee onto the bed, one on either side of me. In this position, at this angle, the object of my desire is one simple tug away.

I run my hand up his thigh, cupping his hard length over the fabric of his boxer briefs, then hook my fingers into the elastic and pull down slowly, exposing him. My tongue wets my lips, the anticipation rising. He fills my mouth and then some. I take his sharp inhale as a positive sign and push him deeper.

"Fuck," he groans on a ragged breath, bending over me. He tangles his fingers in my hair, but his movements aren't controlling. He lets me have my way, licking and sucking for some time, before he pulls away. "I can't take it anymore." He presses me back onto the bed again, this time more forcefully.

He makes quick work of getting his pants the rest of the way off and stands back up, giving me a full view of his naked body. *My god.* The light from the street filtering in casts long shadows on every curve and ripple. He's so much more muscular than I allowed myself to notice. The veins in his arms strain as he reaches for the item he'd pulled from the drawer.

"Do you trust me?" he asks. I nod, unsure at this point if my voice will even work if I try. Declan runs a bit of material between his hands. It looks silky, like a scarf or a tie perhaps. "Put your hands up between the bars of my headboard."

Oh my god. For a split second, my body panics. But the next thing I know, my hands are up, clasping a bar, impatiently waiting for what's about to happen next.

He dips forward, wrapping the length of the fabric around one of my wrists, then the bed, and finally, the other wrist. Somehow, he knows exactly how tight to make it, so that I'm definitely not going anywhere but not in pain, making me think it's not the first time he's tied up delicate wrists.

Declan's eyes meet mine, and he presses kisses to my lips before coaxing my mouth open, taking it fully. He hovers over me, barely touching me. His chest grazes against my nipples and my back arches, pushing my body toward his.

"Cora," he whispers, trailing kisses over my collarbone.

"Yes," I say. It's not even a question.

"I don't want this to be a one-time thing," he says. "I don't want you to hate me anymore." His hand slides down, palming my breast, causing me to moan.

I shake my head back and forth. "No," I breathe. "Definitely not a one-time thing." I arch again, pressing further into his hand. "I don't hate you."

He bends down, pressing the flat of his tongue to my other nipple, the one not covered by his hand. "Are you sure?"

"Yes," I moan. "God yes."

His teeth press into my skin as he gives one deliberate, slow suck. "Are you positive?"

"Yes," I beg. "Declan, please."

His mouth and hand leave me, his weight pressing back on his heels. I watch him through hazy eyes, like I'm fucking drunk. He rips open a condom and rolls it onto himself. My eyes can't look away as I watch his every move.

"Please, what?" he asks, his weight coming back down against me. This time, he positions himself so his dick is pressed against my center. One tiny maneuver and he could be inside me. My body is writhing.

"Fuck me," I beg.

DECLAN

A MOMENT after she murmurs the words, I'm inside her, filling her slowly, inch by delectable inch. I watch her head press back into the pillow, her eyes rolling and closing. God, she looks good like this. *I want to make her look like this every day.*

My mouth covers hers, muffling the unfiltered noises coming out. I press my body against her, rocking back and forth, dragging out of her slowly and pushing back in. Cora hooks her heels over my legs, pulling me into her. She fights against the silk tie binding her hands, and I like that too.

"Do you feel good?" I whisper, pressing my cheek to hers, my lips close to her ear.

"Yes," she moans, her one-word answer coming out strained, spurring me on. My pace increases, as do the noises coming from her.

"Please," she begs. "I want to touch you."

I reach up and tug on the fabric, letting her hands free. Because, if I'm being honest, I want her to touch me too. Her hands go to the hair at the nape of my neck, before scratching down my back. Her fingertips dig into my flesh, but it doesn't hurt. If she scars me, I'll consider it a victory.

Cora clings to me as I palm her ass. *God, she's perfection. Desire personified.* I bury myself deeper inside her, desperate to make her feel good. She feels amazing. It's taking so much concentration not to come before she does. Her thighs squeeze against me and I raise up, pulling her feet over my shoulders.

From this angle, I can look down at her, at everything. She cups her own tits, squeezing and massaging. *I'm about to lose my mind.*

I press the pad of my thumb to her clit, easing into a circular motion as she cries out. Her thighs start to shake against me and I know I've almost got her.

"I want you to feel good," I say. "I want you to come for me."

As if my words drive her over the edge, her body stiffens and shakes. "I'm coming," she whimpers.

I continue to press into her over and over again, through her orgasm. She tightens around me, the sensation driving me wild. Everything is building as I thrust again and again. I'm right on the edge when she digs her fingernails into my forearms, her teeth sunken into her bottom lip.

"Now you come for me," she says, desire dripping from each word. It's enough to send me spiraling, my body unraveling inside hers. I push into her, stilling the both of us as I come.

Then I collapse, right on top of her, careful not to squish her too hard but definitely giving her most of my weight. Her arms wrap around me tightly. We're both breathing erratically, both doing our best to regulate it. The side of my face is pressed to her chest, her heart beating so hard I can feel it against my own. We rise and fall together until our breathing syncs and calms.

She drags her fingertips lightly over my back, in the same places she'd gripped and clawed. It's enough to put me to sleep. My eyelids feel heavier, and a yawn slips out.

"Should I go? Let you sleep?" she asks, her voice uncertain. I can hear the sleep in her own voice.

"Stay with me tonight," I say, more a statement than a question.

It's quiet for a moment, and though it's only a few seconds, it feels like it stretches on for too long. It feels like she might say no.

"Okay," she says, putting my unease to rest.

I lift myself off her and step into the bathroom, disposing of the condom. I stare at the shower, considering rinsing off, but she beats me to the punch.

"Can I take a quick shower before we lie down?" she asks.

"I was literally just thinking the same thing," I say, dropping a kiss to her lips as she steps up beside me.

We shower, mostly innocently. *Mostly.* Sure, we make out a lot. Sure, there's some touching. But nothing that warrants needing a second shower. As we dry off, I'm mesmerized by the way she twists her hair to wring it out, roiling it between the towel and shaking it out. Her damp red locks fall over her shoulders as she paws the towel over her body.

She steals an elastic from my nightstand and sits at the edge of the bed, putting it into a bun on top of her head. The curve of her spine is delicate, graceful. I trace my eyes over it again and again before she slides her legs under the blanket.

"Do you snore? Talk in your sleep? Sweat? Anything I need to be warned about?" she asks, raising a teasing eyebrow at me.

I laugh but try my best to look like I'm deep in thought about her questions. "Not that I'm aware of. There is one thing, though."

"What's that? Terrible halitosis in the morning?" she jokes.

"No, of course not," I say. "I wake up totally minty fresh."

"Then what?" She giggles.

I slide my body flush against hers, hooking my leg over her hips. My one arm wraps around her while the other lazily rests on her side where I cup her left tit. "I like to cuddle like we're on a life raft and there's barely enough room for both of us. You know, like Leo and Kate except better."

Cora wiggles her ass against my crotch, and I feel myself getting hard all over again. "I can live with that." She giggles, wrapping her arm over mine.

Her bottom presses harder against me. *This is torturous.* "You're going to murder me with ass wiggles," I say.

Cora laughs, the sound echoing into the darkness of my apartment. "Oh, come on," she says. "Is that such a bad way to go?"

"Listen, if you want to sleep anytime soon, you should stop. One ass wiggle? Fine. Two ass wiggles? I can't handle it. Three? We'll need to shower again."

"Okay, okay. Truce. For now," she says, tucking her face down. Her entire body relaxes into mine. My lips rest less than an inch from her ear, and I resist the urge to kiss it.

Soon, I feel my own body relax. Having her here, tucked beside me, is soothing. Sleep is coming, the warmth spreading over me as my eyelids grow heavy.

"Declan," she says, her voice barely audible.

I hum out a response, unable to form words.

"I was wrong about you. You're good. You're so good," she says.

That's the last thing I hear before sleep takes me, the scent of peonies filling my senses as I drift off.

You're good. You're so good.

CORA

EVERY NIGHT for the past two weeks has been the same. I get off work. Declan and I either go out for dinner or stay in and cook together. Sometimes we watch a movie or Declan paints while I work on my laptop. And then we go to bed together. Sometimes we actually sleep. Sometimes, we worship each other.

I haven't slept alone since the first night in his apartment. He sleeps in my bed on the mornings I need to go to work early, because it makes more sense rather than hauling everything I need over to his place. On days I can sleep in, we're usually at his place.

When he paints, he prefers to be alone. So sometimes we spend a few hours in our separate apartments then reconvene after. It's quite the little routine. I'm telling this to Lyla via text while at work, when it hits me.

> OMG. Maybe this is what he meant by it being too easy to live so close.

LYLA

> What do you mean?

> I mean, it's only been a couple of weeks and we're already slipping into a routine like we've been together for years.

LYLA

And that's bad?

> It just feels a little fast. Don't you think?

LYLA

I don't think I can be the judge of that. After Gentry and I decided to be together, we moved in with each other. It had only been a couple of months. So...

> You're right. You're bad for this conversation.

LYLA

Does he make you happy? Are you satisfied? Content?

> Yes.

LYLA

Then stop focusing on what's right or appropriate and just feel it.

I nod at my phone, because she's right. I shouldn't be concerned about some imaginary set of rules and what's right or wrong. I'm happy. I'm sated. Nothing else matters. I try to think back to the last time I was this happy in the dating department. Before my two-year spree of bad dates, I dated a guy named Todd for a little while. Claire had set us up, Todd being a friend of Claire's husband. And he was really nice. He really was. But after a few months in, I knew it didn't feel right. The sex was...okay. Not bad. Not mind-blowing, but not bad. I mean, I had an orgasm *most* of the times we slept together. Eventually, I broke it off, eager and hopeful to find something truly magical.

Boy, was I mistaken.

Then again, the last two years of suffering have made me more than grateful for what I have now. Sure, it's still very new. Sure, it could end before it even gets that deep, but what I've been feeling recently is nothing short of worth it.

My phone buzzes again, and I absentmindedly pick it up, thinking it's Lyla again.

DECLAN

You should've played hooky today.

And lose my ability to pay bills?

DECLAN

You're the boss. Long way away from not being able to pay bills.

I have to set a good example for my employees.

DECLAN

You went out celebrating with them and I had to carry you home.

This is such a bad time to bring up such a good point.

DECLAN

Can I bring you lunch?

Yes, please.

It beats the other plan I had for lunch. The frozen dinner I left in the freezer last week will just have to wait a little longer.

DECLAN

Can I be your boyfriend?

If I had liquid in my mouth, I would have spit it out. Instead, I choke on oxygen, which is to say I choke on nothing at all. Or I'm just bad at being a human. My fingers hesitate over my phone screen for a full ten seconds. *Be Declan Walsh's girlfriend?*

Yes. Please.

I smile down at my phone like an idiot, as he responds with a GIF of a kid doing a celebration dance and tells me he'll be here in an hour with sandwiches. *He's such a weirdo.* Sure, I always knew he was a little weird, but it was hard to see behind the jerk façade I painted him in. And that's exactly what happened. He wasn't actually a jerk. It was me. I'm the one who took a single moment, expanded it in my mind, and made it out to be something it wasn't.

Part of me tries to think about what would've happened, where we'd be now had I never done that. But I can't dwell on it too long. The idea that I sabotaged something before it even had a chance to occur makes me ill. Too many *what ifs* play over in my mind.

An hour later, Declan arrives, a brown paper sack in hand and a smile plastered on his face.

"Hello, girlfriend," he says, leaning in to press a chaste kiss to my lips.

Girlfriend. Wow.

"Hello, boyfriend," I say, inhaling his scent. It hasn't gotten old. Each time, my eyes close, my lungs fill with him, and I get a little turned on.

"I think we have an audience," he whispers.

Turning my head, I see my team members jerk their eyes away from us and back onto their work. It's fake, of course. They're still honed in on us. We're not safe here.

"They're harmless, mostly," I tease.

"I'd love to meet them," he says. "I've only met Claire."

Surprised, I nod, then turn to walk him toward Sara in the corner. It's rare anyone is ever interested in anything beyond the bare minimum.

After introducing him to the whole team, and showing him around the office in general, we take our lunch to the bench in the park across the street.

Declan tells me about his upcoming show, how he's both excited and nervous. Apparently, the pieces he's been working on—the ones I haven't seen—are a little different than his other works. No one has been over to his place for him to paint either, which admittedly has made me curious. But he's insisted on keeping the whole thing under wraps.

I tell him about my projects, although they're far less interesting, even to me, than his show. He asks me to accompany him, and of course, I accept. I'll definitely be getting a new dress for that.

"Can you come somewhere with me after work?" he asks.

I do a mental checklist, wondering if I've committed to anything I can't remember, but nothing comes to mind.

"Sure," I say. "Where are we headed?"

"I need to go see my parents," he says.

Oh. Shit.

CORA

I DRESS in the most *meet the parents* appropriate outfit I can find in my closet, attempting to cover my cleavage and of course, the tattoo on the top of my foot. Not to mention I'm making every attempt not to throw up all over myself.

Declan squeezes my hand, apparently quite calm. The smile playing at the edge of his lips relaxes me. Isn't it supposed to be a lot longer before people meet parents? Isn't this reserved for like, really serious couples? The ones who are about to get engaged and shit?

I don't have time to overthink it as we pull up to the front of a two-story colonial in the suburbs. The near pristine white house has a well-manicured lawn and cute black shutters, like something right off the front of a real estate magazine.

"I know this isn't what people traditionally do," he says, holding my hand as we step up the cobblestone sidewalk, "but they're old fashioned. And ever since I mentioned you, my mother has been bugging me."

"So you're just doing this to get her off your back?" I tease.

"More or less," he teases back. He stops us just before we reach the front porch, turning to me and wrapping his arms around me. "But also maybe because I want to."

Before I can lean up and kiss his stupid grinning mouth, the front door clicks open.

"Hello," a melodic female voice says.

I hear her before I see her. *Declan's mom.* The petite woman steps out onto the porch, her pale yellow capri pants and black polka dot top hug her figure well. Her salt and pepper hair is tied back at the nape of her neck, exposing dainty gold earrings. "You must be Cora."

"Yes, ma'am," I say. "It's so nice to meet you."

"Oh, call me Judy," she says, waving her hand dismissively. "None of that *ma'am* stuff."

I nod, sticking out my hand in preparation for a shake, but she embraces me instead, wrapping her delicate arms around me with a surprisingly tight hold.

"You have a lovely home," I say, as she pulls back from her embrace.

"Thank you so much," she says.

Considering the span of time they've lived here, the house is in immaculate condition.

"And who's this out here?" a man's voice booms as he steps out of the front door and onto the porch.

It's not hard to guess. Declan's father looks just like Declan. Or I should say, Declan looks just like his father. The two are spitting images. His father's jet black hair is graying at the temples, and his laugh lines are much deeper. Crow's feet line his nearly black eyes. But there's no mistaking it.

"Cora," Declan says, pushing me toward him. "This is my father, Eben."

I put my hand out once again to shake, but this is a family of huggers for sure. The older man embraces me warmly. It's not one of those awkward hugs you feel forced into.

"It's nice to meet you, Cora," Eben says. "We've heard so much about you."

I deliver a quiet but sharp look to Declan, hoping my facial expression says, *"What the hell did you tell them?"*; but he just smiles, completely content.

"Come on in," Judy says. "Dinner is almost ready."

We step through the threshold and into a well-decorated foyer, then into the living room and open space to the kitchen.

"It smells great, Mom," Declan says. And something about the softness in his voice catches me. It's different with Judy.

"Declan, why don't you give her a tour? I'm sure she'd love to see where you grew up," Judy says, rounding the kitchen's center island to stir something in a pot.

"Come on," Declan whispers to me. "I'll show you around."

We start up the stairs to the second floor of the home, but I stop mid-climb. On the wall, all the way up, are family photos. Declan in a traditional school pose catches my eye. He doesn't have long hair here, nor the cut he has now. His hair is nearly buzzed all the way to his skin. But he wears the same bright smile.

"I think I was in eighth grade there," he says. "It was a terrible fashion year."

I laugh, my attention snagging on the next photo. It's older, black and white. Baby Declan in his mother's arms. He can't be more than six months old, all rolls and wild baby hair.

"You sure were a cute baby," I say. "What the hell happened?"

Declan laughs as he grabs me. "Oh, you got jokes, huh?" He pokes fingers into my ribs until I cry out in laughter.

At the top of the stairs, he points to various rooms, showing me the bathroom, then his parents' room, and so on, but stops in front of the door furthest from the landing.

"And my room," he says. "My mother's kept it the same since I moved out for college. It's like a time capsule in here."

His words make me eager. I'm eager to know younger Declan, to be in his space, see where he slept.

He opens the door slow and wide, allowing me to step in before him, and my eyes dart everywhere. The walls are painted a navy blue, the bright white trim of the windows popping against it. A full-size bed sits on the far wall of the room, covered in white bedding. *Teenager Declan slept there.*

"What were you like as a teenager?" I ask, stepping to his dresser and examining the items on top. I run my hand over some art awards. *Best in Show. First Place. Judge's Pick.* So many medals.

"Uh, well," he hesitates. "That's probably a question better suited for my mom, to be honest." He laughs.

"Well, what do you think you were like?" I ask, adjusting the question.

"Nerdy," he says. "And very much a loner. I took every art class I could get into, including the advanced ones. I always had paint on my clothes."

I press my eyes shut, trying to imagine him walking down the halls of some school, lockers on both walls. Little Declan, sure of himself in an environment that tried very hard to break him down and make him something else. It's a plague, really.

"I would've been your friend," I say, giving him a knowing look.

His eyebrow raises, a smirk beginning to form at the corner of his mouth. "Oh, yeah?" He takes two long strides and places his hand on the small of my back. "I wouldn't have wanted to be your friend," he whispers.

"Why not?" I protest.

"Because my teenage hormones wouldn't have let me stop thinking about kissing you," he admits, bending down and pressing his lips to mine. My arms wrap around him, pulling him to my body. Or pulling me to his. His sheer size alone makes this so.

"Well, I might have let you do that, too," I say, breathy and low. "Especially if you were this good at it. My teenage heart wouldn't have been able to resist."

A low groan comes from the back of Declan's throat as he kisses me once more. "Do you want to make out on my little teenage bed?" he asks, as he backs me up toward it.

I giggle, stepping backward to keep his pace. "Oh my god, what if your parents walk in?"

"Then they'll get a show before dinner," he growls into my ear, "and it'll make the experience more authentic."

My legs hit the edge of the bed and I sink down into the fluffy comforter. Declan lies next to me, half his body on top of me, pressing me down. Just when I think he's about to lean in and kiss me, his head pulls back a fraction, his eyes searching my face.

"You're so beautiful," he whispers, his fingertip grazing my forehead and tucking a stray strand of hair behind my ear. "Everything about you is so beautiful."

Warmth radiates over my cheeks, my throat tight with emotion. "Thank you," I manage. "You're beautiful, too." And I'm not just saying that to him as a forced returned compliment. I mean it. From his thick black hair to his coal eyes, to the dimple that forms on his left cheek when he smiles. From his large, calloused hands to his broad shoulders and the trail of hair from his chest all the way down. The man is a sculpture, something that belongs in a museum.

His lips meet mine, coaxing my mouth open immediately, his tongue exploring and teasing. His kisses are perfection. He's mastered the art of using his tongue. I could do this all day.

"Honey, dinner is ready," Judy's voice calls up the stairs, startling me, causing Declan to laugh.

"See," I say. "We're caught. No way do they think you're still showing me the house."

"Nah," he says. "We're fine."

Back downstairs, with his hand in mine, Declan leads me to the table, depositing me onto a chair across from his parents who are already seated.

"Sorry, Mom," he says. "We were making out."

Oh. My. God. He did not just say that to his mother. I squeeze his thigh under the table while simultaneously covering as much of my face as I can with my other hand.

Judy laughs. "Well, you're nothing if not honest."

What the hell is happening here?

Declan pats my thigh in return, as if to say, "*See, it's fine,*" but I still want to die. I know my face is beyond red, the heat radiating all the way down my chest. I'm probably splotchy as fuck. *Awesome.*

I concentrate instead on the meal in front of me. Roast beef and onion with roasted potatoes and carrots fill my plate. It looks delicious.

"Oh, and here," Declan says, handing me two warm slices of bread from the basket in the center of the table. He winks and I could kiss the man all over again. He doesn't judge my bread addiction.

"So, Cora," Eben says. "Declan says you own your own company?"

"Yes, sir," I say. "That's right. I have four employees at the moment. We're small but mighty."

"That's quite impressive," Judy says. "And at such a young age too."

I smile. "Thank you, yes. I started it nearly fresh out of college. Been building it ever since."

"Do you think you'll still work once you have a family?" Judy asks, and I nearly choke on my roasted potato.

"Mother," Declan warns.

I pat his leg, calming him. "Actually, no. I fully intend to work when or if I ever have children. I come from a family with two strong, independent working parents, and there's no reason to sacrifice one for the other."

I peek over at Declan's face, his smile earnest and wide. He forks a carrot in as he gives his mother a look that says, *take that, Mom!* as he swallows.

"I like her," Eben says, announcing to the whole table. "Keep her."

Judy smiles genuinely at me. Or at least it feels that way. It doesn't seem to be one of those fake, for the sake of manners smiles. She doesn't seem displeased with my answer. It's like I passed some invisible test.

The dinner moves on more quietly, with someone asking an occasional question. Declan's parents describe teenage Declan as *quiet and reserved*, much like he is now, saying only people truly close to him get to know his other side; the carefree, funny Declan.

I consider their words, realizing as the days have gone by, his demeanor around me has become more carefree, and lighter. His smile, while it's always felt genuine, is more relaxed. I can't explain it. He just feels more open. Then, it dawns on me. *Only people truly close to him see his other side.* We're close. Really close.

I suppose I already knew that in a way. Hell, we're sleeping together every night. Wow, this is like, serious. It's only been a couple of weeks, but it feels serious. Should we talk about it? Do I go with the flow until one day we're picking out China patterns and I can't remember how we got so far? *Fuck. China patterns. Calm down, Cora. Calm way the fuck down.*

We say goodnight to his parents, departing around nine. It's later than I expected us to stay, but after dinner, Judy served coffee and dessert, still talking up a storm about all things Declan. You can tell she's a big fan of her son, proud of his artistic abilities and accomplishments. I like Judy and Eben. They're good people as far as I can tell. And if how they raised Declan is any indication, they're good parents, too.

On our way back out, we pass fresh peonies in the hall. I hadn't noticed them before, likely too preoccupied with being here in general.

"Your mother likes peonies?" I ask him, once we're back in the car and settled in for the drive home.

"She's had fresh peonies in the house every week since I was a boy. Since I can remember, really," he says. "The smell of peonies is home to me."

I think back to when he told me I smell like peonies. *The smell of peonies is home to me.* I put two and two together, everything clicking into place.

That's intense.

DECLAN

MAYBE GROWN MEN don't usually bring the woman they've only just begun dating home to meet their parents. Maybe most of them wait a while, really settle into a full-blown relationship. Hell, maybe most grown men don't even do it for a solid year or more, depending on the circumstances.

But my parents are important to me. Cora is important to me. Time has very little to do with connection. We could end things tomorrow, and I'd still be resolved in the fact that she met my parents today. I've only brought home two other women in the past. One during college and the other some years ago. Both felt important to me at the time and in many ways still are. I believe past loves shape the way you love in the future, each one teaching a lesson.

"You're quiet," Cora says, as we pull onto our street.

"Just thinking, love," I say.

"About?" she asks.

I could tell her the truth. I could tell her I'm thinking about how important she feels to me already. I don't think she'd scare away because of it. "I'm thinking about time."

"Time?" she asks, clearly not following my train of thought.

"Yeah," I say. "The way it shapes people. The way there's too much of it sometimes, and other times there's not enough."

"What made you think of that?" she asks.

Putting the car in park, I turn to her. "You did." When she doesn't understand, I go on. "The way I feel like the three years we spent hating each other was both lost time but also necessary. Maybe I wouldn't have appreciated this as much if it had been easy from the beginning." I lift her hand and press a kiss to the center of her outstretched palm.

"I understand," she says. "Time is a strange thing."

We walk inside the building and I step toward the stairs, Cora's hand in mine, but she pauses. When I look back at her face, she's staring at the elevator, contemplation in her features.

"Let's take the elevator," she says.

I stumble back, bringing her closer to me. "Are you sure?"

"Yeah," she says. "I'm done not taking chances."

She presses the button for the elevator as she presses up to her toes and back down. One arm slinks around mine, her cheek resting on the outside of my shoulder. I push my free hand into my pocket and wait with her, sighing with contentment.

When the elevator door opens, she hesitates for a moment before stepping in. I follow, pressing the button for our floor and giving her hand a squeeze. I don't want to miss anything, so I turn us toward each other. Cora's eyes are pressed shut.

She presses both of her hands into mine as the elevator jostles and begins to lift us.

"Open your eyes, love," I whisper. "It's just me."

Slowly, ever so slowly, Cora cracks one eye open, then the other. She exhales slowly and the elevator dings, opening to our floor.

"That wasn't so bad," she says, quickly stepping out.

In this moment, for the simplest thing, I admire her. I appreciate her. I am in awe of her.

"No," I say. "Not bad at all."

"My apartment or yours?" she asks, our routine so ingrained at this point it's a question one of us asks each night.

"Yours," I reply. "You've got your meeting in the morning."

"Oh, right," she says. "I nearly forgot."

As she unlocks the door to her apartment, my phone buzzes against my leg in my pocket. I pull it out when I step inside, noticing I have six texts from Ryan.

I sigh, opening the chat.

> RYAN
>
> Dude, where are you?
>
> RYAN
>
> Look, I know you're working on some secret stuff, but I've got a surprise for you.

The next two are photos of him with Natasha. Her red dress plunges so deep there's no doubt things are taped into place. She's pressing her red lips to Ryan's cheek, his head thrown back in a fit of laughter. Good for them.

> RYAN
>
> Your surprise will be there Thursday at 1PM.
>
> RYAN
>
> Make sure you're there to sign for it. ;)

His winky face is unsettling. He only uses them when he's up to something. His surprise probably isn't even something I want, if history has taught me anything. Ryan is terrible at gifts.

"Something wrong?" Cora asks, filling a glass of water from the tap.

"No," I say. "Nothing at all. It's just Ryan. Let's go to bed."

I slip out of my boots where Cora left her wedges and we walk barefoot to the bedroom. I never bother bringing clothes, opting to sleep in boxers or nothing; in the mornings, I just slide my pants back on to walk across the hall. Although I do have a toothbrush here. Cora got me one after the third time I stayed over and had been carrying mine back and forth.

At my place, she has a toothbrush, a hairbrush, some lounge clothes, and a book she's reading. It sits on the nightstand on the side of the bed she sleeps on. Sometimes, at night, she'll sit and read while I paint in the other room. Or I'll sit up beside her in bed and sketch. I have an immense appreciation for the little things. Those kinds of moments are what make up a lifetime.

Now, we slip beneath her blanket—my arm under her head, her leg thrown over my hips. She runs her hand over my chest, settling into place. My fingertips graze the bare skin of her thigh as I exhale, completely immersed in comfort. But I feel restless. Perhaps there's too much on my mind.

"You okay?" Cora asks, not sounding very tired herself.

"A little more awake than I'd prefer," I say.

Cora presses her leg down, sinking her knee into the mattress and sitting up, straddling me. "I have something for that," she whispers, bearing down against me.

She leans down, kissing my neck, trailing up to my mouth. Her tongue is greedy, taking from me, and I let her. As far as I'm concerned, she can have anything she wants.

Her hand slides down, gripping my dick through the thin fabric of my shorts, causing me to groan. At some point, and ever so slyly, she removed her panties. Her black silk nightgown is pushed up, bunched over her hips as she presses down on me over and over again.

"God," I breathe. "You feel so good."

She sits up, rolling her hips around and around, the movement driving me wild. I tug at the edges of her gown, silently begging her to take it off. She responds in kind, pulling the garment up and over her head, her tits falling free. I palm her nipple, feeling myself harden beneath her.

Small, satisfied moans escape her lips as she rocks back and forth against me. I'm not even inside her yet and I could probably come like this, with her sliding against me over and over again.

She reaches for a condom on the nightstand, dipping one hand into the elastic of my shorts and pulling me out, stroking me. I grunt, my head flying back against the pillow, and I reach for her hands.

"Do you like that?" she asks, her voice low and sultry.

"Yes," I growl. "God yes."

She skillfully rolls the condom onto me moments before sinking herself down on top of me. Her back arches as I fill her, her thighs pressing into my sides. I steady her—one hand on her stomach, just below her tits; the other on her hip, pushing her back and forth. I glide into her again and again.

"There you go, love," I whisper, as she digs her fingertips into the flesh of my chest.

I can already feel myself building, her exquisite motions driving me to the edge. Her hand travels up my chest, settling at the base of my throat. I never would've pegged her for someone who likes to take control but I've learned my lesson. She's incredible at leading. And I'll happily follow.

"I'm gonna come," she whispers, barely able to get the words out between gasps and moans.

I buck up against her, burying myself deep inside her. She runs her fingers over the outside of her entrance as she rolls her hips over me. *There's nothing more satisfying than this*, I think, as I watch her unravel on top of me. Her body stiffens then relaxes, and I feel the final wave of my own orgasm take me. She stills, bearing down on me one final time, before collapsing against my chest. We're panting together, tangled up inside each other, and it's heaven. My version of heaven, anyway.

A few moments later, she slowly lifts herself up and off me, the cool air hitting my chest where she just was. The sudden loss of her warmth makes me reach for her, desperate to have her back.

After cleaning up, we lie back down, falling right back into our positions like before. I pull her to my side, her leg wrapping over me immediately, my head resting against the top of hers. I could spend a lifetime in this position alone.

Then, it comes rushing in; a wave of so many emotions flooding me. But the one I feel most, the one leading the charge, the one filling me with panic and excitement, is also the one that scares the shit out of me.

I'm falling in love with Cora Reed, my beautiful redheaded spitfire neighbor, who's spent the last three years hating me. I'm falling in love with her, and there's not a goddamn thing I can do about it.

CORA

"LET'S go away for the weekend," I say.

Declan looks up from his boots, slipping one on as he studies my face. "This weekend?" he asks.

"Yeah," I say. "It'll be fun. Actually, let's leave Thursday? I can take off work Friday."

"Where are we going?" he asks.

"I don't know, somewhere secluded. Outside the city," I suggest.

After slipping his second boot on, he nods, walking toward me. "Okay, sounds like a plan. You find the place, I'll pack the car."

"Deal," I say. Truth be told, I already have a place in mind. I found it last week while I was distracting myself at work. There's a quaint little Airbnb cabin right outside Boston, that overlooks a lake. The photos were amazing. I don't even want to wait two more days to go, but I will.

Declan kisses me goodbye, walking to his apartment as I make my way to the elevator. That's right, I take the fucking elevator now. I'm all grown up. I sip the coffee he made for me from my travel mug as I hurry to work, eager to catch up on several tasks and book the cabin. The only way I can ensure I'll be ready to take Friday off is if I can really focus these next two days and work ahead of schedule. It shouldn't be a problem, but as the boss, it all falls on me if something slips through the cracks. So I have to be diligent and focused.

Unfortunately, I don't have time to even sit down before the first fire of the day presents itself. Claire rushes me as soon as I walk in.

"Oh my god, it's awful," she says. "We've got a major problem."

I refuse to panic, picking up the pace to my desk. "Tell me what happened," I say, setting my mug down and sliding out of my jacket. I throw it over the back of my chair and boot up my computer.

"The samples we ordered from the vendor to send to Mr. Briggs are all wrong," she shrieks. Mr. Briggs is the point man on the brand-new client account we just obtained, so delivering him the wrong samples would clearly be a bad first impression.

"Wrong how?" I exclaim.

"They're the wrong color and size," Sara interjects, stepping around the corner with one of the brochures in her hand. And she's right.

"Okay, let's get on the phone with the vendor and tell them to replace them," I say. "And tell them we want them expedited at no extra cost, since I assume this is their fuckup."

"It is," Claire says. "I've been on the phone with them all day. They can't expedite a new batch until Monday and these are due to Mr. Briggs by Friday. We can't be late on our first deadline with him."

She's right, too. That doesn't exactly scream *professional* and I refuse to even call him and explain the situation. Though I'm sure he'd be understanding, I won't even broach the topic. This is not the way we operate.

"Sara," I turn in her direction as she joins the conversation, "get on the phone with every vendor we work with and explain the situation to see if we can get the right samples here by Thursday to deliver on Friday," I say. "Claire, get back on the phone with the original vendor. Tell them Monday is unacceptable and that we need another vendor to do it this time. And tell them we want a refund for this order."

Both women nod along, agreeing with the plan for a path forward. Getting this resolved today is the key to my weekend plans, or rather, making sure I still have weekend plans. I will not disappoint a client or ruin my own damn weekend over a vendor screwup.

The two women depart as I sink down into my chair for the first time, inhaling deeply. It's times like this I wish I had a healthy habit like meditation. I'm sure that shit helps people. I've even tried it a few times, but I just end up staring blankly as thoughts race through my mind and I don't think that's the point of the exercise. So I gave up after three sessions.

My inbox shows sixty-three new emails since yesterday. *Sixty-three.* After contemplating a quick cry in the bathroom, I calm myself, determined to focus. Of course, that only lasts two emails in, and then my phone buzzes, alerting me of a text.

> DECLAN
> I miss you already.

My stupid ass grins down at my phone like I just won the lottery. In some ways, maybe I have. Hey, I suffered through nearly sixty shitty dates to get here. I'm not going to deprive myself of the simple joys in having a boyfriend. *Boyfriend. Wow.* The label still shocks me.

> I miss you too. But you're distracting me.

> DECLAN
> From?

> Work. If I want to take off Friday, I have to be a grownup.

> DECLAN
> You're right. I'll leave you alone. Got packing to do anyway.

> DECLAN
> But there's something first.

> What?

> DECLAN
> Any minute now.

The office door opens, catching my attention. A younger man— maybe college age—steps inside, flowers in hand.

"Delivery for Cora Reed?" he calls out to the room.

Setting my phone down, I stand and walk over to him, signing a screen and taking the vase from him. Fresh pink peonies sit inside a clear glass vase, a small white card tied to the base with black ribbon.

Back at my desk, I place the flowers in the corner, untying the delicate ribbon and pulling the card off.

Hope you have a great day,
even if it isn't spent lying next to me.
Love, Declan

I'm smiling like an idiot again, so wide I'm convinced I might chap my lips if I don't stop. He's too much. And he used the word *love*.

Love. Whoa.

I shoot him a quick thank you text, just as Claire walks back over.

"Are these from the boyfriend?" she asks, wagging her eyebrows. She calls him *the boyfriend* now. That's his official title here in the office.

I roll my eyes at her. Hearing her say the word sounds so insane to me. "Yes," I say, pressing my lips together to contain my stupid smile.

"Things are getting pretty serious, huh?" she asks.

"We're going away this weekend," I say. "I won't be here Friday."

"Oh my god," she says. "It's happening. Finally."

"What's happening?" I look at her, confused.

"You having a life outside this place," she says, slapping my shoulder and retreating to her own desk.

I laugh for a moment, realizing she's right. Wow, she's been right a lot today. I haven't had much of a life outside of here. Going on shitty dates can't possibly count. I was a little livelier when Lyla lived here, as she constantly encouraged me to adventure. But since she's been gone, I've settled into a routine of work and reruns of FRIENDS, with an occasional disaster date. But I deserve this. *This is your reward for suffering through that,* I remind myself.

The rest of the day drones on, so busy I barely have time to eat lunch. I survive on caffeine and a strong will to be hulled up in a secluded cabin with Declan all weekend. I do manage to steal away a couple of minutes to book said cabin, but aside from that, it's all business. I haven't even gotten a chance to text Declan after conveying my thanks for the flowers.

But by the end of the day, Sara's found a new vendor to deliver the samples, the original vendor agrees to a refund, and I'm only slightly behind on the other tasks I need to accomplish. All in all, I can't complain too much.

I pack up my work bag, slipping my laptop inside and grabbing my travel mug. The ladies walk by, each one saying bye as they leave. I'm almost always the last person to leave. When the office empties, I shut off a few remaining lights and head for the door, stopping in my tracks at the sight of Declan standing by the front desk.

"What are you doing here?" I ask, stepping toward him with renewed energy.

"I thought I could walk you home," he says. "Carry your bag for you. Seems like you had a rough day."

God, he's sweet.

"I did," I say, my shoulders slumping, my bag sliding down. He reaches for it, slinging it over his shoulder as he leans down to kiss me. Usually, his kisses in these moments are brief, a chaste embrace. But this one is different, deeper, causing me to stumble for a moment.

My eyes meet his, and I see nothing but desire. A hunger brews like a storm in the darkest parts of his irises, awakening my own need. His shoulder slumps, my bag gently sliding down onto the floor next to him. He grabs both sides of my face, licking the seam of my mouth as I open it to him.

My hands explore the expanse of his chest before slipping into his jacket and around his back. Declan pulls back from the kiss for a moment, stepping back and locking the front office door. *Oh my.* I'm not going to lie, I've had fantasies about this. Sure, not with Declan, but in general. Full scenes of fooling around in my office have played out in my mind. Sure, usually it was Chris Evans as Captain America, but it was just like this. Only, this is better.

Returning to my embrace, he breathes hot air over my ear and down my neck.

"Let me make love to you," he says. "Right here. I don't want to wait."

My mouth hangs open, a fit of nerves crawling up my spine. The excitement of it, the naughtiness, makes me hot all over.

Declan takes off his jacket, letting it fall next to my bag, then lifts me off the ground and wraps my legs around his hips. He carries me all the way into the conference room, setting me down on the edge of the long table.

It's a frenzy now as he claws at the buttons of his shirt, untucking it from his pants. I unbutton my own silk blouse, the white lace bra underneath not leaving much to the imagination. He bends to kiss the tops of my breasts as his pants fall to his ankles.

I unbutton my pants, my bare bottom hitting the cold wooden desk beneath me and I blush. I'm going to have to sit here during conferences from now on.

"Fuck," he says. "Wait."

"What's wrong?" I ask, pressing kisses down his chest.

"I didn't bring a condom. I got carried away when I saw you. I didn't plan this out," he says apologetically.

I bite into my bottom lip, contemplating for only a moment. "It's okay," I say. "I'm on birth control." Declan's eyes search mine, clearly hesitant. "It's okay. I want you."

"Are you sure?" he asks.

I nod, desperate for his touch. His mouth lands back on mine as my legs part for him. He rubs himself against my opening, the skin on skin friction so delicious, I can hardly handle the sensation. He pushes against me, teasing, giving me just the tip of himself. My back arches, curving my hips toward him, my body in need of him.

Declan lays me back onto the table, spreading me wider and pulling my ass all the way to the edge of the table. He slides over my sensitive skin, causing me to moan. My voice echoes against the walls of the conference room, and I press my hand over my own mouth to quiet the noise.

Finally, and ever so slowly, he pushes all the way into me, letting me feel every inch, every sensation he's causing, until I'm full. His thumbs dig into my hips as he slides in and out, throwing his head back, his face toward the ceiling.

I shut my eyes, concentrating on the sensations rippling through my body again and again. *This man. This. Man.* He does things to me. Touching me or not, I can't get enough of him. I'm getting fucked on my conference room table for Christ's sake. *What did he ask though? To make love.* There's that word again.

"Cora," he says through gritted teeth. "Cora, I—"

I pull him down to me, interrupting him, pressing his mouth to mine. I don't want to hear what he's about to say. I can't. Not right now. I just want to feel this with him.

My orgasm washes over me, the intensity almost more than I can handle. His own rips through him a few seconds later, overlapping with mine. I look up at him, watching the features of his face tighten and relax just before he collapses over me, his face cradled between my breasts, his breath tickling the sensitive skin of my nipple. I pant and shake, pant some more.

Finally, after a few delicious minutes of simply living in the feeling, he lifts up, sitting me up with him. We're quiet as we dress, not in a tense way. It feels content and relaxed, calm even.

As we leave, he slings my bag back over his shoulder while I lock up. Walking home hand in hand, we stop to grab quick sandwiches to go, and though I offer to carry them since he already has my work bag, he insists.

"Your place again?" he asks, and I simply nod.

"Yes, but at the end of the day tomorrow, we get to leave the city," I say excitedly. "I can't wait."

"I packed and went shopping for a few things, assuming we need to pack our own food?" he says.

I nod. "Yes, perfect. And if you haven't already, bring stuff for French toast, pretty please."

Declan chuckles. "It just so happens I know you and I definitely didn't leave that off the menu."

Ugh. Maybe the perfect man does exist. Maybe he's been hiding under my nose all along. "Did you get any painting done today?" I ask, as we step into the lobby of our building.

Declan shakes his head almost in a circular motion, like he can't decide if he wants to say yes or no. "Not as much as I would've liked."

I squeeze his hand, knowing how hard he takes it when he doesn't have quite as productive of a day as he would have liked.

"I'm sure you can get some in before we leave tomorrow," I say. "Are you going to be okay while we're gone?"

"I'm going to bring my sketchpad just in case," he says. "That way I can at least plan things out if the mood strikes."

Inside my apartment, we scarf our sandwiches down then get in the shower together. My shower is one of my favorite things about this place. It's glass on all sides, tiled, and huge. We have plenty of space, which we take advantage of, fooling around and kissing, taking our time.

We brush our teeth next and crawl into bed, both of us unburdening the weight of the day. Sometime in the night, Declan stirs, and we make slow, sleepy love, falling back to sleep again still tangled up in each other.

Right before the darkness takes over, for a split second, I let the happiness warm me, and I think to myself, *I love this man.*

DECLAN

AFTER CORA LEAVES this morning for work, I head out to do the last bit of shopping needed for our trip. Some of the food requires a cooler, which I don't have. I also want to pick up a few surprises for her, like her favorite wine.

I arrive at my apartment just past noon, and I'm barely through the door when Ryan calls.

"You're home, right?" he asks from the other end of the receiver.

"Yeah, why?" I ask.

"Your surprise is on the way, remember?" he says.

No, I didn't remember. I'd forgotten all about it actually. "What is it?"

"Inspiration, my friend. Inspiration," he says, laughing as he hangs up.

God, I don't like the sound of that.

I make quick work of the stuff I bought, shoving it into my fridge in no particular order, since I'll be packing the cooler in a little while. I finish filling my duffel with the clothes and toiletries I'll need, then there's a knock at my door.

When I pull it open, I expect to find a delivery man of some sort, holding a package and something for me to sign. But that's not the case. Not at all. Instead, Natasha greets me, a playful smile on her face. I think she's trying to be seductive, but I wouldn't know. I'm pretty sure you can only sense that in people you're actually attracted to.

"Hey," she says. "You ready?"

"Ready for what?" I ask, clearly left out of a major plan.

"Oh, Ryan said this is when I could come over to start my painting," she says, stepping past me into my apartment.

By all means, come on in.

"Oh, um," is all I can manage. It's obvious to me Ryan planned this, purposely left me out of it, and told this woman I knew. Judging by the look on her face, she's got every intention of staying until that painting is started. *Fuck.*

"I'll be with you in just a moment," I say, stepping into my bedroom.

> What the fuck?

RYAN
> Great, right?

> I don't want to do this.

RYAN
> Dude, she's paying twice your rate for a custom painting.

> I don't care if she's paying in gold coins from a treasure chest, I told you I didn't want to at the party.

RYAN
> Look, she's there now. You might as well go with it.

I shove my phone back into my pocket and step back into the living room. *Oh, Christ.* Natasha has removed her long coat, her shirt, and her pants, leaving only the smallest set of lingerie I've ever seen. There's more string than actual material. Her nipples are popping out of the center of what I assume is supposed to be a bra; but it just looks like two cups, a shred of lace, and like someone forgot to make the rest of it.

"Is this okay?" she asks, seating herself extremely provocatively on a chair I have in front of my easel.

Goddamn it, Ryan.

"Uh, yeah," I say. "Sure." Truth be told, I don't give a fuck how she sits, what she wears. I just want this over with. I'll paint her in a clown suit if it means she'll leave.

I grab a bottle of water from the fridge, take a drink, and then pull my phone back out. After I've had a couple of sips, I set both the water and my phone down on the counter, then head toward my stool. I can't paint with my phone in my pocket and I can't leave it out near the paints. I've gone through three phones in two years because paint caked into the speakers.

I mix a few colors onto the palette and grab a fresh canvas, setting the one I was working on aside. Then I stare at Natasha for a few minutes. God, she's boring. Bleach blonde hair cascades over her shoulders and nearly covers her fake tits. And they're definitely fake. There's not a lick of genuine bounce to them. I'm pretty sure she's gotten filler in half her face, too. Everything is very plastic-like. I detect no body hair, with the exception of eyebrows. Though, they look mostly drawn on. Truth be told, I feel really shallow assessing her like this. She's fine, I guess. I'm sure many men find her attractive and interesting. I'm just not one of them. And I'm sure the things she's done to her body have boosted her confidence, which is all that matters.

"So," she says, "was that your girlfriend at the party the other night?"

"Yes," I say without a moment's hesitation.

"Are you guys serious?" she asks.

Her tone implies she couldn't care less, but I still hesitate on this one. Because I don't know. I feel like we are. I like to think things are moving in that direction. I mean, going away for a weekend, that's something serious couples do, right? But we haven't exactly talked about it, and I don't like to be presumptuous.

"I think so," I say honestly.

"You think so?" she asks. "You don't sound so sure."

Instead of answering her question, I focus on the canvas in front of me, letting silence take over. I don't owe her any information about my personal life. One thing I know for sure is Cora isn't going to be happy about this. She made it pretty clear she didn't like her, and I said the same. So I doubt her being in my apartment, as nude as she is, is going to sit well. I'd prefer to tell her about this, rather than her show up and see it with her own two eyes.

It's not that I'm trying to hide anything; I have nothing to hide. I'm not even remotely into Natasha. That would be the same whether Cora was in my life or not.

The paint on the canvas starts to take shape, the curves of her petite form beginning to fill out. I start to flesh out the details of her face next, pausing to turn and check the clock on my shelf. Maybe another hour of this and I can send her on her way. I'll tell her to come back next week for the second session.

Another couple of hours and I'll be doing what I really want to do. Holding Cora. Kissing Cora. Looking at Cora. All things Cora.

What's another hour of this hell when that's my prize?

CORA

WORK HAS BEEN HELL. From the moment I walked in until now, it hasn't let up. And I'm leaving an hour early, even if I have to murder someone to do it. But there's been a lot of great successes today too. The new samples came in and they look amazing. Even better than I expected, to be honest. Claire is delivering them to the client tomorrow morning, which I don't need to worry about. I've been fielding calls and emails all day from potential new clients. Apparently, news travels fast and Mr. Briggs is a talker, telling all his corporate friends how impressed he was with our presentation. We have three meet and greets next week alone to discuss various projects with new companies.

It's exciting. And if next week goes well, I'll need to look into bringing on an additional team member. It's the kind of growth I've been hoping would continue.

I check my phone again. I've texted Declan three times today, and no response. *Strange.* He always answers. Even if it's a little delayed because he's painting, he always answers eventually. *He's probably just busy packing, finalizing things,* I remind myself.

I refocus my attention on the color samples in Sara's hand in front of me. She needs me to pick a scheme for another client's campaign.

"You know what?" I say. "I trust you. You give it a run and we'll see how you do." I pat her on the shoulder, confident in her abilities. At some point, I have to start passing decisions down. Otherwise what's the point of having employees?

"Really?" she chirps, eager at the chance to make more decisions.

Hell, she's the point person on this campaign, she should be making most of the decisions and only roping me in when she's stuck. Of course, I get the final say, but we're not there yet.

Forty-five minutes later, I'm finally walking out the door. Declan still hasn't texted me back, but no matter. I'll see him in a few minutes.

"Have fun," the ladies yell to me from their desks.

I feel bad leaving them when we're so busy, but they all insisted I deserve the break. I can't even remember the last time I took any sort of vacation. Last year, I got the flu and couldn't go in all week and it drove me insane. I kept checking my work emails until Claire came and took my laptop. She collected it while wearing a mask and gloves, wrapping it in plastic and vowing to disinfect it and return it when I was back to a healthy state. God bless her. I slept for five days.

I make a quick stop on my way home, picking up this pink silk nightgown I've seen in a window every day on my walk. It's short, falling well above the knees, with lace edges and thin straps. The back dips all the way down, showing off your whole spine. I think it's a perfect surprise for the cabin.

I can't wait to see the look on Declan's face when I wear it.

I make easy work of packing, having snuck into my apartment as quietly as I could. I didn't want Declan to know I got off early, in hopes of surprising him when I knock on his door, completely ready to go and earlier than he expects.

I take one last look around my bedroom, stuffing my charger cords into the side of my bag. After peering down at my packed clothes one more time, I'm fairly certain I got everything I need. Locking the door to my apartment, I turn to see Declan's door opening and a smile spreads over my face for a split second before falling.

Because Declan isn't the one walking out of his door.

Natasha steps out into the hallway, covering her bare shoulders with her coat, a shirt in hand. Declan steps out behind her a second later, immediately registering my presence.

Acting as if she doesn't see me at all, Natasha turns and plants a kiss on Declan's cheek, thanking him for the afternoon. She steps past me, excusing herself as she edges around my duffel bag next to my feet.

Declan stands in his doorway, his hands inside his pockets. "I can explain," he says.

"Is this what you do all day while I'm at work?" I say.

"What?" he asks, his brows furrowing.

"Pretending you're having trouble painting and having Natasha over? Of all people?" I snap.

"This is the first time she's ever been over," he says.

"Is this why you won't let me see any of your new work? Is it of her?" I ask, my voice at a decibel I don't like.

"No." He sighs.

"I thought you didn't like her?" I say. "Or is that what all men say? Do they just lie?"

"Cora," he says. His voice is calm, which only pisses me off even more. "Ryan sent her here for the painting she wanted. I didn't know."

"I wish I could believe you," I snap. "But maybe this whole thing has been a lie. Maybe you do just sleep with all the women you paint."

"Are you serious right now?" he says. "We're back to this? Why is it so easy for you to think I'm a piece of shit? Has nothing I've done these past weeks made you see? You said you trusted me. You said you didn't hate me anymore. Clearly those were all lies."

I turn back to my door, putting my back to him and then slamming my key in the lock. "This was a mistake. I knew this was a mistake."

"Fine," he blurts. "Go ahead. Run away. It's easier for you to do that then put your trust in someone. I can see that now."

I hear the sound of him retreating into his apartment and then slamming the door as I get mine open. I throw my bag inside, slamming my own door. This whole thing was a terrible idea. *God, I'm really going to have to fucking move now.*

I topple to the floor as tears start to stream down my cheeks. *Stupid. This was stupid.*

God, you're so stupid.

My duffel drags behind me, the zippers making a scratching sound as I pull it to my bedroom and dump it out all over the floor. The pink silk nightgown falls last, floating down on top of the pile and taunting me. Ignoring it, I slip my shoes off and crawl into bed, not bothering to change, clean up, or even plug my phone in. The blankets are promptly pulled all the way up over my head, and this is where I'll stay until I have to go back to work on Monday.

That's also when I'll start looking for a new place to live. Maybe it's time to finally buy a place.

Until then, I'll cry all this out and avoid Declan like the plague.

DECLAN

THREE WEEKS AGO, Cora broke my heart in the hallway of our apartment building. Three weeks ago, she showed me that no matter what I do, she'll still have the same false opinion of me, driven by her own past issues. I've tried four times to get her to listen to me, to come over and let me show her I'm not lying. But she won't have any of it. She barely looks at me, and every time she does, her eyes are red rimmed and glossy, like she's been crying. I hate it all so much.

Of course, all this does is break my heart even more. At this point it's absolutely shattered. Do you know what artists with broken hearts do? They hurl themselves into their work, and they don't look back. They paint, write, sculpt all that pain into something tangible, touchable. Which is exactly what I've done since then.

I look at the canvas in front of me. It's the most recent piece I've completed. Delicate lines and monochrome shades of pink and lavender fill the entire canvas. The show I have tomorrow will be unlike anything I've done before. All the original pieces I've been working on will be picked up later today, including this one.

The installation team and I will meet first thing in the morning for setup. Unlike my last show, no other artists are being featured. This one is at a smaller gallery, and it's just me. Although *smaller* doesn't mean worse. Sure, there's less space, but that means the gallery is that much more selective about who they feature. I've been in negotiations with them for months about a solo show. Their one condition was that it had to be all new work, to which I agreed.

I had my concerns, considering I was struggling at the time to find new inspiration. Then Cora happened, completely changing that for me. As I stand back and look at the collection of pieces now, I want to burn them. They're every reminder I don't need right now.

The phone rings, distracting me from my thoughts. I run to it, praying it's Cora, but I'm let down.

"Hello?" I say, into the receiver, the inflection in my voice nearly gone.

"Jesus, man, why do you sound so sad?" Ryan asks.

"Because I am sad," I say.

"Listen, why don't you come out with me and Natasha. She has no hard feelings about you not finishing the painting. And she's got some great friends you can meet," he says.

Ryan thinks his sole job in life is to get me to party when I'm down. He doesn't understand the weight of brokenness.

"No thanks," I say, tone still flat. "I'll pass." What I don't say is that I'll pass on that forever, every time, until the end of time. Natasha couldn't possibly have any friend I'd be interested in socializing with. Not to mention, I'm not dating or even thinking about dating for a long time. Things will be good and dusty before I try that again.

We hang up after I tell him I'll see him tomorrow and I turn back to my studio space, which is actually just most of my living room. I make decent money now. Perhaps I should get a bigger place with a separate real studio now. I survey the paint everywhere and decide it's time. Besides, I don't think I can live across from Cora anymore. It'll be good for me to get some distance. It's been a long time coming, really.

After I sit on my stool, I decide there's one more painting I need to do. I grab one of the smaller size canvasses I have and press my eyes shut. This one is part memory, part imagination. Something I've never really painted before. My eyes open and skim over the white, drawing imaginary lines I'll soon make with brushstrokes.

One might say the sudden inspiration that's come over me is worth the sadness I'm enduring. One might even say I should be grateful for it. But I don't like the people who'd say that. Ryan is one of them.

With each passing day, I contemplate our friendship and business partnership more and more. It seems as time goes on, we grow further and further in opposite directions. What once worked, I'm not sure does anymore. After this show, I'll have to do some serious evaluating.

I press my brush to the canvas, twisting and pushing the paint around until it begins to form vague outlines of my goal. I reach for the stereo remote, flipping on music without a care as to what it is. I just need noise, a tempo, something to move the paint to.

This might be the last time I ever create something in this apartment. So I want it to be something I can be proud of.

CORA

IF SOMEONE HAD ASKED me a few months ago, I'd have said three weeks was nothing. A short amount of time. A blip on the timeline. But now? Three weeks without Declan, without his laugh or kiss or touch, is an eternity.

I cried myself to sleep every night the first week. The second week, he tried talking to me a few times and I ignored him in true Cora fashion, switching back to the stairs and changing up what night I did laundry, just to avoid him.

> **LYLA**
> Why don't you just talk to him? I know you want to.

> No I don't.

> **LYLA**
> Lie to yourself all you want, but don't lie to me.

> There's nothing to say.

> **LYLA**
> So you think he had sex with this Natasha woman?

Yes.

Well, no. Maybe he didn't. I don't know. That's the whole point.

LYLA

You sound insane.

You don't understand.

I put my phone back down on my desk and look up at the vase holding what are now very dead peonies. I haven't been able to bring myself to throw them out. All the water has evaporated from the vase, and the drying flowers are beginning to crumble—much like my life—all over my desk.

"Honey, we need to talk," Claire says. Her hand is on her hip and she has her *I'm not playing any games* look plastered over her face.

"About what?" I ask, thinking something is wrong with her current project.

"About you, you sad sack," she says.

"I'm fine," I say, turning my attention back to my computer screen.

"The hell you are," she says. "You're a lump on a log. This is worse than any bad date you've had in the past."

"So?" I say, sinking deeper into my chair.

"So, why don't you just talk to him?" she asks, leaning over my desk. "I mean look at this." Claire points to the dead flowers, apparently proof that I'm beyond insane for not speaking to him.

"I don't want to," I say.

"You know," she says, "I thought you'd say that. So I give up. But you're coming somewhere with me tomorrow night, and you don't get to say no. It's the price you get to pay for how miserable you look."

"I don't feel like socializing," I say, clicking down harder on my mouse.

"I don't care. I'll be at your place at seven to get you," she says. "Oh, and don't dress like you feel."

Ugh. Friends are the worst. Sure, Claire has good intentions. Distract me, cheer me up, try to help me out of the slump. But I don't really want to get out of it. I want to live in the slump for a while. Wallow in it like a pig in mud. I'm good at making homes out of sadness. I've been doing it all my life.

I check my email; the one sitting at the top, I don't want to open. It's from the owner of the cabin we were supposed to go to, kindly offering—once again—to reschedule. They had to keep my deposit and felt bad after I explained the situation. The elderly woman offered to let me move dates and come for a vacation on my own if I wanted to. Her kindness made me cry too.

I told her I'd think about it, not wanting to give it any more thought. Now she's checking back in with me, saying the offer's still good. Maybe getting away by myself would be good for me. Maybe a little *me time* is exactly what I need.

Emailing her back, I accept, requesting two weekends from now if it's free, before throwing myself back into my work.

I'll get over this. I always get over it. It doesn't matter how bad the date is, how shitty the breakup is, people always move on. It's life. Heartbreak is inevitable.

Time will make it better.

Right now, focusing on myself is exactly what I need to do.

I grab the stack of mail from my mailbox in the lobby, each move I make more quiet than the last. Any moment now, Declan could arrive home. Or hop out of the elevator as he's leaving. Or hear me and come running out of his apartment. The possibilities are endless. Which is why I've taken to mastering ninja-quiet skills when coming home and leaving.

Halfway up the stairs, I hear music coming from his place. There's no way he'll hear me with it at that volume. It's not so loud it would bother our neighbors, but it's definitely loud enough to drown out the sound of me going into my apartment.

The music itself sounds sad; the melody full of melancholy, the lyrics full of regret. I can certainly relate to his music at the very least. Not that I understand why he'd be so sad.

I retreat into my apartment, keeping my eyes on his door the whole time. I'm not sure why. It's not like I have a backup plan or escape route if he were to come out. I would just haul ass getting my door open and pray I'd make it.

I check my phone again before bed, but there's nothing I need to bother with. Declan gave up trying to text me days ago, but I haven't had the strength to delete those either. His name sits a few down from the top. I click on the chat, scrolling back through everything he sent me.

> DECLAN
>
> Please hear me out.
>
> After everything, I think I deserve that much.
>
> I don't understand why you're sabotaging us.
>
> Fine. It's clear you're not interested in fixing this.
>
> I can't believe this is over.
>
> Please talk to me.
>
> I'll be here if you want to talk.

Clicking out of the chat, I swipe left, revealing the red trash can. One click and it can all be gone. I swipe back, unable to do it. *Damn it, Lyla.* Opening the chat back up, I scroll further up.

> DECLAN
>
> Can I be your boyfriend?

I stare at the older text for a full few minutes, tears beginning to brim my eyes yet again. I should be used to it by now. But every time I cry, I'm surprised and angry.

Exiting the chat once more, I click on Lyla's messages. Two unread from earlier.

> LYLA
>
> Just think about it.
>
> Love is worth taking a chance.

I cry myself to sleep, phone clutched to my chest, a pang of doubt in my heart.

CORA

CLAIRE IS at my apartment at seven on the dot, just like I knew she would be. I'm not sure she's ever been late for anything in her entire life; certainly not since I've known her. My little nap earlier didn't last long, but I needed it.

I swing open the door, self-conscious about the bags under my eyes.

"Oh my god, what are you wearing?" she asks.

My eyes follow hers down to where she's looking. Apparently jeans and the T-shirt I have on aren't going to cut it for where we're going. It's not like I knew; she wouldn't tell me anything about it.

"Let's get you changed," she says, as I take in what she's wearing. Her sleeveless dress falls just below her knee, but she's thrown a leather jacket over it, making the whole thing look a bit more edgy and cool.

"How about you just pick," I say. "I don't have the energy."

Claire shrugs, unperturbed by my request. "Sure thing," she says, as she begins digging through my closet. She pulls out my leather pants and a light pink top to match. The off-the-shoulder blouse is flowy, reminding me of the nightgown that's gone unworn since I dumped it back out of my bag.

"Snap out of it," she says. "We're going to be late."

Shaking the depressing thoughts from my head, I make quick work of changing and then Claire twists my hair back into a loose bun, low on my neck. She throws two silver chains of varying size over my head and stands back, admiring her rushed masterpiece.

"Will this work?" I ask, before sliding into my black wedges.

"Oh, yes," she says. "This is perfect."

Claire hurries me out the door, barely letting me grab my clutch and keys.

"Will you slow down?" I say. "I'm going to sprain an ankle going this fast down the stairs."

"Well, if you'd take the damn elevator like a normal person, you wouldn't be in danger, you old bat," she says.

Claire shoves me into the Uber waiting for us on the street, and we're off. To where, I have no idea, but it's clearly important to her.

"Can you at least tell me if I'm going to know anyone where we're going?" I ask, straightening out my top, which rumpled in the scurrying.

She adjusts a compact in front of her face, checking her eye makeup. "Maybe one or two."

Great. Out all night at an event where I may or may not know someone, when what I really want to do is sit at home and watch Rachel kiss Ross for the first time and cry.

Who knows how many minutes later, Claire signals to the driver to let us out.

"But this isn't your destination," he protests.

"It's right around the corner, we can walk from here," she reassures him.

Why isn't she letting him pull up to the place? That's weird.

She opens the door, jumping out of the car onto the sidewalk like there's a fire in here, and all but pulls my arm out of its socket to get me out.

"Oh my god," I say. "Calm down. No one's on fire."

We take a few paces toward the corner but she stops abruptly in front of me, causing me to nearly trip as I rock back onto my heels. "Christ," I exclaim. "Are you on drugs?"

"Listen," she says, spinning around to face me. "You're going to be mad for like a few minutes once you realize what's going on. And you're smart, so that's pretty much going to happen as soon as we make it around this corner. But I need you to keep an open mind and just go with it, okay?"

My eyes narrow at her, fear and skepticism circling my brain. *What has she done?* Exhaling louder than necessary, I reluctantly nod. I trust Claire; she's my friend. Despite our differences of opinion on my personal life, I know she'd never put me in harm's way.

Rounding the corner, I realize she's right. It takes me a total of two seconds to realize where we are and what's happening.

A line is forming in front of an art gallery, one I've never heard of. The small venue sits nestled between two other shops, but its size doesn't seem to affect the crowd.

"What the hell, Claire?" I ask, stopping in my tracks. "I told you I don't want to see him."

"You don't *think* you want to see him," she says. "But whether it's to reconcile or make peace with your decision, you do need to."

"Is he expecting me?" I ask. "Did he reach out to you or something? Are you plotting?"

"I can honestly say he's not expecting you," she says, causing my eyebrows to raise even higher. "But someone else is."

She drags me toward the door, bypassing the people in line as they give us dirty looks and mumble god knows what under their breath. At the door, she gives a man my name, and he calls for someone inside.

"Carrot cake," Ryan says, cutting through the crowd, arms outstretched. "Listen, we need to talk."

I don't think I've ever rolled my eyes so hard at someone. "What do you want?"

Ryan pulls us inside and immediately shoves us into an office near the front. "This is all my fault," he says, shutting the door behind him.

"She was there because of me. He didn't even know I was sending her."

My mouth makes a noise that sounds like a mix between a huff and a snort, because I'm not having any of this nonsense. "That's really not the point."

"You need to understand that his work is his work. Sometimes it's great, and sometimes the clients suck. But money is money," he says. "Look, Declan is the best guy I know. He's never done a shady thing in his entire fucking life. And you're blowing it."

His words come out sharp, a side of him I've never seen. There's a look in his eyes that says he's protecting his friend; he's trying to right a wrong.

"I don't know," I say. "Maybe I'm too stuck in my ways for all of this."

Ryan and Claire sigh at the same time, both shaking their heads at me.

"Fine," he says. "But look, he's in the back talking to a buyer. At least go out front and see his work."

I cross my arms over my chest, furrowing my brow. No part of me wants to go see his new work. I don't want to see Natasha splashed across a canvas. Some of the other women he's painted in the past don't bother me so much. You can see in the way he paints them that it's not sexual. But something about her in particular makes me want to rip her face off.

"Come on, Cora," Claire says. "Let's at least have a quick look."

"Fine," I huff. "A very quick look."

Ryan hands Claire an invitation card with some information on the back before pushing us out the door and back into the liveliness of the party.

Thanks to the gut-wrenching paranoia associated with the thought of Declan seeing me here, I spend the few steps we have to take peering through the crowd, on high alert.

We slide through the people gathered in front of the main gallery wall, where most of his exhibit is located.

And for a full minute, I can't breathe.

CORA

TEN CANVASES ARE MOUNTED to the brick wall in front of me, each with its own light source staged just above it. Claire shoves the invitation card into my hand, backside up.

Zion Gallery Presents:
That Girl, Peony
by Declan Walsh

Tears are already brimming my eyes as I attempt to read through the blurriness. I look back up at the pieces on display.

They're all me.

The one I sat for—wearing his suit jacket—hangs just left of center. But the rest, I don't know.

A smaller piece is just my bright red hair, locks draped over a white pillowcase, twisted and curled. Another is of my hands, the delicate lines doing nothing more than folding a napkin. To the right is another; of my legs, one crossed over the other, a spattering of freckles over the tops of my thighs. There's one of my smile, another of only my eyes. All the canvases have touches of pink and lavender, peony petals and blooms in the backgrounds, sprinkled over parts of me, braided into my hair.

I can't focus on any single one before the next one catches my eye. Until I come to the small piece dead center. It's a bird's eye view of Declan in bed, me lying across his chest, the same way we always went to bed. My naked back exposed, my side profile nestled into him, a white sheet pulled up to our waistlines. His lips rest against my forehead, and it looks as if he's inhaling the scent of my hair even in sleep.

Holy shit. Holy fucking shit. All at once, it clicks. This is what he's been working on. This is why he never let me see it. I can't stop the tears silently erupting down my face.

"I need to go," I whisper. "I can't be here."

"What?" Claire asks, leaning in closer to me. "Are you crazy? Look what he did. For you."

"Excuse me," a voice interrupts us. "Is that you?"

I turn to where the voice is coming from, meeting the eyes of a petite woman holding the same invitation I am. Her eyes dart from my face in person to my face on the canvas and back again. She's pointing at the one of me wearing Declan's jacket, a smile across her face. That is, until she looks long enough to realize I'm sobbing.

"Oh my god," she says. "Are you okay?"

"Um," I say, not certain I feel like sharing anything with this stranger, "I'm fine." I turn away from her, giving her my back and leaning in toward Claire in an attempt to hide my face. "Get me out of here," I whisper to Claire.

Claire sighs, turning to lead me out of the crowd, toward the entrance. I do my best not to elbow anyone, not to make waves, just hoping to disappear like I was never here.

"Cora?" I hear, as his familiar voice cuts through the noise of the room around me.

It's too late. I'm caught. I peek over Claire's right shoulder, and there he is. *Declan.* His sharp black suit has never looked so good. Tonight, he's wearing a black button-up underneath, with a black tie. All black everywhere, doing magnificent things for his dark eyes. His lips part, like he might say something, then press together again.

"Hello," I say, through tears.

Declan's hands are clenched at his sides, a confused and pained look in his eyes, almost as if he's trying to stop himself from reaching for me.

"What are you doing here?" he asks, moving closer through the last few people standing between us.

I stammer, "Uh, I—"

"Ryan had me bring her," Claire says. "He called work looking for her and spoke to me instead."

"I don't understand," Declan says.

"You guys need to talk in private," Claire says. I can hear her words, but they're not registering. My information processing center is in a deep fog.

"Come this way," he says, leading us through the crowd to a utility closet in the back. It's nearly as big as the front office we stood in with Ryan.

Claire stops short of going in, giving me an encouraging look as I trail behind Declan. The door shuts behind us and I can't feel my hands. All of my appendages are numb and tingling, like everything has fallen asleep. I feel like I'm five seconds from a panic attack or heart attack or possibly a nervous breakdown.

"Ryan brought you here?" he asks, clarifying what was said outside this closet.

I nod. "I didn't know where we were until we got here," I say.

"So, you didn't come looking for me?" he asks, disappointment lacing his words.

"No," I manage to squeak out, instead of another sob.

He sighs, the hope on his face dissipating into melancholy.

"I saw your new work," I whisper.

"Yeah?" he says. "Is this when you tell me I had no right? Is this when you demand I take them all down?"

"No, of course not," I say. "I'm sorry I made you feel that way before."

"This is hard for me, Cora," he says. "I don't have the same social skills as others." It feels like one of the only times I've ever heard him call me by my name instead of *love*, and I don't know how to feel about that.

"I understand," I say. "I should've let you show me, I should've let you explain fully."

"Yes," he says. "You should've."

Silence falls around us in this small space, the noise from outside muffled. We're not standing more than a couple of feet from each other, and there's a palpable tension in the air that's beginning to suffocate me.

"I should go," I say. "I've already taken your attention away from your show too long."

"I could give a fuck about this show, Cora," he snaps out. "Don't you understand by now?"

"Understand what?" I say, my voice not quite yelling but definitely louder than normal.

"I love you!" he exclaims, the tone of his voice biting and adamant. "Goddamn it, I love you." The last few words come out softer, almost a sigh.

"No you don't," I say, shaking my head back and forth.

"Yes, I do," he says, grabbing both of my arms. I'm still shaking my head softly back and forth as he tries to still me, looking into my eyes. "Why can't you see it?"

Another moment of silence passes us before I can manage any words. "I'm scared."

Declan's face softens, a small, understanding smile playing on his lips. "Yeah, love. So am I. But that doesn't make it any less true."

A welling in my chest propels me forward, my arms wrapping around his neck as I kiss his lips through sobs. "I love you too," I say, between kisses. "You know that, don't you? I'm so sorry."

He kisses me hard, his arms wrapping me up into him, his hands exploring me like he's searching for something. "I hoped," he exhales. "God, how I hoped."

Another wave of sobs hits me and I can't tell if they're happy or sad or a little of both. This man has my heart and he didn't even know it because I was too stubborn to tell him, to show him.

"What do we do now?" I ask, wiping at the mascara stains all over my cheeks.

Declan lets out a soft sigh, his head slightly bent as he leans into my hair and inhales. His hands grip me, still clinging to me like I might float away.

"Well," he says, "we're going to leave the closet and talk to people about all these paintings of you."

"Okay," I say.

"Then, I want to take you home," he says. "And make love to you." He presses his lips against my earlobe, kissing then nibbling.

"That sounds good." I giggle, still wiping at the makeup under my eyes.

"I just have one question," he whispers softly, sending goose-bumps down the back of my neck.

I lean in, humming, anticipating what he's about to ask.

"My place or yours?" he asks, his breath hitting my ear, the warmth spreading down my neck.

"I don't care," I say. "As long as I'm with you." I press my forehead against his, inhaling him.

I'm in love with Declan Walsh, the artist who lives across the hall, the man I spent three years hating for no good reason.

This is all I've wanted for so long, and I almost let it slip away. But I won't do that again.

Taking a chance with my heart scares the shit out of me. But come what may, I'm ready for it, with him by my side.

EPILOGUE

DECLAN

"HURRY UP," she cries, climbing the front steps of the hospital. "We're going to miss it."

All I can do is trail after her at this point. I don't exactly have a warp speed button or a NOS can hidden anywhere. This is the fastest I've ever seen Cora move, even when there was bread on the line. Not that I blame her. It's not every day your nephew is born.

"It's all right, love," I call up to her, but she isn't hearing me today.

"Declan, I swear if we miss it, I'm punching you for driving like an old man," she yells back.

What did she expect? We drove eighty through the night all the way here as soon as Jensen called with news of Harper going into labor. He assured us it would be a while, but they were heading to the hospital just in case.

I suggested flying but there were no flights direct to Raleigh last night. So instead, we've been in a car for twelve hours. *Twelve. Hours.* I wish I could say we did the smart thing and slept while the other drove, but that didn't happen. The excitement kept Cora up while I drove and Cora kept me up while she drove.

We run straight into the elevator and press the button for the fifth floor, the maternity ward. I had enough sense in all the excitement to tell Cora to call ahead and find out exactly where to go so there were no delays once we made it.

We hit the floor and round the corner, heading straight for the nurses' station. They hand us visitor stickers to adhere to our chests and then point us in the direction of a small alcove lined with chairs down the hallway.

"Oh my god," Cora says. "Lyla!"

She runs up to a woman standing in the area and embraces her. A man seated next to her stands, hugging Cora next. I've heard a lot about Lyla and Gentry, even seen a few photos from their wedding. But this is the first time I've met them and I'm strangely nervous. I know how important they are to Cora. And that makes them important to me.

"Hey, man," Gentry says, sticking out his hand. "Good to meet you."

I have no doubt they've heard about me as well. "You too," I say, returning his shake.

"Cora's told me so much about you," Lyla says, before throwing her arms around me. "I'm so glad you could be here."

I return her hug, getting in my greetings as best I can before the baby talk starts.

"Do we know anything?" Cora asks, looking to the both of them for any sort of update.

"Jensen kicked us out so he could have a private moment with her, but I'm going back before the labor starts. Nan and Paw couldn't be here, and they're devastated. So Harper asked me to be in the room," Lyla says.

"And how's my brother doing?" Cora takes my hand, squeezing. I know she's nervous for both of them. Parenthood is a big deal. Giving birth sounds scary as fuck.

"He's calm as a fucking cucumber, of course," Gentry interjects. "I've never seen the kid sweat anything. I don't understand it."

Everyone laughs, including me. The one time I met the couple, Jensen struck me as the type who didn't get worked up over much.

As if on cue, the door to our left bursts open, and Jensen—decked out in scrubs and a cap—comes strutting out.

"Hey, Lyla, it's time." Jensen crosses the floor and hugs Cora, her hand leaving mine for a few moments. Then he shakes my hand, gives me a knowing grin, and walks back through the door with Lyla, still calm as ever.

"I don't know how he does it." Gentry laughs, shaking his head as he sits back down.

"I agree," I say, taking a seat, Cora next to me. I feel like this is going to take a while.

Some hours later—I can't be sure how many, because I fell asleep—Jensen and Lyla reappear.

"Come on, guys, it's time to meet my son," he says. Even through my sleep deprived haze, I can see he's beaming, bright eyed and happy, like he's the one who just woke up from a nap or got a damn Shiatsu massage.

I step more gingerly than everyone else into Harper's hospital room. It feels like an extremely personal space, and I'm definitely the outsider in this situation.

"This is Jackson," Jensen says, taking the tiny bundle from Harper's arms and turning to show us.

I turn, watching Cora's shoulders begin to shake.

"Oh my god," Cora says. "Hi, baby boy." Her tone softens and takes on a child-like quality. "I'm your Auntie Cora."

I press my hand to the small of her back, looking over her shoulder at the little fellow. His eyes are closed, with some kind of goop spread across them, but aside from that, he's pretty cute.

The whole room takes turns holding him and passing him around. I even hold him for a few minutes. As an only child, I don't have any children in my family, so I think in my whole life this is the third time I've held a baby.

Cora leans into me, the tears dry, her face warm and content. "Harper, you're a rockstar," she says.

She's not wrong there. Harper's sitting up in the bed now, nursing Jackson after he made his way around the room. She looks much less disheveled than I expected and much less tired than I feel. Sure, I could complain about the twelve hours in the car, but Harper is the one who's done most of the work in the past twenty-four hours, and there's no arguing that fact.

"Piece of cake," she says, running her finger over the top of her new son's head. "Jensen was a great coach."

After a few more minutes of admiring the baby and new little family, all four of us leave them to check into a hotel with promises to come back later after Harper has rested.

We follow Lyla and Gentry a few blocks to a place they called ahead to and check into rooms next to one another.

"If you'll excuse us," Gentry says. "We're going to go try to make one of those ourselves."

Cora gives Lyla a look, and she confirms, right before Gentry gently pushes her into the room in a fit of giggles.

"Oh my god," Cora says, as we finally lie down onto a bed. "I can't believe they're trying to have a baby."

"Why's that?" I ask.

"I thought they'd wait a little longer, that's all." She shrugs.

"I don't know," I say. "I think when you know what you want in life, why wait?"

Cora tucks herself into my side, throwing her legs over my hips like she always does. "That's true," she says. "I agree."

"I'm glad you do," I say, reaching over the side of the bed into my well-staged duffel bag.

"Why do you say that?" she asks.

I place a small, white box on my chest in her eye line. "Because."

"Oh my god," she says. "Don't."

"Why are you always trying to reject my love?" I ask, laughing softly.

"Is that what I think it is?" she asks.

"Yes," I say. "Unless you think it's a pizza."

Cora sits up, crossing her legs and staring down at me, her eyes searching mine. She reaches for the box and opens it, revealing the pink diamond engagement ring Lyla helped me pick out two weeks ago. Her hands start to shake and for a moment I think she might start crying again. This woman cries a lot.

"I can't say I've loved you from the moment I met you. I don't think you can say that either," I say. "But I can say from the moment I started falling in love with you, I knew I'd never want anyone else."

"Oh my god," she whispers. "This is really happening."

"And if you let me," I say, pressing up onto my elbows, "I'll spend the rest of my life making sure you never regret taking a chance on us."

Cora's lips tremble, her breathing quickens, and then she presses a soft, wet kiss to my lips. "Yes," she whispers. "Yes, a hundred times over."

I pull the ring from the box and slide it onto her finger. Then, I pull her on top of me, still kissing her lips.

I want to sink into her so deeply I get lost. I want to crawl beneath her freckled skin, taste the salt of her body. I want to make art out of her bones. I want to bleed for her. But I'll settle for loving her. She is the sun and I am the shadow.

ACKNOWLEDGMENTS

First of all, fuck acknowledgments and fuck racism.

Second, I would be no one and nothing in this author world without the love and support of my home bitches, J.R. Rogue and Christina Hart. You two ground me, motivate me, challenge me, and cheer for me. I love you, now and always.

To the only man who's put up with me for this long. Chris, your constant support and devotion to my dreams astounds me. It's in the small things you do. Thanks for making dinner, running to the store, chauffeuring the children, getting me a snack, and all the other tiny things you do so I can do book stuff.

Special shout-out to some of the most supportive fellow authors, bloggers, readers, and book enthusiasts a girl could ask for. There are so many I can't even begin to name them. But you know who you are, and I love you dearly for every book you read, post you like, status you share, review you leave, and general shout-out you give to me.

For my bloggers and reviewers, and #TEAMQUEEN ARC CREW, thank you so much for spreading the word about my books. The work you do is so unbelievably important. I thank you, from the bottom of my heart.

For my kids. Mattie, Kali, and Kaden. As I've said before, you guys really don't do anything to help me. You're like cute and give me hugs and mostly don't bother me while I'm writing. Thanks for sometimes staying quiet and not killing each other while I was in front of my computer sobbing. I love you.

Thank you to every single reader who took the time to read this or any other book of mine. I'm beyond grateful that you'd want to read something I wrote. It's wild to me. Five years into this, and I'm still astonished. You're amazing.

Peace out until the next time I have to write one of these shits.

ABOUT THE AUTHOR

Kat Savage resides in Louisville, Kentucky with her three beautiful children, her hunky spouse, and three spoiled ass dogs. She secretly has hopes of getting chickens one day.

She was driven to write out of a need for distraction and self-preservation after the death of her sister in 2013. Since then, it's snowballed into a full blown passion she can't escape. Even on the toughest days, she wouldn't want to. Her unique brand of storytelling ranges from tragic poetry to swoony rom coms and even a little darkness. She uses her real life experiences to fuel every word she puts on paper. She's published several collections of poetry and multiple novels.

Savage is a natural storyteller, getting better with each book. She tries to give the characters in her novels depth, whether they're serious or comical. Savage builds them in layers with the hope that you see a little of yourself in some of them.

www.thekatsavage.com
Newsletter

ALSO BY KAT SAVAGE

Made in the USA
Monee, IL
28 April 2025

16456976R00381